YUGANDHAR

Shivaji Sawant (1940-2002) was born in a farming family of Ajara village in Kolhapur, Maharashtra. He worked as a teacher for twenty years and afterwards, as an editor with Maharashtra education department's monthly magazine *Lokshikshan* between 1974-1980. Later, he held the post of vice-president at Maharashtra Sahitya Parishad. As a prolific novelist in Marathi, he is best known for his novel on Karna, *Mrityunjay*. He was the first Marathi writer to be awarded the prestigious Moortidevi Award in 1995 from the Bhartiya Jnanpeeth. He has received many other awards including the Poonamchand Bhutodiya Puraskar (1986) and the Maharashtra Shasan Puraskar. His important books include *Yugandhar*, *Chhava*, *Kavadase* and *Ladhat*.

Kadambini Dharap is late Shivaji Sawant's daughter. She writes poetry in Marathi, Hindi and English. She published a collection called *Kinara Houn Aapanach* in 2011. This is her first work of translation.

Madhura Phadke is an avid reader and language enthusiast. She has been a Marathi language teacher, a Japanese language faculty at the University of Pune and a corporate translator. She is interested in mythology, and her ability to translate while preserving the essence of the original has enabled a wider audience to enjoy *Yugandhar*.

SHIVAJI SAWANT

Yugandhar

TRANSLATED BY

KADAMBINI DHARAP AND MADHURA PHADKE

ekadā

First published in Marathi as *Yugandhar* in 2000 by Continental Prakashan

First published in English as *Yugandhar* in 2017 by Mehta Publishing House

Published in 2020 by Eka, an imprint of Westland Publications
Private Limited by arrangement with Mehta Publishing House

Published in 2025 by Ekadā, an imprint of Westland Books, a
division of Nasadiya Technologies Private Limited

No. 269/2B, First Floor, 'Irai Arul', Vimalraj Street, Nethaji Nagar, Alapakkam Main
Road, Maduravoyal, Chennai 600095

Westland, the Westland logo, Ekadā and the Ekadā logo are the trademarks of
Westland Publications Private Limited, or its affiliates.

ISBN: 9789360453749

10 9 8 7 6 5 4 3

Typeset by Jojy Philip

Printed at Nutech Print Services, India

SRIKRISHNA

I must lay bare my heart. I must lay bare my soul today. You seem surprised. Don't be. You have known me as an articulate orator and a deft negotiator. But today, I am not here for any kind of mediation and am certainly not going to offer any clever explanations. What then am I going to speak about, you wonder?

You have been listening to the Gita for ages, and may even have studied my Uddhavagita. But there is another Gita – the Krishnagita – the story of my life, and I want to share it with all of you now. 'There was never a time when you and I did not exist; there will be no such time in the future either.' These were the words that I spoke to my beloved friend Arjuna, in the Gita. They hold true, eternally. Today, science claims that time is infinite. Neither does it have a beginning, nor an end. Aeons ago, I clearly stated, in the Gita, that I myself am time – *kaala*. I am here to help you understand the dynamism of life itself. The material world keeps changing with time – its very nature is undulation. However, this vibrant life is pervaded by weightless energy, which is eternal and boundless, infinite and inexhaustible. And I exist as part of every manifestation of life for eternity. It is this idea that I wish to discuss with you.

In what capacity shall I to speak to you? As the miracle child who effortlessly eliminated asuras and rakshasas? Or as an imp, who inexcusably stole clothes of gopis bathing on the banks of the Yamuna. Shall I speak as the warrior who led the Yadav clan ? Or as the little devil, who, despite the abundance of curd, milk and butter at home, stole some more from the gopis? As the sorcerer who took on many avatars? Or as the conjurer who aided Draupadi on the brink of abject humiliation, by offering her vesture? As the axis around which the epic of Mahabharata revolves? Or as the one who brought on the apocalyptic war? Am I to speak as the sole protagonist of that saga?

Even as I engage in this conversation, I want to lodge a protest. Till today, you have kept me at a distance, turned me into a mere idol.

You have relegated me to being an incarnation of Lord Vishnu. For hundreds of years, I have been saying that I exist inside each one of you, but you just keep denying it.

This conversation between you and me, is, in fact. an internal dialogue. Don't hold me up as Vasudeva – the supreme being – distant and inaccessible. Instead, think of me as Achyuta – the unwavering spirit of divinity – that speaks to you from within the depths of your heart.

It has been ages since we had a heart-to-heart. More than five thousand years. It is time we spoke freely. And I sense you are all ears. But where do I begin? My life is filled with thrilling adventures. Like a sprawling Audumbara tree – branches laden with clusters of raw, green and ripe fruits. Over the last five thousand years, the saga of my life has been buried under several layers. I am determined to scrape them off and reveal my true identity.

Let's begin. What does my Gita contain? Doesn't it ask the most difficult questions? And aren't the answers surprisingly simple?

For thousands of years, I have been answering questions posed by all of you. You deemed me an ingenious philosopher because my answers seemed convincing. And in the process, unwittingly, turned me into a holy avatar. But what has happened of me? Both my ardent devotees and staunch rivals have tarnished my reputation. Innocent devotees termed me God for their own convenience and rivals disposed of me by attributing adjectives like 'deceitful' and 'crafty.'

That is why, today, I must clear away the muck from over the clear blue lake of my life… And so, I am not going to recite the story of Srikrishna that you have been hearing for generations now. As I speak, I am lying under an ancient, dense Ashwattha tree in the precincts of Bhalaka Tirtha in Saurashtra. It is summer. The melodious rustling of the Ashwattha leaves permeates through the forest. My blue body, more than a century old – a hundred-and-nineteen years, to be exact – is resting here, under the shade of luxuriant branches. A fresh Vaijayanti garland, woven with white flowers and twined with bunched lush green leaves, adorns my neck. Along with it, many pearl necklaces, bedecked with divine kaustubh beads and numerous other gold ornaments, lie on my chest. Underneath is the gold-plated iron armour that I have deliberately worn after a long time. My beloved divine white conch, Paanchajanya, which I have blown many times with all my might, and which is usually tied to the blue shawl around my waist, is also resting leisurely beside me on the ground. I clearly feel the warm trickle of sweat running down the golden armlets fastened on both my arms. A few rays of the sun, sneaking through the Ashwattha foliage, are leisurely spread over my yellow silk dhoti. A few bold wild grass blades are glued to my silken shawl. I can clearly see my left leg covered with the dhoti, resting horizontally on the partially bent right knee. Also visible is the rosy sole of my left foot. I can even see the Suchi arrow, shot by the hunter Jara, pierced deep into the tirelessly itinerant sole of my foot. I am deeply aware of the warm drops of blood dripping down my sole. I can clearly see the pool of my blood accumulate around my right heel.

At this moment, the blood gushing from my sole has opened up the cocoon of my childhood memories. The first fragrant memory in the deepest recesses of my heart is connected straight to Gokul!

My beloved Gokul! What was it like? The crescent-shaped holy river, Yamuna, with abundant water, coursed around it in a semicircle. All of Gokul was girded by a robust protective fence of bamboo canes and teakwood sticks – a precautionary measure to protect the cattle from wild beasts. The watchdogs provided additional protection to cattle. Diligent gopas had toiled tirelessly to tame various breeds of these wild canines – some of them reddish and dusky, and others grey.

The main fortified fence had two towering wooden gates on the east and the west ends. Made from the durable, solid wood of the Kikar tree, these sturdy gates were about eighteen feet tall and quite broad. Seasoned carpenters had engraved captivating emblems of gopas on these gates.

There were two plump, young bulls with their tails erect, nostrils flared, copiously slobbering from their snouts, sprinting eagerly to head-slam with their rival carved alongside the gates. Their plump, fleshy humps were tilted towards their right. Their rumpled, flabby dewlaps, drooping close to the ground, clearly boasted their haughtiness. It looked like they were going to pull up their dewlaps and fill the surroundings with thunderous bellows any moment now.

Positioned at the very top of the gate was the image of a full moon; one half was engraved on the left door and the other half on the right. It was the emblem of the Abhirbhanu family of the gopas, a symbol of the Chandravansha. Every evening, when the gatekeepers shut both the doors, the full moon would emerge. The two galloping young bulls would join their heads and prepare to protect the populace inside. Both gates had two huge, cylindrical lead bolts. A small wicket gate was used for nightly transit. Even now I can hear the squeaking of those huge gates. Many of my memories are especially associated with the squeak of the eastern gate.

Every day, hundreds of our cows would leave Gokul from the eastern gate, mooing happily as they plodded along to graze. My beloved Gokul would come alive in the wake of their ebullient mooing, and begin its daily chores in the name of Goddess Ida. The western gate was closer to the river Yamuna's bed. In the evening, the cows, content after grazing, would quench their thirst with water from the Yamuna and return hastily through the western gate, eager to meet their calves.

Adjacent to the main fortification wall, corrals with similar but smaller fences were erected. They accommodated cattle belonging to the eighteen clans of gopas and other castes. The bulls as well as calves had separate corrals. Adjacent to the eastern gate was the largest, most spacious corral containing hundreds of cows and cattle. It belonged to my father, the leader of all gopas in Gokul, Nanda. He was reverently called Nandababa. Other gokuls within Vraja would identify our gokul as Nandagram, by my father's name.

Located in the heart of Gokul was a well-planned colony, abounding in alleys. All gopas had simple, clean and tiled houses, made of mud. Their walls were smeared with red ochre mud. Using limestone, they were decorated with pictures of plump cows; calves swinging their tails and running around freely; plump bulls bellowing and snorting; herds of cows resting under a huge banyan tree and ruminating leisurely. Under the rule of the Yadavas, the gopas adopted the family deity of the Yadavas, Goddess Ida as their own. Various manifestations of the goddess and portraits of Abhirbhanu – the founder of the gopa family and many other gopa kings – also adorned these walls.

It was customary for every house to have a minimum of seven–eight slings to store curd and butter. There also used to be tall, pointed churning sticks fastened with ropes next to big earthen jars used for churning buttermilk. An array of storage bins full of grains like barley, rice and wheat would be arranged on the veranda.

In the heart of the colony was my father's massive house built in stone. A huge courtyard in front of it was the assembly yard for the gopas. A small, dome-shaped stone temple dedicated to Lord Shiva was located at some distance to the east. A shivapindi made of Shaligrama stone from River Gandaki was placed in the inner sanctum. In the front yard, a statue of a seated Nandi – Lord Shiva's mount – was placed with its back facing the entrance. Our founder Maharaja Abhirbhanu's consort was like a mother to us. She was an ardent devotee of Lord Shiva. Due to her, we gopas also became devotees of Lord Shiva. To the west of the house, a wrestling ground was located a few yards away. It contained a spacious gymnasium, fully equipped with wooden and iron clubs as well as the polished wooden Mallakhamba.

Such was Gokul – like a doting dimple on the cheek of the land of Vraja!

Each person here was like a luscious bulbous root, full of pure love, replete with emotions. That's why it is impossible for me to forget these men and women even if I want to. So many people – with so many emotions, and so many dispositions.

My father belonged to the mercantile class. Short of stature, he had a hefty body frame, wheatish complexion and round face. My mother, Yashodamata, was a bit taller than my father, fair, with a face as round as the full moon and always smiling. I had eight kakas – Sunanda, Upnanda, Mahananda, Nandana, Kulnandana, Bandhunananda, Kelinanda and Prananananda. All of them looked more or less like Nandababa. We used to recognise their wives – our kakus – by the names of their husbands and also address them as such – Sunandakaku, Nandanakaku, Kelinandakaku and so on. Each one of my kakas possessed expertise in some skill or the other. One uncle could unerringly identify the seasonal disorders of cows and treat them with effective medicinal herbs. Another could effectively handle my father's job in his absence just as skilfully. Another possessed mastery of the seven musical notes and practised a variety of melodious ragas for hours. Yet another could give wonderful discourses based on the Upanishads. Kelinandakaka was especially proficient in sports, swimming, wrestling and many others. That's why he was my favourite kaka. I also had a stepmother, Rohinimata, mother of my elder brother, Balaramadada. She was a bit taller than Yashodamata, fair and slim.

Balaramadada! Chubby and ruddy, fair-complexioned. A little older than me. He was short-tempered, but would also calm down quickly. To show respect to our mothers, we both called Yashodamata 'Thorali' – the elder mother. Naturally, Rohinimata had become Dhakali – the younger mother!

Both of us had a younger sister, Ekananga, born to Thorali, a few years after my birth. We affectionately nicknamed her Eka. She was the apple of our eyes.

At this moment, more than anyone else, I remember my dearest old grandfather, Chitrasena. Nandababa's father. Chitrasena had a thick, white, mushroom-shaped moustache. Even his thick eyebrows were completely white. He used to keep a roll of betel leaves in his mouth, and chew for hours.

He usually carried a small pouch decorated with tiny bells, to store the betel leaves. A man of robust physique, he always donned a twisted, brick-red turban. A prominent sandalwood mark adorned his forehead. He draped his coarse, woollen blanket loosely around both his shoulders, on top of the special Barabandi dress that he wore. His black-bordered dhoti dyed in red ochre was tightly tucked around his knees. A dazzling silver bracelet, the symbol of our family, hung loose in his hand. A beaded, golden earring dangled from his right ear. Hunchbacked due to old age, he always uttered the name of Goddess Ida while getting up with the support of his sturdy cane adorned with tiny bells.

He was the one who had explained my life's Gita to me in numerous ways in the local language of the gopas.

During my childhood, it was always the three of us – Balaramadada, our sister Ekananga, who was born when we both were about five or six, and me.

At home, we would always hang around grandfather.

As Thorali always said, I was a very chubby baby, constantly giggling, energetic and naughty. I was the apple of everyone's eye. One day while churning buttermilk, Thorali did something very funny. Not on purpose, it just happened inadvertently. Dhakali was also churning buttermilk with her while humming a tune.

All of a sudden, Thorali pulled a fresh, iridescent peacock feather from a bunch kept in a niche. It glowed with such a medley of iridescent colours – blue, purple, green and golden. She quickly stuck it in my thick, curly hair. Since then the peacock feather has been with me forever. Later, it became a significant symbol of my life.

One memory that Yashodamata shared with me is always going to remain with me – just like the hairy calf-shaped birthmark on my chest.

One evening, when I was a little older, while returning from the pasture with the cows, I was lost in a unique tune of Raga Asavari on my flute. In the clouds of dust rising along the hooves of the cattle, my friends and I could barely see each other. With the rays of the setting sun lingering on our backs, all of us entered Gokul from the western gate. The cows returned to their own corrals out of habit. With the help of attendants, Dada and I tethered our cows, put out fodder for them and went home.

I washed my feet and entered Thorali's room as usual. I hung the coarse blanket from my shoulder on the wall peg and put my belled staff carefully in a corner. I put my flute and lunch bag in the alcove. As usual, I bent down to touch Thorali's feet, who was standing in front of me. She quickly held my shoulders and pulled me up. For a moment she gazed deep into my eyes. Her face had a peculiar look that day. The corners of her eyes were visibly moist. It shocked me to see her like that. Holding both her hands affectionately in mine, I hastily asked her, 'What is it, Thorali? Why do you look so strange today? It is as if you are here, but your mind is wandering far away.'

'Were you playing the flute just now?' she asked. I nodded.

'Oh, this peculiar tune of yours has left my heart aching. I regret the apprehension that I harboured on the night you were born. The night of the Abhijeet constellation, the eighth night of the dark fortnight in Shravana! The whole world had blossomed with such vibrant energy on that thunderous, stormy night.'

'An apprehension? What was it?' I asked, shaking her hands fiercely. 'Come now, sit.' She made me sit next to her, and said, 'I had lost consciousness due to agonising contractions on the night you were born. A thunderous, destructive storm had hit that night. Many giant, ancient trees of Gokul collapsed with a loud crashing noise. The cool, fragrant breeze of Shravana coming from Yamuna awoke me sometime in the wee hours. You were right there – by my side, newborn, fresh, wailing ravenously. I gathered you in my arms to nurse you. But the moment I touched you, a dreadful suspicion engulfed my heart, 'This baby is not mine.' I kept gaping at you in disbelief. You were still wailing and kicking. The moment you ravenously started suckling at my bare bosom, a profound feeling of motherhood rushed over me like a flash of lightning. I had never experienced such an emotion before. The first touch of your lips completely transformed my awareness. As if you were silently reassuring me – 'I am the apple of your eye, your dear son, and you are indeed my mother.'

'That memory, lying deep in the recesses of my mind, resurfaced today after hearing the peculiar tune of your flute. Krishna, my dear son, please forgive me for the doubt that I harboured in the past.'

I simply smiled that time. Sometimes, in the jungle, I would hold the bushy tail of my favourite cow and stroke it over my face. Likewise, I held both her rosy palms and, gently stroking them over my cheeks, said, 'Now, now, don't be so silly! Am I even worthy of forgiving you?'

Another memory that she was fond of recollecting was that of my naming ceremony. I still remember it vividly, just as she had described it to me.

All the houses, streets, palaces, temples, gymnasiums and gates in Gokul were festooned with garlands of assorted fragrant flowers woven together with mango leaves. The corral attendants had beautified the horns of all cows, bulls and calves, and adorned their necks with garlands of jingling bells. All animals had their foreheads smeared with vermilion. Kettle drums and trumpets reverberated through town all day.

The inner sanctum of our house was decorated with garlands of champak, hibiscus and assorted wild flowers. At the centre of the hall a magnificent cradle made of rosewood, engraved with delicate tracery patterns, was swaying on wooden crossbars. It was also bedecked with assorted garlands of flowers, pearls and beads. The hall resonated with the chatter of zealous gopis in festive attire. Wrapped in a rich, soft fabric with a tiny dot of kohl on my forehead, I was dressed up in a golden cape. Thorali gently put me in the decorated cradle. At the auspicious moment recommended by the royal priest, she gently whispered my name in my ears – 'Krishna'. The people of Gokul were full of fervent enthusiasm. 'Our Nandababa's precious son, an answer to his prayers, has been named, "Kri…shna…! Ki…sh…an!"'

Krishna – Krishna! The one who attracts like a magnet. The one who mesmerises everyone – charming Krishna! Dhakali gave an affectionate push to the cradle.

Gokul resonated with the sounds of various musical instruments. People of all caste and creed feasted at our home that day. My father was content that he was graced with a firstborn son as an answer to his prayers.

More than six hours had passed. An urgent council was held on the veranda of our home. For this particular purpose, Gargamuni had arrived from Mathura on the previous day. No one knew who had sent him. He was the royal priest of the Yadavas of the Shoorsena kingdom in Mathura, but he was intentionally present for the naming ceremony of the son of Nanda gopa from the Abhirbhanu dynasty. Last night, in the seclusion of the secret chamber, he had discussed something with father for quite some time.

My eight middle-aged kakas, their wives and children, and Chitrasena attended this council. Gargamuni's ascetic, serene eyes glanced at Nandababa, who was sitting to his right with a few selected gopas, and the priest of Gokul, Abhirananda.

Gargamuni had a radiant and calm face. He wore rudraksha armlets around his upper arms streaked with holy ash and had matted hair. The ingenious architect of the Yadavas. The prophetic astrologer of the royal Yadav family. He began speaking with his eyes closed, as if he had reached beyond his subconscious mind, and was clearly visualising something. His profound words poured deep into the ears of the eager gopas as if they were coming from an unknown territory, 'Oh goparaja Chitrasena and Nandaraja, please listen. All gopas, listen carefully to the forecast of your dear, newborn son according to the holy scriptures.

'He will live up to his name "Krishna". With his physical beauty and enchanting mind, he will captivate one and all. He will lead an unprecedented, novel way of life full of love called "Premayoga". All of us spend our lives trying to understand the purpose of our existence, and observe religious practices and penance for the same. But this child is already aware of his identity. Just as clearly as you can see your multicoloured cows every day, he can perceive the Absolute Truth – from every angle. Just as you can recognise your cows in a herd even from a distance, he can easily recognise every person, inside out, with an open mind.

'He will shower his unconditional, pure affection on all of you in such abundance that you will never be able to forget him. He will silently preach the divinity of Love. But…but you won't experience his endearing, affectionate company for long.'

Gargamuni fell silent for a moment. His eyes were still closed. He took a deep breath. His wonderstruck disciple recording the remarkable forecast on a leaf kept gazing at him. All assembled gopas gasped in astonishment.

'He will act as the guardian of nyaya – justice and Dharma – duty throughout his life. He will offer his unconditional support to a banished valiant royal family that had to suffer extreme injustice despite being righteous. To make sure they get the justice they deserve, he will initiate a humongous, unprecedented war that will rock the world. Like precious gems emerging after a laborious process of production, many principles of life will re-emerge from this war, to be protected and cherished by mankind. His invaluable guidance will prove exemplary to the entire human race. It will be held in the highest esteem for ages. It will prove to be eternal.

'Time and again, he will reincarnate on this earth. He will uproot many unscrupulous kings and kingdoms, destroying them completely. He will release the life force of Aaryavarta and let it flow unhindered for years to come. Yet, he himself will never claim authority over any kingdom. His conduct will prove inspirational and guide the future generations of humanity for ages to come. He will have profound understanding of the essence of femininity and exhibit the same in his own conduct. He will honour every woman in his life as an integral part of Nature.

'He will be instrumental in the migration and well-planned rehabilitation of a powerful royal family on the west coast. After witnessing the same royal family forsaking the path of truth and becoming insolent and rude, he himself will destroy them with absolute detachment. The fourteen skills that are often unattainable for a common man will dance at his fingertips. An artist struggles tenaciously throughout his life to master a single art out of the sixty-four art forms, but he will be the sovereign master of all of them. The mellifluous music of Samaveda will always reflect in his personality. In fact, he himself will be music incarnate. He will be recognised by the names of his gurus and his mothers for ages to come. In fact, by being his educators and caretakers, both his gurus and mothers will attain immortality and experience a sense of fulfilment. He will spectacularly exhibit a perfect manifestation of manly charm surpassing all criteria of physical beauty. Befitting his charm will be his celestial speech, as melodious and irradiant as the sound of his flute. Occasionally, it will be as intense and difficult to endure as lightning bursting through the skies. At an opportune time, he will also erect an unparalleled golden city on the shores of the western ocean, which will be worthy of his ethereal beauty. There he will spend an ideal family life, full of love and affection with his eight virtuous wives, children and grandchildren, which will prove inspirational to future generations.

'Dear gopas, don't be blinded by his miraculous acts and don't judge his character by that. That he lives physically amongst you is in itself a miracle of miracles. He will spend most of his life near water bodies. He is also the Jalapurusha – the Lord of Water, which is one of the five essential elements of the universe.

'Just as water never stagnates in one place and courses further to create and develop life, this Jalapurusha will be a traveller throughout his life. He will be a Chakravarti – the ideal universal ruler.

'He is not only the majestic Jalapurusha who knows the Truth, but also a yogi – a proficient practitioner of yoga. The greatest yogi of all.'

While concluding his forecast of the exceptional horoscope, Gargamuni looked like he had transcended his own body and reached the realm beyond. There was a resplendent glow on his face. The final words describing that incredible horoscope made the assembled gopas feel blessed.

'Oh dear gopas, through the power of vigorous meditation, we sages try to understand Ishwar, the god, but so far none of us have been able to explain what Ishwar is; and I doubt anyone ever will be able to do it in future. Don't you think that Ishwar, God, Almighty and Incarnation are all false ideas that beguile the mind and make it go astray? Even I can't tell for sure if He exists at all. But this virtuous son of yours is undeniably the greatest yogi of all – a complete yogayogeshwara – a superhuman in the true sense of the word. He is the great Purnapurusha – the perfect man. Never forget that there is no one else like him. He is unmatched and incomparable. You should rest assured and undoubtedly offer all your ideas of divinity at his feet. Just as Premayoga, or love, is innate in his nature, so is renunciation and detachment. He will never get attached to his own karmas – he will be free from the fruits of his actions – and hence he will never get entangled in their consequences. Like a lotus he will remain pure, untainted, and free from the sinful desires of the human mind. That is precisely why you will find him a divine conjurer.

'He will attain the highest epithet of Vasudeva – the supreme being. He will teach millions what life is; how to live it; and demonstrate the same in his daily life.

'He took the first breath of his life in the confines of Nanda's house, but this Vasudeva will breathe his last of his own accord, under the open skies, in a thick desolate forest, in the shadow of an Ashwattha tree, in complete solitude. With this I conclude the forecast. May all be well!'

Gargamuni fell silent as if he were watching something splendid, glorious, larger than life right in front of his eyes. Bringing both his palms together, he touched them to his forehead and whispered gently, 'Krishnarpanamastu – I submit to you, oh, Lord Krishna!'

Thoroughly content, the spellbound gopas left our house chanting the name 'Kisna, Krishna'. But I – 'Krishna Kanhaiya' of Thorali – was fast asleep in the cradle.

Soon, the innocent days of crawling, running and messing around were over. The days of getting spanked by the elders for our pranks were also past us. Dada and I had grown up to become eight/ten-year-olds.

And then dawned that special day in my life – the day of my initiation as a gopa.

Dada and I were to graze our cattle in the lush pastures on the outskirts of Gokul, near the banks of the Yamuna. Nandababa had chosen this auspicious day for the initiation ceremony.

Every year, to pay the levy, he would make one trip to Mathura, the royal capital of the Shursena kingdom of the Yadavas located on the other side of the Yamuna. This year, from the traders' market of Mathura, he had bought fine silk dhotis for both of us. Such fluorescent colours. A bright yellow one for me and a deep blue one for Balaramadada. Such an accurate selection by our father – the yellow suited my complexion and the pure blue enhanced the crimson fairness of Dada's skin.

Thorali and Dhakali called me Shyam, meaning 'dark'. To be exact, my colour was dusky dark. Yes, I was dusky. Like an evening of Shravana, drenched in sentiment. Let me assure you that I was and still am indeed proud of my complexion! I loved my name – Shyam – from the bottom of my heart.

On the day of our initiation ceremony, both Balaramadada and I got dressed in special gopa attire. Grandfather Chitrasena had tied brick-red-coloured, twisted turbans around our heads. The soft, shiny dhotis were draped neatly around our waists. Our shoulders were covered with woollen blankets made from the soft wool of local sheep.

We carried our refreshments bundled in a cloth in the folds of our blankets. It contained seven–eight rotis with mouthwatering garlic chutney and thick curd in an earthen pot capped at its mouth with a Palash leaf tied with a small piece of cloth. There were also some freshly plucked spring onions.

I had also kept a small sharp sickle in the folds of my blanket.

The rituals began. Our family priest Abhirananda began intoning melodious Sanskrit verses. Dada and I sat on square wooden stools carved with tracery designs. Once all the rituals were over, Nandababa came forward. Gathering up the blanket on his shoulders, he gently removed an octagonal silver medal – the emblem of the Abhirbhanu dynasty-hanging on his chest and held it in his palms. He touched it to his forehead and mumbled something to himself. The next moment he put the medal around my neck, pulled me closer with deep affection and said, 'Krishna, now you have formally become a gopa, my true heir. So far, I have looked after all young and old gopas to the best of my abilities. Today onwards, you and your elder brother are duty-bound to carry forward my legacy. Not only should you take care of all gopas but also guard the cows and the cattle of Gokul.

I looked at Balaramadada sitting next to me. He was smiling while caressing a similar medal that Grandfather had put around his neck earlier.

We got up from our seats and paid obeisance to the family deity, Goddess Ida, sought blessings from the elders in the family and prepared for the day ahead.

We picked up our staves from a corner of the veranda. They were a foot taller than us, carved with tracery and decorated with tiny jingling bells. They were going to protect us in various ways. We were going to use them to our advantage every now and then.

Both mothers were already present at the eastern entrance of our house. They put blobs of thick curd on our palms. I put it in my mouth and closed my eyes for a moment to savour its taste. Even today I feel the lingering sweetness of that curd on my tongue.

About fifteen–twenty of our friends had gathered in the courtyard outside our house. Seeing us, they all got excited and made a din shouting our names, 'Here comes our Kisna – Kanhoba! Krishna – Kanhaiya! Balaramadada – Balidada!'

We embraced each one of them tightly and then immediately all of us turned towards the corrals. We released the cows from their tethers. Within a few moments, a huge herd of zealous colourful cows was on its way, brushing against each other, clattering horns and bellowing freely to their hearts' content. They exited from the eastern gate of Gokul. Holding the blankets on our shoulders and raising our jingling staves, we drove the herd towards the rich meadows on the banks of the Yamuna. In hundreds, the cows then dispersed in the meadows. The bells tied around their necks made a sweet, rhythmic tinkling sound. Slowly, birds like the myna, the black drango and others started landing on their backs. The lush green grass swayed gently to tune of the breeze coming from the

Yamuna. Balaramadada and I were now free to roam around and play games with our friends.

The vast expanse of the Yamuna's shining, blue waters was now visible to us. Leaving behind the cows, all of us ran towards it. As if something was pulling me towards her unknowingly. For some reason, ever since I had laid eyes on the Yamuna, I had felt a mysterious turmoil in my heart. A flurry of questions would arise. About Madhupuri – Mathura – the capital city of the Shursena kingdom of the Yadavas. What kind of a place was that faraway city? Who must be the king of that city? Father, Grandfather and others always had such lengthy discussions about that city. I used to hear so many names – Maharaja Ugrasena, Maharani Padmawati, General Satyaki, Anadhrishti, Kanka – the minister Akrura, the charioteer Daruka, the royal counsellor Vipruthu, Vasudeva in captivity, and his helpless wife Devaki. Devi Devaki. For no apparent reason, just hearing all that made my young heart throb in unknown, unbearable pain. The heartless, diabolical, vicious son of Maharaja Ugrasena, Kansa, who had imprisoned his own father to usurp the kingdom – what kind of a person would he be? What kind of people would the Yadavas of Mathura be?

Glancing from left to right, I feasted my eyes on the Yamuna and preserved her vivacious, rushing flow in my mind. Unwittingly, my palms joined in prayer and I touched them to my forehead to pay respects to her. I felt at peace.

I carefully removed and placed my yellow silk dhoti on the blanket, undressing down to the loincloth. Raising her countless rippling wave arms, Mother Yamuna had been calling me for a long time now. Many birds of different shapes and sizes were gliding freely on her waters. I ran impulsively and entered Mother Yamuna's arms with a passionate yearning. I got shivers all over my body instantly.

Plunging into the water, I started swimming to my heart's content. Soaking myself in the affectionate caresses of the Yamuna's warm waters, I started reminiscing about the many invaluable conversations that I had had with grandfather, father and both mothers. I recalled what Prananandakaka, who was learned in the 'Shastras', had told me. 'Krishna, my dear child, always remember the deeper meaning of the word 'jala'. Dear son, 'jala' is one of the five fundamental elements from which life blossoms and eventually merges into. It is the most important and powerful element of life.'

Reiterating the meaning of 'jala' in my mind, floating on my back, I started basking in the dazzling light of the shining sun. I had completely forgotten myself.

We played in the water for a long time. The ascending sun was almost over our heads now. We dried ourselves, got dressed and started moving towards a big pasture that had a sprawling Kadamba tree loaded with fresh, fragrant flowers and foliage.

Our flock arrived under the Kadamba tree. The intoxicating fragrance of flowers and the buzz of beetles and hovering bees filled the air. Everyone carefully brought out their meal packs.

I was sitting at a distance under the Kadamba tree, resting my back against its trunk. I pared a colourful bamboo cane that I had found earlier into a beautiful new flute. I had barely begun to practise a tune on it, when my friends began calling me. They were shouting my name at the top of their lungs, 'Krishna, Kisna, come on, our meal is ready!'

We finished our meal, laughing, giggling and cracking jokes about each other. Stokakrishna said to me, 'Come on, Krishna, tell us. Which things are among your favourite?' Smiling at him, I responded, 'Stoka, among flowers, jasmine is my favourite, especially the one drenched in dewdrops in the early-morning autumn breeze. Its sweet scent is unmatchable and its tiny orange-coloured stem looks so pretty. Isn't it? Mango is my favourite among the fruits, especially the ones about to ripen, scarlet-coloured. In birds, the peacock, dancing tumultuously to the tune of the first shower of rain, unfolding its rainbow-coloured iridescent plumage, fascinates me the most. My favourite drink is, of course, cow's milk,the chosen drink of all gopas.'

'And you should know by now that soft cooked rice mixed with curd with a pinch of salt is his favourite food, Stoka,' said Sankudada.

Soon after, our friends went to fetch some water from the Yamuna. Standing under the Kadamba tree, Dada picked up the newly made flute and asked me in astonishment, 'Hey, how do you do all this? Not just this, but everything else that you do.' I simply smiled.

I spread my blanket over a tall boulder and lay down. I began playing melodious tunes, one after the other on my flute, my favourite musical instrument. All my friends relaxed wherever they could, spreading their blankets in the shade of various trees. They were engrossed in my music.

It was now time for a series of games. By the time we had finished playing, evening had dawned and it was time to leave. Wild parrots, hawks, cranes, larks, herons and several other birds were returning to their nests, creating a cacophony of sounds. Our cows returned mooing, content after grazing to the fullest and quenching their thirst with the Yamuna's water. The refulgent crimson platter of the setting sun was gently touching the surface of the Yamuna.

I shouted impulsively, 'I have formally become a gopa today. Therefore, I am going to teach you a new game. I am sure you will like it, but for that each one of you will have to finish the tasks that I am going to assign you, as soon as possible.'

'Yes, yes, tell us Krishna, what do we have to do?' all of them shouted together in approval.

'Balaramadada and I will stay here. Vadaja, Sudama, Rudrasena, Bhadrasena and a few others will carry pitchers and fetch as much water from the Yamuna as we need. Some of you will collect fresh white flowers and fresh bela leaves from the woods nearby. A few others will collect fresh warm milk in pitchers. The rest will stay with us. Come on. Hurry up now! Get to work fast!'

Dada and I chose a clean place on the banks of the Yamuna. We started working on the soft, blackish, wet sand. We removed big stones and pebbles and briskly started collecting fine, soft sand and kneading it with water. Whatever we were about to build was going to last the night. Soon enough, all of us erected a waist-high Shivapindi – a symbol of Lord Shiva – along with the majestic Nandi. The *shalunka* base of the Shivapindi was shaped like a kettledrum and its tapering end pointed towards the north. Oh, how neat and elegant it looked!

I told Dada to perform the ritual of abhishek by pouring fresh milk slowly on the Shivapindi. The rest of us did the same. After that, we poured water on the Shivapindi. As per my instructions, all my friends offered white flowers and bela leaves to the idol. We all closed our eyes and brought our palms together in prayer.

The sun had merged completely with the western horizon. After some time, I opened my eyes before everybody else and glanced at the Shivapindi. Only its edges were barely visible. I said to all, 'Dada and friends, the gopas of the Abhirbhanu family line have been the worshippers of Lord Shiva since ancient times. The shalunka base of the Shivapindi symbolises the female yoni, and the lingam represents male potency. Shiva, also known as Shankara, is the one that tranquillises the turbulent mind. If needed, for the sake of peace, he performs his Tandava dance at times to destroy evil. Lord Shiva is the God of Destruction, the destruction of wrong and evil.' Everybody listened to me in awe. I had only reiterated the words I had heard some time ago from the family priest, Abhirananda. Not a single word of my own.

We dispersed and gathered the cows back in a herd. On our way back, I pulled out my flute from the folds of the blanket and began playing various tunes spontaneously. As the warble in my tunes hit the climax, someone came rushing towards me and held my hand effusively. My flute stopped automatically. I opened my partially closed eyes. Standing in front of me was a gopa woman – young, fair and innocent-looking. She was older than me, tall, and had sharp features. An incredibly beautiful woman. I asked my friends curiously, 'Who is she?'

Somebody replied, 'She is Radha, wife of gopa Rayana! She has come to Gokul from Arishtagram, her *mama*'s town.'

By this time, Radha had stroked my cheeks with her fingers and, cracking her knuckles on her temples as a gesture to ward off evil, exclaimed, 'Oh Kanhaiya, such heart-rending tunes you play! It makes me yearn for more.' For a long time, holding the flute in my hands, I stood still as if I was not among friends. Her very first touch was full of affection, like that of my mother's, and full of innocence like my younger sister, Ekananga's. But there was so much more in it that I cannot put in words, and so I will never be able to describe it.

She looked at Balaramadada and just smiled, but did not speak anything as such with him. Putting her hand on my shoulder, she started walking with all of us towards the incline leading to the western gate of

Gokul. While walking, she said to me, 'Kanhaiya, every time I hear your flute, I feel like becoming one with myself.'

The moment she had touched me, I had realised she was part of my body. Unknowingly, I put my own hand in her warm, chubby palm. She held it with such intense passion that it seemed she was going to lead me. Today I had been initiated as a gopa and the very same day I had met her. She was also going to initiate me in another way.

Our cattle had already entered Gokul through the western gate. I let go of her moist palm. She patted me gently on the shoulders and left for her colony. Looking at her fading figure, I recollected the meaning of the word 'dha'. Prananandakaka had explained its meaning to me. 'Dha' means 'moksha' – freedom from the circle of life and death. I racked my brains to recollect the meaning of the word 'ra', but it simply kept eluding me. We tethered the cows and washed our feet. We then entered our house through the wicket gate, changed our clothes and put our gopa dresses in their proper places.

As soon as I entered, I shared two things with Thorali. 'We erected a huge Shivapindi on the shore of the Yamuna today with wet sand. And just now I met Radha. Her voice is as sweet as honey.'

As usual, Thorali gave me a pleasant smile. While arranging our dinner plates in the dining room, she said to me, 'Oh silly Krishna, how long is the sand Shivapindi going to last? And the woman Radha you are talking about – she is gopa Rayana's wife. No wonder she was enchanted by your flute! Sometimes, I, too, get carried away by the sound of it. But you better stay away from Radha as far as possible – her husband Rayana is very short tempered!'

That evening, after dinner, I asked Prananandkaka a question that had been nagging me for a while, 'Pranakaka, what does "Ra" mean in Sanskrit?' He patted me lovingly and said with a smile, 'Kanhaiya, you are usually the giver; you give everything to everybody, especially joy. How come today you are asking about gaining something? 'Ra' means to get, to obtain, and to achieve!'

A melodious tune of the flute flashed through my mind – 'Ra' means 'to obtain'. 'Dha' means 'moksha'. 'Radha' means a being desperately longing for moksha.

There was only one word lingering in my mind when I rested my back on the bed that night. 'Ra...Dha...' – a being eagerly yearning for moksha.

Sometimes, my mind would be flooded with questions.

Balaramadada had crimson fair complexion. Why was I the only one with bluish, dark complexion? Why was I the only one who yearned for the Yamuna? What was the connection between Gokul and Mathura? Who was Maharaja Ugrasena of Mathura? Why had his son Kansa imprisoned his own father? And why did I have frequent and intense urges to visit Vasudeva and Devakidevi detained in Kansa's prison? My mind irresistibly longed to visit Mathura. Why? None of my questions were ever answered. What was my association with Mathura? How come Radha, who had met me only yesterday, had such intense yearning for me?

There wasn't a single house in Gokul that we didn't know. There was not a single dairy storage room in these houses that had escaped our secret raids. Why did we steal from others in Gokul when there was an abundance of milk, curd and butter at our own house? It was because, for us, all of Gokul was one big, spacious house – our own house. I had a strong desire to make others feel the same. It was my intense wish that they shared everything without being possessive about anything. Not a single gopa couple was unknown to me. For Dada and me, all the gopa children were like our own cousins, our Eka.

The more we got acquainted with gokul, the more we enjoyed playing a variety of thrilling games and making mischief, both inside and outside the city. There was no limit to our antics.

Everyone in Gokul was quite annoyed with our pranks. They would come home and complain about us, 'Yashoda, Rohini, should we live in Gokul or not? Or should we just go someplace else? Are you going to control your children at all? Your spoilt, insolent brats have become a nuisance!'

Both our mothers would get weary of pleading with and pacifying them. Finally, they would wield their ultimate weapon saying, 'All right then, we will banish Krishna–Balarama from Gokul and send them to another gokul far away. We are also fed up of their antics.'

These words would do the trick. All gopis would immediately lower their voices and whisper amongst themselves, 'That's not what we want. But the children should stay within their limits. That's all.'

Both Dada and my footprints were now imprinted on each and every grain of sand on the banks of the Yamuna. We were also closely acquainted with every blade of grass from all the meadows on the outskirts of Gokul. Despite being mischief-makers, we were the ones managing any trouble that came Gokul's way.

Once a hideous wild donkey suddenly charged from the woods into the meadows, where our cows were grazing. His deafening brays scared everyone, even the gently swaying grass in the meadows. Seeing him charging at them with flared nostrils, the poor animals were terrified. In panic, they started running helter-skelter, raising their tails high. Our gopa friends began calling out to us in desperation, raising their staves in the air, 'Krishna…Balidada…Run, Kanhaiya…Sankudada…hurry, hurry, run faster!'

We ran as fast as we could from wherever we were, and together we attacked that bulky animal with all our might. After a while, we finally brought him down. The gopas hailed our names in victory and carried us to Gokul on their shoulders with pomp.

The account of that incident spread among other gokuls in the land of Vraja. Meanwhile, on another day, we heard of an enormous serpent living in the deepest part of the Yamuna, tormenting the gopas and their cows all the time.

One day I went alone closer to that part of the Yamuna, to keep an eye on the serpent. It was glaring noon. The serpent came out of the water and crawled into the thick meadows. He must have found a prey there. He gobbled it up and lingered sluggishly. This was the perfect opportunity. I pulled out two flat, rounded flintstones tied in the yellow silk dhoti around my waist. I scraped the flintstone in my right hand against the one in my left. It produced tiny sparks, enough to set the dry meadows alight. The grass flared up instantly, with flames leaping high into the sky. In the glaring heat of the day, this inferno raged. Watching the billowing smoke, everyone in Gokul began running towards the Yamuna. By this time, the terrifying snake came out of the meadows, scorched by the flames, writhing and hissing. After crawling towards the banks of the Yamuna for a while, he lay dead there – tongue dangling loosely out of his mouth.

Thorali came running, panting, beating her chest. Seeing me safe and unharmed, she embraced me tightly. She kept muttering to herself, 'Death to that serpent. He is dead anyway. Come, Kanha, let's go home first.' My friends lifted me on their shoulders. But this joy did not last long. Gokul faced double trouble this time – the attacks of wild animals along with natural calamities. In broad daylight, wild beasts like tigers, wolves and hyenas from the surrounding woods started attacking our grazing cows. Sometimes, they wandered outside the fences with wide open jaws in search of prey. Our trained guard dogs would bark loudly at them but they would be least bothered.

These wild animals kept harassing Gokul. To add to that, there was now a shortage of fodder for our cattle in the nearby meadows. Our usual abode was to be abandoned for the time being. This was the first instance in my life where I had to leave a place very dear to my heart.

For that purpose, a meeting was called under Father's leadership. For an entire week, a few knowledgeable adults surveyed some places and finalised a location. Everybody asked me to suggest a suitable name. This area was packed with small forests, or '*vana*'s'. It was like a team of forests. So I named it 'Vrindavana'. They all loved it.

All families moved to Vrindavana. As the clan leader's family, our family left after everybody else. I was about twelve years old then.

Vrindavana. Doesn't everyone cherish a Vrindavana of sentiments in their heart? Vrindavana was like a jade embedded in the lap of natural beauty.

One day, in the forest of Madhuvana, my beloved friend Radha dragged me away from my friends, and took me under a tree. It was the Kadamba tree, our favourite, proudly displaying its branches loaded with clusters of scarlet blooms. Their intoxicating fragrance diffused in the air.

Radha wanted to gift me something. She had taken extra effort to conceal it in the folds of her dress. I sat down on a big rock. She stood by my side and said, 'Manamohanaa, today I am going to offer you an exclusive gift. That is why I have brought you here, away from the others. Mukundaa, you will like my gift, for sure.' She took out the gift carefully and held it in front of me. It was a crown made of tiny, lush green leaves from wild creepers. Its beauty was enriched by an iridescent peacock feather tucked in the centre. Awestruck, I kept staring at it. Then, with some thought, I wore the crown on my head, smiling, and glanced at her.

Her eyes sparkled with tears. Lost in deep emotion, she instantly closed her fish-shaped eyes and stood still for quite some time. Mesmerised, I kept looking intently at her serene beauty. Evening had slowly crept over the forest of Madhuvana. We both returned to Vrindavana along with our friends, bearing the dusty twilight clouds on our backs.

I had deliberately accepted and worn the peacock-feathered crown gifted by Radha today. The peacock feather was a delicate and befitting symbol of something healthy and perpetual. It was a symbol of the fertile yoni – the supremely sacred virtue of womanhood. I had honoured it with a clean and clear mind at the beginning of my life's journey.

Radha was indeed my first female guru. The one who introduced me to the different emotions and moods of a woman – sometimes loquaciously, other times silently. She had initiated me into a lustless, incomparable Premayoga full of deep affection, pure love and complete devotion. Soon, the silvery, full-moon night of sharad poornima descended gently on Vrindavana. Shining brightly in the night sky, the platter-sized moon began shining its silver light on Vrindavana and Madhuvana. The gopas of the Chandravansha had a sentimental tradition followed by generations, that of the Rasa dance. Under the bright light of the full moon, men and women would indulge in the Rasa dance throughout the night. No other place in Aaryavarta followed such a tradition, except for the eighteen gokuls of Vrajabhumi.

The first batch of children and the elderly got exhausted after dancing for quite some time. Innumerable tunes blossomed with the escalating rhythm under the starlit sky.

The main team of Rasa dancers entered the dancing ring now. It seemed as if Radha was determined to keep the memory of our love alive forever. Today, too, she had brought me a precious gem, hiding it in the folds of her dress. Balaramadada, Radha, our friends and cousins, and I gathered in the dancing ring. Holding my hands in her moist palms, Radha gently pulled me to the centre of the circle.

Radha affectionately pressed my cupped hands tightly with her palms and said, 'Kanhaiya, please accept the gift that I am going to give you today as a gift from my heart. Never separate it from yourself, even for a moment. It should always be with you in the same form that it is now. Will you fulfil this wish of this sentimental friend of yours? Please. Promise me!' She presented her right palm to me. Now, I held her cupped hand in mine and pressed it lovingly for a moment. Putting my right palm on hers, I said to her, 'Certainly, I will fulfil your wish. I give you my word.'

From the folds of her dress she pulled out a thick white garland of fresh flowers artistically intertwined with lush green leaves. Putting it around my neck, she whispered, 'This garland – my Vaijayanti garland – you must wear every day, woven with new, fresh flowers. Kanhaiya, remember its name, VAIJAYANTI.'

The brilliance of the full moon that shone in her eyes blended with the moonlight in my eyes. I lifted the garland so full of sentiment and inhaled deeply to fill my chest with its fragrance. I caressed the knee-length garland with both hands. Just like Grandfather had done, I tossed a fistful of vermilion in the sky.

To commence the main Rasa, I pulled out my flute and played an indicative tune. The kettledrums echoed. Dancing without a break, Radha got exhausted. Beads of perspiration gathered on her forehead. We all got lost in the rhythm of the dance. We had completely lost sense of our bodies. Radha, the gopa-gopis and I, we had totally lost consciousness in the rhythm of dancing. Radha was not a woman any more and I not a man. Radha–Krishna were not two separate entities. We had become one wick of the life-lamp flickering to the beat of Rasa; one entity, one existence!

We had not realised that all the elders and children sitting around us, watching the Rasa, were totally engrossed. Clapping their hands with closed eyes, they were rhythmically chanting, 'Radha–Krishna, Radha–Govinda, Radhe–Krishna, Radhe–Govinda! Radhe–Govinda, Radhe–Krishna.' Listening to their chanting, I felt particularly satisfied about one thing – they had honoured a woman, my friend Radha, chanting her name before mine.

The enchanted days in Vrindavana were soon over. Our original Gokul was lush green again. Father announced our return. It was time to say goodbye to Vrindavana, where every place carried sentimental memories of Radha and me. Apparently, I was used to saying goodbyes like this since birth. It was my destiny. Various melodies of my flute had blossomed and resonated in the ambience of Vrindavana, Madhuvana and Govardhana. The fresh natural beauty around had given me so much during my stay. But my beloved friend Radha had given me much more than that.

Whatever Radha had taught me – sometimes by speaking continuously for hours together, sometimes through silence, sometimes just through the touch of her hand, and at times simply through her communicative eyes – was invaluable. She introduced a woman to me as the Creator's most positive, virtuous work of art that is full of pure love.

A farewell to Vrindavana was a farewell to the matchless and pure emotional love of Radha–Krishna. With heavy hearts, both of us bade farewell to Vrindavana. As we were departing, I told Radha, 'Today onwards, you are the queen of Vrindavana. Wherever men and women will have a Vrindavana of pure affection devoid of lust and lechery, Radha will exist there for sure.' These were the days of approaching youth. The phase of life that steers the chariot of horses of Imagination aspiring for the skies; that harbours the ambition to explore the world to the best of its abilities. That expels the word 'impossible' from the mind.

From Gokul to Vrindavana and back to Gokul – the healthy, life-giving air in the land of Vraja had made us mentally fearless and physically powerful. Our bodies were well built and toned by the rigorous exercise under the meticulous supervision of Kelinandakaka and Prananandakaka. Dada was already looking all grown up, like a tough and hefty wrestler. A glistening moustache had just started growing above our lips, indicating the arrival of youth.

Nowadays, my pestering questions to Grandfather, Father, both mothers, our kakas and kakus had considerably increased. I incessantly asked them questions like, 'How come Maharaja Ugrasena of Mathura has been imprisoned by his own son Kansa? How come nobody has ever tried to liberate Devakimata and Maharaja Vasudeva from the clutches of Kansa? What were the various clans and hundreds and thousands of Yadavas belonging to them doing at that time? Why do I have the incessant urge to go and meet them? Why does my heart revolt to free them from the clutches of Kansa?' My incessant questions would leave all of them nonplussed. I couldn't find a satisfying answer to a single question.

Finally, that day dawned on Gokul. As usual, Dada, our friends and I returned in the evening, along with our cattle. That day we saw an unusual sight – an embellished royal chariot yoked with five strong, shiny, pure black horses stood near the western entrance. Dada and I were startled when we saw the chariot, as there was no one in it. Dada ran frantically towards Gokul. In a short while, he returned with Father. Nandababa, who was always cheerful irrespective of any number of calamities, looked dejected today. Hastily, he said to me, 'Krishna, come immediately. The royal minister has summoned you. He is resting at our house.'

Just as we entered our house, I saw a tall, hefty, bearded man in royal attire, wearing a crown on his head. Upon seeing him, my pace increased unknowingly. For the first time in our lives, we were meeting a Yadava warrior in person.

I moved forward and bowed to pay my respects to him. He instantly pulled me up and embraced me. Father introduced him to me. 'This is Akrura, Maharaja Kansa's minister. He has arrived to invite you to 'Dhanuryaga' – a yajna along with an archery contest. Balarama is invited too.' Father stuttered while speaking. But the royal minister Akrura observed me for a while. After some time, he gathered his thoughts and addressed us, 'Maharaja Kansa desires to see your valour.'

'First, tell me Akrurakaka, how did you bring this huge royal chariot from Mathura across the Yamuna?' I asked him.

'You are observant! One spacious boat carried our chariot and the charioteer. I disembarked in Gokul from another boat on the banks of the Yamuna. Both the boats are still anchored in the river,' Akrura told us, smiling gently. He put his hand on my shoulder and entered the inner chamber.

Akrura stayed back for supper.

His sudden arrival had left all the family members restless. Possessed by innumerable doubts, they were tossing and turning in their beds. We thought that Akrurakaka must be sound asleep as he was exhausted due to the long journey. But at the midnight toll, holding a lantern in his hand, Akrurakaka came out of his chamber and stood in front of Father. 'Nandaraja, I need to speak to you about something crucial, in private.

So please come to my room alone. We will talk first and, later, I will summon both your sons,' he said.

The unexpected invitation, the hearsay about Kansa's tyranny... Father was already disturbed, but he followed the royal minister to his chamber.

Akrurakaka closed the door first, and then, in a low, whispering voice, explained what his vicious king Kansa's actual plan was under the pretext of the Dhanuryaga. He said, 'Oh gopa king Nandadeva, the invitation for Dhanuryaga is a deception, an utter lie. A diabolical scheme to slaughter both your sons has been cunningly hatched in the royal palace of Mathura. Huge intoxicated elephants and wrestlers will attack your sons without any warning. They will be killed either under the feet of huge elephants or in the duel with wrestlers. They need to be cautioned about this today. Go and fetch both of them.'

Father woke us up and took us to Akrurakaka. He looked me in the eye and started speaking.

His words flew like sparks of fire. I had never experienced such emotional turmoil before in my life. 'Krishna and Balarama, listen carefully and calmly to what I tell you. Both of you are the sons of the venerable Yadava Maharaja Vasudeva and Maharani Devakidevi! Under the pretext of Dhanuryaga you will have to face fatal assaults tomorrow. Though you are invited to this yajna as a Yadava, it is not as an ally, but as an enemy.

'Krishna! Son, Kansa has even imprisoned his own parents to seek control of the kingdom. He got terrified and went berserk when he heard the divine utterance from heaven during your mother's wedding ceremony. He is the one who has held your parents captive. Krishna, dear son, he has murdered your six newborn brothers born to Devakidevi by smashing their heads on a big boulder. His gruesome slaying of the newborns has put the entire Yadava clan to shame. Balarama, son, you are the only one who miraculously escaped from his evil clutches. Krishna is your real brother.

'Nandaraja, who is a vassal of Vasudeva, assumed this crucial responsibility of caring for the both of you, only after discussing it with him. Nandaraja knows your origin very well, right since your birth.

'Nandaraja, bid farewell to them tomorrow as your duty calls for you to do so. They have served the Abhirbhanu dynasty so far. I am confident that they will serve the Yadu dynasty similarly in future.'

Overcome with emotion, he pulled both of us closer to him. We paid our respects to Akrura as he left.

Everyone else in the house was fast asleep that night. Vasudevababa is my real father! He had been held captive in Kansa's prison all these years. Kansa is my mama – and yet he gruesomely murdered my six newborn brothers, right in front of my mother. In fact, any mama should love his nephew. Isn't that natural? And all this because of a prophecy. He imprisoned his own parents, the king and queen of the Yadavas, and banished the eighteen families of the Yadava clan from the kingdom for the same purpose. I am also a Yadava. Kansa – the evil, unjust king of Mathura is my mama. Why is he afraid of us? Just because of the divine utterance? How do they look – my father Vasudevababa, Devakimata, Maharaja Ugrasena, the king of the Yadavas, his queen Padmawatidevi?

The next day dawned. The day of bidding farewell to Gokul, probably for good. The day to go to Mathura and live there…probably, forever. It was the biggest and most significant turning point of my life.

Somehow, last night itself the news of our departure for Mathura had spread like wildfire in Gokul. The people of Gokul crowded around our house since morning. Pin-drop silence prevailed despite the crowd. Their faces were drained of colour. From wherever they were, they tried to catch the slightest glimpse of us.

We wore our regular outfits, the yellow and blue silk dhotis. I wore a peacock-feather crown on my head. The new, fresh, thick Vaijayanti garland that Radha had given me hung around my neck. I pulled my flute out from the folds of the blanket and tucked it in the scarf tied around my waist.

We entered our mothers' rooms to bid them farewell. How much their faces had changed in just one night. Thorali gave out a heart-wrenching cry the moment she saw me. 'Krishna…Kanhaiya…please don't go to Mathura, the invitation of that devious king is not worth it. Once he has you his clutches, I will never be able to see you again in my life. Finally, Yamuna did succeed in her evil scheme. Kanhaiya, the day you were born

I doubted just for a moment that you were not my child. Is that why you are punishing me so severely? Please don't desert me, Kanha!'

She put her arms around my neck and sobbed inconsolably, so much so that she could barely breathe. I consoled her, patting her on the back, 'Shush ... Thorali, be calm. Get a hold on yourself.' Finally, they both calmed down and regained their composure.

In the meeting square of our home, Akrurakaka was waiting for us. The entire square was packed with a crowd of sentimental gopas and gopis. Glancing disdainfully at Akrurakaka, quite a few people whispered amongst themselves, 'He doesn't look like 'Akrura' – the Merciful – in the least. He looks like the most merciless, vile creature.'

I turned back to take a final look at the ancient structure of the Abhirbhanu dynasty. I brought my palms together in prayer and paid obeisance to it.

As I turned to leave, I saw her standing right in front of me; my beloved sakhi Radha! Radha, the soul yearning for moksha! She stood still like a statue, but tears were streaming down her face. She looked lost and her eyes were devoid of emotion. And yes, her husband Rayana also stood behind her, sobbing and completely shaken.

Captivated, I stood in front of Radha. Lifting up the Vaijayanti garland slightly, I said to her, 'Radha, I will never forget this loving gift of yours. I am also going to give you a gift of my love today. You will never be able to forget it. Here, take this.' I pulled out my favourite flute from the shawl around my waist and held it in front of her. The same flute that was so dear to my heart, the melody of which resonated in the atmosphere of Gokul and Vrindavana. Taking it in her hands, as she put it to her lips, her body trembled and she started sobbing. While she was sobbing, 'Kanhaiya, Kanhaiya', I gently patted Rayana's shoulders and went forward. Following Akrurakaka, we advanced towards the Yamuna, breaking the circles of sobbing gopa-gopis who were falling at our feet. But now the crowd of disheartened, grieving, young and old gopas and gopis started following us. They cried out loud, 'Oh Krishna–Rama... Kanhaiya–Balarama...please don't leave Gokul, don't leave us. If you go now, we will never be able to see you again. Dear ones, please don't be so indifferent. Krishna–Balarama, please don't go.' We came out of the western gate of Gokul. Akrurakaka's charioteer Ashwadamana had kept the chariot ready. First, Akrurakaka boarded the chariot, then Dada and, finally, I climbed in. As the charioteer cracked his whip, the alert, dark black horses harnessed to the chariot lifted up their front hooves, sprinted forward and neighed. The life-chariot of two gopas started its journey towards Mathura, the Yadava capital.

I glanced back. Near the western gate of Gokul, Yashodama had passed out and Nandababa was trying to revive her, while trying to regain his own composure. A lot of gopas and gopis were wailing loudly, throwing their hands skywards and beating their chests. Not having heard the melody of my flute since morning, many disconcerted cows were mooing and wandering around them. Even they were shedding tears today. The chariot kept advancing towards the Yamuna, leaving so much behind. I turned my back with a strong resolve. Vrindavan, Madhuvan and Govardhan, everything was left further behind. And yes, all my aliases, such as Murlidhara, Shyam, Mohana, Govinda, Damodara, Gopala, Madhava and Milinda, were also left behind. Krishna, the Yadava leader, was now going to enter the battlefield of real life.

I stepped on to the land of Mathura, the capital city of the Shursena kingdom, alongside Dada, with Akrurakaka leading us. On the other side of the Yamuna, only one Yadava was waiting to welcome me with a thick garland of fresh, fully blossomed, scarlet-coloured Kadamba flowers. He was a bit younger than me. The moment he saw me, he excitedly ran towards me. With sparkling eyes, he promptly put the Kadamba garland around my neck. Kneeling on the sand, he rested his head on my feet with utter devoutness and said earnestly, 'Dada, do you recognise this young brother of yours?' Holding both his shoulders, I tenderly pulled him up. I gazed deep into his loving, clear eyes as Akrurakaka introduced him, 'Krishna, this is Uddhava, your cousin. He is the son of Vasudeva's brother, Devabhaga, and Kansaadevi! He has two more brothers, Chitraketu and Brihadbala.' We had already recognised each other – right when our eyes met, like we knew each other from our previous lives and were going to know each other for many more lives to come. Ut – Dhava – means the holy fire of a Yajna – the flame of life that always keeps rising.

I called to him, 'Uddhava…Udho. Dear brother!', and embraced him tight. Now onwards, my life was going to be full of inexplicable emotional ties with Udho. He was going to be the keeper of my sentiments, my confidant. Dada and I started walking on the sands of the Yamuna along with him. Every single step of ours was leading us closer to an unknown future.

Gently patting Uddhava's shoulder, I said, 'Uddhava, would you do me a favour? Nobody else is suitable for this particular task. You go to Gokul right away, and console Yashodamata, Rohinimata and all the gopas–gopikas suffering the anguish of separation from me. Comfort Radha and Eka, just like I would.'

Uddhava looked at me in delight with bright eyes. Instantly he exclaimed, 'As you wish.'

I embraced him. He hesitated momentarily as he walked towards the boat. He was delighted that I had showed such faith in him on our very first meeting, but he was also worried for me.

Soon the towering gates of the temples of Mathura and the domes of the royal palace came into view.

Just like the news of Akrurakaka's arrival had spread in Gokul, the news that Krishna and Balarama from Gokul had arrived in Mathura had spread very fast. Thousands of young Yadava warriors marched on the streets with whatever weapons they could get hold of – swords, spears, hatchets, pestles and maces – along with flower garlands in their hands. It was no longer possible for Akrurakaka to hold them back. Dada and I were definitely not going to.

Within moments, a crowd of Mathura's Yadava warriors gathered around us like the roaring high tide of the sea. They were innocent people, who, for years, had been ruthlessly exploited under the unrestrained, tyrannical rule of Kansa. Their wrath, suppressed so far, had erupted today. It was uncontrollable. Thousands of oppressed, infuriated Yadavas started shouting at the top of their lungs, 'Hail Krishna, Balarama … victory to them … victory!'

Our very first procession in Mathura left the alleys and narrow lanes behind and arrived on the wide royal highway. As Dada and I turned back, we saw the ocean of roaring, determined, excited Yadava warriors following us. Their foreheads were smeared with vermilion. It looked like a whirlwind of blood-red ocean waves rising behind us. By this time, both of us were fully doused in vermilion.

Dada and I were confident when we left Gokul, but now, looking at the thunderous ocean of thousands of Yadavas oscillating behind us, our confidence knew no bounds. Dada and I had just entered the hall of the Dhanuryaga with indignation, when an uncontrollable and inebriated giant elephant, goaded by his mahout 'Mahamatra', attacked us at once. Since morning, he had been made to drink alcohol to intoxicate him. His name was 'Kuvalayapida'. Dada and I instantly removed the flower garlands around our necks and threw them away. Only the vermilion-smeared Vaijayanti garland remained on my chest. On the other side of the arena, Kansa – the heartless, diabolical, arrogant king of Mathura, our mama – was vaguely visible, sitting on the elevated royal seat. Surrounding him were members of his ministry and other honourable Yadavas. Among them were his eight brothers – Nyagrodha, Kanka, Shanku, Suhu, Rashtrapala, Srishti, Sunama and Tushtimana. Also present were his wives Asti and Prapti, and his sisters Kansaavati, Kanka, Shurabhu, Rashtrapalika and Kansaa.

As we quickly dodged the first attack, a round of applause followed. Dada instantly moved towards the straight, tiny tail of that enormous beast. I scurried towards his trunk. Swaying his big neck in jerky motions and lashing his trunk around, the huge elephant let out terrifying, deafening cries.... With a nimble move, I dodged his trunk and went underneath his belly. Holding his tail like a rope, Dada leapt on to his back. After a few moments, Dada picked up the mahout, along with his goad, and hurled him down.

I slipped through the gap of the bulky animal's front legs and stood directly in front of his trunk. Predicting his impending movements by a direct look into his fiery-red, crazy eyes, I began dodging his movements with agility. I provoked him with challenging gestures. Now, the elephant was completely under our control. By this time, Dada landed on the ground and picked up the goad. The frightened mahout had already fled. Dada constantly pricked the elephant with the goad from behind and I dodged him from the front, making him spin around. This thrilling game of gyrations went on for quite some time. It was our favourite wrestling manoeuvre, 'Abhyakarsha', mastered under Pranakaka's guidance. Now the elephant couldn't figure out which way to turn. The Maireyaka drink, coupled with the constant circular motion went right to its head. It gradually got dizzier and collapsed, I moved closer to his trunk and, with a single jerk, wrenched out his arm-long, curvy, white tusk, shouting, 'Victory to Goddess Ida'. Streams of blood spurted out. Using his tusk like a sharp weapon, I briskly kept striking blow after blow on his musth temples. Meanwhile, Dada ensured there was not a single spot on his body that had not been pricked using the goad. Both of us were drenched in sweat and blood.

The first assailant sent by Kansa – the royal elephant Kuvalayapida – finally died in despair. The suppressed, benumbed Yadavas around us hurled their turbans in the air. They fearlessly shouted spontaneous slogans of victory, 'Down with Kuvalayapida, he is dead. Victory to Krishna–Balarama…victory…victory!' Hearing these electrifying slogans, the Yadava crowd waiting outside became uncontrollable and broke in through the huge gates of the royal palace like a torrent of water.

Kansa, the king of Mathura, rose from the royal throne at once and stood erect. His body was trembling with rage, his bushy eyebrows were twisted weirdly and his eyes were breathing fire. He loudly roared, 'Minister! Present those boorish gopas for the Dhanuryaga. Bring them into the pit.'

Right in front of his royal altar was the spacious wrestling pit with red soil. A bow garlanded with flowers was placed in the centre, on a soft, shiny brocade fabric with designs of vines and creepers.

Kansa's minister commanded in a rowdy voice, 'Come on now, show us your archery skills!'

Dada was credulous. He went closer to the bow and started examining it intently. But I stood right next to him, cautiously keeping a close watch all around us. I knew that the Dhanuryaga was merely a deception. Suddenly, we heard a loud thumping of arms around us. Two hefty, muscular royal wrestlers descended in the wrestling pit with their dhotis tucked in.

One of them was Chanura, and the other was Mushtika. Slapping their thighs loudly and raising both their arms while dancing they shouted loudly, 'Hail Maharaja Kansa, the king of Mathura, the invincible great wrestler, victory to him!' A mere look at them sent a chill up people's spines.

Dada was also ready now. Hurling fistfuls of soil, Chanura collided with me, while Mushtika approached Dada. The royal kettledrums strategically kept at various places in the big hall started booming now. Frightening commotion prevailed in the arena.

Chanura struck me near my ear. That first punch itself made me see stars. At that moment, Kelinandakaka's wrestling tips flashed in my mind. His words echoed, 'The moment you hit your rival with such a powerful blow, you will become a true wrestler.' Instantly, my blood flared like corn grains on burning embers. The wrestler in front of me seemed just like the elephant – a trifling pile of flesh. I used a variety of wrestling manoeuvres and kept throwing him down, toppling him like rolling a big rock over with a small crowbar. Exhausted, he fell on his back. Planting my knee on his thick neck, I crushed him with all my might. As my rival lay exhausted, I used the final trick in the bag – the 'Bahukantaka' manoeuvre.

Putting my arm tightly around his throat, I clasped his neck in my firm grip. His tongue lolled out and his eyes rolled frantically. Vomiting blood, he struggled violently to get rid of my grasp. I was not going to give him that chance. Bahukantaka was like the thorny hold of Death itself, fastened tightly around the neck of your rival.

Ultimately, his body went limp and Kansa's giant wrestler succumbed to death. Dada, too, had killed Mushtika in the same manner.

The ecstatic Yadavas were beside themselves now. Applauding continuously and tossing their shawls and turbans in the air, they chanted, 'Hail Krishna–Balarama…victory…victory', and rushed into the wrestling pit. Kansa, who was standing on the royal altar shaking frantically with anger, roared loudly, 'What are you looking at? Minister… Commander… Anadhrishti… Let Toshalaka and Kuta deal with them. Send Shala and Kaushala too.' His brother Sunama suggested, 'Let me get rid of that elder gopa.'

Immediately, Toshalaka and Kuta from one side and Sunama, Shala and Kaushala from the other entered the wrestling pit! The armed attendants drove the crowd out of the pit. The walls of the hall echoed with the loud sounds of the wrestlers thumping on their thighs. Toshalaka and Kuta clashed with me, while Sunama, Shala and Kaushala tussled with Dada. The royal servants had already removed the dead bodies of Chanura and Mushtika from the wrestling pit.

Compared to massive wrestlers like Toshalaka and Kuta, I was like an insignificant, tiny hill standing in front of the twin peaks of Mount Govardhan. Yet, both Dada and I did not feel any pressure due to the size or the number of wrestlers standing in front of us. Our bodies were no longer human – they had transformed into vivacious flames of energy.

One person was cautiously staring at us, standing on the royal altar, watching our every move carefully. The tyrant king of the Yadavas – my mama – insolent Kansa.

The exuberant Yadavas started throwing spontaneous encouragements our way, 'Pull that vile man under your thighs, do not let go of him.' Spontaneous ecstatic cries rent the air.

Our struggle lasted for a good half an hour. Finally, I used the Bahukantaka manoeuvre on Toshalaka and Kuta, and Dada used it on Sunama, Shala and Kaushala. We eliminated all five of them, one by one.

The Yadavas started shouting unceasing, ear-splitting slogans of victory now. 'Krishna, Rama victory…victory, Rama, Krishna victory… victory.' In all the commotion, someone let out a provocative cry, 'To hell with the devil Kansa. Get rid of the devil, get rid of him!'

By that time, I had leapt from the wrestling pit and stood erect in front of the royal altar of Kansa, the self-declared, all-powerful, unjust king of the Shursena kingdom. It seemed as if the stone walls, too, were thrilled to hear the slogans.

I met Kansa's gaze – I recognised fear in his eyes. He realised that he was facing his death. This was the moment to emancipate innumerable repressed lives and give them a chance to breathe freely.

A completely novel, unknown calling of my own spirit resonated in my ears; it was telling me, 'Krishna. Go ahead, proceed. You were born for this very purpose. To crush injustice under your feet. To uphold justice on your shoulders. Always remember that growth and progress are the only signs of life. Remove this obstacle, which is hindering the progressive flow of life.'

I briskly climbed the stairs of the royal altar in front of me and, in a single leap, collided with Kansa. Fear-struck, he gawked at me with eyes wide open. I gave his hand such a strong jerk that he instantly rolled down the stairs and landed on his back. His golden crown tumbled down the stairs and rolled away with a clank. His thick, rough hair was dishevelled.

His cruel, muscular, hairy arms that had crushed my six newborn brothers on a boulder were feeble today.

From the altar, I jumped on him like a lightning bolt and mounted myself on his insolent, plump chest like a tiger. Clutching his thick, rough hair tightly in my left fist, I pulled his impudent neck up and slammed it rapidly on the stairs seven–eight times. I shouted, my eyes bulging with rage, 'Take this, you traitor of the Yadava dynasty', and landed a heavy blow on his chest.

As I repeatedly hammered him, I shouted, 'This one is for killing my first brother – hail Goddess Idamata – this for the second – this one is for the third – hail Devakimata – this one for the ruthless torture you inflicted on my mother – this one for insulting my father – this one for driving the Yadava families out of Mathura. Hail Idamata… Victory to her.'

Finally, he lay motionless. A vicious, ferocious royal storm whirling in Mathura in the form of his rule had finally abated.

Kansa's eight brothers, hesitant at first, rushed towards me with frenzied fury, but Dada confronted them and held them captive with the aid of the enraged Yadavas.

Hearts overflowing with love, the jubilant Yadavas picked up Dada and me on their shoulders. With loud gestures, they proclaimed, 'Hail the king of Yadavas, Krishna–Balarama – victory to them!' They carried us closer to the royal altar. Raising both my hands, I addressed them, 'Calm down, my dear Yadava brothers of Mathura!' Their clamour ceased instantaneously. In that moment, I realised intensely that a divine voice resided deep in my throat. Whenever it manifested, hundreds and thousands were compelled to listen in silence. I had found the purpose of my life.

Standing near the royal altar, to Dada's right, I glanced around and said slowly, 'Mathura is liberated from Kansa's clutches today. She is free and independent now. The Shursena kingdom is free. With your blessings, I am going to visit my parents at their mansion and free them from years of captivity. I am going to visit the royal prison right now and release Maharaja Ugrasena and Maharani Padmawati too.

'Citizens of Mathura, rest assured that only Maharaja Ugrasena will ascend the royal throne of Mathura again. I request the royal chief minister to present himself.'

My determined words got the assembled Yadavas whispering among themselves. Moving aside, the crowd presented a middle-aged Yadava to me.

He approached fearfully with palms joined in prayer, petrified that I would order his execution as he had been Kansa's ally…

'Your name?' I asked him.

'Vi…Vipruthu', he stuttered.

'Don't be scared, minister. I am not going to penalise you. You are not at fault in any way. You acted only as an obedient servant of the king, as a minister always should. The reign of the Yadava commander Maharaja Ugrasena will commence now. Therefore, make the necessary arrangements for his coronation in accordance with the Shastras.'

A terrified Vipruthu was relieved by this unexpected gesture of mercy. He composed himself and said, 'As you wish, Lord. I will never forget that you have spared my life. Any other task for me?'

'Minister, many families of the Yadava dynasty had fled Mathura during Kansa's tyrannical reign. Invite all of them back to Mathura immediately, with due respect. Assist in their rehabilitation, and reinstate their wealth and land confiscated by Kansa, with precise assessment.'

'As you wish, my Lord,' the minister responded.

'Give Kansa a formal cremation, with the rituals befitting a member of the royal family, on a sandalwood funeral pyre near the banks of the Yamuna. As our ancient adage goes, enmity is over with death. And get the army commander here immediately.'

The royal minister beckoned Anadhrishti towards the royal altar. Hefty and broad-shouldered, Anadhrishti soon presented himself. He was wearing an iron armour. I asked him, 'What should I call you? Anadhrishtikaka or commander?'

'All Yadavas call me 'Yadavashreshtha'. I would appreciate it if you called me the same,' he replied fearlessly.

'Take caution in dispatching both wives of Kansa – my mamis – Astidevi and Praptidevi to Girivraja, the capital of Magadha, their father's country. Both of them are not safe here, amongst the foes that their husband created during his lifetime.'

I could not wait even for a moment now. My life's yajna had commenced from this moment. I held Balaramadada's hand, saying, 'Come on, we have to release our parents and obtain their blessings.'

The place where I was born came into view. The vast place was empty now – not a single person was in sight. A big iron lock was hanging on the iron gate.

One of the Yadavas came forward and, with a single strike of his mace, broke the lock open. Balaramadada and I met our mother with tears in our eyes. Our parents hugged both of us.

Along with Vasudevababa, Devakimata and a few chosen Yadavas, we left for the main prison to rescue Maharaja Ugrasena.

When we went to the main prison of Mathura and commanded the attendants to break the iron handcuffs to free the aged Maharaja Ugrasena and Queen Padmawatidevi, the old couple wept openly.

The citizens of Mathura had not seen them for years now. The chapter of Kansa, the first chapter of my life story, was over.

Minister Vipruthu consulted Gargamuni, the royal priest of the Yadavas, to choose an auspicious day for the coronation of Maharaja Ugrasena.

As Maharaja Ugrasena ascended the throne, he glanced at the council with gratitude and said, 'Actually, the right to ascend this throne goes to Krishna, Vasudeva's son. If, for whatever reason, he renounces it, it should be automatically transferred to his elder brother, Balarama. I cannot comprehend why in this old age he has handed me the responsibility of looking after the Shursena kingdom. I bless him from the bottom of my heart and request him to confer his invaluable guidance on the Yadavas, who have come together in this royal council of the Shursena kingdom in such large numbers after so many years.'

I stood up and took in all the present young and old Yadavas. I said, 'My dear Yadava brothers, the tyrant Kansa, too, was a Yadava. I had to execute him, even though he was my mama. The biggest calamity that is going to befall Mathura now is the onslaught of Kansa's father-in-law

Jarasandha, the emperor of Magadha, who will not sit quiet once he comes to know of Kansa's execution. In fact, by now he must be burning with the fire of vengeance. He has imprisoned more than eighty kings in Girivraja to carry out his resolution of sacrificing one hundred kings for 'Shataraj sheersha yajna'. Therefore, you should always stay united, be prepared and take advantage of Maharaja Ugrasena's experience. The royal priest Gargamuni should bless him.'

I leant forward and smiled at Gargamuni. The royal priest stood up. Gathering his soft, silky upper garment, he said, 'As the royal priest, I give my blessings to Maharaja Ugrasena and the maharani from the bottom of my heart. Let me tell you this. I had read the horoscope and predicted the future of Vasudeva's son, Krishna, in Gokul, at the time of his birth. I see that it is coming true. My dear Yadavas, with utmost humility, I am going to pronounce a meaningful title for the first time. A single syllable, 'Sri', like the sacred syllable 'Aum' has been regarded the most prestigious of all titles. It is most appropriate to confer it only upon a supreme personality and only at the right time.

'"Sri" is power, "Sri" is beauty, "Sri" means vast reserves of wealth, and "Sri" is pure intellect. 'Sri' has many more meanings – incredible success is also one of them. Is it not evident that this Krishna, the youthful son of Vasudeva, is the bearer of the wealth of all such supreme qualities? Wouldn't it be appropriate that you honour him with the title of "Srikrishna"? Do you all agree with me? Do you give your consent happily?'

Gargamuni's sharp glance moved around the hall briskly. Instead of answering his question, the Yadavas, full of youth and vigour, cheered in unison, 'Hail Yadava king Srikrishna…victory to him!' The very next day, under the guidance of Gargamuni, my Upanayana ceremony was performed at an auspicious time. As my Upanayana ceremony took place, it was considered my second birth, a 'Dwija'.

There in Girivraja, the royal capital of Magadha, Emperor Jarasandha's royal council had reached a final decision after a long hour of deliberation – that of an armed attack on Mathura with full force.

Two professional wrestlers and warfare experts, Hansa and Dimbhaka, were the commanders of Jarasandha's army. As our informants had told us, the enormous army of Jarasandha, led by Hansa and Dimbhaka, fell upon Mathura with full force.

Hundreds of ships carried their armed soldiers across the Yamuna.

Fortunately, Mathura was surrounded by a wide trench, flooded with water and full of obstacles. All borders of Mathura had robust gates, which were secured with sharp, upended nails set in them. Jarasandha spared no effort to cross the trenches, and burst open the eastern and western gate by dispatching huge elephants to break them. But despite attacks from both sides, there was no clear victory for either.

On the twenty-seventh day, Jarasandha sent his royal envoy holding a white flag in front of the eastern gate of Mathura. As per my orders, he was taken in. He carried a deceptive and astute message, 'Let one of the Yadava wrestlers, equivalent to Magadha commanders Hansa and Dimbhaka, play a conclusive wrestling bout with either of them, and the winner's side will be declared victorious in the war.' The war was going to be concluded based on the result of the wrestling bout.

I recognised Jarasandha's cunning strategy. Taking advantage of the commotion after the bout, he wanted to infiltrate a few of his loyal soldiers through the wicket gate of Mathura to break them open from inside. He wanted to force Mathura into a bloody war within the impenetrable fortification walls. Once the gates were opened, the Yadavas would not stand a chance against the colossal army of Magadha.

I glanced at Dada after hearing the message of the royal envoy. He got up and declared that he accepted the challenge. I looked at him and simply smiled. The royal envoy returned with our message.

We selected expert professional wrestlers to accompany Dada. The wrestling bout was going to take place in a big wrestling pit on the open grounds in front of the main gates of Mathura. Dada chose to wrestle with Dimbhaka.

Balaramadada and Dimbhaka began the fight at the fixed time, surrounded by the tumultuous Magadha and Yadava crowd. Vipruthu himself was conveying all the minute details of the fight outside to me. I did not want to be seen by the Magadha soldiers yet, at least not till the right time.

I spread rumours through my informers beyond the fortification wall of Mathura, 'There will be no war now. The wrestling bout will settle the conflict between the Magadhas and the Yadavas for good. Hansa, believing the rumours and confident of Dimbhaka's victory, boarded the ships with a few chosen soldiers to return to Girivraja. Here in the wrestling pit, Dada and Dimbhaka were fighting vehemently, using various strategies to take each other down. Within half an hour, Dada lifted Dimbhaka high up, then threw him down on the floor, and immediately clasped his throat in his invincible hold. All the spectators held their breath, thinking 'Dimbhaka is going to die now.'

As instructed, Vipruthu immediately conveyed the situation to me. I sent him back with instructions to spread the rumour amongst both the armies that Dimbhaka had been killed by Balarama during the bout. I also instructed him to follow Hansa in a boat and make sure that Hansa received the same news promptly.

He left to implement my instructions. Within a short time, accompanied by Satyaki on my left and Anadhrishti on my right, I stepped outside. As soon as they saw me, a buzz of whispers spread among the Yadavas and the Magadhas, 'He is here. He has come. Make way for him. Move back.' The wrestling bout had reached its climax now. Balaramadada was not going to let Dimbhaka slip out of his grip and would have kept tightening his hold on Dimbhaka's throat until he died. It was imperative to stop him.

Rushing into the wrestling pit, I patted Dada on his sweat-covered back and said, 'Let him go. Even though the wrestling rules say that a bout should end in the death of the defeated, do not forget that a victor also has the right to spare the life of the loser.'

Dimbhaka was on the verge of dying, with his tongue hanging loosely from his mouth and eyes rolled upwards. I signalled to him to raise his fist with his thumb up to indicate surrender. He instantly did so out of fear for his life.

A very upset Dada, his face red with strain and anger, finally loosened his grip while looking at me helplessly. As the Magadha soldiers saw Dimbhaka stand up, they started shouting in delight, 'Hail the Magadha emperor Maharaja Jarasandha, victory to him!' Their words made me laugh.

Hansa, on hearing the news that his dear friend Dimbhaka had been killed, collapsed in shock. Then beating his chest and in an insane fit of sadness, he plunged into the Yamuna.

The accompanying soldiers looked for him to the best of their abilities. Later, they returned to Mathura, announcing the bleak news, 'Commander Hansa has drowned in the river Yamuna!' On hearing this, Dhimaka immediately boarded a boat and set sail on the Yamuna in search of his dear friend. With a wail, he, too, plunged into the Yamuna, at the same spot where Hansa had jumped in.

While I was thinking about Yamuna, the Magadha army was returning to Magadha sailing on her waters, after losing both their invaluable war-expert commanders, and completely losing the battle after full twenty-seven days.

In this very first fierce attack of the Magadhas which lasted for twenty-seven days, our farmlands suffered the most. During the war, lakhs of cavalrymen, thousands of elephant troops and innumerable soldiers ran over our farms.

The battle had destroyed our crops and we realised that the food we now had would barely last a year. Dada and I, along with the other youth, decided to dig an extended channel to lead the Yamuna's waters to our farmland.

By the evening of the same day, we had successfully channelled the life-sustaining waters of the Yamuna towards our farmland.

Dada carried his huge plough on his shoulders and placed it in a large farm. Then he harnessed it to the muscular shoulders of two big bulls with elegant horns. I nudged one of the bulls by poking him with the whip in my hand. My association with animals and the whip began that day. I said to Dada cheerfully, 'From now on, I am going to call you "Haladhara".'

The Yadavas of the Shursena kingdom had barely settled. Yet, they had to face Magadha's attacks four times in four years.

Every time we fought them off with determination. During this time, Dada was blessed with two brothers. Dhakali gave birth to two sons. In a ceremonial function, they were named Gada and Sarana. Gada was two years older than Sarana. Dada himself had named him Gada, after his favourite weapon *gadaa*, the mace.

King Drupada of Panchala sent us information that was of utmost significance. Drupada was a close friend of Vasudevababa. He had highly commended Acharya Sandipani from Avanti, who used to visit his kingdom from time to time.

Sandipani. A great sage of Varanasi, born in the Kashyapa lineage, he had established many ashramas of his own throughout Aaryavarta. Chosen unanimously by Vasudevababa, Maharaja Ugrasena and Gargamuni, he was Balaramadada's and my prospective mentor – Gurudeva Sandipani.

Word was that somewhere far away in the south, he had established an ashrama named 'Ankapada' in the forests of Avanti. 'Anka' means 'to reach'. 'Pada' means 'sublime feet that are worthy of worship'. 'Ankapada' means 'a place to reach the honourable Acharya's sublime feet'. The name was so relevant that I liked it the moment I heard it. When I heard the acharya's name, I had the same inexplicable feeling that I had when I first met Uddhava. His name had a rich rhythm to it – San-di-pa-ni!

The royal council of Mathura, our family heads, and Gargamuni took a decision for the Shursena kingdom – we were to leave for the acharya's ashrama, accompanied by Uddhava. Daruka, the royal charioteer, was to see us safely there.

The auspicious day recommended by Gargamuni for our departure to Avanti dawned. Daruka brought a chariot with four hefty horses of different colours. I said to him, 'Daruka, the horse is my favourite animal. I love its speed, competing with the wind. I have seen you, many times tackling four, even seven horses easily. That is why I like you as much as the horses. Would you like to be my attendant? And for the rest of my life, if required?'

Without a word, he sat down on his knees and placed his head directly on my feet. Instantly pulling him up to my chest, I held him in a deep embrace, just like I had held Uddhava. Dada and I took the blessings of all elders and left for Ankapada, along with Uddhava. The moment we mounted the chariot, I whispered in Daruka's ear, 'Dear friend, I liked all your horses, but not their different colours. When you come again to fetch me after the completion of my education in the ashrama, bring a chariot harnessed with four well-built, tall and well-behaved snow-white horses from different regions. Snow-white and only four horses. Will you remember?'

This was the first long journey of my life. Crossing many rivers in spacious boats, we continued our journey along with Daruka's chariot. I was feasting my eyes on the beautiful nature around us. After a full month, we reached the forest of Avanti – dense, rich with fauna, resonating with the sounds of various animals and birds.

Crossing many big and small rivers, we finally reached the shores of the famous river, Kshipra. 'Kshipra' means 'unobstructed', 'expeditious'. One more precious memory that dwells in my heart. Expansive and wide, she was filled with crystal-clear waters. Compared to the Yamuna, she was small and narrow. I had noted a specific peculiarity about this forest of Avanti – it was full of many big and small lakes along the Kshipra. These lakes were always full of blue, red ochre, white and blood-red lotuses. What a magnificent and captivating sight!

We crossed the Kshipra along with the chariot in an enormous boat. And finally sighted the gigantic wooden fence around the Ankapada ashrama of Acharya Sandipani. We bade farewell to Daruka and walked barefoot to the ashrama. Dawn had just broken and the ashrama was glistening in the golden rays of the morning sun. Before entering the ashrama, the three of us touched the ground with our hands and placed them on our forehead in reverence.

The two disciples sent by the acharya welcomed us warmly. I glanced around, taking in the surroundings of the ashrama. One could see rows of huts all around on the inside. The row near the fence was for former senior disciples who were always in the service of the guru. The middle row was for pupils of the ashrama. These were occupied by hundreds of pupils from kingdoms all over the world. The last row was for assistant educators, who had expertise in various disciplines. The huts of young pupils were in the centre of the ashrama so that the elders could keep a watchful eye on them.

The towering and spacious 'Acharya kuti', the acharya's cottage, was also located in the centre with a triangular white pennant fluttering on top. A thatched storehouse with multiple rooms was located on the left of the main cottage. All foodgrains, clothes, weaponry, medicinal herbs, wooden logs and other ashrama necessities were stored there. The extended corrals for the ashrama cows were located on the right.

As I walked along with Dada, I wondered about the acharya's appearance and how he would treat us.

The acharya was sitting on a wide, elevated seat in the centre of the cottage on a deerskin mat placed atop a grass rug. He was in deep meditation – his right hand holding the rosary was in the air, his wrist resting on the meditation staff. Mesmerised, we kept staring at him. So effulgent, pious and serene his meditating face looked.

So far, I had experienced that many people were attracted to me by some force. However, that day the exact opposite had happened. I moved towards him, bowed down and touched his right foot with my head. He felt my touch and said, his eyes still closed, 'Come, Yadava prince Srikrishna, the saviour of Vrishnis and Andhakas, I have been waiting for you since long. Welcome.' He opened his eyes to look at me. We gazed at each other for the first time, and instantly knew that we had known each other for ages. I smiled. He reciprocated with a smile and said, 'Enough of the prostrations. Now sit.'

Balaramadada and Uddhava, too, prostrated.

The acharya spoke slowly, his voice just as sweet, full of soul and heavenly as the flute that I had entrusted to Radha when I left Gokul.

He said, 'Balarama, Srikrishna, Uddhava, remove your royal attire and wear the ashrama robes. Keep in mind that your life as an ashrama disciple will begin from tomorrow. This is the most significant phase in the yajna of life – 'Bhramacharyashram', or bachelorhood.

'It will last exactly sixty-four days. Others may find it to be insufficient, but you have already been born with such virtues that I feel it will perfectly suffice you. You will not be treated as the royal princes here. Hundreds of students like you are gaining knowledge here. For me, you are simply a disciple of the ashrama just like my own son.'

He closed his eyes for a moment. I could clearly see an inexplicable pain briefly flashing on his face.

He continued, 'You will learn all aspects of life here from the Vedas, the holy scriptures, to Vaadas, the debates. Many expert and experienced acharyas from various cities have volunteered to offer their guidance; they are all as knowledgeable as me. Get yourself acquainted with the daily routine of the ashrama life. You may leave now.' Acharya Sandipani closed his eyes and re-entered the calm meditative state.

On the first night, while sleeping on the dry grass bed, reminscing about everyone back at Gokul and Mathura, I feel asleep.

The ashrama woke up to the sound of conch shells being blown by a few disciples. We could hear the cows in their corrals as they moved around, the bells around their necks making jingling sounds. The rhythmic intonations of the morning prayers could be heard at a distance.

I got up and sat on the grass rug. Holding both palms in front of me, I looked at them for a moment. It was still dark as I stepped out. Dada, Uddhava and I left together for the river Kshipra. The waters were warm. We finished our ablutions and returned to the ashrama.

After drinking freshly drawn warm milk, it was time for the acharya's discourse, which was announced by a unique tune of a conch.

It was getting brighter now as we all moved towards the cottage

We were all ears now, our eyes focused on his face. Acharya Sandipani glanced affectionately at all of us and gave a gentle, sweet smile. I was reminded of the newly blossomed Brahmakamala buds on Manasa Sarovar on an early autumn morning. Then, in his deep, melodious voice, he started talking slowly.

'Dear disciples of the ashrama, there are fourteen vidyas that each one of you is required to be proficient in. I am going to talk about them in detail today. Listen carefully.' The entire cottage fell silent.

'The four Vedas – Rigveda, Samaveda, Yajurveda and Atharvaveda – are considered fundamental, independent vidyas. The first is the Rigveda, replete with praises of Usha and Varuna, in incredibly rich lyrical hymns. The second is Yajurveda, composed with hymns of absolute surrender to the Supreme Soul. It has two clear branches – Shukla Yajurveda and Krishna Yajurveda. The third is Samaveda, adorned with comprehensive melodies of musical notes. The fourth is Atharvaveda, manifested in effective hymns of prayers for the destruction of the enemy and self-protection.

They also contain an ardent call of the soul, to ward off approaching calamities. The Vedas have six sub-sections. The first is 'Shiksha'. It is the study of flawless and melodious pronunciations of the words of the Vedas. The strength of the Vedas lies in the clear pronunciation of words, called Vanis, which are categorised into four types – Vaikhari, Madhyama, Pashyanti and Paraa.

Vaikhari is the simplest form of Vani, used regularly and inadvertently in the daily routine.

Madhyama is the second Vani that comes from the heart after proper deliberation. The third Vani is Pashyanti, which originates from the navel, and is characterised by love and a variety of emotions. The Paraa originates from the core of the being, the Mooladhar chakra. Only the power of self-realisation after penance and introspection gives birth to Paraa. The acharya paused for a moment as he looked at his pupils. He focused his eyes on me and asked, 'Srikrishna, which of the four Vanis do you like?'

I thought for a moment and answered, 'I would like all four. But isn't there a fifth Vani that exists beyond these, Acharya?' I questioned with a smile.

'No, at least according to the scriptures there are only these four.' The acharya smiled deliberately, a mysteriously sweet, soft smile. Then we kept on staring at each other. We had recognised the silent Vani hidden behind our exchange. It was the speech of the supreme soul, the speech of pure love that could not be contained within any part of the physical body. It had neither beginning nor end.

'The second sub-section of the Vedas is "Chhanda"', the acharya continued, 'Chhanda is the study of the principles of musical notes, rhythm and tempo.' The acharya was completely absorbed in the discourse now.

'The third sub-section is "Vyakarana", or grammar. It contains the complete set of linguistic rules for perfect comprehension.

'The Vedas are spontaneous inspirations – hence, they are open to various interpretations. The fourth sub-section is "Nirukta", or the lucid yet relevant elucidation of the Vedas.

'The fifth sub-section "Jyotish", or astrology, discusses the measurement of time, the planets, the constellations and palmistry.

'The sixth sub-section is "Kalpa", in which the religious rites and rituals are discussed thoroughly. Unimaginable pomp and show can infiltrate "Kalpa" any time. One should be very cautious about this, as this can very easily transform into superstition. The one who abolishes such superstitions with determined prowess proves to be a "Yugapurusha", a prophet, and "Yogayogeshwara", the greatest ascetic of all. The one who descends to rescue mankind is called the "Avatar", an incarnation. The one who descends to rescue superstitious people around him from ignorance befits to be a prophet, the greatest ascetic, an epochmaker.' The acharya paused for a moment. Looking at me, he asked pointedly, 'Did you understand, Srikrishna?'

'I clearly understood the part about how religious pretensions transform into superstitions, but Acharya, I did not quite get what you were talking about the Avatar, the incarnation.'

'Did not get it? That's okay. You will, at the right time!' We both laughed so loudly that tears filled the acharya's eyes. Baffled, and wonder-struck, all the pupils kept staring at us. Regaining his compsure, the acharya continued, 'The remaining four vidyas are – Mimansa, Tarka, Puranas and Dharma. Mimansa means critical investigation of a topic of discussion from all angles, analysing and examining it as thoroughly and carefully as possible. There are two types of Mimansa, one is Purva and the other is Uttara. Tarkavidya is the science of logic and reasoning.

'The next vidya is the Mahapuranas. The first amongst these is the Brahmapurana and the last one is the Brahmandpurana. Brahma, Padma, Vishnu, Shiva, Bhagvata, Narada, Markandeya and Agni are the major Mahapuranas. Shivapurana is also known as Vayupurana. Along with these, including the Bhavishya, Brahmavaivarta, Linga, Varaha, Skanda, Vamana, Kurma, Matsya, Garuda and Brahmanda, there are a total of eighteen Mahapuranas. Each one deals with a different aspect of life.

'But the Puranas carry more description of the rituals rather than meaningful discourse. That is why they have remained away from the majority of the populace.

'The last and the most significant vidya is called "Dharma". Try to understand and comprehend its meaning thoroughly, and ponder over it – contemplate about it. The wise men of the society have considered four types of Purusharthas to be the founding pillars. They are: Dharma-Duty, Artha-Wealth, Kama-Desire and Moksha-Salvation. Dharma is that which inculcates the Sanskaras in the living being for its complete development.

'Never forget, to practise true Dharma in daily life, all four Purusharthas are indispensable. Dharma does not mean performing rituals. Dharma, too, can sometimes experience decay. Dharma which is about to perish due to the predominance of Adharma – irreligiosity – needs to be revived with sheer determination.

'It is the foremost duty of the Kshatriyas to protect Dharma. To fulfil that duty, in my opinion, the most important vidya is "Yuddhavidya" – the art of warfare. This vidya has two main divisions: Shastra and Astra. Among the Astras, Varuna, Vayu, Agni, Pashupata, Parjanya, Praswapa, Narayana and Brahmastra are the major astras. I will teach you the transmission of astras with the recitation of their mantras and their obstruction too. The science of archery is also called "Dhanurvidya". Some learned critics have regarded it as one of the Vedas, considering the tremendous velocity and exactness involved in it. Remember that Dhanurvidya is called the fifth Veda. Dhanurveda has four sub-sections: Diksha, Sangraha, Siddhi and Prayoga.

'Diksha is paying respects to the bow before using it by incanting a mantra. "Sangraha" means touching the arrow to the forehead, remembering the guru and, with closed eyes, silently intoning the mantra of launching the arrow and mounting the arrow on the bowstring. 'Siddhi' is the yoga part of it. In the shooting posture, one should breathe in a chestful of air, assessing the direction of the flowing wind.

'"Prayoga" is the actual act of shooting the arrow. Once the archer is ready, the arrow should be shot instantly to hit the target unerringly. Exhaling the air, the chest should be emptied.'

His solemn words intensified the silence in the cottage. 'Just as there are fourteen vidyas, there are sixty-four kalaas (fine arts) that enhance the beauty of life in all aspects and make it complete. Music is the first and foremost of all art forms.

Why is music the most significant among the fine arts? Because it can directly touch the heart of the audience without the aid of an agent.

Yet, music is not regarded as a vidya. Do not forget that it has been regarded as a kalaa, an art form.'

This was just a small glimpse of the depth of knowledge that the acharya possessed. 'The world is what is visible to our sight. What is beyond the world is the infinite universe. Be cautious, understand the clear difference between the Aakash–Sky and Avakash–Space. The sky is clearly visible to us as a blue expanse. Space exists beyond it. Endless and limitless, it is black – the colour of Krishna! Balarama, do you understand?' he suddenly asked Dada. Dada instantly replied, 'That which is Krishna is infinite and endless!' Both the acharya and I looked at him and smiled at the implied meaning of his answer. But his face was just as innocent and curious as before.

The acharya continued, 'To comprehend the truth of life duly, you must also clearly understand one more concept – the concept of "kala", or time. We measure time in the units of day, night, month, year, a tapa and a yuga. A tapa is a period of twelve years. A yuga consists of a thousand tapas. A single day of Brahma consists of a thousand yugas like this. Many such days of Brahma make a "kalpa". In short, a "kalpa" is made up of four-hundred-thirty-two million years!'

Leaving all disciples baffled by the complicated calculations involved in time measurements, the acharya took a breather and smiled to himself. He posed a question and answering it himself, said, 'So is it possible for anybody, any time to measure limitless time in its totality? No. Therefore, time is infinite. It has neither beginning nor end. Similarly, life is also limitless, unending and eternal. The one who knows this truth is a true visionary. And the one who proclaims with full responsibility that "I am kala myself" and "I am life itself" is the greatest visionary of all times. Who knows, maybe such a visionary exists amongst you.'

Suddenly, the acharya asked, in a voice loud and clear, 'Srikrishna, what do you say?'

Looking at me, he gave a meaningful smile. I silently responded with a smile that reflected his. The other pupils looked askance once more.

Changing the topic completely, the acharya said, 'The ego is that which encumbers the total spiritual progress of one's soul. It is multifarious and multifaceted. The pride of one's own authority, power, wealth, beauty and fame never lets a person move forward towards progress.

'Balarama, could you tell us which is the most dangerous pride of all?' Dada, in a dilemma for a brief moment, answered, 'The pride of power, Acharya!'

'No Balarama, the pride of knowledge! The pride of the knowledge of spiritual realisation is the most dangerous of all. A wise, learned person, who is a realised soul, should always be humble like a mango tree bent with the weight of its fruit. Only then will the gold of knowledge obtain the heavenly aroma of the ultimate truth.

'Remember that an animate being always exists in three dimensions – length, width, and height or depth. The one who comprehends and acknowledges the fourth dimension of unending time becomes the greatest of mankind – the Supreme Man – "Purushottama". Some other dimensions also exist. I will share those with you later. *Arpanam astu*.' Closing his eyes, he went into a meditative trance, signalling the end of the class.

Dada, Uddhava and I were housed in a single hut. Within a few days, one more friend joined us – Sudama from Saurashtra. Sudama's arrival transformed our trio into a quartet.

Sudama was a skinny, hard-working, fair-skinned, simple and innocent son of a Brahmin. Based on experience, I had realised that it was not possible to explain in words how and why pure friendship sprouts, grows and strengthens. It is a bond of hearts connected through many lives. One should not try to find its source and one should not imagine its end. It is purely meant to be experienced.

Sudama, who always spoke with spontaneous affection, became a dear friend of ours. We were not four individuals but a quadrangular entity.

The acharya once touched upon the subject of other fine arts. Glancing affectionately at our eager and curious faces, in a melodious, rhythmic voice, he said, 'My dear pupils, the second most significant fine art after music is Aalekha. Aalekha means sahitya – literature, and the art of painting. All the Vedas that I spoke about are examples of ageless and imperishable sahitya. An artist's pure, innocent and capable mind is indispensable for the creation of any art form, whether it is music, literature, a picture or any of the other sixty-four arts. Such a sound mind can only reside in a sound body. Therefore, in the beginning itself, the creators of the Vedas have deemed the body a divine temple of "Vishwadeva". No other vidya except yoga can offer humanity the divine ornament of a healthy body. 'I consider yoga the fifteenth vidya.'

The acharya deliberated on something in his mind and stopped for a moment. Fixing his eyes on me, he ordered in a commanding voice, 'Srikrishna. Get up from your seat, come and sit right in front of me, along with your Dada, Uddhava and Sudama.' We obediently got up and promptly took a seat in front of him. Closing his eyes, he began to chant the Guruvandana, the prayer for the guru, in his deep voice.

'Aum Guru Brahma, Guru Vishnu...' A thought flashed instantly in my mind, 'Really, who could be the acharya of our acharya?'

'Srikrishna...Balarama, Uddhava, Sudama, and all. Now listen very carefully to what "Sankhyayoga" is. It is the most important yoga of life.

'The core, "Mulkanda", of a human being is located near the navel. From the core, seventy-two thousand "nadis" originate and are spread systematically throughout the body. There are six chakras, or vortices of energy, located in the human body. The scarlet-coloured divine Shakti called "Kundalini" is seated firmly facing down, coiled like a serpent in the Muladhara chakra located in the region of the waist.

'There are ten major nadis above and ten below it. Two nadis each above and below run horizontally too. The prana shakti, or vital air, consistently flows through these twenty-four major and minor nadis, in the form of blood.

'The ten major nadis that circulate blood day in and day out are the most important ones. Those are – Ida, Pingala, Sushumna, Gandhari, Hastijiwha, Pusha, Yashswini, Alambusha, Kuhu and Shankhini. Among these, the Ida, the Pingala and the Sushumna are the most significant.

'Ida is the major nadi that is continuously functional and carries many minor veins that run through the left side of the body. The Pingala nadi is functional in the same manner on the right side of the body. The Sushumna nadi is constantly active, running between the Ida and the Pingala, through the spinal cord. The sacred, divine Kundalini force sits face down in the Muladhara chakra at the base of the Sushumna nadi. Very few people realise its existence and if at all they do, it is only due to their spiritual virtuousness. A few of them have the earnest urge to wake her up. A limited number succeed in actually doing so, and only a single Supreme Being, a Yogayogeshwara, with prophetic vision, can actually make it dance at his fingertips with sheer willpower. The science defining the rules for awakening the divine Kundalini is called the "Sankhyayoga". This yoga contains eight stages – Yama, Niyama, Pratyahara, Aasana, Pranayama, Dhyana, Dharana and Samadhi.

'The Sankhyayoga is the most difficult of the scriptures to comprehend, and even harder to practise. A true yogi, however, should never make use of such powers, as it ultimately leads to the ruin of spiritual power.

'The state of Samadhi is said to be achieved when the being ultimately unites with the infinite, endless Paramatma, through the potency of the awakened Kundalini. The one who performs any small or big tasks while in the state of Samadhi is known as "Yogeshwar".

'A being that feels content with the state of Samadhi and leaves the body voluntarily attains moksha, the final salvation. The one who, without any expectation of attaining such moksha, lives his life for the sake of pure love and pure karma; who easily leaves the body simply like a fruit separating from its stem and dropping down from a tree, is called "Yogayogeshwara"! The principles of life that he utters casually prove to be the guidelines for humanity for ages. As these principles are carried forward from age (Yuga) to age, the One who is an authority on them is called "Yugandhar", an epochmaker.'

The acharya, whose eyes had closed while sharing information about Sankhyayoga, opened them now and looked directly at me. For a long time, he silently and steadily kept staring at me. Then throwing a glance around, that was either intended for all or none, he said, 'Who knows, such a visionary, epoch-maker 'Yogayogeshwara' might exist amongst you pupils.' By now, I had gotten used to his mysterious statements, like this one.

We learnt a great variety of things in sixty-four days, the period meant for us to acquire knowledge. We learnt so many subjects in such minute detail. And then the day dawned – the day that I could never forget in my whole life – the day of Gurudakshina, time to pay remuneration to our guru.

The acharya woke up much before sunrise that day. He bathed in the Kshipra, performed morning rituals and returned to his cottage. He sat on the deerskin and started meditating to offer blessings to all pupils for their future life. He had already transcended his body.

It was still dark when we woke up. As we walked towards the river, I noticed Sudama was quiet. I asked Uddhava, 'Udho brother, what was your favourite topic in the teachings of Acharya? Astravidya, Shastravidya or the sixty-four fine arts?'

'What I liked most, Dada, is the unforgettable, profound philosophy of life that Acharya shared with us. I feel that for the Gurudakshina, I should stay right here in the ashrama at the feet of Acharya and keep serving him for the rest of my life instead of returning home.' Uddhava had transformed completely now. Smiling, I patted his shoulder while walking.

I asked Dada, 'Balaramadada, what touched you the most in the company of Acharya?' His chest puffed up with pride as he instantly answered, 'I liked Acharya's teaching of the Yuddhakala, warfare, the most. Here, I understood in greater depth the wrestling that we had learnt from Kelinandakaka.'

Finally, I asked Sudama, 'Sudama, dear friend, from Acharya's teachings, what made the most impact on you?' He did not hear my question at all. He was in a totally different mood, thinking or worrying about something. Shaking him vigorously, I asked, 'Where are you lost, Sudama? I am asking you, what did you like the most from Acharya's teachings?'

He answered stutteringly, 'I…I liked his teachings about the ideal family life.'

By this time, our quartet had reached the big Neel Sarovar. All four of us entered the lake. The water was warmer than usual. Dada asked with the authority of an elder brother, 'How come you brought us here today instead of going to the Kshipra? Your actions are always puzzling.'

'It will be crowded, with all the pupils bathing in the Kshipra today, Dada. Besides, there are no lotus flowers in the Kshipra like the ones in this lake. I am thinking of taking some of these for Gurudeva.'

Far away in the east, the sun ascended through the forest of Avanti. The forest was now awake to the sound of birds.

Near the 'Kashyapa' gate, the main gate of the ashrama on the eastern side, many royal chariots were already waiting in line.

The sun was fully visible now. I could see Dada, Uddhava and Sudama getting into the grassy meadow beside the lake, tired of swimming.

I kept swimming for a long time, intentionally. It was my last day in the forest of Avanti. In my mind, I was constantly going through acharya's teachings, while my arms were moving through the water.

The sun was quite high in the sky now. 'Srikrishna, Dada, dear friend, come out now.' I could clearly hear shouts coming from the meadows on the shore. I circled the lake one last time while plucking off as many blue lotuses as I could, some of them still buds and others partially blossomed. Holding a big bunch of those under my arms, I came out of the lake. Pulling out the peel of one lotus stem up to the petals with my nail, I fastened it tightly around the bunch, and handed it to Sudama.

Meanwhile, Dada and Uddhava were dressed in their royal attire and Sudama had put on his Brahmin dress – an ear cap, a long robe and a dhoti with a red border. Sitting in the meadows, I dried my body thoroughly in the sun. The moment I opened my cane basket, I was amazed at acharya's ingenious foresight. There it was, resting on top of everything – the fragrant Vaijayanti garland, freshly woven with luscious white flowers. A mere look at it brought back a myriad of expressions of Radha, my beloved soulmate in Gokul.

Uddhava gently picked it up and handed it to me. I filled my chest with its fragrance, and tenderly placed it on the green meadows. I tied the shining, bright, soft yellow dhoti around my waist and wrapped a blue silk shawl over it. Then, I wore the ornaments on my arms and hands, and put the pearl necklaces around my neck. Dada came forward and put the decorated peacock-feathered golden crown glistening in the sun on my thick, black, curly hair.

Finally, Uddhava picked up the freshly woven Vaijayanti garland resting on the grass and put it around my neck. At first, the large, intense, clear eyes of my ruddy-complexioned, moon-faced dear friend Uddhava widened, and in amazement he went back a couple of steps. Smitten, he simply kept staring at me.

Then, with an ebullient heart, he spoke rapidly, 'Dada…dear Dada. I cannot take my eyes off you today. It feels like at this moment, even the sun in the sky must be blushing, looking at the splendour of a hundred suns reflecting from your beautiful face. I must drive away the effects of any evil eye. Wait a moment.' He uttered a chant to ward off any evil eye. I instantly laughed at the innocence of his actions.

As we started walking towards acharya's cottage to offer the Gurudakshina, I let Dada and Uddhava go ahead. Lingering behind with Sudama, I affectionately patted his shoulders and asked, 'Dear Sudamana, I have been watching you since early morning. Why do you look so gloomy today? Why are you so quiet?' He stopped and said, 'Friend, I find myself in a quandary today. My poor parents from Saurashtra have not sent any Gurudakshina for acharya. They cannot afford it. What should I offer to acharya ?' Suddenly he stopped walking and in a flash, his face, as fair as a Prajakta flower, darkened with unbearable agony.

'Is that all? Rest assured, Sudamana. I did not give you that bunch of blue lotuses without reason. Have I ever done that before? Offer these flowers at the feet of acharya with full devotion and ask for his blessings.'

Sudama stopped and looked at me. His sadness had vanished.

The sun was almost overhead when we reached acharya's cottage. All other pupils had offered their Gurudakshina and were already on their way home with acharya's blessings. Acharya's cottage was remarkably silent now.

The four of us stood in front of acharya. On my cue, Dada and then Uddhava moved forward. Dada kneeled and touched his head to acharya's feet. As he was about to speak, acharya spoke with his eyes closed, in a meditative trance, 'You are Balarama, the prince of Yadavas!'

Dada was astonished to see that acharya had recognised him with his closed eyes. He bowed down and said humbly, 'Yes, acharya, I am Balarama. My baba, Vasudeva, and Maharaja Ugrasena of Mathura have sent milch cows and a troop of horses, along with ornaments as the Gurudakshina. I have already submitted those in the ashrama store. Please offer me your blessings.'

It felt like acharya smiled slightly. He kept his hand on Dada's head and, with eyes still closed, said, 'Your whole life will be prosperous. The whole world will sing your praises as the 'Elder'. But remember one thing, try to restrain the short temper that overpowers your mind at times. May all your wishes be fulfilled.'

Uddhava moved forward next. He kneeled and touched his head to acharya's feet and remained in the same position.

With his eyes still closed, unmistakably recognising his touch, Acharya said, 'You are Uddhava, son of Devabhaga and Kansaa of Mathura.'

'Yes acharya, it is me, Uddhava.' Big, innocent-eyed, round-faced, fair Uddhava said with utmost humility, 'Acharya, I have deposited clothes in the ashrama store for all the teachers, and foodgrains. Please oblige me with your auspicious blessings for my life's journey.'

Acharya raised his hand and, in a very deep, unique tone, said, 'Uddhava, you are a true devotee. Only you are capable of being a beloved devotee of a visionary, an epoch-maker. You will serve one such loving, visionary yogi. The world will recognise you as his confidant. In your later life, you will have to perform an unpleasant duty, for which you will have to harden your heart. Farewell, son, you have my full blessings.' He put his hand on Uddhava's head.

Only the two of us were left now – Sudama and me. I gestured with my eyes. Moving forward with utmost humility, Sudama put the bunch of blue lotuses at acharya's feet and put his head on the bunch of flowers. He instantly choked, and started weeping. It was the heart-wrenching awareness of his poverty.

His guru was present in front of him, in person, the all-knowing, omniscient guru. He half opened his eyes. Still in a meditative trance, acharya consoled Sudama, patted him with the words, 'You are Sudamana. You are called "Kuchaila" due to the worn-out garments that you wear. But, in fact, you are "Suchail", as your innocent, loving soul is dressed up in the unique outfit of virtues from your previous deeds. The treasure of divine friendship that you possess is one of a kind. You will be recognised in the whole world for that unique friendship. Always cherish that treasure. You have my blessings.'

The sun was directly overhead as I moved forward – as the very last disciple of Acharya Sandipani – as the Srikrishna of the Yadavas. I prostrated in front of him. Without opening his eyes, acharya said with a smile, 'Srikrishna, the most auspicious fruit of the virtuous deeds of "Vrushnis" and "Andhakas" for ages together. The eighth-born of Vasudeva and Devakidevi. The protector of the gopas of Gokul! My most esteemed disciple in the Ankapada ashrama, Srikrishna!' With the touch of my hands, his fish-shaped meditative eyes opened gradually. I stood in front of him with humility. He glanced deep in my eyes. It was a very distinctive look – even I had never experienced it before. He smiled gently.

'Acharya, each and every disciple has offered something or the other as Gurudakshina at your feet and obtained your blessings. But kindly forgive me, for I have absolutely nothing suitable at this moment to offer you as Gurudakshina.' I smiled. My smile must have been different, for acharya momentarily tried to trace it and reciprocated with the same kind of smile. Then he spoke in his usual serene voice, 'I do not need Gurudakshina from you anyway.' He laughed like an innocent child and said, 'You actually lived in my ashrama as a disciple for so many days. What could be better Gurudakshina in this ephemeral world?' He smiled again, like a newborn, an innocent infant. A smile that was a reflection of his spread on my face.

Gazing into my eyes, he conferred an unknown spiritual energy upon me. For a long time, we both were lost in a reverie. Only I know how much and what all I gained as his blessings, from this divine transfer of energy by Gurudeva Sandipani.

He exclaimed, 'My beloved, my best ever disciple – your life will always be prosperous. Oh Yadunandana, visit the sacred city of Prayaga at least once in your future life, whenever possible, and visit Sage Angirasa. Oh, son of Nanda, obtain the knowledge of Brahma from him.

'Just as his name implies, he has undergone severe penance. He is the innate, devout worshipper of Agni, the apt heir of the original Angirasa. Do not forget that his disposition is just like fire. If you stay within your limits, he will be warm enough, but if you transgress, he will be as scorching as fire itself. He will stay in Prayaga only for a short time. After that, he will travel towards Mount Raivataka as a preacher of the religious sect that attracts him of late, to propagate it and spread the same around the world.

'You will come to know of your relationship with him at a proper time. Farewell, Srikrishna. Give him my regards when you visit him.

And accept this gift of mine to you with love, and cherish it always like the "Vaijayanti".'

Since early morning, he had, very carefully, placed a crimson, fully blossomed lotus in his waterpot. It was charmed with a divine mantra. He handed it to me with love, and I accepted it with pure devotion, touching it to my forehead.

Acharya's wife would rarely come out, as she would always be engaged in household chores. But that day, she was present. I bowed down to her, along with the others. She offered blessings from the bottom of her heart and stood still like a statue. The tears streaming down her face instantly revealed the root of her silent agony. Offering solace to her, I determinedly said, 'Oh ashrama mata, I will liberate your dear son, Dutta, from the clutches of Shankhasura and bring him back to you. Oh Mata, this is my promise to you. I have already offered my Gurudakshina to acharya, and he has also given me his blessings. Please consider the liberation of Dutta as my Gurudakshina to you, and give me your blessings to successfully overcome conflicts in life.'

The expression in the eyes of our ashrama mata changed instantly. She wiped her tears and put her hands on my head affectionately.

We retreated respectfully without turning our backs to Acharya and his wife, and slowly stepped out of the cottage.

Sudama was not to be seen anywhere. Dada, Uddhava and I went to the main entrance of the ashrama. Daruka was standing in front of the gate. He scurried forward to touch my feet. I moved forward, and before he could bend down, stopped him halfway and held him in a tight embrace. His face shone brightly. I whispered in his ear, 'Daruka, henceforth you will not be my charioteer or my attendant. You will be my friend, my escort, who will accompany me in all walks of life. I am going to steer the chariot today – not you!'

The three of us followed him to the royal chariot. The bedecked chariot looked exceptionally attractive. It was spacious enough to easily accommodate a number of people, along with their weapons. Four sturdy waist-high spoked wheels maintained its equilibrium. A sturdy yoke made of strong, painted Kikar wood, decorated with engravings, was attached to it. Daruka had harnessed four snow-white, tall, hefty horses to the yoke. On the very first glance, they captured my heart.

The moment I saw them, I was enamoured. Walking briskly, I moved closer to the agile animals. Acharya's words echoed in my ears, 'The horse that outstrips the wind is the first loyal friend of mankind. When a horse stands on three legs and leaves the fourth one hanging in the air, he becomes useless for running. An understanding of the touch and the words of his master that a horse has is sometimes missing even in human beings.'

I lovingly patted the nape of the horse standing in front of me. He swished his tail in excitement, pricked his ears and neighed with joy.

I asked Daruka, 'Where did you obtain such purebreeds from?'

He answered with a smile, 'I searched the entire region of Panchanada to obtain this breed. He is from the valleys rich with meadows between the rivers Chandrabhaga and Iravati. As hefty as he is, he also runs quite swiftly, and is very obedient too?

'Well done, Daruka. I would like to call him "Shaibya". What do you think of the name?'

'How can he disapprove of the name given by you?' Balaramadada said with a smile and patted the horse.

I went to the next horse. I momentarily ruffled his thick mane and just as I used to put my arms around Uddhava or Sudama's neck, I put my hands around his thick, flexible and muscular neck.

Uddhava said, 'Dada, you suggest a suitable name for this horse too.' I laughed and looking at his ruddy, sincere face, said, 'Uddhava, my action has already suggested a name for him. He is the "Sugriva" of our chariot!'

Sugriva – the one with the beautiful neck. Uddhava simply kept staring at the Vaijayanti garland around my neck and Sugriva's white neck with his beautiful full mane, and said, 'Dada, I cannot tell if the white Vaijayanti garland on your bluish body looks more beautiful or your bluish hand resting on the white mane of Sugriva's thick neck.'

'Master, I have brought this thick-necked, cautious horse from the well-known country of Kambhoja.' Daruka humbly provided further information.

The three of us moved to the next horse. He snorted a bit. He was pure white.

'Master, this horse has been brought from the faraway country of Gandhara. For that sole purpose, I went to Pushkalavati, its capital,' Daruka stated.

'We should call him "Balahaka". Balahaka means a flying, white crane,' I suggested. I was now inspecting the last horse. All the four horses were white, but this one was whiter than the others. His colour was like the frothy snow-white water of a river cascading off the Himalayas. Gently patting his snout, I said to Daruka, 'Surely you must have brought this horse from somewhere in the Himalayas.'

'That is right! I had to go far away to Pragjyotishapura of the Kamarupa kingdom,' Daruka said with a smile.

'We should call this one nothing else but 'Meghapushp'. He looks like the flower of a snow-white cloud just touching the Himalayas. Does he not? Garuda, the king of birds is the emblem of the Yadavas' zeal for conquest. Spreading his wide, robust wings, he soars high in the sky. The pennant on this chariot commemorates Garuda, the king of birds. I humbly pay obeisance to Acharya Sandipani at this moment, and in front of my dear ones, I announce the formal name of this royal chariot – Garudadhwaja.' Dada, Uddhava and Daruka unanimously cheered, 'Beautiful! Extraordinary! Garudadhwaja, Garudadhwaja!'

'All of you get into the chariot,' I said, jumping into the charioteer's seat.

As I turned to take a final look at the ashrama, I was startled to see a thin lone figure in white, approaching slowly. It was Sudama. He was walking along the fence, carrying his sack on his shoulder. His neck was hanging low as he dragged his feet.

He was to travel farther than us, to Saurashtra. But no carriage or even a person had come to fetch him. Turning to Uddhava, I said, 'Udho, get my dear friend Sudama here.' Soon, Sudama boarded the chariot.

My life's chariot had begun its non-stop pilgrimage of Karmayoga.

Daruka and I started a dialogue about Sarathyayoga charioting.

I asked him, 'Daruka, do you know how innately intelligent horses are?'

'Yes, if a horse rider gets lost in a forest, all he needs to do is let loose his horse's reins, hold his seat tightly, and his horse will unmistakably bring him back to his original place,' Daruka replied.

'Right. He closes his eyes in a desert to avoid getting the dust into his eyes; and still carries the rider on his back in the expected direction. He specifically understands even the smallest pressure of his rider's thighs, and on cue changes direction while he is running. His ears are very sharp and alert. He catches even the slightest of the wind breeze with precision. He has excellent understanding of his master's spoken language, as well as his touch.

'Daruka, a horse never sleeps sitting on the ground or lying on the floor. In fact, he never sleeps as such. He takes a nap in a standing position. A horse is the supreme yogi among animals and has the boon of innate self-control. They are my friends. I will tell you more about it at a suitable time later. Who knows, maybe in the future, I may have to demonstrate flawless charioting skills to you? What do you think, Daruka?' I steered his mind's horse somewhere deep and left it hanging there.

After travelling for a long time, we reached a fork – one of the roads led to Mathura and the other to Saurashtra. I stopped the chariot.

'Are we not going to Mathura?' Dada asked, pointing in the direction of the city.

'No, Dada. We will go to Saurashtra first, drop off Sudama and then return to Mathura.' I tugged at the reins and saw Sudama smiling broadly.

We soon reached the outskirts of Sudama's town. He looked at the familiar dusty, winding trail leading home and said, 'Milinda, dear friend, let us stop here. I will walk the remaining distance.'

The moment had come to bid farewell to a dear friend. I alighted from the chariot while Uddhava, Balaramadada and Daruka waited.

Gathering his bag at his shoulders, Sudama said, 'Dear friend, Srikrishna, remember this poor Brahmin boy. I consider that our learning together in acharya's ashrama is the result of ties in our previous birth. Could you please do me a favour?' His voice became heavy.

I grabbed both his shoulders, looked deep into his eyes and said, 'Speak, dear friend, Sudama. I will never forget you. Speak freely with me.'

He hesitated momentarily before saying, 'Srikrishna, I did not even realise how time flew in your divine company in the ashrama. To keep those memories alive in my heart, please give me something, a gift, as a symbol of our loving friendship. I will cherish it for the rest of my life.'

I smiled and said, 'Friend, did you not hear what I told Acharya on the day of Gurudakshina? I said I do not have anything suitable to offer to him as Gurudakshina, and yet, you are asking for a gift from me today as a token of our friendship. What can I give you?'

He looked at the peacock-feathered golden crown on my head, the beaded necklace around my neck, and then at the golden ornaments on my lower and upper arms.

Finally, his eyes lit up with joy as they caught sight of my sandalwood slippers. He held my wooden slippers tightly in his hands and said with ardent intensity, 'This is what I would like to have as the token of our friendship. It is perfect.' He put his head on my wooden slippers. Without a word, I pulled my feet out of the slippers while Sudama put them in his bag. He was thrilled, as if he had been offered the realm of the three worlds.

Pulling him up immediately, I held him in a deep embrace and bid him farewell. I looked at his slowly disappearing figure for a long time.

Mathura welcomed us with great pomp and vigour. The entire city was decorated with garlands and festoons. The citizens of Mathura welcomed us with lighted oil lamps and showered us with flowers. Kettledrums were being played at every intersection.

We arrived at the square in front of the royal palace of Mathura. As soon as we saw Maharaja Ugrasena, Vasudevababa and Devakimata at the landing, the three of us briskly climbed the steps towards them. We bowed down to pay obeisance to Vasudevababa first, then to Maharaja Ugrasena. Maharaja looked tired. He said, 'Gadadhara, in your absence we resolutely fought Jarasandha's army seven–eight times, forcing him to retreat. Now that you have returned, my worries are over.' While bowing down to pay respects to Devakimata, I strongly felt the absence of Rohinimata. I asked her, 'Rohinimata is not to be seen anywhere. Where is she?' Smiling broadly with pure affection, she said, 'She has just delivered a baby. You have been blessed with a sister. She resembles Balarama – rosy fair, plump and chubby.'

'Tomorrow is the naming ceremony of your sister, Srikrishna,' said Maharaja Ugrasena. We now understood the real reason for why the city had been decorated. It was because of the ceremony that I found out how big and widespread my extended family was in Mathura and the Shursena kingdom. I had a very big family here, including uncles, aunts and cousins, just like my family in Gokul.

Everyone had especially gathered here for the naming ceremony of the first girl child born to Rohinimata. Amongst those, Uddhava's father, Devabhagakaka, had already formed a special bond with us. The rest of them were going to interact with us in the future, circumstantially. I had freed some of them from Kansa's imprisonment in the first week after his execution and had offered them suitable positions according to their capabilities.

I had often wondered what these people were doing when their brother Vasudeva was in prison.

On this day of the naming ceremony of Rohinimata's blessed daughter, four significant royal envoys had arrived in Mathura from different countries with royal gifts. Vasudevababa gave us minute details while introducing them, since these royal envoys had come from the capital cities where his own sisters, our aunts, lived. One of them was from the country of Chedi. This aunt had just one son, about the same age as me, named Shishupala. My spies had gathered information that he was totally under the control of Jarasandha. Keeping in mind his rivalry with the Yadavas, Jarasandha had appointed Shishupala the commander of his army. He was going to be a big nuisance in my life. The second royal gift was from the kingdom of Avanti. This aunt of mine had two sons, Vinda and Anuvinda, who were fellow disciples in Acharya Sandipani's ashram. During that time, we had hardly got acquainted with each other.

The third royal envoy had come from the country of Karusha.

The fourth gift had not been brought by a royal envoy, but dispatched at the hands of a sage from a forest. Therefore, I carefully heard all the details provided by the sage and stored the information in my mind forever. He had arrived on behalf of Aunt Kuntidevi. Though she was the queen of Hastinapura, she had unfortunately, been, living in the Gandhamadana forest along with her husband Maharaja Pandu as a result of a curse by Kindama rishi.

Vasudevababa's eyes were filled with tears as he related her story since birth, 'Sister Kunti has three sons of her own, Yudhishthira, Bhima and

Arjuna. She also treats Nakula and Sahadeva, the twins of Maharaja Pandu's second wife Madri, as her own. Kunti and Madri's five sons are known as the "Pandavas" by the name of their father. Srikrishna, whatever misfortune your mother and I suffered during our imprisonment by Kansa is nothing compared to what Kunti has endured since birth. When you meet her, treat her with due respect.'

During the naming ceremony, the priest said, 'What should we name the baby?' Rohinimata looked straight in my direction and simply ordered, 'Srikrishna, you suggest a suitable name for your sister.'

I immediately said, 'I brought back a lot of "Bhadra", or fortune, from Acharya's ashrama. I am going to call her "Subhadra".'

That night, when I went to bed after my prayers, my mind was preoccupied with thoughts of Kunti and her sons.

But the first task Dada and I had was the liberation of our guru's son.

All the informers that minister Vipruthu had sent to various countries had returned by now. The informer returning from the west had arrived with good news. Dutta had been kidnapped and was secretly being held captive on a faraway island in the ocean, along the western coast near Mount Raivataka, also known as Mount Ujjayanta. A mammoth asura called Shankhasura was responsible for the evil act. The locals in the region also knew Shankhasura as 'Panchjana'.

I brought Balaramadada and Uddhava to the banks of the Yamuna and discussed the delicate matter with them. Shankhasura was not going to surrender easily. He had hired a small army of select asuras and lived fearlessly inside a sheltered cavern on an island. After deliberations, Dada and I decided to launch an armed attack on Shankhasura. We decided to carry small boats on the backs of elephants, in case we had to encroach islands.

I declared our decision in front of the Yadava royal council with Maharaja Ugrasena's consent. For this mission, brave and sinewy Yadava warriors were selected, including Satyaki, Uddhava, Kritavarma, Shaineya and Avagaha.

Our fourfold army consisting of elephants, cavalry, chariots and infantry marched out of the western gate of Mathura with grandeur. This was our first extended journey after we had returned from Acharya Sandipani's ashram. After travelling for two whole months, our army reached the western coast. This was the first time in my life that I was viewing an ocean.

The towering Mount Raivataka stood close by.

Our skilled informers dispersed in all directions in the ocean in small boats. By evening, they had reached the island and located Shankhasura's cave. We could not have used any war tactics after dark. Therefore, we erected small tents on the ocean shores and camped through the night.

The very next day, our warriors crossed over to Shankhasura's island. We could not estimate the size of the asura army inside the cave. We started dispatching wave after wave of armed troops.

Our soldiers kept coming back in despair after fighting and getting exhausted. Some of them lost their lives while slaughtering the enemy. Not just for a day or two, the battle continued for an entire week, with no result in sight.

On the ninth day, while I was offering oblations to the Sun god rising from the western ocean, a huge fish sprang out of the water and disappeared like silver lightning flashing momentarily. Shankhasura should be forced to come out of his cave, I thought. Sending our troops in there will not work. But if the cave is filled with torrents of smoke, he will come out like a snake slithering out of its hole. That was it. The first thing we did was withdraw our troops.

We collected wooden logs and dry leaves in a heap and ignited a huge fire right in front of the cave's entrance. This strategy worked perfectly. At first, the troops of sweaty and wounded asura warriors rushed out of the cave, screaming, wheezing and coughing due to the smoke. Following them, the mammoth Shankhasura came out roaring, with his big red eyes wide open. He was holding a sparkling, wide-blade sword in his hand. In his hairy left hand, he held a very big, pure-white shining conch. As per our plan, Dada challenged him to a wrestling bout. Both of them put their weapons down to prepare for the bout.

On the sandy beach of the island, thumping their thighs loudly, they confronted each other. Before they began, Shankhasura blew the conch in his hand very loudly and sent tremors through the surroundings.

There is a proper technique to blow a conch but he did not even know the basics and simply threw it aside. Wrestling was not merely an art or a skill for Dada now – it had become his very breath. Soon, Dada put Shankhasura to death. 'Hail Yadava warriors, Srikrishna, Balarama! Victory to them!' The slogans of our warriors matched the roar of the ocean.

I moved forward and bending down, gently picked up Shankhasura's pure-white, beautiful and auspicious conch, which he had treasured in his life but had thrown away casually in the sand.

It possessed precisely every quality of an auspicious conch. Not merely a conch, it was an invaluable jewel. An unparalleled truth. Dada, Uddhava, Daruka and Satyaki had already gathered around me in curiosity. The sun was setting on the western ocean.

Along with the others, I entered the foamy waters of the roaring western ocean till they reached my knees. My heart was filled with an indomitable, unnamed self-confidence. Dada, Uddhava, Satyaki, Vipruthu and Daruka – everybody was offering oblations to the setting sun with the water of the ocean itself. Reading my mind, dear Uddhava poured a trickle of ocean water on the conch. I blew the divine conch with my entire being. Instantly, each and every pore on my skin experienced goosebumps. Fish sprang out of the water to hear the sound of the conch – they momentarily sparkled in the moonlight and disappeared.

Yadava warriors, excited by the inspiring sound waves of the conch, started dancing with joy, and chanted, 'Hail Srikrishna, king of the Yadavas, victory to him!' It was a divine conch that chased Untruth and annihilated it. The piercing, rhythmic sound of that conch was unbearable for the imprisoned asura warriors. They tore open the ropes tied around them and ran away, fearing for their lives.

I ordered Satyaki, 'Commander, enter the cave and rescue our Guru's son, Dutta, and bring him out with honour.'

Satyaki entered the cave with a few chosen armed warriors.

I gave instructions for the formal cremation of Shankhasura. Our warriors named the place 'Shankhoddhara', meaning deliverance of the conch, and we sailed out.

Moving along with Dutta, our army's first sojourn was to the foot of Mount Raivataka. It was under the rule of King Kakudmin of the Raivata dynasty. The royal capital Raivatanagara was located on the summit of the mountain. Our plan was to rest here for a while. Nobody had imagined that our stay here was going to be extended. We were eager to move towards Acharya's ashrama in Avanti. As per our promise, we were supposed to deliver Dutta safely to his mother and obtain her heartfelt blessings. The next day, while our army was performing morning rituals, a royal envoy from King Kakudmin descended from the mountain and brought me the king's message. The king had invited all of us with honour and delight to visit his royal capital.

I instructed our commander, Satyaki, to continue his journey with Dutta and wait for us near the banks of the Kshipra. Along with the royal envoy of the Raivatakas, Balaramadada, Uddhava, Vipruthu, a few chosen warriors and I started climbing the tall mountain full of thick forests.

King Kakudmin welcomed us with open arms. After the royal meal, he offered us gifts of jewellery, cows and horses. As Vipruthu was the eldest among us, the king put an unexpected proposition to the minister, 'My beautiful, humble daughter Revati is of marriageable age. I request Balarama, the elder prince of the Yadavas, to accept her hand in marriage.'

The minister was completely baffled with this unexpected proposal. He did not even know what to say. He stuttered 'How – how – can I – I – take this decision?' Dada looked at me and gave a gentle smile. It meant that the matter was in my hands now.

'Dear Raivatakas, the Yadavas are pleased to accept your pure love. This marriage will surely take place. We are going to need your support in the future. In my opinion, Dada should meet my future sister-in-law at least once,' I said.

King Kakudmin's eyes glowed with joy. He quickly gave orders, and within a few moments, Revatidevi, the princess of the Raivatakas, dressed in fine royal attire, stood in the great hall in front of us. She was a perfect match for Dada.

All our family and Yadava relatives were in Mathura. King Kakudmin suggested that they carry out just the basic swayamwar ceremony, as per the Raivataka tradition. We could perform the formal wedding ceremony later in Mathura.

While we were climbing down the long, curving road, I constantly kept feeling in my heart that I was going to foster a firm bond with Mount

Raivataka some time later. I will have to come here again – but I could not tell for what purpose. I did not know it myself then.

Along with a few warriors who had accompanied us from Raivataka, we met Satyaki, who had camped on the shores of the Kshipra. We entered the ashrama. Mother and son embraced each other while the former wept profusely, overjoyed at meeting her son after many years of separation.

I was very eager to show Acharya the rare, divine conch that I had brought with me. At dinner time, before saying our regular prayers, I expressed my biggest concern to him. 'The Magadha empire is enormous. Our Shursena kingdom is very small in comparison, almost negligible in size. Jarasandha, Kansa's father-in-law, has been fuming with anger since Kansa's execution; he does not let the citizens of Mathura live in peace. We have had to fight off his armed attacks nearly fifteen times so far. Could you please suggest a way out of this situation?'

Acharya smiled like a child and said, 'Srikrishna, you have just returned from visiting the ocean. Would you not like to live in its company? Anyhow, are you not going to show me the divine conch that you have brought from the Shwetasagara ocean?' He digressed on purpose from the topic, smiling instead. I understood and reciprocated.

I had safely secured the shining, divine conch in the blue scarf wrapped around my waist. Carefully releasing the knot, I took it out, touched it to my forehead and placed it gently at Acharya's feet. Picking it up, as if it were a Prajakta flower heavy with morning dew, he closed his eyes.

In his melodious voice, he said, 'Srikrishna, this is another invaluable jewel, as precious as the Vaijayanti garland around your neck. It will be known as 'Paanchajanya'. You have fulfilled your promise of the Gurudakshina. I am going to give you another precious gift today.'

Acharya's wife brought out a curvaceous bow decorated with beautiful garlands of Madhumalati flowers and a quiver full of arrows. Stepping forward, Acharya balanced the bow in his hands, and twanged the bowstring once. Acharya holding a bow! It was a very rare sight. He said, 'This meritorious bow is named 'Ajitanjaya'.' I got up, touched it to my forehead, and accepted the gift humbly.

In this moment of bliss an amusing thought entered my mind. Looking intently at Acharya, I implored, 'Gurudeva, if you will, can you blow the conch once? Exonerate it forever of all the blemishes it has acquired in the company of asuras. Purify the Paanchajanya completely.'

Acharya, holding his chin high up towards the ceiling of the cottage, blew the divine conch with such passionate intensity that it made the veins in his throat protrude. Instantly, his fair face flushed. All of us experienced goosebumps.

This time, when we returned to Mathura, I had three priceless jewels with me. The Vaijayanti garland, Paanchajanya and Ajitanjaya. Well, I could say that our sister-in-law, Revati, was the fourth jewel!

Maharaja Ugrasena himself came to receive us. The citizens of Mathura showered us with flowers and welcomed Revati with joy. The entire city was decorated with festoons and flowers to welcome her. I feasted my eyes upon the river Yamuna encircling Mathura in a crescent shape with her waters. Remembering Vasudevababa and Devakimata, who were waiting for me in the royal palace, I bowed down. Then, on the border of the Shursena kingdom, I blew the pure-white Paanchajanya for the first time with all my might.

Since the moment I had held this conch in my hands, I had been transformed completely. As if the old Krishna had vanished. The sound waves seemed to convey the deepest meaning of my present and future plans.

We were welcomed into Mathura with fanfare. But Jarasandha, the tyrant emperor of Magadha, was not going to rest until he had annihilated the Yadavas of the Shursena kingdom. In Girivraja, the royal capital of the Magadhas, his daughters and Kansa's wives – Asti and Prapti – would not let him think of anything else except 'the destruction of the Yadavas and Srikrishna's execution at the earliest'.

Following the political adage, 'an enemy of an enemy is a friend', he had formed a political alliance with Dantavakra, the king of Karusha, and Shishupala, the son of the Chedi king, Damaghosha, my paternal cousins. But they had surrendered to and joined hands with the more powerful Jarasandha. The trio of Shishupala, Dantavakra and Jarasandha had also succeeded in convincing several other kings to join them. Jarasandha had invited all his vassal kings to the royal capital of Girivraja. All our nemeses had gathered together to obliterate the Yadavas. Within a week of our arrival, we had to face the challenge of the Magadha invasion again.

This was the seventeenth attack by Jarasandha. A giant army crossed the Yamuna in a large number of boats and reached Mathura. Compared to earlier invasions, this was the ultimate, conclusive invasion. Jarasandha himself led the army as the commander. A Yadava council was organised under the leadership of Maharaja Ugrasena and Baba. Along with me, Dada, Commander Anadhrishti, Yuyudhana–Satyaki, Uddhava, Akrura, Kritavarmana, Satrajita, Shini, and all my kakas, mamas and the Yadava leaders gathered together with determination.

Compared to the mammoth Magadha army, the Yadavas would have appeared like a mouse in front of an elephant. Yet, I silently listened to the resolve of the fervent Yadavas. The short-tempered Yadavas were not going to learn to be cautious unless and until they had learnt from experience. I gave my silent approval. As proposed unanimously in the council, the Yadavas got all geared up to fight the Magadhas.

Based on the previous experience, the frontiers of Mathura were secured by sealing all gates on four sides. Thunderous sounds of war drums and kettledrums echoed in the air. A long, violent, unpredictable war had begun.

The Magadhas started propelling huge rocks and burning torches inside Mathura's enclosure continuously. About eight days passed by. The battle was still inconclusive, and it was not going to end any time soon. Outside, the farming land of the Shursena kingdom was getting destroyed under the feet of elephants, camels and horses.

Jarasandha's armed riders started attacking the towns close by, badgering the citizens of the Shursena kingdom. They also extorted foodgrains and money from the people. After ten days, I offered a pragmatic suggestion to Maharaja Ugrasena. I discussed a secret decision with him in private, and proposed to arrange the Yadava royal council immediately.

Maharaja Ugrasena convened the royal council. Looking at the burning torches in the council, he said, 'We Yadavas have determinedly faced the constant armed assaults of the giant Magadha army and if required, will do so again in the future. I can see that Srikrishna is the only Yadava leader in our kingdom today with the capability to evaluate a situation correctly and take a suitable decision accordingly. In my opinion, you should all listen to him and comply with his decision. Srikrishna believes that this war should be brought to an end. If the Magadhas are not ready to do so, then the Yadavas should do it from their side.'

'What does this mean? We have fought with them staunchly sixteen times before; why surrender now? That is not possible,' Satyaki burst out with his usual vigour. Many others supported him. There were two views and no one was willing to come to a conclusion. I sat silently, listening to their debates.

Finally, Vikadru, the oldest and most senior Yadava in the council hall, stood up. His pure-white, thick beard trembled with his wobbly neck. Raising both his arms, he roared in a commanding voice, 'Silence, everyone keep quiet. Using my authority as the most senior and experienced person, I demand that all of you listen to me carefully and do as I tell you.'

He continued, 'What is all this ruckus about? It is all in vain. Do you even know the actual reason for the wrath of Jarasandha, Kansa's father-in-law? Are you ever going to take that into account? He has no reason to be hostile towards the Yadavas. He is your kith and kin, and he never had any enmity towards you before. Isn't Srikrishna the only reason for all this? Kansa sent many deadly executioners to kill him because he thought that Srikrishna was the one who was going to destroy him. Srikrishna survived all the attacks astutely and killed him. As Kansa's father-in-law, would Jarasandha not want to avenge his son-in-law? He wants to inflict vengeance on Srikrishna. It is just for this purpose that, time and again, he has assaulted Mathura with his army. I see only one solution that will benefit all Yadavas from this situation. I think Srikrishna and Balarama should not stay in Mathura even for a moment. They should go somewhere far away to live incognito. That will give some peace to the citizens of Mathura. Isn't this the only solution to this problematic situation?'

The piercing and experienced words of an aged Yadava left all those gathered aghast. This was totally unexpected, unthinkable.

Getting up quietly, I briskly glanced around the fully packed Yadava council. I said, 'I am well aware that the powerful Jarasandha, whose son-in-law I executed, is my arch enemy. I am going to leave Mathura today itself, along with Balaramadada.

'I know that due to my actions today, future generations will loathe and mock me as "Ranachhodadasa" – a runaway warrior. I am happily willing to bear that dishonour, that stigma on my character. It is better than the whole Yadava clan perishing in vain.'

I glanced around the hall. I could clearly see a lot of faces distressed and agitated at the thought of me leaving Mathura. It was the same look that the gopas and gopikas of Gokul had on their faces when I had left Gokul.

Maharaja Ugrasena stood up and said, 'I think Srikrishna is not easy to understand – for you, me or anybody for that matter. It is not in his nature to remain in one place anyway. Does water or air ever remain stagnant in one place? Do the rays of the sun ever stay in one place? But wherever he goes, I implore him that his emotional bond with Mathura always stay alive in his heart, at least as long as I am alive.'

The special council of the Yadavas was over. That very night, by a secret passage, Balaramadada, Uddhava and I, along with Vipruthu and a few chosen Yadava warriors, reached the shore of the Yamuna. We sailed towards the south in large ships.

While we were sailing, our infiltrators spread rumours among the Magadha army base that Srikrishna had escaped. It was certain that after hearing this news, Jarasandha was obviously going to follow us. As soon as his army started retreating from Mathura, select armed Yadava troops were going to join us at a certain place in the south. At present, Mathura was going to be battle-free.

We wondered where we could go – I had already pondered the question. According to our spies, there were four more Yadava kingdoms in the south. These had been established by the four sons of our founder Maharaja Yadu, born to his Naga wives. One of them, located on the banks of the Narmada, was known as Mahishmati. King Muchkunda had established the kingdom to the south of Mount Hrikshawana.

The second was the kingdom of Padmawata near Mahabalishwaram, established by Yadu's son Padmawarna on the plateau of Sahyadri near the banks of the River Venna. Famous since Vedic times, it was ruled by a vassal king named Shrigala of the Naga dynasty. Karvir, a city on the banks of the Panchganga, was also known as 'Dakshinakashi'.

The third royal city of Kraunchapura established by Yadu's son Sarasa, was located to the south of Karvir. This city had red soil and fertile land.

The fourth kingdom, founded by Yadu's son Harita, was located on the coast of the western ocean. The skilled fishermen there were expert ocean divers, adept at pulling out sea shells that contained pearls, sea corals and conches from the ocean's belly.

Minister Vipruthu had already dispatched our emissaries with messages to these four kingdoms. We had also received news that sage Jamadagni's son, Bhagwan Parashurama, along with select disciples, had come to the Padmawata kingdom. We decided to visit Parashurama first.

During this expedition to the south, we faced the biggest challenge of Dandakaranya. A challenge of the mountain ranges of Vindhya, Satpuda and Pariyatra.

There was only one narrow path to go through this forest, known as 'Dakshinapatha'. It was so narrow that even one person, while holding the reins of his horse, could barely walk one step at a time. We took along an experienced forest dweller as our guide, who knew the way.

Finally, after a month, we reached the other end of the forest, along with our horses.

We crossed River Godavari along the border of the Vidarbha kingdom and descended into the Ashmaka kingdom. We also crossed River Bhima and finally came to the border of the Padmawata kingdom.

I sent a messenger to Bhagwan Parashurama with the news of our arrival. We rested at the border for a day. We left the next morning to meet him.

First, we bathed at the confluence of the Krishna and the Koyana to enter the area near River Venna. Parashurama had sent two of his disciples to receive us. With shining axes on their shoulders, they welcomed us. We soon reached the tall, wooden gate of the Bhrigu ashrama.

The son of sage Jamadagni himself stood at the entrance with a smile on his face and arms wide open. This completely wiped out the image that I had built of him in my mind for the last month and a half. I was stunned. Just as I was enamoured by Acharya Sandipani, I was drawn to him the moment I saw him. Moving forward, I laid myself prostrate at his feet to pay obeisance with the utmost respect and humility. Dada followed suit. He instantly picked me up, held me in an affectionate embrace and uttered blessings in a gentle rhythm, 'Victory to you, revered Yadava.' Dada was blessed the same way.

In Gokul, my restless urge for the Yamuna would get quenched the moment I would view her. Since we had left Mathura, I had longed to meet Bhrigushreshtha Parashurama. That thirst of mine which nobody else would understand got quenched only when I saw him in person.

He had a thick, full and snow-white beard. His garments were simple white clothes. Rudraksha garlands were tied around the matted hair on his head. Despite his age, he had a glow on his face and serene eyes that seemed peaceful. He said, 'Your arrival here has emancipated this land. I know who you are. Come into the ashrama. Take some rest and have some fruits first. Then we will talk.' After we took rest, Bhrigu Parashurama enquired about our journey with genuine interest. I explained my anxiety over Jarasandha's assaults on the Yadavas in its entirety to him.

As he heard about my journey to the south, and about Jarasandha, he became lost in thought. Closing his eyes for a few moments, he went into a meditative trance, and said, 'Oh Yadava king Srikrishna, your decision to leave Mathura was the right one. You will never stay put in one place, leave alone Mathura. You are a "Chakravarti". Wherever you put your feet, that land will be blessed. Therefore, you will constantly be on the move, and you should. Jarasandha will come looking for you wherever you go. Therefore, I would suggest that you, along with your people, go to the strong and secure, naturally beautiful Mount "Gomanta". Once your Yadava army gets there, you should wipe out Jarasandha completely. After your triumph on Mount Gomanta, come and visit me again. I have been saving an exceptionally precious gift for you for many ages now. I will be relieved once I hand it over to you with my own hands.'

Meanwhile, Balaramdada, who had not participated in our discussion but was impressed with acharya's foresight, gathered his courage and said, 'Bhagwan, it may seem disrespectful, please forgive me, but I am in a dilemma whether to ask you or not.' Dada brought both his palms together and leant humbly in front of Bhrigu.

'Go ahead, Balarama, do not hesitate,' the Bhrigu replied with a serene smile.

'Bhagwan, we did not see your shining axe, usually resting on your shoulders, when we met you. How come? Have you changed your mind about your vow of destruction of the Kshatriyas? Or has our Kshatriya status been eradicated since Maharaja Yadu, as is believed?' Bhrigushreshtha looked at the plough with the golden blade that Dada had taken down from his shoulder and gave a wide smile for a moment. He said, 'Not I, but Srikrishna will give a convincing and pertinent answer to your question.' With his serene eyes, he looked at me purposefully. As our eyes met, we both smiled.

I replied, the way Bhagwan Parashurama would have. 'The axe is a mere symbol. It cleanses the intellect of the weeds. Bhagwan never had any enmity with the Kshatriya clan. He was against the vile attitude of the arrogant, blind and thoughtless powers that obstructed growth and development – the basic attributes of life in the name of the Kshatriya Dharma. Once his mission was over, he took the axe off his shoulders. Dada, tomorrow you, too, will take your plough off your shoulders once your life's mission is accomplished. Yet, it will be associated with your name forever. You will be known as "Haladhara" to future generations.

'Now, to speak about our Kshatriya status, it is not characterised by birth, but by innate valour. I think for the same reason, Bhagwan has blessed us suitably. Maybe he has kept my precious gift with him for the same reason.'

'Perfect. I knew he would speak correctly. Srikrishna, Balarama, I confer many blessings on both of you. Krishna, Rama, may victory always be with you.'

He hugged us and patted our shoulders affectionately. His touch had a comforting warmth. We stayed there for two days before leaving for Mount Gomanta.

Gomanta. It was spread long and tall, and was challenging to cross. Many dense forests of tall and thick-leafed teak trees had spread for many yojanas at the foothills. An open plateau was located at the summit of the mountain. It was also covered with grass and scattered trees. The Gomantaka kingdom of the Kadamba dynasty was clearly visible from this plateau on the western side.

By evening, we reached the summit. Our troops immediately built a few strong huts on the plateau using their axes and sickles. That night, standing on the tall boulder, I feasted my eyes upon the silver waterline of the western ocean visible far away on the horizon. Dada stood next to me. I said to him, 'I do not know why I was drawn to the Yamuna when I was in Gokul and why am I irresistibly drawn to the western ocean ever since we came here to kill Shankhasura.'

Looking once at the line of water in front and then at my eyes, Dada said, 'You are drawn to the ocean that is abound with water, but people like me get attracted to your ocean-like eyes. We have come a long way from Mathura, have we not?'

For a long time, Dada and I kept chatting on the boulder.

Within a week's time, Dada and I wandered and surveyed as much of the mountain as we could. We checked all possible paths for descending the mountain and memorised them.

A variety of juicy fruits, clean water rich in iron, and the cool breeze of the western wind made Dada and me fall deeply in love with the mountain. We did not even realise how our blissful days began and how they ended.

Our joy started escalating when troops of armed Yadava warriors from the southern kingdoms of Mahishmati, Padmawata, Vanavasi and Harita began assembling on the mountain. Our delight reached its peak when the expert charioteer, Satyaki, joined us with his troops. The entire mountain was transformed into a huge military camp.

While passing through the forest of Dandakaranya, meeting Bhrigushreshtha Parashurama, and since arriving here there, was a lurking feeling of things to come. Some spectacular event was going to take place here that would be eternally memorable for future generations.

That is exactly what happened. Barely a month had passed that we had come here. One day, along with the rising sun, a tumultuous cacophony of war tabors and kettledrums flooded the thick forests... Birds and animals cowered in fear as the shrill sound of the drums kept mounting.

Dada, Satyaki, the commanders of the southern Yadava kingdoms and I surveyed the bottom to see hordes of elephants, horses and infantry from the Magadha army moving about at the foothills. Rows of triangular, scarlet Magadha pennants were spread around. Behind them rows of silver Chedi flags were visible.

It was obvious that vengeance had taken over prudence. Jarasandha was determined to exact revenge. He had followed me, along with Shishupala, the Chedi king, and reached here.

We had to take quick action. I divided the whole army according to the disposition of the mountain, taking a strong defensive stance. The Magadhas of Jarasandha never knew patience and composure. Without any thought, they entered the dense forests, where our Yadava army, already hidden, counter-attacked fiercely and slaughtered them. A long and arduous battle had begun.

Every day, Jarasandha and Shishupala started thrusting fresh warriors with strong mettle into the teakwood forests, most of whom were slaughtered by our army.

Jarasandha had become impatient to capture me. He was dreaming of slaughtering me with his mace, but for now he was stuck here. He would move restlessly, shouting at his commanders as he was frustrated that he had been unable to fulfil his mission.

To lure Balaramadada and me out of the mountains and on to open ground, he decided to set the entire Mount Gomanta aflame. He ordered foot soldiers to hold burning torches in their hands. I realised his ploy and instructed everyone to leave the mountain by any way they could find, and gather on the western plateau at the base of the mountain.

Like a pile of camphor, the trees started burning, and soon, bright yellow flames of the inferno rose sky-high.

Animals ran for their lives, many getting burnt in the process.

It was chaos all over, as everything in the forest was getting consumed by the raging fire.

Even Jarasandha's Magadha warriors at the frontline could not bear the blasts of hot air coming from the blazing mountain and retreated a few metres in fear.

Jarasandha and Shishupala, sitting in their tents, were happy, and had already started guzzling down pots of Maireyaka wine. They presumed we must have burnt to death in the blazing fire of Mount Gomanta like sweet potatoes roasted in a fireplace.

Dada and I had left the mountain after getting all the Yadava warriors to safety from the western side. Just like an arrow shot out of the bow stops on its own only when its speed dies, the wildfire on Mount Gomanta was going to stop on its own, sometime. Jarasandha had started the fire but putting it out was not in anyone's control.

Our army joined forces with those from the south and this united Yadava army encircled the mountain completely, and assaulted the intoxicated and unwary Jarasandha and Shishupala with the battle cry, 'Hail Goddess Ida!' The attack began even before the Magadhas and Chedis could get hold of their weapons. The mammoth Magadha army was stunned by the surprise attack and ran like headless chickens.

The very first king Dada encountered was King Darada. Within moments Dada had pulled him down from his chariot, putting his Samvartaka plough around his neck, and with one strike of his Saunanda pestle, had executed him.

What had never happened before, happened on this day – Jarasandha retreated. He turned his back and started running. His army followed him. Our fervent, victorious army began chasing the Magadhas now. Finally, we drove them out of the borders of the Vanavasi kingdom, and came back as the evening was setting in.

We returned and camped on the same spot where Jarasandha and Shishupala had camped before. The mountain was still burning. Our troops rested for the night.

The next day, our victorious army began marching towards Bhrigu Parashurama's ashrama. The news of our victory over Jarasandha had already reached him. I was eager to see the venerable Parashurama. How wisely he had guided me to go to Mount Gomanta. What if Jarasandha had caught up with us on the open plateau?

Many months had passed since we had left Mathura. During the recent eventful period, we had not got any news of Mathura. So, I was trying to extract as much as possible from Satyaki. He said, 'Maharaja Ugrasena and all the Yadava leaders of Mathura are tired of these consecutive wars. Though you and Balarama have left Mathura, they are still worried that the Magadhas will return.'

'Commander, Jarasandha, his allies and the Magadhas will never assault Mathura again now. I have also taken a firm decision. After this journey through the south, when we return to Mathura, I am going to present it to the Yadava royal council. The situation in which and the way I left Mathura is a matter of anguish for Yadavas. That guilt needs to be removed. I will do it myself at the right time.' I consoled Satyaki, patting him on the shoulder.

Bhrigushreshtha Parashurama himself came to receive us with all his disciples. And yes, this time a six–even-inch-wide axe was shining on his shoulders. Dada, Satyaki and I – we all prostrated respectfully at his feet.

Walking towards his cottage, he kept his hand on my shoulder and said lovingly, 'You felt deep regret when Jarasandha burnt down Mount Gomanta, a beautiful creation of nature that came into existence after hundreds of years of penance. And you are right to feel the pain. But I clearly foresee that even you will be compelled to take such a decision in the future, to burn down a forest even thicker than this. And you will have to do it for the sake of humanity.' The elderly Bhrigu smiled through his thick, white beard.

We arrived at his cottage. Parashurama sat on a tiger skin on a tall, wooden seat.

Parashurama said, 'Rama–Srikrishna, only Srirama, the son of Dasharatha, along with Lakshmana, had crossed the Dandakaranya, the southernmost tip of Aaryavarta before. Now you have come, and even I got a chance to meet you.

'I am much more experienced than both of you as I am older in age. Based on that experience, I can clearly foresee the purpose of your life. I am going to sum it up for you briefly. Listen carefully.

'The essence of true Kshatriya Dharma is the protection of the life and rights of the weak. That is the true meaning of Purushartha.

'Though I am a Brahmanakumara by birth, I have dutifully practised the Kshatriya Dharma. I annihilated the supercilious and arrogant Kshatriyas who blocked the flow of life. I never had any desire to possess any royal throne. I have been building Bhrigu ashramas throughout Aaryavarta and have devoted my life to the duty of giving knowledge to others as a Brahmin.

'Let me tell you the meaning of life in short as I have comprehended it. Jnana, Vijnana and Prajnana are the three basic realms of life. Jnana is complete cognisance of our surroundings and nature.

'Vijnana is special knowledge. The detailed knowledge of a particular subject. I obtained Vijnana by acquiring the knowledge of the Brahmastra.

'Prajnana is the thorough knowledge of all facets of life, including the knowledge of self. Prajnana is the quest for the eternal energy that resides within oneself and within the animate and inanimate.

'Whatever I am telling you now is very significant as it is from beyond the realms of Jnana and Vijnana. It is from the realm of Prajnana.

'Rama–Srikrishna, though you are born in the Yadu dynasty, you do not belong only to the Yadava dynasty, not even to the Shursena kingdom, and not just to the Aaryavarta, which ends at the borders of Dandakaranya. You are the eternally burning lamps on the banks of the perpetually flowing Ganga of human life. You cannot be contained within the limits of a dynasty, a place or time.

'With a specific vision in my mind, I travelled and worked all my life. Srikrishna, I see that you are my true heir in terms of my life's mission, and, therefore, I am going to present you with an invaluable, divine gift today. I can see that you are fully capable of understanding its essence, activating it at the right time and immersing it when necessary. You are the only one who solely and truly deserves this.'

He closed his eyes gradually and went into a meditative trance. Mantras of initiation began shooting out of his mouth like rapid arrows. They resembled the sound of my Paanchajanya conch. I had never heard these mantras before. But they were swiftly getting inscribed in my memory. Each particle of my body blossomed like never before.

In a moment, acharya's cottage was filled with various melodious sounds. Within a few moments, the cottage was filled with a dazzling light that would put the brilliance of millions of suns to shame.

In the glowing bright light, Parashurama raised his right index finger in the air, where it stayed for a moment or two. A shining, divine chakra with twelve spokes, swiftly revolving around its axis, appeared magically on it. Its divine light blinded everyone in the cottage. Dada squeezed my hand tightly, mesmerised by the spinning chakra. Only I could see it clearly.

The spinning divine chakra, carried by Bhrigu. To me that blinding divine light looked and seemed like the cool moonlight in Gokul on the night of Paurnima and the Rasa dance.

As Bhrigushreshtha signalled with his eyes, I got up and walked towards him. He uttered a few mantras in my ears and said to me, 'Experience the power of this "Sudarshan" chakra yourself.' He closed his eyes and chanting the mantra, released the chakra. Within a trice, it crossed over the river Venna, touched the faraway mountain ranges and swiftly came back to his finger. Spinning around itself, it gradually disappeared, just as it had appeared.

With his eyes closed, Bhrigurama released the sacred water from his water pot on my right palm and said, 'Take a sip of it.' I did as instructed. He further said, 'Yadava king, son of Vasudeva, Srikrishna, from today onwards you have the authority over this chakra of brilliance called "Sudarshan", which was with me for many years. Achyuta, you already know the story of the birth of this chakra. However, let me repeat it just to refresh your memory.

'Many eras ago, Lord Shiva himself created this divine Sudarshan chakra to destroy the malicious powers of the demon Tripura. Lord Vishnu himself...' Bhrigu stopped short before saying something. He opened his eyes and looked at me. His eyes, which looked like the burning pit of a yajna fire some time back, now looked very serene. His mysterious smile seemed to me like my own. The thought made me reflect his smile.

Closing his eyes again, Bhrigu said, 'Who is Lord Vishnu? Do I really need to explain it to you? You know everything. So then, "our" Vishnu offered Shiva a thousand lotuses with utter devotion to obtain the Sudarshan chakra. Then, it was given to Agni. Agni gave it to Varuna. From Varuna it came to me. I never made use of the chakra in my life as I never felt the need to do so. My axe was more than enough to accomplish my life's mission.

'From today, you have become the complete master of the divine Sudarshan chakra. Launch it only when you find it absolutely necessary to do so. You have to protect Truth, Justice and Dharma. Balarama will have to accompany you like your shadow and protect you.

'Remember, oh sons of Yadavas! Using Balarama's plough, you have to plough this land of the Aryas and sow the seeds of the truths of life that will be cherished for ages. And, you have to protect them with the Sudarshan chakra.

'My life's mission is over now. Srikrishna, in my opinion, you are the only one suitable to carry forward my mission. I will give my final discourse to the disciples in Shurparaka ashrama and then head directly to the Himalayas, for Vanaprasthashram.

'As the senior leader of all Bhrigus, I give you all our blessings. May victory be with you Srikrishna, Balarama…!'

Since I obtained the mantras of Sudarshan, I have been completely transformed. Listening seemed better than speaking now. My vision was always thirsty to foresee the faraway future. I constantly felt that I had gained the miraculous power of reading a person inside out. I felt that this power was beyond the body, the mind, and even beyond Kala, time.

Dada, Satyaki and I were sitting in our tent, discussing our return journey and the hurdles we would be facing. I was, of course, only a listener.

Meanwhile, our head of surveillance team ushered in a man who bowed and said, 'I am from Karvir city in the Padmawata kingdom. I am here to protest against the injustice we are being subjected to.'

He continued, folding his palms together, 'Maharaja Srikrishna, do we have to leave the Padmawata kingdom and find another place to live? King Shrigala is a brute, and is forcefully seizing our women, wealth and land. Many citizens have suffered his wrath. Some have fled from the kingdom.

'We have heard that you executed Kansa, the tyrant king of Mathura, even though he was your own mama. We do not see anybody else who can penalise King Shrigala. Please do something, save us from the clutches of this vicious king.'

I stood up and went closer to him. It amused me that he had called me 'Maharaja'. I gently patted his shoulder. Immediately dropping on his knees, he put his head on my feet. With that touch, the same sacred sound that had echoed before the manifestation of Sudarshan resonated through my entire body. Holding his shoulders, I pulled him up and comforted him. I commanded Satyaki, 'Commander, plan our troops' return journey via Karvir.'

Our army reached the border of Karvir. Shrigala's kingdom was a tiny vassal kingdom, contained within the larger Padmawata kingdom. It was located on the banks of River Panchaganga. But the arrogant and insolent Shrigala considered himself to be an invincible, powerful emperor. He did not even recognise the authority of King Padmavarna.

He had built a strong, protective fortification on the banks of River Panchaganga. Using a herd of elephants, we broke open the gates of Shrigala's royal fort. Our troops collided with those of Shrigala. I stood at the bottom of the staircase leading to Shrigala's palace, carrying only the Ajitanjaya bow on my shoulders, the Paanchajanya conch tied around my waist and the Vaijayanti garland around my neck. Shrigala was a tall, hefty and armed warrior. Standing on the highest step, wielding his huge, shining, round iron mace, he roared, 'You lowlife cowherd of Vasudeva who ran away from Mathura. You may have forced Emperor Jarasandha to retreat using the wildfire on Gomanta to your advantage, but this is Karvir, the city of invincible wrestlers. You better go back the way you came. Otherwise I will tear you to pieces and eat you raw.'

His poisonous words had no effect on me at all. The divine mantras of Sudarshan had been echoing deep in my mind for long. Only I could feel the barely audible, unrestrained, bright waves of those mantras coming from my lips. Blazing, radiant particles started moving about through my entire body, like embers being tossed around. My eyes closed involuntarily. I was no more Srikrishna Vasudeva Yadava – only a pillar of bright, radiant, pure light! My right hand rose slowly. Following an ear-splitting, tumultuous sound that filled Shrigala's palace, the radiant Sudarshan chakra with twelve spokes manifested, revolving swiftly around itself on my right index finger.

I aimed the chakra at my target. Sudarshan had been launched for the first time. In a trice, unmistakably cutting through Shrigala's arrogant, thick neck, the radiant chakra leapt forward. His tall, hefty, insolent, armoured torso tumbled down the stairs, splattering blood all over. His bloody head followed. The iron mace came tumbling down and lay near my feet. The moment his blood touched me, the chakra retreated swiftly. Settling on my index finger, it revolved around itself for a moment and gradually vanished.

The city of Karvir had been liberated from the clutches of Shrigala. Shrigala's queen, Padmawati, only had one son named Shakradeva, a young, strong man, barely in his twenties. He was wounded while fighting with our army. Our warriors presented him to me as a royal prisoner, tied in ropes. We had no intention of capturing the throne. We wanted to formally declare Shrigala's son as the royal heir of Karvir. But that young prince kept staring at us with sheer hatred and contempt. I sensed that the young man could be steered in the right direction.

I loosened the ropes tied around him and freed him, but he continued to glare at me. Looking directly into his fearless eyes, I patted his shoulders and said, 'Oh son of Shrigala, never follow your father's destructive ways. It will not be helpful in any way. We are entrusting you with the responsibility of the Karvir kingdom. Build a kingdom here, for the welfare and happiness of your subjects. In memory of your father, declare a new name for Karvir – Kolhapur.'

His stance changed immediately and, bending down, he put his head on my feet. Pulling him up, I embraced him. That night, we had a lovely feast. After a week, the citizens of Karvir, along with Shakradeva, gathered on the banks of the Panchaganga and bade us farewell. 'Hail Lord of Mathura Maharaja Srikrishna, Balarama! Hail Lord of Karvir, Maharaja Shakradeva!' We left for Mathura after this.

We camped near the border of Vidarbha after a few weeks. Kundinpura, the famous city of Vidarbha, was only a few yojanas away. King Bhishmaka had, much earlier, collaborated with Jarasandha against us. His son Rukmi was as impatient and short-tempered as Satyaki. During this sojourn, Satyaki asked me, 'Should we send our messenger to Bhishmaka and ask for his consent? There is a huge, ancient temple of Goddess Ambika here. We can pay obeisance to the goddess.'

'No, not right now. We are going to pay obeisance to the goddess at the right time.' Smiling, I declined Satyaki's suggestion.

We reached Dandakaranya again on our way back. After a month's gruelling journey, we finally crossed Dandakaranya and arrived in the Bhojapur city of the Avanti kingdom. This was the city of King Kuntibhoja, the foster father of our aunt, Kunti. Here, we unexpectedly met Gargamuni. He had come to visit King Yavana of Ajitanjaya city on the western coast. I was curious about the name of the city – Ajitanjaya and the name of the king, 'Yavana'. My bow had the same name as the city and 'Yavana' were the people living in the faraway region of Gandhara. All said and done, they were outsiders. I asked Gargamuni, 'What is your relation with King Yavana?' He did not give a clear reply, answering vaguely. He was the royal priest, as revered as our guru. Therefore, I did not vex him any further.

After many sojourns, we reached the border of Mathura.

The news of our triumph over insolent Jarasandha had reached the Shursena kingdom long back. All the citizens of Mathura had gathered at the border. Uddhava was there too, right in front, along with his brothers Bruhu and Chitru.

We were given a traditional welcome meant for heroes. Meanwhile, seeing me, Uddhava eagerly came forward and said, 'Dada, your face looks more radiant than ever. I have never seen it so bright before. I am proud of you for defeating Jarasandha. But I am quite upset with you about one thing.'

Asking Uddhava to get in the chariot, I asked him, 'Udho, what are you so upset about?'

'Because you left without any warning and did not take me with you.'

'Is that it? As a dear brother, I had shown you the previous three precious jewels immediately after I got them. I thought you would ask me what I have brought with me today.'

'I know you have brought the most precious yet invisible jewel this time,' Uddhav exclaimed.

'How do you know?' I asked him.

'From the expression on your face. Your face is emitting extraordinary splendour today. Tell me, what have you brought with you?'

I said, 'I have brought a jewel that gives a healthy acceleration to the life cycle of the universe. Can you guess what it is?'

'To the life cycle of the universe? You have formally obtained the holy mantras of the divine Sudarshan chakra. Tell me, where did you meet Bhagwan Parashurama?' With uncontrollable joy, Uddhava embraced me tightly. I had never seen him so excited before. After dinner, in the family room, I noticed Vasudevababa was lost in thought. He said, 'Dear son Srikrishna, I get a chance to meet my three sisters and your aunts Shrutashrava, Rajadhidevi and Shrutadevi once a while, but my beloved sister Kunti has been alienated from me since childhood.'

'Father, I can see that Aunt Kunti is really your favourite sister.'

'Srikrishna, your aunt has been bravely facing her tough destiny. After the death of her husband Maharaja Pandu, she has returned to Hastinapura from Mount Gandhamadana in the Himalayas. Her five sons are with her. I do not know how she is going to bring them up in Hastinapura.'

I lovingly held both his hands in mine and said, 'Baba, your dear son Srikrishna will never keep away from his beloved aunt, Kunti. I have never seen her sons, the five Pandavas. But they are as beloved to me as they are to you.

'In the name of the infallible power that I have obtained, I promise you that I will see to it that Aunt Kunti and the Pandavas get justice. They have my full support for the rest of my life.'

'I was sure you would say the same. That is why I shared my anguish for Kunti with you,' Baba said.

I immediately dispatched a messenger and called for minister Akrura. As he arrived, putting the responsibility of this mission on his experienced shoulders, I said, 'Akrurakaka, you are to immediately leave for the Kuru kingdom's royal capital, Hastinapura, and meet with our aunt, Kunti, and her sons.'

'As you wish. After returning from Hastinapura, I will present the details to you.' Looking at his disappearing figure, a clear vision of the royal palace of Hastinapura, far away on the banks of the Ganga, swam before my eyes. Despite his blindness, Maharaja Dhritarashtra was dreaming of the coronation of Duryodhana – the eldest of his one hundred sons.

Maharani Gandhari's crafty brother, Shakuni, who had come from the Gandhara kingdom, was willingly feeding him cunning, political machinations in his sweet tongue. The royal gurus Drona and Kripa were occupied in edifying the royal princes in warfare. The only person with a sense of justice that I could see was the royal minister of the Kurus, Mahatma Vidura. I had instructed Akrurakaka to meet him too. The responsibility of the Kuru kingdom, which was located far away on the banks of the Ganga, lay on the shoulders of the senior Kuru Bhishma. Hearing his life's story from Baba, I had developed a natural affection for him. It was the same feeling that I had for Uddhava.

My father held my hands and said in a melodious tone that reminded me of Acharya Sandipani and Bhagwan Parashurama, 'Srikrishna, every valiant warrior from the eighteen royal families of the Yadavas has always kept one aspiration in life – of obtaining the highest epithet of the human race, the epithet of "Vasudeva" – the Supreme Being. My dream of becoming a "Vasudeva" was never fulfilled. Dear son, would you make that unfulfilled dream of mine come true? I can clearly see all the essential divine qualities and traits amalgamated in you to achieve that status. Will you accomplish this unfulfilled wish of mine?'

Looking into his eyes with an immense and incomprehensible self-confidence, I said, 'Surely Baba. I will become 'Vasudeva'. Working diligently to achieve that goal, I will travel all over the world, and spread love that goes beyond discrimination. I will treat all like they are part of my own existence, and will diligently strive to gain the knowledge to spread love around me. I will act in a neutral, detached way that befits only the 'Vasudeva'. Your son Srikrishna will attain the epithet of 'Vasudeva', and you will surely witness it with your own eyes.'

I bowed and paid obeisance to my parents, determined to fulfil my promise. That night, while walking towards my bedchamber, the divine mantras of Sudarshan chakra kept resonating in my mind. Lying in bed, while observing the symbols of the conch, fish, flag, swastika and chakra on my rosy palm, only one word kept revolving around – 'Vasudeva, Vasudeva!'

The very next day, in the royal council of the Yadavas, minister Vipruthu made a significant announcement in the presence of Maharaja Ugrasena. Pointing to Father, who was sitting on the right of the Maharaja, he said, 'Vasudeva's sister, wife of the Chedi king Damaghosha – Shrutashravadevi – has arrived in Mathura from the city of Shuktimati to meet him. She has come to discuss something of utmost importance. Please allow me to present her in the council.'

Dada and I kept looking at each other after hearing that. We were going to see Father's eldest sister for the first time.

The minister reverentially presented the Chedi maharani in the council. Shrutashravadevi presented royal gifts to Maharaja Ugrasena, offered salutations to him and, addressing the Yadava council, especially our father, she said, 'I am the daughter of Mathura. My son Shishupala is beyond my control and that of the king. He has associated himself with the Magadha emperor Jarasandha... He recently chased Srikrishna along with Jarasandha and conceded humiliating defeat on Mount Gomanta. He has returned home barely saving his own life. I implore the Yadavas, Vasudeva and especially Srikrishna, to forget and forgive the recklessness of my son.'

This was completely unexpected for Maharaja Ugrasena. Utterly perplexed, he could not even respond properly to her plea. He kept looking expectantly at Vasudevababa. I could clearly see Baba caught in a predicament due to blood relations. This stalemate had to be broken. I had to intervene. By now, I had enough practice in putting forward ideas to others in a way that was easily comprehensible to them.

I got up immediately, glanced around the council hall and said, 'Yadava warriors, the maharani of Chedi is the daughter of Mathura, so the Yadavas should accept her plea without a doubt. I readily accept it. On behalf of all present here, I promise our revered aunt that I will patiently tolerate one hundred offences of her son, my cousin Shishupala. Nonetheless, he will never be able to commit the hundred and first offence. He should be watchful not to commit that mistake. Otherwise, he will have to suffer the consequences of his actions. My dear aunt should be content with this promise. I request her to accept our hospitality and convey our regards to Maharaja Damaghosha.'

She went back satisfied. Nowadays, for no reason, I had started reminiscing about Gokul in Vraja. Though it was near, it was not possible to pay a visit to it. I knew I would not be able to come back if I were to go there. I had been transformed since I left Gokul, therefore the gopas and the gopikas of Gokul were not going to be able to bond with me like they had before. The 'Srikrishna' in me had no right to shatter the image of the 'Gopalkrishna' in their hearts.

I said to Balaramadada, 'Dada, you should go to Vraja one of these days and meet Nandababa, Yashodama, Eka, all our childhood friends, Radha and the gopa–gopis, and bring news of their wellbeing to us.

'And do one thing. Do not wear the royal costume when you go. Wear the simple gopa dress of Vraja and visit them as one of them. Only then will they recognise you, and open their hearts to you.'

Dada went to Vraja and brought news of well-being of all people there.

Mathura, too, was free from worries at present, now that the threat of Jarasandha and Magadha's assaults had been warded off. Days were passing joyously. Taking the chariot, I would usually go for a ride with Dada and Uddhava on the shores of the Yamuna. During one such ride, Dada asked me a tricky question, 'Brother, you entangled me in the chains of marriage, but what about you?'

'I have never been approached with a proposal by any king like you were, Dada. Otherwise, I would have thought about it too.' I dismissed his question casually.

That day, after returning to the royal palace, minister Vipruthu presented a very peculiar news to our family. His head hanging low, he said, 'Bhishmaka, also known as Hiranyaroman, the king of Vidarbha, has organised the swayamwar – wedding ceremony – of his daughter Rukmini, but he has not invited the Yadavas of the Shursena kingdom!'

Maharaja Ugrasena asked Vipruthu, 'Minister, what could be the reason?'

Minister Vipruthu answered hesitatingly, 'The princess is still young anyway. And Mathura is so far away from Kundinpura. It is possible that they may have forgotten our royal family by oversight.'

'How is that possible, minister? We have just recently passed by their kingdom after executing Shrigala, the southern king of Karvir.' Balaramadada firmly emphasised his point.

'I know why the king of Vidarbha has not invited the Yadavas. It seems our forefather, Maharaja Yadu, was cursed by his father Yayati. Everyone believes that since then, the Yadavas have lost their Kshatriya status. The royals of Vidarbha do not consider the Yadavas their equals,' I said, bringing the discussion to the point. The minister was startled.

'...Therefore, only for that purpose I have decided to attend the swayamwar ceremony even without any invitation. Dada will stay behind for the protection of Mathura. I will bring the princess of Vidarbha to Mathura in the presence of King Bhishmaka, Jarasandha's ally, his son Rukmi – the disciple of Bhrigushreshtha Parashurama, and his brothers. Initially I will try to reconcile with them and if that does not work, as the last resort I will abduct her by force as per the great tradition of the Kshatriyas.' I spoke with a certain resolve. Hearing my words, the royal council calmed down.

A few days before Kartik Paurnima, our troops left the borders of Mathura, moving towards Dandakaranya again. Once before, I had passed through this dense forest with the intense urge to meet Parashurama. This time I was going to pass through it again, for obtaining the Vidarbha princess whom I had not seen so far.

After a month's time, we entered the Vidarbha kingdom of the Aandhrabhrutya dynasty.

Kundinpura. The royal capital of the Aandhrabhrutyas. Kings, invited for the swayamwar, had set up camps on the outskirts. Among those were Jarasandha, Shishupala and Shalva. Also, kings of southern and eastern kingdoms like Panchala, Vatsa, Matsya, Videha, Kosala, Anga, Vanga, Tripura and Uttkala had assembled. The name of the Yadavas of the Shursena kingdom was not even being mentioned in any of the camps. If at all the subject came up, it was instantly rejected by bringing up the old curse, and the subject was changed. We got hopeful news from only one camp – the camp of King Krathakaishika!

He did not approve of the fact that we were being excluded from the swayamwar. He dispatched his minister and invited us honourably to his city. There, in the presence of Satyaki and Anadhrishti, he bestowed his kingdom upon me. In the presence of everyone in the royal council, he crowned me in a proper ceremony at the hands of the royal priests.

I could not reject his offer, for it would have insulted the Yadavas accompanying me. Therefore, I accepted his offer. For once in my life, I sat on the royal throne. Honouring Krathakaishika's earnest affection, I became a formally ordained king, and returned to the frontiers of Kundinpura.

Now, we were officially eligible for participating in the swayamwar ceremony of the Vidarbha princess. We were waiting in our camp for the next day's ceremony.

In reality, the swayamwar did not take place at all. That very night, Jarasandha, Shishupala and Shalva spun a conspiracy. They organised a council of all assembled kings and vilified me intensively.

After the council, they sent a message to Bhishmaka's son Rukmi, 'If Srikrishna, a cowherd who was defeated in war and who was made king by somebody else, is treated in the same way as us at the swayamwar ceremony, we will never approve of it. Srikrishna is not a Kshatriya. He is a worthless, lowlife cowherd. He has no right to be in the ceremony at all. His participation is the swayamwar is an insult to us.'

King Bhishmaka got utterly confused by this message. Rukmi advised him, 'Order Srikrishna to go back, and organise the swayamwar ceremony for the rest of the kings.' He was on the verge of convincing Bhishmaka to do so. But King Krathakaishika presented our side and the Yadavas were invited to the swayamwar.

As that news spread among the assembled kings on the outskirts of Kundinpura, they lost their temper. Jarasandha and Shishupala were the first ones to abandon their camps and return. Following them, Shalva and all other kings left their camps.

We were the only ones left on the desolate land of Vidarbha – the Yadavas of the Shursena kingdom and our closest ally, Krathakaishika. That day at our camp base, I was at a loss for words. How obstinate the kings of Aaryavarta were. Finally, with resolve I said to our strongest supporter, Krathakaishika, 'Dear friend, let us return to your royal city now. Let our warriors take some rest. Then we will return to Mathura. From today onwards, you have become our closest ally.'

On our return to Krathakaishika's kingdom, the first thing I did was reinstate his royal crown and return his kingdom to him in a formal ceremony. The burden on my head was released and I felt so liberated at that time. While returning in the embellished chariot gifted to us by Krathakaishika, I said to Uddhava, 'Udho, you always admire me and feel so proud. But see how he was humiliated by the trio of Jarasandha, Shishupala and Shalva.'

'Whatever you say, only you can take such a decision of returning Krathakaishika's kingdom to him, and it befits you perfectly. You did not let anything tarnish your pure reputation. I am indeed proud of you.'

At this time, deep down in the recesses of my mind, the mantras of Sudarshan chakra were resonating vaguely. But on the surface, only two names were revolving in my mind. One was of Krathakaishika and the second was of the not-yet-seen Vidarbha princess, Rukmini. What did she look like, and how was she in person, I wondered.

On our return to Mathura, we faced a very bizarre situation regarding our elderly royal priest, Gargamuni. Even I did not know what or how to ask him. Gargamuni was the father of our foremost enemy, and that bitter truth had come to our notice only now.

Jarasandha had repeatedly failed in his attempts to uproot us from Mathura. So, he had played a very astute game this time. He had formed an alliance with Shalva, the ruler of the Saubha kingdom. To annihilate the Yadavas, rather to destroy me for good, he had summoned Kalayavana, our enemy from near the faraway kingdom of Gandhara, to Aaryavarta.

Shalva owned a high-speed aircraft, a sky-travelling machine that could easily travel thousands of yojanas. It was named 'Saubha' in honour of his kingdom. He had flown to the Gandhara kingdom in his aircraft and invited Kalayavana.

Kalayavana used to reside in his state within the Gandhara country for some time and, at other times, in the southern kingdom of Aaryavarta in the Ajitanjaya city with his foster father Yavanaraja. He was, in fact, a biological son of our royal priest, Gargamuni.

How did all these shocking, improbable things come to be? During one of Gargamuni's travels, the Yavanaraja of Ajitanjaya city approached him, and served him humbly to obtain his blessings. Gargamuni gave him the blessing of a son. Despite the blessing and even though he had many wives, the Yavanaraja did not have any progeny. When he brought the fact to Gargamuni's attention, he felt bewildered at first. Then he said to the king with determination, 'My word will never be untrue. You will obtain a son. Though you cannot become a father yourself, you will be the foster father of my own son.'

To keep his promise, when a gopa woman named Gopali gave birth to his son in Mathura, Gargamuni gave away his son to Yavanaraja right after his birth. Kalayavana was that very son.

Just as calmly as he had done all this, he told us the whole story. How was it possible to get irate with him? We put forth the complicated situation about his son, Kalayavana. He said, 'The day I gave him away as a foster child to Yavana, he became Yavana's family. I gave up my right as his father. As Yadava leaders, you are free to take any necessary action against him. I will raise no objection. I have always been loyal to the Yadavas and will remain so in future.'

Gargamuni was an exemplar for us. The most erudite person, he was an expert in horoscope-reading and architecture. For many years, he had imparted all-round knowledge of life to the young and the old Yadavas. It was impossible for us to blame him or do anything that would hurt him.

We got ready to face any kind of ordeal. Jarasandha was not going to be content unless and until he had uprooted all Yadavas, along with Dada and me. His ego was now badly hurt due to the humiliating defeat on Mount Gomanta. He had expanded his circle of allies by inviting Shalva and Kalayavana. Along with my paternal cousins Shishupala and Dantavakra, he was now getting assistance from his new ally, Kalayavana. Bhishmaka was also going to assist him secretly.

Assaulting us from three sides – Shishupala and Jarasandha from the east, Shalva from the west and Bhishmaka from the south – they were going to slaughter Mathura. Jarasandha felt that the Yadavas were an obstruction in the path of his Naramedha – a yajna that involved human sacrifice. He was only fifteen kings short of completing the required number of hundred captive kings for the sacrifice.

We started getting news of various powerful armies of our enemies assembling in Girivraja from all sides. Accompanied by minister Vipruthu, Uddhava, Dada and I immediately approached King Kakudmin of Raivataka kingdom. With his assistance, along with a few divers, we thoroughly inspected the ocean from the Prabhas region of the Aanarta kingdom to Kushasthali for one week. For hours, we scrutinised the expanse along the ocean coast till the island where Shankhasura was executed.

Fortunately, in the region of Mount Raivataka, we came across an undisturbed large island near Kushasthali. Covered with trees, the green island looked like an emerald fixed in the blue socket of the ocean. It was not a single island. In fact, it was one of twin islands attached to each other by means of a tabor-shaped passage in the ocean. It was easily possible to reach the Kushasthali island by crossing the distance of a yojana through the ocean creek. A perfect place to keep a watchful eye on the ocean.

The twin islands were convenient to get in touch with the Aanarta, Saurashtra, Bhrigukachchha, Marusthala and Avanti kingdoms located at the rear. Adjoining these islands on the north, there was a desolate region that stretched for thousands of yojanas – the desert land of Kachchha. It meant that from three directions – the south, the west and the north – no assault was possible on these islands. The western ocean had spread around all the three sides. Only from the fourth direction, the eastern side, these islands were connected to the land of Saurashtra.

We sat on a huge boulder at the centre of the Kushasthali island. It had survived the surge of the sun's heat and the impact of ocean water for millions of years. I went into the meditative trance taught by Acharya Sandipani.

For a long time, I silently communicated with the continuous sound of the ocean. The mantras of Sudarshan and the sound of the ocean fused into each other. I had a ceaseless and unbreakable bond with it. No, in fact, it was my own sound. The sound and I were not two separate entities! The resonating, rhythmic Sudarshan mantras within me and the sound were one.

That eternal sound was speaking to me with a roar now, 'Srikrishna! This is your Karmabhumi! Oh, son of Vasudeva. Erect the first glorious, majestic golden city of the Aaryavarta. Raise the first harbour of Aaryavarta that will become home to many magnificent ships. Right here, on the coast of the vibrant ocean. This is the place of your duty, your ascetic abode, and your ultimate accomplishment.

'Arise, oh descendant of Vrushnis and Andhakas, the son of Vasudeva, Achyuta – make such a firm, sky-high resolution that the whole world will remember it forever. Take a vow right now to build a mammoth, formidable, organised, secure golden city for the Yadavas on the land of Kushasthali.'

I opened my eyes peacefully, and automatically stood up as if entranced. I untied the Paanchajanya conch tied in a scarf around my waist and held it in my fist. Momentarily touching it to my forehead, I raised my head high towards the sky and blew it to pronounce my resolve. Its hair-raising sounds mingled with the roaring sounds of the western ocean. Many a huge silver fish sprang out of the ocean water, glistened and disappeared.

Uddhava, who possessed great presence of mind, rushed forward and promptly brought a palmful of water from the western ocean and let it trickle on the gleaming, white Paanchajanya; it dripped on the land of Kushasthali. He then rapidly uttered some mantras for land worship. We all prayed humbly. A promise was made to erect a secure, grand and inhabitable golden royal city of the Yadavas on the land of Kushasthali on the coast of the western ocean to raise a new, powerful welfare state.

The next day, Uddhava sought out a knowledgeable elderly priest from Saurashtra, who was well versed in the Vedas. Under his guidance, we performed a formal ritual of land worship by chanting mantras. Then we returned to Mathura.

Soon I called for a Yadava royal meeting in Mathura. For many prominent Yadavas, this was going to be the last meeting there. As per my suggestion, Maharaja Ugrasena was going to appoint Gargamuni as the chief guest of the meeting. After the meeting, all the Yadavas were going to make loyal efforts for all-round prosperity of the new city. The meeting was overcrowded like never before and began in a solemn atmosphere.

I greeted everyone warmly and said, 'Dear Yadavas! I have delightful news for all of you. Soon a new royal city will be erected for the Yadavas. I have selected an auspicious location for the city, thoroughly examining it with Dada and Uddhava. I have returned only after sanctifying that location. This land is located far away on the coast of the western ocean, near Mount Raivataka in the Aanarta kingdom in Saurashtra – the name is Kushasthali.

'Gargamuni, the greatest architect of the Yadavas, will design and raise this spectacular city. I am quite sure that he will raise a city befitting the reputation of the Yadavas. All the craftsmen amongst you – architects, ironsmiths, carpenters, masons and goldsmiths – will have to use your expertise for the construction of this city. Many skilled workers from other kingdoms invited by minister Vipruthu will assist us in the mission. Tomorrow itself we will all have to leave for the site in bullock carts. This city will belong to all Yadavas. Therefore, all citizens should strive to assist through day and night.

'As Mathura is our original kingdom since the time of Maharaja Yadu, we cannot desert it completely. Therefore, as per his wish, Maharaja Ugrasena will stay back in Mathura for some time, along with a few warriors. All others – young, old, men and women – will take off for the western coast. Starting from tomorrow, there should be a constant flow of Yadavas travelling from Mathura to Aanarta, Saurashtra. Do you all agree?' I raised my right fist high in the sky and appealed emotionally to the overcrowded council.

'Agree, we absolutely agree, revered Yadava! We all will leave Mathura tomorrow itself. Hail Yadava leader, Maharaja Srikrishna!' There was not a single soul that did not respond spontaneously to my appeal.

A few days passed. The news of a total solar eclipse predicted by Gargamuni and other royal priests of various kingdoms spread everywhere. As per tradition, the ritual to ward off the ill effect of this eclipse was to be carried out. For that purpose, the kings of major kingdoms in Brahmavarta and their royal ministries were going to assemble at the holy place, Kurukshetra, on the shore of Sanneth Sarovar near the Suryakunda. The Yadavas were also going to attend. We dispatched a few troops ahead to set up our camp. As it is, our Shursena kingdom was experiencing a total eclipse – a destructive concord of three powerful arch enemies – Kalayavana, Shalva and Jarasandha.

An auspicious day for our departure was selected. A few chosen people like Dada, Uddho, both commanders – Akrura and Satrajita – and I left for Kurukshetra. Kurukshetra. A holy place, brimming with lakes! Generations of various Kshatriya dynasties like the Yadava, Kuru, Matsya, Chedi, Panchala, Panchanada and Virata assembled here without fail, at the time of every solar eclipse, and offered alms in charity at the shore of the Sanneth Sarovar.

We were also going for the same purpose. I had been hearing the divine mantras of Sudarshan in my mind ever since I had been blessed with it. But this time, all I could feel was the raucous sound of the ocean's high tide and the shrill cry of female lapwings. Why was this happening? I found myself asking the same question countless times, but could not find a satisfactory answer. Finally, smiling to myself, I simply shook off all questions. Looking at my smile, Uddhava said, 'Dada, what were you thinking about for such a long time?' Pointing towards Sanneth Sarovar in front of us, diverting his attention, I said, 'Uddhava, we have reached our destination, Kurukshetra, the land of Dharma! Let us get down.'

The Yadava camp was set up on the northern side of the Suryakunda. As per Gargamuni's instructions, we finished our bath and stood in the Suryakunda. We offered oblations to the Sun god. As the bright disc of the sun began to get shrouded, my entire body started shaking. I lost sense of everything around me – my relatives, the minister, the sages, Sanneth Sarovar and even Kurukshetra. My eyes closed inadvertently. For a moment, it felt like I myself was getting eclipsed. Then everything went blank. Bit by bit, I got completely eclipsed.

After a few moments, Uddhava shook me forcefully. Wide-eyed, he commented, 'How horrible you looked during the time of the eclipse, Dada – horribly dark! Please tell me at least once, who are you exactly?'

I diverted his attention by saying, 'Will you please first listen to what Akrurakaka has to say?' Then I simply laughed like nothing had happened at all. Akrurakaka humbly said, 'I just met Vidura, the royal minister of the Kurus. From Hastinapura, your aunt Kuntidevi has also arrived here to offer charity, along with her five sons. They have just finished their offerings. As soon as they came to know about your arrival, they started for Kurukshetra.'

I said to Dada, 'Dada, our charities are already paying off. What a great day and moment to meet them. Let us go ahead to welcome them.'

We had barely crossed a small distance of the lush green meadows spread around us, when we saw Aunt Kuntidevi. She had a round moon-like face. She was a little plump, wearing a soft, bright white saree with a bare forehead. She was walking slowly and graciously. Two of her sons were on her right. And the one on her left was tall, strong and hefty. Behind her stood two sons looking like a pair of elegant royal swans of similar build and height. Behind this royal family of the Pandavas was Mahatma Vidura, the minister of the Kurus. He was the same age as our minister Vipruthu and had a similar virtuous disposition.

Just as I had been drawn towards Acharya Sandipani and Bhrigu Parashurama, I was drawn to Aunt Kunti. Walking forward briskly, I approached her. Dropping on my knees to the ground, I put my head on her feet. For a few moments, my head remained on her feet involuntarily. Two warm teardrops slid down my cheek. My whole body shook just the way it had during the solar eclipse. Words that she had held back for ages followed: 'Oh, Krishna! Rise!'

I stood up and my eyes momentarily met hers. We instantly felt the connection of our hearts that had existed since several births. Her eyes were unique. I had never seen such eyes. The very next moment, my dear aunt held my arms and embraced me tightly. Emotionally overwhelmed, her body trembled and she sobbed for quite some time.

After a while, she regained her composure. Holding my shoulders tightly, she made me stand in front of her eldest son. Like the proud and experienced Kshatriya lady she was, she spoke in a clear, determined voice now, 'Yudhishthira, this is your cousin, the son of my elder brother Vasudeva and his wife Devaki. The world calls him Srikrishna, but for me he is only Krishna.'

I stepped forward to bow and pay obeisance to Yudhishthira. He did not let me do so, and simply said, 'No no, let it be. Let it be.'

Meanwhile, Dada and Uddhava had already obtained blessings from Aunt Kunti. She held the upper arm of the hefty, fair-skinned son standing on her left, pulled him forward and said, 'My son, Bhima. To restrain him is like restraining the stormy wind. Apart from me, he may listen only to you some day.' Recognising his mother's gesture, hefty Bhima pulled the two brothers standing behind him, made them bow down to me and said, 'Yadava, they need your guidance more than me. My dear brothers, Nakula and Sahadeva.' Nakula was the more handsome of the two, with his sharp nose, well-built physique and ruddy fair complexion like Uddhava. The only difference was that Uddhava would have seemed gentler, only to me. Bhima held me in a deep, loving embrace. His face looked peaceful now, like a lion whose hunger had been satiated.

In a single glance, I admiringly observed the faces of my cousins and noted all their qualities subtly in my mind. Yudhishthira was tall, broad shouldered, fair and sharp-nosed, with a raised chest. His face was calm. His thick neck was high above his shoulders. His long, thick eyebrows reached almost upto his ears. His ears were big and long, with fleshy lobules. He was probably just a little older than me.

The edges of Bhima's eyes were reddish. He looked like a mountain and a lion both at once. His thick, curly hair was elegantly resting on his sturdy shoulders. Even while speaking normally, his voice sounded like the thundering clouds of the Mriga Nakshatra. He, too, was older than me.

Nakula and Sahadeva were coeval, of similar height and physique – like a pair of male pigeons. Both looked muscular and fresh. They were a little shorter than me. Bhima was a little taller than both of them, but a bit shorter than me. On this very first meeting, I noticed that none of them wore crowns. Especially today, on their visit to this holy place, they were wearing the traditional twisted turbans of the Kurus.

Finally, turning towards Aunt Kunti, I asked her, 'How come your fifth son is nowhere to be seen? The one I want to meet.'

'He was right here somewhere.' She simply kept smiling at me. I had no clue what was happening. Till today, I used to make fun of people around me, but Aunt Kunti's smile was teasing me. I then understood that he was standing right behind me. Slowly, I turned. The bright Kuru warrior standing in front of me, who had been waiting for quite a while to see me, moved rapidly. In the blink of an eye, he kneeled on his left knee and took the Virasana pose. Such elegance and grace – it completely astonished me. Like the graceful king of the birds, the royal swan, fluttering his pure white wings, while gently alighting on Manasa Sarovar. Like the elegant white pigeon sitting on the dome of the Yadava royal palace in Mathura. No! In fact, he did not look like anything else. He looked only and solely like himself.

I caught him by his strong, muscular shoulders tightly but gently pulled him up with warmth and looked deep into his eyes. He smiled momentarily. We recognised the bond connecting us since several previous lives. He was the same height as me, with a similar complexion, fish-shaped eyes, and a sharp nose like the tip of an arrow. Thick-necked, like my horse Sugriva. He was an exact replica of me! For a moment, I thought that I was looking at my own reflection in a mirror. The next moment, I recognised the slight difference between the both of us. I laughed to myself. He also reciprocated with the same smile. I had a double-tooth near my right chin, and he had a double-tooth near his left chin. Aunt Kunti stepped forward and, putting her hands on both our shoulders, she gently pressed them. Before she could say anything, I spoke up, 'Aunt, this is your son Arjuna. The one who acquires whatever knowledge he comes across. The one who considers virtue as wealth and earns it. Dhananjaya, Partha, isn't it?' Looking into his eyes, I questioned him.

'Oh Hrishikesha, you are the one who has conquered all the senses since birth. You need no introduction. And as far as I am concerned, I have already showed you what you mean to me, by taking the Virasana stance at your feet the moment we met,' he said. The next moment, I held the handsome, muscular man in a deep embrace. I heard my dear aunt whispering a few words again, 'They look so alike. Cannot figure out who is who. Just stay like this always – inseparable. My blessings to you. May you have a long life; may you be victorious.'

A tranquil night descended on the shore of Sanneth Sarovar in Kurukshetra. I intently listened to Aunt Kunti's trying, turbulent life story. Throughout the night, she kept narrating the gripping story of the Pandavas' childhood, full of joy and sorrow. I kept listening to her, holding back the divine mantras of Sudarshan rising in my mind again and again. The only witness was Arjuna, smiling sweetly in between. He was Gudakesha, the one who had conquered sleep. All others had fallen asleep.

Just like a few select Yadavas, the four horses of my chariot, the western ocean, charioteer Daruka, friend Sudama, dear Uddhava and the sun in the sky – which had been eclipsed a few moments ago – felt like a part of my existence, so did Arjuna. I met my soulmate Radha in Gokul, Uddhava was my favourite cousin, but this one was my friend for life, distinct from all others.

I was an Ashwattha, an upside-down tree. But Arjuna was the straight shadow of the upside-down tree. I was a figure of energy – a brilliant flame of life. My young friend Arjuna was the shadow of the same divine flame. Can a flame ever have a shadow? Yes, it can. That, too, so bright! Dark-complexioned Arjuna seemed like that bright shadow to me. I was striving to achieve a particular mission in my life with a relinquishing sentiment. Only 'Premayoga', pure love, could help me achieve this mission. Therefore, I was looking for a valiant man with utter devotion and loyalty towards me as a medium. I found that man in Arjuna.

We bade farewell to the Pandavas and returned to Mathura.

Upon arriving in Mathura, Commander Satyaki presented a disciple from the ashrama of Bhrigukachchha before me. The news he had brought was not going to give us any time to relax. Kalayavana's sizeable army had assembled on the western coast. Coming from the royal city of Girivraja, Jarasandha's enormous Magadha army had unified with it. From the royal city of Martikavati on Mount Arbuda, Shalva had also joined in. Bhishmaka had already left with his army from Kundinpura. The trio's united army had spread along the coast of the western ocean. They planned to surround Mathura from all four sides and annihilate us.

Parashurama's follower in Bhrigukachchha had immediately conveyed the news to us. Dada and I quickly instructed our army. Mathura now echoed with the cacophony of war drums. Our golden chariots, bearing orange pennants with the Garuda emblem, were equipped for war, and left for the western ocean through the western gate of Mathura. Only a few million Yadavas were warriors. The rest were engaged in daily chores. Several had already been dispatched to Kushasthali island to assist in the construction of the new royal city.

After many sojourns, we reached the western coast, near Mount Arbuda in Marusthali. We received information that the rival army had settled in a huge encampment at the base of a mountain near Dhaulpura. As we were approaching Dhaulpura, I presented a strategic proposal to Dada. Had we launched only a one-pronged attack, we would have never succeeded. The combined army of the trio was thrice as big as ours. The western ocean on the one hand, the massive rival army on the other, and the widespread Marusthali region in between – such was the scene. I convinced Dada and both commanders that it was inevitable and beneficial to divide our army into three sections. Dada would attack Shalva and chase him to Mount Arbuda. Both commanders would con Jarasandha to chase them and divert him towards the Magadha kingdom itself. With selected troops, I would directly face Kalayavana.

Dhaulpura. A city surrounded by desert on all four sides. Here I was going to show Kalayavana that although he was Yavana, I was going to be his 'Kala' – Death. As planned, Dada confronted Shalva from one side. From the other side, our valiant commander duo challenged the Magadha army. Kalayavana was left alone on the desert base of

Dhaulpura. Amidst the cacophony of war drums, I directly attacked Kalayavana.

Within moments, my Garudadhwaja caught up with Kalayavana's chariot. First, we fought a thrilling battle, propelling rocks at each other. The chariots and horses around us were barely visible in the deluge of rocks from both sides. But our chariot was sturdy, as it was made of iron. Controlling the four horses of our chariot, Daruka rotated it like a spinning top around Kalayavana's chariot. Both chariots were out of rocks. The bow-and-arrow battle began now. Kalayavana was a skilled warrior. His charioteer was probably an expert too. As the arrows in our quivers ran out, we began the javelin war.

Daruka was handling our horses exactly as per my instructions. A single tug of the reins, and all of them would fold their front legs to sit down in unison. With each tug they were dragging the chariot awkwardly around, giving the impression that we were struggling. All of a sudden, I ordered Daruka to haul my chariot out of the battlefield. He skilfully steered our dragging chariot out. With a certain idea in mind, I pulled out the Paanchajanya, raised my head skywards and blew it with a strange, terrifying sound. It was a signal for our army to retreat from the war. The Yadava army under my command was well acquainted with it. Our army began retreating.

Kalayavana instructed his charioteer in the Yavani tongue. His chariot, with seven sand-coloured horses, began chasing me. So far everything was going according to plan. My expert charioteer Daruka kept our chariot ahead. Kalayavana was thrilled to see us running away from war fearing for our lives. His eyes, already red from drinking the Gandhara wine, became even more red while screaming at me in rage. He pulled his charioteer by the collar, and himself took the reins of the hefty Gandhar horses. Screaming something viciously in his incomprehensible Yavani tongue, he began chasing me.

Yavana chasing Kala – such was the spectacle on the battlefield of Dhaulpura. I smiled to myself. By this time, Daruka had skilfully drawn Yavana many yojanas away from the battlefield.

Now the next phase in the drama of this combat began. As I signalled, Daruka pulled all the eight reins in his hands in a specific way and at the same time made a peculiar sound with his mouth, warning the horses to come to a halt. Picking up their front hooves, they neighed loudly, folded their knees and sat on the ground instantly. As if our chariot, in which we were escaping, had broken down. Daruka swiftly jumped on to the ground, and immediately untied Sugriva. Shaking his tail, with his ears pricking up, he stood up, snorting. I jumped on to the ground, mounted Sugriva and prodded him with my heel. That auspicious white animal understood my signal perfectly. Rearing up, he neighed much louder than before and sprinted forward swiftly.

In front of us stood Mount Dhaula – average in height, composed of layers of sand amassed over the years and surrounded by small trees and short bushes. Sugriva kept galloping towards the mountain. After travelling quite a distance, I looked back. Kalayavana, burning with the fire of vengeance, was still after me. He had also untied one of the horses from his chariot and was riding it. He was not going to stop at any cost. I smiled again. This was an excellent opportunity indeed. We rode our horses till we perspired. We reached the summit of Mount Dhaula. Now I let Sugriva go, and started walking on foot. The blazing sun was scorching my skin. The hot, barren desert was spread out everywhere under my feet. I could see the mouth of a cavern in front of me, about nine–ten feet tall and covered with small creepers. I muttered to myself, 'This is the place of Rajarshi. This is the place where this war drama is going to end.' I evoked our family goddess Ida, and entered the cavern. I was certain Kalayavana was going to chase me here too. I kept walking, turning left and right through the dark passage. After a long time, I reached the spacious central part of the cavern. This was, in fact, a safe, auspicious place of meditation for many sages of Marusthali. It was dimly visible due to a few sun rays peeking through holes in the roof.

My searching eyes saw an indistinct figure in the corner. It seemed as if he had been there for ages. It had become possible for him only because he had acquired control over his breathing through severe penance. An anthill had formed up to the throat of his supine body. He was the royal sage Muchkunda, the forefather of one of the branches of the Yadavas in the south. Thinking of something, I laughed to myself.

Stepping forward, I humbly put my head at his feet, which were covered with mud from the anthill, with utmost respect. Untying the long blue scarf around my waist, I held it in my hand, and opened the knot that held the Paanchajanya. Touching the divine conch to my forehead first, I put it near the feet of the royal ascetic. Then, with caution, I gently spread the shawl on his body without disturbing his meditation. Paying obeisance to him again, I squeezed my body into a corner and hid there. After a while, a few intimidating Yavani words echoed through the cavern. They meant, 'How far are you going to run, you cowherd of Mathura? Where can you hide?' Deep, heavy breaths followed. Within a moment, Kalayavana, who I was only able to hear, appeared. Dark, tall, red-eyed, with a ferocious face. I realised there was no resemblance between him and Gargamuni.

Furiously moving around, blabbering constantly, the tall, giant Yavana got excited when he saw my blue scarf. His loud, roaring shriek reverberated in the interior of the cavern, 'Sleeping? You, shameless cowherd. Get up. Are you going to get up or not? Get ready for a duel.' Shouting at the top of his lungs, thinking it was I who was sleeping there, he threw a single hard kick. Breaking the anthill around, his kick reached the chest of the royal ascetic, Muchkunda. He stood up as his prolonged sleep, Yoganidra, had been interrupted. The light in the cavern seemed brighter. He picked up the Agnikankana weaponying at his feet – he had kept it there before beginning his Yoganidra. He roared, 'Insolent Yavana, you have interrupted my Yoganidra. Now pay for it.'

Instantly, he turned his Agnikankana weapon with such speed that when its sharp edges pierced Kalayavana's skull, he screamed in agony. The royal sage then struck Yavana on the chest, the arms and wherever else he could. Kalayavana fell down and died. I came forward and put my head on sage Muchkunda's feet. Pulling me up, he embraced me. As we were related through the Yadava lineage, he commanded me, 'Srikrishna, pick up your life-saver Paanchajanya conch. Then go to the entrance of the cavern and blow it with your soul in this barren land. I would have handed it to you myself but my hands are soiled with a Yavana's blood.'

I picked up the Paanchajanya, and came to the entrance of the cavern. Raising my head high, I blew that divine conch effusively. Its inspirational sound resonated in the air of Dhaulgiri, Dhaulpura, Arbudagiri,

Marusthali and the nearby expanse. Kala had finally taken the Yavana. One storm of a foreign invasion on Aaryavarta had been pacified.

We dispatched Kalayavana's immeasurable treasure to the Kushasthali island. It mainly contained hefty Gandhara horses, and plenty of camels. It also had many bullions of gold that Kalayavana had amassed by ransacking many kingdoms along the west coast after coming here.

Acharya Sandipani and Gargamuni chose an auspicious day for performing the formal rituals of land worship to commence construction of the royal city on the Kushasthali island.

The enormous undertaking of constructing the new royal city had now commenced officially. Gargamuni invited Maya, an accomplished asura architect, for assistance in the project. Vishwakarma, a creator from the Kurujangal region, was also summoned. In a chamber on the shore of the island, both of them created a clay replica of the city with the aid of many experts from various kingdoms. Dada and I went there ourselves and examined it thoroughly. Simply ingenious, it was creativity at its best. Impressed with the replica, I put my arm around Maya's shoulder and said, 'I will be looking forward to seeing my residence in the royal city. Especially my spacious resting chamber, connected by a special stairway, as I want it. I have a special design for the stairway – a "Krishnasopana" – in my mind, leading to the resting chamber in the upper section of the residence. It is going to be the most significant part of this design.

'I want this stairway built mainly from the broad planks of the Krishnashisam wood. These wooden steps will be covered in gold-plated, thick copper sheets. To begin with, this stairway will have only twenty-five steps. The first eighteen steps in memory of the eighteen royal families of the Yadavas. The next four will be for both my fathers and mothers. The next two will be for Dada and his wife. The remaining one will be for Acharya Sandipani. Thus, initially there will be only twenty-five steps of the Krishnasopana.'

'Only twenty-five? Your life is going to begin here. Many more people will come into your life. What about them?' Gargamuni asked. Smiling at him, I said, 'For that, sufficient space will be left between every two steps. Steps can then be added in that space as needed. Besides, the top passage will be raised higher as and when necessary. Probably you yourself will have to complete that task!' For a long time, I provided details of the Krishnasopana design in my mind to Gargamuni, Vishwakarma and Maya. I clearly read the question reflecting in their eyes. They were wondering – in this enormous undertaking on the twin islands, I had not shown any interest at all in the royal palace, the royal council, the queens' residences, or the temples and gymnasiums; then why was I so focused on this particular stairway? Before they could ask me any more questions, I distracted them by saying, 'Today onwards, Dada and I will travel frequently from Mathura to Kushasthali. We will supply the necessary materials on time. Let the project begin.'

Many seasons passed by. The enormous undertaking of creating the royal Yadava city lasted several years. One fine day, Gargamuni and Maya communicated a much-awaited message, 'The construction of the royal city has been completed. Maharaja should choose an auspicious day for his coronation. He should come with the senior Yadavas and take a look at the city. If he observes any defects those will be fixed as per his instruction. We are sure he will not find a single defect. Actually, we are confident that when Srikrishna sees the "Krishnasopana" that he has desired, he will surely give us a pat on our backs. '

We left for Kushasthali.

What an unbelievable sight it was! At first glance, the golden fortification spread from one end to the other, glistening in the sunrays, dazzled our eyes. The island's long, yellowish, reflection in the water did not stay steady even for a single moment. It kept dancing on the waves. As a narrow strip of land had gone under the water in the ocean, the twin island on the right could not be seen. All of us arrived in large boats dispatched by Gargamuni. After walking for some time, we stood in front of the gigantic, golden main entrance on the east. It had two doors covered in thick gold-plated copper sheets with beautiful engravings. It was difficult to keep one's eyes open in the bright light reflecting from it. The majestic, graceful Garuda on its surface, spreading its golden wings as if about to soar in the sky, was eye-catching. It had sharp, golden talons. It had effortlessly balanced the golden replica of the full moon on its head. It was the motivational insignia on the Yadava pennant. Onlookers would halt right in front of the gate in awe. It was the emblem of the Yadavas of Somavansha. On the right door, the little golden star, Arundhati, was shining next to a crescent moon. The remaining surface was covered with golden figures of weapons used by Yadavas – the sword, the chakra, the mace, the trident, the pestle, Bhrushundi, Agnikankana, and the bow and arrow. A single fearless, serene, healthy cow and a lion looking at her could also be seen.

After we finished observing it, the gatekeepers opened the gigantic gate. To pay obeisance to my karmabhumi, I touched the land with my right hand, then touched it to my chest and head. Dada followed suit. We followed Maya, Vishwakarma and Gargamuni to the top of the stairway near the gate. Gargamuni and Maya opened two in-built eye-shaped windows on the right and left sides of the golden fortification wall. Offering information about it, they said, 'If at all there is any concern of assault on our royal city, it is only from the eastern side. The other three directions are protected by the western ocean. These two eyes for surveillance of the eastern direction are a precautionary measure. From here, one can see a ten-yojana stretch of the ocean and land in a single glance.' Upon hearing that, I commended Maya for his creativity and put forth some more food for thought, 'There must be a western gate on the opposite side of this gate. We must select a perfect place for surveillance of the ocean from that gate. Not on the island, but in the ocean, by locating a huge boulder in the ocean itself.'

'I did not get it. A watch post in the ocean?' he asked.

'For what?' Dada, too, asked out of curiosity.

'Dada, this is not going to be merely a new royal city of the Yadavas. Remember, Kalayavana came by way of the ocean. We will have to protect this city by building a new naval force. A few kingdoms are located on the west side of the ocean too. To communicate with them, we will have to develop a harbour in the city. To guide ships towards the harbour, we will have to erect a lighthouse. We will have to keep a tall torch of oil constantly burning in the lighthouse after sunset. During the day, of course, its golden dome, shining in the sun, will be visible from afar.'

I was engrossed in thought about what suitable name I could announce for this eastern gate in the first royal council here.

I looked at the temple on the left. The orange pennant fluttered on its golden dome. It was the temple of our family goddess Ida – much grander than the stone temple in Mathura. We entered it along with others. Standing in the heart of the temple, Goddess Ida with ten hands, holding weapons in each of them, was vividly visible from the square outside. The temple had not yet been inaugurated officially.

Looking at the large corral for the cows, I asked Gargamuni, 'How many more gates does the city have?' He answered, 'Three more gates in the three directions. Each main gate has wicket gates too. Besides, considering the structure of the island, some small gates have also been built at various places.' Satisfied by the well-built cow corrals, I asked the craftsmen leaders around, 'It is excellent that you have raised the corrals, but what about grazing the cattle?' A Yadava leader from the group answered zealously, 'We have grazing prairies beyond the trench outside the fortification wall. If those fall short, we can sail our cows in boats to the land of Saurashtra.'

'How are the cows going to cross the trench every day?' I questioned.

'For that, we have built wide, floating bridges,' an expert woodcutter replied.

Looking at Dada, I winked and asked the next question to the sentry of the fortification, 'Can the same floating bridges not be used by the enemy to cross the trenches?'

'Not at all. The floating bridges can be removed in case of an attack by the enemy. Once that is done, the island will be completely cut off from the outside world. Besides, the deep and wide trench inundated with salty water is also secured. Meshes of thorny water creepers are spread throughout the trench. Also, huge alligators and crocodiles captured from the ocean have been trapped in by placing iron grids between the trench and the ocean. They cannot return to the ocean. Roaming around in the trench, they feed themselves on the small fish that swim in through the iron grid. In addition to that, after the craftsmen finish their meals, the remainders are also tossed into the trench to feed them. These huge alligators and crocodiles are, in fact, the real protectors of the trench.' The sentry answered proudly.

We came to the southern gate. The dark black boulders bathing in the pure white foam of the ocean water on this side of the coast looked so wonderful. For a long time, all of us kept looking at the foamy waves colliding with the boulders.

From there, we left for the western gate. From this direction, the deluge from huge rain clouds caused by the ocean winds was going to descend upon the island. As soon as we reached here, I looked at a huge boulder visible far away in the ocean. Pointing at its peak with my forefinger, I said to the royal minister, 'On that rock the lighthouse for this harbour will be raised.' While everybody was thinking about it, Dada asked a relevant question, 'What about the deluge of rain that will thrash this western gate?'

I smiled at Dada. Putting my hand on the royal minister Vipruthu's shoulder, walking towards the northern gate I said, 'Minister, there are heaps of sun-dried Kusha grass spread all over the island. Get thick dry grass sheets made and cover the wings of the golden eagle on the western gate well in time.' Now the last gate, the northern gate, was in sight. Only this door was going to connect this island to the twin island with the queens' residences by way of sea. Standing at the gate, I was immersed in my own thoughts for a long time looking at the gulf stretching before us. I said to Dada, 'Somewhere far away in the north, even beyond Kurukshetra, there lies the monumental snow mountain reaching high up in the sky – Mount Himavana. Kailas, the residence of the greatest ascetic Shiva, is located on that mountain.'

As I had anticipated, there was indeed a golden Shiva temple with a dome. Shiva was our deity in Gokul, as the deity of the Abhirbhanu dynasty. In Mathura, our Yadava family deity was Ida. Creative Gargamuni had wisely founded the temples of both deities in this city. In my mind, the deluge of some unknown rain began pouring. Pure white and uncontrollable. The Sudarshan mantras also echoed momentarily. I stopped Dada, Uddhava, Viprutha, Gargamuni and the others and started talking rapidly, 'The main eastern gate with the watchtower will be named "Shuddhaksha". The southern gate witnessing the rocks bathing in the foamy ocean waves will be called "Pushyadanta". The western gate bearing the deluge of the ocean rain with a smile will be known as "Aindra". This northern gate witnessing Shiva will be called "Bhallata".'

The Yadavas around me kept listening and I kept talking, 'Dear Yadavas, we can see the edifice of the royal assembly with the glistening dome in the centre of this island, encircled by the royal palaces. No other kingdom in the entire Aaryavarta possesses such a unique edifice for the royal assembly. This assembly will be called "Sudharma" – that which protects all that is true, beautiful and righteous! I have not thought of a suitable name for this city yet. But I will do that soon, and announce it in the royal assembly at the right time. Come, let us go there.'

We started walking towards the royal assembly by the royal highway passing in front of the northern gate. On our way, we saw dancing water fountains in many places. On both sides of the road, a variety of trees were planted artistically. Behind them were well-planned markets with a variety of shops. There were also fenced parks at places. The empty space between two parks had been utilised to build armouries, treasuries and stables for horses, camels and elephants. While observing all that, I asked Maya, 'What about the physical exercise of the Yadavas?'

Dada immediately asked his favourite question, 'Where are the wrestling pits? Where are the grounds for the elephant fights? Where are the areas for the Yadava warriors' competitions of horses?'

To satiate his curiosity, Gargamuni answered, 'Those are built in many open places between the two royal highways.'

We reached the east-facing door of the royal assembly. This was where my life's 'karmayoga' was going to take place. I touched the first step of the royal assembly with both hands. I brought both my palms together and prayed with my heart full of emotions and moved forward.

Looking at the circular structure of the royal assembly, I was dazzled for a while and stood still. Everything here was shining golden and bright. In the western direction was our elegant insignia. The huge golden Garuda spreading its wings, effortlessly bearing the shining, full moon on its head, was ready to soar high into the sky.

Two majestic golden thrones were positioned on the highest plane in such a way that the tops of their backs were almost touching the curled talons of the golden Garuda above. These were designed for the maharaja and maharani – for my father and mother. Both the chairs had their hand rests designed in the shape of lions with their jaws wide open. Not a single inch of these thrones was left without a decorative design and the royal emblems. Located almost near the base of these two thrones were two seats smaller in size. These were for the crown prince and his wife, my dear Dada and his wife. A little below that, on the next plane to the right, was a seat with a plain wooden back, no hand rests and covered with deerskin. This was for Acharya Sandipani. A similar seat on the left had been placed for Gargamuni, the royal priest. Below that, on the next plane, there were ten seats in a semicircle, five on the right and five on the left, for ten royal ministers. At the centre of this ring, a large seat had been elevated for the chief minister, Vipruthu. On his right, there was a tall, stone socket to place the magnificent, golden, jewel-studded royal sceptre of the Yadavas. Touching the base of the royal sceptre were two seats, one on either side, for the two commanders of our army – Yuyudhana, also known as Satyaki, and Anadhrishti, who were Satyaka's sons and Shinee's grandsons. On the plane below, there were two long half-circular rows of seats for spies, envoys, army leaders, the treasurer, the armoury chief, the chiefs of horses, elephants and camel troops, and many more.

There were two seats located high on the right, clearly away from the rest of the seats, somewhat parallel to Maharaja Vasudeva's throne or to Prince Balarama's seat. These were also golden but simple, without any decorative engravings on them. Yes, the right seat among them was for me and the left seat was for my future wife. Right now, it was empty.

This seating arrangement of the royal assembly would certainly inspire awe amongst spectators. In front of these royal seats was a huge square. It was for citizens, guests and people seeking justice from the Maharaja – this was the real 'Sudharma' assembly. There were separate sections for men and women. For other royal ladies, separate sections of galleries were located on both sides, parallel to the royal throne. Next to those were sections for other female guests and learned female invitees.

I checked each row leisurely with Dada and Uddhava. In this circular structure of the royal assembly, designated platforms for armed sentinels had also been built. Near the eastern gate, a huge, round time-disc was dangling. Right next to it, a long hammer was placed in a groove – this was to ring the time-indicating tolls. Both were made of iron and polished with gold. We left the Sudharma assembly satisfied. After looking at the well-built mansions of the prince, the royal priest, the chief minister and the commanders, etc., we finally arrived at my residential mansion.

I was eager and extremely curious to see how Maya and Gargamuni had built the 'Krishnasopana'. The moment we entered the mansion, we saw the huge, long, spacious Srikrishnasopana, with glistening golden stairs right in front of us. It was exactly the way I had envisioned it. Moving closer, I stood near the lowest step, touching it and tightly holding the railing on the left. My gaze moved sequentially from the first step upwards and reached the twenty-fifth step eventually.

Questions flooded my mind.

'How far up do I have to climb the staircase of my life yet? How many more men and women am I going to meet at every turn? How many such turns have I left behind? My beloved Gokul, my Baba and Mata there, friends, the gopas and gopis, Eka and Radha. Gokul? No, a childhood. Doesn't everyone have a Gokul of their own childhood?'

We climbed up the golden staircase, visited the resting chamber and the bedchamber on the upper level and came down. I walked through the complete mansion, checking all the big and small rooms and passages. While leaving the mansion with a contented heart, I handed a pearl necklace to Maya and said, 'Maya, we saw Kushasthali, and loved it. It does not have a single fault in it. You will be duly honoured in the special royal council. Tomorrow we will visit the neighbouring Shankhoddhara island to see the queens' residences.'

That day we stayed at Kushasthali. The next day we woke up before sunrise and performed our morning rituals. Standing waist-deep in the ocean water, the three of us offered oblations to the sun. Instead of travelling by way of the channel connecting the twin islands, we sailed in boats to arrive at Shankhoddhara island. Even here, there was a trench and fortification like Kushasthali. It was a little smaller in circumference. It also had four big gates but not as big as Kushasthali's. Here, too, various facilities had been built. Cow corrals had been constructed and grazing meadows were reserved for cattle. The boulders near the fortification on the sandy shore of the western ocean were shaped like seats. The Yadava pennant was fluttering in the air on a platform at the centre of this island.

The chariot assembly on this island was quite spacious. The path connecting both islands was narrow and long. Communication between the two islands by this way was possible only by chariots and horses.

If commuting by water was required, it was only possible through boats, rafts, etc. Both modes of transportation were already in use. The queens' residences had eight grand palaces – four on both sides, facing each other. While observing those edifices, I asked Gargamuni with the usual playfulness, 'Why are there exactly eight of these edifices? And for what?' He took a moment, then with a slight smile, said, 'Even though the Yadava prince may have only one wife, surely the fragrance of her reputation will disperse in all eight directions. These eight edifices are a symbol of that. ' I kept looking at him in amazement.

We also checked out the mansion for Balaramadada's queen. Spending the night on that island, the next day we returned to Mathura.

The invitations for Vasudevababa's coronation were dispatched to various kingdoms in Aaryavarta. I sent off Uddhava again to invite Nandababa, Yashodamata, Ekananga, Radha and everyone from Gokul. But he returned with a sentimental refusal and a few gifts. Yashodamata had refused to come, saying, 'If we see you after so many years now, we won't be able to return to Gokul. We cannot leave Gokul forever, like you have left Mathura. Come to visit Gokul as per your convenience. Come to meet dear Eka. See how she has grown. Come and meet your friend Radha too, at least once. Till then we will meet the Gopalkrishna in our hearts every day.'

Almost all the Yadavas of Mathura left the city to attend the coronation. Only a select few stayed behind. Acharya Kashyapa Sandipani planned the complete agenda for the coronation. Kushasthali island, glistening with golden gates, royal palaces and the fortifications, was now fragrant with various kinds of garlands. In the presence of all sages and hermits from various kingdoms, Sandipani and Gargamuni first performed a religious ceremony at the hands of Vasudevababa and Devakimata to begin the function. Idols of gods and goddesses were formally installed in many temples. Plenty of charities were distributed. Then the actual coronation ceremony began with vibrant sounds of various musical instruments. At the exact moment of sunrise, with various ascetics from holy places like Kashi, Prayaga, Ahichchhtra, Kurukshetra, Panchanada, Hrishikesha and many more coming together to chant the holy mantras, the rituals of the ceremonial 'abhishek' began. Vasudevababa and Devakimata's faces were shining with unlimited, unparalleled radiance today. Their loving eyes silently reflected the serene satisfaction of their lives' fulfilment.

The sun rose. His first rays bowed down to touch the feet of venerable Yadava Maharaja Vasudeva and Maharani Devakidevi. At that moment, hundreds of sages and ascetics began continuously intoning mantras from the Vedas. Five priests performed the holy abhishek on Mother and Father's heads with the holy waters of the Ganga, the Yamuna, the Sindhu, the Narmada and the Kaveri – the holy rivers of Aaryavarta. That was followed by an abhishek using the five holy liquids – milk, honey, golden water, lotus water and sandal water. The waters of the three oceans protectively surrounding Aaryavarta on the three sides were also offered. The concluding abhishek was performed with the waters of seven rivers. Mother and Father wore elegant royal costumes and ornaments.

Similar rituals were performed for Balaramadada and Revati to proclaim them as the crown prince and princess. They, too, wore shining royal costumes and ornaments. I took the holy bath along with Uddhava and all my maternal and paternal cousins, and performed the necessary rituals. I wore my usual yellow dhoti.

As usual, the precious Paanchajanya conch was tied in a blue scarf around my waist. I put my peacock-feathered crown on my head. I did not forget to wear the Vaijayanti garland around my neck over a pearl necklace studded with a kaustubh jewel. I wore gold-plated iron armour on my chest. My Ajitanjaya bow and arrows were on my shoulder. I fastened the Nandaka sword at my waist and held the Kaumodaki mace in my hand. Uddhava handed me a fully blossomed red ochre lotus flower.

As the auspicious hour approached, we left the royal palace to go towards the Sudharma royal assembly. Leading us was Chief Minister Vipruthu, holding the royal sceptre. Behind him were Acharya Saandipani, Gargamuni and many sages. Behind them was Baba, wearing the Yadava turban on his head, and Devakimata, in her royal costume. They were followed by the crown prince and princess, along with Rohinimata, in their royal costumes. I followed them. On my right were Uddhava, his brothers Chitraketu and Brihadbala, and many maternal and paternal cousins. On my left were Satyaki, Anadhrishti, Akrura, Satrajita, Vikadru and many ministers of the royal council.

As soon as our royal procession entered the Sudharma assembly from the eastern gate, a cacophony of drums and trumpets ensued. Following that, hundreds and thousands of excited Yadavas, standing on both sides, showered my dear Mata and Baba with various flowers. Walking on the red carpet, our royal panel reached the royal altar on the east side. As per the instructions of the five priests, Baba gently put his right foot forward on the footrest of the royal throne and, making a cautious effort to not let his foot touch the royal throne, seated himself in an elegant posture. Devakimata followed suit and took her seat. At that moment, each corner of the Sudharma assembly resonated with the exhilarating sound of non-stop applause.

As the coronation was barely a few moments away, the head of the five priests moved forward to remove the Yadava turban from Vasudevababa's head. The main rituals of the coronation commenced now. In a clear voice, the five priests began non-stop incantation of the mantras. Many hymns from the Vedas singing the praises of Rajadharama – imperial duties and rights – poured from their mouths like a waterfall gushing incessantly.

Time-measuring vessels had been kept in big, round, golden tubs near entrances on the four sides. Capturing the exact moment of the coronation, all the vessels simultaneously sank in the water inside the golden tubs. The timekeepers on all gates simultaneously struck powerful time-indicating tolls on the discs. Their sounds echoed together – 'Tha…nn…nn.' At that moment, on the royal altar, the five priests picked up the crown in their hands. The traditional golden, grand royal crown of the Yadavas was gently placed on my father's grey-haired head. After that, they installed a smaller golden diadem, suitable for a woman's delicate face, on Devakimata's head. Seeing that, two tears appeared in the corners of my eyes.

Similar rituals were performed for the crown prince and princess. After that, the royal priests declared minister Vipruthu as the royal chief minister, and officially handed over the pride of the Yadava clan – the golden royal sceptre embellished with diamonds and jewels – to him.

Now that their religious rituals had concluded, the royal priests settled in their own seats. The chief minister was now in charge of the royal assembly. As he raised the royal sceptre in his hand, the entire assembly hall rose to their feet. As it was brought down, everybody sat down. There was absolute silence. Vipruthu spoke with authority, 'Dear Yadavas, and honourable invitees, now, the venerable leader of the Yadava clan, Maharaja Srikrishna, will felicitate the creator of this precious royal city – the architect Maya and his associates Vishwakarma, Gargamuni and Twashtta.'

I smiled and glanced at Uddhava sitting in the royal council. First, I bestowed rich garments and platters of jewellery upon the aforementioned architects and felicitated them. Then I began to speak, 'All my dear Yadava men and women, we consider our guests as gods, and I welcome all our guests. I am extremely happy today that the Yadavas, who have endured suffering and humiliation for so long, now have their own royal city and palace. This was a divine dream that they carried forward in their hearts for ages. This royal city has been erected with the blessings of the Ocean God, and the conscientious, diligent efforts of millions of Yadava brothers. While inaugurating this city, I am overwhelmed with unparalleled joy that cannot be expressed in words.

'The perfect name that comes to my mind for this royal city of the Yadavas is Dwaravati – Dwarika – Dwaraka.

'My dear Yadava brothers, the chief representatives of the sixteen major kingdoms of Aaryavarta are present here today. Some have not come. I am well aware that those present today have brought invaluable gifts for Vasudevababa and for the Yadavas. But more than that, they have brought their heartfelt blessings. We, the citizens of Dwaraka, are looking forward to a future full of peace and harmony with other kingdoms along the ocean coast. I have complete faith in the universal truth of love.

'I have declared the name of this royal city with the permission of Maharaja Vasudeva. I presume that Aaryavarta will certainly acknowledge Dwaraka as the seventeenth kingdom of the region. Everyone is welcome in this city.'

By this time the Sun god, a witness to the very first coronation in the golden city of Dwaraka, was about to set. The emissaries of various kingdoms offered their royal gifts to Maharaja Vasudeva. No gifts arrived from Jarasandha, Shishupala, Shalva, Dantavakra and Bhishmaka; nor were they expected. The southern Yadava kingdoms of Vanavasi,

Kraunchapura, Padmawaat, Mahishmati, Purika, Ratnadipa and Harita had offered us many exclusive gifts, including substantial amounts of gold, silver, diamonds and pearls, along with copper, lead and iron jars full of honey and liquor, and closed containers of extracts of medicinal herbs.

'Dada, Vasudevababa's coronation today was an extraordinary event. Everything went smoothly. Nothing bothered anybody. I am the only one to ask you – when are you going to fill the vacant seat on your left? Who is going to be our, lucky, virtuous sister-in-law?' Uddhava asked.

Soon the Yadava kingdom in golden Dwaraka settled into a routine. Warriors, attendants, artisans and civilians started commuting easily between both islands. The sounds of the tolling temple bells began blending with the sounds of the ocean. Most of my stay was in my residence adjoining the royal assembly hall. I began living in the resting chamber above the golden staircase. Uddhava used to attend to my needs. One day, he and the minister presented a middle-aged, lean and bearded Brahmin in my resting chamber. It was clearly visible that the Brahmin had made a long and arduous journey. His originally neat clothes were now torn at places and soiled. His fair complexion was tanned due to the journey on foot in the scorching sun. As he approached, he instantly prostrated in front of me. Holding his shoulders, I pulled him up and comforted him. He handed me a soft, silk pouch that he had carried carefully in the shawl on his shoulder and said briefly, 'Maharaja Srikrishnadeva, it is only in your hands now to save the precious life of our princess. Her father and brother have arranged for her wedding against her wish. It will take place very soon. You should immediately leave with your army for our city Kundinpura in Vidarbha.'

Kundinpura. The moment I heard that name many white swans of reminiscence fluttered in my heart. The image of Rukmini floated in front of my eyes – the one whom I had never seen before, the daughter of King Bhishmaka and Maharani Shuddhamati. Pages of an emotional epic that could not be put into words instantly fluttered in front of my eyes. The name of the city Kundinpura and the name of Princess Rukmini were blended in that flicker. Hearing these two names, the deeply rooted divine mantras of the Sudarshan chakra spontaneously resonated in my mind.

'Your name?' I asked the humble servant.

'I am a Brahmin; my name is Sushil. I am the priest for the daily religious rites performed by Vidarbha princess Rukminidevi,' he answered.

I seated him on a chair. A Yadava attendant offered him fruits and a glass of milk. The courteous envoy was reluctant to eat anything in my presence. I comforted him again. He then finished the fruits and milk. I collected all precise details about the princess's wedding. I instructed the minister to take care of him and to arrange for the Brahmin to rest.

As Jarasandha had been unable to defeat the Yadavas, Dada and me on the battlefield so far, he had conspired again to fulfil his devious motive. Inviting Bhishmaka's son Rukmi from Kundinpura to the Magadha capital Girivraja, he had honoured him in a royal assembly by offering him a gold-hilted sword, a large shield and silken royal vestments.

Ruddy-complexioned like our Uddhava, Rukmi was impatient and quick-tempered like Balaramadada and Satyaki, but also valiant like them. He was good-looking like his sister. As his father Bhishmaka, also known as Hiranyaromana, was getting old, the eldest son Rukmi was running the kingdom.

Jarasandha was trying to corner me by forming an alliance with Rukmi. He had sent Rukmi to Shuktimati, the royal capital of my paternal cousin, Shishupala. Rukmi had proposed that Shishupala wed his sister Rukmini, and Shishupala had eagerly accepted. Both of them had persuaded King Bhishmaka to fix a date for the wedding. Magadha emperor Jarasandha had astutely designed the whole plot from his capital Girivraja. He had an axe to grind. So, he wanted to pull Bhishmaka and his sons on his side by keeping them under obligation using Shishupala as bait. They did not take into account Rukmini's wish or choice at all, for she was merely a woman to them.

I began reading the letter, written on birch parchment, delivered by Sushil. It was not merely an epistle, but the ultimate lamentation of a sensitive and effervescent Kshatriya lady who had the earnest wish to get married to me without even seeing me. She had openly expressed her emotions in her own handwriting using a peacock feather, 'Oh Srikrishna, the most enchanting one of the three worlds, those who perceive your superiority are relieved of all their grief instantaneously. Those who see you with their own eyes and place you in their hearts are blessed for their lives. Ever since I have heard your acclaim, I have been yearning for you unabashedly. I simply cannot help it. I am penning this epistle, surrendering my modesty at your feet.'

The very commencement of her letter gripped my mind in an unbreakable hold. She was imploring me for pure, genuine love. And what else had I done in my life so far? What was I going to do in future? Offering pure, genuine love without expectations was the essence of my life, after all. Was it not?

Curiosity got the best of me and I started reading further, 'Madhusudana, everything about you is exceptional – your character, lineage, age, lustre, wealth, beauty, power, eloquence – everything. You enchant the universe, so it is no wonder if a lady of marriageable age like me surrenders her life like a Prajkta flower at your feet.' I smiled to myself in appreciation of her brilliance and continued reading, 'Oh beloved, you can say whatever you wish about me, but I have already surrendered myself to you in the heart of my hearts. Therefore, please leave no stone unturned to do whatever is necessary at this time.' The articulate emotional rendition in her epistle amazed me further, 'You are the lion, the monarch of millions of Yadavas. But if you delay even a bit to take your share, then a jackal named Shishupala will lay his hands on it. It will be like a crow grabbing the share of an eagle, won't it?'

She had skilfully used striking words that would instigate the pride of any true Kshatriya. I could clearly sense the dynamic beauty of her intellect along with her physical beauty. She would not let the reader stray from the topic. Even while realising that, I laughed to myself. She had written further, 'You might think it my audacity to write a message like this. But only for your sake, I am ready to sacrifice my family, my womanly modesty…everything I have.'

Her brilliance, evident so far in her words, reached its zenith in the contents ahead. 'You may be concerned that there could be trouble when you enter the wedding hall, but rest assured about that. The Bhoja dynasty has a familial custom of the bride visiting the temple of Goddess Ambika on the outskirts of the city. Be present and ready with your chariot at the time of my visit to the temple. The moment I come out of the temple, take me into your captivity and abduct me. As I have been wedded to you in my heart, your character will not be tarnished by the sinful abduction of an unknown woman. You have no reason to harbour such doubts!' Her clearly suggested solution produced a dimple in my cheek. Overly curious about how she had concluded, I read further.

'Oh lotus-eyed Hrishikesha, after all this, what if you decide to turn down my request? In that case Manamohana, Madhusudana, have no doubt that I will end my life remembering you. Hopefully, you will be my husband in the next life, if not in this one.

'Oh Srihari-Sridhara-Srikrishna! I desperately await you. Do not forget Anandakanda, Mukunda, Govinda, that even a moment's delay will be the end of this world. Just drop everything and leave urgently!'

I said to Uddhava, seeing him observe me intently, 'Udho, you always ask me who is going to occupy the seat on my left in the Yadava royal assembly. She is the one who deserves that honour. Rukmini!' I handed over the birch parchment to him and I could see he enjoyed reading it thoroughly!

'Go Udho, hurry. Dispatch a scribe, royal envoys and the cavalry chief immediately. Order the treasury chief to keep a few platters of royal gifts ready. Tell Daruka to take along the four white horses of the Garudadhwaja chariot, their backs covered with decorative garments. The chariot will stay behind. We will only take the horses with us. I will leave for Kundinpura this evening itself, along with Sushil. Tell Dada to follow me along with the army, and you come with him too.' I dismissed him with instructions.

An ecstatic Uddhava scurried away promptly. A scribe showed up within a few moments; I dictated four letters for the four Yadava kings in the south to meet up with us directly at the border of Kundinpura with their armies. The sealed missives were dispatched with the royal envoys. I ordered the cavalry chief to be at the ready with a few nimble horses and combative Yadava warriors. We had learnt a lot due to the experience of travelling twice through Dandakaranya. Dwaraka to Kundinpura was a long journey. We had prepared special troops to assist us during this journey. All of them were ordered to be at the ready.

The wheels turned fast. We bade farewell to all and received some customary curds and blessings from Devakimata. By this time, the news of our departure to Kundinpura had spread through the royal families of Yadavas. Everybody knew only this much – Maharaja Srikrishna is leaving for Kundinpura to attend the wedding ceremony of the Vidarbha princess Rukmini.

This time we crossed through Dandakaranya within two weeks, and immediately dispatched a royal envoy with the news of our arrival to King Bhishmaka. He dispatched his minister Rukmavarma to welcome us. He tried his best to persuade me to enter the city along with the army. After offering several excuses, I cleverly declined his invitation. Our encampment was set on the outskirts of the city. The wedding ceremony was going to take place the very next day in the royal assembly hall. Many southern kings had arrived for the ceremony. From the north, Jarasandha, Shalva and Dantavakra had arrived together. Shishupala, the bridegroom-to-be, had already arrived. Many other kings had arrived with their armies either because they were in awe of Jarasandha or due to his coercion. From the south, the four Yadava kings – our kith and kin – had camped on the southern boundary of the city as per my instructions. Skilfully, I had gathered succinct information about all those who had arrived, from minister Rukmavarma.

Convinced by Shishupala, his prospective brother-in-law, this time too, Prince Rukmi had not invited us Yadavas for the wedding ceremony considering us lowly cowherds. He had become wary due to the fact that we had arrived for the wedding ceremony despite that. He had sent spies to our camp disguised as servants. I had to design a counter-strategy to keep an eye on his informers and plan our course of action accordingly.

King Krathakaishika had camped on the southern boundary of Kundinpura. I requested for his embellished royal chariot to be dispatched to our camp. As per my instructions, it was yoked with four hefty black horses.

As expected, Rukmi had received news during the night itself that a black-horsed royal chariot had arrived at our encampment. He called for his secret service chief and warned him, 'Keep a close eye on the black-horsed chariot of black Krishna! Surely, he will plot some dark scheme and do anything any time!'

Immediately after my arrival here, I had sent a message with the brahmin, Sushil, to the Vidarbha princess – 'I have arrived. Do not worry. Rest assured. Be patient.'

The day of the princess's wedding dawned on Kundinpura. Their royal palace resonated with holy sounds of various instruments. Family members clad in royal attire gathered around the wedding platform. Shishupala stood near the wedding platform, with the twisted gold-bordered turban on his head. After the wedding, he was going to wear his formal Chedi golden crown. He was going to crown Rukmini with the Chedi diadem meant for the maharani, with his own hands. He was daydreaming about his blissful wedded life. His mother Shrutashrava and father Damaghosha stood behind him. Jarasadha's son Sahadeva stood as the groom's best man. Rukmi and his four brothers, clad in flashy royal costumes, strutted about with golden crowns on their heads. Due to the terror of her armed brothers, Rukmini was first going to place the wedding garland around Shishupala's neck as her 'own wish'! In the packed hall, Rukmi was keeping an eye out only for me, so that he could banish me from the ceremony. It was a well-planned scheme. As the time of the wedding ceremony drew closer, I began my strategic movements swiftly on the northern boundary of the city. First of all, I started dispatching troops of Yadava warriors towards the royal palace of Kundinpura, with my royal gift platters. They would go till their destination but not enter the palace and participate in the wedding ceremony. In fact, from there, they were going to disperse and return to our base.

The selected warriors who stayed behind let loose the black horses of Krathakaishika's chariot, yoked the four white horses of my Garudadhwaja that we had brought along, and hoisted the Garuda pennant on the chariot.

The most exciting moment of my life so far, the moment of my wedding, that was going to be reminisced for ages to come, lay ahead. Daruka brought the chariot to the front of my pavilion. Dropping the reins, he descended from it. Walking swiftly, he approached and bowed to me and Uddhava standing on my left. I verified with him, 'Everything ready? Anything missing?'

'Everything is in place. Arrows, the Ajitanjaya bow, chakra, the Agnikankana, the Kaumodaki mace, the Saunanda pestle, the Nandaka sword in its scabbard – everything has been kept at the rear of the chariot.' He answered promptly, giving me a pleasing smile.

'Both of you stay right here. I will visit the Aandhrabhrutya goddess Ambika's temple and be right back along with her blessings.' In a single leap, I was on the chariot and took the charioteer's seat. Unfastening my beloved Paanchajanya conch from the blue scarf tied around my waist, I held it in my palm and momentarily touched it to my forehead. At the boundary of Kundinpura, pointing it towards the sky, I blew it till my veins bulged. I could feel that I had never blown it with such intensity before. I held the reins of my dearest friends, the four horses, in my hands. I hollered from the core, 'Megha, Shaibya, Bala, Sugriva, go!' Responding to my voice, the horses neighed exultantly and sprinted forward.

Within a short while, navigating several twists and turns, I brought my Garudadhwaja chariot in front of Goddess Ambika's temple located at the base of the dense mountain range. I positioned it under a Champaka tree at a little distance from the temple. The priest and the attendants of the temple were stunned. Briskly climbing the steps, I crossed the central square and entered the temple. Bowing down to Goddess Ambika, I put my moist forehead on her holy feet. Slowly walking around the idol of the goddess, I spread my right palm in front of the temple priest to receive the holy water. Still baffled, with his eyes wide open, he kept staring at the peacock feather tucked in my golden crown and the pure white Vaijayanti garland around my neck. I removed a pearl necklace from my neck, placed it gently in his hands and asked him, 'How come you did not go to the city for the princess's wedding?'

'The princess-bride herself will soon be here to receive the blessings of the goddess. After offering my blessings to her, I will go to the city to receive the royal gift.' The priest answered with a smile.

Looking at the pearl necklace in his hands, I whispered, 'This is my gift to you.'

The entire city had gathered at the wedding hall. Only a few people stayed behind at the temple. I strolled around the temple to take a look at the place that was going to be a memorable part of my life. Descending the steps, I returned to my chariot and sat leisurely in my seat. I was lost in thought. Within a few moments, the rhythmic galloping sound of horses was heard. Following that was a cacophony of musical instruments. I became cautious and stood up. Soon, armed horse riders surrounded the temple. It was the cavalry for the protection of the princess. Following them, many bearded hermits and anchorites clad in saffron and white arrived, clacking their wooden slippers on the floor. They were intoning Vedic hymns, blowing their conches in between. They directly entered the temple. Behind them was a bevy of bridesmaids. They carried platters of fruit, garlands, ornaments, garments and other materials as offerings for the goddess. After them, the royal female relatives of the bride, dressed in rich, vibrant costumes, alighted from their chariots. Behind them were grand, embellished chariots of the bride's five brothers. At the very end was the tallest, grand royal chariot of Rukmini, the princess-bride. The white pennant of the Bhoja dynasty fluttered atop it.

Headed by a bevy of maids that carried platters of charity, the chattering royal ladies entered the temple. The five princes began climbing the temple steps with the commander and a few armed escorts. They entered the temple. Now they were out of sight. The maharaja and maharani remained behind to perform some rituals. Rukmini alighted in the end.

The indistinct sight of her feet from a distance stirred an irrepressible, unknown emotion in my heart. Waves of the Sudarshan mantras sprang up from deep within the recesses of my mind. Automatically, my hand moved towards the Paanchajanya conch. Instantly putting it to my lips, I blew the large, white conch from my very core with passion.

When she heard its novel sound, she was baffled, and stopped in her place momentarily. She quickly flung back the dupatta that covered her face and stared in the direction of Garudadhwaja chariot. She was like a fully blossomed lotus in the moonlight. That is how her face looked – vibrant and blooming with youth. When she saw the Garudadhwaja pennant fluttering on the golden flagpole of my chariot, her face lit up with a tide of joy. The next moment, she smiled, pulled the dupatta back on her face, and started walking towards the Ambika temple, firmly and fearlessly.

My job was done. She had received my signal.

Within moments, the rituals of worship began. The sound of innumerable bells resonated in the surroundings, the sound of conches blown by the sages blended with them. The rituals inside the temple continued for about half an hour. Now the groups of bearded sages and anchorites came out of the temple. No one realised that the bridal procession had not come out of the temple in the same sequence it had in. Sushil had done his job perfectly, according to my instructions. Breaking the sequence of the procession, the princess herself came out adorned in bridal attire, with only a few maidservants by her side. Her eyes were looking for just one thing – the golden pole with the Garuda pennant. Meanwhile, I had turned my chariot around and pulled up right in front of the temple steps.

She came! Like a moving sculpture in marble, delicately climbing down the white steps of the temple brightened in the sunlight. Like an autumn dawn, fresh with the fragrance of Prajkta flowers. Like a streak of lightning amidst grey clouds at the beginning of Aashadha. The moment she reached my chariot, she flung off her dupatta. Our eyes met for the first time. Time stood still. In silence, our eyes spoke volumes to each other. The next moment, her big, bright, dark black eyes fell on the peacock feather in my crown. For a moment, they were glued to the inviting iridescent colours. But in an instant, she blushed demurely. For a moment, her eyes met mine, recognising our eternal love for each other. Again, her face was swept by unique royal modesty. Then her beautiful fish-shaped eyes moved from the Vaijayanti garland resting on my chest and settled on my feet. Only a few select people had given me the feeling of such closeness, as if they were part of my body. I felt the same about her. Yes, she was the most important organ of my body – the heart.

The tears that she had restrained so far began streaming down her face. She surged forward and put her head on my royal golden striped sandals and whispered, 'Achyuta, Madhava, how long did I have to wait for you? Take me away, far away from here, never to return – do not waste another moment now.' Holding her fair hand in mine, I promptly pulled her gently into the back of the chariot. In a single leap I took the seat of the charioteer. Pulling the reins of the four horses, I signalled them to run. Raising their front hooves high in the air, all horses neighed together loudly, indicating that they had understood, and sprinted ahead immediately.

As per Rukmini's wish, I had officially abducted her, a widely accepted practice that Kshatriyas considered honourable.

I brought the chariot near the northern boundary of Kundinpura. Uddhava and Daruka were already waiting there for me. Balaramadada had just arrived from Dwaraka, along with the army, and was resting in his pavilion. I descended from the chariot, and Daruka took his place as charioteer. I climbed into the back of the chariot along with Uddhava. We left in the direction of Dandakaranya. Dada was supposed to stay behind to keep the other kings at bay and defeat them. I had the mammoth cavalry – ours combined with the southern Yadava cavalry – with me.

In Kundinpura, total bedlam had erupted. Prince Rukmi, boiling with rage, was not going to sit quiet after this. We travelled faster and arrived near the southern side of Dandakaranya. Now the question was what could be done with the chariot, as it was not possible to enter Dandakaranya with it. It was not even possible to return the chariot to King Krathakaishika. Daruka and Uddhava were pondering the situation, when I offered a solution. The chariot should be offered to the Vanavasi king in the vicinity. In return, we should ask for some honey, long-lasting wild fruits and some holy, medicinal herbs. Rukmini was the only lady among the Yadavas at the time, so we also asked for an enclosed palanquin and a few female attendants to accompany her on the way. We also imposed the condition that they fight against Rukmi, who was chasing us, to keep him at bay as far as possible.

A troop leader met the Vanavasi king on our behalf and got all our conditions approved. We crossed Dandakaranya as quickly as possible. Our cavalry arrived near the city of Avanti. A few royal chariots and select elephant troops coming from Dwaraka to welcome us met us here. Acharya Sandipani was in Dwaraka now with his family. But our Ankapada ashrama, well looked after by his successors, was in the vicinity, near the banks of the Kshipra. It had become much more active now and had prospered. Rukmini implored me to let her visit the ashrama at least once. I gave in, and with Uddhava and a few armed soldiers, sent her to visit the ashrama, along with a few royal gifts.

On the border of Avanti, near the banks of the Kshipra, we awaited Rukmini and Uddhava. It took them two days to come back. The ashrama disciples had welcomed them with great joy and urged them to stay overnight. They returned in the afternoon the next day. We were getting ready to move towards Dwaraka. Just then, a cacophony of war drums was heard from the south side of Avanti. Within moments, our camp was surrounded by horse riders. It was Rukmi. His face was red with anger. He was fuming with rage over the abduction of his sister.

Barely halting his robust, sturdy horse, he alighted from it directly next to my chariot. In a moment, he tucked in his dhoti tightly and got ready. He indignantly pulled out his massive club from the leather case hanging on the horse's back and directly charged at me.

He roared in an emphatic voice, 'You runaway cowherd! You fiendish thief! You abducted my dear sister Rukmini, the grace of the Bhoja dynasty, in front of everybody. I dare you to a duel right now. Better accept my challenge if you do not want to see bloodshed on both sides. If you think you are gallant enough, accept this challenge. If you want to take away my sister, it will have to be over my dead body. Or else I guarantee you that I will kill you myself in the duel. I will certainly take her back to Kundinpura, and get her married to Shishupala, whom we have chosen as her groom. I have taken a vow that if I do not fulfil my promise, I will not set foot on the ground of Kundinpura again. You coward, get down if you have any courage!' Swirling the massive club around himself, he took a fighting stance.

It was mandatory that I accept the duel now. As a Kshatriya, I had acted in line with one tradition – that of the abduction of the bride. Now, I had to comply with this norm too – to accept the challenge of the duel. I also tucked in my yellow dhoti tightly, patted my upper arms and prayed in memory of Kelinandakaka. Lifting my huge Kaumodaki mace from the back of the chariot and roaring the war call of victory to the Yadava goddess Ida, I leapt out of the chariot. Rukmini tried to stop me, but only the shawl on my shoulders remained in her hand. I brandished my club to accept the challenge.

Our maces collided instantaneously in the meadows on the borders of Avanti. A crashing sound exploded and fiery sparks flew around. A deadly duel commenced. Warriors on both sides became spectators, holding their breaths, agape. Keeping an eye on Rukmi's foot movements, I was anticipating each and every move and the direction of his next strike. I was blocking his strikes accurately and dodging his deadly attacks. Both of us were perspiring profusely, drenched in blood due to the hard blows of our maces. The hand grips of both our maces ultimately got twisted, and we had to cease the mace duel. Throwing a contemptuous glance at Rukmini in the chariot, Rukmi dropped his mace to the ground. I also threw down mine.

He pulled his shining wide-bladed sword out of the hilt tied to his waist in rage and challenged me to a sword fight. I had nothing in my hands. Nimbly leaping towards my chariot, I caught my Nandaka sword that Daruka promptly threw towards me.

We began fighting swiftly, clashing our swords against each other. At times, we tried to strike each other through the air, aiming towards the neck, and at times we blocked each other's strikes coming from down below in the direction of the calves. Rukmi was a master sword fighter. For about half an hour, our blood-tingling sword fight continued, destroying the grass under our feet. Both of us were quite wounded and blood-soaked by now. We both looked like the Palash tree in the summer – dreadful and blood red. Fully engrossed in the challenging duel, we had completely forgotten about our surroundings. The Vaijayanti garland around my neck was drenched in blood. A few drops of blood had splattered on the peacock feather on my head. My silk dhoti was wet with blood and sweat, and was stuck to my body at places. But the duel was still inconclusive.

Ultimately, I struck a firm blow right at the centre of Rukmi's sword, breaking it into two. He was terrified now. He knew too well what the outcome of the duel would be. Barely blocking my blows with his broken sword, he began retreating one step at a time towards my chariot. In a trice, his sweaty red face turned black with the fear of death.

With firm resolve, I picked up my sword to strike the last blow to decapitate him, but no matter how hard I tried, I could not bring it down. It was Rukmini. Standing in my chariot, she had held my sword's blade tightly in her hands, like her life depended on it. Her palms had already started bleeding. She did not utter a single word, but her eyes spoke volumes, 'Oh my dear Lord, are you going to take me to Dwaraka as your bride after killing my brother? He has made a mistake. Are you also going to make the mistake of not sparing his life?' The deep, yearning compassion in her eyes touched my heart deeply; I caved in.

Slowly, I brought my sword down. I could never forget that look of compassion in Rukmini's eyes for the rest of my life. I composed myself, got into the chariot and instructed Daruka while wiping my sweaty forehead with the end of my dhoti, 'Put some medicinal herb extract on her wounded palms. First take the chariot to the banks of the Kshipra. We will leave for Dwaraka only after a bath.' Meanwhile, Balaramadada had defeated all the kings who had engaged in war with him in Kundinpura and joined us with his army. Defeated Rukmi, who had been spared, went back fretting and fuming from the borders of Avanti. The joyous populace of Avanti named the place of our duel 'Gopalapur'.

Along with Rukmini, we arrived at the shores of the Kushasthali and dispatched a messenger to Dwaraka with news of our arrival. Within a single day, the entire city was decorated. The buildings were decorated with lamps. Arches embellished with flower garlands were raised. Chief Minister Vipruthu welcomed us along with Baba, both matas and a mammoth crowd of Yadavas.

Gargamuni and Acharya Sandipani soon decided upon an auspicious day for our wedding. On that day, in a spectacular ceremony, my wedding to Rukmini – the daughter of Vidarbha – took place in front of all Yadavas.

It was the most memorable event for the populace of Dwaraka, after Baba's grand coronation ceremony. This time too, we received countless gifts from friends and relatives. The treasury of Dwaraka was flooded with riches. Rukmini literally proved to be 'Lakshmi', the goddess of wealth, for the Yadavas of Dwaraka.

A few days passed. The queens' mansions on the twin island were yet to be inhabited. Therefore, along with her maids and friends, Rukmini lived in the royal palace, in my chamber connected to the golden staircase. The first time, while she was climbing the shining staircase along with me, she paused and questioned, 'So many steps on the staircase. Why?'

She possessed an unparalleled intellect to go with her matchless beauty. I had already realised that when our eyes had met for the first time. I had to give her a convincing answer. I smiled and said, 'Life itself is a staircase, dear. We keep climbing it without stopping, without resting. Take it as a symbol of that. You may consider these steps similar to the flight of stairs that one finds along the banks of rivers like the Ganga and the Yamuna, for resting. What do you think?' She did not say anything at that time.

I wanted to surprise her with a beautiful gift. Climbing the stairs, I arrived in the lobby of the resting chamber. As per my instructions, the palace attendants had already arranged wicker baskets in a line along a wall. They were covered with round wicker lids. The maid scurried inside to announce my arrival to Rukmini. I took a seat on a golden chair and waited for her.

In a moment, I could hear the delicate tinkling of her golden anklets. Soon enough, the pleasant perfume of sandalwood paste wafted in the air, floating on the ocean winds of Dwaraka. The next moment, a ruddy fair foot came out from the sheer veil in the chamber, and halted for a moment. It wore a golden anklet embellished with tiny golden bells, reminding me of a ripened mango – plump, fresh, pinkish and golden bright.

In a moment, Rukmini stood in front of me, arranging her thick, black, open hair wrapped in a white cloth. She looked so different, exceptionally beautiful and radiant today. I playfully said to her, 'As it is, you are good-looking, but today you look exceptionally gorgeous. Your bare feet are looking more beautiful than your face.' She simply smiled demurely.

She was indeed exceptionally brilliant. Ignoring my mischievous comment, she said to me, 'Enough of your mischief now. First show me what gift you have brought.'

I went to the wicker baskets, laughing, and picked up one of the lids. It was filled with big pearls to the brim. The Yadava fishermen had taken those out of the shells. I picked up a handful of pearls, and came closer to Rukmini. Emptying my palms into hers, I said, 'You are an original beauty. Wear some ornaments made from these pearls – it will enhance your beauty. The lustre of gold and the fragrance of sandalwood will be united then.'

Her cheeks flushed red. She kept staring at the pearls in her palms for a moment. Then, shaking her head as if she were talking to herself, she said, 'No, my lord, these pearls look more beautiful in your palms than mine.' She dropped the pearls from her hands into mine, and gave me a mischievous smile while glancing at me from the corner of her eye. Looking at the pearls in my palms, I asked her, 'I did not get what you said just now. A whip or a sword will look good in my hands. Maybe the Paanchajanya conch, but the pearls…?' She gave me an innocent smile, and fluttering her thick, long eyelashes, she said, 'You should observe the pearls in your hands carefully, my lord. They reflect the bluish colour of the sky in your hands. In my hands, they reflect a mere crimson fair shade. The blue colour of the sky assimilates all other colours in itself. Do I really need to explain this to my lord?'

So, that was it then! Before I could say anything, she turned briskly, pushed the veil aside, and disappeared. Why did she leave so hurriedly? It was because she knew that only by looking at her feet, I had come to know that she was having her menstrual cycle. Our family life had begun.

With Rukmini's arrival in my life, a colourful chapter of 'family life' had begun. As per my instructions, the artisans had inserted one more step into the golden staircase. A fifth step was added after the steps of both fathers, and both mothers. In the name of Rukmini.

Rukmini's arrival made my heart's dwaraka blossom with iridescent colours of emotion. It reflected the same marvellous freshness that Rukmini's feet reflected today.

RUKMINI

A woman's life is a potential core with tremendous power. She never looks back in life once she realises her inner strength. I am Rukmini – formerly known as the daughter of Vidarbha, the princess of the Bhoja dynasty. That Rukmini was left far behind at the border of Avanti during the duel between Rukmidada and Sri. The one who evolved here in Dwaraka is the Rukmini of the Yadavas, seasoned by being subjected to the tests of time every now and then, with the sounds of the western ocean as her witness. Rukmini of Dwaraka. Rukmini of the entire Aaryavarta.

My husband is worshipped by the entire world, but you see, how easily I call my husband 'Sri'. I usually addressed him as 'Lord', 'Aarya', or 'Yadavaraja'. But in private, while talking intimately to him, I would unwittingly end up calling him 'Sri'.

I am now going to relate the story of my life that was in perfect harmony with Sri's. There is only one problem. His life was just like the vast ocean surrounding Dwaraka. My mind is flooded with countless waves of his memories, just like the continuous and countless ocean waves. As soon as the first one subsides, the next rises.

Putting them in a sequential order is quite a bewildering task for me. It does not matter anyway. I am going to narrate as much as possible, as I recall, from the bottom of my heart – in my own words. I know it from experience that how much ever I talk about Sri's life and accomplishments, I will still not be able to cover everything.

I have just returned after performing a major duty. Our first-born son, Pradyumna, has arrived with his new bride, Rukmavati. I have just returned from welcoming Rukmavati, the first daughter-in-law of Dwaraka. Pradyumna is extremely handsome, muscular and well built. Rukmavati is my own niece – Rukmidada's daughter. Now, she has become my daughter-in-law. It was obviously Sri who wisely arranged this union.

So far, I have been hearing that I am the only one who possesses extreme beauty. But I was disillusioned when I saw Rukmavati, the first daughter-in-law of the Yadavas.

Sri stood with Rukmavati, Pradyumna and the Yadava army. I kept staring at the three of them.

In Kundinpura, Rukmidada and I were always at loggerheads. We were six siblings in all, and I was the youngest. All my brothers always complied with me, probably because I was their only sister, except for Rukmidada. Rukmidada was an egomaniac. He was plain arrogant. All my brothers were golden-complexioned and handsome, .just like our father Bhishmaka.

We had only one uncle, Aakrutikaka. He was the master of a rare skill, snake charming. His remedial intonation of mantras was a fast-acting antidote for any kind of snake venom.

Since arriving in Dwaraka, I had not visited Kundinpura even once. But whenever I remembered Aakrutikaka, an amusing thought always crossed my mind – that my dear Sri was also a master charmer. Sri could easily sway someone hell-bent on opposing him without that person realising it. That was how Rukmidada, who had once fought a deadly duel with Sri, had given his beloved daughter Rukmavati in marriage to Pradyumna and made her Sri's daughter-in-law. It was the effect of Sri's charm and his ambrosial words.

My father, Rukmidada and the other brothers were against my wedding with Sri. My mother Shuddhamatidevi stood firmly by my side, though. She was as innocent and pure in thought and action as her name denoted. She loved me unconditionally, and always gave me courage. Even she did not get the chance to see her son-in-law, the Yadava king Srikrishna, before our wedding. But she readily approved of him, as he was her daughter's choice. Later, I could keep in touch with her only through the priest Sushil, whom I had first sent to Sri with my letter.

Except for Shuddhamatimata, all others wondered, 'How did she choose Srikrishna as her husband without even seeing him?' That question was never answered.

It was a secret. I might as well share it with you, now that I am sharing everything openly. I had actually never seen Sri before our wedding – only heard of his renown across the corners of the world. But more so, his infamy from Rukmidada's mouth. How did I take such an important decision, then? It was during the first swayamwar ceremony that Dada and Baba had organised, where they vilified Sri for not being a Kshatriya and called him a mere cowherd.

Right in front of me, Rukmidada agitatedly announced his rejection. He kept shouting at the top of his lungs, 'We are the descendants of Mahabhoja, the forefather of the Satvat dynasty. We are Kshatriyas. Krishna's family has lost its status as Kshatriya, right from the time of Yayati's son, Yadu. He is a mere cowherd. We would rather die than get Rukmini married to a cowherd. She must be married to Chedi king Shishupala, a Kshatriya.'

He completely forgot that his sister, too, was a Kshatriya lady. That it was her wedding, and not his own. That was the moment I resolved in my heart that I would get married to that cowherd, to Sri.

When I arrived in Dwaraka, I was quite befuddled. No one from my parents' home had accompanied me here. The acclaim of golden Dwaraka had spread all over the world and so had stories of the quick-tempered nature of the Yadavas. I was bedazzled the first time I saw Dwaraka. 'How am I going to survive here?' I wondered. A volley of questions arose in my mind, 'How will the senior royal ladies welcome me? How will they accommodate me in their circle?' But soon, all questions and doubts vanished. I cannot, till today, forget the spontaneous welcome I received when I arrived here. Devakidevi, my elder mother-in-law, held me in a deep embrace and affectionately whispered in my ear, 'Welcome, Rukmini, my dear "daughter". I have been waiting for you.'

Revatidevi, too, displayed great affection and embraced me. The first year after our wedding flew past quickly, like the ocean wind. It left behind a medley of colourful reminiscences. Some of them were quite unpleasant, though.

Especially the memory at the time of Pradyumna's birth is so unpleasant that even today its very remembrance gives me the feeling of a gargle with salty ocean water.

At that time, I was living on the island housing the queens' mansions, in my large golden palace. While he was still in my womb, Sri and I had decided to name him 'Pradyumna'. More than me, Sri was quite sure that our child was going to be a son, that too, an exquisitely handsome one.

I had very peculiar cravings during that pregnancy. I constantly felt that instead of listening to the unceasing sounds of the ocean, I must go to a dense forest far away and live alone in peace. In the next instant, my mind would crave the cacophony of musical instruments. Then, suddenly, I would have an urge to wear bizarre, loose dresses like the asuras.

The eighteen families of Yadava royalty arranged an exceptionally memorable baby shower feast in my honour at this time. Countless people from various Yadava clans feasted on both the islands. A new scion of the new kingdom of the golden city of Dwaraka was to be born. Balaramadada, whom I had unwittingly started calling Dada, already had two healthy sons, Nishatha and Ulmuka. They were the apple of everybody's eye, especially Sri's. But this child was going to be Sri's first-born. Dada was more excited about it than Sri himself. Dada would always say, 'My brother does not know anything at all. I know him too well. He is always engaged in the royal council, meeting the sages, engaging in warfare, politics and what not. You should not rely on him for anything. Whatever you need, feel free to ask Revati.'

No matter how hard I try to forget the day of Pradyumna's birth, I cannot. The entire week, in fact. Pradyumna was born exactly at midnight. All the old and young Yadava royalty had eagerly amassed outside my delivery room. They wanted to record the exact time of Sri's first son's birth. To capture the precise time of birth, several golden vessels full of water with time-measuring golden cups afloat, were placed outside the delivery room. Skilled priests and astrologers sat alert under the guidance of Gargamuni.

At the exact hour of midnight, the timekeepers gave clear time-indicating tolls on the time discs. At that exact moment, the newborn Yadava let out his first cry.

At the midnight hour, the island of Dwaraka looked as bright as broad daylight. There was not a single inch of the city without a lit lamp. Citizens danced to the rhythm of various musical instruments. Maharaja, Rajmata, Dada – everybody donated fistfuls of gold coins.

No one – not even Sri or the members of the royalty – was allowed to enter the maternity room to see the newborn during the postpartum period. That was the custom. Everybody was going to see him only after the first ten days. He was chubby, with thick, curly black hair and had a peaches-and-cream complexion. 'Pradyumna' – we had chosen the perfect name for him. it means the bright sun.

The fifth day dawned after the baby's birth. In the last five days, Dwaraka, the royal Yadava capital, was drenched in happiness. The fifth night descended. Yadava astrologer Gargamuni was frantically preparing, as he had invited many expert astrologers from Anga-Vanga to Kapisha and Kamboja.

The sixth day brought a nightmare with it. From the direction of the baby's bedecked cradle my nurse Vetra came running to my bed, screaming at the top of her lungs and beating her chest frantically, 'Maharani...! Terrible news. The baby prince has vanished from his cradle. Save me, save me!'

Her loud wailing startled me awake. Upset as I was sleep-deprived for the last five days, I yelled at her, 'What is it, Vetra? Why are you screaming like all Hell has broken loose?'

'Indeed, Devi. Hell has indeed broken loose. The baby Yadava has vanished from his cradle. ' Her words struck me like lightning. Instantly throwing my blanket away, I rushed towards the baby's cradle. I frantically tossed around all the baby blankets in the cradle. The baby was not there. Lightning had indeed struck. Sri's first baby, his newborn, had been abducted within a few days of his birth, despite the tight security.

'Oh, Ambika Mata...! Ida Mata...!' I screamed, lost consciousness and collapsed on the floor. Within moments, the distressful, heart-breaking news spread rapidly in the royal family and around the entire city. The city that had been drenched in joy for the last five days turned dark in grief. The Garudadhwaja pennant fluttering atop the Sudharma royal assembly was lowered halfway in the morning itself. Batches of Yadavas started arriving on the island to console me. The royal minister and both commanders kept them at bay.

Sri came with Balaramadada to visit me in my room. I was lying in bed, listless. My head was numb and still aching. Sri sat by my side, and lovingly put his hand on my forehead. His affectionate touch gave me courage and hope. As I opened my eyes, Sri gently smiled at me. He said, 'Get a hold of yourself, Rukmini. Be assured that nothing has happened to him, and nothing will happen. He will return at the right time. Trust me.' I put complete faith in his words and composed myself. During this period, Dada's loving sons Nishatha and Ulmuka came closer to me. They helped me recover faster. Of course, it was Sri's idea to keep them in my chamber all the time. Gradually, I pushed aside the sorrow of my first son's abduction. The citizens of Dwaraka did the same. Time is the biggest healer of any kind of pain. Is it not?

Apparently, the citizens of Dwaraka forgot about the abducted baby, but I could not. After all, I was his mother. He was my first-born. I did not even get a chance to hold him close to my heart and nurse him. His own father, Sri, had not even got the chance to see him properly. I constantly kept wondering about who could have abducted him. Why? Such wild guessing would eventually make my head ache, but I could not find a single clue. Exhausted, I would then just lie in bed. Yet, the thoughts of the baby would keep whirring in my mind like a buzzing beetle, tearing my heart apart.

The Yadavas were never ones to surrender easily. They had come to Dwaraka after courageously and dauntlessly fighting the Magadha emperor Jarasandha seventeen times. They strived hard to erect this magnificent city from practically nothing. They left no stone unturned in search of the abducted baby. Skilled informers in numerous disguises left in all four directions to gather clues.

During the period of the search for the baby, inadvertently we all forgot about the Shursena kingdom of the Yadavas. It was our original kingdom.

Six months after the baby's abduction, an untoward event took place in Dwaraka. The royal ministry of the Sudharma assembly had an honourable Yadava minister named Satrajita. His wife was Viravati. Satrajita had a twin brother, Prasena, who looked exactly like him. He had a stern disposition. Both brothers were prominent members of the royal assembly. Satrajita was staunchly devoted to the Sun god. Religious rituals were conducted at his grand residence all the time.

His ardent devotion to the Sun god had earned Satrajita the invaluable Syamantaka jewel. It possessed exceptional qualities, like that of the Paras stone. The place where it remained automatically flourished with vigour and prosperity. When worshipped with proper rituals and the right incantation of mantras, it would turn any piece of iron into gold. On the strength of this gold, Satrajita had become a wealthy aristocrat. All his children grew up pampered. All of them were healthy and beautiful. His eldest daughter, Satyabhama, was the most pampered, extremely beautiful and very stubborn. The acclaim of her beauty had not only spread in the Dwaraka-Saurashtra and Aanarta regions, but also reached the distant kingdom of Madhyadesha.

Hridika's son, Shatadhanwa, a Yadava king of the Bhoja dynasty from the original Shursena kingdom, had come to Dwaraka and requested Satyabhama's hand in marriage. He was also the brother of Kritavarma, who was a member of the royal ministry of Dwaraka. Satrajita had denied his request, vaguely saying, 'Our daughter is not of marriageable age yet; we will see about it after she is ready'. Shatadhanwa took it as a probable affirmation and returned to his kingdom.

Sri did not know a single thing about all this. There was no reason for him to. Dwaraka was flourishing due to Sri's and Dada's mettle. Its opulence kept growing everyday. In Mathura, Maharaja Ugrasena was managing the kingdom with the remaining Yadavas. Due to frequent battles, the condition of their treasury was not as strong as it should have been. It essentially needed a boost.

One day, Sri decided on something and went to visit Satrajita at his palace, along with Uddhava and chief minister Vipruthu. Sri put forth a proposal to Satrajita, 'Satrajitakaka, could you do me a favour as my elder? All Yadavas basically belong to Mathura. Old Maharaja Ugrasena is desperately trying to preserve the city. We have received news that their treasury is in bad shape. All of us should assist them to recover from these conditions. Therefore, I have come up with a proposition for you.'

'Tell me, oh Lord of Dwaraka. What kind of proposition?' Satrajita vaguely suspected the proposal of another matrimonial alliance for his favourite daughter, Satyabhama.

'Could you please hand over the invaluable Syamantaka jewel in your possession in front of the Sudharma royal assembly? I will dispatch it with Uddhava and Gargamuni to Maharaja Ugrasena in Mathura.' Satrajita was perplexed. He said, 'What kind of request is this? Even you would not have agreed to such a demand, Lord of Dwaraka, if you were in my place. Forgive me, but this is not possible.'

Sri heard that clearly humiliating reply, and yet responded with an aloof smile, 'All right. As you wish.' But Uddhava was hurt deep down by the treatment meted out to his brother. They were all ready to leave the chamber. Just then, a royal lady entered the hall hastily, arguing with the groom of her horse. She had just returned from a horse-riding lesson. She was startled to see Sri in person at her residence. With lady-like modesty, she composed herself and silently left the scene. The sensational drama of the Syamantaka jewel had begun.

A few days passed. The royal city of Dwaraka was busy with its routine. Meanwhile, Satrajita's brother Prasena began preparations for a hunting expedition. He left with his hunting troops and sailed for Aanarta. Prasena had the urge to wear the Syamantaka jewel on this day. He wore it around his neck, strung in fancy gold chains. His hunting troops entered the thick, dense forests of Mount Hrikshawana. This mountain had a large colony of lions, just like on Mount Raivataka. Brandishing his spear, Prasena began chasing an excited wild boar with huge tusks. He was so engrossed in hunting that he lost track of time.

Suddenly, a huge roaring lion pounced on him from among the dense foliage. A breathtaking tussle took place between them. How long could a mere human, albeit brave and muscular, stand against a wild beast like a lion? The lion tore into Prasena's body within half an hour. The Syamantaka jewel that Satrajita loved with his own life lay in the pool of blood in the dense forest of Mount Hrikshawana. A Nishadha king called Jambavan was making his way through the forest along with his Bhilla friends. He came across the lifeless, mutilated body of Prasena, but none of them could recognise him as the 'Yadava warrior of Dwaraka'. One of them washed the Syamantaka jewel in the nearby spring water and handed it over to Jambavan. They prepared a funeral pyre in the forest and cremated Prasena's remains.

Weeks passed and yet Prasena did not return. Satrajita was concerned at first and eventually got suspicious. Rumours started spreading around his palace that Prasena had been treacherously killed by Srikrishna, the

Lord of Dwaraka. And that he had secretly appropriated the Syamantaka jewel that he wanted.

Satrajita put forth a demand to Maharaja Vasudeva to summon a special session of the Sudharma royal assembly. In front of Maharaja Vasudeva, an infuriated Satrajita directly accused Sri in sharp, offensive words. He burst out, 'Maharaja, are you going to exempt this crime only because the criminal happens to be your own son and the Lord of Dwaraka? My dear brother Prasena was captured alone in the forest and gruesomely assassinated. The auspicious, divine Syamantaka jewel in his possession was cunningly snatched from him. Your younger son Srikrishna, who puts on airs of being the only one shouldering the responsibility of the Yadavas' welfare, has committed the heinous act of robbery. He has also murdered a Yadava! He is the assassin of my brother. This royal assembly should prosecute him in a just and impartial manner. He better return my Syamantaka jewel to me. The criminal should be punished severely.'

The entire royal assembly trembled at this vehement verbal assault. Only because Satrajita was a senior royal minister and extremely opulent could he dare to accuse Sri of such a heinous crime. The Yadava assembly was abuzz with discussion. Commander Satyaki rose first, holding the hilt of his sword, looking contemptuously at Satrajita with his flashing eyes. Balaramadada tightened the grip on the handle of his mace.

'This is a lie. Srikrishna himself is the jewel of the Yadava clan. How dare a mere possessor of a single jewel accuse him of such an atrocious crime? He should take the accusation back with an apology, or get ready to face the consequences. Down with him!' Angry remarks were hurled from all sides.

The eyes of the entire assembly were fixed on our seats now. I was rattled by this unforeseen spectacle in the royal assembly. A storm of doubts and questions arose in my mind. Knowing well that I was shaken, Sri looked at me with his usual cheerful glance and rose quietly with a smile.

'Oh, Yadava warriors, calm down! First, let me congratulate respectable Satrajitakaka, a senior minister of the Sudharma royal assembly.' This unexpected and strange beginning to his speech instantly silenced the assembly.

'I congratulate Satrajitakaka, for he has laid the foundation of a fearless, new tradition in matters of the state today, that of speaking out against injustice clearly and without fear, in a fully occupied assembly, even against a person of high rank. My guru, Acharya Sandipani, has essentially taught me the same. It is my privilege that he is present in this assembly today.

'In the presence of Acharya Sandipani, I pledge in the name of Maharaja and Rajmata that I have not committed the atrocious crime that I am being accused of. Nor will I ever commit such a crime in my life. I do not wish to possess any precious, divine jewels at all. I have no reason to harbour such temptation.' Sri purposefully stroked the Kaustubh diamond on his chest.

He continued, 'Warriors of Yadavas, in memory of Maharaja Yadu and Kroshtu, and with a promise in the name of the family deity Ida, I announce that I will search and obtain the Syamantaka jewel of Satrajitakaka that is as dear to him as his own life, from wherever it is, even if it has reached the Netherworld. I will present it to him in this same assembly hall.

'I did not wish to do this, but since I have been accused in front of the entire royal assembly, I must disclose a truth that is unknown to the assembly.

'I had requested Satrajitakaka to present the Syamantaka jewel to me. It was not for my sake at all, but to improve the dire economic conditions of the people of Mathura. It is due to the misconception of my actions that he is accusing me of this crime. At this time, I want to make it explicitly clear that there have been many misconceptions about me before, and there will be many in future too. What am I going to gain by stealing the Syamantaka jewel anyway?'

'Nothing at all. You better apologise, Satrajita!' the impatient Yadavas roared. Sri raised his hand to calm them down and said, 'That is not necessarily the entire truth, my friends! I am going to be hugely benefited from the Syamantaka jewel. Even Satrajitakaka himself does not know it yet. But eventually everyone will.'

It was crucial that the promise made to Satrajitakaka in the assembly was fulfilled. Sri immediately gave necessary instructions. The very next day, he landed in the forests of Mount Hrikshawana, along with both commanders, maharathi Satyaki and Anadhrishti. A week passed.

News like 'he has reached Mount Hrikshawana', 'the informers are spreading throughout the forest and a thorough search for Prasena is under way' began to reach Dwaraka. Around the end of the second week, finally, news of Sri's return came. Sri, who never settles for anything less than success, was returning with the precious and auspicious Syamantaka jewel.

The entire city of Dwaraka assembled at the Shuddhaksha gate to welcome Sri. Satrajita was among them.

Ecstatic slogans of victory erupted from millions of Yadavas gathered at the gate, 'Victory to the triumphant leader of the Yadavas, Maharaja Srikrishna!'

I came forward and performed a ritual to cast away evil. Oh, how radiant and triumphant his face looked. A hero, my husband had undauntedly cleared himself of the charges of appropriating the Syamantaka jewel. Oh, how proud I felt of Sri.

A mischievous smile with a dimple, which I was so familiar with by now, momentarily flashed on his face. I became alert.

Holding the arm of a dark-complexioned, healthy woman standing behind him, he pulled her forward and casually said, 'One more jewel of a lady has come along with the Syamantaka. Not I, but the Syamantaka has brought her with itself. Syamantaka could not have reached here if she would not have come with it.' As usual, Sri threw a web of a riddle at me.

I looked at the shy, bewildered, youthful lady standing in front of me. She was a beautiful, curvaceous lady with a dark complexion and thick, long hair. Looking at her dress, I immediately assumed that she was a woman of the forest – a young native woman. She was bewildered by the opulent riches of Dwaraka. Fluttering her thick eyelashes, she kept staring at me like a scared bird.

'Rukmini, I have brought her as your companion and my wife in a Gandharva wedding, only because I had full confidence in you. Her name is 'Jambavati'. She is the daughter of the Nishadha king Jambavan from Mount Hrikshawana.'

He had said it casually, as usual, but for me it was another moment like my first-born son's abduction. For a moment, the Shuddhaksha gate spun around me rapidly. But only for a moment. The next instant,

I composed myself and said, 'Come, Jambavati, my dear sister, give me a hug.' I spread my arms open to make the wild beauty comfortable. She immediately clung to me as if she were eagerly waiting for that moment, and whispered, 'I do not understand anything here. Please take me under your wing.' I patted her back affectionately to calm her down.

Sri introduced everybody to her father Jambavan, who had come along. When I held Jambavati in my embrace, the people of Dwaraka accepted her as Sri's second queen. That very moment, I noticed Sri letting out a sigh of relief.

Jambavati entered Dwaraka amidst slogans of millions of ecstatic Yadavas, 'Hail Yadava queen Jambavatidevi!'

It so happened that on Mount Hrikshawana, Sri had discovered that the Syamantaka jewel was in the possession of the Nishadha king Jambavan. He had hidden it securely in his cave in the forest. The Yadava army surrounded the cave. Commander Satyaki and Anadhrishti presented Nishadha king Jambavan to Sri, as a criminal, tied up with wild creepers. When Sri demanded the Syamantaka jewel from him, the latter got perturbed and said, 'I do have that jewel, but I would not hand it over to you just like that, even at the cost of my life. I want an assurance from you.'

'What kind of assurance?' Sri was pleased with the fearless reply of the Nishadha king. Jambavan caught him in the trap of a Nishadha tradition and said, 'I have a gem of a daughter – Jambavati. She is my only daughter. If you accept her hand in marriage, I will bring out the hidden Syamantaka jewel. Otherwise, I would rather die than give it to you.'

For reasons best known to Sri, he accepted the bizarre condition. A Kshatriya from the Chandravansha accepted a tribal woman's hand in marriage. Such a thing had never happened in Aaryavarta before. I was surprised at myself while embracing Jambavati. A strange thought flashed through my mind. Would any of the kings gathered for my swayamwar in Kundinpura, including the self-proclaimed Emperor Jarasandha, who had humiliated Sri as a mere cowherd, have had the courage to act so? Would at least one of them have accepted a tribal lady as his wife?

Jambavati's blessed sylvan feet brought such things in my life that I would never have imagined. She had a clean, innocent mind like a wild stream. She did not have a clue whatsoever about the Yadava royal assembly, their Rasa dance, the hunting, the royal games, their festivals, their weddings, their traditions, costumes, jewellery, social etiquettes and so on. Yet she instantaneously picked up whatever I told her about the royal life with her innate sagacity. I began enjoying the hours I spent in teaching her the niceties of royal life.

I was enjoying it because, while chatting with me, she was also unknowingly sharing the rare subtleties of the forest with me.

On seeing me smile, she would cut short her talk and say, 'I like your smile very much.' Her words would instantly arouse Sri's memory in my mind and I would say to her, 'Jambe, my smile is nothing. You should closely observe your husband's smile. You will see many shades of that captivating, infectious smile.' Both of us would then giggle like silly young girls.

Now that Sri had obtained the Syamantaka jewel, he instructed minister Vipruthu to summon a special session of the Sudharma royal assembly. Addressing the special council, the royal minister said, 'Valiant citizens of Dwaraka, Srikrishna, the Lord of Dwaraka, has made each one of us proud today. Senior Yadava Satrajita had wrongfully accused him of abducting the auspicious, divine Syamantaka jewel, in the same assembly hall.

'First of all, we all should honourably recognise Jambavatidevi's status as the second wife of Srikrishna after Rukminidevi.' The royal minister raised the jewel-studded royal sceptre to alert the assembly. The assembly erupted in slogans of acclaim, 'Hail Queen Jambavatidevi! Hail Nishadha king, Maharaja Jambavan! Hail Maharaja Srikrishna! Hail Maharani Rukminidevi!'

The minister continued, 'The Lord of Dwaraka is going to present the Syamantaka jewel to the senior Yadava Satrajita, in the presence of this royal assembly.'

Sri stood up. In his hand, he held a small decorative wooden casket containing the Syamantaka jewel. From the circle of royal ministers, Satrajita approached him, trembling. Smiling his usual gentle smile, Sri handed over the casket to him and humbly bowed to offer him his respects. Amidst a thunderous round of applause, the Sudharma royal assembly reverberated with slogans of acclaim, 'Hail Goddess Ida. Hail Maharaja Vasudeva, Maharani Devakidevi!'

Satrajita was feeling contrite now, remembering his imprudent accusations in the same assembly hall. He was ashamed. He held the casket in his trembling aged hands and said in a shaking voice, 'As I am old in age and his senior, Srikrishna should forgive me in front of this royal assembly. I do not have appropriate and enough words to express my feelings. But, as a father, I can do only one thing. At this moment, I am offering my beautiful daughter Satyabhama's hand in marriage to Srikrishna. I humbly request that he graciously accept her as his third queen, along with the Syamantaka jewel.'

'Oh Lord of Dwaraka, Maharaja Srikrishna, please accept this second gift along with the Syamantaka jewel. You deserve it rightfully,' combatant Yadavas in the assembly started shouting continuously in unison. I was sitting next to Sri. He just kept looking at me intently. So many questions were hidden in that look. As if he were silently asking me, 'What should I do? What do you suggest? Should I accept both the jewels? Do I have your approval, beloved?' I nodded in affirmation. He shook his head as if in disagreement with something. Then he rose peacefully. The Sudharma royal assembly echoed with thunderous applause and victorious cries of acclaim.

Sri spoke slowly and determinedly, 'Dear Yadavas, have no illusions. I accept not both but only one of the jewels – the jewel-like lady. I never had any longing whatsoever for the Syamantaka jewel, and will never do so in future either. I am honourably returning it in the presence of the Sudharma royal assembly, acknowledging Satrajitakaka's rightful ownership of the same.' Thus the second act of the Syamantaka jewel drama concluded and Sri's third wife came into our lives.

I could easily take Jambavati under my wing. But it was the toughest job to do so with Satyabhama. After all, she was the daughter of a Yadava. As the daughter of an affluent father, she was greatly pampered at home and had grown up to be an opinionated, stubborn Kshatriya lady. Indeed, she was incredibly beautiful and bold. That is why she was so full of pride. Notably, she was not even aware of her pride. That was the most difficult task for me. She would never listen to anybody – sometimes not even to Sri. But, somehow, in front of me, she was always compliant.

I had understood quite clearly that it was not going to be easy for Sri to handle her. I also came to acknowledge that I would have to take the initiative to mellow her down. It was my duty to do so as the maharani of the Yadavas. I was also confident that she would never answer me back.

Three edifices on the twin island of the queens' mansions were now occupied by the three of us. They were now alive with the constant coming and going of attendants. I had come to realise that the other five edifices were still vacant. Both of them had not yet realised that. It was also up to me to take the initiative and make them aware of this fact at the right time.

When I first bowed to pay obeisance to the architect Gargamuni, he had suggestively blessed me, saying, 'Senior Maharani of the Yadava dynasty, may your life be full of fortune. May you be blessed with eight sons. It is your right, after all. But I would like to give you a special blessing – may you be the guardian of the eight mansions of the queens!'

He had erected the eight mansions on this island with the future in mind. It was a well-organised colony of palaces, with two rows of four palaces facing each other and a towering, grand palace for Sri at the centre. All the palaces had a view of the ocean. We did not see Sri for months when he crossed the ocean and went out of Dwaraka. Our life would be on hold then, waiting for him and listening to the sounds of the ocean.

Sri's daily routine on both islands was fixed. Half an hour before the 'Brahma Muhurta', bards would begin reciting hymns and eulogies from the four Vedas, accompanied by melodious tunes of rudravinas. Sri would rise exactly at the 'Brahma Muhurta'. After waking up, he would first gaze at his palms with his expressive eyes. He would observe the lines on his rosy palms. His face would instantly reflect many subtle shades of smiles while he looked at the royal symbols like the pennant, the chakra, the lotus, the fish and the swastika on them. Next, he would look at the floor and, addressing the earth with innate humility, say, 'Forgive me for stepping on you'. Then he would dip his fingers in the fresh water in the golden chalice and run them over his eyes. Sitting on his bed in the Padmasana posture, he would meditate for some time. At the same time, he would recall the divine mantras of the Sudarshan chakra in his mind. At such times, I would occasionally get a rare glimpse of him. How radiant his face looked while meditating with closed eyes. Then he would clean his already white teeth with the powder of medicinal herbs mixed with neem leaves, and rinse his mouth with water made fragrant by khus grass. For some time, he would do some asanas for the whole body, practising control over his breath. A few of his loyal male and female attendants would serve him at that time.

His bathing was a big ritual. In huge golden vessels, hot, warm and cold water from various rivers in the Aanarta region would be filled. Many small and big golden bowls would be filled with a variety of aromatic cleansing powders. Nourishing red soil was brought from the mines of Govardhan, and sifted and kneaded in buttermilk and oil. Dark black stone chips were brought from the bed of the river Gandaki to scrub his neck, chest and heels thoroughly. After applying the cleansing powders and the soil on his body, he would bathe in the water blended with khus grass. Then, immediately, on his wet body, he would get a shower of freshly drawn milk from the cows from Kathiawar, mixed with gold water. In the end, the attendants would give him a shower of aromatic, cool water from a golden jar while singing folk songs of Saurashtra.

Many a time, I have heard his bathing attendants whisper among themselves, 'Maharaja Srikrishna looks like the Shivapindi in the shrine of the Somanath temple while receiving the abhishek.'

To me, he often looked like the Sun god rising from the western ocean, especially when I saw him like this – fresh after a bath, wearing his royal attire, and a freshly woven, fragrant, white Vaijayanti garland on his chest, bearing the peacock-feathered golden crown on his head.

After the bath, he would first visit his parents and the other elders. Then he would perform the Sandhya prayer and drink freshly drawn milk to his heart's content. As the priests chanted mantras, he would offer oblations to the fire. Next, he would worship the rising Sun god visible from his meditation chamber. He would sit on a grass mat and, with full concentration, humbly recite the Savitru mantra. Then the holy Tarpan water would be offered with mantras to the gods, forefathers and sages of the dynasty. After that, the offering of charities would begin. Initially, only I would sit by Sri's side during the charity offering session. Then I came to realise that I should make both Jambavati and Satyabhama also participate in that session. Two additional golden seats were then arranged for them at the time of the charity session. Then, Sri would dress up in the royal armed attire of the Sudharma assembly. At such times, he would carry the Ajitanjaya bow on his shoulders. On his back would be the quiver full of arrows. Sometimes, he would carry the polished, dark-black, tall Saunanda pestle made of wood. At times, there would be the gold-plated, rounded, elegant Kaumodaki mace made of iron. At other times, he would leave with only the Nandaka sword in its scabbard tied around his waist. I loved watching him dress up in a variety of armed attires – it gave me immense pleasure.

Before leaving for the Sudharma assembly, both of us would follow the ritual of looking at the reflections of our faces in a mirror of liquid ghee placed in a big golden platter. Then we would take our seats on the porch outside and listen to the complaints of citizens, servants, warriors and troop leaders. We would resolve matters and satisfy their demands according to their needs.

During this meeting session with citizens, I would always strongly sense an exceptional quality in Sri – that of an abundance of love, that of unconditional affection.

After performing the morning routine and rituals, he would leave for the original Dwaraka to go to the Sudharma assembly. I would not accompany him every time. His dear charioteer Daruka would bow down to him and request him to board the chariot. Before he could touch his feet, Sri would take Daruka's hands in his palms with warm affection and hold him in a deep embrace. Then he would call the four pure-white horses of his chariot by their names – Meghapushpa, Balahaka, Sugriva and Shaibya. The horses would immediately respond by pricking up their ears. Sri's bluish muscular hand resting on the nape of the pure-white horses' necks would look captivating.

Once Sri would board the chariot and signal by raising his hand in the air, Daruka would pull the reins and give an inspiring call to the horses. My mind would then fill with an inexpressible yet strong gloom in anticipation of the dullness that would engulf the island of the queens' mansions till the evening. The Yadava king would be busy for the entire day in the daily routine of the Sudharma assembly.

In the evening, many tweeting ocean birds would return to their nests. The sun would be about to set. The sound of the ocean that was surrounded by a variety of other sounds during the day would become clearer now. Sri's chariot would return to the island. Sometimes Sri would have some political predicament on his mind. At such times, he would tell a Yadava fisherman to take a small boat out into the sea. Usually Balaramadada, Vipruthu, Satyaki, Anadhrishti or Kritavarma, whoever was associated with that particular problem, would accompany him at that time. In any case, Uddhava would accompany him without fail. A pure-white, triangular pennant visible from far away would fly atop that boat. The sound of a conch akin to the sound of the ocean, blown by the fisherman before pushing the boat into the western ocean, would reverberate in the vicinity of the island. It would clearly indicate that, 'The Lord of Dwaraka is busy in an important, secret political council'. The details of such council would never be revealed to anybody else.

On other evenings, he would practise sword fight, archery, horse riding, elephant riding and charioteering. At sunset, he would again sit on the grass mat for the evening prayers. After the prayer to Goddess Ida, the traditional prayer of the Yadavas, Ishastavana, would begin. Following that would be his dinner time. He loved dishes made from curd and milk. No matter what kind of dinner it was, he would personally make sure that others were served plenty of delicious dishes. He himself, however, would never eat a single morsel extra.

After dinner, he would converse with family members and share their joys and sorrows. He would exchange views in detail about any topic as per the occasion, such as the Vedas and Vedanta, the Shastras–Puranas, dance–music, etc., with acharyas and priests.

As soon as the timekeeper in the central square of the island would indicate the beginning of the second quarter of the night, wherever Sri would be, he would give a sweet smile to the people around him, join his palms together, and say, 'The Karmayoga of this day has come to an end. I am not yours any more.' His smile would be so enchanting that he would never need to say anything more. While going towards his bedchamber, there would be no tinge of happiness or sadness whatsoever on Sri's face of the joyous or doleful events of the day. At least to me, he seemed like the Sun god at dusk, about to immerse itself in the ocean.

All kinds of amenities and luxuries were always available at our fingertips here but, for me, looking at Sri's face every day was the greatest joy of all. The company of Jambavati and Bhama was assuring. Both were like sisters to me. Still, the memory of our lost son would occasionally flash through my mind like the sharp wail of a female lapwing. 'Sri has told me that nothing has happened to him. I have full faith in his words. He will return at the right time. Then where is he now? How old is he now?' I would be overwhelmed by questions like these. But I never talked about my heartache with my two new companions.

Sometimes, Revati would come to my palace, along with her sons Nishatha and Ulmuka, who were not far apart in age. She would always talk a lot about her Raivataka kingdom and more so about Mount Raivataka. She was very loquacious, simple and good-natured. We were very fond of Subhadra, as she was the youngest among the ladies. She was indeed admirable. Sri himself had suggested the name Subhadra, knowing her qualities. She was the apple of his eye. He always respected her feelings. Sometimes, he would tell her stories of his other favourite sister in Gokul – Ekananga. He would insist, 'Subhadra, you should go to Gokul in Vraja with Dada, and meet Ekananga; chat with her freely, and bring her with you when you come back.' Simple Subhadra would listen to him, and just nod her head in affirmation. But when I heard Sri telling the same thing to Subhadra a few times, I interrupted, saying, 'Why should Dada alone accompany Subhadra? You should take her to Gokul, and visit all your beloved people once. You yourself should bring your dear sister Ekananga to Dwaraka.'

Sri would unmistakably deduce that my words were pointing towards Radha and say with a smile, 'How can I ever go to Vraja now? This enormous kingdom of Dwaraka needs me.' He would usually be in a jolly mood, but if there was even a fleeting mention of Gokul, a momentary sense of loss would become apparent on his face. I would strongly feel at those times that Sri must go and visit Radha there. See Nandababa and Yashodamata, who nurtured him in his childhood.

One day, an unbearable, heart-breaking news reached Dwaraka, shaking the cheerful city to its roots. 'Rajmata Kuntidevi, along with the five Pandavas, has fallen prey to wildfire in the Varanavata forest. Six charred bodies of a mother and her sons, which are beyond recognition, have been found in the burnt-down house where they were residing. As they were in no condition to be brought to Hastinapura, they have been cremated in Varanavata itself. The corpse of Purochana, their only faithful attendant, was also found in the same house. He has also been cremated there. With Prince Duryodhana's initiative, the present Maharaja, Dhritarashtra, will perform their funeral rites on the banks of the Ganga.'

This news brought the Yadavas' mighty pennant Garudadhwaja halfway down on the flagpole. A mournful Sudharma royal assembly was held. Nobody was in their right minds to talk about anything with anybody. Sri said to me in a low but firm voice as we prepared to attend the royal council, 'Rukmini, I do not think there is any truth in this news. Maybe this is some kind of cunning, unsuccessful political machination by Duryodhana and Shakuni in the name of Maharaja Dhritarashtra. No, I simply cannot visualise the fiery flames that can burn the mace maestro Bhima alive.'

In the Sudharma royal assembly of the Yadavas, minister Vipruthu raised the royal sceptre and put forth a brief proposal, 'Due to the sad demise of Kuntidevi and her sons, this royal assembly will now observe the mourning period. On behalf of all Yadavas, Prince Balarama and Srikrishna, the Lord of Dwaraka will leave for Hastinapura to attend the funeral rites. This assembly is dismissed now.' The royal assembly was dismissed within minutes. Dada and Sri immediately left for Hastinapura, along with Daruka.

One week passed. I kept thinking about the doubt that Sri had expressed at the royal assembly. 'There is no truth in this news about the Pandavas and their mother.' Why would he say such a thing? And if he believed that there was no truth in this news, then why would he keep all the Yadavas of Dwaraka in the dark about this? I just could not understand.

Only recently we had received news that Guru Drona had organised a grand championship contest of the Kauravas and the Pandavas in spring.

During that contest, the young and gutsy Kauravas and Pandavas had performed extraordinary feats. Guru Drona had put the championship garland around Arjuna's neck. Suddenly, a radiant youth had entered the contest arena and challenged Arjuna to a duel. That was Karna, a charioteer's son. Drona's brother-in-law, Kripacharya, raised a question, 'How can there be a conclusive duel between a Kshatriya and a charioteer's son?' Duryodhana immediately took action and instated Karna as the king of Anga. The rivalry between the Kauravas and the Pandavas had deepened even further.

This was Sri's first visit to Hastinapura. I spent that entire week thinking about what would happen during this visit. One day, Bhama entered my chamber, wailing loudly, beating her chest with both hands in a manner that sent shivers through my body. The human mind is so susceptible to apprehensions. I momentarily had a terrifying suspicion, numbing my entire body. My heart froze. 'Did something happen to Sri?' Initially, I did not even understand what Bhama was saying. She lamented continuously, 'Betrayal…Yadava Maharani. What should I do now?'

I held both her arms tightly and chided her, 'Bhama, get a hold on yourself! Tell me what has happened.' She momentarily suffocated due to her uncontrollable sobs. Then she said, 'That traitor has viciously murdered my father in his sleep. He broke into our palace, stole the Syamantaka jewel and escaped from right under the nose of our warriors and commanders. If he wanted to steal anything at all, that scum should have only taken the Syamantaka. Why did that creep murder my Baba, despite being a Yadava?'

I was at a loss for words. While breathing a sigh of relief that Sri was safe, my breath choked for Bhama. Never before had such a heinous crime taken place in our newly built kingdom – the murder of a Yadava. Within moments, unknowingly, the maharani in me rose. I held Bhama's arms tightly again and, shaking her vigorously, asked her, 'Who is the culprit? When did it happen?' She embraced me tightly and spoke slowly, 'Shatadhanwa. Last night.'

I went numb. I was truly proud of every small and big heroic exploit of the Yadavas and their tenacity while facing Jarasandha's seventeen attacks. Many Yadava warriors had sacrificed their lives in those wars.

Sri was the reason and inspiration behind their sacrifice. It was a shock for me that any Yadava, no matter who he was, could commit such a heinous crime – theft and murder at the same time. Indeed, I felt it very deep as the consort of Sri and as the maharani of the Yadavas.

My usually operative intellect was not of much help while consoling Bhama. I kept patting Bhama with great affection, and felt lost as if Satrajita was my own father. I simply kept saying to her, 'Be quiet. Calm down. Behave like the courageous Yadava daughter of your father. Stay calm. Let Sri come back to Dwaraka. Believe me, he will definitely punish that scoundrel severely.'

'My whole body is burning with fury. I just cannot wait. Send Vipruthu with me. I am directly going to Hastinapura. I will return to Dwaraka with him.' Bhama said determinedly, controlling her emotions. Nobody was going to be able to stop her now.

I gave proper instructions to Vipruthu and sent him with her. She left, along with a troop of guards. She entrusted me with the responsibility of performing the final rites of Satrajita.

This unforeseen calamity that had befallen the Yadava royal family made one thing clear to me. I came to know what kind of an iron-willed, resolute Kshatriya lady Bhama was. A few days passed and Bhama returned with Sri, as she had resolutely said. I immediately presented myself at the Shuddhaksha gate to welcome them. Due to the recent events in Dwaraka, we were not going to be able to talk at length. The moment our eyes met, he gave me a smile that could only mean one thing. Aunt Kunti was safe, along with her sons.

While walking towards the Sudharma royal assembly, he asked Anadhrishti, 'Commander, were the final rites of Satrajitakaka performed as per tradition? Spread rumours everywhere that I am still in Hastinapura. Within four days, I should receive all minute details of Shatadhanwa's whereabouts. Send his brothers Hardikya and Kritavarman to meet me immediately; send Akrurakaka too.' Only those two had not come to receive Sri at the Shuddhaksha gate, as they usually did. Sri had unmistakably noticed it. It clearly meant that both of them were up to something. It was also clear that no matter where Sri went, he was always receiving minute details of each and every event happening back here.

Indeed, he was the 'Lord of Dwaraka', though he was not enthroned on its royal seat.

The hunt for Satrajita's assassin began in full swing. First, Sri called Kritavarman in his private chamber and enquired about the Syamantaka jewel. Kritavarman was Shatadhanwa's brother. Both were the sons of the senior Yadava Hridik. He was an honourable man in the royal ministry of Dwaraka. Shatadhanwa was meddlesome. He lived in the distant Shursena kingdom. He had desired the valiant and beautiful Satyabhama, though he was not worthy of her. He had put forth the marriage proposal to her father. Satrajita had astutely avoided it. Sri knew nothing about this. Shatadhanwa felt deeply offended by the fact that she was married to Sri and had resorted to the heinous act of murdering Satrajita.

Kritavarman was well aware of the consequences of what had taken place. He entered Sri's chamber, determined to present whatever facts he knew. Sri welcomed him hospitably and offered him fruits and milk with saffron. After having a general chat, he asked Kritavarman directly, 'Kritavarma, it is quite possible that our maharaja and the Sudharma assembly will entrust you with the charge of looking for the Syamantaka. What are you going to do?' Kritavarma was caught off-guard. He blurted, 'I know who has the Syamantaka now. My brother Shatadhanwa has thoughtlessly murdered Satrajita. At present, he has sought asylum with the king of Kashi. He had handed over the Syamantaka jewel to Akrura for safety, in my presence. You should ask for him and seek out the truth.'

Sri had got another clue leading to the truth of Satrajita's assassination. It was an unexpected, shocking truth that the Syamantaka had gone into Akrura's possession for the sake of protection. A more shocking truth was soon revealed. As soon as the honourable elderly Akrurakaka, who now possessed the Syamantaka jewel, heard that Sri had invited Kritavarman to visit him, he quickly absconded from Dwaraka, along with the jewel.

There was no way of knowing how many problems this Syamantaka jewel was going to create now, and how many people were going to be affected by it.

By this time, Satyaki had become a close, loyal maharathi and was among Sri's trusted few. It was as if there was an unwritten arrangement between him and Anadhrishti about the responsibility of the army.

Anadhrishti took charge of protecting both the islands of Dwaraka. He vigilantly kept an eye on the borders of Dwaraka up to Saurashtra, Bhrigukachchha and Aanarta. Satyaki would accompany Sri within the Dwaraka kingdom and outside throughout Aaryavarta. External military strategies were designed under his guidance.

As soon as Sri came to know of the whereabouts of Shatadhanwa, he left Dwaraka again, along with Satyaki and the army. Balaramadada accompanied him as usual. Soon they had travelled along the banks of the Narmada and passed through the city of Mahishmati in the Avanti kingdom. Sri then reached the Chedi kingdom along with the Yadavas, crossing River Vetravati. Though it was the kingdom of his aunt, Sri skipped Shuktimati, the royal capital of Chedi, keeping in mind Shishupala's fanatical behaviour, and travelled further ahead.

Finally, news arrived. Sri had reached the borders of the kingdom of Kashi and beheaded Shatadhanwa in battle. Shatadhanwa had formed an alliance with Subahu, the king of Kashi, and had arrived at the border from Varanasi. The king of Kashi surrendered after his defeat. As a tribute, he offered a lot of riches at Sri's feet. At Kashi, once again, an undesirable dramatic event took place due to the Syamantaka jewel.

Balaramdada was never interested in wealth and riches as such. He never even visited the treasury at Dwaraka. But that troublesome Syamantaka jewel had bred irresistible curiosity in the mind of this valiant Yadava warrior. As Sri appeared in front of him, he smiled and said, 'Krishna, let us at least see that Syamantaka jewel once. We have followed it over such a long distance from Dwaraka. Now all hurdles in our path have also been cleared. Our Satyabhama has lost her father for the sake of that jewel. A look at it would make her feel better. Come on, show me the jewel.'

Sri shrugged his shoulders, smiled and said, 'I do not have it. It is with Akrurakaka. First, we will have to find him, and obtain it from him. Only then will you and I be able to take a look at it!'

Usually, Balaramadada never had any misunderstanding with Sri. Unfortunately, it happened that day. He kept saying again and again, 'Just show me that jewel, only once. I have no desire for it.' Sri kept trying to convince him, 'I really do not have that jewel with me at this moment.'

Suddenly, Dada lost his temper and said angrily, 'That mere stone of a jewel means more to you than your respectable elder brother! Keep it with you then. I am leaving right now, and will go wherever my feet take me. I do not want to see your face any more.' And just as he said it, Balaramadada picked up his mace and left the base in a fit of fury. His Yadava followers went after him. They crossed River Ganga, River Sharayu and reached the banks of the Gandaki. He directly reached Janakapuri of Mithila.

For no fault of his, the Syamantaka jewel had given Sri a solid emotional blow.

After punishing Shatadhanwa, victorious Sri returned to Dwaraka. But this time, Balaramadada was not with him. Even the troublesome Syamantaka, which was the reason for the rift, was not with him. I just could not comprehend the fact that Dada had left in anger. I could not stay without meeting Revati immediately. But it was she who consoled me. She instantly reduced the heavy burden on my mind, saying, 'You are worrying for no reason, Rukmini. The prince will not go anywhere. He will return soon. He cannot live without his younger brother.'

Amidst all this, minister Vipruthu presented Sri with news. The minister spoke of his meeting with a group of women from the Kamarupa kingdom to the east of Aaryavarta. They spoke of dire life conditions for the women of Kamarupa and the surrounding countries. In Pragjyotishapura, the royal capital of that kingdom, the life of women, especially the beautiful and healthy ones, was in danger. The king Narakasura alias Bhaumasura had forcibly imprisoned nearly 16,000 beautiful women from Kamarupa to use and exploit physically to satisfy his own lust. New women were being added every day to the prison.

'Is there any saviour at all, in the entire Aaryavarta, for thousands of these innocent women? Is there any valiant man who will protect these powerless women?' They asked such heart-piercing questions and demanded an audience with Sri.

'I will go to the Kamarupa kingdom, to Pragjyotishapura, to emancipate my sisters,' he said.

In a council meeting, Sri expounded his views about the essence of femininity. He said, 'My dear Yadava warriors, no matter what accolades virility achieves, it is conceived in a woman's womb. A manhood that cannot honour and respect the feminine is futile. Narakasura has been brutally abusing women. That is precisely why I have taken the decision to attack him, along with the fourfold Yadava army. I am confident that you all will comply with my decision.'

A public announcement was made in Dwaraka, 'Yadava king Maharaja Srikrishna is planning a military attack on Narakasura, the brutal, arrogant king of Kamarupa.' Fearless young men from the regions of Saurashtra, Bhrigukachchha and Aanarta were recruited to the Yadava army. Training camps guided by expert commanders and troop leaders were organised throughout the kingdom. The size of the combative Yadava army, already numbered in millions, kept burgeoning. The proficient spies of Dwaraka had spread out in kingdoms such as Avanti, Chedi, Dakshina, Kosala, Magadha and Videha, which were located along the way from Dwaraka to Pragjyotishapura. Secretly keeping in constant touch with each other, they had started collecting information about the enemy's capacity and promptly conveyed it to Dwaraka.

The Yadava craftsmen got just as busy as they had been at the time of the construction of Dwaraka. This was a vast undertaking, quite challenging, and was going to test the limits of the Yadavas. Dwaraka had no association whatsoever with the Kamarupa kingdom. This was preparation for a war to protect an eternal truth, to fight for the protection of womanhood that was oppressed, anywhere. Sri constantly travelled throughout the kingdom, along with both commanders and other companions. He got absorbed in getting the fourfold army thoroughly equipped and ready for war.

The only person missing was Balaramadada, but I had full faith that Sri would win this war and return victorious. Uddhava and Satyabhama wanted to accompany Sri on this mission.

Though he was brave and a Yadava, Uddhava was not a warrior by nature. In fact, he always fearlessly propounded that conciliation was better than war. It surprised everyone that he had insisted on going with Sri on this particular mission, but I was not. I knew that he was going only to fill Dada's absence. I also felt a bit envious when I heard Bhama's decision. I felt like joining him too. It was indeed my right as the maharani of Dwaraka. I expressed that wish of mine to Sri in private. As usual, he gave me a lovely smile and said, 'Maharani, Satyabhama is coming with me, but not because she has come closer to me than you. She is skilled in charioteering. She thinks that I have done her a "favour" by punishing Shatadhanwa. She is going to repay that debt as a Kshatriya lady by serving me in the war. Do you know how to drive a chariot? If so, you can come with me too. Do you consider any of my actions as a "favour" done to you? If so, you can come too. Do you consider yourself an "indebted Kshatriya lady" like her?'

Realising that he was going to whip me with such questions and drag me along, I stopped him and said, 'That is enough. I am not interested in being a Kshatriya lady like her. Both of you go and come back safely.'

With smiles on our faces, we bade them farewell. The huge army crossed the island creek in large ships and united with the neighbouring army that was already camping on the ocean shore.

In the absence of the commanders and Balaramdada, my responsibility as a maharani had increased considerably. It was necessary to assist the aged maharaja and Devakimata in looking after the kingdom. Therefore, I appointed Jambavati as the caretaker of the island of the queens' mansions and came to original Dwaraka. Here, too, I had a palace for me as the maharani. I began keeping a keen eye on the execution of the Sudharma royal assembly operations, along with Revati and Rohinimata. Within fifteen days of Sri's departure, a warrior sent by Satyaki arrived at the Shuddhaksha gate, along with a royal lady guest. She was Mitravinda, the princess of Avanti, the daughter of the Avanti king Maharaja Jayasena and Sri's aunt Rajadhidevi, and a sister of princes Vinda and Anuvinda.

Sri's army had entered the Avanti kingdom during their journey. At the same time, the Avanti king had organised the swayamwar ceremony of his beautiful daughter. They assumed that the Lord of Dwaraka had arrived for the swayamwar! Prince Vinda and Anuvinda sent a humiliating message to Sri through their emissary, 'You cannot participate in this swayamwar. You have lost your Kshatriya status. That is exactly why you have not been invited.' God only knew if the Yadavas were ever going to clear such familial complications.

Sri possessed the innate diplomatic skill of turning any messy situation to his advantage. He sent a return message to Vinda and Anuvinda.

'We have not come here for the swayamwar at all. We are going to Kamarupa to attack Narakasura. It is essential to obtain the blessings of our elderly aunt and her husband.'

Sri ushered his team towards the royal capital of Avanti. At the last moment, he entered the swayamwar pandal, along with chosen warriors. While all the invited guests kept gawking at him, he forcefully abducted Mitravinda and brought her to the chariot. Powerful Satyaki and Anadhrishti took on the infuriated Vinda and Anuvinda, and kept them engaged in battle. Sri immediately dispatched the Avanti princess Mitravinda to Dwaraka, along with a troop of armed warriors and faithful charioteers. I welcomed my third co-wife, Mitravinda, with a smile.

Mitravinda had a temperament that was a combination of Jambavati's and Bhama's. Since she was a Yadava, she was proud, but her pride was not as blatant as Bhama's. She was perceptive like Jambavati, but not as inquisitive and innocent. Like Jambavati and me, she, too, began awaiting Sri's arrival. At last, after two months, the news that we had been desperately waiting for arrived at the victorious Shuddhaksha gate of the Dwaraka kingdom. All of Aaryavarta was thrilled.

'Maharaja Srikrishna has executed Narakasura. For that, he had to fight a thrilling battle with four governors of Narakasura and his commander, Mura.' This victory was a culmination of Sri's warfare skills. Under the leadership of commander Mura, the asuras had laid a sturdy safety net in the thick meadows of Pragjyotishapura, the royal capital, and 6,000 hidden snares with weapons. Mura himself stood guard, all armed with weapons and 'astras', to protect this net, along with his sons. This very first wall of defence of his adroit war strategy was difficult to break. As gallant Yadava warriors stepped forward, the invisible contrivances under their feet automatically released javelins hidden in the net that was spread in the meadows. Those javelins struck the warriors. Pierced by javelins, the Yadava warriors were quickly falling down in the meadows, without any resistance. Tall, towering mountains stood behind these nets. Hiding in the mountains were Narakasura's armed governors Hayagriva and Nishumbha, along with the army. That was the second wall of defence. Beyond it, two more governors, Virupaksha and Panchjana, were hiding on the Maniparvat, along with their armies, all set to give Sri a tough fight. This was the third wall.

For the entire first week, gallant Yadava warriors fought desperately to break the deceptive first wall of security. Many sacrificed their lives. Courageous Satyaki, Anadhrishti, Shini and Avagaha also became disheartened. They did not know what to do. In the encampment, everybody sat in front of Sri, hanging their heads in worry. For quite some time, many strategies of counter-attacks were discussed. Bhama was also involved in the discussion. Even here, at first, Uddhava did not say anything. Finally, he said, 'Dada, I do not need to say this. I do not understand why you are not making a decision. Mura is using a deceptive strategy to fight this war with you. Every day Yadava warriors are losing their lives in vain due to the hidden javelins. Why don't you project your divine Sudarshan?'

Everybody in the camp looked at Sri with hopeful eyes. Sri eyed Uddhava with a smile and closed his eyes. His face blossomed like a sunflower. He had recited the unique, divine mantras of Sudarshan. Instantly, a divine instrumental melody began echoing in the encampment, leaving everybody entranced. Sri stood erect, with his eyes closed. He raised his right hand gradually. In a trice, a rapidly revolving, dazzling radiant chakra with twelve spokes appeared on his index finger. Its extraordinary brilliance blinded everyone. In the rising incantation of mantras, Sri projected the divine chakra. It left, buzzing with the thrilling rhythm of music to destroy the magical net of weapons. It destroyed the hidden weapons in the thick, grassy meadows. It beheaded commander Mura as well as his six sons, and returned. It came back on Sri's index finger and steadied itself. And just as it had appeared, it disappeared. All those present there were never going to forget this and the way Sri looked. Bhama was indeed fortunate and a blessed consort of Sri, as she was the first among his wives to see his divine form, holding the Sudarshan chakra. Having overcome Mura, Sri called to the Yadava army, along with Satyaki and Anadhrishti. They broke down the next two walls of defence. They beheaded the governors Hayagriva and Nishumbha. At Odaka, on the Maniparvat, the governors Panchjana and Virupaksha, the third wall of defence, confronted them fiercely. Sri beheaded them too and ended their opposition. These four governors and commander Mura were Narakasura's major defenders. Once the Yadava army broke through the three defence walls, the war reached a fever pitch. Bhama herself steered Sri's chariot and brought it right in front of Narakasura's. Daruka stood next to her. Bhama wore iron armour and war attire today. She did not look like a woman, but like one of the Yadava warriors! A fierce battle took place between Sri and Narakasura. This was the ultimate battle of Justice against Injustice. It was not going to conclude very soon. First there was a deluge of rocks through the Bhrushundi rockets. Then there was a fierce battle of bow and arrow between Sri and Narakasura. The day kept progressing hour by hour, but as both warriors were powerful, neither of them backed down. Finally, both of them descended from their chariots for the final decisive duel. A hair-raising mace duel began. Sri had tucked in his yellow silk dhoti tightly and balanced his Kaumodaki mace easily; he roared 'Hail Goddess Ida', circled gracefully and attacked Narakasura. Both of them forgot about the surrounding battlefield and warriors. They looked as fearless as soaring falcons. Spellbound and transfixed, Bhama and Daruka stared at the thrilling battle in front of them.

It was almost evening. The white, long-winged birds – himapakshi – were returning to their nests on Mount Mainaka.

The sun, touching the distant mountains, was about to set. This was the time for Sri's daily prayer. For a few moments, under the pretext of taking rotations while balancing the huge mace, Sri had a good look at the sun. The next moment he planted his feet firmly on ground, took a stance and feinted at Narakasura in such a way that he was not able to see the cowherd in front of him. He did not realise when the cowherd went behind him. As the mace struck him hard on his stout, demonic back, that had supported innumerable evil deeds, he fell face forward. For an instant, the brightness of many suns flashed in front of his closed eyes. He turned on his back while moaning. That day, with the setting sun of Kamarupa as his witness, Sri's first decisive strike pounded on his unjust chest, shattering it. It was followed by several others.

Fountains of demonic blood spurted out. That was the fourteenth day of the dark fortnight of the month of Ashwin.

Triumphant Sri left with Satyaki and Anadhrishti on either side, followed by Uddhava and Bhama. Troops of ebullient and victorious Yadavas accompanied him, shouting war slogans. All of them arrived at the prison – the pivot of Narakasura's base of abuse. The armed soldiers there had already vanished. Only the clamour of the women confined behind the sturdy fence was lightly audible. As Sri gave him a smile, Satyaki moved forward and struck his mace on the wooden gate of the strong fence. Following his actions, the victorious warriors broke it down with whatever weapon they could get hold of. That sound caused the clamour of the women inside to stop completely, as if someone had pressed a thumb on their throats. The terrified women inside thought that, as usual, this was an onslaught of Mura and his governor friends, led by the shaggy Narakasura.

They were completely baffled when they saw the remarkably radiant Sri in the circle of Yadavas, standing in front of them. Understanding their bafflement, Sri raised his blue, muscular arm in assurance without saying a word. He just glanced at Uddhava. He promptly came forward. Raising both his arms, he said, 'My dear sisters of Kamarupa. Do not look at us with fearful eyes. The despotic Narakasura, who had been oppressing you for years, has been killed today. This dear Dada of mine has killed him. This is the Lord of Dwaraka, the leader of the Yadavas, Maharaja Srikrishna. With his consent, I assure you and declare that from today on you are free to go wherever you want.'

It took them some time to digest the fact of Narakasura's death. For a while, they did not even realise that they were free.

Uddhava, who had the knack of reading people's minds, realised it. He declared again in a loud voice, 'You really are free. Not prisoners any more. You are free to go anywhere. Narakasura has been killed.' The women were slowly coming to their senses. Some of them whispered amongst themselves, trying to convince each other, while pointing at the broken gate and at Sri. Their words were vaguely audible, 'Free... released...to go anywhere.' A bold young woman among them stepped forward. Raising her arm, she let out a cry of freedom... 'Hail, Lord of Dwaraka, Maharaja Srikrishna!' Thousands of women joined her,

'Victory...victory!' Within moments, these women, for whom prison life had become unbearable, left joyously, chattering in groups, through the broken gate. The women held captive in the royal prison were also freed.

After releasing all the women from both prisons, Sri arrived at the open square in front of the royal palace of Pragjyotishapura, along with the royal council. Here the infantry troop leader presented a young royal prisoner of war in front of him. He was Narakasura's son, Bhagdutta. He was scared to death due to the unexpected precipitous events that had taken place. As usual, Sri had already gathered information about him. He was not at all involved in the subjugation orchestrated by his father and his commanders. He was righteous from birth. But now he was terrified, thinking that he was going to be executed. Sri discussed him with Uddhava. Then he stepped forward and affectionately put his hand on Bhagdutta's shoulder. He immediately bowed down and held Sri's feet. Sri patted him, pulled him up, held him close to his generous heart, and said, 'Bhagdutta, let go of your fear. You are the one who is going to look after this kingdom. Not the way your father did, but in your own way. Cremate your father on the banks of the Brahmaputra.' Sri gave orders to the army commanders, 'Since the asuras do not follow the tradition of the mourning period, organise the coronation of this asura king, Bhagdutta, tomorrow itself in the main square of the city. He is going to be crowned king in presence of asura citizens. Announce this all over the city.'

That night, after dinner, Sri was resting and discussing things with Uddhava and Bhama in the capacious encampment erected on the banks of the Lohitganga. Oil torches were burning dimly inside. Armed guards were walking outside. Uddhava said, 'Dada, you will easily forget it, but I will never forget this blessed day.'

Just then, the whispering of seven–eight women was heard, followed by the intimidating words of Yadava guards attempting to stop them. Sri only glanced at his brother. Uddhava immediately stepped outside and returned with a group of women. 'They have something to say. I have heard it. Their problem is difficult indeed. Dada should hear it directly from them,' he said.

The young woman who had courageously stepped forward earlier said, 'Maharaja, we all are indebted to you and can never repay it. You have given us the light of freedom that we never even imagined. You have kind-heartedly given us the freedom to go anywhere. But…but…' she hesitated. She did not know how to say what she wanted to say.

'But what? Do not hesitate to speak freely. Do not be afraid,' Sri comforted her.

She gasped and gathering courage, said, 'Some of us live here, in the city of Pragjyotishapura itself. When you freed them, they joyously rushed back to their homes. But…' she stopped again.

'But what? Speak…' A subtle crease, never seen before, appeared on Sri's forehead.

'But Maharaja, their own family is not ready to accept them because they are disgraced, defiled. You freed them, but their own families are not accepting them. If society does not accept us, where should we go? We cannot even go back to the asura prison, as it has already been destroyed. Where should we go? How should we face the world? What should we do?' She was Kasheru, the sixteen-year-old daughter of King Twashtta. She lowered her head and started sobbing in agony.

Sri went around in the pavilion with his hands behind his back. He muttered something to himself. Then with the same beautiful smile on his face, he said to his brother, 'Udho, present all these women tomorrow in the main square of the city, at the time of the coronation. Let us offer justice to them too. The problem that you perceive is not a problem at all. It will be solved in my own way. Take them back to their group.'

The next day, the central square of Pragjyotishapura was packed with men and women from Kamarupa. At the centre of the square, a spacious coronation altar had been raised under a tall canopy. All the material needed for the ceremony was neatly placed on the altar. Citizens had come out in great numbers to welcome the new young king. Half an hour before the designated time, musical instruments reverberated in the air. As per Uddhava's instructions, the 16,000 women liberated from the prisons were also present. The mammoth crowd was encircled by Yadava warriors. As the muhurta of Bhagdutta's coronation drew close, Sri arrived in his chariot, along with Bhagdutta. As the high-pitched instruments began playing to welcome them, the murmur died down. With Bhagdutta on his right, Sri began walking on the carpets spread out on the ground, offering greetings to the citizens of Kamarupa with utter humility. Behind him were Uddhava, both commanders and Bhama. Citizens standing on both sides showered flowers on the royal league walking towards the altar.

Sri ascended the altar along with Bhagdutta and the others. A welcoming round of applause followed.

The priests began intoning mantras in deep voices. The moment the first jar of sacred water was poured on Bhagdutta's head, he felt purified inside out. No one in his asura dynasty, including his father, had had such luck.

After the abhishek, Bhagdutta donned the traditional royal costume of the asuras.

The royal priest brought Bhagdutta near the elevated royal seat placed at the centre of the altar. The time-measuring earthen cups, floating in copper vessels placed in the four corners of the altar, were about to sink. The chief priest who carried the platter with the traditional crown of the asuras came to Sri and bowed before him. Sri got up and approached the elevated royal seat at the centre, adorned with garlands. Before picking up the crown, he held the Paanchajanya, tied skilfully in the shawl around his waist, in his lean-fingered hands. He raised his head high and, with all his might, blew such a divine tune that the asura priest chanting mantras and the local instruments stopped immediately. The crowd inadvertently moved towards the altar. As the time-measuring vessels were sinking, Sri placed the royal crown of Kamarupa on Bhagdutta's head. While showering fistfuls of flowers over the altar, millions of voices cheered, 'Hail Lord of Dwaraka Bhagwan Srikrishna Maharaja! Victory! Victory! Hail King of Kamarupa Bhagdutta Maharaja – victory – victory!'

Bhagdutta sat in the Virasana pose near Sri's feet in front of everybody. He took off his crown, humbly put it down at Sri's feet and, overwhelmed with emotion, put his head on Sri's feet.

Sri picked up the crown in one hand and pulled him up with the other. He put the crown on Bhagdutta's head and embraced him.

Bhagdutta's minister moved forward and, raising both hands, silenced the crowd. He said, 'Bhagwan Srikrishna Maharaja will now give his blessings to our new maharaja. We have only heard a lot about him, especially about his ambrosial speeches. At this auspicious moment, we request him to give us the privilege of hearing it and feeling grateful and blessed.'

Sri casually rested his hand on the golden lion head that was engraved on the right hand rest of the royal seat and stood up. He started speaking in a voice as melodious as the vina, 'Brothers and sisters of the Kamarupa kingdom, I am officially pronouncing this great asura, Bhagdutta, your new king from today. You have all experienced and know very well how brutally and dissolutely his father ruled the kingdom. I believe that this new king of yours will never follow that route. He will hold high the ideal of the high mountains of the Kamarupa kingdom. He will look after his subjects like his own children, with the understanding that growth and progress are key attributes of life. My blessings will always be with him. The Dwaraka kingdom will also support if required.

'Oh citizens, I consider Bhagdutta to be like my own son. Therefore, right from this moment, I consciously and gladly take it upon myself to rectify whatever sinful act his father Narakasura has committed. The Yadavas and I have freed thousands of Arya women whom Narakasura had forcibly imprisoned and who have suffered innumerable atrocities at his hands. I have come to know that the society, obsessed superstitions, is not ready to accept them. It considers them disgraceful, unchaste and shameful. What is their mistake in all this? Nothing at all. Therefore, at this moment, I, Srikrishna, the son of Maharaja Vasudeva of Dwaraka from the Vrushni-Andhaka dynasty, am publicly granting an assurance of safety to all of them.

'With the assistance of the Kamarupa minister and warriors, my dear brother Uddhava stayed awake the entire night and made thousands of mangalsutras with a single black bead woven into a thread. I will touch the platters full of these mangalsutras, declaring that I have accepted all of them as my wives, and assure them safety. With the assistance of the warriors, brother Uddhava will give one of those to each one of you. Wearing it around your neck, you should fearlessly tell anybody anywhere in the entire Aaryavarta with your head held high that you are the wife of Maharaja Srikrishna, the Lord of Dwaraka!

'You belong to Dwaraka from today. Consider it your own parental home and live freely. Just as I rehabilitated millions of Yadavas in Dwaraka,

I am doing the same for you. Indeed, from today, right from this moment, you have become truly free and will remain free.'

Huge ships, full of Kamarupa women, began crossing the creek and arriving at the Shuddhaksha gate of Dwaraka.

The leader of the troop of guards accompanying them had already shared this news in detail with me. As the maharani and Sri's wife, I accepted these women and proved that the faith which Sri had placed in me was right. Prior to this, I had already welcomed three women as my own sisters. With that same affection, I welcomed these thousands of women now. As per Sri's message, I braced myself and got engrossed in the mission of their rehabilitation.

Now I was waiting to see Sri in person. I was eager to meet Bhama and hear all about Sri's heroic exploits. But the troop leader who came brought news that I would have to wait one more month to meet Sri. He had gone to the Kosala kingdom of King Nagnajita along with Bhama. From there, he was directly going to Himavana. He was going to fulfil his long-cherished desire to visit the self-existent Himalinga in the cavern of Amaranath. I could understand that he was going to see the Himalinga. But why he went to the Kosala kingdom was a puzzle. I tried to dig some information out of the troop leader, but he, too, did not know the reason.

I had heard a lot about the Shivalinga of Amaranath. I, too, had a strong urge to see it at least once. Now, as a wife, I was going to have to see it only through Satyabhama's eyes. After a fortnight, news of Sri's heroic feat in the Kosala kingdom arrived in Dwaraka. He had not gone there for no reason. Nagnajita had dispatched an exclusive royal envoy to Pragjyotishapura and challenged Sri's status as the Lord of Dwaraka. His message was, 'It is easy to marry 16,000 imprisoned women, especially after emancipating them. But it is challenging to win the princess of Kosala after fulfilling the condition of the swayamwar. The challenge is for a brave Kshatriya who can put a nasal bridle on the seven robust bulls of my kingdom in front of all the citizens and yoke them to a bullock cart. If you have the guts to fulfil this condition, then come to Shravasti, the royal capital of the Kosalas on the banks of the Gandaki.'

Sri was not going to stop after hearing such a message. He dispatched his own messenger along with the Kosala envoy and sent a message to

Nagnajita, 'From childhood, I am used to reining in robust, intoxicated bulls. I am a gopa-cowherd inside out. How can a cowherd be afraid of a bull? I have also put reins on many impudent male bulls among citizens since becoming the Lord of Dwaraka. I am a gopa in that sense too.'

Sri reached the Kosala kingdom along with his army, passing the Vanga kingdom on the left and crossing the river Kaushiki. The Magadha kingdom was just adjacent to it. Sri had kept a keen eye on the military movements of Jarasandha there. He had astutely avoided the Magadha kingdom, passing by its borders, while going to and returning from Kosala. During the reign of Shrirama, the Kosalas' royal capital was Ayodhya on the banks of the Sharayu. Moving to the east, it had now become Shravasti, on the banks of the Gandaki. The Gandaki was also called the Sadnira.

The news of Sri's arrival to fulfil the condition of the swayamwar of the Kosalas' daughter Satya reached the open-air game arena marked for the occasion. At once, the men and women of Kosala who had gathered there hurried towards the Garudadhwaja chariot, as if pulled by some force, to take a look at Sri.

Sri entered the swayamwar arena surrounded by the roaring crowd of Kosala citizens. Bhama and Uddhava were also in the chariot. A big-wheeled, sturdy bullock cart adorned with garlands stood at the centre of the rink. Ten–twenty nasal bridles made with saffron-coloured ropes, decorated with designs of creepers made with golden threads, were laid on the colourful seat of the cart. Near the vacant cart with its yoke resting on the ground, seven hefty, humped Kosala bulls were bellowing and moving around insolently, ready to ram into anybody they saw. Sri instantaneously tucked in his yellow silk dhoti. While everybody watched flabbergasted, he descended into the secured arena, shouting, 'Hail Goddess Ida!' He charged at the seven bulls. Then the only thing visible was the fierce fight between the fleeting lines of charging bulls of different colours like white, red and black, and a single bluish line dodging them with agility. The citizens of Kosala got a glimpse of how Dada and Sri had defeated the giant Kuvalayapida elephant of Kansa in Mathura. No one understood how the nimble, blue line in front of them dodged each bull swiftly and exhausted them one after another. Nor did they realise when the nasal bridles, lying on the seat of the cart, were inserted in their already drooping, dripping and fretting nostrils.

Within half an hour, Sri had put the nasal bridles on all seven bulls. As he yoked them to the bullock cart standing next to them, and went around the game arena at top speed, thunderous applause and inspirational shouts reverberated. 'Hail Srikrishna – gopa king of Gokul, Lord of Dwaraka – the macho one among kings – victory to him! The son-in-law of Kosala, venerable Yadava Srikrishnadeva, victory…victory!'

Satya, the daughter of Kosala, put the white garland around the neck of the gopa of Dwaraka.

Obviously, I had to fulfil the duty of welcoming Sri's fifth wife. How did this Kshatriya lady, Satya, from the foothills of the Himavana look like, behave, and how would she get used to life in Dwaraka? Such thoughts kept rising in my mind constantly.

One fine day, a specific tune of kettledrums and flutes, reserved for Sri's wives, was played in the welcoming chamber of the Shuddhaksha gate.

I surmised that Satya had arrived.

Just two days ago, I had arrived in original Dwaraka from the island of the Queens' mansions, along with Jambavati and Mitravinda. We arrived at the Shuddhaksha gate, with great curiosity, to welcome Satya. I was astonished to see Satyabhama herself assisting Satya in getting down from the chariot. Satya was expected but how had Bhama come with her? She was, in fact, going to Amaranath. This puzzle was not easy to solve.

I instantly brushed aside all questions and welcomed both of them. As soon as she saw me, Bhama threw her arms around my neck. Satya kept staring at both of us. I was really eager to ask Bhama so much about so many things.

After we arrived at my palace in original Dwaraka, Bhama told me at leisure why she had returned without going to Amarnath with Sri. The Amaranath cave is located on a high peak of Himavana, way higher than the Kosala kingdom. The initial phase of the journey was going to be along the base of the Himalayas. They would have had to go through snowy regions sometimes and at times through thick forests. Immediately after completing this first phase, the second phase of sharp ascent of Himawanta would begin. It is full of difficult twists and turns of snowy passes. Sri had convinced Bhama initially by telling her, 'It is possible to win the world with an army, but not Mount Himawanta!', and afterwards by saying how the arduous journey would not be possible for a woman. I stopped her in the middle and asked her teasingly, 'He may have done his best to convince you, but how come you let go of your usual attitude of being insistent and conceded only in this matter?'

She said, 'Maharani, I tried my best, telling him that I would not bicker, that I would bear all the difficulties patiently, and that I do want to go to Amaranath! He said, "Bhama, it looks like you really do not want me to go and see the Himalinga. It is better that I just cancel my plans to go there. But…but I feel…" I got confused when he said he was cancelling his plan. Still, I asked him with determination, "But what is it that you feel?" Then, as usual, smiling sweetly, he gave me the perfect reason which made me refrain from my stand. What do you think he told me?'

Even I began thinking. Really, what kind of intelligent move had Sri made that had left Bhama speechless and forced her to retreat? After some time, I snapped my fingers and, as if talking to myself, I said, 'Let me tell you, Bhama, he must have said, 'If I would have told the same thing to Rukmini, she would have agreed immediately. She would not have raised any objections ever. My mistake, I should have known that you are not Rukmini."

Hearing that, Bhama widened her large eyes in astonishment. She held both my arms tightly and screamed in wonder, 'That is exactly what he said! That, too, in exactly the same words! How did you guess it so perfectly?' I just smiled.

I kept talking to her at length about the many events that had taken place since she had left Dwaraka. While talking to her, I felt deep in my heart that it was only Uddhava who was the most beloved to Sri among the Yadavas. After all, he had left out even Bhama and taken only Uddhava to Amaranath with him.

A few days after Satya's arrival in Dwaraka, the senior commander Anadhrishti returned, along with the Yadava army. He had brought along the enormous herd of animals that Bhagdutta had offered, which included 20,000 male elephants, 40,000 female elephants, 18,000 horses, and 18,000 milch cows, safely to such a faraway distance. Dwaraka was now full of bustle, with millions of Yadava men and women already living here, thousands of Kamarupa women and thousands of domestic animals.

In no time, Satya became part of the royal ladies' circle. She had a speciality – she was very proficient in dance. Even though she was a princess, she had never missed a single day's practice.

A month passed. Sri reached the borders of Panchala via the shores of the river Ganga, crossing the rivers Sharayu and Gomati. He dispatched the entire Yadava army sailing in ships to Kampilyanagar, the royal capital of the Panchalas. He himself selected a few assiduous Yadava warriors who would be able to survive in the cold of Himavana to go along with him. With the assistance of the Panchala king Drupada, commander Satyaki was going to arrange for the army to cross the Yamuna towards Saurashtra through the Kuntibhoja kingdom. He himself was going to return to join in Sri's service. Maharathi Satyaki left as decided.

The borders of the Kuru kingdom that Sri frequently referred to in his talks were also going to fall on the way. But Sri was not going to visit their royal capital, Hastinapura, as the Pandavas no longer lived there. In fact, he took all precautions to prevent the blind king Dhritarashtra from receiving any news of his passing by the kingdom. It was easy for him to keep this secret, as the enormous Yadava army was not accompanying him. On the way, they reached a juncture in the Himalayas from where there was a turn leading to Mount Gandhamadana. During their stay at that spot, Sri looked at the summit of the towering Himaparvat and said to Uddhava, 'Uddhava, if possible, I would have gone right away to Mount Gandhamadana with you. I do not know why but I get a strong feeling that there is a deep-rooted connection with this mountain. Srirama, the pride of Ayodhya, had resided on the banks of the river Alakananda that originates from this mountain. Notably, all the Pandavas of Aunt Kunti were born on this mountain.'

The brothers and some select Yadavas crossed the Ganga from the borders of the Kuru kingdom, travelled along its coast and reached the holy place of Hardwar. As decided, they camped there, waiting for Satyaki. The commander arranged for the Yadava army to leave for Dwaraka and, along with a few warriors, united with Sri's troops. Now this troop consisted of three chief Yadava warriors and a few tough companions.

Eager to see the Himalinga in the Amaranath cave, Sri now crossed the river Saraswati and descended into the Mattamayura kingdom. Finally, he reached the Kashmir kingdom of the Gonardas and arrived at the base of the steep ascent of the Himawanta. The tough Yadava warriors that Sri had taken with him dropped one after the other on the first few twists and turns. In the sojourn during the second phase of the journey, while Sri was looking at the sun on the snow-clad eastern horizon, he suddenly smelt a strong, sweet and enchanting fragrance. Sri closed his eyes and, breathing deeply, filled his chest with that fragrance and made a precise prediction about it. In that desolated snow-clad region, he said, 'Udho, brother, somewhere in a nearby lake the flowers of Brahmakamala must have bloomed recently. If you could go with Satyaki and collect some Brahmakamala buds and a few flowers, we can worship Shiva with elaborate rituals. These flowers are not ordinary. Take a garment with you to cover your nose. The intoxicating fragrance of these flowers is so strong that it will not allow anyone to come close to pluck them. It leaves one unconscious. To pluck a Brahmakamala in full bloom and offer it to the self-existent Himalinga while chanting Shiva's hymn is indeed an exceptionally rare opportunity. These fully blossomed flowers will last for a minimum of one month. They disperse their fragrance continuously. Nature itself has gifted these unique snow flowers with such power.

Uddhava took two Yadava warriors who had so far sustained this journey in the snow and started towards the lake following the trail of the sweet fragrance. Everybody had covered their noses well with garments. Still they could smell the strong fragrance of the snow flowers. By evening, Uddhava returned with some fully blossomed and some half blossomed Brahmakamalas wrapped in a shawl. Sensing the fragrance of the Brahmakamalas approaching his tent, Sri was already standing at the door with his hands on his waist. Seeing Uddhava return successfully, he moved forward and said with a smile, 'Uddhava, my heart is telling me that in the final phase of this journey towards Shiva, only you will sustain and remain with me.' Satyaki, who was resting in the tent, could not have heard this dialogue.

Finally, it happened just as Sri had said. The two or three Yadava warriors who had resolutely sustained so far and even, Maharathi commander

Satyaki, retreated in the last phase of the journey to Amaranath. Only the two brothers kept going. It was getting strenuous for Uddhava to climb the ascending, winding turns as he was holding the bunch of wet lotus flowers wrapped in a shawl under his arm. Sri offered him the support of his hands and they climbed together. Ultimately, surmounting all trying twists and turns in the last patch of Himavana, both brothers finally stood in the Amaranath cave in front of the self-existent Himalinga, about six feet tall. Uddhava let out a big sigh of relief. As Sri saw the crystal-white, moist, dripping self-forming Shivalinga, he took out the Brahmakamalas from the shawl and offered them one by one to the Himalinga. In the desolate cave on the towering Himavana, the Lord of Dwaraka remained in a meditational trance for a long time in front of Lord Shiva, with his palms joined in prayer. Uddhava joined him. After feasting their eyes on Shiva to their hearts' content, both brothers started on their way back. On the first turn itself, Sri said, 'Do not run, Uddhava. Hold my hand. Stay with me. Tell me, what did you feel about the Shivalinga of Amaranath? What did you ask Shiva for?'

Uddhava, who had gone ahead, stopped on hearing that. Staring continuously at his Dada, he said, 'I was excited while looking at the fresh, six-foot-tall Himalinga dripping with snow water. My eyes closed automatically when you sang Shiva's hymns. I could visualise only one scene – that of a towering, snow-clad white mountain summit penetrating the cerulean sky. It had merged into the sky. Both had become one. That scene made me forget completely that I was supposed to ask Shiva for something, and also that I wanted to tell you something.'

While returning, both the brothers took along the Yadava companions who had stayed behind at various camps and started towards Dwaraka. News of their progress towards Dwaraka kept reaching the Shuddhaksha gate. Finally, Sri stood at the Shuddhaksha gate, along with Uddhava, with a triumphant look on his face, after completing the famous mission of Narakasura's annihilation. A large army of warriors who had been gifted to him stood behind him. I was already waiting eagerly for Sri in original Dwaraka. My four sisters – Jambavati, Satyabhama, Mitravinda and Satya – had joined me from the island of the queens' mansions. The entire city of Dwaraka was delighted. Citizens erected decorative flagpoles atop their houses, hung festoons at each intersection of the royal highway and flung fistfuls of vermilion in the air. I threw a glance around and strongly felt the absence of Balaramadada and Akrurakaka.

Because of Narakasura's annihilation, the acclaim of Sri's fame was reverberating through Aaryavarta. This event in the eastern kingdom of Kamarupa had already reached Mithila. It had reached sullen Balaramadada, who was residing in the city of Janak. From Pragjyotishapura, Sri had immediately descended to the Kosala kingdom. He did it intentionally, hoping that since the Mithila kingdom was adjacent to it, he would surely meet Balaramadada at Satya's swayamwar. But that did not happen at all. Balaramadada was unrelenting. Even if Sri were to be acclaimed as the lord of the three worlds, Balaramadada would not return to Dwaraka.

It constantly bothered me. It made me feel gloomy. That is why, in the resting chamber of my palace, after dinner one night, I decidedly broached this subject with Sri. 'Wait, Rukmini, listen to me before you present your request. Today itself I have dispatched minister Vipruthu and Uddhava, along with Chitraketu and Brihadbala, out of Dwaraka on a special mission,' he said.

'Such missions of Sri will never be over. I am quite aware of your habit of keeping others around you constantly engaged. I am the maharani of Dwaraka, only for name's sake. Here I have become a mere hostess who welcomes Sri's special guests. But I will feel true joy in welcoming only one person, something I have not felt in receiving anyone so far,' I said.

'At least listen to me, Maharani. Minister Vipruthu has gone to the kingdom of Mithila. He is going to bring Balaramadada along with him on the strength of his brilliance and convincing skills. To make this difficult task easy for him, I have played a small trick. Of course, I am not as intelligent as the Maharani. Could you guess what could be the one thing that I have sent with the minister? I have also sent a small message with it – what could that be?' I was confused. I thought for a few moments and said, 'Sri must have sent the prince's favourite mace along with the minister. And the message must be that this mace looks worthless without him. The prince's throne in the Sudharma council looks desolate. Come back with the minister to honour both.'

He smiled and said, 'Oh, where do I have that kind of intelligence? The thing that I have sent with the minister is just my favourite peacock feather in a closed casket! The message is that I have kept it in the casket since you left. If you come back and tuck it back in my crown, only then will all Yadavas get to see it. Or else this golden coronet of the Lord of Dwaraka will remain desolate without the peacock feather. Please remember the days in the Ankapada ashrama and come back right away, along with this peacock feather!'

Now I realised that Sri had indeed not worn his peacock-feathered crown ever since Dada had left.. Wonderstruck at his intellectual genius, I kept staring at him. I asked cautiously, 'Then where have you dispatched Uddhava along with his brothers? And why? I had thought of suggesting his name as the most appropriate person for this job.'

'You are wrong. Dada would not have liked it if I had sent Uddhava, who is even younger than I am. That is why I have chosen the senior Yadava minister for this task. Through him, this is an appeal to the prince who resides within Dada. He will never be able to deny it. Or else I will have to go to Janakpura myself.'

'Then where have you sent Uddhava? And for what?' I was baffled now. But he smiled affectionately as usual, as if nothing had happened, and said, 'Uddhava has gone to the kingdom of Kashi. To convince Akrurakaka, who has the Syamantaka jewel. In his own sweet way, he is going to convince Akrurakaka that he himself should present the jewel in the Sudharma assembly just once to convince everyone that it is not in the possession of the Lord of Dwaraka. After that, if he wishes, he can return to Kashi. Dada insists that he should spend the rest of his life in Dwaraka. But Dada should not be forced go to the Kashi kingdom again only for the sake of the mere jewel!'

I was stunned to hear that keen diplomatic manoeuvre of getting this done in a roundabout manner. I tenaciously asked one last question, 'Then why has Sri sent Uddhava's brothers, Chitraketu and Brihadbala, along with him? Or does the Lord of Dwaraka intend to keep an eye on Uddhava himself for the sake of the Syamantaka jewel?'

'Wrong again, Maharani! Akrurakaka will never give the Syamantaka jewel to Uddhava. I anyway never yearned for it at all. I know Uddhava better than anybody else. He is less of a warrior and more of a philosopher. Therefore, I must take precautions for his safety. Uddhava's brothers are older than him. They are expert warriors. I have told them whatever is necessary.'

A month passed and an envoy brought news that minister Vipruthu and Uddhava had succeeded and were returning. Balaramadada and Akrurakaka were also returning with them. Though the end of monsoon was approaching, Dwaraka blossomed again. I was happy for two reasons. The first was that Sri's staunch supporter, our dear, mighty Dada, had let go of his anger and was returning to Dwaraka. The second was that Sri would be cleared of the accusation of stealing the Syamantaka. Except for Bhama, all four of us had never got to see that jewel. Now we were going to see the Syamantaka jewel that begot one dramatic event after another, in person. At this time, I was also curious about one thing. Whom would Sri entrust this jewel to after it returned?

The Yadavas of Dwaraka gave a grand welcome to Uddhava, both his elder brothers, Balaramadada and Akrurakaka. At the Shuddhaksha gate, in the presence of their father and mother, when Sri bowed down to touch Dada's feet, he did not allow him to do so and passionately held him in a deep embrace. The moment Balaramdada met Sri, thousands of emotionally overwhelmed Yadavas roared ecstatically, 'Hail Balarama–Srikrishna!' I felt contented.

The very next day, a grand Sudharma royal assembly was held to welcome Dada and Akrurakaka. The minister introduced the agenda for the meeting to the council of the Dwaraka kingdom, 'Honourable Yadava ministers of the Sudharma council, today's special meeting has been organised to honour the joyous occasion of the return of two distinguished senior Yadavas back to the kingdom. This kingdom honourably welcomes Prince Balarama and minister Akrura. Valiant Yadava prince Balarama wishes to give a gift to the Lord of Dwaraka for their reconciliation after such a long time. I request him to carry out his wish.' Now the assembly hall got curious about what gift Dada was going to give Sri.

Dada got up from his seat carefully, holding the wooden, decorated casket in his hands. Even more delicately than that, he lifted the fresh, iridescent peacock feather as big as a palm from the casket. I could clearly see his big, innocent eyes fill with tears. Holding it in his strong, muscular hands, he raised it higher and moving in a half-circle, he showed it to all his Yadava brothers. Leaning forward, Dada tucked it into Sri's shining golden crown. At that moment, Sri also got up from his seat amid a loud round of applause that pierced the roof. Sri had beautiful eyes, but rarely did they get teary. Today Sri's eyes were moist while looking at his dear brother. He was about to bow down to obtain Dada's blessings when Dada held his broad shoulders tightly and pulled him in a deep embrace. He patted Sri's shoulders with affection. At that moment, the royal council exploded with continuous applause and unrestrained cries of joy. Dada touched his dear brother's golden crown to offer his blessings and returned to his seat without saying a single word. Interlocution was not his forte after all.

The minister introduced the most important topic of the day's council after pounding the royal sceptre. Akrurakaka, who used to sit in the minister's circle before, sat awkwardly as a common Yadava guest on a mat in the guest square in the front. He himself was the cause of his downfall. He had brought the casket of the Syamantaka jewel along with him in the Sudharma council. In Mathura, he had witnessed Sri pulling down his own mama, Kansa, from the royal altar. He was quite petrified of the verdict that Sri would pronounce.

Minister Vipruthu pointed towards him and said, 'As per the command of the Lord of Dwaraka, I also welcome former senior minister Akrura. Something that should not have happened has happened due to a mere jewel. Due to a misunderstanding, a disagreement arose between our venerable Lord of Dwaraka, who is as good as the most precious Kaustubh jewel for thousands of Yadavas, and his elder brother, Prince Balarama. Akrura should show the jewel to the entire Yadava assembly from his seat itself. That way, everybody will be convinced that it was never with Maharaja Srikrishna. He should submit it at the feet of the Lord of Dwaraka in front of everybody. That is its rightful place.' Following this command, Akrurakaka got up. From his location, he turned around in a half-circle and showed the radiant jewel to the council once. Then he approached Sri and put the casket at his feet. He bowed to Sri and went back to his seat. The minister continued, 'Now, whatever verdict the Lord of Dwaraka pronounces about the Syamantaka jewel will be acceptable to the Sudharma assembly. I request him to offer his invaluable guidance to this assembly, not just about the Syamantaka jewel but also about wealth in general.' As Vipruthu pounded the royal sceptre, thousands of honourable Yadavas fell utterly silent with extreme curiosity. The only sound audible was that of the western ocean.

Before getting up, Sri threw a glance at me. How bright his fish-shaped, dark black eyes looked with the brilliance of his illuminated self. He smiled slightly. The next moment, he got up, easily handling the casket with both hands. Casting a hawk-eyed glance casually over the assembly, Sri began his melodious speech,

'My dear Yadavas! This is a very important day in your life, more than in mine. In the same assembly, my late father-in-law, senior Yadava Satrajita, had accused me of a contemptible act – of stealing the Syamantaka jewel. This extraordinary jewel also raised a doubt in my dear elder brother's mind.

'Both these doubts have been cleared today. I never longed for the Syamantaka jewel. Not just this, but I will never have any desire for any other jewel either. Wealth is a mere means to assist the running of life. It can never be the only goal of life. When that happens, one has to face unimaginable calamities. Society sees an upsurge in inconceivable crimes. Then the kingdoms associated with such people face staggering hurdles. The real wealth of mankind is in intellect. A healthy intellect disciplined properly by ethics is the real jewel, the real wealth. That is what takes life forward even if by an iota. That is what develops life.

'This Syamantaka brought many a storm in our new kingdom. I was intently following this Syamantaka jewel only because I wanted to clear the misunderstanding it had caused in my elder brother's mind. The misunderstandings of elders are even more damaging than the worst curse. Now all misunderstandings have been cleared. That has made me happy.

'Right now, as your Lord of Dwaraka, I need to make it clear that I disapprove of the selfish actions of the senior Yadava Akrurakaka and Kritavarman. They conspired against a senior and experienced Yadava like Satrajita, who was a valuable member of Dwaraka's advisory ministry, and got him killed by a distant Yadava like Shatadhanwa by coaxing him. I give both of them a strong warning against such an unforgivable offence.

'It is beyond comprehension, especially as to why Akrurakaka behaved so strangely after getting hold of the jewel. He was the one who had cautioned me the night before bringing me from Gokul to Mathura to visit Kansa. I have never forgotten that kindness of his in the past and I will never forget it in future. Why would the Yadava minister who cautioned me that time behave so recklessly himself? Clearly, it is due to greed for wealth. Therefore, it is necessary to tell you all right now that this new kingdom will never survive on greed. No matter what heights of puissance it reaches, it will sink due to uncontrollable greed. It will survive only on unlimited sacrifice – on boundless devotion towards duty.

'To give him that opportunity, on behalf of everybody, I request Akrurakaka to leave his seat and come to sit among the ministers again. I have intentionally kept his seat vacant since the day he left. He should accept his post again and also the Syamantaka jewel. He himself should look after it as a trustee, so that henceforth no conflict will arise among the Yadavas due to this jewel. He should donate all the wealth he has obtained from the Syamantaka to the Kashi kingdom, and maintain his sublime title of a "philanthropist". He should never forget that due to the presence of the Syamantaka and charity, Dwaraka will remain opulent.' Sri gave the casket in his hands to an attendant and sent him towards Akrurakaka.

Overwhelmed, Akrurakaka got up amidst a thunderous round of applause. He walked slowly towards his vacant seat among the ministers and sat on it again.

All Yadavas treated my second pregnancy as if it were the first, and organised a feast to celebrate it. A long time had passed since the abduction of my first son. The Yadava relatives felt the agony of it even more than me. They had organised flewless celebrations. Sri told me that the name of the son to be born should be 'Charudeshna'. I asked, 'What does Charu mean?' He smiled as usual and said, 'Charu means "beautiful"'.

'And what if a daughter is born?' I teased him.

He said, 'No, it will be a son. And his name will be Charudeshna. In case a daughter is born, we will answer that "what if" question at that time.' But I was preoccupied in thought as to what the name would be if a daughter were born.

Sri was never wrong – I had realised that long ago.

I delivered a son indeed. He was named Charudeshna. He looked as beautiful as his name denoted. He removed the pain from everybody's heart caused by my first son's abduction. After me, Bhama delivered a son. Fair like his mother and radiant like the sun. He was named Bhanu. Within a fortnight, Jambavati also delivered a child. She came as Sri's wife before Bhama, but became a mother after her. Jambavati and Sri both had darkish complexion, but the son born to them was fair. Though he was a son, he looked like a daughter. Jambavati's father's deity was Shankara. He was called 'Samba' in his wild form by the people in the forest. In his memory, this son of Jambavati was also named 'Samba'. Soon, Avanti's daughter Mitravinda also delivered a son. He was named 'Vrika'. Towards the end of spring, Satya from Kosala also gave birth to a son. He was named 'Vira'. Sumptuous gifts from the parental homes of all four of my sisters arrived in Dwaraka, congratulating them on their deliveries. I was not going to receive any gifts from Kundinpura. I did not even expect it. My family members were still upset with me.

While all five of us were engrossed in nurturing our children, important news reached the Sudharma royal council. The infamous, gluttonous and hideous demon named Bakasura residing in a jungle called Vetravan in the Panchala kingdom near the Ekachakra city had been killed by a Brahmin boy just as huge as him. While delivering this news, Daruka also told me a subtle thing that he had noticed. He said, 'As soon as Sri heard this news, his face lit up. He called for the surveillance chief and ordered him to dispatch a pair of expert spies to Vetravan immediately.' I did not understand why he immediately sent spies so far away for such news. A lot of his dealings were incomprehensible to most of us. Due to Dada and Sri, the Dwaraka kingdom had now achieved a respectable status in the Kshatriya circle. Because of that, a significant invitation had arrived in the Sudharma royal council of the Yadavas. It was for the swayamwar of Panchala king Drupada's daughter, Yajnasena, also known as Draupadi.

I had heard a lot about this Yajnasena and her Yajna brother, Dhrishtadyumna. Word was that Yajnadeva, who himself manifested from the fire of the yajna pit, had offered both these children to King Drupada and his wife, Sautramani. They also had a son named Shikhandi, born before the yajna, and eight more sons born afterwards. The glory of Draupadi's dark-complexioned, fragrant beauty and luxuriant hair had spread in the entire Aaryavarta.

Located beyond the Yamuna, the Panchala kingdom was enormous. For the sake of convenience in governance, it was divided into two parts – southern Panchala and northern Panchala. The royal capital of the northern Panchalas was Ahichchhatra. The boundary of this kingdom had extended through Brahmavarta in the north and directly touched the boundary of the Hastinapura city of the Kurus. The royal capital of southern Panchal was Kampilyanagar. This was where the swayamwar of Draupadi was going to take place. This swayamwar was going to drastically change the destiny of Aaryavarta. Many kings of Madhyadesha did not know it then, but an intense desire for the elegant Draupadi had taken hold of the heart of every king participating in the swayamwar. It would be a wonder if the Yadavas did not try their best to win such a lady. Balaramadada, both the commanders, Uddhava, many Yadava warriors and, yes, Sri himself were excited to leave for Kampilyanagar. While all this was happening, a completely unexpected and unimaginable event took place, which filled Dwaraka with euphoria.

One day, unexpectedly, my first son, who had been abducted many years ago, stood at the Shuddhaksha gate of Dwaraka. He had many asura warriors with him. He had come from Yadava's original kingdom, Shursena, from the thick forests of Mount Govardhan. Holding some kind of a grudge, Shambarasura had abducted my newborn son on the sixth day of his birth, several years ago. Shambarasura and his wife Mayavati had vigilantly raised him while instilling asura values in him. They had taken thorough precautions against letting him know about the Yadava family.

But all their efforts had failed. The moment he came to know that he was a Yadava from Dwaraka and the son of Sri himself, he had fought a fierce battle with Shambara and had come only after killing him. He had left Mayavati and, taking a few loyal asuras along, had directly reached Dwaraka.

This son of mine had been attractive since birth. Madan incarnate! As he had grown up in the carefree atmosphere of the forest of Govardhan, he looked exceptionally tall, healthy and so handsome that he could become anybody's envy. Sri himself went with Dada to the Shuddhaksha gate and welcomed him. He held his strong, broad shoulders tightly, stared deep into his blue eyes, regarded him with a scrutinising eye and only then took him in a deep embrace. I was baffled when, after so many years, my first-born son bowed down to seek my blessings. I could not believe that he was my own son!

I held him in a deep embrace. The tears that I had restrained for twelve years flowed effortlessly. Exactly at that time, Sri's visionary, prudent words fell on my ears, 'First of all, it is difficult to be a mother. Rukmini, you have to take up the toughest task of wiping out asura sanskaras from his mind. Just like you transformed Jambavati into a Yadava royal lady, with her assistance, transform this son of yours into a Yadava maharathi.'

The royal priest of the kingdom performed a formal naming ceremony for our first son. In everybody's presence, he was named 'Pradyumna', just as we had planned before. The Yadavas left for Kampilyanagar, along with the fourfold army for Draupadi's swayamwar. The young, handsome Pradyumna was a new addition to the already selected Yadava team. Sri had purposefully taken him along. The intention was to show him the Kshatriya tradition of swayamwar in person. But that circulated a rumour among the Yadavas in Dwaraka and other kings around that the Lord of Dwaraka was going to Kampilyanagar for Pradyumna. However, while leaving, he clearly told me, 'The Panchala invitation is for the Lord of Dwaraka! Who knows I might have to step in to fulfil the condition of the swayamwar. The condition is very bizarre. It is going to thoroughly test one's archery skills.'

After hearing that, I said, 'I am all ready to welcome the Panchala daughter as my fifth sister! But what is this test of archery that even Sri finds tough?' Sri usually did not utter words like impossible and difficult. My curiosity was awakened.

Sri presented a detailed picture of the swayamwar pandal and the condition to be fulfilled, set by Drupada and Dhrishtadyumna. 'The Panchalas have dug out a spacious, neat circular stone pond at the centre of the pandal. It is filled to the brim with water from seven holy rivers. A narrow path going east to west leads to the centre of the pond. A round seat for the archer is located at the point where it begins. Adjacent to the seat is the groove for a huge Shiva bow that the Panchalas worship, adorned with garlands. Near that is the seat for quivers. Many quivers full of Suchi arrows will be placed there. Shooting only five of these arrows, the archer has to pierce the eye of the fish rotating in a device near the roof. With only five arrows. The eye has to be pierced indeed. That, too, with one out of five arrows only, not by looking directly up at the rotating fish, but by looking at its reflection rotating in the pond – looking downwards but piercing the eye up, by showing unparalleled expertise of skills.'

Seeing my confusion, smiling mischievously, Sri added, 'At least for now, only one warrior of Hastinapura has such skills – Karna, the charioteer's son. Karna had performed all the feats that Arjuna performed in the spring contest organised by Guru Drona, and had also challenged him to a duel. Frankly, only Arjuna had the capacity to fulfil this condition. But…but…' His big, smooth forehead wrinkled momentarily, which happened rarely, only while solving a complicated problem. Then he left, saying, 'Goodbye'. He left one question hanging in my mind. He had mentioned the names of two archers who had the ability to pierce the fish eye. But he had not mentioned himself as the first one. However, I was fully confident that no matter how hard it was, Sri was the one who was going to fulfil the condition. The sixth palace on the island of the queens' mansions was going to belong to the Panchala daughter.

I was, at heart, sentimental and credulous, no matter how much Sri himself called me an intelligent maharani. I wondered what Draupadi looked like in person. I had heard of the fragrant Brahmakamala in the description of Sri's travel to the Himavanta. Word was that she was fragrant too. What would this fragrant lotus of a lady look like? It is said that she was very proud. This sister of Dhrishtadyumna – Yajnasena – Shyama. How would she treat me? Like Bhama or Jambavati? The number of Panchalas at her parental home alone would be equivalent to the manpower of my four sisters' parental homes put together. The other four arrived after me. They respected and treated me as the maharani from the bottom of their hearts. Would she behave similarly? Or would she overpower me?

Who knows, maybe eventually she herself would become the maharani of millions of Yadavas. As it was, she was extremely beautiful, statuesque, with long and thick hair. And to top that, fragrant like the Champaka flower, a Kshatriya lady born out of a yajna. Could she be more intelligent than me? Sri has bluish-dark complexion, she was dark-complexioned too, both were brilliant – seemed like a perfect match.

A month passed. The Lord of Dwaraka returned with Dada and Uddhava. Panchala daughter Draupadi had not accompanied them, as I had surmised. How did this happen? I was extremely curious. To verify it, I caught Sri in his chamber while he was alone.

As he saw me, he scurried forward and, exuberantly holding both my arms tightly, he said, 'Rukmini, Maharani of the Yadavas, the Pandavas are alive. Virtuous, serene-faced Yudhishthira; his incomparable, muscular, wrestler of a brother Bhima; the winner of the swayamwar, invincible archer Arjuna; our Pradyumna's lookalike Nakula; the horse expert Sahadeva, who reminds me of Daruka – all the Pandavas are alive. I have returned after meeting them, along with Aunt Kunti and Draupadi, at a potter's house in Kampilyanagar. Maharani, Arjuna is alive. Many of my resolutions will be accomplished.

'Dear Rukmini, understand well that a new chapter in my life has begun because of this swayamwar. Your dear Uddhava will provide you with details of the happenings in Kampilyanagar.'

That night, Uddhava came to pay obeisance to me and put forth each small detail of the Draupadi swayamwar, as if drawing a picture of the whole event. He said, 'Duryodhana had come to fulfil the condition of the swayamwar, along with his brothers, Dushasana, Durmarsha and Dussaha. To compete in the swayamwar on his behalf, Karna, the king of Anga, had come with his brother Shona and son Sudamana. Gandhara king Shakuni, his eleven brothers, Magadha king Jarasandha, Shishupala, Dantavakra and Paundraka, who identified himself as the real Vasudeva, Shalya, the king of Madra, Saindhawa king Jayadratha, Balhika and Chitrangada were also present. About one hundred kings had gathered in Kampilyanagar for the swayamwar.

'On behalf of the Panchalas, Prince Dhrishtadyumna welcomed all the kings, along with their commanders and armies. He vividly described his sister's beauty and merits, and presented the purpose of the swayamwar. He explained the necessary details and rules that demanded the fulfilment of the difficult condition.

'Along with the fish, its reflection also began rotating rapidly in the serene water of the pond. Many kings came forward, puffing their chests proudly, accepting Dhrishtadyumna's challenge. Some even failed to pick up the heavy Shiva bow of the Panchalas, while some picked it up but were unsuccessful tying the bowstring to it. Many caved in. Hours passed. Even Madra king Shalya and Jayadratha were unsuccessful. Whispers started spreading in the pandal. One could hear the words 'Magadha emperor Jarasandha!' echoing through the gathering. At that point, weighty, muscular Magadha emperor Jarasandha rose from his seat. The golden, royal medallions and laurels on the royal attire on his muscular chest were shining. With a loud round of applause, his Chedi and Magadha supporters in the pandal gave out continuous ecstatic cries of 'Hail invincible Magadha emperor Maharaja Jarasandha… Victory… victory! King of Girivraja, invincible wrestler, master of archery, Emperor Maharaja Jarasandha, victory to him!' A few impatient Magadha citizens also pushed in joyous cries of 'Hail Magadha queen Yajnasenadevi!'

'The moment he got up, the first thing the Magadha emperor did was throw a contemptuous glance only at Dada, the Lord of Dwaraka! As if he was there not to wed the sister of Dhrishtadyumna but the sister of Srikrishna, the Lord of Dwaraka! And he wanted to tell him silently, "You, runaway coward of Mathura, a cowherd, I will put Draupadi on my shoulders and take her to Girivraja in front of your eyes. You escaped from the inferno at Mount Gomanta. But after this swayamwar, I am going to strap you with a rope and take you to Girivraja too!"

Jarasandha reached the Shiva bow, stomping his feet on the narrow path, with his chest puffed up with pride. He sat in the Virasana pose near the Shiva bow, held it at midpoint and picked it up. So far nobody had succeeded in doing that before him. Therefore, Magadhas got excited and the Panchala pandal reverberated with their ecstatic shouts. "Victory… victory!" Still in the Virasana pose, Jarasandha pulled an arrow from the quiver and touched it to his forehead. He was about to mount it on the bowstring when he lost balance and collapsed from his seat with a loud thud. The entire pandal stood at once in shock. The spectators, who were anxiously waiting to watch Jarasandha win Panchali's swayamwar, helplessly watched him trapped and struggling under the heavy Shiva bow. That powerful tyrant who kept more than eighty kings confined in his prison was himself weighed down by the heavy Shiva bow. There was a moment where it looked like he was going to die struggling.

'As Karna, the king of Anga, stood up at that moment, Dada looked at Pradyumna sitting next to me and smiled. They both looked so similar. Karna smiled at Duryodhana and slowly walked to the Shiva bow. He also sat in the Virasana pose. He picked up the Shiva bow very skilfully, just like he would pick up his Vijay bow. Jarasandha was free. He picked up the Magadha crown that had tumbled down, put it on his head, went back to his seat fretting and fuming and sat down quietly. The moment Karna picked up the Shiva bow, the pandal reverberated with victorious cries in his name, "Hail Karna, the king of Anga! Victory, victory!" I kept staring at him. He looked exquisitely handsome, just like our Pradyumna. Maybe I was hallucinating. Even in that pose, he was staring only at Dada's feet.

He easily mounted the arrow in his hand on the bow. He gracefully turned his neck like a pigeon and began searching for the fish eye in the pond. The entire swayamwar pandal held its breath and waited for him to pierce his target. Just then, Draupadi, who had her head turned down till then and was holding the white lotus swayamwar garland in her hands, raised her head for the first time. The scathing, determined words of a Kshatriya lady tartly resonated like lightning, leaving the pandal atremble, "Wait! You cannot participate in this swayamwar! I will not be the wife or the daughter-in-law of a charioteer. Never!"

'The Shiva bow held high in Karna's muscular hands trembled momentarily. His Virasana pose broke in an instant. At once, the arrow mounted on the bowstring was shot. Taking many twists and turns, it pierced Dada's big toe. Dada still smiled and pulled it out. Karna laughed out loudly, raising his neck towards the sky. The kings in the pandal got terrified by his laugh. The next moment, he violently threw the bow down and went back to his seat next to Duryodhana.

'The fish in the device kept revolving, provocatively teasing all macho Kshatriyas. The atmosphere in the pandal was extremely tense now. Dhrishtadyumna, the yajnason, got up again. Glancing at all the assembled kings, he roared, "Am I to take it that not a single eminent king of Aaryavarta possesses the strength to win my yajna-born sister? Is it that all archers here are devoid of valour? Is the elegant, virtuous Draupadi, dear daughter of the Panchalas, not going to have a suitable match in her life? Why have all these kings gathered here? Is it for the Kumbha mela or for the chariot race? Are they here to surrender in front of a mere fish device? Shame on the Kshatriyas of Aaryavarta who boast of their sky-high gallantry. Shame on those who claim to be the descendants of the Suryavansha and Chandravansha." Indeed, these were no simple words by Dhrishtadyumna, but fiery sparks from a blazing yajna pit. Some of the kings actually covered their ears with their hands and some felt so insulted that they were about to draw their weapons.

'Now, my dear Dada, sitting on my left, stood erect. The moment he stood up, Yadavas, several assembled kings and other invitees shouted ecstatically, "Hail Yadava leader Sharangadhara, Lord of Dwaraka, Srikrishna Maharaja, victory!"

'It was as if the roof of the pandal was going to blow off with ecstatic victorious cheers. Meanwhile, making his way through the assembled kings, a tall, extremely radiant Brahmin youth came forward, walking with his head held high, and chest puffed up, and stood near the pond. No one in the pandal knew his name, or who he was and from where he had come. But he came with such agility and confidence that the din in the pandal stopped instantly. I observed the youth dressed up as a Brahmin with a keen eye. For a moment, I thought Dada himself was standing near the pond in a Brahmin dress. How was that possible? Now I, too, began looking at him intently. He moved forward in the same slow gait and with full confidence. He went close to the archer's seat located at the centre of the pond. He had emphatically grabbed the attention of everyone in the pandal.

'He took an elegant, spectacular Virasana pose, and a big round of applause resonated through the pandal. I, too, stood up at once, clapping. Then I heard Dada's familiar whispering words, "Udho, brother, this is the same Virasana. The one that I saw at Kurukshetra near the Suryakunda on the day of the solar eclipse. Udho, he is no one else but the son of

Pandu and Kunti, Arjuna himself!" I kept staring at Dada, wonderstruck. Now he had forgotten himself and was joyfully clapping away, lightly and rhythmically. I had never ever seen him like that before.

'Meanwhile, the saffron-clad Brahmin youth had picked up the Shiva bow, mounted an arrow on the bowstring and checked the reflection rotating in the pond. In a flash, he pierced the fish eye in the very first shot. The fish device stopped. Right from that moment, the wheel of improbable, innumerable events began rotating. Panchala daughter Draupadi moved forward and, with a demure smile, put the white lotus garland around the neck of the Brahmin youth. Exactly at that moment, Dada patted my shoulders and whispered vaguely, "She is the third one! The first one was of Gokul, the second one of Dwaraka, this is the third one from Kampilyanagar!" I was confused to hear that. I could not resist asking him, "Third who?"

'He gave me a very affectionate smile and said, "The third sister. In Gokul, there is Ekananga, in Dwaraka there is Subhadra, and Yajnasena from Kampilyanagar is the third one."

'Only he could act and speak like this. My brother, who was about to participate in the swayamwar a moment ago, easily took the fragrant, elegant Kshatriya lady for his sister.

'The moment Draupadi put the garland around the neck of the Brahmin youth, the Kshatriyas in the pandal got agitated. Jarasandha roared, "Is this ordinary Brahmin going to take away a Kshatriya lady, the Panchala daughter, in our presence?"

'Many kings supported him and brandished their bows, maces and swords. Within a moment, the pandal of the swayamwar had transformed into a battleground. Another hefty youth came closer to the pond to protect the Brahmin youth. Immediately, Dada said to me, "Uddhava, this is indeed mighty Bhima, the son of Vayu!" Dada unmistakably recognised the three young men who followed him. They were Yudhishthira, Nakula and Sahadeva. They were the sons of Pandu – the Pandavas.

'The Panchala king Drupada raised both hands and tried to control the unruly invitees in vain. With one arm, Dhrishtadyumna was trying to restrain the invited Kshatriyas. With the other hand, he held his sister Draupadi's arm tightly to keep her from getting caught in the ruckus.

'I was surprised to see that Dada was extremely calm. He brought his face close to my ear so that I could hear clearly amidst the furore in the pandal and commanded, "Uddhava, the Pandavas are going to win this swayamwar battle for sure. Once it ends, Draupadi will follow her husband out of the pandal. Follow both of them, and find out exactly where the Pandavas and Aunt Kuntidevi are staying."

'It happened exactly as he said. In the ongoing battle, Karna's young son Sudamana got wounded and collapsed from a moon-faced throat-piercing arrow of Arjuna's. Karna immediately threw away his bow and rushed to Sudamana. Sudamana had been killed by Arjuna's arrow. All the kings encircled Karna, who was sitting dispirited next to his dead son.

'Arjuna offered his respects to King Drupada and Maharani Sautramani and started leaving the pandal with his four brothers. When Draupadi's parents and brother gestured her to follow them, Draupadi started walking behind Arjuna with her face turned down. She had formally become his wife, as he had fulfilled the condition of the swayamwar. I intently observed young Arjuna, who was full of the radiance of a Kshatriya. He and Dada are so similar. Their complexion, figure and height are exactly the same. I am quite sure that even you would get confused between them if you saw them from behind. While observing keenly, I felt that Dada may be a tiny bit taller than him. He must be!

'As per Dada's command, I, too, left the pandal and followed the Pandava brothers. They were staying at a potter's place on the border of Kampilyanagar. No one had recognised them so far, as they had disguised themselves as Brahmins, immediately after leaving Varanavata, and had taken precautions not be seen together ever.' Uddhava had been narrating the events in such an expressive way that it made me feel as if I was present in the pandal itself. Now, an irresistible curiosity about how Draupadi, who was the cause of all this, looked. With girlish curiosity, I asked sweet-spoken Uddhava, 'Then how did both of them actually meet? Please tell me something.' As if pacifying me with both his hands, he said, 'Have patience! Aunt Kuntidevi was completely taken aback when she saw Dada standing in front of her. She did not even let him pay obeisance properly and at once holding him in a deep embrace, she said, "So, now you remembered us…hmm? I heard that you went to

Hastinapura and performed our final rites too. What blessing should I give you for such a heroic feat?" Thus, she rebuked Dada as soon as she saw him. Dada, who otherwise would never oblige anybody, pinched both his ears and said, "My mistake, dear aunt! Forgive me for that. But the Dharmashastra that I have heard says that if final rites are performed for persons who are actually alive, they live longer and successful lives! Besides, it was a diplomatic strategy too. Performing your final rites was going to keep you safe." Dada had asked for forgiveness in his own style indeed. Aunt Kuntidevi, who was initially jubilant to see Dada, showed a bit of anxiety and said, 'Srikrishna, I have committed the biggest blunder just now.' Arjuna returned with his wife and said, 'Mother, I have brought stupendous alms today!'

"Hearing the zest and excitement in his voice, I surmised that he had brought food as usual, but in larger quantity.

'While I was still inside, I said, "If it is stupendous, then share it among all of you."

'My obedient Arjuna and his brothers have taken my wish as my final decision. They have decided to share this Panchala daughter Draupadi, among themselves as their wife. I have a nagging feeling that I have made a mistake. I am feeling restless.

"Have I done injustice to her, whether knowingly or unknowingly, despite being a woman? You travel throughout Aaryavarta. You easily solve challenging problems for others. Tell me whether I am right or wrong. Put yourself in place of Arjuna and tell me the truth after due consideration."

'She expected Dada to stumble and hesitate. But he instantly said, "Arjuna has taken the right decision. Besides him, all four sons of yours have developed a desire for her. When you said 'share the alms amongst all five of you', that was not said unknowingly at all. You are so attached to the joys and sorrows of these five that unwittingly your mother's heart spoke the truth prudently.

"Now, you yourself think carefully about it and answer my question, oh mother of the Pandavas. Tell me the truth – if you put yourself in place of your elder son Yudhishthira, would you not have desired this Panchali?"

'Now it was the experienced, mature aunt's turn to get baffled. She said, "Definitely, I would have desired her. Arjuna and these four have indeed taken the right decision."

"Now, that's like my aunt! That is exactly what I wanted to say. Only if these five brothers are united like a powerful fist and stay together both physically and in thought, can they raise their voice and get others to listen to them. They will establish their legitimate rights even if they need to snatch them out of the jaws of death.

"This ravishingly beautiful Draupadi could have first become the cause of a rift and then a ravine of disparity among these five. That is what you have prevented from happening. Only you could think of such an instruction of sharing the alms. But I am thinking about this Panchala daughter Draupadi."

He asked, "Draupadi, do you agree, from the bottom of your heart, to accept these five as your husbands? If yes, how exactly did you arrive at that decision?"

'Now all five Pandavas, along with Kuntimata, listened expectantly, wondering what could the answer be. I noted that even Balaramadada's face displayed curiosity.

'Draupadi's answer suited her character. She said, "Hrishikesha, I accept these five brothers as my husbands from the bottom of my heart. Madhava, you know well that they appear to be five but exist as one from within. Even I believe the same. They may be five to the world, but for me they are one.

"Achyuta, I have heard a lot about you. I feel it is my great luck to see you in person today. Now I would like to ask you what you think of me."

'Now all of us stared at Dada in curiosity, wondering how he was going to answer that question. Without wasting a moment, he said, "Friend, my beloved friend! The world will call you my sister. I already have Subhadra as my sister. But you are my friend!"

'Draupadi also nodded in affirmation. She moved her eyes from the peacock feather to Dada's feet and, in a clear voice, said, "Then give this friend of yours a suitable blessing." She instantly touched Dada's feet. Till today, he had been quickly answering many difficult and puzzling questions. He raised his right hand to bless her. "You will reach the zenith of conjugal purity and chastity, despite being the wife of five husbands! Your name will be worth remembering in morning prayers for ages to come. Just like the boundless sky becomes clear after the rain showers of Mriga, your purity will be maintained in the service of your five husbands. It is only you who will grace the lives of these five sons of Pandu, just as the Shivapindi looks sublime adorned with Bela leaves, and my crown looks elegant with the peacock feather. Your mother-in-law will be like your mother and, at an appropriate time, you will experience that. All seven of you will be remembered forever.'"

After a few days, Sri had to go to the Panchanada region. King Brihatsena of the Madra kingdom in Panchanada had organised his daughter's swayamwar, possibly taking inspiration from the Panchal king Drupada. Her name was Lakshmanaa. The condition to be fulfilled for the swayamwar was the same as Draupadi's swayamwar – piercing the eye of the rotating fish in the roof while looking at its reflection in the water below. The invitation for this swayamwar also arrived in Dwaraka. One of Vasudevababa's sisters, Shrutakirtidevi, had been married to the Kekeya king – Maharaja Dhrishtaketu – in this region. The Panchanada region, inclusive of Vahika, Kekeya and Madra, was well known for its invincible, pugnacious warriors. Due to the recent Draupadi swayamwar, there was hostility between the Kurus and the Panchalas. To discuss the invitation, the Sudharma council of the Yadavas was held. In this council, Balaramadada, minister Vipruthu and commander Anadhrishti were of the opinion that if there was going to be any probability of enmity arising during the swayamwar, it would not be wise for a new kingdom like Dwaraka to offend the pugnacious region of Panchanada. Our foremost enemy was the insolent, self-proclaimed emperor Jarasandha of Magadha, who had uprooted the Yadavas from Mathura completely. Therefore, it would be wise not to attend this swayamwar.

Some Yadava warriors were of exactly the opposite opinion.

As the council was divided into two groups with regard to the invitation of Lakshmanaa's swayamwar, Acharya Sandipani and the royal priest Gargamuni implored Vasudevababa to take the final decision as the king. Maharaja Vasudeva, who had suffered many hardships in life, was experienced and mature, and resolutely presented his royal decision,

'I think that as your leader, the Lord of Dwaraka should respect the invitation of Madra king Brihatsena. As my son, Srikrishna should visit my sister Shrutakirti, who lives in the Girjaka city in this region. I would get the satisfaction of meeting my sister, if not in person, but through my son's eyes. I will also get to know about her welfare from him.'

Sri stood up. This time he spoke just a few words, 'My dear Yadava warriors! I absolutely respect the maharaja's command. Hence, I will go to Shakalnagar for sure. Along with Balaramadada, you all should accompany me without any doubt in mind. I am going there for a prospective mission while keeping the pugnacious warriors of Panchanada in mind. On coming back, I will also deliver news of the well-being of the Maharaja's sister – Shrutakirtidevi.'

The Yadavas left for Panchanada fully prepared. The disciplined fourfold army accompanied Sri, Uddhava and many senior Yadavas. Sri had especially taken minister Vipruthu along with him on this journey. He had appointed young Pradyumna in his place and had instructed him to faithfully follow the advice of the acharya and the royal priest, along with Vasudevababa, me and all the elders.

Till this day, Sri had travelled from Karvir and Gomanta in the south to Pragjyotishapura of Kamarupa in the east to the Himalayas. He had also visited Kampilyanagar. Hearing his acclaim as the Lord of Dwaraka, many kings along the way had offered him plenty of gifts wherever he reached, and had welcomed him joyfully. Everyone longed for Sri's unconditional love.

But in the Matsya kingdom, the exact opposite happened. Sri summoned Uddhava and the minister to his tent and instructed, 'Uddhava, you go with the minister to Viratanagar with two gift platters. Offer one to the Matsya king Virata and send the second with the minister as a gift to his commander Kichaka. Talk to Virata and tell him, "I am Uddhava, brother of Srikrishna, the Lord of Dwaraka. Consider that it is not me but Lord Srikrishna himself who has come here, and accept the gift." Always keep relations of the Matsyas strong with the Yadavas of Dwaraka.'

He instructed the minister, 'You should offer the second platter as a gift to commander Kichaka, and talk to him yourself. In your communication with him, mention the numbers of elephants, horses, camels and infantry and do not forget to tell him that the gift is from the entire Yadava army!'

Both of them returned, completing their tasks successfully. The Yadava army reached the banks of River Saraswati after crossing the Yamuna twice. This river was as divine as the divine land of Kurukshetra through which it flowed. The three brothers bathed in the holy bed of her crystal-clear waters, and gave away charities. The mammoth Yadava army now descended on the Mattamayura kingdom. They rested there for two–three days after a long stretch of travel. In the end, crossing river Vipasha, along with Sri, the triumphant, invincible Yadava army reached the Vahika kingdom. This was the beginning of the Panchanada region. This is where Sri began executing his agile, diplomatic military strategy. He dispatched various competent emissaries with missives of cordial relations and platters full of valuable gifts to the royal capitals of Ambashtha, Trigarta, Audumbara, Kulinda, Madra and Kekeya. The most proficient emissary went to Brihatsena's Shakalanagar. Minister Vipruthu himself went to Kekeya king Dhrishtaketu. He presented gifts to Sri's aunt Shrutakirtidevi and her husband Dhrishtaketu in the name of Vasudevababa and Devakimata. He did not forget to deliver the message, 'The Lord of Dwaraka will come to visit in person.'

The main emissary who returned from Shakalanagar provided Sri with detailed information, 'Preparations are going on in full swing for Madra daughter Lakshmanaa's swayamwar. Magadha king Jarasandha is coming to participate in this swayamwar, along with the king of Ambashtha. Master archer Arjuna is also coming with his four brothers. They have left from Viratanagar and are travelling to Hastinapura.'

Hearing that news, Sri smiled mischievously as usual, and naughtily said to Uddhava, 'He will not be participating in the swayamwar. He will not get that chance. I will be the very first one to participate. If at all the Madra bow falls on my chest, he will come forward to pick it up and free me.'

Uddhava was such a mind reader that from that sojourn itself, he dispatched a carrier with a message for me, 'Madra daughter Lakshmanaadevi is coming home as one more sister of yours. Be prepared to welcome her!'

The swayamwar took place in Shakalanagar, located on the banks of River Chandrabhaga. Most of the kings who were present for Draupadi's swayamwar were also present for this one. New kings from Panchanada region like Ambashtha, Trigarta and Audumbara were also present. No one had arrived from the Kurus of Hastinapura. The reason for their absence was unknown. As a matter of fact, the Kurus of Hastinapura, especially Duryodhana and his brothers, would never decline such a challenging invitation. Dhritarashtra, the blind king, looked after the kingdom of Hastinapura. The eldest Kaurava, Duryodhana, had become insolent, arrogant and deceitfully ambitious. He hungered for the kingdom and power, and hence did not respect anybody. He was turning a deaf ear to the affectionate and valuable advice of his own mother, Rajmata Gandharidevi, who had chosen to blindfold herself for the sake of her husband. He was also disregarding the valiant, sacrificing, noble and virtuous Grandsire Bhishma, who was the last Kuru. He was not paying attention to the austere, pious and duteous Mahatma Vidura. He did not even take notice of Gurudeva Dronacharya – the master of archery – and the senior family priest, Kripacharya. Like an insolent bull, he was discarding cautious warnings and advice given by all repeatedly. His mama Shakuni's word was final for him in every aspect of life, including politics, warfare, justice and family disputes.

Shakuni held this live ember of the Kuru dynasty named Duryodhana in his fist so skilfully that it was out of sight for others. King Brihatsena welcomed all the kings invited for the swayamwar and on the auspicious day, ordered the craftsmen to turn on the fish device. Madra daughter Lakshmanaa modestly stood next to her mother and father, holding the swayamwar garland in her hands. In this swayamwar, Sri did not give anyone an opportunity to raise any objections at all.

Sri was the first to walk towards the pond of water. He picked up the Madra bow easily. He took the Virasana pose near the edge of the pond, his neck as graceful as that of a pigeon. He mounted the Suchi arrow on the bowstring and pulled. This was the very first arrow. The eyes of hundreds and thousands of people of Panchanada kept moving up and down between the tip of the arrow and the eye of the fish rotating rapidly on the roof. All invitees held their breath, eagerly waiting to watch the unerring shot that would pierce the eye of the fish. For some reason, Sri lowered the bow, causing a furore in the audience. He gently put the Madra bow down. He took off the golden crown on his head, and momentarily put it in his lap. He gently removed his beloved peacock feather out of the groove in his crown. He eyed it with a smile once, and placed it gently on the edge of the pond. He placed his crown back on his head again, and picked up the Madra bow just as easily as before. He took the elegant Virasana pose again.

After that, nobody knew when he twanged the bowstring and mounted the Suchi arrow on it, when he filled his chest with a deep breath, when he shot the Suchi arrow, and how and when it pierced the eye of the fish.

A big round of applause followed when the rotating device stopped. After that, a round of victorious acclaim echoed, 'Victory to the invincible master archer of Aaryavarta, Sharangadhar, Lord of Dwaraka, and groom of Madra daughter Lakshmanaa, Maharaja Srikrishna…! Victory to him…victory!' Tossing their shawls in the air, and raising their hands high, many citizens of Madra hurried towards the pond to offer their congratulations.

Maharaja Brihatsena brought Lakshmanaa near the pond, where she put the white swayamwar garland around Sri's neck. Uddhava softly picked up the peacock feather from the edge of the pond, wiped it delicately and tucked it again in the groove of his brother's crown.

Sri bent down to pay obeisance to the elder Pandava Yudhishthira, but Yudhishthira did not allow him to do so. In the meantime, Arjuna, who was innately polite, had already touched Sri's feet. Even in that hubbub, Sri sincerely enquired about Aunt Kunti aatya and Draupadi. All of them were leaving for Hastinapura.

Sri instructed them to meet him in his pavilion at the border of Shakalanagar.

Uddhava was done with the account of Lakshmanaa's swayamwar with all its details. But I still had one question. 'Uddhava, why did Sri put down the bow and remove the peacock feather from his crown?'

'The peacock feather was keeping Dada from piercing the eye of the fish. The reflection of the peacock feather was wobbling continuously over the reflection of the device and obstructing his view,' Uddhava explained.

Hearing those words, I let out a sigh, and unknowingly said, 'A mere peacock feather obstructed Sri. Did it not?'

Immediately correcting me, Uddhava said, 'Yes, a peacock feather indeed, but not any ordinary peacock feather. It was from Dada's crown!'

The Madra son-in-law stayed in Shakalanagar along with the army for one week. Maharaja Brihatsena showered generous hospitality, in Panchanada style, on everyone.

Sri left to keep his promise made to the senior Pandava Yudhishthira in the swayamwar pandal. He arrived at the Pandava base on the border of Shakalanagar to meet Aunt Kuntidevi. Aunt Kuntidevi herself came with her new daughter-in-law, Draupadi, to welcome Sri. The five Pandavas stood behind them. Sri enquired about his aunt's health and touched her feet. Draupadi, who had met Sri for the first time after Kampilyanagar, also bowed down to pay obeisance to him. At that time, Sri insisted, 'Draupadi, I call and consider you my sakhi, my dear friend. You need not follow these formalities every time we meet. You should always talk and behave freely with me, just like Subhadra.'

Then, at the base, on the shores of Madra's Chandrabhaga, Sri had a special council with the Pandavas, their mother and his sakhi. The main topic of discussion was the justified right of the Pandavas over the Kuru kingdom of Hastinapura.

Maharaja Pandu had inherited the kingdom of Hastinapura. Due to a curse inflicted by a sage named Kindam, Maharaja Pandu had to renounce the kingdom and live in a forest. Since his elder brother Dhritarashtra was blind since birth, the royal ministry of the Kurus had disqualified him from inheriting the royal throne before.

Maharaja Pandu went to the forest. The royal ministry was left with no choice but to request blind Dhritarashtra to take charge of the Hastinapura kingdom as guardian. Grandsire Bhishma, who was selfless, veracious and celibate for life, was actually the last scion of the Kuru dynasty. He had to hand over the royal authority to blind Dhritarashtra, according to Mahamantri Vidura's advice.

Duryodhana, the eldest of the hundred sons, Dushasana, who was like his shadow, Durmarsha and his many brothers, his wicked, conniving mama Shakuni, and his eleven brothers who always supported him and obeyed his every word – all had joined hands. Destiny had brought together minister Kanaka and valiant Karna, who had become Duryodhana's friend after he was made the king of Anga on the occasion of the Vasant Paurnima contest. On the strength of all this, blind Dhritarashtra had grown a hundred eyes dreaming of making the impossible possible. Valiant Bhishma and Mahatma Vidura were gradually being sidelined in Hastinapura.

It was not easy to help the virtuous, valiant and noble Pandavas, who were suffering due to circumstances, to acquire their fair right over the kingdom. Keeping that in mind, Sri cautiously began taking measures. He commenced the current meeting, saying, 'Kekeya king, Maharaja Dhrishtaketu, is my aunt's husband. He has earnestly invited me to his royal capital, Girjaka, along with the army. Therefore, I will be going there.

'Yudhishthira, you brothers are also his nephews. But the Kekeyas have no idea that you have come here. The news about the swayamwar in Kampilyanagar must have, of course, reached them. You will have to gather support from all big and small powers to protect your rights in Hastinapura. I propose that you come with me to Kekeya's royal capital, Girjaka, to visit aunt and the Kekeya king and obtain their blessings, even though you are not officially invited.'

Throughout the night, a lot of deliberation took place. The Pandavas had never disobeyed their mother Kuntidevi's word. She concluded the council with a single sentence, 'My sons and their wife will obey Srikrishna. We will leave for Girjaka along with the Yadavas tomorrow.'

While taking leave of the Madras, Sri gave a confusing instruction to Uddhava. 'Uddhava, send your special messenger to Dwaraka. Give a message to your dear sister-in-law that two more guests are coming! Get ready to welcome them.'

Two special people arrived in Dwaraka eventually. Kekeya daughter Bhadra arrived in Dwaraka as Sri's wife following Lakshmanaa.

Aunt Shrutakirtidevi was overjoyed when Sri arrived in Girjaka along with the Pandavas. She was expecting to see only the nephews from the

Yadava side of the family. But the Pandavas, her nephews from the Kuru side of the family, had come too. She welcomed her sister Kuntidevi along with everybody else. She talked to Sri, and convinced him in her own Yadava style, 'Srikrishna, your Dwaraka kingdom is new. Our Panchanada kingdom has more manpower. We have formed strong familial relations with every neighbouring kingdom here. If Dwaraka also forms such a bond with us, the entire Panchanada region will automatically support Dwaraka.'

She continued, 'Srikrishna, why don't you become the son-in-law of the Kekeyas? Then, automatically, you will be the son-in-law of the entire Panchanada. I want to get our daughter Bhadra married to you.' Sri lovingly held both her hands and said, 'Your wish is my command. Now I understand why you urgently sent a special messenger to Vasudevababa in Dwaraka when you came to know that we were going to visit Panchanada. And why he asked me to visit you in any case.'

They raised a grand pandal on the banks of River Iravati, which flowed around their royal capital, and got their daughter Bhadra married to Sri with grandeur.

Bhadra was Sri's seventh wife.

Lakshmanaa and Bhadra, both daughters of the Panchanada region, arrived together in Dwaraka. The populace of Dwaraka offered them a ceremonious welcome. Now the chapter of the Pandavas in Sri's life had begun in the true sense. He had sent Lakshmanaa and Bhadra directly to Dwaraka from Viratanagar of the Matsyas. Sri himself had proceeded towards Hastinapura along with Balaramadada, Uddhava, Vipruthu and Satyaki, taking Aunt Kunti, the Pandavas and Draupadi and a select Yadava army with him. They crossed the Yamuna near the thick Khandavavana and reached Hastinapura in the east, located near the banks of River Ganga.

From the borders of the Kuru kingdom, precious gift salvers were dispatched to Maharaja Dhritarashtra through minister Vipruthu and Uddhava. Uddhava was given cautious instructions to meet with Mahamantri Vidura, Grandsire Bhishma and minister Vrishavarma in private. He was told that he should astutely observe their exact reactions and that of the citizens of Hastinapura about the fact that the Pandavas were alive and actually coming to Hastinapura. He should check if the citizens of Hastinapura had forgotten Maharaja Pandu or if they still remembered him. He was to collect exact information about the people's opinion of the Pandavas' mother, Kuntidevi. He should also meet Maharaja Dhritarashtra, the eldest Kaurava Duryodhana, Shakuni Mama, all the brothers of both of them, Kanaka, Guru Drona, Drona's son Ashwatthama, Acharya Kripa, chief charioteer Sanjay, and Karna, the king of Anga.

The minister and Uddhava returned after successfully accomplishing their political mission as per Sri's wish. During this important visit, after a long time, the Pandava women – Kuntidevi and Draupadi – were going to stay in the chamber of Maharani Gandharidevi. By nature, Gandharidevi was truthful and tenacious. She still loved Kuntidevi and the Pandavas as dearly as before. She was eager to meet all of them. It was the ill luck of the Kuru dynasty that Duryodhana was born to her and all his brothers considered him their ideal.

The news of the Pandavas' arrival produced conflicting opinions among the royal family of the Kurus. Maharaja Dhritarashtra's psyche had become most complicated. The blind maharaja of the Kurus was clearly divided into two Dhritarashtras. The first was the pretentiously dutiful Maharaja Dhritarashtra and the second was the selfish father who always kept hatching political machinations for the love of his own son.

He strongly felt that he had been deprived of the royal throne despite being the eldest son only because of his blindness, and that was indeed an injustice. Now that Maharaja Pandu had passed away, and he had become old, it was his firm belief and opinion that due to his seniority, his eldest son Duryodhana should be the rightful heir. Time and again, whenever he got the opportunity, he tried to convince Mahamantri Vidura and Grandsire Bhishma. But those dauntless royal men were not giving in to him at all.

They were of the opinion that Yudhishthira was the first-born among both Kauravas and Pandavas. His father, Maharaja Pandu, had temporarily appointed Dhritarashtra to look after the kingdom. Now, as per his royal duty, Dhritarashtra should honourably return the kingdom to Yudhishthira – the eldest son of Pandu – who was now an adult. Yudhishthira must be crowned the prince. Yudhishthira should be offered the throne of Hastinapura after Dhritarashtra. That was just and according to Dharma.

The news of the Lord of Dwaraka, the leader of the Yadavas, Maharaja Srikrishna bringing the Pandavas with him spread throughout the city. Hastinapura came alive with a vibrant energy. Thousands of Kuru men and women heartily welcomed the Pandavas along with Sri, with showers of vermilion and flowers.

Sri had been to Hastinapura once before. But that was a sad occasion, for the last rites of the Pandavas. A mammoth crowd of Kuru men and women assembled at the western gate, along with Grandsire Bhishma, Mahatma Vidura, Chief Minister Vrishavarma and minister Sanjaya, to welcome the Yadava–Pandava warriors. But Maharaja Dhritarashtra, his sons, Shakuni Mama and Kanaka were not present in the welcoming congregation. Vidura had come as he loved the Pandavas and Sri. Actually, only one representative of the entire Hastinapura kingdom was present there – that was Chief Minister Vrishavarma, who had come to deliver the order of the king!

Sri stepped on to the land of Hastinapura from the Garudadhwaja chariot. The one who received him was the incredibly valiant, tall and well-built Grandsire Bhishma, with his thick, white beard pulsing on his broad chest. As Sri saw him, he started to bend down to touch his feet with respect, when moist-eyed Bhishma spread his muscular arms wide and held him in a deep embrace, saying, 'Vasudeva, I am meeting you after so many days. May your feet bring joy and peace to Hastinapura, this royal capital of the Kurus! Achyuta, it is now only up to you to guide all of them on the right path. I am tired.'

Uddhava was the first to realise that the son of Ganga, disciple of Parashurama, the one and only Kuru by blood, Grandsire, had addressed Sri as 'Vasudeva'. Amidst acclamations and flowers showered by the citizens of Hastinapura, Sri started walking towards the royal palace of the Kurus along with Bhishma, Vidura, Sanjaya and the Pandavas.

The royal party of the Yadavas and the Pandavas stayed at Mahamantri Vidura's residence. Sri enquired about Maharaja Dhritarashtra's welfare and sent a message to him through minister Vipruthu, 'The sons of Pandu have arrived, along with their mother, to claim their fair share of the kingdom. I request you to organise a royal council of the Kurus to listen to their appeal. Make your judgement impartial so as to avoid any long-term enmity among the family of Kurus.'

The maharaja sent a reply through his minister Vrishavarma. It, too, was loaded with political sagacity. It addressed Sri as 'Vasudeva' just, like the Grandsire had called him, and enquired about the welfare of Vasudevababa, Devakimata and the royal family of the Yadavas. It also offered the explanation that he could not come to the western gate of Hastinapura to welcome them only due to his blindness and also gave a clever justification that minister Vrishavarma was sent in his place. There was no mention of Duryodhana and Shakuni at all. It contained a hypocritical promise that the Pandavas, who were regarded as his own sons, would be judged impartially in the royal council of the Kurus. Sri heard the message with a smile.

That night, the ancient skies of Hastinapura heard two different discussions in two parties, with a detached and stoic mind. One party was that of the maharaja of Hastinapura, Dhritarashtra himself. The political deliberation in his council chamber lasted till midnight. The attendees were Shakuni and his brothers, Kanaka, Duryodhana, Dushasana and a few other brothers, and the minister Vrishavarma. Grandsire Bhishma, who shouldered a major responsibility in the Kuru kingdom, was not involved in this council. Even Mahamantri Vidura was not part of it. Though he was Duryodhana's best friend, even Karna, the king of Anga, was not part of the discussion.

Finally, at midnight, the political deliberation reached a conclusion – that of coercing the Pandavas to accept the desolate region of Khandavaprastha and Khandavavana, which had thick forests full of wild beasts. It was decided to take thorough precautions to avoid their association with the royal capital of Hastinapura in any way.

Kanaka, who was an equal match to Shakuni in matters of the state, seconded the idea. He said, 'Khandavavana is so thick that it will be one big war-like task to make the sunrays reach its land. The Pandavas will fall prey to wild beasts while fighting that war. Even if they are spared from that, the wild tribes of Khandavavana, like the Nagas, the Asuras, the Danavas, the Nishadhas, the Vyadhas and the Barbaras, will kill them for sure. In the council arranged under Sri's leadership at Vidura's residence, the same topic of the Pandava's fair share in the Hastinapura kingdom was up for discussion. The major attendees were Mahamantri Vidura, Balaramadada, Uddhava, Satyaki and minister Vipruthu. The highlight was that the Pandavas' mother, Kuntidevi, was also present along with her five sons. In the discussions, minister Vipruthu and Vidura were insistent on dividing the kingdom along the shores of River Ganga, which coursed through Hastinapura. As the Panchala kingdom, related to the Pandavas, was located on the eastern side, Yadava commander Satyaki suggested a division with the eastern side coming to the Pandavas and the western to the Kauravas. As Sri was present in the council, all the five Pandavas listened silently.

Finally, at midnight, Sri gently tapped Arjuna on the shoulder, and said while leaving, 'Our discussions are not relevant to what is going to happen in the royal council tomorrow. Grandsire Bhishma, who is the last senior Kuru, will be making the final decision. I am going to accept his offer. May I? What do you brothers think?'

'As you say, Vasudeva.'

The next day, the royal council of the Kurus was held in Hastinapura. The news that Sri would be present in the royal assembly with the Pandavas had spread like wildfire. Therefore, the citizens of Hastinapura had gathered in groups. They were all eager to see the virtuous Pandavas and their courageous mother, along with Sri, in person. After many years, the royal assembly of the Kurus was fully occupied.

Silence prevailed as Chief Minister Vrishavarma pounded the royal sceptre. First of all, on behalf of Maharaja Dhritarashtra and Maharani Gandharidevi, Mahamantri Vidura welcomed Sri, the Pandavas, their mother, and the assembled citizens. He announced the purpose of the council in a few words. In that speech, he earnestly reminded everyone of the valour of his dear brother Pandu in a picturesque manner. He made everyone aware of the complicated problem the kingdom of Hastinapura was facing. In the end, he said, 'The one and only senior heir of the Kuru kingdom, Grandsire Bhishma, should present the final and just decision around this problem in front of the assembly. Everyone should honour it.' Vidura fulfilled the duty of an experienced Mahamantri.

Bhishma said in a firm voice, 'Venerable Yadava Vasudeva's son Vasudeva, Lord of Dwaraka, Srikrishna is present in this ancient royal assembly of the Kurus for the first time, along with his elder brother Balarama and younger brother Uddhava. I feel that this is the moment of greatest honour for us Kurus of the Chandravansha. I welcome him with joy.

'The last time he visited Hastinapura, he did not come to the royal assembly. He asked for my blessings at that time, which, had not given then, deliberately. Yesterday, too, I did not give him my blessings. It is true that I am senior to him in age. But just seniority of age does not indicate quality of life. Accordingly, I am not senior to him in any other capacity except age.

'Even though he lives far away in Dwaraka, he knows very well in his heart how highly I regard him. That is why with that respect in mind, at this critical juncture of life, I am going to speak from the bottom of my heart about this kingdom of Hastinapura that I have nurtured devoutly with my life. I request everybody to listen to it quietly.

'First of all, I am elated that the Pandavas, who have suffered a lot, are alive. I am going to perform rituals to ward off all ill effects that must have been caused due to the Tarpana rites performed for them. At this moment, my mind is brimming with innumerable joyous memories of their father, Maharaja Pandu. Valiant, victorious Maharaja Pandu, who spread Kuru's reputation throughout the world. Today, the Pandavas have returned with their mother to the royal capital of their late father. I welcome them from the bottom of my heart and offer them my blessings.

'All the Pandavas and Kauravas should come together. If that happens, then, under the guidance and support of venerable Yadava Srikrishna, the Kurus can teach a good lesson to the self-proclaimed emperor Jarasandha, who has put eighty Kshatriyas in his prison. I have no doubt at all that under Yudhishthira's composed leadership, with Srikrishna's eternally pragmatic advice and by getting associated with his kingdom Dwaraka, my 105 Kurus themselves will achieve the glory of being honourable emperors.

'The valiant sons of Maharaja Pandu, officially crowned king of this kingdom, have returned now. Yudhishthira, the eldest of the Pandavas, is the rightful heir. King Dhritarashtra, who was taking care of this kingdom of Hastinapura as a guardian after Pandu, should honourably restore it to Yudhishthira now.

'All the remaining Pandavas and all Kauravas should come together under his leadership and keep the pennant of Hastinapura's glory fluttering forever. This is my final and impartial verdict as the last senior Kuru. As a king, Yudhishthira should appoint the eldest Kaurava, Duryodhana, as the chief commander and both should establish new standards of valour in future.'

The entire royal assembly of the Kurus fell silent as they heard the clear-cut decision of the just and truthful Bhishma. Maharaja Dhritarashtra was dumbfounded to hear his final decision. Tightly clasping the lion faces carved on both sides of the royal throne, he went through unbearable anguish for a moment. He muttered as if he was talking to himself, 'You mean to say that I – I – should get down from this – this royal throne?' Noticing his agony and hearing his murmuring, Duryodhana got up from his seat at once. He shouted, 'Looks like the Grandsire has forgotten the service of the maharaja to the royal throne so far. There is no question of appointing the prince till he is alive. As it is, the undeclared princehood already belongs to the Kauravas – the eldest among them, meaning me. What the Pandavas can do at the most is ask for their share of the kingdom. If the maharaja is ready to offer it to them, then they should silently accept whatever he offers.'

Shakuni, the son of Subala, who always supported his nephew vigilantly, stood up suddenly. He spoke in his usual sly, sarcastic, deceitful tongue, 'The Grandsire is indirectly suggesting that the maharaja go to the forest for Vanaprasthashrama. The truth is that his beloved Pandavas were born in the forest. They are fond of forests. Therefore, my advice to the Kuru royalty is that if at all they wish to give the Pandavas a part of the Hastinapura kingdom, they should offer them the region of Khandavavana. As long as the guardian maharaja is alive, there is no question of appointing a new king or prince!'

'Shakuni, nobody has asked for your advice. King Dhritarashtra should announce whatever his decision is,' the Grandsire desperately tried to restrain Shakuni. Now the assembly hall was abuzz with whispers. It went on for quite a while. Duryodhana stood up and stopped the whispers with his booming voice, 'The Pandavas have nothing to do with the royal throne of the Kurus in any way! They may be the sons of Kunti and Madri, but in no way are they Pandavas – the sons of our kaka, Pandu! All the citizens know very well why our kaka Maharaja Pandu left Hastinapura. Grandsire need not support the Pandavas so openly. He should not ask for the entire or half of the kingdom for the Pandavas at all. The Pandavas should quietly accept whatever part this Kuru assembly offers them.'

Now Sri clearly realised what Duryodhana was getting at. He was referring to the Pandavas' birth by the Niyoga custom. Till today, he had solved the problems of the Shursena kingdom of Mathura, the kingdom of Karvir, Pragjyotishapura and many more, in a perfectly righteous manner. But this dispute of the Kuru kingdom was indeed tricky. It was apparent that Duryodhana was going to make a big issue of the Pandavas' birth and deprive them of the fair share of their venerable father Pandu's kingdom. At that point, Sri rose from his seat determinedly. Immediately, the Kuru council fell silent. All attendees were well aware of the power of Sri's speech, as they had heard about it. Shakuni and all Kauravas, including Duryodhana, panicked. They thought that with his eloquence and mesmerising speech, Sri would persuade Maharaja Dhritarashtra within moments. But the unexpected happened. Sri spoke calmly and deliberately, 'Dear Kurus! I agree with the impeccable thoughts of the Grandsire about the kingdom of Hastinapura, but whatever he has said may not happen. Listening to Duryodhana's speech, I have come to realise that the unity of the Kauravas and the Pandavas is an improbable prospect, like that of day and night coming together.

'Shakuni Mama has unerringly noticed the merits of the Pandavas. It is true that they are very fond of forests. Forests are dear to me too. I have complete faith in the dauntless capability of the Pandavas. On behalf of the Pandavas, I declare to Kuru maharaja Dhritarashtra, all the Kauravas, Shakuni Mama, all his brothers, and all the members present here, along with venerable Grandsire Bhishma, that the Pandavas are ready to accept the region of Khandavavana that Maharaja Dhritarashtra is so generously offering them as the share of their father!'

The Kuru council, including Grandsire Bhishma, was astonished at this firm decision of Sri that was so unexpected, even to the Pandavas. There was only one person in that fully occupied assembly who was not astonished, not startled at all. It was Kuntidevi, the mother of the Pandavas! The Pandavas had given complete power to Sri to take a decision on their behalf, as decided in the council the previous night. And yet, Bhima grumbled. There were whispers among the Pandavas trying to console him. To contain those whispers, the cunning minister of the Kurus, Vrishavarma, raised the royal sceptre in his hand and, firmly pounding it, said, 'Venerable Pandava Yudhishthira, do you accept the region of Khandavavana as your share of the kingdom? Any complaint later will not be tolerated.'

Following a nod from Sri as a signal, Yudhishthira rose quietly and said, 'I agree to accept the region of the kingdom offered by the maharaja of Kurus as our father's share of the kingdom. I hereby humbly accept the region of Khandavavana.' Very politely, he added, 'All we want are the invaluable blessings of all. Citizens of Hastinapura should feel assured that in memory of Maharaja Pandu, with the blessings of the Lord of Dwaraka Vasudeva Srikrishna, and Kuntimata, we will raise a new and prosperous kingdom in Khandavavana.'

Many had surmised that there would be a lot of feuding in the royal assembly of the Kurus. But Sri had accepted the region of Khandavavana on behalf of the Pandavas and concluded this most important council very skilfully, leaving everyone astonished. During this visit to Hastinapura, Sri stayed for a couple of days at the residence of his staunch devotees Mahatma Vidura and minister Sanjaya, and gladly accepted their hospitality. The Grandsire attended one of the meals at Vidura's residence on the outskirts of the city. Though Mahatma Vidura was Maharaja Dhritarashtra and Maharaja Pandu's brother, he was an illegitimate son born to a maid. He was a simple and unselfish person. Though he was a minister in the royal assembly of the Kurus, he lived in a simple house with his wife Parasavi and his family, on the desolate border of Hastinapura. He was well known everywhere for being a staunch devotee of Sri, even more than being famous as the minister of the Kurus and as a noble person in Hastinapura and the region around it. However, nobody knew where he and Sri had first met. Even I did not. But just as Sri had deeply embraced Uddhava, Daruka and Arjuna on their very first meetings, he had embraced Vidura too.

Similarly, Sanjaya, the special minister of Maharaja Dhritarashtra, was also a devotee of Sri. He was the chief of the special charioteer troop of Dhritarashtra. Sanjaya also possessed a rare skill – a vidya that allowed him to see distant things. He would go into a meditative trance while sitting. The exact picture of whichever events and places he would think of, even if being hundreds of yojanas away, would take form in front of his meditative eyes. He could pass on minute details of the scene that he visualised with his inner eye, in his melodious voice. After leaving Hastinapura, Sri went along with the Pandavas to survey Khandavavana region. A small town named Indraprastha was located here. Sri got a spacious, sturdy cottage built for the Pandavas on the outskirts of this town. While leaving Hastinapura, Sri also arranged for the Pandavas to get some plasterers, woodcutters, ironsmiths and architects with the assistance of Vidura and Sanjaya. He had also urgently dispatched special envoys and ordered famous architect Mayasura, his assistants Taraksha, Kamalaksha, Vidyunmali and the one and only master architect Twashtta to be present in Khandavavana immediately. They already had the experience of creating Dwaraka.

During this period, Sri used to go to River Yamuna, which flowed through the thick forests of Khandavavana, for his bath and morning prayers. On one such beautiful morning, he came to the stone steps on the banks of the gently flowing Yamuna, along with Uddhava and a few select Yadavas. It was the time of daybreak. Sri saw a woman in the Yamuna, standing in waist-high water, like a sculpture. She had tightly tied her thick, black hair on her head with a string of white jasmine flowers. She was wearing a white vesture with a white bodice. The reflection of her fair and graceful upper body that was above the water was gently undulating on the waters of the Yamuna. Sri stood transfixed as he saw her. He said to Uddhava, who was with him, 'Udho, brother, who is this jalakanya? Go, find out everything about her.'

Uddhava went up to the river and slowly descended the stone steps, but could not bring himself to disturb the jalakanya engrossed in meditation. Just then, a long-winged wild peacock came from somewhere and produced a high-pitched cry. Fluttering his long plumage with golden, blue, green eyes, he gently alighted on the banks of the Yamuna, and began drinking from its waters. The fluttering of his plumage broke the trance of the jalakanya. Ripples appeared on the Yamuna's water. The jalakanya prayed to the Sun god, smiled at the peacock and stepped out. She picked up an earthen pot full of water from the step near the shore, carried it on her waist and began walking. Uddhava moved forward at that moment and said, 'Forgive me, Devi. Who are you? Where are you from? Do you come here every day? Who do you meditate on and worship?'

The jalakanya from Khandavavana got startled for a moment or two. Then, looking at Uddhava's innocent face and polite expression, she smiled and said, 'I am Kalindi. I live here, in Khandavavana. I am awaiting Krishna of Dwaraka ever since I remember. I meditate in his name, and worship him. I have offered my entire life to him. Who are you?'

'I am Uddhava. The one whom you worship and in whose name you meditate is my elder brother, Srikrishna of Dwaraka, and he has come here in person. Look there!' He pointed to Sri standing on the topmost step. The eyes of the jalakanya and the jalapurusha met. Sri slowly climbed down the stone steps. Kalindi gradually climbed up the steps of life on the strength of her worship.

The king of birds, the peacock, flew far away with a joyous cry.

I had to go to the Shuddhaksha gate to welcome my seventh and last sister, after Sri's Hastinapura visit. While taking her into my embrace and patting her, I let out a sigh of relief. Sri wed Kalindi on the banks of the Yamuna itself through the Gandharva tradition of marriage. She was quite different from the seven of us. The last palace on the island of the queens' mansions raised by Gargamuni was occupied with her arrival now. Though she was a daughter of a Kshatriya, she looked, seemed and talked like a Brahmin daughter. She easily mingled with the seven of us.

Dwaraka had transformed into a populated Gokul now. I had noticed that since meeting the Pandavas, especially after bonding closely with Arjuna, Sri's mood had changed quite a bit. He always looked happy.

Each task that he performed was with brimming enthusiasm. He breezed through the palaces of the eight of us as easily as the fragrant air in a garden. I do not know if my seven sisters felt the same, but to me it felt as if he was always in my palace, even if he was elsewhere.

Nowadays, when Sri talked, not a single moment passed without mention of the Pandavas in some or the other context, and without their praise. Especially when he was speaking about Kuntidevi, he spoke with tireless and exceeding enthusiasm. He was well aware that she had suffered a lot in her life, and Vasudevababa regretted it deeply in his heart. That is why, in his sweet tongue, Sri would describe how Aunt Kunti's third son, Arjuna, possessed all possible good qualities. He would say, 'He looks, talks and behaves exactly like me. He is even more valiant than me. His name itself is Arjuna – the one who gathers all the knowledge that comes his way and stores it. When people see us together, they cannot figure out who is who.'

While speaking, Sri would sometimes unwittingly refer to him as Dhananjaya, sometimes Partha or Kaunteya, and at other times, Gudakesha. I would get lost in his words about Arjuna. Sometimes, to me, Sri himself would seem like Arjuna. I would pinch myself and come back to my senses. An intense urge would well up in my mind to meet Sri's dear Dhananjaya at least once.

Sakhi Draupadi occupied a bit more space in Sri's heart than Arjuna. Only I knew that with all the details. Radha from Gokul was also Sri's sakhi. But there was a subtle difference between the two of them. And I was the only one who was aware of that. Radha was lovely, fragrant like the bud of a Champaka flower. Draupadi was like the enticing bud of a Brahmakamala. Radha was like the silent streak of lightning that flashes in the sky from one end to the other after the rain of Mriga. Draupadi was like the roaring, thunderous lightning that resounds through the firmament during the downpour of rain in Mriga. Both were equally dear to Sri. Maybe that was the reason that I felt an uncontrollable urge to meet both of them.

Sri would talk about the other Pandavas in few but precise words. He would say, 'Yudhishthira is the perfect elder brother of the Pandavas. The other four Pandavas are like roaring, foaming oceans. Around them is the quiet shore of Yudhishthira's controlled and broad mind. All the other Pandavas respect Yudhishthira absolutely. Bhima is like a catastrophic, gigantic ocean of mammoth strength. He appears to be quiet and peaceful, but, in his mind, he keeps bubbling constantly. His hunger and sleep patterns perfectly suit his burly body. Though Nakula and Sahadeva are twins, there is no similarity in their disposition. Nakula looks extremely handsome, like our Pradyumna. Our Uddhava also looks like Nakula and Pradyumna, but he has a completely different nature. He is like the high peak of a snow-capped mountain that has pierced the sky and has attained peace. Sahadeva possesses unmatched skills of assessing horses. He is alert and cautious.

'The Pandavas are like the five fingers of a hand. Five fingers with different shapes and skills, that are always active. Draupadi is the rare woman who brings these five fingers together like the Aadishakti. Kuntimata is the supreme power that inspires their unity. Each word uttered by her, each dream...'

I just loved to keep listening to Sri when he talked about the Pandavas with such intensity. He had tested the Pandavas in every possible way he could think of. He would compare the Pandavas' family priest Dhaumya Rishi to Gargamuni of the Yadavas. He would give an upper hand to Dhaumya Rishi for his excellence. And then to avoid any misunderstanding, immediately place him lower than Acharya Sandipani.

A new chapter in Sri's life began as the chords of his emotions got entangled with those of the Pandavas. That chapter was the Pandavaparva. Now Sri had only one thing on his mind, and that was to raise the puissant, populated royal capital of the Pandavas, Indraprastha. He immensely loved such constructive, creative Karmayoga. Now, he focused his attention on the creation of Indraprastha, from Dwaraka itself.

One day, a horse rider arrived in Dwaraka with Yudhishthira's message from Khandavavana. The Pandavas were struggling to clear the thick forests but were not getting expected results. At this pace, it would take twelve years just to clear the forests of Khandavavana. The five brothers had reached a point of frustration and thought of Sri, not knowing what to do. Sri immediately left for Khandavavana, taking with him special troops of diligent Yadavas who had been trained during the

Dandakaranya expedition. This time he neither took Balaramadada nor Uddhava along. Instead, he was accompanied by young Pradyumna and his troops. Satyaki, too, was part of this expedition. This undertaking of the construction of Indraprastha lasted for a long time.

In the meantime, many seasons passed. On the banks of the Yamuna, Indraprastha, the royal capital of the Pandavas, was flourishing. Here in Dwaraka, Sri's Yadava family was blossoming. Sri's only daughter, Charumati, and sons Charudeva and Sudeshna were born to me. Charumati was beautiful, just like her name denoted, and since she was the only daughter, she was doted upon. She was Pradyumna's favourite sister. My delicate daughter Charu was not to be seen in my chamber very often. One or the other of my seven sisters would pick her up and take her to theirs. Sri would hold her in his arms and lovingly pull the tip of her nose, saying, 'You are just like our Eka in Gokul.'

During this time, Satyabhama also bore three sons – Subhanu, Swarbhanu and Prabhanu. These three sons of Bhama had a radiant complexion, just like their mother.

The palaces of the Panchanada daughters, Bhadra and Lakshmanaa, were also blessed with sons. Bhadra gave birth to three sons – Sangramajita, Brihatsena and Shura. One of them, Shura, was named after his great grandfather, Vasudevababa's father Shursena. Meanwhile, Lakshmanaa, too, gave birth to three sons – Praghosha, Gatravata and Urdhwaga. Jambavati also bore a daughter during this time. But she was born after the birth of two sons, Sumitra and Purujita. She was called Girija. Satya also gave birth to three sons during this period. They were named Vira, Chandra and Ashwasena. Mitravinda had also become a mother to three sons. She went to her parental home in Avanti to give birth to each child. Her three sons were named by the people of Avanti – Vrika, Harsha and Anila. Khandavavana daughter Kalindi's three sons were named Shruta, Purnamasa and Darsha.

One day, my priest Sushil said, 'A Brahmin from Saurashtra has arrived at the Shuddhaksha gate. He is scrawny and very tired, as he has travelled from so far. He is pleading to see the Lord of Dwaraka. What should we do?'

As the maharani of Dwaraka, I was used to this. I told the priest, 'Arrange for him to stay in the guest chamber. Look after all his needs properly. Tell him that Sri will meet him once he returns to Dwaraka.' Sri returned within a few days of completing the construction of the Pandavas' royal capital in Khandavavana. But this time, he arrived in Dwaraka at night, using boats. All of Dwaraka was asleep when he arrived. Sri had instructed the chief minister and other assembly members who had come to receive him at the Shuddhaksha gate to refrain from organising a formal welcome and to keep it quiet. Even I did not come to know when Sri arrived in Dwaraka at night.

The next morning, I performed all morning rituals and sat for the daily charity offering with Sri. My seven sisters had taken their seats by my side. Sri looked delighted as the construction of the Pandavas' royal capital in Khandavavana had been concluded to his satisfaction. He said, 'Rukmini, the royal city of the Pandavas has been built splendidly. Pradyumna's young troops cleaned the thick forests of Khandavavana with the assistance of Agni. Indraprastha is indeed slightly superior to Dwaraka. Arjuna and I had to fight a furious battle with Varuna, the king of the forest. Varuna attacked us fiercely with his army, saying, "This forest is our residence, we will not let you Kurus–Yadavas burn it." The cut-throat battle lasted for many days. Ultimately, he had to concede defeat. He acknowledged Arjuna's prowess, and happily offered Arjuna his auspicious bow, named Gandiva, along with a quiver that has an inexhaustible supply of arrows, and his well-built, well-balanced chariot, named Nandighosha.'

While Sri was picking up a handful of pearls from the cane basket, I gently said to him, 'A Brahmin from Saurashtra is here. He is pleading to meet you. He is waiting in the guest chamber.' With an astonished look in his eyes, he asked, 'Who? From where did you say he has come?'

'A Brahmin – from Saurashtra.' As Sri heard my words, his handsome face blossomed with ecstasy. His fish-shaped eyes sparkled; he let go of the pearls in his palms and muttered, 'That's him, my dear Sudama!' He instantly began walking towards the guest chamber, saying, 'I will be back soon, Maharani! You finish the rest of the charity session.' We soon saw Sri and Uddhava gently supporting the scrawny Brahmin, holding his arms on both sides and bringing him into the charity chamber. He had a gaunt frame and a shabby appearance; he was wearing a Barabandi dress from Kathiawar, a red-bordered dhoti covered his legs halfway, a cap covered both his ears, and there were dots of sandalwood paste on his forehead between the eyebrows and on his cheeks. He held a crooked, dry staff of the Bela tree in his hand, his untidy shoulder bag reached down to his waist, and he was barefoot. Dumbfounded, all of us gawked at him. I was utterly speechless.

Both the brothers carefully brought their friend and made him sit on Sri's golden seat. That completely flustered the Brahmin from Saurashtra. He just kept staring at everything with his eyes wide open.

Sri ordered Sushil, 'Please bring the golden salver that is used for daily worship. Also get some Prajakta flowers with it.' A big golden salver consisting of big and small gold plates used for worship was placed near the small golden footrest in front of the seat on which the Brahmin was sitting. Sri was so engrossed in attending to the Brahmin that he was not aware of who had gathered around him. He put a golden salver on the footrest in front of the Brahmin, and requested his dearest friend to put his soiled feet on it. He let a stream of Gangajala fall on his dear friend's feet and wiped them gently with his shawl. He adorned them with a dot of sandalwood paste. He picked up a fresh garland of white lotuses from the big worship salver, put it around the neck of his dear friend and glanced at Sudama with such affection that he got overwhelmed with emotion. Sri pulled him up and held him in a passionate, deep embrace. Sri picked up the golden bowl in the platter, took a small piece of the sweet saffron-and-ginger-flavoured delicacy made of milk and put it in his dear friend's mouth.

Now, the entire chamber of charities was overcome with emotion.

Sri released his friend from his embrace and looked at me. I was well acquainted with the silent language of his eyes. I immediately stepped forward. Asking Sudama to sit down, I requested him to put his feet in the platter on the footrest. I also worshipped his feet in the same way that Sri had done. After me, the remaining seven wives came forward in order of seniority. They also did the same for him. After that, Sri affectionately asked his friend, 'Sudamana, friend, you have not been speaking at all and your left arm is constantly touching your shoulder bag. Tell me, what is in that bag?'

'What else could be there?' Saying so, Sudama put his hand in the shoulder bag. The curiosity of all the gathered Yadava men and women heightened. Everyone's eyes were fixed on his shoulder bag. Sudama instantly pulled out a pair of sandalwood slippers, about nineteen inches long. In a moment, he touched the sandalwood slippers to the tilak of the sandalwood paste on his forehead with loving respect.

I had heard that Sri and Sudama had been disciples of Acharya Sandipani in the Ankapada ashrama. I obviously thought that those were the acharya's slippers. Acharya himself was present in the chamber. Sudama was so overwhelmed that he had not even noticed him yet. He handed over the wooden slippers to me. I touched them to my forehead, believing that they belonged to the acharya, and returned them. Sri was simply watching all this with his mischievous smile. Meanwhile, Sudama noticed the acharya and his wife. He approached them and put his head on the acharya's feet. Acharya momentarily patted his lean shoulders and put his hand on Sudama's head to offer blessings. The acharya was honourably brought towards the golden seat. Acharya had closed his eyes. He had already gone into a meditative trance. Sudama's left hand still kept moving towards his bag. With his gaze fixed on the acharya's face, Sri brought both his palms together in prayer and said with utmost respect, 'Acharya, I hope to hear something precious at this moment.'

Acharya's white beard and moustache quivered momentarily. He smiled and, with eyes still closed, said, 'Yes Srikrishna, I will. First, let Sudama complete a formality. Oh Sudama, friend of Srikrishna, without hesitating or feeling diffident in the presence of all, give your friend the gift of love that you have brought in your bag.'

Everyone's eyes were now fixed on Sudama's bag. Sudama's right hand went into his bag twice, and came out empty. Then the guru spoke again, 'Sudamana, poverty is not a flaw – but poverty of the heart is indeed a fault. Just give your gift!'

Sudama pulled out a small bundle from his bag. It was tied in a soiled cloth. With trembling hands, he put it on the rosy palms of the Lord of Dwaraka.

Sri gently opened the bundle. There was plain, dry puffed rice in it. It was a simple gift of love that his wife had packed in a hurry when Sudama had told her, 'I have to give a gift to my friend, pack something.'

Sri's eyes, sparkling like the Pushkaraja jewel, stared at the dry puffed rice in his palms with utter joy. Looking at that incredible gift of love, his fish-shaped bright eyes brimmed with tears. Sri picked up a couple of grains of the puffed rice and first offered them at the acharya's feet. Then he relished a couple of grains fondly while smacking his lips and held some out for me. I also picked up a couple of grains and put them in my mouth. They were indeed delicious. Acharya Sandipani then spoke. He said very little, but it was remarkable. He said, 'Oh citizens of Dwaraka! Today is a golden day in the life of Dwaraka. Srikrishna and Sudama, both are best friends and my best disciples. I have already told them this. Today, I repeat it for your sake: pride of any kind – of power, wealth, beauty, strength or knowledge – ultimately destroys the human being. The pride of power, authority and wealth is bad. But, above all, the pride of knowledge, of spiritual knowledge, is the worst.

'Srikrishna, Sudama, I am proud of both these disciples of mine. The essence of life is love. You should cherish and spread it throughout your lives. Just like the loving gift that Sudamana has brought and Srikrishna has distributed!'

Sudama stayed in Dwaraka for a week. Immediately after that, Sri called for minister Vipruthu in the discussion chamber. He must have been giving him a lot of instructions about something. When I went there, I just heard fleeting words, '...Once everything is completed, announce the name of the city as "Sudamapuri". Also, announce the same in the kingdom of Dwaraka.' I surmised that a new city like Indraprastha was going to be built in the name of Sudama.

On another occasion, the drums at the Shuddhaksha gate boomed to announce the arrival of a special guest. I wondered who this special guest could be, since the Lord of Dwaraka himself was going to receive him.

I was even more stunned when I reached the Shuddhaksha gate to find everyone, including Acharya Sandipani and his wife, there, all waiting to receive this special guest.

A tall, white-bearded, white-haired, radiant elderly man wearing a white loincloth descended from a ship. He had covered his lips with a white strip of cloth and tied it securely at the back of his head. The moment his feet touched the land of Dwaraka, Sri promptly moved forward along with Acharya Sandipani. Both acharyas embraced each other. Sri knelt down and put his head on the divine feet of Ghor Angirasa. Ghor Angirasa immediately held his shoulders, pulled Sri up, and embraced him, saying, 'No…Hrishikesha.'

The story of this great rishi's life that I had come to know from Acharya Sandipani was indeed amazing.

He was originally a Yadava from Mathura and was related to Sri distantly. In his youth, he had left his home and family to become an ascetic and had gone to the Himalayas. He had humbly submitted himself at the feet of the renowned rishi Angirasa, become his disciple and performed severe penance. The older Angirasa had thoroughly assessed him through difficult tests and appointed him the heir of his family ashramas. After him, this Angirasa had set up many ashrama branches at various places in Aaryavarta. His disciples knew him by both names – Ghor Angirasa and Arishtanemi.

A grand procession was organised to welcome Ghor Angirasa.This venerable rishi stayed in Dwaraka for one whole month. Sri had arranged his stay in his own chamber near the Krishnasopana. Every day, the venerable rishi and Sri spent hours in discussion in Sri's chamber. The great rishi possessed divine knowledge. That was indeed something Sri would never miss. Sri would pester him with questions on a variety of subjects.

Initially, Acharya Sandipani and Uddhava would also participate in these discussions. Afterwards, both of them would just listen. During Ghor Angirasa's stay in Dwaraka, neither did Sri pay attention to any administrative duty, nor did he leave the island of Dwaraka.

Sri was quite influenced by the discussions with him. Sri had urged him to visit Dwaraka only to become his disciple. He once raised the subject in the presence of Acharya Sandipani and Gargamuni. Holding both his palms together, Sri said to the rishi with utmost humility, 'Bhagwan, I have spent more than half my life in performing all Kshatriya duties with dedication. Now I feel like surrendering the divine Sudarshan at the feet of an appropriate person and beginning my search for the ultimate essence of life. I humbly request you to take me as your disciple.'

At that point, Ghor Angirasa laughed like a small child and said, 'The ultimate essence of life? And am I the one who should teach it to you, Achyuta? Looks like your mischievous, impish disposition from Gokul has not vanished yet! If you say so, I will become your guru; that too, for my eternal fame. But not now – sometime later – when the time is right.'

Sri organised a grand ceremony in the Sudharma assembly to felicitate and honour Acharya Ghor Angirasa, to show all the Yadavas in Dwaraka how a Yadava amongst them can reach the zenith with intense penance.

Notably, Sri also declared his heartfelt wish to become the disciple of Acharya Ghor Angirasa in the fully packed assembly.

Even Acharya Angirasa, who had such a balanced disposition, and had reached far beyond life, was moved by Sri's humility. He set aside the reserved attitude that went with his white vestures and responded in his candid language, 'Dear Yadava brothers, I belong to you indeed. It is because of your virtuous deeds of many lives that you have obtained a remarkable, exceptional mentor like Srikrishna. I earnestly advise you never to disobey him, even by mistake. It will never benefit you.

'He is imploring me in front of all of you, to accept him as my disciple. It is only with his blessings that I am telling you that although I am senior to him in age, I have not yet reached the status of making "him" my disciple. But whenever the time comes, I will certainly fulfil that duty.'

Acharya Angirasa bade farewell to Dwaraka and proceeded towards the north, leaving everybody desolate, including Sri. With his conduct, he had compelled the hot-headed, volatile Yadavas to think about life in a new light. The people of Dwaraka kept talking about him even a month after he had left the city.

Once again, the ensemble of musical instruments at the Shuddhaksha gate resounded, just as it had for welcoming the rishi. For a moment, the citizens of Dwaraka wondered whether Ghor Angirasa had returned. But that was not the case. Venerable Pandava Dhananjaya – Arjuna, whose acclaim I had been hearing – was entering Dwaraka for the first time, along with Dhaumya rishi. Sri left his palace to welcome Arjuna without waiting for anybody. But Partha did not give him that chance and presented himself promptly at Sri's feet. I hurried with my maids to see him in Sri's chamber. I was baffled to see him in the Virasana pose at Sri's feet. For a moment, I thought that Sri himself was sitting in the Virasana pose.

Even I could not make out who Sri was and who Arjuna was when both of them embraced each other.

As he walked towards me, I found a quirk to correctly distinguish both of them from each other.

Arjuna walked balancing his shapely body on his robust feet, like a warrior. Sri always walked easily like a zephyr. As if drifting gently, like a tune of the flute.

Within moments, Partha stood in front of me; he knelt down and putting his head on my feet, said, 'You need not have climbed the Srisopana. I was coming to visit you.' At that moment, I smiled broadly. I had found another quirk when I heard him speak. Arjuna's voice was loud and clear, like an arrow hitting a rock. Sri's voice was sweet and charming, like a flute. No matter when and how many times one heard it, one was never satiated. They indeed had distinct voices.

Arjuna had come to Dwaraka to formally invite all Yadavas to his elder brother Yudhishthira's coronation.

The Yadava royal circle, ministers, all troop leaders and Yadava men and women packed in the Sudharma assembly were impressed and fascinated by the strong resemblance between Pandu's son Arjuna and Sri. One Yadava lady, sitting in the royal ladies' chamber behind the soft curtain, was mesmerised. In that moment, she chose him to be her husband. She was Sri's sister, Subhadra. My dear Bhadra.

Arjuna stayed in Dwaraka for a week. During this time, the citizens of Dwaraka witnessed many of his wonderful and extraordinary feats with the Gandiva bow. As soon as the gaze of all ladies seated in the women's spectator gallery shifted from each arrow that Arjuna shot, it would automatically turn to Subhadra, who was cheering with a speed faster than the arrow itself.

Dwaraka was now full of excitement about the coronation ceremony of Yudhishthira, the eldest of the Pandavas.

Vasudevababa was going to stay back in Dwaraka. For the protection of Dwaraka, my brave, handsome son Pradyumna was going to stay with him too.

The chariots of Balaramadada, Sri, Uddhava, Vipruthu, and commanders Satyaki and Anadhrishti were going to leave last. As usual, Sri and Uddhava, Bhama and I were going to travel in the Garudadhwaja chariot, and Daruka was going to steer it. Daruka had adorned Garudadhwaja exquisitely even without any instructions from Sri.

Along the way, we halted at a few kingdoms, including Marusthala and Dasharna. One such stopover was on the borders of Viratanagar in the Matsya kingdom near Mount Arbuda. Everybody thought it would be a short one, but it was extended for two days on Sri's command. In Viratanagar, he went to meet King Virata along with Dada and Uddhava, carrying gift salvers. Balaramadada immediately noticed it, though nobody else realised it. As usual, pulling his dear brother's leg, he asked, 'My dear Lord of Dwaraka, are you thinking of becoming the son-in-law of the Viratas too?' Sri smiled sweetly as usual and said, 'Now, it is only the fulfilment of duty that I am married to. Who knows, if not the Yadavas, maybe the Pandavas will get connected to the Viratas through familial relations some time in future? Dada, everybody walks on the well-trodden path. Very few explore a new one.'

Sri was duly welcomed in Viratanagar. I met a new friend in Virata's wife – Maharani Sudeshna. Our last halt was on the banks of River Yamuna in the Indraprastha kingdom.

I was wonderstruck when I stepped on to the holy land of Indraprastha. To welcome Sri, Rajmata Kuntidevi was present in person, along with all five Pandavas and Draupadi, their family priest Dhaumya rishi, Panchal king Drupada, Maharani Sautramani, Prince Dhrishtadyumna, commanders of both armies, the chief minister and sages Yaaja, Upayaaja and Asitadevala, along with their many disciples. Sri took a good look at everyone with his keen eyes. Not a single Kaurava of Hastinapura was present.

The ensemble of Indraprastha's musicians raised a loud chorus of musical instruments to welcome Sri. Rapturous citizens of Indraprastha showered vermilion and flowers on Sri, Dada, Uddhava and Daruka.

Spellbound, I simply kept looking on both sides as we started moving in our chariot. Indraprastha. The royal capital of the Pandavas! An unmatched sculpture raised by indomitable prowess! Well-built, lofty edifices, capacious temples with decorative domes, special practice arenas for various kinds of combats, stables full of horses and camels, fenced pits for goat and cock fights, well-polished iron statues of valiant warriors in different costumes and different war poses located at intersections, gardens bustling with sprawling trees covered with creepers and the cacophony of chirping birds adorned the city. I found this royal city a tiny bit better than Dwaraka itself.

There was only one thing lacking here – the continuous roaring sound of the ocean. That is why I felt that Indraprastha was very quiet. The formal coronation ceremony of Yudhishthira lasted an entire week. During this time, many kings from various kingdoms stayed in the Pandava royal palace. The wide bed of the Yamuna was full of boats. Many royal pennants with different colours proudly fluttered atop their masts.

I had met and talked with Draupadi as soon as I had come, but that was not enough for me. On our first meeting itself, I felt strongly that though dusky, she was indeed extremely beautiful, statuesque and graceful. She had thick hair, fragrant skin, a sharp and determined voice, and bright, black, large eyes.

The day of of Yudhishthira's enthronement dawned. The five valiant brothers entered our chamber together to meet Sri and me, and seek our blessings.

After seeking our blessings, while all the brothers were engaged in pleasantries with us, the commander of Indraprastha came rushing. He said, 'Venerable Lord of Dwaraka, Grandsire Bhishma from Hastinapura has arrived in Indraprastha to offer blessings to the eldest son of Pandu. Mahatma Vidura and minister Sanjaya are also with him.'

Sri asked further, 'Who else has come?'

'Only the select army of Grandsire. Nobody else.'

Sri smiled sweetly, as usual, and exclaimed, 'Commander, let us welcome him.'

The coronation took place in the royal assembly of Indraprastha. The family priest of the Pandavas, Dhaumya rishi, removed the twisted turban of the Kurus from Yudhishthira's head and replaced it with the royal golden crown engraved with tracery, amidst loud chanting of the mantras. A small triangular diadem was placed on Draupadi's head. At that moment, the royal assembly reverberated with the sound of many royal instruments. Assembled guests and the jubilant men and women of Indraprastha showered the king and queen with flowers and vermilion. An acclamation in honour of the new king arose, 'Hail the Lord of Indraprastha, the pride of the Pandava clan, Maharaja Yudhishthira!' Thousands of voices repeated it.

It was time for everyone to return. Though Maharani Draupadi was occupied in bidding farewell to all, she kept meeting Sri under some pretext or the other. She kept asking him many questions like a small girl.

I immediately realised one thing through their conversations. Draupadi was talking to Sri freely and addressing him simply without attaching an honorific. In Sri's case, only the elders could do that. I could have never talked to him like that, leave alone my other sisters in Dwaraka.

Just as I had deduced about Arjuna and Sri in Dwaraka, so also did I about both Radha and now Draupadi here in Indraprastha. Radha, whom I had never met, was the pleasant image, in Sri's mind, of the ideal hard-working village woman. Draupadi was the pleasant image of the ideal royal woman.

Draupadi always honoured and respected me earnestly. And I, too, often met with her during our stay in Indraprastha, always accompanied by our beautiful and playful Subhadra. Draupadi greatly admired her as Sri's sister. If at all, for any reason, any elderly woman spoke a little harsher with playful Subhadra, Draupadi would immediately stand up for her and silence the other woman. I would smile at such times, and say to Draupadi, 'Oh Pandava Maharani, please do not praise this Yadava daughter so much. Sometimes things appear simpler from a distance than they actually are. I invite you to come to Dwaraka once with your archer. Then you will see her qualities.'

Sri's councils with Pandava maharaja Yudhishthira and Rajmata Kuntidevi automatically increased before leaving for Dwaraka. In one such council, Sri put forth a proposal to Kuntidevi and all the

Pandavas – a simple one and agreeable to all. Sri said, 'Now the acclaim of the Indraprastha kingdom will pervade through entire Aaryavarta. You gallant brothers should embark on a world conquest and expand the glory of Indraprastha in all directions. Leave it to your new maharaja to decide who will go in what direction.

'A grand ceremonial coronation of a kingdom's ruler is not sufficient. The royal throne should be honoured everywhere. There is only one way to achieve this – grand heroic exploits. For that purpose, Dwaraka will always be here to supply Indraprastha, which is a close ally of the Yadavas, with a fourfold army, elephants, horses, weapons and wealth.

'The most important thing right now is the protection of your newly built kingdom. That is why I am presenting a proposal with foresight. I have no doubt that all of you are valiant. Yet, the responsibility of the protection of Indraprastha is eventually going to fall more on the shoulders of only two – Arjuna and mighty Bhima.

'Therefore, to become incomparably skilful in mace-fighting and wrestling, Bhimsena, who is already well versed in those skills, should be sent right away to Dwaraka as the disciple of our Balaramadada'

On that, Maharaja Yudhishthira glanced at Rajmata Kuntidevi in the council, in expectation of a decision. As she nodded, Maharaja gave his word to the Lord of Dwaraka, 'As per Srikrishna's wish, Bhimsena will go to Dwaraka. We will leave Indraprastha for the world conquest as soon as he returns after completing his training. I request Balaramadada to train my brother. Also, I request Srikrishna to give us his blessings for the world conquest.'

We bade farewell to all in Indraprastha and returned to Dwaraka. A mammoth crowd, bigger than the one that had come to see Arjuna, awaited us.

Till today I had respectfully regarded Balaramadada as incomparable in physical strength. But looking at Pandu's son, the mighty Bhimsena, I felt that just like Arjuna was Sri's shadow, Bhimsena could become Dada's. To see both of them together was like seeing Mount Kailas and Mainaka in a single glance. As soon as they saw the mighty, muscular, ruddy fair physique of Bhimsena, the already eager Yadavas excitedly showered flowers on him.

Now it was as if the entire Dwaraka had turned into a grand wrestling pit and a huge battlefield of mace fights.

In Indraprastha, the entire Pandava family settled down after the coronation ceremony. The Pandavas, along with Kuntimata and Draupadi, had decided upon the rules of conduct for the family in a secret council. One of the rules stated which days Draupadi would spend with which husband in privacy. During that period, none of the remaining four brothers would be permitted to enter the private chamber. At one such time, while Yudhishthira and Draupadi were in the private chamber, a Brahmin's cows were being abducted. Arjuna needed his Gandiva bow to protect the cows. He had no alternative but to enter the private chamber to obtain the Gandiva bow. But he now had to face the consequences. He had to go on a pilgrimage for a year. The news of Arjuna's departure from Indraprastha as a pilgrim arrived in Dwaraka. Sri became solemn initially on hearing the news. Then, with a charming smile, he said to me, 'Surely, Arjuna will visit us within a year now.'

Sri was now having continuous discussions with commander Satyaki and Anadhrishti in the Sudharma assembly. As per what Uddhava had conveyed to me, those discussions were only about Jarasandha – the Magadha emperor of Girivraja. Both brothers were not paying any attention at all to their sister Subhadra, who had come of age. Both were still treating her like an innocent young child. It became my responsibility to make them realise that she was of marriageable age and that it was necessary to find a suitable groom – a life partner for her at the right time. To me, Subhadra was like my daughter Charumati. Therefore, I sincerely took the task upon myself.

After the meals, I found an opportunity and decided to take full advantage of it. I said, 'Our Subhadra has come of age. What about her swayamwar? Is anyone among you ever going to get some time to pay attention to her at all?'

As he heard my appeal, Vasudevababa immediately said, 'What Rukmini says is right. But we are tired and old. Now Prince Balarama should take the initiative to get this done. He should choose a suitable groom for Subhadra. Srikrishna should help him in every possible way to that effect. Srikrishna will definitely look after her welfare. Our blessings are with him.'

By this time, Balaramadada, who had been laughing loudly so far, turned pensive. With determination, he said, 'Subhadra is our favourite sister. Vasudevababa need not worry about her wedding. I have already chosen a perfect groom for her. I am sure Rukmini will also like and approve of him. And once she approves, there is no question of Krishna objecting to it. Right, Srikrishna?'

Naïve Dada put Sri in a quandary in front of all without even mentioning the name of the groom. But Sri was one up! Without any delay, he smiled and asked a counter question, 'Dada, you are seeking my approval without even mentioning the name of the groom.' Dada put forth another question. 'The groom is from the Kuru family. He is valiant. Now you tell me – who could he be?'

'From the Kuru family? Valiant? Who else could it be but one of the Pandavas?' Uddhava interrupted.

'When you speak, Uddhava, I take it that Srikrishna has spoken through you. The groom that I have chosen for Subhadra is from the Kuru family, but not one of the Pandavas. He is one of the Kauravas – the prince. Soon, he will be formally crowned king of Hastinapura. The groom I have chosen for Subhadra is the son of Maharaja Dhritarashtra – Prince Duryodhana!'

Hearing Dada's choice, the entire family fell silent. Dada continued further under the misconception that everybody was bedazzled after hearing the unexpected name, 'Duryodhana is my disciple in mace-fighting. He came to Mithila and obtained this vidya with diligence and humility after serving me well. In my opinion, if at all I understand anything about mace-fighting, then Duryodhana is an unmatched mace warrior in entire Aaryavarta. Dwaraka will gain more strength if we form familial relations with the Hastinapura kingdom. I have complete faith that my favourite disciple Duryodhana will never disobey my word. Therefore, as a suitable match for my dear sister, I have chosen Duryodhana as her groom. What do you say, Srikrishna? Share your honest opinion about the groom with all, in this council itself. I want no confusion later. I am a wrestler from the red soil, outspoken and open-minded. You are a wrestler of diplomacy – crafty and cunning!'

Dada's direct question left the family council shaken and silent. Everybody stared at Sri in anticipation of how he was going to answer that question. Only Sri said with a smile, without getting disturbed at all, 'Dada, how can your choice of groom for our dear sister be wrong at all? After all, you are the senior – the prince; your choice is bound to be perfect. How can we disobey your word? Even I have heard that the valiant Kuru warrior Duryodhana is the ultimate in mace-fighting. He is unmatched in entire Aaryavarta. But it is Subhadra's swayamwar – not yours or mine! Taking the meaning of "swayamwar" into account, shouldn't we at least ask her if she has anybody in mind for a groom? If it is the Kaurava prince Duryodhana, then there is no problem at all. In that case, we will get our dear Subhadra married with great pomp right away. What do you say?' Everyone spoke in unison, responding to Sri's perfect solution, saying, 'What Srikrishna is saying is right.' News of Subhadra's wedding spread throughout Dwaraka in no time. Somehow, the news reached Subhadra too. She stormed into my chamber and said, 'Sushri, what is all this that I hear? Are all of you going to forcibly marry me off to that insolent, egotistical son of a blind man? Have I become that much of a burden to the Yadavas?

'Sushri, I am explicitly telling you to tell both my brothers firmly that I will never go to Hastinapura as the daughter-in-law of the Kauravas. If such a time ever comes, I will take shelter in the womb of the western ocean.'

In Indraprastha itself, I had recognised that she had given her heart to the archer – Dhananjaya. Still, acting as if I had no clue, I said, 'Subhadra, why are you acting so silly? You will be the Maharani of Hastinapura tomorrow. Have you even realised how wealthy and powerful you will be?'

Usually she would talk to me with respect, but since I touched her sore spot, the 'Yadava' woman in her awoke. She stared at me and said, 'Then why didn't you choose to be the maharani of the Chedis? Why did you choose to spend the rest of your life with a cowherd?' She spoke intensely in her outburst, and then realised that she had called her dear brother a cowherd. Instantly, she hid her face in her palms and began sobbing.

I affectionately embraced her and said while patting her, 'Bhadre, be calm, be quiet. Your heart's desire will be fulfilled. Do only one thing – if Balaramdada asks you, tell him that you will get married to whoever your Srikrishnadada approves. Do not keep cry like a weakling henceforth, and stay closer to Sri. Listen carefully to whatever he tells you and follow it precisely. Your wish will be fulfilled for sure.' She became sentimental now and embraced me.

The drama of Subhadra's wedding, the beauteous and virtuous daughter of all the Yadavas, got more and more intriguing.

Soon, Bhimsena's training was over. The Yadavas felicitated him in a grand celebration in the Sudharma assembly to bid farewell to him. Muscular, mighty, well-built Bhimsena was honoured in an overcrowded hall. Sri himself put a six-foot-long, fresh red-lotus garland around his muscular neck. Dada had got a huge mace, just like his, moulded and charmed with the chanting of mantras that imparted energy. Amidst the continuous applause of thousands of Yadavas, he put the shining mace on Bhimsena's shoulders and embraced him deeply. Dada, who usually did not speak in the assembly, could not hold himself back today. He signalled to Sri and got up. He said, 'Pandu's son Bhimsena, my disciple, has successfully completed training in wrestling and mace-fighting. Actually, Duryodhana, venerable Kuru prince, the son of Dhritarashtra, is my first disciple. There is no doubt that both of them are equally proficient in these skills. Yet it is true that as my first disciple, I love Duryodhana a bit more. Soon I am going to forge a bond of relations between the Yadavas and Hastinapura. I believe that Duryodhana and Bhimsena will always support the kingdom of Dwaraka. I give my heartiest blessings to valiant Bhimsena for the journey of his life. May all be well with Pandu's son Bhimsena, may victory be with him!'

This time Sri was not going to speak, but the eyes of thousands of Yadavas were stuck only on him. As soon as Sri raised his right hand and lifted the index finger, the assembly fell silent. 'Dear Yadava brothers, as long as our dear mace warrior and wrestler Balaramadada is here, I do not think Dwaraka will ever be in need of Bhimsena's assistance. On the contrary, the newly built Indraprastha kingdom may need Dada's valour, if at all. I can understand Dada's inclination towards Duryodhana as his first disciple and as a prince like himself. At this moment, I wish to say only this much – mighty Bhimsena's invincible strength will always be required, but for a very different reason. Hence, I have a plan for a future bond of relations with Indraprastha. Even today, Bhimsena is our relative. Soon he will be much more closely related to us. For that, I give him my heartiest best wishes. Hail Bhimsena! May victory be with you!'

Bhimsena bade farewell to the Yadavas of Dwaraka and left for Indraprastha.

Balaramadada had now reached the decision of forming a matrimonial alliance with the Kuru kingdom of Hastinapura. He had shut his eyes to Sri's frequent, straightforward or indirect suggestions of 'seeking Subhadra's approval'. He had already dispatched minister Vipruthu and his loyal brother Gada to Hastinapura to get Subhadra betrothed to Duryodhana.

I immediately realised how stifling the situation was for Sri. We had to find a way to halt the Duryodhana–Subhadra wedding. Otherwise, our virtuous, dear Bhadra was going to droop in the company of Duryodhana and his ninety-nine brothers like a delicate creeper slumping in a windy storm.

Restless, Sri once said to me, 'There is no clue where that master archer Dhananjaya is wandering throughout Aryavarta for his pilgrimage. Our best spies have hunted for him in all directions.'

What was I going to suggest to him, after all? I could not keep quiet and said, 'You always visit the holy place of Prabhas for your peace of mind. You should try it this time. The charities and bathing in the holy place will calm your mind. Then you will be able to think better.'

Hearing my suggestion, Sri laughed cheerfully, and said, 'Rukmini, you are such a mind reader! Even I was thinking about the holy place of Prabhas.'

Sri gave orders to prepare for the journey to the holy place. Then Sri went to meet his brother and urged him, 'Dada, you must also come to the holy place of Prabhas. Subhadra's royal wedding is due. So, let us offer some charities and bathe in the holy water.'

Dada lovingly patted his shoulders and said, 'You go and perform all the rituals on my behalf. I cannot move from here. Prince Duryodhana will be in Dwaraka any time now for the betrothal ceremony.'

Sri left alone for Prabhas, along with select Yadava warriors. I had estimated that he would not be back for at least a fortnight. But something unexpected happened. He returned immediately from Prabhas, with complete peace of mind! As soon as he came, he met me in private in our inner chambers and said, 'Rukmini, I met Partha at Prabhas. Everything has become easy now. He is dressed up as an ascetic in saffron vesture. He is not easily recognisable, as he has grown a beard. I have instructed him to come immediately to the Shiva temple of Somanath near Veravala. Uddhava will leave tomorrow itself for Somanath. He will return with joyful news for the citizens of Dwaraka that an ascetic "Shivayogi", who has performed penance in the cave of the Himalayas, has arrived in the Shiva temple of Somanath to make up for the lack of such an ascetic here. The citizens of Dwaraka will believe this blindly, as it is going to come from Uddhava. Men and women will form queues at Somanath to visit the Shivayogi. You should also go with Subhadra to meet him. How does that sound?'

The drama of Subhadra's wedding was now going to take place across the region of Prabhas, Somanath, Dwaraka and Raivataka. The main stage of this drama was going to be Mount Raivataka and the family deity temple of the Raivatakas.

Now I started getting a very rare glimpse of Sri that I had never seen in my life. He was the courageous one who determinedly punished the unjust and insolent ones. He was an expert ruler who immediately put his plans to action. A brilliant philosopher who discussed philosophy with great sages. A premayogi who loved all young and old people of Dwaraka from the bottom of his heart. Was there any quality that he did not possess? He was a brave commander, a maestro of music, an expert in the war of maces, daggers, bow and arrow, an inspiring orator who left the audience spellbound and captivated. He was an accomplished expert of all fine arts, skills and vidyas. But these days, in matters of our delicate, familial issues, he had become a fine actor. Even I was astonished to see that.

He would welcome Balaramadada in our chamber with a broad smile on his face. He never explicitly told Balaramadada, 'You are making a big and irreversible mistake by betrothing Subhadra to Duryodhana'. Had he said so, it might have been a blow to the honour of his elder brother. He did not want that to happen at all. He had already realised that Subhadra had given her heart to Arjuna. Her life was to be saved from getting nipped in the bud. He already knew in his heart that Arjuna was the perfect groom for his sister.

I went to the Shiva temple at Somanath with Subhadra as per Sri's plan. I visited and paid obeisance to Lord Shiva. Subhadra visited and paid obeisance to Lord Shiva as well as the Shivayogi. I waited outside the temple so that both could talk freely. I recalled the urgent epistle that I had sent from Kundinpura so many years ago. Subhadra, too, was standing at a similar crossroads in her life. But I had full faith that Subhadra was indeed going to be Arjuna's wife.

As per the Yadava tradition, Subhadra was to travel to Mount Raivataka as the new bride-to-be. She was to visit the mountain goddess and seek blessings for her future life. That was exactly when Arjuna was supposed to abduct her. The Raivataka king Kakudmin was going to be a major hurdle in this process. Kakudmin was renowned for unerringly capturing huge roaring lions alive in hidden traps placed by his hunting troops. It was impossible for saffron-clad Arjuna to escape from his army. Above all, ascetic Arjuna did not even have the much-needed armed chariot that he could have placed at the base of the mountain to abduct Yadava daughter Subhadra. He did not have any armed guards essential for this thrilling act. The distance between Mount Raivataka and Indraprastha was also quite a bit.

Sri, as always, had figured out everything and had solutions in place.

News arrived that Prince Duryodhana had begun his journey for Dwaraka for the betrothal ceremony. The mammoth fourfold army of the Kurus was accompanying him. Dada did not let Satyaki and Anadhrishti rest even for a moment and gave exhaustive instructions to ensure a grand welcome. Sri casually presented an idea. He said, 'Balaramadada, sometimes we miss the big things inadvertently; things easy to think of while otherwise taking care of every small detail. Once the time has gone, however, we end up regretting not doing them.'

Balaramadada smilingly said, 'Why are you talking in riddles? Whatever it is, just say it freely.'

'I have a humble request. I think we should invite your father-in-law, Raivataka Maharaja Kakudmin, along with his army, to welcome Duryodhana. He will be elated.'

'You are right. I am not good at such subtleties. I will send Satyaki with the invitation to Raivataka today itself.'

Sri gave a very charming smile and said, 'Also convey my humble obeisance to Maharaja Kakudmin through him.' The very next day, after confirming that commander Satyaki had left for Raivataka, carrying gift salvers for the Raivataka king from the prince's chamber, Sri also dispatched his special informers in two directions. One of the troops left to visit all those kingdoms lying between Raivataka and Indraprastha, which Arjuna and Subhadra would be passing through in a chariot. They were going to offer gift salvers sent by the Lord of Dwaraka to kings of Aanarta, Dasharna and Matsya, and deliver a special message to them. The message was, 'Our cousin Arjuna, along with our sister Subhadra, is passing through your kingdom towards Indraprastha in a chariot with the Kapidhwaja pennant. Please offer your heartiest support to him and strengthen the friendship with Dwaraka.'

The second troop was led by Sri's most loyal brother – Uddhava. It was going directly to the Shiva temple of Somanath, with an embellished, armed chariot with Arjuna's Kapidhwaja pennant on its flagpole. The chariot also carried royal attire and weapons for Arjuna.

Sri told me all this in detail. I invited Subhadra to my chamber and explained it to her thoroughly. Subhadra had transformed a lot in the meantime. Her face glowed with resolve. When I saw her, I wondered if I had looked similar when I had sat in the chariot with Sri. Sri had planned everything thoroughly; and yet I was getting more and more anxious every moment, all due to a single fear. Once Balaramadada comes to know of all this, would Sri once again be left bereft of his love like before? Maharaja Kakudmin arrived in Dwaraka. Now the climax of the drama began. News arrived that Prince Duryodhana would soon be reaching. Subhadra also left for Mount Raivataka along with Revati, a bevy of maids and a troop of guards. The ascetic devotee of Shiva in the temple of Somanath blessed all devotees and changed his saffron clothing. The year of his pilgrimage was also over. During this time, although he was a pilgrim, he had wedded the Naga daughter Uloopi by the Gandharva custom of marriage, on the banks of the Ganga in the north. Uloopi was the daughter of Naga king Kauravya, and she was a child widow. Her father-in-law, Airavata, had granted permission for the Gandharva marriage. Arjuna was also wedded to Chitrangada – the daughter of Chitravahana, the king of Manipura. Notably, Arjuna had conveyed all these details to me through Uddhava. He had also not forgotten to request that all these details be conveyed to Subhadra and see if she was still ready for this marriage. I shared all these details with Subhadra in private. After hearing all this, she fell silent for a moment. She was lost in thought. At that point, alerting her, I said, 'After all, Arjuna is your Sri Dada's cousin. More than that, he is Sri's favourite disciple. What else is he going to do but follow in his guru's footsteps? You are lucky, that he has only three previous wives. Like me…'

At that point, she immediately raised her head and breaking her silence, said, 'Sushri, I am not worthy enough to be compared to you. I have considered only you as my idol in my life. No matter what, I will get married to the son of Pandu.' She had no doubt at all.

The temple of Raivataka's family goddess was at the base of the mountain. Subhadra paid obeisance to the goddess and was coming out of the temple when, as per Sri's instructions, the Brahmin priests surrounded Revati for donations. Arjuna grabbed this opportunity and blew his Devadutta conch from his chariot, raising his head high. Subhadra picked the signal of the conch and, keeping her eyes on the Kapidhwaja, briskly walked towards the chariot. Arjuna also leapt down from the chariot, approached her and lovingly offered his hand to gently take her into the chariot. Instantly, he tugged at the reins and signalled the horses to run. Immediately, the four bright white horses galloped towards Indraprastha.

Subhadra's abduction was successfully carried out without any hurdle. I breathed a sigh of relief when news of the successful mission arrived in Dwaraka. But a furore erupted amongst the Yadavas. Still, Sri climbed on to the charity platform to offer gold jewellery and cows in charity on the occasion of the wedding of his sister. Kuru prince Duryodhana, who was travelling towards Dwaraka and had reached Saurashtra, was uncontrollably furious. He could not send any harsh message to Dada, who was his guru. Therefore, he just sent a message, 'We are returning to Hastinapura', and returned along with his army, fretting and fuming. Enraged, Balaramadada roared furiously at Sri, 'What is all this drama? Who do you think you are?' He could not even speak further as he was shaking with anger. Sri quietly gave him a charming smile as usual. He touched Maharaja Kakudmin's feet and then Dada's, and pulled out his ultimate weapon, leaving everybody stunned. Looking at Maharaja Kakudmin with a smile, he said, 'Respected Maharaja, I request you to explain to this prince of the Yadavas that Subhadra has selected a groom of her own accord. Master archer Dhananjaya has abducted her as per the tradition that the Kshatriyas are proud of. I have nothing to do with this – I am not at fault at all. Still, of my own accord, I am going to leave Dwaraka before he gives me any punishment as the prince. Just as he had abandoned me and gone to Mithila, I am going to Indraprastha, leaving Dwaraka and him, forever. Henceforth, for any kind of problem, he should consult you as his father-in-law.'

This strong dose abated Balaramadada's royal fury instantly. He was totally shaken. Aged Maharaja Kakudmin moved forward, patted Sri's shoulder and said, 'Oh Lord of Dwaraka, only you have the sole right to offer any consultation to your prince-brother. We, the Raivatakas, approve of Subhadra's choice. I will return today itself, and send gifts to the newlywed couple. I believe that this will help resolve the dispute among you brothers.' He silently preached Dada on how to treat his brother. Dada did not speak a word and, mutely accepting Subhadra's abduction, went to his chamber.

Now our Subhadra was going to receive a grand welcome on the borders of Indraprastha. I was confident that Subhadra, who had found her inner feminine strength, was going to obtain an honourable position among the Pandavas.

DARUKA

I am Daruka. Just a charioteer of the Lord's Garudadhwaja chariot. The first time I met him was in Mathura, after the execution of Kansa. Even today, I remember that moment very clearly, as if it happened only yesterday. Before meeting the Lord, I was just an errand boy. Since meeting him, I have transformed gradually, unbeknownst to myself.

I was a charioteer but just in name. The Lord was the real charioteer. He always said – a chariot of thoughts gallops along with every human being at all times, even in slumber. I was fortunate enough to be the charioteer of this epoch maker, who steered the thoughts of millions.

The chariot of the Lord's life resembled his own, Garudadhwaja. He just loved speed. He used to say, 'Remember, growth and development characterise life.' I ended up asking him once impatiently, 'Doesn't growth itself mean development?' He gave a charming smile as usual and said, 'Daruka, growth is outward – the increase in the size of a body – whereas development is the broadening of the mind through sanskaras.' I thoroughly experienced this life principle of his.

The Lord silently initiated me into the habit of going to the depth of things in any quest. That is why I tried to find out everything about the roots of our family as much as possible before starting my duty as a charioteer in the Shursena kingdom of the Yadavas. Those clues led me to the region around River Ganga in the Magadha kingdom. Whenever I said, 'The horse is the fastest animal', the Lord would smilingly correct me and say, 'Brother Daruka, the human mind is faster than the horse. Disciplining the human mind and keeping it under control is true charioteering. Do not forget that horses also have minds of their own. They express their feelings through their eyes, ears and by swishing their tails. To understand that language is true charioteering.'

My wife Hayamati accompanied me through my life like a shadow. She was the loving mother of our sons – Daruki, Hayaketu, Hayagriva and Darukaksha. Our eldest son Daruki was a little older than the Lord's first-born son Pradyumna. He became the charioteer of Pradyumna later.

We had only one daughter named Darukaa. She became a close friend of the Lord's daughter Charumati.

It was due to the Lord's way of thinking and affectionate demeanour that everybody would get drawn to him automatically. He was striving to make the newly built kingdom of Dwaraka well renowned all over. For that purpose, he constantly travelled in the Garudadhwaja throughout entire Aaryavarta – from Sindhu-Sauvira in the east to Anga-Vanga in the west, from Kashmir to Vanavasi, from north to south. I was fortunate enough to offer my services as a charioteer during this journey, and because of that, came to know how thoroughly pure and flawless Maharaja Srikrishna – the Lord of Dwaraka – is. Just as there is a difference between charioteering for a daily seashore ride, covering the distance between the royal capitals of two kingdoms at a constant pace, and steering a chariot on the actual battlefield, in the same way, the Lord's life has different shades as a family man, as a social leader, as a great Yadava on the battlefield and as a disciple of Acharya Sandipani lost in contemplation on philosophy, in the company of sages and hermits.

The rain descends in many rhythms – coming down heavily as if from a jar, drizzling and swaying in the wind, playing hide-and-seek with the sunrays, and many more. The life of Lord Srikrishna was like that too.

I am going to try to hold all the reins of this narration in my hands and see if I can steer this chariot. Will I be able to do it? I must try, though. Oh, how can I catch the epoch maker Yadava with my charioteer's eyes? He is as vast as the sky. I am going to attempt to see as much as I can of that sky-high man through the window of my charioteer's life. Whatever I see, I will present before you. It will only be a small glimpse of the Lord. He himself had convinced his beloved wives Rukminidevi and Satyabhamadevi at the time of his 'suwarnatula', when he was weighed against gold, that, 'If offered with true devotion and piety, even a leaf of holy basil can weigh me out.' This narration is just like that leaf of holy basil.

Rukminidevi had a nature and disposition that was distinct from the other seven queens. The moment I would see her, I would automatically be reminded of the Lord. She was like the shadow of the Lord. 'Love' was the innate mantra of the Lord's life. As his wife, the innate mantra of Rukminidevi's life, too, was 'love'.

The island of the queens' mansions was full of bustle with the chatter of the Lord's sons and daughters. By this time, his eight queens had begotten ten sons each. The number of Yadava children had surpassed eighty. Charumati had also got a few half-sisters.

Since the first time my Lord met the Pandavas and their mother Kuntidevi at Kurukshetra on the day of the solar eclipse, his behaviour changed drastically. He had been safeguarding the Pandavas much more than his own eighteen families of Yadavas. As an important part of that policy, we recently travelled from Dwaraka to Upaplavya. From there, along with the Lord, commander Satyaki and I went to Hastinapura of the Kurus, accompanied by a troop of chosen warriors. I can never forget the enthusiasm with which the citizens of Hastinapura welcomed us this time. This visit of the Lord was very valuable. This was the moment that could have led to war due to the disagreement between the Kauravas and Pandavas on the burning topic of the division of the kingdom. This visit of the Lord was for the royal mediation in Hastinapura. He was almost besieged by the citizens of Hastinapura, who had gathered in large numbers. Not just the Kurus and the Yadavas, but people from all other countries of Aaryavarta too were eagerly awaiting the result of this arbitration.

I escorted the Lord to the assembly hall of the Kurus and waited outside in the impenetrable circle of commander Satyaki and the armed warriors. I could not know the proceedings of the assembly on that day. But after about half an hour, my Lord came out, along with the venerable Kurus – Grandsire Bhishma, Mahamantri Vidura, minister Sanjaya, maharathi Karna and minister Vrishavarma. His face looked very different today. As if he had taken a stern and difficult decision. Usually he would walk easily, like the gentle breeze of wind. Today he walked like Bhima the wrestler, balancing his body, planting each step on the ground. I pulled the Garudadhwaja chariot near him. The Lord signalled commander Satyaki to board the other chariot at the back. Unexpectedly for all, the Lord, who was sitting in the chariot, stretched his left arm and held it in front of Karna – the king of Anga – saying, 'Come, I want to talk to you about something.' Maharathi Karna also boarded the chariot readily. Then the Lord ordered me, 'Daruka, take the chariot to the outskirts, and do not stop anywhere now.'

The chariot sprinted forward. Commander Satyaki and the other warriors followed us. I had already guessed that the Lord wanted to say something important to Karna. He was looking for privacy. I dropped off both the gallant warriors under a sprawling banyan tree on the outskirts of Hastinapura. I waited far away in the shade of a tall Khadira tree.

After some time, both the valiant men returned. The Lord looked at me and ordered, 'Daruka, drop the king of Anga at the assembly hall in the royal capital.' Now the philanthropist held the Lord's hand and pressing it for a moment or two, said, 'No need, Madhava, I will walk.' He turned his back and started walking.

My Lord whispered, like talking to himself, 'The war is indeed inevitable now! Daruka, let us go.'

I have been thinking since the Lord returned after meeting Karna. How all these twists and turns came to be between the Kurus, the Pandavas and the Yadavas.

The most significant turn in this journey was the execution of Jarasandha, the self-proclaimed emperor of Magadha.

I am talking about the time when the Pandavas had settled down in Indraprastha. It happened while the venerable Pandava Yudhishthira was planning to organise the Rajasuya yajna. By this time, the valiant Pandavas had returned after finishing the conquest in all four directions of Aaryavarta. We had heard the news of the victories of all the Pandavas in Dwaraka. Indraprastha had now become a prosperous, booming royal capital. Dwaraka had also rejoiced with the expansion of the Pandava family. Maharani Draupadidevi had begotten five gallant sons, one from each valiant Pandava. They were Yudhishthira's son Prativindhya, Bhimsena's son Sutasoma, Arjuna's son Shrutakirti, Nakula's son Shatanika and Sahadeva's son Shrutakarmana. Later, another son was born to Arjuna, and Dwaraka celebrated that event ecstatically. He was the son of Subhadradevi and Arjuna. As per the Lord's command, I myself had escorted Subhadradevi to Dwaraka for her first delivery. He was the very first offspring born of the firm familial relations between the Pandavas and the Yadavas. The Lord and Balaramdada were ecstatic to see him for the first time as his mamas. My Lord himself named him Abhimanyu with love.

Since his arrival from Indraprastha, my Lord had rarely been to the Sudharma royal assembly. He would mostly go to the western gate, Aindra, in his chariot with Uddhava Maharaja. Sitting on the boulder there, he would discuss the Pandavas with his brother for hours on end. During these talks, they would discuss the subject of the Rajasuya yajna and the possible interference of the self-proclaimed invincible Magadha emperor, Jarasandha.

On one such evening, the Lord was returning with Uddhava Maharaja from the western ocean after offering evening oblations to the Sun god. I was awaiting them in the chariot. Suddenly, an elderly Brahmin approached him from somewhere. He stood courteously in front of them, with his palms joined in respect. The Lord instantly removed the pearl necklace around his neck and held it in his hands to offer it to the Brahmin. At that point, the Brahmin said, 'Oh Lord of Dwaraka, I am not here to ask for charity. I am here only to see you. One may not understand the feeling of being blessed by meeting a selfless and valiant Kshatriya in person unless one is a Brahmin.' Saying thus, the contented Brahmin prostrated in front of both of them. Both of them pulled him up affectionately and bade farewell to him. I noticed that the Lord was lost in deep thought. After a few moments, he lovingly patted his brother's shoulders and muttered to himself, 'Brother Udho, finally the solution for Jarasandha's problem is in sight.' Then they both kept talking and I kept steering the chariot.

The very next day, the Lord travelled to Aanarta along with Uddhava Maharaja, in a ship with the Garudadhwaja chariot, crossing the creek of Dwaraka. I was with him, obviously, and so were chosen Yadava troops. We approached the borders of Indraprastha. As news of our arrival had been sent in advance, the Pandavas and their sons were present to welcome us, along with Kuntidevi and Draupadidevi. We came to the royal palace of the Pandavas. Dhaumya rishi came to visit the Lord. The Lord whispered in his ear, 'Dhaumya rishi, please train Bhimsena and Arjuna in the daily routine of a Brahmin with all its subtleties in a day or two with immediate effect. Leave no error in their training. No one had no clue as to what he was planning.

We stayed in the royal palace of the Pandavas in Indraprastha for an entire week. Whatever I came to know was indeed inconceivable. Only four of us were involved in the first phase of the scheme that the Lord had planned for the destruction of Jarasandha – wrestler Bhimsena, archer Arjuna, the Lord of Dwaraka himself and I.

I was perplexed on hearing the plan. Entering Jarasandha's war-hungry royal capital Girivraja as a group of four was like entering the jaws of death willingly. Jarasandha had forcibly captured and imprisoned eighty-six kings from nearby kingdoms in preparation of the Shatashirsha yajna of kings. Expert informers from Hastinapura, Indraprastha and Dwaraka used to enter the kingdom of Magadha to retrieve news from the kingdom, but never return. The royal capital Girivraja was located in a valley of seven mountain ranges. No one could get there. That was the place where the kings captured by Jarasandha were imprisoned.

The Lord himself had planned the scheme of taking only two of the Pandava warriors with him to Girivraja. We were to plant informers during each sojourn of the journey. All three warriors were going to drop their royal vesture and disguise themselves as Brahmins before entering Magadha. They were going to enter Girivraja as formally appointed priests of Kashi, invited by the Magadha king himself for the Shatarajashirsha yajna. I was to be disguised as a Magadha charioteer and would have to take them as close to the royal palace as possible. The three gallant warriors were tactfully going to collect information that no informer had been able to gather till date. I was going to stay in the Magadha stable itself. Once the task was completed, I was going to be informed. Then one day, I was supposed to present myself to the Magadha royal priest and deliver a message, 'Please send the three priests of Kashi back, as they are needed to perform an important ritual at the main ashrama in Kashi.' The three warriors were then going to leave Girivraja just as they had come. Then, the Indraprastha kingdom of the Pandavas, Dwaraka and their allies were going to unite. They were going to appeal to the citizens of the kingdoms of all those kings Jarasandha had captured, seek support from them and strike the final conclusive blow. This was the second phase of the campaign. The main goal was to release the eighty-six kings who had been imprisoned. For that purpose, it was essential to destroy Jarasandha.

Crossing the Yamuna, we entered the Panchala kingdom. Then, crossing rivers like the Ganga, the Gomati and the Sharayu, we reached

Mithila. This was our last sojourn before entering Magadha. This was the city of Janaka, the father-in-law of Srirama, who had been born a few generations ago. Jarasandha had captured the Videha king, a descendant of Janaka. The subjects of Videha were tired of waiting for him. The Videha commander and chief minister had asked the young prince to ascend the throne and were taking care of the kingdom.

Finally, we reached the borders of Magadha. As planned, I had disguised myself as a Magadha charioteer. I wore a brick-red large twisted turban on my head. In Mithila, we had already mastered the colloquial Magadha dialect. My Lord, Partha and mighty Bhimsena got dressed as Brahmin priests of Kashi, with sacred threads clearly visible on their chests. The three warriors looked completely different now, with bald heads except for small tufts of hair at the back, moustaches shaved completely and foreheads smeared with stripes of sandalwood paste. No citizen from Indraprastha would have recognised Arjuna and Bhimsena in this disguise. No one from Dwaraka could have recognised my Lord either. I, too, was getting confused when the two of them stood in front of me. Sometimes, I just could not figure out who my Lord was and who Arjuna was. The citizens of Mithila had gifted us a small chariot with five horses. We made sure to keep Bhimsena's huge mace, Arjuna's Gandiva bow and arrows, the Lord's Ajitanjaya and Sharanga bow and the Nandaka sword in the back of the chariot, hidden under covers. We passed by many Magadha surveillance posts on the way to Girivraja, playing our roles quite artfully. In Indraprastha itself, the Lord had outlined the protocol of conduct for this journey. The three of us were supposed to obey each and every word of his, not violating it even if our lives were in danger. We were not supposed to counter-question him. Girivraja was the invincible royal capital of the Magadhas located inside the natural ramparts of seven mountain ranges. All seven mountain ranges had surveillance posts with armed Magadha warriors. The gate on the eastern range was called Chittagiri. One could see wild cheetahs roaming around, roaring loudly even during broad daylight. The Shailagiri gate was located in the north and the Udayagiri gate in the south. The gate on the western side was called Sonagiri. Girivraja was surrounded by a river named Panakan. We went across the western mountain range known as Gorathagiri and arrived at the huge Sonagiri gate of Girivraja. This gate was even taller than the Shuddhaksha gate in Dwaraka. It was covered with sharp and strong iron nails. That is why it would not have been possible for even a couple of hundred mighty warriors to break it open by bashing it with huge Kikar wood pillars. Mammoth elephants could not have attacked the iron nails. The upper half was inscribed with images of a lion, a boar and wild buffaloes.

The moment we crossed this gate, we immediately began putting our plan into action. The three warriors descended from the chariot, climbed the tall staircase near the gate they reached and entered the great drum room with huge kettledrums. All of Girivraja suddenly reverberated with sounds of the kettledrums One of those drums sounded much louder, as if it were roaring and telling not just Girivraja but also the Magadha skies overhead, 'I have come! I am here!' Bhimsena, the son of Vayu, was beating that kettledrum.

The citizens of Girivraja had never heard such unusual cacophony of kettledrums before. Many scared citizens and curious soldiers gathered at the base of the drum room. They created a racket below since they could not understand how to climb the staircase leading to the drum room. Mighty Bhimsena had climbed last and blocked the entrance to the room with a huge boulder. Some soldier reported this to the four commanders of Jarasandha who were supposed to guard the four directions. They came to the base of the drum room carrying their wide-blade swords on their shoulders. Jarasandha was under the influence of liquor and engrossed in performances by female dancers in the inner chambers of his royal palace. As he heard the unnerving sound of the kettledrums, the chalice in his hand slipped and fell. With wide eyes, he commanded, 'Who is beating the drum in such a weird way? Bring him here.' The emperor's order reached the commanders. By this time, the four commanders had laboriously removed the boulder with the help of about a hundred soldiers.

All the four commanders were utterly confused, wondering why Brahmin priests would be saying, 'We have come from Kashi for the Shatashirsha yajna' while beating these drums so loudly. Within a short time, they presented the three Brahmins to their emperor. The emperor's inebriation had waned considerably now. He fixed his gaze on the mighty son of Vayu and asked him menacingly, 'Who are you, and why have you come here?'

The answer came from my Lord, in a scared, faltering voice, 'Oh Maharaja, we have come from the holy place of Kashi, hearing about the Shatashirsha yajna that you are going to perform. All three of us are well versed in the four Vedas. We know all the subtleties of the yajna rituals. If granted permission, we will smoothly perform the Maharaja's yajna with the precise rituals. We will accept whatever donation the Maharaja will offer and give our blessings to the Maharaja and his family and return to Kashi.'

'Then why did you beat the drums so loudly instead of meeting our royal priest?'

'Maharaja, we have heard the acclaim of your invincible glory in Kashi,' Arjuna said in between.

'Besides, we have been fortunate enough to attend many religious ceremonies of Maharaja Kansa in Mathura. This brother of mine beat the drums loudly so that news of our arrival would reach you directly without wasting time in formalities. It was a mistake indeed. Please forgive us. Though we are the masters of Dharma, this is the first time we are asking for anyone's forgiveness. It would unleash Rudra's wrath if the emperor himself does not forgive the Brahmins.' The Lord wove a web of charming words around the emperor in his enchanting sweet tongue, joining his palms together.

Whatever intoxication was left in Jarasandha's system vanished completely as he heard the name of his family deity Rudra, and yajna. Looking at his commanders disdainfully, Jarasandha roared, 'Do you think you have set a record by capturing these innocent Brahmins? Instead, if you had brought three kings to help complete the required number for the yajna, I would have felicitated you. Take them with you. They have come here from distant Kashi. Arrange for their lodging in the guest chambers. Go.'

Our campaign was set in motion smoothly. Bhimsena and Arjuna began meeting various troop leaders of the Magadha army under the pretext of the yajna and started gathering precise information. My Lord began charming people with his sweet talk and hence could roam around the imperial palace without any restrictions. His observant eyes detected the strengths of the Magadhas silently. The information that the three of them gathered was then conveyed to me. I began delivering that information to Satyaki and Anadhrishti through our informers planted in kingdoms like Mithila, Kampilyanagar and Kuntibhojpura. An entire week passed. Meanwhile, the Lord had befriended Jarasandha's son, Sahadeva. He had also got well acquainted with all major ministers in the Magadha ministry. The Lord, who readily gave references from all four Vedas and Upanishadas in Sanskrit during casual conversation, was revered by all. I would meet Arjuna in the morning, Bhimsena after lunch in the afternoon and the Lord at the time of evening prayers. Then we would whisper in our Saurashtriyan language and exchange information.

One fine morning, the Lord of Dwaraka conveyed that we would leave soon. We were to begin the second phase of the campaign. I temporarily bid farewell to the now – well-acquainted Magadha citizens, and told them, 'Our guru is going to perform a similar yajna in the original ashrama of Kashi. We will attend it and return in a fortnight.'

But…I will never forget the evening that descended on the mountain ranges of Girivraja that day. Jarasandha came to know that the three self-proclaimed priests from Kashi were secretly meeting troop leaders and roaming freely in the army, and he got suspicious. So, along with his minister and the four commanders, he arrived in person at the Magadha guest chamber.

As soon as he entered the guest chamber, he roared, 'Where is that runaway cowherd of Mathura, the one that duped me on Mount Gomanta? What kind of yajna is he going to perform here? I am going to commence my Shatashirsha yajna by chopping his head off. Till now, I have chased him up to Mathura and Mount Gomanta. Now, he has come into my clasp on his own. Commander, present him to me, along with his companions.' One of the commanders went to the inner chamber and pulled the three priests of Kashi outside.

The emperor of Magadha stood in front of Arjuna first, and shouted, 'Tell the truth. Who are you? Are you a citizen of Kashi or Indraprastha?'

Archer Arjuna courageously answered, 'I am a priest of Kashi, here for the emperor's yajna as instructed by my guru.'

At that point, the emperor moved forward, caught Arjuna's right hand and pointing to his right thumb and index finger, roared, 'What are those calluses on your hand? Did you get those by offering grass bundles in yajnas? Liar, you are the self-proclaimed archer – the insignificant younger brother of Yudhishthira of Indraprastha.' The emperor tossed Arjuna's hand away in contempt, and holding the sacred thread on his chest tightly, he shook him violently and burst out, 'You, childish archer of Indraprastha, are you ready to fight a deadly duel with this emperor?'

'Certainly. If my guru permits me to do so.' Courageous Arjuna answered calmly while straightening the sacred thread that had been crumpled.

Then the emperor stood in front of Bhimsena and, pointing to a blotch on his naked right shoulder that was caused by carrying the mace, shouted, 'What is this black patch on your shoulder? Is that caused by carrying baskets of sacrificial sticks for yajnas? Who are you fooling, you voracious Bhima of Indraprastha? Are you ready for the duel?' He pulled the shawl that Bhimsena had wrapped around his neck and questioned him.

Bhimsena grabbed the throat of the emperor standing in front of him violently. He could not control his anger, just as he could not control his hunger. The Lord of Dwaraka pulled Bhimsena's hand back and, smiling as usual, said to the emperor, 'Oh valiant warrior, the one who captured eighty-six innocent kings for a yajna sacrifice in spite of being a king himself! You self-proclaimed invincible warrior beating your own drums throughout Aaryavarta, I am the one who is your actual culprit – son of Vasudeva, Srikrishna of the Yadavas. Are you going to challenge me too to a duel?'

My Lord had cast a question to him, anticipating his answer fully well. He had quickly whispered in Bhimsena's ear while Jarasandha was challenging Arjuna for a duel and told him, 'When I stroke the Vaijayanti garland, take the clue and challenge him to a duel.'

That insolent emperor who attacked Mathura seventeen times to destroy the Lord said haughtily, 'I will not spare your life today, you lowlife cowherd who killed my son-in-law. Not just you, in fact all three of you will not be able to get out of Girivraja now. You wicked, black leader of the cowherds – yes, I challenge you to the ultimate duel. My ancestors will not get salvation unless you are killed.' He thumped his shoulders in front of my Lord. This was a critical moment since we arrived in the kingdom of the Magadhas. Even at this moment, the Lord smiled and said, 'Is the king going to fight the duel with all three of us at once or what? Or should I say that the king does not even know the basic rule of a duel?'

Jarasandha was a bit confused. Yet in a loud voice, he asked, 'What rule are you talking about, cowherd?'

'The rule is that a deadly duel can be fought only between two people at a time. I am ready to fight a duel with you.' The Lord stroked the Vaijayanti garland around his neck with a smile. Now Bhimsena, who was fuming and waiting precisely for this moment, came forward and thundered, 'What kind of an invincible wrestler and emperor is this? He calls you a runaway, but he himself is a big runaway – what else did he do on Mount Gomanta? I, Bhimsena, the son of Kunti, challenge him to the ultimate duel. He will accept it if at all he is the emperor that he claims to be and if he has the power that he boasts of. Or else, he should just surrender and accept defeat.'

Fuming and grinding his teeth, Bhimsena thumped his well-toned muscular arms, hard like steel and shouted, 'Hail Goddess Ida! Kuntimata! Goddess Bhavani!'

No one had ever looked in the eye of Jarasandha of the Magadhas and directly challenged him. Fretting with uncontrollable fury, Jarasandha thumped his arms and gave a counter-challenge in a roaring voice, 'You glutton of Indraprastha, I accept your challenge!' Meanwhile, Bhimsena had already thrown away the shawl wrapped around his neck. He tucked in his red-bordered dhoti and was at the ready. The muscles of his burly thighs twitched. Both wrestlers retreated a few steps to prepare for the stance before the attack. Now both of them looked like stocky, bellowing bulls.

The Lord had unmistakably caught Jarasandha in his web. Jarasandha had accepted the provocative challenge of Bhimsena.

No one could tell what was going to happen next. Both wrestlers, with drops of sweat on their foreheads, were going to transform the guest chamber into a wrestling pit. They began to dare each other while thumping their arms and thighs.

Immediately, the Lord of Dwaraka moved forward, stood firmly in between both of them and smilingly said, 'Both of you are master wrestlers. Both of you know very well the consequences of a duel – either victory or death. It should not be fought like the daily practice.

'For that, a formal wrestling pit should be prepared in front of the royal palace of Girivraja. Seating arrangements should be made for the Magadha citizens to watch the bout. Expert judges should be appointed to announce an impartial decision in this historical fight. Therefore, both of you will have to wait till tomorrow morning. It is not about what you wish. These are the fixed rules of a wrestling bout.'

The emperor of Magadha was arrogant but when he heard my Lord's irrefutable words, he calmed down a bit. The news that Bhimsena, the son of Vayu, and Jarasandha, the Magadha emperor, were going to fight a conclusive duel spread like wildfire not only in Girivraja but throughout the Magadha kingdom.

Next day, began rising, the populous ocean of Magadha men and women assembled around the wrestling pit in front of the royal palace of Girivraja, to witness the thrilling, breathtaking, historic duel. A racket of varied noises burst out. As the citizens of Mathura were fed up of Kansa's injustice, so also the citizens of Magadha were sick and tired of Jarasandha's atrocious, brutal regime. Around the wrestling pit in the section for royalty, Kansa's wives Asti and Prapti were sitting with their select attendants. Young prince Sahadeva, who had courageously stood up against his own father's unjust regime, was also present. It was because of this resistance that he had been disregarded in his father's kingdom. The troop leaders of Jarasandha's mammoth army were moving around among the assembled crowd with weapons like swords, maces and pestles. Though they were more in number, they were unable to stop the chattering of the crowd even for a moment. This day was indeed going to be an unforgettable day in this royal capital. Invincible emperor, unequalled wrestler Jarasandha, the son of Brihadratha, stood in front of his royal circle, facing the west. He was wearing only a brick-red loincloth. The sinewy muscles of his calves, thighs, shoulders and burly chest had been massaged with oil; they were glistening and wiggling smoothly in place like a coiled snake. He warmed up his body by doing a few squats. It made the muscles in his entire body expand, just like a lump of clay expands in water. This was indeed a rare sight for all. He hailed the name of his family deity, shouted loudly and demonstrated his vigour. His widened eyes were breathing fire and he was staring at Bhima with utter contempt. The sight of his massive body was indeed horrendous.

The Lord of Dwaraka was sitting on a somewhat taller wooden seat in front of me. Archer Dhananjaya was sitting on his left. Both of them were still dressed as Brahmins. Still, their indomitable self-confidence and radiant faces captured the attention of thousands. I stood behind them. Just like everybody else, I was extremely curious to see the final result of the duel.

We were on the west side of the wrestling pit, facing Bhimsena. We were facing the east. Even we had not seen our 'wrestler' Bhimsena like this before. His complexion, like a ripe lemon, was glistening spectacularly due to a coat of oil. The toned muscles of his calves, thighs, shoulders and chest were contracting and expanding with even the slightest movement.

He did a few squats to warm up his steely strong body. His body began expanding within moments. He looked almost twice his regular size. He moved forward and leapt inside the pit. He circled around the pit and humbly bowed to the citizens of Magadha. A roar of applause followed from all sides after the display of his humility.

Bhimsena roared in a sky-piercing voice, 'Hail Kuntimata, hail Goddess Bhavani!', and challenged Jarasandha, thumping his arms loudly. Jarasandha also thumped his arms.

The five chief priests handed some soil to both the wrestlers to indicate the commencement of the duel. They moved away immediately. Again, the sounds of thumping thighs and arms rose from both sides. The heads of both the wrestlers, round like pumpkins, met each other. Both gave hard blows on each other's necks, trying to assess the strength of the other. A thrilling, hair-raising wrestling war had begun. The ruckus quietened, everyone held their breaths and innumerable people became witness to this war.

It was the first day of the lunar fortnight in the month of Kartika. The dense fog that had covered Girivraja had now completely lifted. One question still lingered in my mind – what could be Jarasandha's political motive behind accepting the challenge? He had not insisted on fighting this bout with Arjuna or my Lord. He was convinced that Bhimsena was the main protective armour of the remaining two. He had full confidence in his wrestling. On the strength of that, as soon as he had broken that protective armour, he wanted to arrest Arjuna and my Lord. Then he was going to dispatch an envoy to Indraprastha and Dwaraka with a special message, 'If you want to see your black cowherd and his disciple alive, then both your kings – Yudhishthira and Vasudeva – should come to Girivraja in person.' Both of them were crowned kings, and therefore fit to be sacrificed in his yajna. Yudhishthira, the king of Indraprastha, and our Maharaja Vasudevababa would have been compelled to come to Girivraja after hearing this message, as they both loved Arjuna and my Lord. Once they arrived in Girivraja, he was simply going to put them in the prison where he had kept other captured kings, to complete the required number of kings for his Yajna.

The sun was shining right overhead now. First, the cacophony of the Magadha kettledrums arose. As the referee moved quickly out of their way, the two master wrestlers began their gripping fight like two roaring lions. They began fighting, thumping their thighs in between and grabbing each other's thick necks in strong grips.

They spent the entire first day employing a few chosen manoeuvres only. As the flaming red sun, as big as a platter, touched the mountain summit on the west of Girivraja, the referee blew a huge conch facing the sky. It was the signal of the end of the day. Both wrestlers came to their senses only after hearing the conch a couple of times, and separated.

The next day, at daybreak, the wrestling bout resumed amidst the cacophony of kettledrums, tabors and trumpets. The news of the previous day had spread throughout the Magadha kingdom. As a result, more men and women were present. The moment the heads of both wrestlers collided, the chatter in the audience died down. Both of them thoroughly knew each other's strengths now. They cautiously avoided yesterday's mistakes. Grinding their teeth, biting their lips and shouting loudly, they attacked each other using different strategies. Now the audience was automatically divided into two groups – the supporters of Bhima and the supporters of Jarasandha. They were going berserk, alternatively shouting various encouragements to inspire their chosen wrestler. All eyes were fixed on both of them. Even today, as evening descended on the wrestling pit in front of the royal palace of Girivraja, the wrestling bout remained inconclusive.

Not a day or two, this combat continued for thirteen consecutive days. The number of spectators kept growing every day, just like the rising water of River Shona in the great flood. It not only filled the arena around the wrestling pit but also the area outside. As usual, as if out of habit, the moment the heads of the wrestlers collided, the cacophony of various instruments that were being played since dawn would stop instantly. I wondered about only one thing – even though Bhimsena and Jarasandha were tenaciously fighting each other for the last thirteen days, neither of them looked even a bit tired or exhausted. All the five referees looked exhausted now after continuously covering the sweaty bodies of Jarasandha and Bhimsena with sweat-absorbing ash.

The thirteenth day also turned out to be inconclusive. Every household in the royal city had only one thing to discuss – the inconclusive, long-drawn battle and who was likely to be the winner. Every night, in the guest chamber, I got to view a rare scene that nobody else could ever get an opportunity to watch. Every day, the Lord of Dwaraka would demonstrate to Bhimsena where he fell short in the duel on that day. Listening to him, Bhimsena would widen his large eyes and say, 'Srikrishna, you are talking exactly like my gurudeva, Balarama. I have never seen you practise wrestling, then where did you learn all this from?' The Lord would then smile and say, 'You will have to go to Gokul to know that, and meet Kelinandakaka.' During this time, Arjuna, who would be rubbing Bhimsena's feet with oil, would listen attentively to both of them. After a cold bath for about half an hour, scraping off the layers of soil and ash on his body with a stone chip, a frazzled Bhimsena would lie on his bed, close his eyes and just start snoring. The Lord of Dwaraka and I would rub his shoulders, thighs and chest on each side. That would escalate the rhythm of his snoring. The Lord of Dwaraka would shake him vigorously and try to wake him up at midnight. But he would only turn to his other side and ignore him. Then the Lord would tell me to fetch the Paanchajanya conch that would be wrapped in a cloth and hung on a hook on the wall. He would look at me, wink and, with a smile, blow the conch loudly. Immediately, the snoring Bhima would wake up. Looking at his own body, he would realise that his cousin, the Lord of Dwaraka himself, had massaged his body. He would feel ashamed and say with childlike shyness, 'Srikrishna, if you massage my body again, I will not fight this duel at all. I will simply surrender and accept defeat.' The Lord would say to Bhimsena, 'It may be okay for you, Bhimsena, but not for me! I have to get many things done from you. Besides, Draupadi – the beloved wife of all you brothers – is my sister, my friend. Would she accept it?'

Bhimsena would shake his head in negation. Then my Lord would hold a large pot full of a cold, sweet, nourishing drink prepared by him. Holding the pot in his hands, Bhimsena would guzzle it, his Adam's apple bobbing up and down. He would then laugh loudly. The Lord of Dwaraka would let Bhimsena finish his drink and then teasingly say, 'Hmmm… Bhimsena, I see that from your gurudeva you have also picked up this art of laughing in an unrestrained fashion while throwing your head back.' During this campaign of Girivraja, I came to witness anew a couple of qualities in the Lord. He would never lose his unwavering spirit and his fresh sense of humour, no matter how tough the situation was. My Lord always believed in doing his duty – without any expectations.

The fourteenth day of the sensational wrestling duel dawned. The duel began amidst thunderous sounds of thigh-thumping and loud challenges. Bhimsena and Jarasandha collided against each other, roaring loudly like two intoxicated wild elephants. Though lakhs of spectators had gathered, there was utter silence. Both of them used new manoeuvres today that they had not used before and reserved only for special occasions.

Lakhs of spectators watched their subtle moves without even blinking an eye. With the hour, the rivalry intensified. Spectators had started whispering amongst themselves, 'Is this duel ever going to end?' The sun had now descended to the third quarter of the day. Even the five judges who were tired after continuously putting fistfuls of ashes on their bodies were sitting in a squatting position in the wrestling pit, wherever they could find a place.

The Magadha chief minister whispered in Prince Sahadeva's ear, 'We should bring chosen wrestlers of the royal circle in the wrestling pit one by one, get them to surround Bhimsena and imprison him directly. Otherwise, something dreadful will happen here, just like it happened in Mathura in case of Maharaja Kansa.' The Magadha ministers seconded him, saying, 'The chief minister is right. The chosen wrestlers should be brought to the pit immediately.'

The sun was about to set now. The Lord of Dwaraka immediately noticed the restlessness among the Magadha royal circle. He stood up and gently caressed the Vaijayanti garland pulsing on the shawl around his neck. In the last fourteen days, Bhimsena had not bothered to glance at anybody except the Lord of Dwaraka whenever he could steal a moment. He understood the meaning of this action. All at once, Bhima stopped his nimble actions as if struck by lightning, and let Jarasandha attack him. Jarasandha was duped, and felt that Bhimsena was tired and burnt out. He moved lithely and touched his huge back to Bhimsena's chest, dripping with sweat. With the Rajakaprushtha manoeuvre, he threw Bhimsena's mammoth body on to the soil with a loud thud. I stood up at once on seeing that. The entire field full of spectators too had the same reaction. Some of them felt sorry for him and moaned with grief, while others tossed their Magadha turbans in the air and shouted ecstatically, 'Hail Magadha emperor, invincible wrestler, Maharaja Jarasandha! Victory to you always, victory…victory!' Arjuna was already out of his seat. Seeing his dear brother caught up in a critical situation, he began breaking into the wrestling pit in a fit of rage. The Lord grabbed his shoulders and with great effort held him back. Meanwhile, Jarasandha reached Bhimsena, who was lying deathly still. He held both of Bhimsena's legs in his strong hands and began pushing them apart with all his might. At that moment, Arjun screamed with unbearable rage, as if his own life was at stake, 'Srikrishna…let me go! He is going to split my brother into two.' The Lord of Dwaraka glared at Arjun and said in a very quiet voice, 'Dhananjaya, just watch what happens. Be witness to this historic duel. I am also compelled to do the same. Bhimsena is not Jarasandha to lose and back off.'

Jarasandha could not stretch Bhimsena's legs apart even an iota, as Bhimsena had gathered all his strength into his thighs. For a moment, Jarasandha got confused and stopped to wipe the sweat off his forehead. He was inattentive. At that exact moment, Bhimsena moved swiftly like a fish, and crossed his legs around Jarasandha in a scissor-like hold. He wrenched Jarasandha so hard that he fell face down in the soil. The Lord of Dwaraka was waiting for exactly this moment. He pulled out the Paanchjanya from the shawl around his waist and, raising his head high, blew the auspicious conch. Taking a cue from that, Bhimsena tightened his arm around Jarasandha's neck in the deadly Bahukantaka manoeuvre. Bhimsena closed his eyes tight and continuously increased the pressure of his steely strong arms in the decisive Bahukantaka hold. Jarasandha's words were muffled; he was rolling his eyes and struggling in the soil in the wrestling pit. The Paanchjanya kept reverberating in the air. The spectators did not even realise when the invincible Magadha emperor died.

Bhimsena let go of the Bahukantaka hold on the lifeless throat and stood up at once like a streak of lightning. Uncontrollable cheers erupted from all sides, 'Hail Pandu's son, invincible wrestler Bhimsena…victory…victory! Hail Bhimsena, the son of Kunti!'

In the wrestling pit, Bhimsena was roaring, dancing on one foot, 'Hail Gurudeva Balarama…victory…victory! Hail Kuntimata, Goddess Ida Bhavani!' The three of us started running towards Bhimsena. The sun set on the mountain summit of Girivraja. As soon as Jarasandha was defeated, my Lord's face turned radiant. Everybody was curious to see what steps he was going to take next. It was mandatory to follow royal custom, since Jarasandha was Kansa's father-in-law, and therefore a relative. His body could not be cremated unless his successor had been formally announced. Therefore, the Lord invited Sahadeva, the terrified son of Jarasandha, by reassuring him through the chief minister. He announced Sahadeva as the successor of Magadha in the wrestling pit itself. While advising him, the Lord said, 'Sahadeva, we have no enmity against the kingdom of Magadha. We are against unjust and vicious attitudes in general.

'Soon, the Pandavas of Indraprastha will perform the Rajasuya yajna. You are to dispatch a gift suitable to the status of the Magadha empire, consisting of attendants, useful animals, wealth and foodgrains along with us right away. You yourself should cordially attend the yajna. Who knows, maybe you will form a blood relation with the Pandavas? You may have to support them with your army in the future.'

Sahadeva was expecting a harsh punishment for himself like his father. Instead of that, when he received complete impunity and invaluable advice, he was overwhelmed with emotion, forgetting the grief of his father's death. He grabbed my Lord's feet and sobbed momentarily with mixed emotions. The kind-hearted Lord pulled him up and embraced him. He signalled to me and Arjuna to get going and, holding Sahadeva's hand in his, started walking. The ecstatic Magadha citizens were bathing Bhimsena in showers of vermilion. As the Lord gestured, Bhima broke the loving circle of his fans and approached the Lord. Arjuna embraced Bhima tightly. The Magadha chief minister carried Jarasandha's corpse with the help of some attendants and moved aside. Bhimsena put his mace at the feet of the Lord. When he tried to bend down to prostrate in front of the Lord, despite being senior in age, the Lord prevented him from doing so and embraced him tightly with great pride. That made the vermilion on Bhima's body spread on the bluish body of the Lord. His body looked like the crimson blue sky on an autumn evening. Ecstatic Magadha citizens cheered, 'Hail sons of Kunti – Bhima and Arjuna…victory…victory! Hail Devaki's son Maharaja Srikrishna…victory…victory! Hail Nanda–Yashoda's son, the Lord of Dwaraka…victory…victory! Hail Vasudeva's son Bhagwan Vasudeva…victory…victory!' The Lord was surrounded by both the Pandavas, the Magadha commanders and ministers, and many sentimental Magadha citizens who were drawn to him. I also walked alongside, my chest puffed up with pride. I had just witnessed a historic event taking place for the first time in Aaryavarta.

We arrived in front of the tightly sealed prison of Magadha. Everyone stopped short, looking at the huge lock hanging on the prison door. The Lord deliberately glanced at Bhimsena. Moving forward, Bhima struck just one powerful blow of the mace on the lock. All the imprisoned kings were now free.

All the prisoner kings, wearing the uniform of Magadha prisoners, could not believe that they were free and kept staring at their emancipator, who was walking briskly towards them. They all automatically gathered in the prison square. Many of them touched my Lord's feet and touched their foreheads with the soil beneath with gratitude. A couple of kings amongst them were very old. They brought their palms together and implored the Lord, saying, 'Oh Lord of Dwaraka, Vasudeva, we had heard your acclaim disseminating through the universe. Today, we have got to see you in person. Our eyes feel blessed. Now do us a favour and make our ears feel blessed too.' As the Lord raised his hand, all the kings sat on the ground in front of a stone platform. My Lord walked slowly and climbed on to the platform. For a few moments, he moved his glance, which was an ocean of love, over everyone.

His face glowed. His melodious speech began flowing, thrilling even the stone walls of the Magadha prison.

'Dear kings of various kingdoms of Aaryavarta. You have experienced first-hand how horrible an innocent prisoner's life can be. You have suffered the unbearable imprisonment of your valour. Power is like a double-edged weapon. It can be used for constructive as well as destructive purposes. The emperor of Magadha imprisoned you under the delusion of being invincible. He was going to brutally sacrifice all of you on the altar of the Shatashirsha yajna once your number reached hundred!' The mere utterance of these words from the Lord's mouth aroused restless murmurs among the kings. The Lord further said without letting the unrest intensify, 'What kind of yajna is this? What if it had indeed become a reality? I know well that none of you are afraid of death. But what would have happened to your subjects after your death? It is my duty to go wherever life gets stuck in one place. It is my life's mission to release life whenever it is obstructed. You are free from today. The credit of this valiant feat goes to our wrestler, warrior Bhima.'

My Lord possessed an innate quality – that of solving any problem. He looked at Sahadeva standing next to him, and said, 'This is Maharaja Sahadeva – the emperor of Magadha. He will provide each one of you with a chariot full of provisions, wealth and weapons, and a charioteer along with it. Once you reach your kingdom, I am sure you will surely send royal gifts to the Indraprastha kingdom of Bhimsena. I am sure that you will remember your emancipation and the bond of friendship which has been formed with Indraprastha as a result. Keeping that gratitude in your heart, you will offer instant support to them whenever needed. On behalf of the Dwaraka kingdom, I offer you best wishes for your future life. May all be well.' He stopped talking while we all wished that his speech would continue.

The next day, the Lord went to the outskirts of Magadha along with Maharaja Sahadeva and bade farewell to all the kings who were departing in different directions.

My Lord's campaign of Magadha had been successfully executed. We stayed in Girivraja for an entire week. When we left Girivraja, millions of Magadha men and women, along with Maharaja Sahadeva, saw us off. A row of bullock carts full of various gifts from the people of Magadha followed our chariot. When we had come to Magadha, the Lord and both Pandavas were dressed as Brahmins. Now, they were wearing fine royal costumes. I was dressed in the uniform of Dwaraka's charioteer.

The execution of Jarasandha spread the acclaim of our Dwaraka and the Pandavas' Indraprastha kingdom throughout Aaryavarta. The major obstacle in the path of the Pandavas' Rajasuya yajna had been removed. After enjoying the hospitality of the Pandavas in Indraprastha for a week, we returned to Dwaraka. On our way back, the Lord was welcomed by the kings and subjects of all kingdoms who had breathed a sigh of relief due to Jarasandha's execution. But the welcome that the Lord received in Dwaraka was the grandest. Jarasandha's execution was an accomplishment even bigger and more significant than the killing of Kansa. That is why, to welcome the Lord, Maharaja Vasudeva had arrived in person at the Shuddhaksha gate, along with both rajmatas. The Lord's seven queens were also present, along with Rukminidevi. Youthful and handsome Pradyumna stood at the gate with a fistful of Prajakta flowers, along with my son Daruki, with both commanders and ministers standing behind them. The eighty sons of the Lord's eight queens stood behind them. Golden-bordered grand pennants with the Garuda emblem fluttered atop all four gates. Arches thickly decorated with assorted flowers were raised everywhere. The men and women of Dwaraka had donned dresses reserved for special occasions and chattered with unending exuberance. Prince Balarama approached the Lord holding a coconut that was covered in golden strings. As soon as he saw the royal circle standing in front of him, the Lord walked briskly towards them and touched the feet of all the elders. The Lord accepted the coconut offered by Dada with shining eyes, and began to bend down to seek his blessings.

Dada did not allow him to do so, held him in a deep embrace and muttered, 'You took me with you to Mathura at the time of the Dhanuryaga for the killing of Kansa. This time you avoided me. Yet, victory is mine. After all, it was my disciple Bhimsena who killed Jarasandha.'

The Lord smiled playfully while releasing himself from Dada's tight embrace, and said to him, 'It is true that your disciple Bhimsena killed Jarasandha, but it is also equally true that he is the elder brother of Arjuna, who is our Subhadra's husband.' Both brothers laughed loudly at the perfect answer and embraced each other again.

Revatidevi welcomed the Lord with bright lamps and a smiling face. With eyes much brighter than those lamps, Rukminidevi welcomed him.

These celebrations of victory went on for an entire week. One day a disciple of Dhaumya rishi arrived at Dwaraka along with the chief minister of the Pandavas to deliver an invitation for the Rajasuya yajna. The yajna was going to take place in Indraprastha but the hustle and bustle began in Dwaraka, on the shores of the western ocean.

Select men and women were supposed to go with the Lord and Rukminidevi for the Rajasuya yajna. Obviously, Balaramadada was included in the list with Revatidevi. Uddhava Maharaja, Chief Minister Vipruthu, Minister Akrura, and from the younger generation, Samba, Brahmagargya and my son Daruki were also included.

Thousands of people gathered to bid us farewell. About a month later, we arrived at the Avanti kingdom. This was the kingdom of Mitravindadevi. The attitude of her brothers, Vinda and Anuvinda, had simmered down a bit by now, after the Lord's acclaim had spread in all four directions. They came to the borders of the Avanti kingdom to welcome the Lord. From Avanti, we crossed the river Charmanvati and entered into the Kuntibhoja kingdom. This was where Kuntidevi had lived in her childhood. We came to the royal edifice in the palace where she had served the short-tempered, whimsical sage Durvasa for a particular yajna. All five Pandava brothers came to the border to receive us when we reached Indraprastha. Rajmata Kuntidevi, Maharani Draupadidevi and our own Subhadradevi, along with Naga daughter Uloopidevi and the daughter of Manipura – Chitrangadadevi – also accompanied them.

The royal capital Indraprastha gave us an unprecedented grand welcome. All the royal paths and squares in the kingdom were fully occupied by invitees from various places. The fame of the five Pandava brothers had spread throughout Aaryavarta due to their victorious conquests. Their royal priest, Dhaumya rishi, had gone to Himavana and invited many sages and hermits from various ashramas to Indraprastha. A grand pandal was raised on the confluence of the rivers Ikshumati and the Yamuna for the Rajasuya yajna. Indraprastha, as the name denoted, had indeed surpassed the divine royal city of Indra.

The capacious pandal, about one yojana in circumference, was skilfully erected on many pillars. My Lord examined the entire yajna pandal with keen eyes. He said to Maharaja Yudhishthira, 'Oh venerable Pandava, your yajna is going to achieve such renown in Aaryavarta as never before. There are no flaws at all.'

In the Lord's heart, River Yamuna was associated with cherished precious memories. In the evening, he climbed down the neat ghat on the Yamuna to offer daily oblations. I was with him too. A few people like Uddhava Maharaja, Dhaumya rishi and Gargamuni also accompanied us. The Lord entered the Yamuna. He was wearing only a yellow vesture around his waist. Uddhava Maharaja followed him in.

Both of them offered oblations to the evening sun. While everyone was coming out of the waters with a contented mind, a long-feathered peacock alighted on a Kadamba tree nearby, fluttering its wings. It gave out a cry that attracted everyone's attention. At that moment, the Lord and Uddhava Maharaja glanced at each other and smiled sweetly. I surmised that the Lord must have smiled thinking of the peacock feather that he always wore in his crown. Only both of them knew what the truth was.

I scurried down the steps in order to offer my services to my Lord to get dressed. At that moment, he smiled sweetly as usual and said, 'Daruka, this is Kalindidevi's parental home. I will visit them once. Just remind me about that.'

The Lord left for an important meeting after finishing the evening worship rituals. Only Uddhava Maharaja was with him. Balaramadada was still occupied in the pandal with his disciple Bhimsena in making arrangements for the invited kings. Word was Maharishi Vyasa had arrived with his disciples and was staying in the special settlement of thatched huts erected far away on the banks of the Yamuna. He was visiting Indraprastha many years after the coronation of Maharaja Yudhishthira. He was accompanied by his wife, Mata Ghrutachidevi, for this all-important yajna.

I drove our chariot to the front of the thatched hut settlement of Maharishi. He and his wife were standing in front of the main hut to welcome the Lord.

With affection, the maharishi took both the brothers by their hands and guided them inside the hut. He sat on a raised seat covered with a grass mat. His wife sat on his left, but on the ground, on another mat. Clad in fine royal attire, both the exceptionally handsome Yadava brothers stood in front of them with their palms joined. As the maharishi signalled, they sat on grass mats. The disciples of maharishi stood wherever they could find a place. I also stood among them.

First, Maharishi enquired about the well-being of Maharaja Vasudeva, Devakimata and Rohinimata. Then the three of them had a profound discussion on various subjects such as royal precepts, justice–injustice, truth and untruth, and proper respect for womanhood. Even the maharishi's wife participated in those discussions. While concluding the visit, Maharishi Vyasa said, 'Yadunandana Srikrishna, this Rajasuya yajna of the Pandavas is indeed going to be a memorable event. The eldest Pandava asked for my recommendation about who should be bestowed with the honour of Agrapooja in the yajna. Who else is suitable for this task but you? I have full faith that with your blessings and your Agrapooja, this Rajasuya yajna of the Pandavas will be accomplished properly without any obstacles. You will certainly take care of any problem, if at all that arises.' Maharishi Vyasa smiled earnestly, reminding us of Acharya Sandipani.

The day of the Rajasuya yajna dawned. The pennant of Hastinapura fluttered on the army camp of the contingent which had come from there. Prince Duryodhana and a few of his select brothers, the king of Anga – Karna – his brother Shona and his commander and chief minister Shakuni Mama and a few of his brothers, and the royal adviser Kanaka had arrived from Hastinapura. Grandsire Bhishma and Mahatma Vidura had come along with Vrishavarma, the chief minister of the Kurus. My Lord was staying in the royal palace of the Pandavas, along with Rukminidevi. Both of them knew beforehand that they were going to have to perform various rituals as part of the Agrapooja. Therefore, they had taken a holy bath and were fasting – without consuming even a sip of water.

From the camp of the Kurus, Grandsire Bhishma and Mahatma Vidura visited the Lord after completing their morning rituals. Panchala king Drupada and Dhrishtadyumna also paid a visit. Notably, Rukmi, the prince of Kundinpura, who had learnt his lesson after the killing of Jarasandha, had also come with his brothers. The Lord's best friend, Sudama, had also arrived from Sudampuri along with his wife.

As news of the Mayasabha, which Maya had constructed in front of the royal palace of the Pandavas, had spread across all camps, huge crowds of spectators were drawn to it. They were wonderstruck after watching the miraculous optical and auditory illusions that Maya had created.

The news of a peculiar incident reached the Lord's pavilion as evening approached. Duryodhana, who had visited the royal palace out of curiosity to take a look at the Mayasabha, had been humiliated. Due to optical illusions, he had mistaken a water pond for a floor carpet and fallen into it in front of everyone. Karna had helped him recover and pulled him out of the pond. While this was happening, the Pandavas' wife Draupadidevi had ridiculed Duryodhana from the balcony. Duryodhana had got furious when he had come to know about it later.

We came out of the inner chambers. All five Pandavas were waiting outside. Rukminidevi arrived from the ladies' chambers, surrounded by maidservants. She was wearing a light orange attire. She was also looking radiant. As the prince of the Yadavas, Balaramadada ascended the chariot along with Revatidevi.

Ahead of all, I took a seat as the charioteer of the Garudadhwaja chariot. In the back of the chariot sat the Lord, Rukminidevi, and his brother Uddhava Maharaja.

I steered the chariot to the main entrance on the eastern side. Dhaumya rishi approached the Lord with his palms joined. The Lord descended from the chariot, smiling, and affectionately held Dhaumya rishi's right hand in his own. Maharishi Vyasa stood behind Dhaumya rishi, smiling gently. The Lord humbly touched their feet and took their blessings.

He began walking slowly and steadily towards the yajna pandal, bowing gently to all. Many auspicious musical instruments played in unison at that time. His blue body, like the blue Anjani flower, was dazzling in the soft rays of the setting sun. As soon as we entered the yajna pandal, Grandsire Bhishma approached the Lord immediately along with Yudhishthira and took him in a deep embrace. Draupadidevi and the other Pandava wives welcomed both of them with lamps. On behalf of the Kurus, Sanjaya and Mahatma Vidura put thick white lotus garlands around their necks. Both of them touched the feet of the rajmata with humility and sought her blessings. Everybody in the pandal arose automatically out of respect now. Only two people continued to sit – Chedi king Shishupala and Kaurava prince Duryodhana.

Maharaja Yudhishthira seated the Lord and Rukminidevi on the golden royal seats near the yajna altar. I remained standing behind them. After the Lord took his seat, everybody in the pandal sat down. Now the sages and hermits sat in the Padmasana pose on their tiger-skin mats. Maharishi Vyasa sat right at the front, on a separate high seat.

Maharaja Yudhishthira stood near the yajna pit and started speaking, 'Respected Maharishi Vyasdeva, Mata Rukminidevi, Bhagwan Vasudeva Srikrishna, honourable Uddhavadeva, venerable Grandsire Bhishma, Yadava prince Balarama, motherly Revatidevi, Gurudeva Drona and Kripacharya, Kuru prince Duryodhana, Shakuni Mama, Karna, the king of Anga, Chedi king Shishupala, Madra king Shalya Mama, honourable sages, invited kings and citizens! On behalf of my brothers, I cordially welcome you all to Indraprastha with a great deal of happiness. We are performing this yajna for the prosperity and peace of our kingdom. It is our great fortune that Bhagwan Srikrishna is present here today with his wife as the yajnavetta of this grand yajna. Maharishi Vyasadeva, who is not partaking in any of the yajna rituals, has come here today along with his wife only to give us his blessings. As the formally crowned king of Indraprastha, on today's auspicious day, I am going to wash the feet of the yajnavetta couple as part of the commencing rituals. The first holy sacrificial stick of bela will be offered in the yajna fire at the auspicious hands of the yajnavetta in your presence. I have confidence and full faith that with your blessings, our Indraprastha kingdom will scale new heights.'

Agnihotri rishi incanted the mantras. Pandava Maharaja Yudhishthira indicatively glanced at his chief minister. He brought a golden jar full of water made auspicious by the chanting of mantras, from various rivers of Aaryavarta, and a big golden platter. Yudhishthira himself put the golden platter at the feet of the Lord; gently picked them up and put them in the platter. After washing the feet of the yajnavetta, the king of Indraprastha sipped a few drops like holy water. He gently wiped the Lord's blue feet with his exclusive, fine royal garment with ardent devotion. He also washed the feet of Rukminidevi.

The Lord arose from his seat amidst the escalating chant of mantras. Rukminidevi followed him, and both of them walked towards the yajna pit. The Lord glanced around the yajna pandal. In the next instant, he smiled and bent to pick up a small bunch of bela sticks.

Rukminidevi touched his hand holding the sacrificial yajna sticks. The Lord muttered something and was about to offer the sacrificial sticks into the yajna pit when the Chedi king Shishupala, sitting in the section of invited kings, suddenly stood up. He pulled up the huge mace in his hand and put it on his shoulder. He objected loudly, 'Stop…!'

Everybody stared at him, terrified and shocked. He looked around the pandal. Finally, his eyes locked with those of Maharaja Yudhishthira. With flared nostrils, he roared loudly, 'Oh Yudhishthira, descendant of the highly esteemed Kuru dynasty, how come you honoured this lowlife son of a cowherd to be the yajnavetta of this grand yajna? Yudhishthira, have you invited all the valiant Kshatriyas of Aaryavarta only to humiliate them?'

Balaramadada, Bhima, Arjuna and Satyaki stood up in fury, brandishing their weapons.

The Lord threw the bunch of sacrificial sticks back on to the pile and with a mere gesture of the hand, restrained all of them.

Shishupala, who noticed that nobody was objecting, walked briskly towards the yajna altar, leaving his seat, and began speaking even more furiously. 'What were you thinking while disregarding so many warriors in this pandal, way more gallant than this cowherd? How did you come to wash the feet of this runaway in front of such gallant warriors like Grandsire Bhishma, Prince Duryodhana, Shalya – the king of Madra –

Sindhu king Jayadratha, Shakuni – the son of Subala – Matsya king Virata, and Panchala king Drupada?'

Grandsire Bhishma stood up as he heard Shishupala mention his name. Trying to control Shishupala, who had clearly lost his faculty of discretion, he said, 'That is enough! Control yourself and be seated.'

Shishupala, who harboured the pain of the killing of Jarasandha, the one who had made him a commander, and the torment of his broken engagement with Rukminidevi, was in no mood to listen to anybody. He simply discarded the Grandsire's experienced words of caution. Instead, he retorted insolently, 'Son of Ganga, you have become old now. You better sit down.' Grandsire Bhishma sat down, humiliated and dejected. Then Shishupala became uncontrollable like an insolent bull that had broken free from its tether. Looking at Maharaja Yudhishthira and the Lord alternately, he shouted again, 'Didn't you notice the splendid scholarly Brahmins in the pandal like Paila, Dhaumya, Yaaja, Upayaaja, Drona, Kripa, Vidura and Ashwatthama? Instead of them, how could you wash the feet of a black cowherd? Oh, son of Kunti, how come you did not feel even a bit of remorse while performing such a low act of putting the glory of the Kuru dynasty to shame? If you are impressed by his black-blue complexion, how come you missed gallant Karna, the king of Anga, much more attractive? He also possesses the impenetrable golden kavachakundala from birth, the one who is a philanthropist?'

Shishupala waited momentarily to see if there was any objection. Karna stood up and warned him. 'Oh, king of Chedi, you are going overboard. Gather yourself. Be calm.' Shishupala screamed, 'I am not a cowherd like this one, to listen to a charioteer like you. You better sit down.'

Now going completely berserk, Shishupala's blood-red tongue went loose, jabbering uncontrollable indignations. 'Yudhishthira, how could you forget all the elder and valiant people in the pandal? How dare you assign a cattleman that wanders in the forest as the yajnavetta of such a grand yajna today? What else is this if not utter humiliation of all present?' I could not bear his utter nonsense now. Sitting on the northern side of the pandal, Grandsire Bhishma, Vidura, Sanjaya and Karna were boiling with rage; Balaramadada, Satyaki, Uddhavadeva, Bhima, Arjuna, and Nakula and Sahadeva, who were sitting in our section, stood up at once. But the Lord made all of us sit down with only a single stern glance.

Completely demented, Shishupala went on ranting insanely. Intoxication by the idea of revenge is even stronger than by liquor. One would agree with this after watching Shishupala. He wanted revenge as the commander who went up to Mount Gomanta, and as the humiliated rival who returned empty-handed from Kundinpura without becoming Rukminidevi's bridegroom.

He began using all possible vulgar words that he could think of, publicly defaming the Lord in a way that nobody had done or heard of before. 'You traitor – you murdered your own mama. You are a runaway deserter who turned tail and fled, unable to face Magadha emperor Jarasandha's mettle. You are only fit to deliver cow's milk from the cowshed of Mathura for this holy yajna organised by the Kshatriyas and sages, get paid for it and walk away. Why didn't you do that? How dare you sit at all on the divine throne reserved for the yajnavetta? Did you not feel ashamed of yourself while getting your dirty feet washed by an elite Kshatriya?'

With each word that came out of his mouth, the audience got more and more anxious with fear. My Lord's head was gradually rising like the hood of a cobra. He put his left hand on his waist and, to warn Shishupala in time, said in a stern, resolute and calm voice, 'Shishupala, I have tolerated ninety-nine offences of yours till this moment. I have promised your mother – my aunt – that I will condone up to a hundred offences of yours. Every moment henceforth is bringing your life closer to its end! Beware, and control yourself.'

'You coward, teaching everyone useless philosophy, if valour is the true Dharma of a Kshatriya, and if you are a true Kshatriya, then come here to the centre of the yajna pandal and agree to a wrestling duel with this king of Chedi. Or else just get lost from this holy place.' He threw away the mace in his hand, and thumped his arms.

I wanted to scream out loud and tell that arrogant, insolent, disoriented Kshatriya, 'Shishupala, your life is over!'

At once, the yajna pandal began trembling with a loud cacophony of thousands of instruments unheard before. Nobody could figure out from which direction it was coming. My sight got drawn towards the

Lord's face and rested there. His body looked like a thousand-petal red lotus flower resting on a tall blue stem. His face, which had looked like a blue lotus a moment ago, now looked blood-red. His rosy lips began uttering a divine mantra. The unintelligible words of the mantra that I had never heard before kept increasing every moment. They filled the entire pandal. The Lord's right hand rose gradually. Within moments, a serrated, radiant, vajra-centred, swiftly revolving chakra with twelve spokes manifested on the index finger of that hand, dispersing circles of brilliance. The words that came out of Lord's divine mouth were so intense and sharp that they broke through the cacophony of thousands of instruments, loud enough to put thundering clouds to shame. It directly penetrated the heart of every single spectator in the pandal. By this time, surmising that something inconceivable was going to happen, the entire pandal was on its feet. The Lord's words fell on their ears like they were coming from the skies, 'Shishupala, your limit of one hundred offences is over. Henceforth, you will not be able to commit the hundred and first offence at all. You will not get such an opportunity.'

The Lord opened his eyes. In the next moment, he projected that rapidly revolving Sudarshan chakra towards Shishupala.

The entire pandal was now fully aware that the Lord of Dwaraka, Bhagwan Vasudeva, had launched the Sudarshan chakra, which he rarely did. Many invitees started running helter-skelter, raising both hands in the air, shouting, 'Run…help…Sudarshan is coming…Sudarshan…' At this moment, the Lord looked as radiant as millions of suns. The effulgent glow on his face was too much to look at. I realised that he was indeed far away from us, like the Sun – the Lord of the sky. I immediately raised both my hands and prostrated in front of him. I said in my mind, 'Oh Lord, please forgive me, give me shelter at your feet. Indeed, I have no ability to be your confidante. Oh, Lord Vasudeva, save me.' I prayed to him from the bottom of my heart. Shishupala began shaking with fear now, and his face turned black. Pandemonium had broken out in the entire pandal. Unbearable brilliant bright light had spread everywhere. Making a whirring sound, the Sudarshan chakra moved towards Shishupala.

Shishupala tried to block that brilliant radiance with his hairy hands. He tried to hide behind the seats of the kings in the pandal to avoid the blazing glow of the chakra. The leader of the Chedis, who had called my dear Lord a deserter only a moment ago, was running for his life now. Not a single king could stand in front of the blazing chakra even for a moment. Shishupala tried in vain to dodge and hide. With an uncontrollable and cacophonous sound, the Sudarshan followed him everywhere, just like an agile eagle that goes after a snake.

He stumbled over his own mace and fell with a loud thud. There was no Chedi warrior or commander to help him get up. Not even his lord, Jarasandha, whom Bhima had already finished.

In the end, with his muscular chest heaving up and down, Shishupala reached Karna. The king of Anga was standing quietly. Looking at him, Shishupala suddenly stopped and thought, 'When this chakra cannot do anything to a charioteer, then why is it chasing a Kshatriya like me?' He swiftly turned around and, without thinking, touched the Sudarshan chakra. But it charred his hand. The thick hair on his hand turned to ashes. As Shishupala stared at his charred hand, eyes wide with fear, his bravado shattered.

He realised that there was no one who could save him from the Sudarshan and scampered like a horse to reach the eastern gate of the pandal. He dashed out of the gate and started running for his life desperately. He tried in vain to seek shelter behind a boulder in his path, the trunk of a huge tree, anything he could find. But the Sudarshan would not leave him alone even for a moment. Its loud whizzing kept escalating every moment. By this time, many men and women were already safely back in their camps in Indraprastha. A few courageous people, who had stayed back, were stunned and watched the hide-and-seek of life and death between Shishupala and the Sudarshan. I was looking at the Lord, standing near the yajna altar. His eyes were still closed – like in a state of meditation.

Shishupala entered the river Ikshumati in front of him, realising that there was nowhere he could take refuge. To avoid the swiftly revolving chakra, he kept going into the deep waters of Ikshumati. Once the water reached up to his throat, he stopped and closed his eyes determinedly. He got ready to face the truth of his death. Within moments, the chakra chopped off Shishupala's head, which disappeared, floating on the waves of Ikshumati. Shishupala's life was over. I looked at the section in the pandal reserved for the royals. The Lord's beloved wife, Rukminidevi, had not moved from her seat at all in spite of the stirring events. I wondered what she must have felt after witnessing the terrifying drama. I realised that she was indeed the one perfectly befitting the Lord. Another person who sat in his seat without moving was Grandsire Bhishma. He was discussing something with Mahatma Vidura now.

I looked at the yajna altar. My Lord stood there – smiling. I had never ever seen that smile on his face before. After making sure that the chakra had indeed disappeared, kings of various kingdoms hurried back to the pandal and surrendered at the Lord's feet. Dhaumya rishi – the head of the yajna – controlled them with great effort with the assistance of his disciples. He was worried about the Rajasuya yajna, for which preparations had been made with laborious effort. The Lord said to him, 'Oh Dhaumya rishi, find another auspicious time, and plan the yajna soon again.' So many people were gathered around the Lord, but no one dared to speak a single word. Everyone was dumbfounded. We came out of the pandal from the eastern gate. I had tied all four horses in the shade of a sprawling tree. I untied them, patted them and brought them close to Garudadhwaja. Only the Lord got into the chariot. I took the seat of the charioteer. The Lord bade farewell to all, and we left. No sooner had we passed some distance along the bank of the Yamuna, than he questioned me, 'Daruka, how come you did not ask me where to go, as you always do? Come, we are going to Kalindidevi's maternal home. To convey the well-being of their grandchildren.'

I was speechless. My Lord, as tall as the sky, the one who had, only moments ago, launched the Sudarshan chakra, was now going to meet his parents-in-law to deliver news of their grandchildren's well-being!

As per the Lord's instructions, the Rajasuya yajna of the Pandavas took place at another auspicious time, without any obstruction.

The Lord returned to Dwaraka along with all the Yadavas. As soon as he arrived in Dwaraka, he had to hear shocking news. While we were in Indraprastha, Shalva, the king of Martikavati, had attacked Dwaraka with his army. Our valiant Pradyumna had fought him fiercely for twenty-seven days along with his brothers and forced him to retreat.

This was the very first direct attack on Dwaraka since its inception. In his heart, the Lord was deeply offended, but he did not disclose his feelings. He called his master architect Gargamuni in his chambers. While giving him important instructions, he said, 'Oh Gargamuni, a few stairs should be added to the staircase leading to my chambers. It should mainly include steps in honour of Aunt Kuntidevi, beloved sakhi Draupadi, and the five Pandavas, respectively. Below these stairs, add one more step, for my loyal attendant and dear friend, charioteer Daruka!'

When I got to hear this from Uddhava Maharaja, my heart was overwhelmed with the utmost gratefulness for the Lord.

Shalva's armed attack on Dwaraka was not a thing to be overlooked at all. First of all, it was necessary to assess the power of the army and the weaponry that he had used in this assault. For that purpose, the Lord called young Pradyumna to his chamber. He asked Pradyumna a lot of questions. Only one conclusion could be drawn from the information that was gathered – Shalva's real strength lay in his aircraft called 'Saubha'. He could easily travel anywhere in Aaryavarta on the strength of this aircraft. It was with the help of this very aircraft that he had invited Kalayavana from a distant kingdom to Aaryavarta before. It was necessary to destroy his Saubha. But it was safe with his army in the royal capital Martikavati, located on Mount Arbuda in Marusthali.

The venerable Lord of Dwaraka instructed Chief Minister Vipruthu to hold the Sudharma assembly of the Yadavas. There were two points of discussion – controlling Shalva, the owner of Saubha, in time and the decision on who would go to Hastinapura with gift platters for the Vishnuyaga yajna.

Everyone kept looking expectantly at the Lord. He politely addressed all Yadava members of the assembly, 'I will go to meet Shalva myself, provided all of you grant me permission to do so. Because of that, I will not be able to attend the Vishnuyaga yajna of the Kurus in Hastinapura. The chief minister and commander Satyaki should go there, along with select warriors.'

When the Lord, who had so many exploits to his name, politely asked for permission from the Yadava members of the council with his palms joined, instead of speaking at length, the entire Sudharma assembly was touched.

The Yadava warriors, who were moved by his humility, responded in unison, 'Oh Lord of Dwaraka, it is you who should command.'

The fourfold army consisting of lakhs of Yadavas got ready in a week's time. The pugnacious Yadava warriors crossed the ocean creek in huge ships and descended on the borders of Saurashtra. In this expedition, the Lord was accompanied by Balaramadada, Satyaki, Kritavarman, Uddhava Maharaja, Shini and Avagaha. Notably, he also summoned the great architect Mayasura, who was still in Indraprastha. He planted expert spies from Dwaraka up to Mount Arbuda much before leaving. Through them, he made arrangements to spread news that 'the Lord of Dwaraka has received an invitation from Kamarupa king Bhagadutta and has left for Pragjyotishapura in the east. He has taken all major Yadava warriors with him. Pradyumna is in charge of protection of the Dwaraka kingdom with his stepbrothers.'

The news that he was going to Pragjyotishapura was a rumour spread to mislead Shalva. The Lord had also sent detailed instructions to Bhagadutta of Kamarupa, telling him the sequence of actions to be followed.

In reality, it was Shalva on whom the Lord's eyes were. Shalva was living in the region of Mount Arbuda in the Matsya kingdom in the far west of Aaryavarta and was difficult to reach. Was the Lord himself going to go there with his army? Not at all. He was tactfully going to use the Avanti and Kuntibhoja kingdoms in Madhyadesha, belonging to his kith and kin, to his own advantage. He had already instructed the family of Mitravindadevi in Avanti and Aunt Kuntidevi's relatives in the city of Kuntibhoja to keep his arrival a secret. The last sojourn of our army was in the Kuntibhoja city in Madhyadesha. Here, the Lord had a detailed talk with Mayasura. He was the one who had gone to the city of Martikavati long ago and had built the Saubha aircraft for Shalva. The Lord got detailed information about the aircraft from him – its speed, from how far away the whirring sound of the aircraft could be heard, the way it landed on the ground, and so on.

In the region of Mount Arbuda, Shalva's informers had presented news to him, 'Srikrishna of Dwaraka has gone to the Kamarupa kingdom along with the army and select Yadava warriors. The kingdoms of Uttkala, Vanga and Tripura have made grand preparations to welcome him.

Only Pradyumna is in Dwaraka, along with aged Vasudeva. A few of his brothers and select Yadava warriors are with him. This is the right time to strike again and humble that nuisance of a Dwaraka kingdom that has been meddling in unwanted matters. Dwaraka has already become feeble due to the attacks during the previous battle that lasted for twenty-seven days. We can even dispatch part of our army through the kingdom of Sauvira, and they can enter Dwaraka by way of the ocean.'

All this was just as my Lord had anticipated. This is how his military strategy was – beyond the grasp of those around him. Our army took rest and enjoyed the hospitality of the Bhojas in the city of Kuntibhoja in Madhyadesha, for an entire week.

As news arrived that Shalva had descended from the dense forests of Mount Arbuda and was on his way to Dwaraka along with commander Kshemadhurti, our fourfold army, resting in the city of Kuntibhoja, began moving. Balaramadada, Satyaki, Kritavarman, Shini and Avagaha speedily cut across the kingdom of the Dasharnas in between and surrounded Mount Arbuda. This blocked Shalva's path back to the city of Martikavati now. I descended into the Sauvira kingdom along with the Lord, Uddhava Maharaja and select Yadava warriors. This was the westernmost end of Mount Arbuda. Just as the Lord of Dwaraka had constructed a planned harbour at Dwaraka and erected the Kroshtu lighthouse in the ocean, the rulers of Sauvira had built a port on their western border. They had also erected a lighthouse. Along with the Lord and Uddhava Maharaja in the chariot, I began steering the Garudadhwaja towards the port of Sauvira. A few select armed Yadava warriors followed us. Now the Lord was neither in Dwaraka, nor in Pragjyotishapura, nor in the siege around Mount Arbuda. Nobody had any clue as to where he actually was. As soon as we reached the port of Sauvira, the Lord cautiously used a strategy. The island of Dwaraka was closer by way of the ocean through this port. He arranged to convey news to Shalva, who was trying to enter Dwaraka, that the mammoth Yadava army had surrounded Mount Arbuda to destroy the city of Martikavati. He was to get the news before he reached the Shuddhaksha gate, and that would surely cause him worry.

Now Shalva, who had reached close to Dwaraka, was immediately going to return to protect his royal city. He was going to send his army back by way of land, and he himself was going to descend in Sauvira using the Saubha aircraft. From there, he was going to assess the siege and the strength of our army and plan further. All this was going to happen sequentially, just as the Lord had prudently anticipated.

The sun overhead had begun its descent towards the western ocean. The Lord would sometimes restlessly cast an intent gaze far away in the southern direction on the western ocean, holding his left hand over his eyebrows. The boats of Sauvira fishermen with tall sails could be seen returning. Evening was fast approaching now. We could see flocks of chirping ocean birds with long wings and tails returning home.

Suddenly we heard a whirring sound. None of us had ever heard such a sound before. It kept increasing every moment. From the southern end of the western ocean, an eagle-like figure in the sky was slowly moving in our direction. The whirring kept increasing as it came closer. Spellbound, we kept staring at it. That diverted our attention away from the Lord. The Lord had completely closed his fish-shaped eyes; he seemed in a meditative trance. He was whispering something. A terrifying cacophony of war trumpets was heard. The whirring sound that we had heard before was nothing compared to this sound. The Lord's face had turned red. We could hear mantras vaguely. The right hand of the Lord was raised. The bright Sudarshan chakra, emitting millions of rays of light and revolving rapidly around itself, manifested instantly on his right index finger.

The western ocean stretching in front of us glowed in that brilliance. Because of the loud, piercing sound being emitted from the radiant chakra, we were unable to hear the sound of the ocean and the strange whirring that we had heard a few moments before. The Lord's raised right hand flexed forward a little bit. The radiant Sudarshan chakra had been projected. It shot in the direction of the approaching eagle-shaped aircraft. Within moments, the two collided. A terrifying, deafening sound of a blast reverberated. The next moment, that eagle tumbled into the frothy waters of the western ocean with its broken wings and shattered body. And that was the end of Shalva and his Saubha aircraft. By this time, we all had dropped down on the ocean sand. Nothing was visible. My brain was completely numb from the loud boom and the bright light. All I could see vaguely was that the chakra had returned. It did not settle on the Lord's index finger as usual. Instead, with a roaring sound, it moved in the direction where the Lord had pointed his index finger. In the direction of Hastinapura. Meanwhile, the sun had touched the western ocean and was slowly sinking in the water. Throughout the night, the ruins of the Saubha aircraft bobbing on the waves of the western ocean were going to drift away southward. They were going to deliver jubilant news to the citizens of Dwaraka and valiant Pradyumna – 'The ungrateful traitor Shalva, who collaborated with Shishupala and Jarasandha and invited Kalayavana from abroad to Aaryavarta, has been finished.' With tremendous reverence in my heart, I looked at my Lord and found myself speechless yet again.

The Pandava family in Indraprastha had also expanded now. In addition to Draupadidevi, each Pandava had either one, two or three wives. The second wife of Maharaja Yudhishthira was Pauravidevi. They had a son named Devaka. His son Prativindhya, born to Draupadidevi, was the first-born in the second generation of Pandavas. He was the future prince of Indraprastha.

The son born to the second Pandava, venerable wrestler and mace warrior Bhimsena, and Draupadidevi, was named Sutasoma. He was well built just like his father. Just as the Lord had married Jambavatidevi, the daughter of tribal king Jambavana, Bhimsena had married a rakshasa daughter, Hidimba. But Hidimbadevi lived in the jungle at her maternal home. Her son's name was Ghatotkacha. He was the most powerful among all sons of Bhimsena, with rare qualities suitable for war. After the execution of Shishupala, the Lord wished that the Chedis have good relations with Indraprastha. He did not feel that it was right for the Chedis to stand up against the Pandavas and Dwaraka. Therefore, he convinced Bhimsena to accept Shishupala's sister, Kalidevi, as his wife. She remained at her parents' home in Shuktimati. Her son's name was Sarvagata.

The Lord's favourite Pandava was master archer Arjuna. He called Arjuna his 'sakha'. The Lord's favourite, gallant Partha, had two more wives, besides Draupadidevi and Subhadradevi, named Uloopidevi, who was a Naga daughter, and Chitrangadadevi from Manipura. This was a rare blood relation between the Pandavas and the Nagas. Uloopidevi's son was Iravan and Chitrangadadevi's son was Babhruvahana.

The Lord had urged Nakula, the fourth Pandava, to accept the hand of Shishupala's daughter, Karenumati, as his second wife. This couple's son was Niramitra. As Shishupala's sister was married to Bhimsena and his daughter was married to Bhimsena's brother Nakula, the two Pandavas had now become father-in-law and son-in-law. This entire emotional concord and act was indeed due to the intellectual genius of the Lord.

The last Pandava, Sahadeva, was a connoisseur of horses. He had an alert mind, just like that of a running horse. He was the only one besides the Lord who would talk to me at length about horses, chariots and taking care of horses for hours on end. I had close emotional ties with two of the Pandavas. The first was Arjuna, who was as dear to the Lord as Uddhava Maharaja, and the second was Sahadeva. The disparity in our status was never apparent during our discussions. Sahadeva's second wife was Vijayadevi, the daughter of his mama Shalya, the king of Madra. They had a son named Suhotra. Sahadeva's third wife was Bhanumatidevi. As she belonged to a Yadava family, the Yadavas had formed a firm bond with the Pandavas through this marriage. This couple had no children yet.

Just as the Lord and Balaramadada's families had expanded in Dwaraka, so had the Pandavas' family in Indraprastha. Both these royal strengths had come close firmly due to relationships formed by matrimonial alliances. No matter how hard their enemies tried, nothing was going to break this bond ever.

The Dwaraka kingdom, for which my Lord strove throughout his life, had now been established. Throughout Aaryavarta it was renowned as 'the Dwaraka of Srikrishna'. Populated by lakhs of pugnacious Yadavas, no one would now dare to confront the Dwaraka of Bhagwan Vasudeva, who had eliminated many insolent, arrogant rulers with a captivating display of his intellectual genius.

But lakhs of Yadavas and I were to be proved wrong. One day, a royal envoy arrived from a distant eastern kingdom in Aaryavarta. He had not brought any gift for Dwaraka, but an arrogant message. A daring missive that directly challenged the Dwaraka kingdom and its leader, my Lord. That envoy was from the eastern kingdom of Pundra. He delivered the message of his master, Paundraka, to my Lord, amidst a fully occupied

Yadava royal assembly. He said, 'My master, the ruler of Pundra, who is the one and only real Vasudeva in entire Aaryavarta, has sent a message for you…'

No royal envoy had ever behaved like this in the Sudharma assembly before. His actions left all Yadavas in the council stunned.

'The message is that, "Just because he dons the same royal attire like me; wears the same Vaijayanti garland around his neck as me; and bears a peacock feather in his crown, no cowherd who still exudes the strong odour of cowdung can ever become a Vasudeva. Any Kshatriya of Aaryavarta who imitates me and calls himself Vasudeva should fight a duel with me – Paundraka – the real Vasudeva. This is my direct challenge to the warlock of the Yadavas, who calls himself the Lord of Dwaraka and Vasudeva."' That envoy was indeed loyal to his king, and fearless. While delivering his master's message 'as is' to the royal assembly, he literally trembled with rage. The very next moment, a ruckus arose among the Yadavas, 'Throw him out – capture him – kill him.'

The Lord would usually take his time standing up, but this time he stood up at once, not because of the insolent and arrogant words of the royal envoy but because he believed that only he could control the violent Yadavas at this critical moment. He raised his arm high and roared loudly, 'Wait! Drop your weapons and take your seats quietly.' I had never heard such intimidation from him before. I thought something untoward was about to happen. The Lord would probably close his fish-shaped eyes and project the Sudarshan chakra on the throat of the royal envoy. I was terrified that for the first time, our royal assembly was going to witness a bloodbath, and kept looking at the Lord in fear. But…but…

'Oh Yadavas! This royal messenger is not at fault at all. He is only a dutiful, patriotic servant of his master, just like my Daruka and each one of you Yadavas. Calm down, and try to understand.

'All of you should learn an unforgettable, invaluable lesson from this royal messenger-friend of mine! That of loyalty to the master.'

The next moment a command was given to the chief minister that left everyone stunned, 'Vipruthu, please present a platter of my royal attire to be dispatched with this royal messenger as a gift to the real Maharaja

Vasudeva of Pundra. Do not forget to keep a bright and large peacock feather on top of it.'

'Your wish is my command,' said the chief minister of the Yadavas and was about to leave, when the Lord issued another command. 'Please present one gift platter of fine apparel even for this royal attendant of Pundra. He has obeyed his master's command to the word by jeopardising his own life. I will definitely visit his master.'

Within a few moments, two salvers were presented in the Sudharma royal assembly. The royal messenger felt deep regret and realised that instead of receiving fatal punishment, he had received the royal gift of honour, that too from a great person who was revered as the Lord of all the people. Tears of guilt flowed down his eyes.

Now the royal capital of Dwaraka was aroused by the 'Paundraka Vasudeva campaign'. The Lord had conquered the western region of Aaryavarta by killing Shalva. Now his target was the eastern region. The Pundra kingdom was located near the eastern ocean, at the confluence of the rivers Kaushiki and Ganga. Paundraka's kingdom was adjacent to the Karusha and the Vanga kingdoms. Paundraka had dispatched his royal envoy to Dwaraka with careful thought and foresight. He had put up a front as if it was only him who was provocatively challenging the Lord of Dwaraka by calling him a duplicate Vasudeva. But he had secretly formed a political alliance with Dantavakra and Viduratha of the Karusha kingdom and the ruler of the Vanga kingdom. This challenge by the so-called real Vasudeva was not a challenge of his small Pundra kingdom alone. It was a challenge by the alliance. He had no clue that he was dealing with the Lord of Dwaraka, who could turn the tables with his intellectual genius.

Even before the royal envoy of the Pundras could reach his kingdom in the east, the Lord's best informers had met with Bhagadutta of Pragjyotishapura. Detailed information about the three kingdoms – Pundra, Karusha and Vanga – started reaching Dwaraka. It was understandable that the self-proclaimed Vasudeva, Paundraka, had gone against the Lord. But I could not comprehend why the Lord's two paternal cousins had chosen to enter the thorny forests of enmity. The Lord easily understood everything that I and many others could not comprehend.

The background of this expedition to the eastern kingdom was a bit complicated. The Lord's paternal cousins, Dantavakra and Viduratha, belonged to the Karusha kingdom. Among them, the elder brother, Dantavakra, was the ruler of the Karusha kingdom, and Viduratha handled military operations outside the kingdom. He was one of the kings who had returned empty-handed from the unsuccessful swayamwar of Rukminidevi, and held a grudge against the Lord. He was also an ally in the conspiracy of the trio Jarasandha, Shalva and Shishupala to destroy the Lord completely. He had earlier joined hands with Jarasandha on behalf of Shishupala, who was his maternal cousin. Naturally, he was furious with the Lord because all three had been killed.

The Lord crossed the creek of Dwaraka and the army headed east. Many experienced and trained informers from the adroit and efficient surveillance team of the Yadavas were dispersed in eastern kingdoms around the Pundra kingdom. Those included the kingdoms of Uttkala, Magadha, Anga, Kamarupa and Manipura. From among these, the Magadha kingdom because of Jarasandha's son Sahadeva, and the Kamarupa kingdom because of Bhagadutta had now turned into our allies. The Manipura kingdom was also our ally, as Arjuna's wife Chitrangadadevi belonged to that kingdom. So, we needed to befriend only the Uttkala kingdom till the successful completion of this mission. The Lord had already managed to do that by sending royal apparel and gifts to Kalinga and Bhuvaneshwara – the royal capital of Uttkala.

My Lord had experienced the Dakshinapatha of Mount Pariyatra quite a few times while travelling to Rukminidevi's city Kundinpura in Vidarbha. Therefore, we were now travelling towards the east by going around it, camping on the banks of River Narmada. After a few days, we arrived in the Mahishmati city on Mount Vindhya.

The citizens of Mahishmati welcomed Balaramadada, the Lord and Uddhava Maharaja with joy. We rested for a week in this beautiful city. We crossed the big river Shona in the southern Kosala kingdom and reached River Damodara in Magadha. Sahadeva, who was now the ruler of Magadha, gave the three brothers a hearty welcome. They offered sacks of foodgrains, fodder for animals and medicinal herbs for the army. Well-prepared, capacious boats were also given to us to cross the huge river, Damodara. Using those boats, our special troops crossed river, along with chariots and elephants. We pulled the boats out of the Damodara, mounted them on the backs of elephants and reached the banks of River Ganga, with the Uttkala kingdom on our right and the Anga kingdom of Karna on the left. River Ganga flowed into the eastern ocean near the Vanga kingdom through many mouths. The sight of the Ganga reminded the Lord intensely of the western ocean of Dwaraka, roaring continuously. In the end, we were united with our mammoth army on the borders of Pundra. By this time, the Pundra leader was completely misinformed. Based on the information that he was receiving from his informers, he believed that the mock cowherd of Dwaraka had come to visit him as his vassal. But he was taken aback by the mammoth army on the borders. He panicked when Dantavakra and Viduratha, who had come for his support, deserted him to protect their own Karusha kingdom. Still, putting on false bravado, he sent a message with his chief minister. It said, 'Remove the crown on your head before coming to visit. A vassal of the real Vasudeva has no right to bear the peacock-feathered crown. Though there has been a delay, send the remaining customary gift salvers with your messenger.'

Now this had gone beyond Balaramadada's tolerance limit. He shouted at the chief minister of Paundraka, 'Tell your Vasudeva, we both are coming in person to meet him as a gift.'

They met on the banks of the Kaushiki, on the battlefield. The notable thing was that Paundraka Vasudeva, who rode in a canopy on the back of an elephant, had actually come wearing the same attire as my Lord. He got down from the canopy and challenged the Lord to a battle of swords. His commander fought with Balaramadada. It was amusing to see the Lord brandishing the Nandaka sword, shouting slogans of family deity Ida, colliding with Paundraka, dressed in the same attire as him. It was indeed a unique experience to see him in action on the battlefield. The sword in Paundraka's hand broke due to the Lord's Nandaka sword. He contemptuously looked at the broken remains of the sword in his hand and threw it away, and took a huge mace. I swiftly pulled out the Lord's Kaumodaki mace, which was even bigger, and handed it to him. The clanging sounds of the clobbering maces echoed and dispersed on the waves of Kaushiki's waters. The river Kaushiki was witnessing a very rare spectacle, which was rare even for the gods. The Paundraka sun was about to set. In the setting sun, the Lord smashed the chest of Paundraka. He lay on his back, lifeless, on the banks of the Kaushiki. Balaramadada had already killed the commander. The Lord delicately picked up the peacock feather in his crown that lay aside, and gently wiped the fresh stains off the duplicate Vasudeva's blood with the edge of the dhoti tied around his waist. He put that peacock feather in my hand and said, 'Daruka, immerse this in River Kaushiki! Whatever he was, he was a brave warrior who constantly reminded me of my being the 'Vasudeva' even if he did that by linking the word 'duplicate' to my epithet! He was the only king after me in the entire Bharata who tucked a peacock feather in his golden crown!'

That day the sun set with a contented heart.

Now the target was Dantavakra, the king of Karusha who had attended the council arranged by Jarasandha on the borders of Kundinpura at the time of the first swayamwar ceremony of Rukminidevi. And Viduratha, who had participated in Shalva's conspiracy of inviting Kalayavana.

The most inexcusable atrocity by these two brothers was that they had themselves captured many kings and sent them to Girivraja for the Shatashirsha yajna that Jarasandha had been preparing for. Shishupala committed only a hundred crimes, but these two brothers had committed way more than that.

The triumphant Yadava army penetrated the borders of the Karusha kingdom, shouting acclamations of Balaramadada and the Lord. The Lord sent a message to Dantavakra from the borders of Karusha, 'Balarama–Srikrishna, the cowherd sons of Gokul's Nanda–Yashoda, have come to visit the king of Karusha and his brother Viduratha. As Sahadeva, the current ruler of Magadha, is a close ally of the Lord of Dwaraka, he will not come to the Karusha kingdom this time. Maybe the son of Kalayavana of the Gandhara kingdom will come to assist you. So, do call that alien for your assistance now.'

The message was clear – get ready to fight with the cowherds of Dwaraka now. Dantavakra understood it. Along with his brother Viduratha, he arrived at the border with the army, ready to fight.

This was the very first instance in the Lord's life so far where he had to meet his own cousins on the battlefield. The Lord, standing tall in the back of the moving Garudadhwaja chariot, pulled out the Paanchjanya conch from his shawl and blew it with full force. That inspirational sound prompted thousands and lakhs of armed Yadavas to attack the Karusha warriors with sky-piercing war shouts of 'Hail Idamata...victory!' Towards the evening, the Lord pierced the chest of Dantavakra, unerringly shooting five arrows in a row with the Sharanga bow.

Balaramadada killed the commander of Karusha and many Karusha warriors with severe blows from the Saunanda pestle and Samvartaka plough.

Viduratha got enraged when he heard the news of his brother Dantavakra's death. Shouting loudly, 'Show me that warlock cowherd', he brought his chariot rapidly in front of the Lord's Garudadhwaja. In this battle, many Yadava warriors and I saw the Lord's outstanding bow-and-arrow skills. He was not just a master of the life-threatening Bahukantaka manoeuvre in wrestling, or just the master of Sudarshan who projected the brilliant chakra and left spectators bewildered, but it was also a master archer, who equalled the expertise of Dhananjaya of Indraprastha and the king of Anga – Karna of Hastinapura. He swiftly handled bows like the Sharanga and Ajitanjaya as if they were toys. First, he made Viduratha immobile in his chariot by restraining him in a cage of arrows so tight that he could not move at all. Then within a moment, he pushed Viduratha on to the ground along with the cage of arrows around him, and left him without a chariot. Viduratha was indeed a master 'rathi' (charioteer), as his name denoted, but at this moment he was left without a chariot. The Lord chopped his head off with a moon-faced arrow without giving him a moment's respite.

Thus, with the fall of Dantavakra and Viduratha, the eastern region was also set free. The entire eastern side of Aaryavarta was now emancipated from kings like Narakasura of Kamarupa, Jarasandha of Magadha, Paundraka Vasudeva of the Pundras, and Dantavakra and Viduratha of Karusha. Entire Aaryavarta had come to know about the Lord's life mission of removing obstacles in the flow of life and letting it flow freely. The Lord would casually say, 'Growth and development are the characteristics of life.' This was indeed the all-pervading truth.

The next day, after performing morning rituals, the Lord entered the royal city of Karusha along with Balaramadada and Uddhava Maharaja. He had sent a messenger ahead and requested for a visit with Maharaja Vriddhasharmana and Aunt Shrutadevi. Everybody thought the aged royal couple would deny the request, but the opposite happened. They sent a reply, 'Sure, come and meet us. Do not hesitate. We have a lot to speak about.'

As they came into sight, the Lord briskly walked forward leaving all of us behind, and put his blue forehead on the feet of Maharaja Vriddhasharmana and Aunt Shrutadevi. With her trembling hands, Aunt Shrutadevi pulled up her nephew, whom she was meeting for the first time. The Lord wiped the tears rolling down her eyes and said in a voice full of sweetness, 'Oh Aunt, consider Dada and me like your own sons Dantavakra and Viduratha.' Hearing those words, Maharaja Vriddhasharmana, who was silent so far, said in a trembling but sharp voice, 'It is easy to say so. If you two would have been killed, would such words have been enough to console your mother and father?'

'I have not come to console both of you at all. My battle is against the ruthless rulers of any kingdom – against their unfair, lopsided views. Injustice – whoever imposes it on another, for whatever reason, is always terrible. But the injustice imposed by the ruler of a kingdom whose forefathers have sacrificed their blood to protect it is the worst injustice of all. I have not committed a crime by killing my cousins. Yet, if you want to curse me instead of giving me your blessings, go ahead and do so. I will accept that readily too.'

Maharaja Vriddhasharmana held the Lord's shoulders tightly and stared in his eyes for a moment. The venerable maharaja then said, 'Vasudeva's son Srikrishna, we do regret the death of our sons. But we have realised that you had no issue of personal honour or dishonour. I kept telling my sons time and again, "Go to Dwaraka once. Visit Balarama and Srikrishna." Their mother got exasperated trying to persuade them. But both of them never went to Dwaraka to visit you because of their pride. Instead, they turned to Jarasandha in Girivraja.

'Vasudeva, probably you sensed the desire of our hearts and came to visit us. That makes us feel better. Convey our regards to Maharaja Vasudeva and both the maharanis.'

Witnessing this incident, my mind was tangled in confusing thoughts about the Lord. That night, while trying to relax after dinner in the Karusha royal palace, I was restlessly thinking about the Lord throughout the night. I could not sleep however hard I tried.

The next day, our Yadava army bid farewell to the Karusha kingdom and left for the Uttkala kingdom. I picked up the reins in my hands. Looking at the Lord, I said, 'Shall we leave, my Lord?' Looking at me, he affectionately said, 'Daruka, you take the seat in the back. You have not had enough sleep last night. Put a few drops of cow's cold milk in your eyes during our very first sojourn. You will be able to sleep better. I will steer the chariot.'

The Lord's wish was indeed my command. Sitting in the back of the chariot, I kept thinking about his keen observation. Just with a glimpse of the mildly reddish edges of my eyes, he had unmistakably conjectured that I had been deprived of sleep the whole night.

The news of the killing of Dantavakra and Viduratha had already reached the Uttkala kingdom. They welcomed the three Yadava brothers with delight. But the Lord was not ready to stay in any city of the Uttkala kingdom. He was eager to lay his eyes on the eastern ocean of Aaryavarta.

The Lord reached the shores of the eastern ocean along with the king of Uttkala, his commander and army that had come to receive our triumphant Yadava army. Here, our army camped for a full fifteen days.

When we were leaving the shores, and going towards the Kashi kingdom of Dandapani, a mammoth crowd of Uttkala citizens gathered to bid farewell to the Lord of Dwaraka and his brothers. The Uttkala king bent down to offer prostrations to the Lord. Holding his shoulders, the Lord pulled him up. The king, who was impressed to see the various facets of the Lord over the fortnight, bent forward a little and said humbly, 'Oh Lord of Dwaraka, Prince Balabhadra, Uddhavadeva, this small town will always cherish the memories of your heavenly visit. From today, we will call this nameless small town Jagannathpuri, in your memory. You are indeed Jagannatha – the saviour of the world. Every year, on this particular day, there will be a similar Rathayatra – a chariot procession – in your memory.' Listening to his words, the Lord smiled with affection and said, 'Oh king of Uttkala, you should always remember this big brother of mine – Balabhadradada. That will be enough for me. No need to remember me separately at all.'

We arrived at the borders of the Kashi kingdom. Here, Dandapani, the king of Kashi, came to receive us with his army. Along with him, the Lord directly went to the immaculate temple of Kashivishweshwara located in Varanasi, on the banks of River Ganga, without taking any stops in between. In the Vishweshwara temple of Kashi king Dandapani, the temple priests had made thorough preparations for the abhishek worship in sixteen different ways. The three brothers sat on a mat near the immutable Shivapindi to perform the rituals.

Our mission in the eastern region was successful. We bade farewell to Dandapani, the king of Kashi, and returned to Dwaraka.

This time, too, the Lord had a grand welcome in Dwaraka, but something was amiss. So what exactly was amiss in this welcome of the Lord in Dwaraka? It was that the old, yet physically strong Maharaja Vasudeva had not come to the Shuddhaksha gate as usual with a smile on his face. He pulled Chief Minister Vipruthu aside and asked him, 'Maharaja is not to be seen anywhere, minister? Is his health okay?'

Chief Minister responded promptly, 'Maharaja is fine physically, but…but…'

'But what?' The Lord's blue face, round like a sunflower, never reflected distress. His large forehead, adorned with a vermilion tilak, never showed a single crease. But today, I saw that crease on his forehead very clearly. It got me worried too. Uddhava Maharaja also became restless.

'The Lord of Dwaraka should take some rest first. I will present all the details in front of him later.' The chief minister said promptly.

After having lunch and taking some rest, the Lord sent me to invite the chief minister.

Before the Lord asked anything, Vipruthu patiently put forth each detail of the inconceivable drama of the human mind that had taken place in Hastinapura, which none of us could ever have imagined. He said, 'Oh Lord of Dwaraka, something untoward has happened in Hastinapura. I am in a quandary as to how to share it with you. You, and all eighteen families of the Yadavas can suffer the loss of a few, or maybe hundreds of lives on the battlefield and recover from it after a while. We can understand the calamity, but when a kingdom is annihilated from its roots, then one loses one's wits, and does not know what to do.'

Hearing these words, the Lord went near the chief minister, put his hand on his shoulder, and gently patted him, saying, 'Chief Minister Vipruthu, please tell us everything without any inhibitions. What has happened in Hastinapura?'

He was still hesitant. He said, 'The Pandavas had received an invitation in Indraprastha to 'attend the Vishnuyaga yajna' from the Kuru king Dhritarashtra of Hastinapura.'

The chief minister continued, 'As per the invitation, the Pandava maharaja Yudhishthira went to Hastinapura with his brothers Bhima, Arjuna, Nakula and Sahadeva, and a few select warriors. Maharani Draupadidevi and Rajmata Kuntidevi also accompanied them. But... this invitation of the Kurus was not only for the Vishnuyaga yajna. Prince Duryodhana, Shakuni Mama, who always fanned Duryodhana's pride, and Kanaka had hatched an evil political conspiracy in the guise of the invitation. They tried very hard to involve Karna – the king of Anga – in this conspiracy too.

'Prince Duryodhana dared Maharaja Yudhishthira to a gamble even before the yajna. He invited Yudhishthira to a gambling hall as grand as the royal assembly. This cunning invitation was sent on purpose, knowing fully well that Yudhishthira loves gambling. It was bad luck that he accepted. He should have just declined, giving some reason or the other. '

The Lord said, 'I have always admonished and cautioned the eldest Pandava about his obsession for gambling. I have always alerted him that his thoughtless gambling will lead him on the path of destruction. He has always brushed it off with a smile, offering the justification that gambling is an honourable game that befits royalty.' The Lord stared at us and said, 'Let me tell you, Chief Minister, Yudhishthira must have gambled in Hastinapura for sure.

'And I can also tell for sure that the expert gambler and Pandava-hater Shakuni must have stroked his royal ego. Shakuni is a perfect judge of human character. He is an astute conspirator. I would not be surprised if Karna – the king of Anga – did not participate in their machinations at all. He is different, after all.'

'So, Chief Minister, what was the final result of this gambling competition? What profit did Yudhishthira reap from this gambling session?'

'Profit? Not at all, oh Lord! In fact, he suffered a tremendous loss. A loss that was even more humiliating than death for a Kshatriya. Yudhishthira got so carried away with his obsession of gambling that he lost all his senses. First, he lost all the wealth in his treasury, and then all the animals – elephants, horses and camels – of his army. In anticipation of winning the next game and recovering his losses, he insanely kept playing further. As soon as he lost all the animals in the first bet, he gambled the troops of his army. When he lost them too, he gambled the Indraprastha kingdom, which has been erected by his own people and the people of Dwaraka.'

'What? The Indraprastha kingdom?' I could not restrain myself. His hands clasped behind him, moving around in disquiet, the Lord was lost in deep thought. 'Go on, Chief Minister, tell me what else he put at stake after losing the kingdom. What did he do?'

'He was adamant, not accepting defeat. He put each one of his indomitable brothers – Nakula, Sahadeva, Bhima and Arjuna – at stake too, one after the other.'

'What? My beloved friend Arjuna too?' The Lord, who was moving around restlessly, stopped in his tracks. He kept staring at the chief minister in disbelief.

'Yudhishthira lost all these bets too. Nobody could think straight. None of the Pandavas could understand why even once the dice did not show the numbers that Yudhishthira called out. Why was it happening? How come the dice turned up against them every single time? The wicked duo of Duryodhana and Shakuni had secretly retrieved the bones of Jarasandha from Girivraja and got the gambling dice created from them. Except these two, no one else in the game arena had any idea about this. That was the reason these two had astutely kept Karna out of the game arena till the last game. Had he been present in the game arena at the time of each throwing of the dice, the Kauravas would have lost the game. That was because Karna had once defeated Jarasandha in a duel but had spared his life. It was the name of Karna that had the most fearful impact on the bones of Jarasandha. Also, the reason why the Pandavas were losing all dice throws was due to Bhima's loud shouting. When Bhima spoke every time they were thrown, the dice, made of Jarasandha's bones, trembled weirdly with fear, and the result of the dice throw would be the exact opposite of what the Pandavas wanted. Then all the five brothers would stare in dismay at the dice made of Jarasandha's bones. Every moment, it was getting increasingly unbearable for powerful Bhima.' The chief minister kept talking. The scene in the gambling arena of the Kurus appeared vividly in front of my eyes.

'Maharaja Dhritarashtra was seated on the ancient royal throne of the Kurus along with Gandharidevi. Grandsire Bhishma was also present, and Drona, Kripa, Vidura and Sanjaya were sitting next to him. I wondered why Karna, the king of Anga, was nowhere to be seen in the game arena.

'In the end...Yudhishthira also forgot his coronation ceremony that had taken place in front of all the major kings of Aaryavarta. He did not even remember that a crowned king is answerable to his subjects. And he put even himself at stake.' The chief minister bent his head in shame.

'What? The venerable Pandava Yudhishthira put himself at stake in a game of gambling?' I could not help asking. As per my knowledge, nobody in Aaryavarta had, so far, put himself at stake in a game of gambling.

'Indeed. The venerable Pandava Maharaja Yudhishthira put himself at stake in a game of gambling due to his insane obsession with it. And unfortunately, he lost that bet too.'

I was completely shaken on hearing that harsh, bitter truth. But my master, the Lord of Dwaraka, was still calm. I was surprised to see his composure.

The Lord walked towards the chief minister slowly and calmly. The Lord looked into his terrified eyes and asked him with the same demeanour, 'Chief Minister, what happened next? Tell us without any inhibitions. One should always accept the truth like the rising sun – as it is. Speak freely.'

The chief minister kept staring in the void in front of him as if he was watching a great, thrilling battle. He even forgot that the Lord and I were standing next to him. He said, 'Yudhishthira lost himself in the bet. Shakuni leapt with joy and shouted, "The Pandava king and his brothers have become slaves of the Kurus today. Do you still want to gamble with us, slave?"

'When Shakuni called him a slave, the eldest Pandava's head dropped in unbearable shame, and he said, "Yes, I would have still played, but what more do I have to put at stake now?"

'Then Duryodhana stood up in excitement and shouted, "Mama, tell that slave to put the gambling board away now. What else is he left with now?"

'At that point, Shakuni got up shamelessly and whispered something in the ear of his nephew. Hearing that, Duryodhana's eyes widened with excitement and he said, "You slave, you still have one more thing with you. Will you put that at stake?"

'The venerable Pandava raised his head and asked, "What?"

'"Your wife Draupadi."

'Bhimsena leapt up with intense rage, screaming, "No…!" Looking at his brother, Sahadeva, he said, "He will surely put Draupadi at stake. I cannot bear this. Sahadeva, get me some fire. I will burn the hands that played this game. Brandishing the mace on his shoulders, Bhimsena ran towards Yudhishthira instead of towards Duryodhana. Arjuna controlled him with a great deal of effort. "If we lose this bet, we will return everything that you have lost to us so far. My brothers and I will serve you. We will obey every command of yours."

'Again, with the help of Shakuni, Duryodhana provoked the gambling addict in the venerable Pandava. Nobody in the gambling arena had heard anything like this before, and almost all of them stood up. Only two people were sitting – the blind Maharaja Dhritarashtra and Kuru Maharani Gandharidevi, who had blindfolded herself for the sake of her husband. In the commotion of the gambling arena they did not understand what was going on.'

I was speechless to hear the name of Draupadidevi. Still, the Lord looked calm. He said, 'Vipruthu, what happened after that?'

'The venerable Pandava placed the last bet and Shakuni threw the dice for it. At the exact same time, Karna, the king of Anga, entered the arena, attracting the attention of everybody present. As the venerable Pandava lost the last bet too, Duryodhana lost his senses and shouted ecstatically, "Maid…Pandavas' wife Draupadi has become the maid of the Kurus! Maid! Fragrant maid!" Hearing that chant, the insane brothers of Duryodhana tossed their shawls in the air, and shouted, "Maidservant…maid…"'

I looked curiously at the Lord to see his reaction. He was staring at the roof, as if he was not present with the two of us!

The chief minister kept talking as if he was present in the gambling arena of the Kurus.

'Now Duryodhana, who had gone insane in the delusion that he had indeed become master of Draupadidevi, ordered his attendant and manager Pratikama, 'Go, Pratikama, and present that maid of the Kurus in our service. Immediately!' Pratikama left. The entire arena was wondering if he was indeed going to present the maharani of Indraprastha as a maidservant.

'The servant Pratikama returned alone. With his head bowed, he said to his master Duryodhana, "Master, she cannot come to the gambling arena. She is wearing a single layer of clothing – she is menstruating."

'Then Duryodhana rebuked the servant harshly and said to his brother Dushasana, "This is not an attendant's job. My dear valiant brother, Dushasana, you yourself go to the inner chambers and bring that maid to the gambling arena, whatever condition she is in. If she protests and says no, then drag her by force!"

'"Your wish is my command, Dada," said Dushasana and went to the inner chambers. Within a few moments, loud screams were heard from the direction of the inner chambers, which left the entire gambling arena shaken. "Leave me. You scoundrel, let me go! Remember, you also have a mother and sisters."

'As the Pandava noble lady screamed and shouted desperately, Dushasana dragged her into the gambling arena. The entire gambling arena stood up at once and stared at Dushasana, wondering what was going to happen now.'

Even I kept staring at the chief minister, wondering what was going to happen. My brain had gone numb. I had never heard such abominable things in my life. I looked at the Lord, thinking that he must be enraged to hear about the horrendous humiliation of his dear friend. I was shocked to see that he still sat calm, with his eyes closed. I did not understand what exactly he was seeing with his closed eyes.

The chief minister kept talking, 'The Pandava's wife Draupadidevi was dragged over the carpet in the gambling arena. Her hair dishevelled, she demanded justice from Maharaja Dhritarashtra, "Maharaja…you are the venerable senior in the Kuru family, my respectable father-in-law. Tell these gambling addicts, did my husband have any right to put me at stake as his wife after he had lost himself in a bet? Did he not lose the right of being my husband the moment he became a slave?"

'Unable to answer her, the Kuru king Dhritarashtra squirmed in his seat. Meanwhile, Duryodhana remembered his insult at the Mayasabha at the time of the Rajasuya yajna and actually ordered Dushasana, "Dushasana, strip this maid of the Kurus naked in this fully occupied gambling arena. Pull that fragrant sword out of the scabbard dangling at the hips of the weak Pandavas. Let her understand well that a blind father's sons are not always blind. In fact, they wish to see and can see things that even her sighted husbands cannot. Dushasana, strip her naked and make her sit on my lap." Duryodhana pulled his dhoti aside and thumped his bare thigh. Bhimsena could not bear this indignity and shouted, "Duryodhana, I will smash the thigh that you have exposed so impudently in this arena full of people, with a single strike of my mace. When time comes, I will rip off and toss skywards the dirty hand of the scoundrel Dushasana that followed your commands like a puppet and touched my dear wife." Bhimsena did not just roar these words but brandished his mace and ran towards both of them. But he had to return and sit in his place, fuming with anger after hearing his elder brother's command, "Back off, Bhima!"

'Dushasana walked to Draupadidevi like a burning inferno moving towards verdure. He directly put his hand on the vesture that she was wearing. Draupadidevi turned around like an infuriated serpent and bit his strong hand vehemently. Dushasana withdrew both his hands in agony. She ran around in the arena. Dushasana chased her to try and get hold of her vesture. Beating her chest, her hands spread out, hair untied, the wailing lady implored all the major warriors in the gambling arena. Who wasn't among them? Everyone, including Maharaja Dhritarashtra,

Maharani Gandharidevi, Grandsire Bhishma, Guru Drona, Kripa, Vidura and Sanjaya were there. "Maharaja…Grandsire…Maharani…save my honour. I will sweep the gambling arena of the Kurus as a maidservant. I will wash the royal family's vesture. But do not humiliate me like this, by disrobing me."

'No one could respond to her. The next moment, she was standing in front of Karna. He stood up at once at that time. But, for some reason, she did not make any request to him. Lamenting loudly, and cursing everyone, including her husbands, Devi ran around the entire arena. She got exhausted, but got up and ran again, to avoid Dushasana coming closer to her. She began shouting loudly, "Tell me, is there a single gallant warrior in this ancient gambling arena of the Kurus who has the courage of a lion and stands by Truth? Does anyone here today care about the lineage of Maharaja Yayati, Yadu, Puru, Hasti, Ajameedha, Samvarana, Janhu and Kuru at all? Isn't any one of you aware that you are the descendants of Maharani Tapati, Nalini, Bhumini, Sudakshina, Viraja, Devayani, Ganga and Satyavati? An assembly without elders is no assembly, and elders without the sense of justice and injustice are no elders.

'"Do you think that a woman's honour is merely for gambling? Is it a piece of dice that can be held in one's hand and thrown out as per one's whims? Do you think that the society or the kingdom that humiliates a woman in such a horrendous way will not be destroyed? Are you even conscious of the fact that you are born from a woman's affectionate womb? I beg you to tell me, is there at least a single son in this gambling arena today who still honours his mother's milk?"

'For a moment, dead silence prevailed. Even Dushasana's hold on the royal lady's vesture went loose.

'Only one valiant Kuru in the entire gambling arena stood up with resolve, and told Dushasana, who was his elder, "Dushasana, do not even touch Panchali. Members of the assembly, remember this is the assembly that has been honoured by royal ladies from Maharani Tapati to Satyavati. Abusing a royal lady here is like trampling on an idol of a goddess to be worshipped.

'"Though I am younger, I dare to ask all the elders here whether their swords that shine on the battlefield are corroded today. Why are the

Grandsire, Maharaja, Mahatma Vidura, Acharya Drona, Kripa, all the ascetics, the wise and the hermits dead silent as if struck by lightning?

"'I, Vikarna, the son of Dhritarashtra, would like to tell you, the sobs and wails of a devoted wife will carry the terrifying music of doom with them. The hot tears streaming down her face will assume the form of a thundering, tempestuous Ganga and run wild. None of the seats which you are sitting on now will last then. Injustice to a devoted wife is like injustice to chastity itself. Her humiliation is the end of all chivalry."

'His words set the assembly abuzz. Even demented Dushasana, who was till now hysterically trying to grab the royal lady's vesture, hesitated for a moment.

'Karna stood up and said, "Vikarna, you are a fool. Even the elderly Grandsire, Maharaja and Mahatma Vidura, who are present in the assembly, have not said a word. You are straining your vocal chords in vain, portraying that the mantle of Dharma is resting only on your shoulders.

"'A devoted wife? What kind of devoted wife is this? The woman whose trumpet you are blowing as a 'devoted wife' is no devoted wife at all.

"'She is a mere seeker of carnal enjoyment with five husbands. She is impure. An adulteress. A harlot. A whore! This kind of woman prefers hundred and five husbands rather than just five! A maid is at least modest enough to cover her body; she at least has humility. But an adulteress does not. What does it matter whether she comes dressed or undressed in the assembly?

"'Vikarna, do not meddle in matters that you know nothing about. Sit down! Dushasana, strip this maid naked!"

'Everyone in the arena was aghast on hearing these appalling words from the valiant philanthropist. Hesitant Dushasana regained his composure and came forward. Grabbing the hem of Draupadidevi's vesture, he pulled it forcibly. Covering the bodice on her chest with her arms, the wife of the Pandavas cried out in agony, leaving all benumbed, "Oh Milinda…Madhava…Madhusudana…hurry. Gopala, Ghananeela, Achyuta…Keshava…Srikrishna…help! Become the earth and split yourself open to swallow this ill-fated Draupadi. Come to be the fire in the yajna pit and reduce this yajna-born Draupadi to ashes. Take the sizzling ashes of her remains and smear them on the temples of these blind, despicable scoundrels. Dunk the drunken heads of these men in the tidal waves of my defenceless tears and drown them to suffocating death. Burn these venomous serpents lurking in the thick forests of the Kuru dynasty with my scorching sighs. Blow out the giant lamp of the sun today itself and bury this dark slave of the Kauravas in that pitch darkness. Or else, run, come from the expanse of the blue sky, from the void of the netherworld, from the ten directions. Run, rush and save me..."

'And...suddenly a cacophony of musical instruments and mantra incantations were heard from the roof of the gambling arena of the Kurus, like no one had ever heard before. An aura of unbearably brilliant light filled the arena. The next moment, a rapidly revolving circle of blinding light was seen there. I saw something like your shawl coming out of that light and touching the vesture that the royal lady was wearing. The unbearable brilliance made me dizzy and I collapsed. I do not know anything about what happened next.'

Even while narrating this, the chief minister covered his eyes as if he was trying to protect them from the brilliant light. The Lord moved forward, patted his back, removed his hands from his face and said, 'Chief Minister Vipruthu, calm down. No need to share further details now. I have understood everything.'

Since that episode, the Lord began thinking only about Hastinapura. He started looking gloomy like never before. Quite often, he would take Uddhava Maharaja with him and go to the Aindra gate in the west. Sitting on the stone seats there, he would listen to the continuous roar of the rising waves. He appeared lost in some distant thought. If at all he spoke, it would be just a sentence or two with Uddhava Maharaja. I was the only one who accompanied them all the time. I had become so close to my Lord by now that I clearly understood that his mind was roaring just like the western ocean. I could automatically feel the countless thought waves rising in that ocean even without speaking to him.

Despite being such a thinker, the venerable Pandava Yudhishthira had not learnt any lesson from the first gambling episode in Hastinapura. He had even accepted a second invitation from Duryodhana. Within eight days of the first game, he played the second with Duryodhana and Shakuni in Hastinapura itself.

In this game, he lost the Indraprastha kingdom that the Pandavas and the Yadavas had erected. The last bet in this gambling game was that either Duryodhana with all his brothers would have to spend twelve years in a forest and one year incognito, or the Pandavas would have to do the same. Yudhishthira lost this last bet as well.

News arrived in Dwaraka that Yudhishthira had left for Kamyakavana along with the other Pandavas and Draupadidevi to live in the forest. I felt dejected after hearing the news.

The Pandavas, who were the rulers of Indraprastha, were leaving for the forest from the Kauravas' Hastinapura itself. As many men and women of Hastinapura still respected the Pandavas' father – world conqueror Pandu – they had gathered at the borders of Hastinapura to bid them farewell. All the five Pandavas had changed from their royal attire into plain white vesture.

Draupadidevi was also dressed in simple attire. Her brother Dhrishtadyumna had also come to bid farewell to them. He was going to take all the sons of the Pandavas to the Panchala kingdom for inculcation of sanskaras and further education. Our Subhadradevi's son Abhimanyu was to stay behind, because Kuntidevi was going to stay at Mahamantri Vidura's residence in Hastinapura. She was not going to the forest.

The Lord felt hurt that Yudhishthira had gambled again, even after all that had happened. But he was even more hurt that Yudhishthira had left directly for the Kamyakavana, with all Pandavas and his dear sister, Draupadidevi, even without meeting him. Yet, he never deterred from his duty. He went to Indraprastha along with Uddhava Maharaja and me. He explained to Subhadradevi, in a very loving and affectionate way, on how she could face the current situation. He returned to Dwaraka along with Subhadradevi and his infant nephew, Abhimanyu. It was obvious that Shakuni and Duryodhana had taken back the area of Khandavavana that Maharaja Dhritarashtra had so kindly offered to the Pandavas in the presence of my Lord.

The royal capital Indraprastha had completely lost its charm. The cultured royal family of the Pandavas had scattered in all directions. All the Pandavas, along with their wife Draupadidevi, were in the Kamyakavana, the Pandavas' mother Kuntidevi was in Hastinapura, Subhadradevi–

Abhimanyu in Dwaraka, Arjuna's wife Chitrangadadevi in Manipura with their son Babhruvahana, Uloopidevi on the banks of River Ganga at her parental home with their son Iravana, and Bhima's wife Hidimbadevi in the forest with their son Ghatotkacha.

Many of the dreams that my Lord had seen about the Pandavas were wiped out. Now, the foremost urgency was to visit the Kamyakavana – to rekindle the lost courage of the Pandavas, to console Draupadidevi. As per the Lord's instructions, I took him to Kamyakavana. Balaramadada and commander Satyaki accompanied us. As I was occupied in tending to the horses and the chariot, I did not come to know about the discussions that took place with the Pandavas during this visit. The Lord returned after spending two days in the forest.

These days, the Lord of Dwaraka had almost stopped going to the Sudharma royal assembly and the island of the queens' mansions. He would spend hours on end on the shores of the western ocean, along with Uddhava Maharaja. Or he would visit the Shiva temple of Somanath, crossing the creek and then riding in the chariot along with Uddhava Maharaja. It was only in the morning and the evening that the Lord met Maharaja Vasudeva, Devakimata and Rohinimata, Balaramadada and Revatidevi to pay obeisance. If at all, commander Satyaki, Anadhrishti and various troop leaders came to seek his guidance regarding the growing Yadava army, he would only listen to them. Without saying anything, he would ask me to take them to Balaramadada.

If he spoke, it would be a lot with his own sons, whom he would call to his chambers. Some of his sons were brilliant. They would pose their questions to the Lord of Dwaraka to get their doubts cleared. Some were simply warriors. They would gather more information about warfare. A few were born humble and shy. They would only listen. The Lord would often be cheerful and laugh freely with his sons. It had been six months since the Pandavas had gone to live in the forest. Many people of Dwaraka had almost forgotten them. But my Lord, Balaramadada, Uddhava Maharaja, Maharaja Vasudeva and I could never forget them. The Lord met Acharya Sandipani more frequently these days and had discussions with him. I could strongly sense the change in the Lord's demeanour day by day. He was reluctant to perform any of his duties. The Lord, who otherwise participated in any activity enthusiastically with pure love, strongly preferred silence and seclusion. And finally, that day dawned. In a very calm but firm voice, he said, 'Dear brother Udho and Daruka, after much deliberation I have taken a firm decision. I had left Mathura once, now I am going to leave Dwaraka too, for good. I am going to an ashrama far away in the north to peacefully spend time in contemplation of the almighty God. It is up to you to decide whether you want to join me. Balaramadada and I have stayed together since Gokul. But this time I am not taking him with me. He left me once in anger. Now I am going to leave him, but with respect and love for his seniority in my heart. I have no choice. As he is the formally installed prince, the kingdom of Dwaraka holds more authority over him than me. He will remain here, to serve and protect Dwaraka. If you also decide to stay back, my love for you as my "confidants" will not reduce even a bit.'

Both of us simply kept staring at him. For a moment, it was not clear to us what he was talking about. We were stunned, perplexed and did not know what to do. He realised that we were just mutely staring at him. Laughing innocently like a child, he said, 'Dear friends, can you not take such a simple decision? How must have I taken so many decisions in my life? I assure you that whatever decision you take, I will readily accept.'

'Dada, I cannot even imagine living without you. Can there be breath without the body? Is this what you have judged me to be? Of course I am coming with you, whether you consider me your friend or not,' Uddhava Maharaja responded promptly, leaving no doubt at all.

'Oh Lord, I am your shadow, after all. How can one separate it from the body? Wherever the Lord of Dwaraka will be, Daruka will be too.' I also conveyed my firm decision in clear words. Now it was going to be his choice, whether to take me with him or not.

He got a firm, clear response from both of us. Then he looked deep into our eyes once and, coming closer, put his arms around our shoulders. Patting us gently he said, 'Remember, nobody should know where we are going. Uddhava will be fine as he is unmarried. But Daruka, your wife also should not know a single word of this. If that happens, I will leave both of you here and go someplace else all alone. Uddhava, maybe I will go towards the Himalayas, which, with a smile, bears many holy places like Amaranath, which we visited!'

'Oh Lord, you have shown your faith in Uddhava Maharaja. I take a vow in your name that my wife will not know anything about this.'

'Then go, get ready.' The Lord dismissed both of us.

While leaving his chambers, I said to Uddhava Maharaja, 'Now I understand why the Lord never accepted any royal throne.'

Uddhava Maharaja looked at me and, smiling just like the Lord, said, 'Daruka, it's nothing special. Just now, he told you to not tell anything to your wife, which obviously means that he is not going to tell anything to Rukminidevi and the other seven wives either. But I do not know how to leave without telling Rukminidevi. Still, I will go – just as he has told me, without telling anything to anybody.'

The preparations for our departure from Dwaraka were all done. We were only going to take the Garudadhwaja chariot with us. The back of the chariot was filled with minimum necessities like foodgrains for the journey, cooking vessels and a few clothes. The Lord had given us strict instructions to not take any weapons with us.

A week before our departure, the Lord got everybody mentally prepared through Acharya Sandipani. Acharya said, 'My dear disciple, the Lord of Dwaraka, is going to a faraway region in the south to obtain a very rare vidya on my instructions. The Lord may take a Yadava or two with him if he wishes to. His new guru himself has instructed him not to bring anybody else along. Therefore, even Prince Balarama will not go with him. With the assistance of Gargamuni, I am looking for an auspicious time for the Lord's departure.'

After all such preparations, the Lord was ready to depart from Dwaraka – only with us, his two friends. With a signal of the hand, he summoned only two of the men from among all who had gathered to see him off at the Shuddhaksha gate, on the Garudadhwaja chariot that was already loaded on a boat. Those two fortunate men were chief minister Vipruthu and Acharya Sandipani.

We crossed the island creek and descended on the borders of Saurashtra. Then the Lord took the chief minister aside, bade him farewell and said, 'Chief Minister, I may not come back from where I am going. I pulled you aside from amongst all and have brought you here only to tell you that you have to convey my message gradually and gently to all my wives, sons, Vasudevababa, both matas, the prince and Revatidevi, their sons, sister Subhadra, her son Abhimanyu and all citizens in a manner that they can digest it. But not today – only after fifteen days. We will be going to an ashrama near the rivers Krishna and Kaveri in the southern region that we have not seen before. Do not try to come there to find us. It will be in vain.' For the first time, he embraced Chief Minister Vipruthu too, who was baffled by the action. The Lord put his head on the feet of Acharya Sandipani. Acharya pulled him up with genuine affection and held him in a deep embrace immediately. Bringing both his palms together in front of his guru, the Lord humbly said, 'I am going to see the same guru whose name you had suggested in the Ankapada ashrama. Acharya, so far, I have tried to follow your teachings as much as I could. Please forgive me kindly if I have committed any mistakes.'

I took the charioteer's seat on the Garudadhwaja. In the back of the chariot were the two venerable Yadavas whom I have held in high esteem throughout my life – the Lord of Dwaraka and Uddhava Maharaja. Our very first halt was at Nageshwara, a holy place of Shiva's worship. During our journey so far, we had realised that because of the royal attire of the Lord and Uddhava Maharaja and my attire as a charioteer, and also due to the embellished chariot, the men and women meeting us on the way were recognising us very easily. They were running after the chariot, trying to halt it by spreading their hands. It was necessary to stop this. Nageshwara was one of the twelve holy places of Shiva in Aaryavarta. When we arrived at the Shiva temple here, the Lord shared his plan with me. He said, 'Daruka, we should get rid of the royal attire and put on simple clothes like ashrama residents. We should dispatch our royal attire to Balaramadada in Dwaraka, along with our crowns, through the temple priest here. Otherwise, this journey will take very long. Besides, the course of our journey will be known back in Dwaraka.'

In the temple of Nageshwara, we changed from royal attire to the plain clothing of ashrama residents. We removed all royal insignia from the Garudadhwaja chariot, even the well-known pennant atop the chariot with the Garuda emblem, and replaced it with a plain saffron pennant. We also removed the fine caparison on the backs of all four horses, and changed their golden reins too. We handed over all this to the temple priest. The Lord gave him strict instructions on what to do. The appearance of the chariot was radically transformed now and so was ours.

In the temple, we were told that if we continued our journey in the same way, we would safely reach the expected destination of the holy place of Prayaga in the northern region without any obstacles. Before leaving, we devotedly offered a palm full of white flowers and Bela leaves on the grand Shivapindi in the shrine of the temple. All three of us brought our palms together in prayer and closed our eyes. The hymn of Lord Shiva automatically resonated in our minds. Now, in our journey ahead, everything that was 'Shiva'– auspicious in the world – was going to be with us.

We passed Stavatirtha, crossed over River Mahi and entered Avanti through the Malava kingdom. This was the kingdom of Vinda and Anuvinda, who were the Lord's aunt's sons. But during this journey, we did not want to give anybody the slightest inkling of our arrival. Therefore, we decided to seek shelter in the charitable resthouses for travellers at Vishnu temples and Shiva temples located on the borders of various kingdoms on our way. Therefore, the citizens of Avanti did not get wind of the fact that the Lord of Dwaraka was travelling through their kingdom, along with his brother. During this journey, the Lord and his brother would tuck their dhotis in and groom the four white horses of the chariot with the thorny creepers that I fetched from the forests. Both of them used to be engrossed in the act. At this time, they would discuss various topics. I had already seen both of them picking up the soiled dishes of invitees during the Rajasuya yajna. Now, I was also witnessing them feeding all four horses, even occasionally picking up horse dung, without any reservation. Whenever we came across any forests or plateaus, both brothers would talk about various aspects of life from all angles. They would also include me in their discussions. But both of them would strictly keep silent whenever we approached a town and could see the people of that town. Then it would be my duty to speak and collect information for our journey ahead. I would also do this very cautiously.

After passing cities like Vidisha in the Nishadha kingdom, Padmavati in the Dasharna kingdom and Sagar in the Pulinda kingdom, we crossed River Karnavati. This river was named after Karna, the king of Anga. One of our sojourns was at the bottom of Mount Chitrakuta, where Srirama, Lakshmana and Sita had stayed once upon a time. Finally, we travelled through Pampapura and arrived at the holy place of Prayaga.

This place was a holy confluence of the three big rivers in Aaryavarta – River Ganga flowing through the Hastinapura kingdom of the Kurus; River Yamuna, which nurtured my Lord's delightful childhood with her waters and that came flowing from the Indraprastha kingdom; and the invisible River Saraswati.

We arrived at the famous Sangam ghat of Prayaga. I left the chariot on the ghat, in the shade of a sprawling mango tree, and gave fodder to the horses. We began climbing down the steps of the Sangam ghat one at a time. At that time, I strongly remembered the Srisopana in Dwaraka. It had also become huge like this.

All three of us kept our dry vesture on a step near the edge and entered the waters of the confluence, dressed only in our loincloths. I feasted my eyes upon the Lord standing in front of me, drenched completely in the waters of the Ganga and the Yamuna, shining brightly in the sunrays. His radiant face showed no sign of fatigue even after such a long journey. I brought the Garudadhwaja chariot in front of the wooden east gate of the ashrama of Acharya Ghor Angirasa, which was close to the Sangam ghat. While descending from the chariot, Uddhava Maharaja instructed me, 'Daruka, go to the ashrama and inform the acharya of our arrival.'

I had had an opportunity to visit the Ankapada ashrama of Acharya Sandipani in the Avanti kingdom. The Angirasa ashrama had been designed exactly in the same way. The tall, capacious cottage of Acharya Angirasa stood in the centre of all the cottages. Only one thing was different here. That was the square yajna pit in front of the acharya's cottage that was aflame throughout. Uninterrupted worship of Agni was a religious vow taken by the sage Angirasa clan that had been continued for hundreds of years. Even in the rainy season, the yajna pit would be kept ablaze under a tall roof of grass by sheltering it on all four sides with shields made of grass.

Acharya Ghor Angirasa, who was surrounded by his chosen disciples, came out with me and approached the Lord and Uddhava Maharaja, spreading both his arms wide. I immediately noticed that all disciples were wearing saffron vesture but only the acharya's vesture was pure white. He had covered his mouth with a clean white strip of cloth. The strip was tied behind his ears with two strings. That strip easily covered most of the acharya's face and his thick beard. At the back of their heads, a long tuft of hair at the centre, surrounded by four more tufts around it, was clearly visible. These five long tufts of hair and the yajna pit were distinctive features of the Angirasa ashrama. All Angirasas had five long tufts of hair at the back of their heads to signify that the human body came into existence with the enigmatic combination of the five basic elements. They were identified throughout Aaryavarta due to the five tufts of hair and their love of Agni. As they lived constantly in the company of fire, most of them had darkened and radiant fair complexions. Their eyes reflected a radiant streak of fearlessness, just like the eyes of the Bhrigu disciples.

As soon as the acharya stood in front of them, both the brothers knelt down. Acharya immediately pulled up both the brothers and held them in a deep embrace.

'How was your journey? You came without prior notice – I could not believe it.'

This acharya was also a former Yadava of Mathura as per my knowledge. He was betrothed in Mathura. But before the wedding, he became disinterested in worldly matters and directly went to the Himalayas. He had met the main Angirasa of the Angirasa rishi clan. In ancient times, the founder of the Angirasa clan had spontaneously composed a few hymns of the Rigveda. It was followed by Athararva Veda, that had five kalpas, of which one was known as 'Angirasa Kalpa' in his name. Since then, the Angirasa clan was considered to be the 'Vajrakula' among the various clans of rishis. Their main ashrama was in the Himalayas. Many branches of their ashrama, like the one in Prayaga, had spread throughout Aaryavarta. Renowned forefather Maharaja Yayati from the Lord's dynasty had been in the company of this Angirasa clan. He had also composed a few hymns in the Vedas.

This was a unique meeting of the Yadava dynasty and the 'Vajrakula' of the Angirasas.

This sage Angirasa had obtained formal initiation. He had acquired his guru's blessings through severe penance and meditation. Pleased with his severe penance, the guru had given him the name of Ghor Angirasa, and had appointed him as the successor and the chief of the Angirasa clan after him. He had realised that by living in the distant Himalayas, it would not be possible to expand the 'Vajrakula' of the Angirasa clan. Therefore, he himself had started a branch of the ashrama near the confluence of the three rivers at Prayaga. He still had a strong urge to start another branch, much bigger than the main ashrama in the Himalayas, near Mount Kailas.

In this Ghor Angirasa ashrama at Prayaga, our new daily routine began. My Lord and Uddhava Maharaja were used to this kind of ashrama life, since they had lived in the Ankapada ashrama of Acharya Sandipani, their former guru. But I was new to this. Still, I was not afraid of it at all. Both the Yadava brothers stood behind me like rocks and were quite capable of handling the situation in case I made any mistakes.

On the first day, after our formal initiation ceremony, the acharya introduced us to disciples from various kingdoms. In very few words, he said, 'This is Srikrishna – the son of Maharaja Vasudeva of Dwaraka – this is his brother Uddhava, and this is his friend Daruka.'

As soon as he finished the introduction, a big commotion arose among the disciples. Clear, rapid words came to our ears – 'What? Srikrishna? The slayer of Kansa – Shrugala – Kalayavana – Narakasur – Shatadhanwa – Shishupala – Shalva – Paundrak Vasudeva – Dantavakra and Viduratha? The possessor of the Sudarshan chakra? The disciple of Acharya Sandipani, the Lord of golden Dwaraka? We hope this is not a dream!'

The commotion kept increasing every minute. Acharya raised both his hands and ordered silence in clear, loud words. Acharya recognised the sentiments of his disciples and said, 'Dear disciples, he is no Srikrishna of Dwaraka now. From today, he is your ashrama brother. You have learnt a variety of yogas till today, but he has initiated a new yoga in Aaryavarta – that is Premayoga! You will experience it more and more here onwards. Let us first get to know why he has come here. I am also curious to know the reason, because he has not come here like you, who are unmarried and followers of Brahmacharyashrama. He is married, a family man, bound in relations such as father, son, husband, brother and mentor to many. And still, I have initiated him as my disciple. I have also initiated both his friends as my disciples. It is because I had promised him before that I will be his guru at the right time. In my opinion, that time has come now, as he has arrived here. I ask him in front of all of you. 'Tell me, Srikrishna, why did you feel like coming so far away to me, despite having your dear Acharya Sandipani with you? What prompted you to do so? Why have you have become so disinterested in life?'

Quite impressed, I started looking at Acharya Ghor Angirasa. He had directly asked the Lord of Dwaraka all the questions that had arisen in my mind several times. I was curious to see how the Lord was now going to answer the acharya's questions.

My Lord got up from the grass mat. He was modest, as usual. Acharya did not feel it was necessary and so he immediately signalled and said, 'Achyuta, you can speak while sitting.' Hearing Acharya's words, the Lord looked at him with intense affection and smiled. 'Venerable Acharya and all ashram brothers, all of you are wondering why I came here. Probably my dear brother Uddhava and close friend Daruka are also wondering the same. Therefore, I am humbly stating this in the presence of the acharya who is the ultimate master of Brahmavidya in entire Aaryavarta.

'It is not in my nature to stop in one place. From Gokul I came to Mathura, from Mathura to Dwaraka. From Dwaraka I travelled throughout Aaryavarta. I did whatever and as much as I could.

'I established the Pandavas of the Kuru dynasty of Hastinapura in Indraprastha. I met not one or two but literally thousands of men and women. I loved each one of them as much as I could.

'I was involved with my heart and soul in Indraprastha, even more than the golden Dwaraka. I chose the five Pandava brothers from among the many men whom I came across, not because they were my cousins, but because they possessed rare qualities.

'But – but I am deeply saddened by only one thing. A golden city can be erected on the roaring ocean; a grand royal city can be raised in the thick forests; evil powers obstructing the flow of all life can be destroyed determinedly. All this can be done, but for what purpose? We do not understand what goes on in the mind of even our dear ones. I am extremely sad as to why it is not possible to shape it even with great efforts.

'The virtuous, truth-loving eldest Pandava, Yudhishthira, who has endured suffering due to the circumstances, went astray. Even when he had the a golden opportunity to show his prowess. Why? And how? One can create everything from nothing. How should one shape a mind, which is basically shapeless, with sanskaras? Rather, how futile is the pride that "I am the creator."

'I had envisioned a certain picture of entire Aaryavarta based on the exceptional qualities of the Pandavas. I had much higher expectations from Indraprastha than from Dwaraka.

'A formally crowned king like Yudhishthira, who is responsible for his subjects, went astray due to addiction to gambling; put the kingdom, his brothers, along with his wife, at stake. The descendants of the royal dynasty of Hastinapura dared to drag a lady having her menstrual cycle into the gambling arena to fulfil their perverse desire for revenge. They dared to touch the vesture on her body in front of all venerable elders in the arena. Maharathi Karna, who is such an exceptional devotee of the Sun god, who, at that time, should have saved her honour by taking off his body armour and covering her with it, wished to disrobe her in front of all. All these are countless expressions of many human minds that are unfathomable to anyone.

'The eldest among my beloved cousins played the same kind of gambling game once again, even after losing everything in the first game. He lost everything that he had achieved and that was dear to him. He has accepted living in the forest and staying incognito. He left for the forest without meeting his close friend, like me, that, too, with my dearest, most virtuous friend Arjuna.

'Even Arjuna left without meeting me, as he could not explain his brother's idiocy to me. My dear sakhi Draupadi, who I consider my dear sister and because of whom all these unimaginable, despicable events took place, also left without meeting me.

'All such things happen due to the illusions of the mind. Unless a man's mind is moulded, he does not become a man. These bitter experiences of life have brought me here. It is futile to dream about anything. It is impossible to mould human minds.

'I have studied many yogas, like Dhyanayoga, Sankhyayoga and Jnanayoga, devotedly in the ashrama of Acharya Sandipani. I considered Premayoga as the essence of my life. I am heartbroken that all this is just useless, and therefore I have turned my back on all and come here at the feet of the acharya, to find complete peace of mind. He should now expound to me what is right.'

The entire cottage filled with an uneasy silence. All eyes were now on Acharya Ghor Angirasa, who was sitting on the high seat with his eyes closed.

Acharya exclaimed without a moment's delay, 'This is what is called Vishadayoga – melancholy. As beyond the sky, there is the endless, dark space which one can never see, the Vishadayoga of the mind is endless. Srikrishna, I know very well that you are aware of what Vishadayoga is. You are way beyond it. I will explain exactly why you have come here.' Stunned, we pricked up our ears, along with the other disciples.

'You have come here to make all around you, and the future generations, understand what the melancholy of the mind is, with your own example. The experience of the night makes us realise the importance of the day. The exposure to darkness helps us realise the value of light. Grandsire Bhishma himself has addressed you as Vasudeva. I say that Bhagwan Vasudeva, you are the Light that every being is in quest of.' Acharya muttered something vaguely like 'Arpanam astu' and went into a meditative trance. Our first day at the Angirasa ashrama was over.

On the very first day, my Lord had won over the hearts of everyone in the Ghor Angirasa ashrama of Prayaga.

Our days in the Prayaga ashrama were becoming increasingly memorable. All three of us missed Hastinapura, Indraprastha and Dwaraka every single day. But each one of us made sure not to mention it in our discussions.

The days in the ashram got more engaging. All of us disciples would look forward to the acharya's discourses and could not wait to hear the signalling sound of the conch. It had been one month since we came here. Day after day, the acharya's discourse about Brahmavidya was getting more elaborate and profound. While talking about the important subject of Bhaktiyoga, the acharya got entranced. He said, 'An ardent devotee of the Almighty wonders whether it is better to worship the Lord in the form beyond attributes or in a manifest form? The only answer to this is – both are equal. The worship of god beyond attributes takes one closer to the Almighty easily. The worship of a manifest form, without any expectations, also reaches the same height as the worship beyond attributes. Even that takes one close to the Almighty.' While presenting such thoughts, the acharya would forget even about lunchtime. The disciples, too, would feel full with the extraordinary thoughts they had just heard.

A month and a half had passed since we came to the Angirasa ashrama. The five tufts on our heads had grown considerably long now. We had completely become one with the ashrama now.

It had been sixty-three days since we had come to this ashrama. This was the sixty-fourth day. I had heard many times in the discussions of the Lord and Uddhava Maharaja that they had stayed for exactly the same period at the Ankapada ashrama. It was not in his nature to get stuck in one place. He was indeed a Jalapurusha – always flowing like water.

I was lost in thinking about how my Lord's future life would be in this ashrama. A tranquil evening had descended on our ashrama at the holy place of Prayaga near the banks of River Ganga. I saw huge eagles making shrill sounds and returning to Mount Mainaka in the west. I had just returned to our cottage from River Ganga after offering evening oblations to the setting sun. All three of us were getting ready for evening prayers, when we heard some commotion at the western gate of the ashrama. We could vaguely hear words like – 'What – Srikrishnadeva's brother? Mace fight expert Balaramadada? Sankarshana Balarama himself? And the chief minister of Dwaraka?' After hearing those words, I rose at once from my mat and started running towards the western gate of the ashrama. Hefty Balaramadada had descended from the chariot and was standing at the western gate of the ashrama, along with Chief Minister Vipruthu. The huge mace on his shoulder was shining in the rays of the setting sun. He shouted loudly as soon as he saw me, 'Daruka, this Prince of Dwaraka would have found you even if you were hiding in the netherworld. Where is my younger brother?' He laughed loudly, throwing his head back. With that the mace on his shoulder shook. He could not hide the euphoria of finally finding both his brothers. His appearance always inspired energy. Today, I felt it even more. I moved forward and touched his feet. Balaramadada had become impatient to see the Lord now and embraced me tightly as if embracing his own brother. He said, 'Come, take me to my brother. I have come to take him to Dwaraka with me.'

I came to our cottage along with Dada and chief minister. The Lord and his brother were in the cottage. I offered fruits collected from the forest to them. Balaramadada felt refreshed and said to the Lord, 'I have come to take you back to Dwaraka. How could you and Uddhava desert us like this? Poor Rukmini, she has been in so much distress after you left. Father and both the mothers are asking for you every day and night. You should quietly come with me now, along with Uddhava.' Dada clarified the purpose of his sudden visit while sitting down on the mat. The chief minister, standing nearby with his palms joined in request, said earnestly, 'Oh Lord, please do not try everybody's patience now. Come to Dwaraka along with Uddhavadeva.'

The powerful prince of Dwaraka and chief minister kept looking at the Lord with a pleading look in their eyes. But he was completely peaceful. He resolutely said, 'Dada, it is not possible now. I have taken the decision to come here after considerable thought. Now I will live here. You can take Uddhava and Daruka back if they are ready to go with you.'

A few stifled moments passed. Uddhava Maharaja instantly said, 'Balidada, I will go wherever my big brother goes. You can take Daruka with you. The three of us had stayed together in the Ankapada ashrama of Acharya Sandipani in Avanti. In fact, I would have asked you to stay here as well. But as the formally initiated prince, you have the responsibility of Dwaraka on your shoulders.'

Both brothers were trying to make me a scapegoat in front of Balaramadada's powerful mace strike. How would I listen to that? I also said quickly, 'Oh prince, I consider myself the Lord's shadow. I have never gone anywhere without him, and never will.'

Intellectual artfulness and politics were not Balaramadada's forte. Still, he was lost in thought. Within a moment, he decided on something and said, 'Let us do one thing – we will take Acharya Ghor Angirasa's opinion on this matter.'

'Sure. We are his disciples. His command will be respectfully honoured by us.'

After having meals and taking some rest, the prince left for that acharya's cottage, along with the three of us. Acharya was sitting outside, offering sacrificial sticks into the yajna pit that blazed day and night. We approached and paid obeisance to him. First, he enquired after Vasudevababa, both matas, Acharya Sandipani, his wife and son in Dwaraka. Then he affectionately asked Balaramadada, 'How come you arrived without any notice, Prince? Is it that the separation from your brothers has become unbearable?' Gurudeva smiled.

'You are omniscient. Do I need to articulate the purpose of my visit?' I had sensed the difference in Balaramadada's attitude since he had arrived here. He had come with a determination to take his brothers with him. He simply glanced at the chief minister.

'Gurudeva, the kingdom of Dwaraka without the Lord of Dwaraka is like the sky without the sun. The prince has been earnestly imploring him to return to Dwaraka since he has come here. But the Lord of Dwaraka has firmly declared that he will stay here forever. And you already know how firm his decision can be.' The chief minister said plaintively.

'Oh, Chief Minister of Yadavas, it is indeed true. My beloved disciple Srikrishna is another name for Determination. He would not have come to my ashrama leaving Dwaraka behind had he not had that resolve of mind. His wish is the ultimate.' Gurudeva supported his disciple.

Again a few silent moments passed. We all kept staring at the prince, wondering what he was going to do now. He removed the golden royal crown from his head with his own hands and put it on the ground at the feet of the guru. He leaned forward in front of the acharya and joining both his palms, said, 'Gurudeva, it is my innate duty as an older brother to take care of both my younger brothers. If both of them are not ready to come to Dwaraka, then you should initiate and accept me as your disciple and offer me the ashrama attire. Send this royal crown of the prince that was put on my head in a formal ceremony back to Dwaraka at the hands of the chief minister. I have full faith that the king of Dwaraka – Maharaja

Vasudeva – both rajmatas – Devakimata and Rohinimata – will accept your decision readily.'

Acharya Ghor Angirasa kept offering sacrificial sticks into the yajna pit, which was the symbol of his Angirasa clan. The yajna pit of his inner mind came ablaze as he came to a decision. The yajna fire flared. Again a few stifled moments passed. Then he uttered each of his words as if he were uttering hymns from the Vedas – 'Prince Balabhadra, I cannot accept you as my disciple. You are a formally crowned prince of a kingdom, blessed by sages and hermits. Only two things will happen unavoidably if you decide to live here for the sake of your brothers.'

Acharya continued while offering sticks into the yajna pit, 'Once the old king of Dwaraka – Maharaja Vasudeva – comes to know the whereabouts of you brothers, he himself will come here with both his wives. The newly built kingdom will be left without a king. I will have to leave this ashrama, as I will be the reason for all this. Then this new ashrama will also be left without an acharya. Therefore, in the given situation, I can take only one decision – to tell Srikrishna to return to Dwaraka along with Daruka and Uddhava. I have fulfilled my ordained duty to teach him the Brahmavidya, for which he had come here. It is his duty to take the Aatmavidya that I have taught him and make it his life's mission. I have faith that he knows it thoroughly and does have the capacity to fulfil it. In front of this fire of the yajna pit that is the symbol of the Vajrakula of the Angirasas, I command that Srikrishna – the Lord of Dwaraka – now return to Dwaraka along with his brother Uddhava and friend Daruka. I wish you a safe and happy journey.'

As soon as we heard the command, all three of us bent down. While touching the acharya's feet together, we said in unison, 'As you wish, Gurudeva.'

Extremely pleased with our words, the acharya held the crown of the prince of Dwaraka in his hands. He stood up and, going closer to Balabhadradada, put it back on his head. He blessed him, saying, 'May all be well.'

We took the blessings of Acharya Ghor Angirasa and finally got the five tufts on our heads removed. We returned the ashrama clothes to the ashrama store. We bade farewell to all ashrama brothers and left from the Prayaga ashrama. We now wore the vesture and ornaments that Dada had brought with him. After three weeks, we came close to the creek of the island of Dwaraka. As Dada had sent a messenger ahead with the news, I got to watch a scene that I had never seen before. Within no time the ecstatic, chattering men and women of Dwaraka gathered around the Garudadhwaja like fresh flowers spread under the fully blossomed Prajakta tree. They began falling at the feet of the Lord of Dwaraka with moist eyes and heavy voices. 'Oh, Lord of Dwaraka, please never leave us like this again.' Their implorations blended in with the roaring of the ocean.

The Lord started to bend down and pick up the citizens of Dwaraka one after the other. Patting them, he said, 'No, I will never go. Forgive me that I went without meeting all of you.'

The Lord's entire extended family stood anxiously waiting at the Shuddhaksha gate, adorned with festoons and flower garlands. Every single person was present there. As he saw his father, Vasudevababa, my virtuous Lord separated from us and walked briskly ahead with his heart full of love. He knelt in front of his father and put his forehead on his feet. A few silent moments passed by. The gathered crowd simply kept watching with teary eyes.

The old father effusively pulled up and held his beloved son – who was a Chakravarti, a world conqueror, the possessor of the Sudarshan chakra, the one who had left him to become an ascetic – in a deep embrace. Some sentimental Yadava from amongst the gathered crowd hollered jubilantly, 'Hail the disciple of Ghor Angirasa, the son of Vasudeva, Bhagwan Vasudeva Srikrishna…!' Everyone responded spontaneously in unison, 'Victory! Victory!'

The Sudharma royal assembly that was convened the very next day was unforgettable. That day, the conduct of both the brothers, who were my co-disciples at Ghor Angirasa's ashram, got engraved permanently on my mind.

Chief Minister Vipruthu raised the jewelled golden royal sceptre of the Yadavas and announced the purpose of the assembly in the overflowing council hall, 'He who erected the grand golden royal city of Dwaraka with his intellect and hard work himself gave it up in a moment without informing anybody and without meeting anyone. He went to the faraway ashrama in Prayaga at the feet of sage Ghor Angirasa. Brave warriors of our kingdom and expert spies tried their best to find him everywhere, but no one could find any clue as to his whereabouts. We all were feeling despondent. Nobody knew what to do. In the end, Prince Balarama found out his whereabouts unmistakably. Even today I do not know how. I request him to share it with the assembly today.'

Today, Balabhadradada astounded the Sudharma assembly. He had never spoken more than a word or two. But today he spoke, even though nobody expected him to. It was indeed a splendid, unforgettable speech. He raised his hands and said, 'All Yadava members of the Sudharma royal assembly, in front of Maharaja Vasudevababa, let me tell you about my dearest brother Srikrishna – he and I played and grew up together. We are like the eyes of our father and both mothers. Any picture can be seen in its entirety only by using both eyes. I cannot imagine the kingdom of Dwaraka and this Sudharma assembly without dear brother Srikrishna in it. Vasudevababa is the ruler of this kingdom and I am the prince. But my brother Srikrishna is still the Lord of Dwaraka. He was the Lord of Dwaraka yesterday, he is so today and will remain so tomorrow. Many kings and princes will come and go, but there was, is and will be only one Lord of Dwaraka.

'I received news from Acharya Sandipani that Srikrishna is in the Angirasa ashrama at Prayaga. I promptly left for the holy place of Prayaga without a moment's delay. In my hurry, I even forgot to take the crown of the Lord of Dwaraka with me.

'I had once forsaken him due to a misunderstanding over the Syamantaka jewel. Now he has returned after forsaking me. At that time, I had tucked the peacock feather in his crown in the presence of all. Today, I have placed the royal crown with that same peacock feather on his head in the presence of you all.

'He is younger to me. But today, in spite of being older than him, I request him to let go of his status of being the younger one and forgive this Yadava prince. I love him as my brother as intensely as Vasudevababa and both mothers love him as their son, and Uddhava, Daruka, Grandsire Bhishma, Vidura, Sudama, Sanjaya, Arjuna, Radha and Draupadi regard him as their best friend. He knows it very well.

'He is not only the Lord of Dwaraka but the Lord of many more things. That is why I am imploring him.

'What if we had been unable to find his whereabouts? If he would not have returned to Dwaraka, then I would have also abandoned it. I would have worn saffron clothes like him and wandered from ashrama to ashrama in entire Bharatavarsha. Some time or the other, he would have met me during this journey. The credit for the fact that he met me and all of you goes to Acharya Sandipani. I request him to come forward and explain the mystery behind all this to the assembly.'

Balabhadradada's speech moved the entire Sudharma assembly.

As per the prince's request, Acharya Sandipani rose from his wood-backed seat. He had never spoken anything much in the Sudharma assembly before, but he spoke today. His pure-white beard reaching down to his white upper vesture quivered momentarily. Utter silence prevailed in the assembly hall. Acharya said, 'Everybody is mistaken that my dear disciple Srikrishna went to the Angirasa ashrama in Prayaga without telling anybody. It is not so. I myself had advised him to go to Ghor Angirasa to master the knowledge of Brahmavidya, which was essential for him. While leaving, he had genuinely requested me for a favour that until any important person came asking for his whereabouts, I should not voluntarily disclose it to anybody.

'I regarded his request as a command, and so I did not tell anything to anybody. I could see the frantic rush of Yadava commanders through the informers. I could feel the heart-rending anguish of Maharaja Vasudeva and both the rajmatas. That is why I went to their chambers from time to time and tried to console them with certitude, saying, "Be patient. Do not worry."

'I was worst affected by this quandary while listening to my wife's words. She frequently said, "Where could he have gone? Will we ever see him again?" At times, I felt that I should use the right of being his guru and disclose the secret. But I would control myself determinedly. His request seemed very simple to me when I heard it. But it tested even the guru's mettle. This was a completely new experience for me.

'It was Srikrishna's wife Rukminidevi who rescued me from this predicament. She came to my residential cottage once, out of the blue, along with Jambavatidevi. She did not ask me any question at all. Instead, she made a clear, certain statement. I was highly impressed to hear it. The regard that I had for her doubled. She had unmistakably surmised what no one else could even think of. She said, "My Sri would never leave anywhere without visiting his guru and taking his permission and blessings. Please do me a favour and tell me where has he gone."

'Keeping my word given to Srikrishna, finally, I told his whereabouts to her. She conveyed it to the prince and due to the prince's prompt actions, this golden day has dawned in the life of Dwaraka.

'I used to feel great agony wondering whether indeed he would ever come back. When that pain became unbearable, I would intensely feel the urge to get up and go to the Prayaga ashrama directly. But I could not do it, because then I would see the faces of Maharaja Vasudeva and both the rajmatas in front of my eyes.'

Now all eyes in the Sudharma royal assembly turned to Rukminidevi. She was calmly sitting next to her husband. I thought for a moment how tough it must be to be the Lord's wife. For us, Rukminidevi was indeed a devi who was a dutiful wife, and brilliant! She directly went to Acharya Sandipani during intense agony, to enquire about the Lord. What if she had not done that?

The entire Sudharma assembly was now completely charged only by my Lord's name and his presence. So much so that Chief Minister Vipruthu completely forgot to request the Lord, as per the custom, to say something to the citizens of Dwaraka. He simply kept gazing at the Lord.

The Lord rose, without anyone requesting him. He spoke very little this time, but it was indeed unforgettable. In his sweet, flute-like voice, he said, 'My dear brothers and sisters of Dwaraka. I did not go secretly or stealthily to the holy place of Prayaga at the feet of venerable guru Acharya Ghor Angirasa. I did not go there in the gloom that the Pandavas left without meeting me. Sometimes, deep melancholy engulfs the human mind. I went there to seek guidance from the guru to find out where the root of melancholy lies, and how to eliminate it. In short, I went there to revise the knowledge of Aatmavidya–Brahmavidya thoroughly.

'Who knows, maybe in the future, entire Aaryavarta might need it. Whatever my intention and however grand it was, you all had to suffer for it. For that, my brothers and sisters, I genuinely ask for your forgiveness.

'I promise that I will never leave my Dwaraka. And if at all such an occasion arises, I will never come back. Therefore, at this moment, I request all of you to forgive me kind-heartedly and accept me as your own.'

As the Lord bowed down, held his palms together and implored everyone earnestly, the entire Sudharma royal assembly was touched.

That evening, I brought the Lord in the Garudadhwaja chariot to the shores of the western ocean near the Aindra gate to offer evening oblations. Uddhava Maharaja also accompanied him. It was an exclusive and unique experience for me to see both of them standing in the ocean with their eyes closed and offering oblations to the setting sun. A single thought kept cropping up in my mind while staring at the sinking platter of the sun. 'No matter how hard I try, I do not understand who exactly the Lord is.'

DRAUPADI

I am Draupadi! The daughter of Panchala king Drupada. I was also called Yajnasena, and rightfully so. My brother Dhrishtadyumna and I were born out of the Putrakameshti yajna performed by my father Drupada.

It was due to this yajna that Sautramanimata was utterly neglected by all. Is the one who gives birth to you your real mother? What about the one who nurtures and moulds your mind? Is she not significant at all? I became Draupadi as I was named after my father Drupada. But like the fire burning in the yajna pit, I became the dauntless, fiery and proud woman that I am because of my mother. At the mere mention of her name, the Panchala royal city, Kampilyanagar, and our grand royal palace appear vividly before my eyes. It also reminds me of our brother Shikhandi, born before us. Word was that he had become impotent due to a curse. That was the reason why my father had performed the Putrakameshti yajna. After our birth, eight more sons were born to our parents. They were named Sumitra, Priyadarshana, Chitraketu, Suketu, Dhwajaketu, Veerketu, Suratha and Shatrunjaya. I was thus the only sister to ten brothers. Though I had ten brothers, how come Yadava Srikrishna of Dwaraka came to be my only brother? It is a never-ending story.

Almost everyone, including his close relatives, called him 'Srikrishna'. Only a few of us called him 'Krishna' with loving affection. He also genuinely liked it. Those select few people included my mother-in-law – the mother of the Pandavas Kuntidevi – Bhishma – the Grandsire of the Kurus – Vidura, Sanjaya and a few others.

How do you exactly measure someone's worth? Two questions need to be asked for that. First, what if that person was not born at all. And second, what if that person wouldn't have met you in your life's journey? Indeed, what if my Krishna had not been born? What if he would not have come into my life at all? I cannot imagine what kind of twists and turns my life – the scorching life of Yajnasena – would have taken then.

Just as I was addressed as Draupadi and Yajnasena, I was also called Panchali, Krishnaa and Shyamaa, as I was dark-complexioned.

But Krishna addressed me as 'Krishnaa' for the first time. More than a brother, he was my best friend. Whenever I go back in time trying to figure out when my friendship with him began, my swayamwar ceremony in Kampilyanagar flashes before my eyes.

At my swayamwar, Dhrishtadyumnadada and father Drupada had put the condition of piercing the fish-eye, which was quite difficult to fulfil. Many renowned archers and kings had failed. As Dada had severely lambasted the warriors assembled at the swayamwar pandal, it was bubbling with tremendous tension. So many questions arose in my mind at that moment. What if nobody succeeded? Was I going to remain a maiden in the royal palace of the Panchalas? In spite of having ten brothers, what kind of pitiful life would I lead as the unfortunate unmarried sister?

At exactly that moment, my sakha stood up. Whispers arose in the pandal – 'the Lord of Dwaraka, the master of Sudarshan, owner of the Sharanga bow, executor of Kansa ...' – oh, how many goosebumps arose on my body when I heard those words. So far, I had been looking at the ground with feminine modesty, holding the wedding garland in my hands. But now, I raised my head to take a good look at the Lord of Dwaraka. He was indeed 'Sudarshan' – good-looking. The first thought that came to my mind was – what if he indeed pushes aside the Shiva bow and pierces the fish-eye with his own Sharanga bow and fulfils the condition this instant? How would my life in Dwaraka be, as his wife? I had heard a lot about his first wife, Rukminidevi. Would she accept me? How would she treat me?

But whatever was supposed to happen, happened. Master archer Arjuna, disguised as a Brahmin, fulfilled the condition. I put the wedding garland around his neck amidst roaring applause, and glanced at 'Sudarshan' Srikrishna. There was no indication in his eyes whatsoever of the desire of winning my hand in marriage that had been there only a few moments ago. His face shone with crystal-clear brotherly love. I tried my best to analyse it but was unsuccessful.

After the ceremony, he came to meet me and Arjuna at the potter's place. An enigmatic smile that I had never seen before blossomed on his blue face and he casually said to me, 'Krishney, this is my dear cousin – master archer Arjuna. Have a happy married life with him.' The moment

I heard him call me 'Krishney', I realised that he was my sakha – my best friend.

So, how were my five husbands?

What kind of a person was my eldest husband Yudhishthira? He was the formally crowned king of the Pandava reign in Indraprastha. As his conduct always abided by Dharma, he was also known as Dharma. This first husband of mine always spoke the truth. Compared to his truthfulness, my best friend would be deemed an outright liar. But that was not the case. During the toughest times of my life I experienced that one views truth according to one's own perception.

After my swayamwar, at the potter's house in Kampilyanagar, without looking at me, Rajmata Kuntidevi had said, 'If you have received big alms, share it amongst all of you.' But when she saw me, she felt extremely guilty, and repeatedly said, 'How can the lady of a family be called alms and be shared by many? Oh, how foolishly I uttered my words! I take them back.'

At that time, this truth-speaking, Dharma-following son of Pandu did not take a stand as the eldest brother of the Pandavas and say, 'You are right, Mother. A lady of a family should never be treated as alms. Only Arjuna had won her hand after successfully fulfilling the condition of the archery contest. The remaining brothers have no right over her.' At that time, I kept looking at him expectantly. But – but I did not see any sign of maturity in his eyes. All I saw was absolute, bare lust. I could not forget that look in my eldest husband's eyes for the rest of my life. That is why I could never forgive him.

On our very first meeting, he did me the biggest injustice due to his own desire. At that time, my best friend Krishna advised me, helped me survive. That was the first time I experienced his friendship. Due to my innate nature, I would have strongly opposed the sharing of my life. But at that time, Krishna gave me an extraordinarily friendly smile and said, 'Shyamale, Krishney, you have such matchless beauty that your own allure will bring the onslaught of lecherous men upon you. Therefore, you are indeed in need of the combined protection of Bhima and Arjuna. It is best for you to regard my aunt Kunti's words and comply.' That smile of his was befitting of only him. It said so much more than his words.

This eldest brother of the Pandavas did not just stop at disrupting my life. But he literally disrobed me of the invaluable womanly honour that any Kshatriya should protect with his soul and life – that, too, in the crowded gambling hall of the Kurus. He put me at stake after losing himself. For him, the allure of gambling was greater than his own wife. At that time too, my best friend Krishna came to my rescue. Since the gambling incident, I unmistakably realised that wherever he may be, my best friend Krishna always resided in my heart. My faith in him strengthened.

Each one of my five husbands would address me by different names in privacy. Yudhishthira inadvertently called me 'Sugandhe'. My body emanated a gentle fragrance like sandalwood paste or the one dispersed from the pollen of blue lotus flowers. It was this fragrance that the formally crowned king loved very much. In that, too, I could detect the pride of a king. He never praised any of my other innate qualities openly. He always threw his weight around as the eldest brother.

Yudhishthira had a turtle-like mind. Sometimes, he would hide under the shell of being the eldest brother and, at other times, of his kingship. He was much less valiant than his younger brothers, and overcame that deficiency with his fanciful philosophy.

It was because I became the Maharani of Indraprastha that I strongly noticed such prominent flaws of the eldest Pandava. Yet, due to his reserved nature, some of his qualities were unseen. Those qualities suited only him. The first ideal quality among those was that he never did anything without seeking advice from his venerable mother. Rajmata would not have accepted anybody else as the eldest Pandava. Just as he tried to practise his authority as the eldest brother on his younger siblings, he also politely respected the authority of his elders. I have no doubt that if Rajmata would have been there at the time of the gambling, this eldest husband of mine would have simply tossed away the gambling dice for his mother's word. As the Maharani of Indraprastha, he always treated me with due respect in front of citizens.

From Kampilyanagar I came to Hastinapura, and then to Indraprastha. I never visited my parental home after that. I got all the news about Sautramanimata, Father Drupada, all my brothers and major Panchalas, in Indraprastha itself. Krishna's support in raising the royal city of Indraprastha was the greatest.

After we came to Khandavavana, my five husbands decided upon a code of conduct in my regard. They lived with me in privacy in the same sequence that they were born in. According to that, after coming to Khandavavana, I begot the first son from Yudhishthira. Rajmata named him Prativindhya. As he was the first-born of the Pandavas' third generation, he was going to be the future prince. Everyone looked after him vigilantly. All his kakas showered this first son of mine with a lot of affection. I taught him to address everyone as 'Father'.

My second husband was the mighty Bhimsena. He was the tough protective armour of the other four brothers. Bhimsena had an unmatched powerful physique – exactly like friend Krishna's brother, Balarama. What a vast difference there was between Yudhishthira and Bhimsena. Bhimsena could not control three things – hunger, sleep and anger. He looked healthy due to his tremendous appetite and sleep. Like the mace on his shoulder, his rage was a weapon. Though he was such a great mace warrior and wrestler, he politely obeyed the commands of three elders – his eldest brother Yudhishthira, Rajmata Kuntidevi and my best friend Krishna. He would not speak much in the royal council of Indraprastha. Speaking in public was not in his nature. But on the battlefield, while defiantly provoking his enemy, his words would automatically get an exceptional edge of valour.

It was my friend Krishna who had first addressed him as Bhimsena. The word 'fear' did not exist in his vocabulary. All my husbands loved me dearly. But as a woman if anybody asked me to rank them, the first rank would go to Bhimsena, followed by Arjun. And yes, the very last rank would go to Yudhishthira.

Bhimsena, who could not be controlled by others, would quietly listen to Krishna. This is one of the main reasons why Bhimsena became my favourite.

There are many incidents in our life in the Kamyakavana that let me experience Bhimsena's invaluable love for me. A husband can fulfil any wish of his wife when he has a kingdom at his disposal and many attendants to obey his commands. But to fulfil her wishes while living in a forest certainly needs the deepest feeling of love. Once, while travelling in the Kamyakavana along with the five brothers, I reached the shores of a lake. Beautiful red ochre lotuses had blossomed at the centre of that lake. The moment I saw them, I shouted, 'Such beautiful lotuses!' Hearing my words, the eldest Pandava Yudhishthira said, 'Your abundant hair with a blue tinge, almost reaching your heels, look more beautiful than those flowers. Those flowers will look very beautiful in your hair. Once we reach our cottage, we will send a forest dweller to fetch these flowers!'

I listened to him and looked at master archer Dhananjaya. My glance directly meant, 'What are you going to do, Arjuna?' He gave me the expected answer, 'I don't have my Gandiva bow with me right now, or else I would have shown you the magic of my archery, which could even pierce the fish-eye, right here.'

Nakula–Sahadeva also gave me similar responses. I do not even remember today what they said. In the end, I looked at Bhimsena. He did not say anything in response at all. He surmised my question with his eyes, and tucking in his white dhoti, he said, 'Wait a moment. Let me go and get your favorite lotuses!' He leapt into the lake while all his brothers watched. Briskly moving his muscular arms through the waters, he reached the beautiful, red ochre lotuses and swam around them once. Holding the bunch under one arm and using the other to swim, he came back. Then he laughed loudly and said, 'Arjuna, adorn her hair with them!' A woman comes to know the true nature of her husband in privacy during lovemaking – and I had five husbands. Each one had a different attitude in privacy. I am saying all this because I want to unravel my entire life. That is why I have to speak about this without any reservation. To tell you the truth, when it was Bhimsena's turn to spend time with me in privacy for the first time, I was quite scared. But on the first night itself, I found out that my mighty husband Bhimsena, who thunders like clouds and roars loudly with rage, also possesses a sensitive, tender heart like the petals of a lotus. He was never rough with me. That is why, as a woman, I found him the ideal husband. Yes – even more so than Arjuna, who had won me at the swayamwar!

I bore Bhimsena a son. Krishna himself named him – Sutasoma. He was healthy like his father and quite naughty too.

After Bhimsena, it was the turn of Arjuna – my third husband, master archer Dhananjaya, valiant Partha. He had shot the very first arrow unerringly into the target and won my hand in marriage. The one thing I could never approve of when it came to him was the silence he maintained, unfitting of a valiant warrior, when the decision that I be shared by all was made. He justified his silence many a time later, saying he complied with the command of his mother and the wish of his elder brother. But I was never convinced. At that moment itself, I realised that he might even surrender his Gandiva bow at a crucial moment and throw it to the ground.

After the swayamwar, I wondered several times about what would have happened if Srikrishna had been in Arjuna's place at the time of the decision. What would he have done? Would he have remained silent? Certainly not. At that very instant, he would have spoken out clearly and pointed out his elder brother's faults. That is why I have always found Arjuna's silence at that time unforgivable. Only Krishna had the power of admonishing him at such times with stern words.

As a woman, I never felt any hesitation while talking to Krishna about my husbands. That was also a corroboration of my friendship with him.

All my relatives thought that Arjuna was my favourite husband. The citizens of Indraprastha also believed the same. And every time I saw Partha along with Purushottama Vasudeva, I, too, felt the same. They looked like reflections of each other. And the most important reason, above all this, was that my best friend Krishna had considered only Arjuna his sakha – confidant – among all the Pandavas.

Nakula–Sahadeva were more like friends to me than husbands. I had to take the initiative of changing their bashful natures. There was one thing very special about them. Both of them had observed and felt exactly the same things about the three elder Pandavas that I had. Just as they were younger to their brothers, so also were they younger to me. But I never let them feel it. I bore five sons, one each year, from my five husbands. The son I bore Arjuna was named Shrutakirti. This name was also given by Srikrishna. He came from Dwaraka specifically for that purpose.

The meaning of his name was 'the one whose renown is heard by all'. The sons of Nakula and Sahadeva were named Shatanika and Shrutsena.

The Pandavas, the Kurus and the Yadavas – all shared a major custom – polygamy. They justified it as 'a necessity for the Kshatriyas'. Almost all of them had more than one wife. The only exception was Uddhavadeva. That is why he was respected by all. As the Pandava Maharani, I considered Rukminidevi my ideal. But Krishna? I had considered him my sakha as he was my ideal for the whole life.

I frequently had to face the polygamous relations of my five husbands. Yudhishthira later got married to a lady named Pauravi. They had a son named Devaka.

Bhimsena already had a forest-dweller wife named Hidimba, from before our marriage. They had a son named Ghatotkacha. He was the first-born in the third generation of Pandavas. Hidimba never came to live in Indraprastha or Hastinapura. She lived at her maternal home in the forest beyond River Ganga. I came to know about all this after the swayamwar ceremony. Krishna's guidance came to my assistance yet again in this situation. On his first meeting at Indraprastha, he affectionately asked me, 'Krishney, are you happy in the company of your five husbands? Any discord with anyone?' I discussed the topic of Hidimba, saying, 'If Ghatotkacha appears tomorrow saying that he is the first Pandava of the third generation. What then?' He smiled playfully as usual and said, 'Shyamale, do not worry at all. In fact, it will be Ghatotkacha who will save all the Pandavas from trouble. After all, he is the first-born son of Bhimsena. And, you see, my beloved wife Jambavati is also like Hidimba.' I was left nonplussed. It was his speciality that no one could guess what reference he would put forth and when. Amongst all the valiant men around me, he was a genius. I also liked to pick an argument with him. At such times, he would finally say, 'Panchali, you are indeed brilliant, even more than my beloved wife Rukmini. That is why I love you as a friend. Do me a favour. Never share this opinion of mine with her.'

Bhimsena's third wife was Baladharaa. She was the daughter of the king of Kashi. Her son's name was Sharvatrata. Bhimsena's fourth wife was Kali. She was the daughter of Krishna's aunt Shrutashrava and her husband Damaghosha. She was the sister of Shishupala, Krishna's cousin, who detested him throughout his life. Krishna himself took the initiative of arranging this marriage.

Let me again talk about my third husband, Arjuna. Once, he broke the code of conduct that we had all agreed upon and therefore had to go on a pilgrimage for a year. Before returning to Indraprastha, he married thrice. The first marriage was with Uloopi – the Naga daughter. She was the daughter of a Naga named Kauravya who lived on the banks of River Ganga. In her childhood, she was married to the son of a Naga named Airavata. But he died young and Uloopi had become a child widow. This third husband of mine got married to her on the banks of the Ganga in a 'Gandharva' swayamwar. Later, she gave birth to a son, who was named Iravana by the Nagas. Uloopi lived at her parental home of Kauravya Naga.

This husband of mine further travelled to Manipura during the pilgrimage, and got married to Chitrangada, the daughter of King Chitravahana of Manipura. Her son was named Babhruvahana by the citizens of Manipura. Chitrangada had come to Indraprastha along with her son at the time of our Rajasuya yajna.

Arjuna was my favourite as he was dearly loved by Krishna. The three of us had our own triangular emotional bond that was incomprehensible to all others. Arjuna transformed it into a square bond – by abducting Subhadra. Subhadra was his fourth wife. I treated all my co-wives with affection, especially Subhadra. It was because she was Krishna's sister. As my co-wife, I accepted her as a sibling, just like Krishna. My dear sister Subhadra also bore a son. Krishna named him Abhimanyu. Notably, all the other Pandavas besides Arjuna pampered Abhi genuinely. I had quite noted a subtle difference in Arjuna's feelings towards Abhi. Arjuna would unknowingly favour him a little bit more. I could not understand it, no matter how hard I tried. Arjuna addressed me as 'Surekhaa…Shyama' in solitude. There was a tinge of darkness in our complexions – Krishna, Arjuna and I – hence the name.

My fourth husband Nakula was exquisitely handsome. I had never seen Madana, who was supposed to be the most handsome man that ever existed, and had no desire to see him. But everyone called Nakula Madana incarnate. Nakula was an expert in tunnels and horses. After Shishupala's execution, his daughter Karenumati was married to Nakula.

She had a son named Niramitra.

Nakula called me 'Yajnaseni' in private.

My fifth and last husband was Sahadeva. He had an obsession for fortune telling. But he never predicted my future. He was an expert on cows and horses. He had three more wives. One of them was Vijaya – the daughter of Madra king Shalya, the mama of the Pandavas. Her son was named Suhotra.

One more daughter of the Yadava clan of Dwaraka came into the Pandava clan, just like Subhadra. She was Bhanumati – the daughter of King Bhanu. This also took place due to Krishna's initiative. She did not bear any sons.

Sahadeva's fourth wife was the daughter of Jarasandha – the Magadha emperor of Girivraja, the sister of Jarasandha's son Sahadeva. It meant that this Magadha lady had a husband and a brother with the same name – Sahadeva.

Sahadeva addressed me as 'Panchali' in private. Maybe because he was number five.

Yudhishthira – the eldest Pandava – my first husband, was indeed the perfect elder brother. He preferred the company of sages, hermits and Brahmins. He would have prolonged discussions with Mahatma Vidura, Uddhavadeva and sages like Vyasa. After such discussions, this eldest Pandava, who otherwise considered his mother's word as the ultimate, would explicate a few fundamentals of life to her too. He never got angry - as if he had given his share of anger to Bhimsena. This is where he was different from the mighty Kaurava, Duryodhana of Hastinapura. Duryodhana had absorbed the anger of all his brothers within himself. With the exception of a couple of Kauravas like Dushasana and Vikarna, each one spoke the same language as Duryodhana. But each of my five husbands had distinct personalities.

The gift of compassion that this first husband of mine possessed was phenomenal. It was because of this noble compassion that the citizens of Indraprastha called him 'Dharmaraja'.

My second husband Bhimsena was incredibly powerful and modest at the same time. Many people had the misconception that Bhimsena was mighty powerful and therefore not intelligent. I came to know later about the words that he uttered at the time when Yudhisthira gambled me away. He had said, 'Sahadeva, bring me some fire. Let me burn these hands that gamble.' Aren't his intellect and presence of mind apparent from these words? He commanded only his youngest brother. And even in that rage, he did not seek to burn Yudhishthira, just his hands.

Our daily routine was full of examples of Bhimsena's presence of mind. Who could say that Bhimsena – who brought the red ochre lotus flowers for me from the lake, who told Bakasura, 'Let me eat first and take care of you later' – had no restraint or brains? His unmatched strength was the impenetrable shield of our family. But he himself never made any claims about that. Oh, such humility. Every powerful man has some obsession that leaves others in a state of wonder. Bhimsena had that kind of obsession with sleep and hunger. He did not simply gobble down his food, he savoured it. It was a pleasure to watch tall and hefty Bhimsena talking humbly with his comparatively short and lean mother.

Bhimsena would take every possible care to not hurt me as a wife. In his company, I always felt like I was taking shelter under the mighty pinnacle of the Himalayas.

My third husband Arjuna was also called Partha and Dhananjaya. Krishna also addressed him as Gudakesha. Gudakesha is a man who is alert and has total control over his sleep. He was the master of Pratismrutividya or Indrajaala. This husband of mine had two gurus in weaponry – Drona and Kripa. But apart from them, he had two gurus who taught him the real meaning of life – the first one was Yudhishthira and the second Krishna. In the company of these two, he silently learnt a lot. He became the master of weaponry from two expert gurus and mastered the art of understanding life from Yudhishthira and Krishna. Krishna's sister Subhadra was his last wife. Krishna used to tease me playfully, saying, 'Krishney, Arjuna's real love is only Subhadra. The hearts of warriors are like a stack of hay. No matter how tight one tries to bind it, together with one string, when another string is tied to bind it the first string slackens.' I would return his taunt with a smile, saying, 'Who told you that hearts of warriors are like a stack of hay? They are actually like the bed of the Yamuna!' He would give me a naughty smile and tease me again, 'I agree. The hearts of warriors are like the Yamuna, unrestrained!' I would dismiss his words, saying, 'Like the Yamuna that flows while flourishing both the shores equally!'

Whenever Krishna came to Indraprastha, Shrutakirti and Abhimanyu were overjoyed. Both of them would linger around him, calling him 'Mama'. He would also talk to them for hours on end. My other sons would also join them. The one who would badger Krishna with maximum questions was our Abhi.

Abhimanyu had become the favourite among all sons of Pandavas even in Indraprastha. It was not only because of his own virtues but also due to people's love for Krishna and Arjuna.

Sometimes I would feel the urge to probe my husbands about their additional marriages. Maybe it was just my feminine tendency to guess what kind of women my co-wives were. Whenever I would ask Yudhishthira, it would always be with a little sarcasm. I would say, 'All of you Pandavas revere Krishna very much. You consider him your mentor. He has rehabilitated not one or two but thousands of Kamarupa women. Why don't you follow in his footsteps and do the same?'

He would get perplexed at my question and say, 'Maharani, I do not understand what you are implying. None of us can do everything Krishna does. How can we bring thousands of such women into Indraprastha?' Bringing him to the point, I would say, 'Not thousands, only a few. Each one of you brothers has many wives in addition to me. I hear a rumour that they are not coming to Indraprastha because they are scared of me. What if you bring Pauravi to Indraprastha first?'

At that direct question, the maharaja would fall silent. Through this, I would tactfully gather all possible information about my co-wife, who may never come to Indraprastha. Who knows, she might be useful to us in future sometime. I did all this inadvertently as per Krishna's advice.

Just like Yudhishthira, I would probe Bhimsena about his other wives – Hidimba and Kali. Laughing loudly, he would say, 'If we bring Hidimba here, then we will have to transform Indraprastha back to Khandavavana, which is not possible now, even for your friend Krishna. And Kali of the Chedis would never come to Indraprastha. Here in Indraprastha you will have only two co-wives – of the Yadava clan – Subhadra and Bhanumati. And since both of them are from Dwaraka, they are more like sisters to you than co-wives.' I would also probe Arjuna about his other wives, Uloopi and Chitrangada. He would say teasingly, 'Both their kingdoms are far away in the eastern region. They will come for sure, but on one condition.'

'What condition?' I would ask. He would smile and say sarcastically, like his guru Krishna, 'Subhadra will have to be sent back to Dwaraka!' Hearing that, I would feel dumbfounded. The very first thought that would strike me was what Krishna would feel if Subhadra was sent back to her parental home. I would keep silent. Then Arjuna would grab the opportunity to tease me further, 'Before that they would impose one condition about you. Because you are the first wife, the Maharani. You must have by now reckoned what that condition would be!'

I would keep quiet. Because I would have already reckoned that the condition must be to send me back to Kampilyanagar.

After my experience with Arjuna, I decided not to probe the two younger brothers about this subject ever.

The people and my distant relatives knew only one thing – the half-truth that the Maharani of Indraprastha, Draupadi, has five husbands. Not many people knew that she also had not one or two but ten co-wives. Except two of them, all others stayed out of Indraprastha and the two who were in Indraprastha were related to Krishna and so had become more like sisters to me.

During my life in Indraprastha the two women with whom I formed a close bond were my mother-in-law Rajmata Kuntidevi and sister Subhadra. Whenever I met Subhadra it felt like I was meeting Rukminidevi herself. In the beginning, Rajmata Kuntidevi seemed to me like a mother-in-law. Her speech sounded like the sweet resonance of bells in the temple of Shiva. It had the sweetness of maturity that comes from facing the hardships of life. She ardently talked only about my husbands' virtues. She had deputed the duty of informing me about their faults to Krishna. He fulfilled this duty very tactfully.

All my husbands were evidently devoted to their mother. They were ready to sacrifice their lives for their mother's word. Rajmata took me under her wing as a daughter, and immediately filled the vacuum in my life due to the absence of Sautramanimata.

The kingdom of Indraprastha kept flourishing every day. The kingdom of the Yadavas of Dwaraka and my maternal home, the Panchala kingdom, were the two main allies of Indraprastha. After Jarasandha, the threat of the Magadha kingdom had reduced considerably. The acclaim of Dwaraka had spread throughout Aaryavarta. Its renown had reached kingdoms beyond the ocean with the end of Kalayavana. Dwaraka was now being recognised as a well-planned harbour. Many mammoth ships of the kingdoms from the western ocean docked at this harbour. Krishna had now gained renown as Srikrishna. That Srikrishna had then become well known as Vasudeva and Bhagvan. Yet I called him Krishna because of my deep attachment. I never felt there was anything wrong about it.

The layout of Indraprastha was quite similar to that of Dwaraka. The Pandavas had unanimously named the royal assembly 'Sriprasada' in honour of Krishna. Krishna's favourite river, the Yamuna, encircled Indraprastha. Expert architects had built the royal assembly of the Pandavas parallel to the semicircular line of the Yamuna, guiding cool gusts of wind flowing from the river to directly reach the Sriprasada royal assembly.

Many a time, Krishna urged me to visit Dwaraka. I wanted to meet Rukmini and her seven sisters at least once. But no matter what I did, I could not achieve it.

The only times we met were when Krishna came to visit during the construction of the royal city of Indraprastha in Khandavavana. It was at our coronation ceremony that I met Rukmini for the first time. I was smitten by her. She was indeed an exceptionally beautiful lady. On the very first meeting, while chatting for hours together with her, I strongly felt that I should visit Dwaraka at least once. Rukmini also spoke about one more woman – Krishna's best friend in Gokul – Radha – Radhika. What kind of a person would she be? What kind of a place would her Gokul be?

After the first meeting with Rukmini it became my hobby to probe Krishna about Radhika in many ways whenever we met. He was so clever! He would say to me smilingly, 'Why don't you go to Gokul once and meet her in person? Draw all the information from her with your brilliant questions.' He would leave me nonplussed. He knew very well that I would never go to Gokul. Later, I would try to create an imaginary figure of Radhika in my mind, but I was never able to complete it!

Three incidents in my life were very significant. First – my swayamwar ceremony. Later, I came to know from Arjuna that it was because of this swayamwar that he was going to to face his biggest enemy. It was Karna – the king of Anga – whom I had rejected. In the war that broke out after the swayamwar, his son Sudamana was killed in the pandal itself, that, too, by Arjuna's arrow. Furious Karna had taken a vow to kill Arjuna. Arjuna knew the gravity of that vow but never seemed to be afraid of it. During the construction of Indraprastha in Khandavavana, Krishna came often from Dwaraka to Indraprastha. On every visit, of all my five husbands, he would chat with Arjuna alone. They would go to the faraway banks of River Yamuna in Krishna's chariot. After each of these visits, Arjuna looked more determined and radiant than before.

The second significant turning point in my life was the coronation of Yudhishthira. Many kings and queens had come from distant kingdoms to attend the ceremony. Krishna had come with key members of the Yadava clan, Rukmini, Subhadra and both his brothers. Our coronation was celebrated with much grandeur.

Now, there were three mighty kingdoms in Aaryavarta – Dwaraka, Hastinapura and Indraprastha.

The third turning point in my life was the Rajasuya yajna. At the time of the coronation ceremony, Maharishi Vyasa had prudently advised me, 'Never forget that you are also the daughter-in-law of Hastinapura.' But I forgot his advice. There is no convincing explanation as to why someone forgets something. An error is an error, even if it takes place unknowingly. I made such an unforgivable mistake during the Rajasuya yajna in the Mayasabha chamber raised by Mayasura. Prince Duryodhana, who had come from Hastinapura, entered the chamber. It was for the first time after the swayamwar that I saw Karna – the king of Anga. The moment I saw him, a wild thought erupted in my mind. 'Had it been in my destiny to be the wife of this possessor of kavacha-kundala, so many fountains would have blossomed in the garden of my life.' In the meantime, Duryodhana stepped on to the optical illusion of a carpet, which was actually a rangoli design drawn on the surface of the water, and fell into the pond, making a loud splash. I was standing on the balcony along with my maids. I could not resist laughing, seeing the Kuru prince bob up and down in the water. While laughing, I said to my maids, 'Are the sons of a blind father also blind?' My maids, too, laughed at the scene and at my words. Leaving his crown and mace in the pond itself, he stared at me with fiery red eyes, muttered something to himself and stomped out of the Mayasabha chamber.

I immediately realised that I had made a mistake. But it was of no use now. If it had been somebody else, it would have been possible to apologise to and console the person. But never with Prince Duryodhana. Such an unforgivable mistake committed in a fleeting moment keeps continuously pricking at a cultured heart afterwards. That is what happened to me. Duryodhana never forgave me, but even I did not forgive myself for those thoughtless, idiotic words.

At the Rajasuya yajna, I actually saw Krishna using the Sudarshan chakra on Shishupala. The world always told me, 'You are the daughter of fire, born out of a yajna pit.' At that moment, I realised that he was not merely a brother or a friend, as I considered him. He was so much more that could not be expressed in words; he was inconceivable and one who could not be weighed on any scale. It was only possible to experience him, rather than try to understand him.

The Rajasuya yajna, that was of great significance for us Pandavas, was accomplished without any problems. Indeed, it was because Shishupala had a secret purpose in humiliating Krishna in the yajna. He wanted to start a war in the yajna pandal, just like the war that had erupted after my swayamwar. One way or the other, he did not want the Rajasuya yajna of the Pandavas to be accomplished. If the Rajasuya yajna would have been disrupted, it would have brought tremendous shame to the name of the Pandavas. Shishupala would have had the satisfaction of avenging his best friend Jarasandha, who had made him commander. That is why I was quite gratified that the yajna was conducted smoothly. In fact, the pennant of Krishna's and Pandavas' acclaim was magnified due to Shishupala's execution.

I would wonder which of the men and women of Dwaraka, Indraprastha and Hastinapura had different kinds of divine qualities. Among those, the prominent ones were Krishna and Arjuna. Both of them had a blue complexion. If they both stood chatting with each other, people could figure out who was who only because of the peacock-feathered crown and the fresh Vaijayanti garland resting on Krishna's chest. People who knew Arjuna would recognise him due to the Gandiva bow that he carried on his shoulder.

In Hastinapura, there were two other prominent men who were blessed with divine gifts. One was the devotee of the Sun, Karna – the king of Anga, who was born with the impenetrable kavacha-kundala, and the other was the guru's son Ashwatthama, who was born with a fleshy mole on the crown of his head.

I had never seen Bhimsena's first wife Hidimba – a daughter of the wilderness. But I had heard that her son Ghatotkacha was born with some extraordinary powers. Among the women in all three places, I was the only one who was yajna-born, fragrant and long-haired.

I had heard it from many people that my mother-in-law Rajmata Kuntidevi had obtained a divine mantra called Devahuti from Sage Durvasa many years ago. These five brothers carried the effect of that mantra's power in their personality. Yudhishthira carried the effect of the earth or Prithvi, Bhimsena carried the effect of the wind or Vayu, for Arjuna it was water or Jala, and for Nakula–Sahadeva it was light or Prakash. These two brothers were like Usha – the dawn – and Nisha – the night – connected to each other with a thin line of light. I never tried to probe into the deeper meaning of this Devahuti mantra. I did not find it necessary. Nobody ever tried to probe deeper into Dhrishtadyumnadada's and my birth from the yajna. Nobody ever found it necessary.

Among the three centres of power – Hastinapura, Indraprastha and Dwaraka – my friend Krishna was the only one who possessed the authority over the radiant chakra, Sudarshan.

'Why he does he not use the Sudarshan chakra frequently?,' was a question that occurred to me and several others often. So, I asked him once directly, 'Krishna, when you have such a powerful Sudarshan chakra, why don't you use it everywhere? Are there any restrictions?'

He smiled and said, 'I knew you were going to ask me this question. The Sudarshan chakra has been bestowed upon me by Bhagvan Parashurama. As per his instructions, I am not free to use it arbitrarily.'

After hearing his reply, I got even more curious. I asked him, 'Doesn't this mean that when you project the chakra, you get that intuition directly from your inner self?'

'You are indeed extremely brilliant, Draupadi. You have accurately guessed the secret of the chakra. Uddhava also knows it. If I try to use the Sudarshan chakra arbitrarily, I get a very strange experience.' If Krishna himself couldn't use the divine power of the Sudarshan chakra at will, what about the others? From the centres of power like Indraprastha, Dwaraka or Hastinapura, none of the men or women having divine powers were free to use them to their own advantage. I knew I had developed an ego due to my matchless beauty. Krishna had tactfully and clearly made me aware of it from time to time without hurting my feelings. While doing so, he always used to smile and say, 'Krishney, humility befits beauty. If an extremely beautiful lady is also humble, it is as good as gold with the fragrance of a Prajakta flower!'

My days were passing delightfully as the Maharani of Indraprastha. I was engrossed in nurturing my six sons and cultivating their characters. Yes, I considered Subhadra's Abhimanyu as my own. Indeed, I couldn't ask for more in life.

Prince Duryodhana of Hastinapura was never going to take the unmatched prosperity of the Pandavas lightly, or tolerate their incomparable acclaim spreading throughout Aaryavarta and their friendship with Krishna. In reality, he was not the prince of the Kurus of Hastinapura. As soon as the Pandavas left Hastinapura, he had assumed the position of the prince. He would make his blind father Dhritarashtra dance to his tunes. Indraprastha became a thorn in the flesh for Duryodhana. He had not come to his senses even after returning from the Rajasuya yajna and witnessing Shishupala's chilling execution with his own eyes. The Kuru prince, who was still full of hatred for Krishna, would mention my dear friend as 'a cowherd with feet soiled by cow dung and urine'.

A man always behaves according to his nature. An arrogant man never lets go of his arrogance. If such a person comes to power, his ego inflates. And Prince Duryodhana was actually using two kinds of powers – of the royal throne and emotional blackmail. Since childhood, he was used to keeping his ninety-nine brothers under his thumb. Hastinapura was a mighty kingdom due to the wealth, military power and old alliances with other kingdoms. Duryodhana was now getting extremely jealous of the prosperity of Indraprastha. He had begun arranging meetings with his political advisers and planning incredible schemes to bring Indraprastha down. According to informers, Duryodhana and Shakuni were trying their best to get Karna into their inner clique, but had been unsuccessful. Karna, the king of Anga, was strongly against any kind of political machination. He had only one yearning – to directly challenge the Pandavas to war, and fight a conclusive battle with them. This persistence had got me worried. It is true that I had once felt an unknown attraction for him, but it was not lust. He was an ardent devotee of the sun and I was a fire-born daughter. I feel that it was an attraction due to this connection. He had impenetratable armour and, only recently, after vowing to conquer the four directions of Aaryavarta in front of Grandsire Bhishma had fulfilled it successfully.

Duryodhana's seizure of Hastinapura was sheer injustice. Yet my husbands had accepted the region of Khandavavana and had worked hard to erect Indraprastha. Any calamity befalling Indraprastha was unacceptable to me. Duryodhana was astutely going to take advantage of world conqueror Karna who had been wounded by my words during the swayamwar ceremony. But now I had firmly decided not to be afraid of anyone when I had my best friend Krishna supporting me. I had strong faith in his friendship.

One day Chief Minister Vrishavarma of the Kurus of Hastinapura arrived in Indraprastha with a royal invitation. 'Grandsire Bhishma and Maharaja Dhritarashtra of Hastinapura have invited all Pandavas for Vishnuyaga. An invitation for the Yadavas has also been sent to Dwaraka. Maharaja Srikrishna will certainly come for the yajna to Hastinapura, along with Prince Balarama. You all should come too. Please do not miss the opportunity to attend the religious ritual in the original abode of your clan.'

I sent a message to Dwaraka for Krishna with a special messenger. It said, 'You must come to Hastinapura.'

Indeed, he came to Hastinapura at the right time but in such a different form.

I do not even want to remember the incident that happened in Hastinapura at that time. Narrating it is impossible for me.

Some events are indeed difficult to explain in any way, no matter how hard you try. My virtuous, righteous eldest husband, who would not even think of committing a sin, lost his mind. He became delusional and a slave to addiction beyond any kind of justification. His gambling addiction threw the Indraprastha kingdom, that had reached the apex of glory within a short time, into a deep chasm of destruction in an instant.

He played the game of dice with the Kauravas even before the Vishnuyaga. He put the kingdom of Indraprastha at stake, along with the military, maids and servants, wealth and animals, and lost all of it. Then he put his four brothers at stake and lost them too. He forgot that he was a formally crowned king of an established kingdom and therefore responsible for his subjects. He put himself at stake and lost that bet too. In the gambling hall, he was disgraced by the criticisms of the Kauravas, who were laughing hysterically in the frenzy of victory. He became so insane and irrational that he put me – his wife – the Maharani of Indraprastha – too at stake. And lost.

Fortunately for the Pandavas, none of the Kauravas came up with the idea of challenging Yudhishthira to put his widowed mother at stake. I am quite sure that he would have done that too.

I am not saying this just because I am overly emotional. On that day, with encouragement from the Kauravas who had lost their minds, shameless and mean Dushasana touched the saree I was wearing. Dushasana, who was eager to disrobe me, had lost his senses even more than Yudhishthira, who was playing the dice game.

In that ancient gambling hall of the Kurus, I implored them desperately to protect my honour, beating my chest and crying out loudly. None of them except Vikarna got up; no one said anything. Karna, the king of Anga, intimidated him and made him sit down. I lost my mind and had no clue as to what I was saying or where I was. Only an iridescent peacock feather with bluish, purplish, greenish, golden shades kept spinning in front of my tearful eyes.

When I regained consciousness, the only thing I heard was an unfamiliar tune of the flute fading away. Grandsire Bhishma was taking me out of the gambling hall, covered in a heap of sarees.

My honour was saved. I understood clearly who had done it.

When I entered my chambers and saw Rajmata Kuntidevi, I could not control my tears. I ran to her, put my arms around her neck and started crying uncontrollably. She did not say anything except 'be quiet, my daughter', and simply kept patting my back with deep affection. Her words 'my daughter' were engraved on my heart forever. That touch was exactly like the touch of the peacock feather, and her words were like the tune of the flute that I had just heard. I had found my mother again!

Did my eldest husband Yudhishthira learn a lesson and control himself even after the unprecedented heinous events in the gambling game? Did he act like a human being? No! When Shakuni and Duryodhana provoked him, he played another game of dice – Anudyuta – and lost yet again. And the second time, he lost the most valuable wealth of all – Time. As per the bet, all five Pandavas would have to go to live in the forest for twelve years along with their wife, followed by one year of living incognito.

The news that we were leaving for the forest spread everywhere. It was obvious that we could not go back to Indraprastha. Arjuna implored his eldest brother for quite some time to go to Dwaraka at least once. Bhimsena seconded him. I, too, felt that I must meet Krishna, who had saved my honour. If we were going to a forest, we should go to one in the direction of Dwaraka. But I could not say anything. Yudhishthira kept reiterating only one thing – 'I will not go there. All of you can go if you want, only if Duryodhana permits you to do so.' I could not even understand what had gone wrong with my eldest husband. Duryodhana's and Shakuni's intention in offering Khandavavana to the Pandavas was that they fall prey to the attacks of wild tribes, that they be devoured by wild animals. Now, we had to face a life of wilderness for twelve whole years.

We put on plain, white attire and began fasting to get used to starving, as we might have to go without food occasionally. That is why, within two days, everybody's faces started looking gaunt. While bidding farewell to Rajmata Kuntidevi, they became miserable and dark. She was now going to live with Mahatma Vidura in Hastinapura until our return. She kept saying only one thing again and again, 'I am used to living in the forest. Let me come with you.'

This request was presented to gambling expert Shakuni. He said she had not been put at stake. She could not go to the forest even if she wanted to.

My husband Bhimsena was the one who seethed the most at Shakuni's response. But he just could not do anything. Sometimes even mosquitoes get miraculously powerful!

We got ready to face all kinds of odds that came our way.

We were now facing the thick and green darkness of the forests. We started walking from the western side of Hastinapura and reached the Bhagirathi. We woke up early in the morning, even before sunrise, and continued on our journey after bathing in the river. All six of us were barefoot. Fearless, mighty Bhimsena was leading us. The only thing he had in his hands was a sharp hatchet to cut the branches of trees and thorny bushes along the way. By evening we reached Kurukshetra, which was surrounded by lakes. Arjuna said to Yudhishthira, 'We are going towards Sanneth Sarovar. During my world-conquering mission, I lived here at Kurukshetra for one whole month. Every day I used come to this Suryakunda for bathing. This place is also called Dharmakshetra.'

We felt refreshed after drinking the waters of rivers like Drishadwati and Saraswati, and lakes like Brahmakunda and Jyotikunda, and crossed the forests in the west, finally reaching the Kamyakavana. Here, Nakula, the land expert, chose an open space on which we built a cottage, near a crystal-clear stream of water. All five brothers raised a neat and beautiful east-facing cottage by the evening. It had a separate chamber for me, a bathroom and a kitchen. Bhimsena chose some fine sticky clay and kneaded it with his feet. The pots, jars and platters that Bhimsena created were indeed beautiful.

Meanwhile, in the front yard of the cottage, Arjuna had created five beautiful bows from supple wooden sticks. Far away in the distance, horse expert Sahadeva had tamed a wild horse that he had captured. He had mounted it and was making it run in circles at a constant pace. Nakula had created neat arrows from bamboo sticks and copper.

The blue sky above, a crystal-clear spring in front of the cottage with a continuous flow of gurgling water, thick forests with various creepers climbing up the tall trees and tangled in each other, various birds on those trees making distinct chirping sounds since sunrise – such was our charming 'Pandava abode' in the Kamyakavana. We lived here just as happily as in the palace of Indraprastha.

Our days in the Kamyakavana started becoming more and more interesting due to the daily chores we shared. Every day, one of my five valiant husbands would keep me company in the cottage. The other four would go to the forest to hunt for food, and collect materials for daily worship, firewood and fodder for the wild cows that we had domesticated.

Dhaumyarishi, with whom we had ageless close bonds, came to the forest along with his disciples, of his own accord. They also raised their huts near our cottage. Just as columns of smoke from the yajna pit used to rise through the roofs of huts in our Pandava colony every day, the ambrosial Vedic mantras incanted in the clear voice of Dhaumyarishi and his disciples too began renting the air at Kamyakavana. While performing daily chores in the cottage, I would invariably remember Krishna.

I should clearly mention one thing, though – I did not remember anybody else as much as I remembered him during our stay in the forest. For the first few days after coming here, I missed my sons, who had gone to Kampilyanagar with Dada, a lot. My only consolation was that they were under the care of their loving grandfather, grandmother and a dutiful mama. I had no doubt in my heart that they were all going to exceed these five Pandavas in valour.

I had not seen much of the other sons of my husbands. But as Subhadra and Arjuna's son Abhimanyu was in Indraprastha, he had become my favourite. The main reason for that was that while speaking in his sweet tongue he would unwittingly remind me of his mama, Krishna. I also remembered Rajmata Kuntidevi a lot.

But in the later period, Krishna, and only Krishna, occupied my heart inside out. My heart ached due to one bitter truth. We had not even been able to fulfil our duty of meeting him at least once before coming to the forest. What would he think of me? He must have labelled me the most selfish person. Such thoughts would leave me disturbed. My eyes would be moist with profound memories of Krishna. At such times, Bhimsena, who would have returned from the forest, would drop the bunch of wooden logs from his hefty shoulder near the cottage wall and sit by my side. He would wipe my eyes with his shawl and say, 'Panchali, be patient, have faith. Krishna himself will come to this forest to meet you. My heart tells me.' Just him sitting by my side would console me a lot.

I did not have to wait long. One day Bhimsena entered the fence of the cottage, shouting loudly, 'He has come! The Lord of Dwaraka – Krishna – has come!' He stood panting and said, 'Krishney, Krishna has come. I recognised the saffron-coloured golden-bordered pennant of his chariot. There are two more chariots.'

My beloved friend descended from his Garudadhwaja chariot harnessed with four white horses. Charioteer Daruka and Uddhavadeva followed him. From the chariot behind, my brother Dhrishtadyumna descended. Behind him were the commander and the chief minister of the Panchalas. From the last chariot, only the charioteer got down. That chariot was overflowing with household goods required for a family.

Leaving all his brothers behind, Arjuna walked briskly towards Krishna. He leaned forward and was about to touch his feet when Krishna pulled him into a deep embrace. He started sobbing dejectedly on Krishna's strong and bare shoulder. Krishna patted and comforted him. The other four brothers followed and touched Krishna's feet. I was still watching from the door. His long fish-shaped eyes kept turning towards the door. It became unbearable for me to stand there any more and I went into the inner chamber of the cottage. I just did not know what to say to him and how.

My heart was overflowing with mixed emotions. Sages and hermits, venerable kings, citizens of many kingdoms – everyone considered him omniscient. Then how come he did not understand my humiliation? Instantly, my heart was filled with rage for him. The next moment it was filled with joy that he had come to meet me. I did not know what to say.

I presumed he would immediately come in, but he did not. This was his nature that left me and many others disconcerted. He was the one who understood sentiments but was not at all sentimental. He could get one with everyone's emotions but would never get carried away with them. At dusk, our meeting in the forest commenced in the front yard of the cottage on grass mats. One seat was reserved for me. No one spoke. The searing rage that I had kept suppressed in my mind so far burst out.

Looking sternly at Krishna, I said, 'The sages, hermits and yogis consider you as the manifestation of forgiveness and Truth. They say that you existed even before the world that is perceptible to the eyes, that you are the creator of all animate and inanimate beings. Everybody says that you are the universe that consists of the three worlds, all the nakshatras, the ten directions, the sky, the sun and the moon. Then does this universe of yours not include my hair that has been kept untied? Each one of these strands of hair carries a trauma at its root. Don't you see that?

'Tell me, oh Purushottama, who am I? Am I really the beloved wife of these five so-called valiant husbands? Tell me, what if a similar calamity had befallen Rukmini, who is dear to your heart!'

All my husbands dropped their heads and just kept listening. I looked at Krishna. He kept smiling gently as usual. It enraged me further and I said, 'Was it appropriate that the perverted Kauravas dragged me, the wife of these five brothers, your best friend, the sister of Dhrishtadyumna, by pulling me by the hair in a hall full of people? Krishna, I was dressed in a single saree, in my menses! Was it proper that during such a condition, the Kauravas, romping with joy, put me to shame in front of all? Guru Drona, Kripa, Grandsire Bhishma, Vidura and Sanjaya kept mum as if their lips were sealed, since they are slaves of wealth. Is money so destructive? Is wealth so powerful?' I realised that even he did not have the answer to a single question of mine, yet I could not stop pouring out my heart's discontent. The anger that I had kept suppressed so far erupted like a volcano. 'The person who tolerates injustice without resistance is as guilty as the person who inflicts it. Why blame the Kauravas? These five husbands of mine – in spite of being powerful warriors – silently kept watching the injustice meted out to their wife. They never disappoint anyone who surrenders to them. Then how come they kept quiet when I sought refuge? I have borne each one of these husbands one radiant son. How are they going to stand up to the next generation and confess that they were unable to protect the honour of their mother?

'The Kauravas played a deceptive game of dice. They swindled the kingdom from the Pandavas and made all of them their slaves. Of what use is Arjuna's Gandiva and Bhimsena's mace? Shame, shame to the power of Bhimsena and the valour of Arjuna. How can despicable people like Duryodhana and Dushasana remain alive even for a moment when Arjuna and Bhimsena exist? Arjuna had won me in the swayamwar but I became the wife of five as per my mother-in-law's instruction and the wish of the elders. Pointing to that fact, the Kauravas laughed loudly and shamelessly, asking me in a hall full of people, "What does it matter if you belong to five husbands or a hundred and five?"

'As if we had not been demeaned enough, this so-called glory of the family, the eldest Pandava, played another game of dice. Why? With the greedy expectation that he would win back all that he had lost. Krishna, didn't you ever sense that this foolish, destructive greed has been present throughout his life?'

That omniscient Krishna was not answering a single question. He was sitting silent in that forest meeting. His silence became unbearable for me. In a fit of anger, I said, 'These five are not fit to be my husbands. I have no husband. I am neither a wife, nor a daughter-in-law, nor a daughter to anybody. And yes, oh Krishna of Dwaraka, you are neither a brother to me, nor a friend. You are nothing to me. I am all alone – lonely!' With overwhelming grief, I buried my face in my palms and began sobbing uncontrollably.

I could barely speak between my sobs, 'Krishna, you, too, are not mine, which is why the shameless Kauravas could humiliate me. I have to live in a forest even though I am the Maharani of Indraprastha. Karna called me a prostitute in the presence of all elders and laughed disdainfully. Oh Krishna, the fire that his actions have flared in my heart never calms even for a moment.

'You consider me a sakhi and call me so. I worship you ardently as well. You possess indomitable and mighty power. When I was being disgraced in the gambling hall, I surrendered only to you from the bottom of my heart. I desperately invoked only you. Even today I do so and will continue to. Oh Krishna...tell me clearly, are you going to punish these sinners who have disgraced my honour or not?'

Everyone in the meeting was thoroughly shaken by my fiery words. Only Krishna spoke then, very little but reassuringly, 'Krishney, my beloved friend, all those who are the target of your anger, all those who disgraced you in front of the elders will be killed by Arjuna's arrows and

Bhimsena's mace. And I will be a witness to that. I will do everything possible for the Pandavas and you. Just as you live your life grief-stricken, with your hair untied, the wives of the Kauravas will also lament for their husbands. I did not take any vows in my life, but today I am taking one. Only for your sake. Krishney, stop crying. Have faith, Draupadi, that these words of your Krishna will never prove to be false. The Pandavas will become kings again, and you will be their maharani.'

Arjuna, who felt revitalised by Krishna's words, could not keep quiet and said, 'Draupadi, everything will happen just as Krishna has said.'

Now my brother Dhrishtadyumna also said with courage, 'Oh Bhamini, I will kill Drona, who has insulted our father and who helplessly and silently watched your humiliation despite being a guru. Our Shikhandi will destroy Bhishma at the right time. And mighty Bhima will break Duryodhana's thigh as per his vow. Master archer Dhananjaya will decapitate Karna – the son of a charioteer who called you a prostitute. With the backing of Bhagvan Vasudeva Srikrishna, we will always be invincible!'

Krishna said, 'Krishney, had I been in Dwaraka, I would have come to the Vishnuyaga yajna, just as I came to Indraprastha for the Rajasuya yajna. I would have never let that destructive game of dice take place. I would have compelled Maharaja Dhritarashtra to open the eyes of his mind by describing Dushasana's actions to him. I would have forced him to speak. If that would have been unsuccessful, I would have appealed to the femininity in Maharani Gandharidevi and compelled her to pull down the cloth strip from her eyes. Had that, too, proved futile, I would have certainly invoked the divine mantras of the Sudarshan, just as you invoked me. I am certain that I would have clearly recalled the mantras and would have annihilated those who touched the saree on your body, and called you a prostitute.

'But Yajnaseni, I was engaged in a war with Shalva at that time, on the coast of the western ocean. Chief Minister Vipruthu told me everything after returning to Dwaraka. I immediately came here after hearing what had happened. Yudhishthira, I do not hold any resentment in my mind that all of you came to the forest without meeting me. Henceforth, my life's mission will be to seek justice for you.'

Krishna and the others stayed with us in Kamyakavana for a few days.

With the help of attendants, we properly arranged all the weapons, such as Arjuna's Gandiva bow, Bhimsena's mace, Nakula's sword and Sahadeva's pestle, and other useful things that Dhrishtadada had carried in his chariot, into the cottage.

They bade us farewell and were ready to go back. My heart became heavy with the thought that Krishna was leaving. I said to him, 'Tell Subhadra that I am taking good care of her master archer. Do come to meet me with Abhimanyu once.'

Before leaving, he had clearly stated what he was going to do, which had given me great peace of mind. Because of his promise, even our life in the forest became carefree and delightful. We had to live in the forest not for a short time, but for a good twelve years.

During this time, which tested our mettle, we lived in three different forests – Kamyakavana, Dvaitavana and Gandhamadana. For the first six months, we lived in Kamyakavana. Due to the commotion while hunting, the daily routine of hermits from other ashramas was getting disturbed.

Due to this, we decided to leave Kamyakavana and go to Dvaitavana.

During our stay in the forests, one incident considerably reduced my anger towards Arjuna and Bhimsena for sitting mute in the gambling hall at Hastinapura.

Jayadratha, the leader of Sindhu-Sauvira, attempted to forcefully abduct me – a married woman – in broad daylight. None of my husbands were on guard at the cottage that day. Utterly helpless, I was whimpering, 'Help Achyuta…Madhava…Milinda…help.' Jayadratha, laughing wickedly, said, 'That low-life cowherd is in Dwaraka. Let your five husbands stay here in the Kamyakavana collecting wood. Come, I will make you Maharani of the Sindhu-Sauviras. A diamond like you only befits the crown of the Sindhu leader. Your life is not for collecting wood in the forest. I have come all the way here looking for you after hearing the fame of your fragrance.'

My mighty husband Bhimsena was the first to return to the ashrama. As soon as he heard the news of my abduction from Dhaumya Rishi, he did not waste a moment. He climbed on to the stone platform on the west of the ashrama and shouted, sending a signal for Arjuna to hurry. The next moment, Bhimsena mounted a sturdy horse and started galloping in the direction pointed out by Dhaumya Rishi.

The son of Vayu had such a loud and harsh voice that it would scare the wits out of the person at the receiving end. He started roaring at the top of his lungs, 'Jayadratha, you rotten creature, wait! How dare you think that you would be able to pluck the fragrant lotus flower of the Pandavas while I am alive? Wait! You, sinful soul!'

Jayadratha's chariot had to come to a halt as there was a river ahead of us. While his charioteer was looking for a boatman, I heard Bhimsena's cries, which gave me courage. Jayadratha grabbed my wrist firmly and started dragging me towards a boat visible far away. His armed charioteer went to stop Bhima. Bhimsena was unarmed; he began throwing stones at the charioteer and kept shouting, 'Jayadratha, you wretched man… Wait! I dare you to fight a wrestling bout with me if you are the true leader of the Sindhus.'

Even Arjuna, who was following with his Gandiva bow, could hear the screams. By this time Bhimsena had killed the charioteer. He had grabbed the sword from the charioteer's hand.

Soon, Arjuna came into sight, standing next to Bhimsena.

Jayadratha got nervous on seeing both the sons of Kunti chasing him. Leaving me on the spot, the mighty Kshatriya, so-called leader of the Sindhus, disappeared into the thick Kamyakavana.

Due to the prompt actions of my husbands, Bhima and Arjuna, my honour had been protected. More than feeling happy about my honour being saved, I felt satisfied to see the return of Bhima and Arjuna's valour, that had as good as vanished. Yudhishthira was the one towards whom I had the most ire. I was still not ready to forgive him. He was the reason that I was shared by five husbands. He was the one who shamelessly played the game of dice, putting me at stake. It was because of him that Dushasana had dared to touch my saree in front of the venerable elders.

The valour of two of my five husbands had been awakened and now it was the turn of the others. Otherwise, their valour would get extinguished like sparks of fire on a boulder in the forest.

The Kauravas had now usurped Indraprastha. They had imposed the administrative system of Hastinapura on Indraprastha. They had dismissed all the commanders and chiefs of our fourfold army, and replaced them with arrogant leaders from Hastinapura. It was not only the Pandavas and I who suffered due to being condemned to the forest. The citizens of Indraprastha, who had lived happily under our rule, also suffered.

It was now six years since our arrival in Kamyakavana. In the meantime, Arjuna, who had gone to Mount Himavana, had returned after obtaining the Pashupatastra, a divine weapon, from Shiva. During this time, occasionally Chief Minister Vipruthu, sometimes commanders Satyaki or Anadhrishti, and at times Krishna's most handsome son Pradyumna would visit us on his behalf. Balaramadada also came to visit us occasionally. He and Bhimsena would stay together till the time of their departure.

The rainy season that had thrashed Kamyakavana was now over. Rivers had returned to their normal flow. Fog, announcing the severe cold of winter, began covering the forest. Now it was necessary to leave Kamyakavana as soon as possible. Bhima and Arjuna built two neat and beautiful boats with their brothers' assistance. All five brothers were going to take turns carrying these on their shoulders. Wherever we were going we were going to build a new cottage and begin a new life there. On the chosen day, all of us met Dhaumya Rishi and sought his blessings. He was also going to follow us to the new forest, along with his disciples.

We reached the Dvaitavana after crossing many rivers. Here, too, Bhima and Arjuna raised a spacious cottage to our liking. It was even bigger than the previous one. My five husbands built a circular, sturdy, protective wooden fence around it, and raised a small colony of big and small huts nearby for the rishi and his disciples. Dhaumya Rishi was going to bring our cows and cattle with him later. Within a couple of months, our Pandava colony in the Dvaitavana was inhabited and running smoothly. Then Yudhishthira invited Dhaumya Rishi through Nakula.

The Lord of Dwaraka – Krishna – came to Dvaitavana to meet me. Daruka had brought his embellished grand chariot to the ashrama entrance. Krishna descended from the chariot first. As I saw him help Bhama gently get down, I, too, ran forward. This was the second time Krishna was coming to visit us in the forest. I realised that though he was the lord of opulent Dwaraka, when he visited us, he came in a very simple manner with a few select people, leaving his army, chariots and elephant troops behind. He had never done anything in his life without a purpose. He had one intention in coming to visit us in a simple manner – of respecting our way of living in the forest and our Kshatriya pride. With Krishna's arrival, our ashrama was filled with joy. He first went to meet Dhaumya Rishi. Usually, Dhaumya Rishi would be in a trance once he started his meditation. As Krishna stood near the rishi, he automatically opened his eyes with a smile. Krishna moved forward with agility and knelt down in respect. The rishi smiled and offered his blessings, 'May all be well. Arise, oh, Lord of Dwaraka.' Krishna sat in front of him on a grass mat, with Uddhavadeva and Bhama on either side. Then for quite some time all of us chatted about various subjects.

Krishna stayed for a few days. My heart was filled with gloom that Krishna was going back to Dwaraka. Now the period of six years of staying in Dvaitavana, too, was coming to an end. After that we had to go incognito for one year. An urgent meeting was convened in the meeting room of our cottage. Krishna sat on an elevated seat covered with a grass mat.

All of us sat in front of Krishna. Daruka stood at the door of the cottage, holding a whip in his hand. He was not going to let any of Dhaumya Rishi's disciples or servants into the cottage. This was a very important Yadava–Pandava meeting arranged secretly, with a lot of precaution. Our upcoming mission was to live strictly incognito for one year. The smallest mistake from any one of us during this period would banish us to another round of residing in the forest and living incognito as punishment. Krishna said, 'Oh valiant Pandava brothers, a very critical testing period in your life is about to begin – the period of living incognito. During this time, each of you will particularly have to forget that you are five brothers. Though you have been living in the forest, Draupadi is still your queen. Henceforth, you and she will have to forget your past life. She will have to play the role of a maid. Each one of you will have to play the roles of different kinds of attendants. I have thoroughly and deeply pondered what kind of roles all five of you can play efficiently. If you are thinking that you could go to distant forests and quietly spend your time of living incognito there, it is simply not going to be possible. Even before your period of living incognito begins, Duryodhana's skilled informers will be infiltrating all forests of Aaryavarta. They will form an alliance with the tribal kings of each of the forests and thoroughly search them. We will have to plan some gimmicks so that Duryodhana and his secret agents from Hastinapura continue to keep searching for all of you particularly in the forests. For that purpose, five Yadavas and a woman will live in some of the forests in your disguise. Their body structures will resemble yours. The woman will be disguised as Draupadi.'

We kept looking at him mesmerised. He continued, 'Even this strategy will not work for long. Once the duplicate Pandavas in the forests are exposed, we will have to immediately withdraw them from there. In the beginning, we will have to deceive them into believing that you brothers have dispersed and are living separately.

'I am expecting that the first three months will pass in all this. After that we will have to plan something else. The entire Aaryavarta clearly recognises two of you – Bhimsena as the mace warrior and Arjuna as the master archer. People know the remaining three more by their nature than by the weapons they use.

'The second phase in my planning will be to deceive them by making them believe that each of you is in a different forest. First, a duplicate of the mighty mace warrior Bhimsena will emerge in one forest. The acclaim of his mace expertise will automatically reach Duryodhana–Shakuni in Hastinapura. A joint troop of mace warriors and wrestlers will leave from Hastinapura to wipe out that Bhimsena. Kauravas are well acquainted with all the habits of Bhima. The duplicate Bhimsena will have to vanish before they can find him.

'We will use the same trick for Arjuna. By this time, the first half of the year would have passed by.

'For the remaining six months, loyal Yadavas disguised as Yudhishthira, Nakula and Sahadeva will surface in different forests in service of respective tribal kings. But these three Yadava warriors dispersed in three different forests in three directions will not get caught by the tribal kings. They will vanish just as they surfaced, like mushrooms. One after the other they will return to Dwaraka. But the warriors of Hastinapura will keep searching for them in the forests, believing they are still there. By this time, the second half of the year of living incognito will have been over.

'During this entire year, the secret agents of Hastinapura should think that you are hiding in one of the forests only. The success of this mission majorly depends upon this deception. My expert spy team of Dwaraka will successfully carry out the difficult task of convincing the Kauravas that you are hiding in a forest for living incognito – that, too, in the eastern region. You should rest assured about that.

'You are not going to live in a forest during this year. Instead, you will be living in one of the renowned royal cities. That, too, in the western region. You are not going to live in hiding during this time but openly. I am aware that this involves great risks. But sometimes in life such situations arise when one has to play a game of hide-and-seek with everything that one has, putting one's life on the line. I have full faith in the courage that each one of you possesses. I believe in your indomitable self-control and obedience. Listen very carefully to what I am going to say now and follow my instructions to the letter cautiously throughout the year.

'During this year of living incognito, you are going to live in the western region of Aaryavarta, in the royal city of King Virata of the Matsya kingdom, as the attendants of the royal family of King Virata. It is necessary that under all circumstances all five of you get in touch with each other with caution.'

Now he fixed his clear gaze on Yudhishthira and said, 'You have the biggest responsibility during this period. You will have to play your own role to perfection and keep a keen eye on the other five. First of all, you will enter Viratanagar of the Matsyas from the eastern gate two months before the period of living incognito begins, as a Brahmin named Kanka who possesses expertise in the Vedashastras, the Puranas, the Upanishadas, and all religious rituals. You will have a code name, "Jaya", for the convenience of keeping in touch with your brothers. All you brothers will have to give your best to achieve "Jaya" i.e. victory, in this mission. You will have to astutely pretend that you have thorough knowledge of astrology. First, you will have to win over the Matsya King Virata's heart. So, let me tell you about the members of the royal family of King Virata. Listen carefully. Sudeshna is the Maharani of Virata – she is a very loving, religious and virtuous lady who keenly observes rituals. The royal couple has two sons and a daughter. The eldest son is named Bhuminjaya, also called Uttar. In spite of being born in the Kshatriya clan, he is extremely timid. The second son is Shweta, who is still young. Their sister is Uttaraa.

She is exceptionally beautiful, loving, intelligent and a virtuous lady who possesses rare qualities and is very sociable. The commander of the Viratas is Kichaka, giant in size and very powerful. As Maharaja Virata is old and his son Uttara is incompetent, Commander Kichaka holds the reins of the people of Virata.

'Once you win over Maharaja Virata with your knowledge of astrology, you will have to skilfully make him aware of the inadequacies in his kingdom, one at a time. The first shortcoming you will bring to his notice will be the lack of a master chef with skills of preparing delicious food suitable for each season.'

Now the Lord of Dwaraka fixed his eyes on Bhimsena and said, 'Bhimsena, you will be master chef of the Viratas. Your name will be "Ballava". You, who usually carry a huge mace on your shoulders, will have to enter Viratanagar from the western gate carrying a perforated ladle instead. Looking at your bare and weird appearance, the children on the streets may ridicule you occasionally. If it continues for the rest of the year, it will be safer for your stay there. You should look comical and not gallant due to your huge physique. As you will be the royal chef on Yudhishthira's recommendation, your voracious appetite will be automatically taken care of. Your physical strength, which is a major support for your family will not diminish during this time. In fact, it may increase further. You should take only one precaution. Unless there is an emergency, never show yourself in front of Commander Kichaka even by mistake. That expert commander will instantly recognise you for sure. Your code name will be "Jayesha".'

Krishna shifted his gaze from Bhimsena to Arjuna and said, 'Dear Arjuna, you have to play the most difficult role during this period. You will enter Viratanagar from the main gate and that, too, disguised as a woman. The entire Aaryavarta knows you as an indomitable, master archer, and regards you as the best among men. You will have to completely transform your manly handsome appearance, that immediately stands out. Only then can you remain anonymous. You will have to play the role of "Brihannadaa" – the dance and music teacher of Virata's daughter, Uttaraa. Your code name will be "Jayendra". Instead of bearing the Gandiva bow, you will have to dress up like a woman.

You will have to put a vermilion dot on your forehead in the name of your husband, who is in a faraway country. You will have to adapt a feminine gait and speak like a woman. This is going to be very difficult for you. For that, you will have to make Panchali your guru. So far you have been her husband – now you will have to be her disciple.' He was not just surprising us, but also leaving us shocked. How was Arjuna ever going to agree to disguise himself in a woman's attire? Instead, he would prefer to come out of hiding and appear in front of Duryodhana. Krishna surmised the hesitation in his mind unmistakably. He rose from the grass mat and approached Arjuna. Putting his hand on Arjuna's shoulder, he said very affectionately, 'Dhananjaya, this disguise of yours as a woman will be remembered forever. The chapter of your manly achievements is going to begin from this chapter of feminine disguise. Play your role with such perfection that even your wife Draupadi is unable to recognise you.'

Arjuna touched his feet and said, 'Achyuta, everything will be done exactly as you say.'

Krishna went back and took his seat on the grass mat. Fixing his keen, visionary glance on Nakula, he said, 'Nakula, you will enter Viratanagar from the southern gate as "Granthika". Your code name will be "Jayatsena". As you are an expert in horses, you will skilfully bring the stable of Viratas under your command within a month. Remember, bringing the horse troops of a kingdom under your control is almost like bringing half the kingdom itself under your control.'

'As you wish, Madhusudana. I will successfully complete the task assigned to me.' Nakula replied with a smile that suited him.

Fixing his bright eyes on Sahadeva, Krishna said, 'Sahadeva, you will enter Viratanagar from the northern gate as "Tantipala". Your code name will be "Jayadbala". You have acquired deep knowledge of Tanta – the tethers for cows. As an expert cowherd, you will bring the cattle of the Viratas under your control. You will have to teach them minute details of how to nurture and protect the cattle. Remember that your knowledge is going to prove significantly beneficial to the Viratas in the near future.'

'As you wish, Gopala. Everything will happen as per your wish,' Sahadeva also responded in the affirmative.

Uddhavadeva, who was silently listening so far, smiled and expressed a doubt, 'Dada your plan is to disguise Arjuna as a woman. Now only Draupadi is left. Are you going to tell her to dress up as a man?'

'Brother Udho, wait a bit. The role that I have chosen for Draupadi is an appropriate one. She will stay in the chamber of Maharani Sudeshna and Princess Uttaraa as "Sairandhri". Sairandhri is a maid especially assigned for helping the royal ladies in adorning themselves. For the convenience of all, her code name will be "Malini". Dear Pandava brothers, you all can meet twice a day in the kitchen of the Viratas at the time of lunch and dinner. Draupadi can go to the kitchen any time under any pretext. Sakhi Draupadi can always keep the five of you united by skilfully using your code names.

'Draupadi…sorry, Sairandhri, no Malini – remember one thing always. You, too, should particularly avoid going in front of Commander Kichaka. If that happens, any kind of disaster may befall you. In that case, only Bhimsena will be able to protect you! I won't be there.'

While talking to me, he had intentionally pretended to make a mistake. By making that mistake, he wanted to warn me about Kichaka. He wanted to inscribe the name Malini on my mind. Malini means a flower girl. He had given me this name suggestively. Any woman's chastity is like a flower. I was to protect it and not let it wither.

He asked, 'Any doubts, Draupadi?'

I asked, 'What should I do about the fragrance emitting from my body?' My five husbands, along with Uddhavadeva, kept staring with their eyes wide.

My best friend Krishna was different from anybody else. He imagined himself in my place, living as a Sairandhri for an entire year, and said, 'The fragrance of your body can be taken care of by using a new Ketaka leaf in your thick, curly hair, daily. But during this period of living incognito, you will have to tie your thick, long hair that you have left open so far. For that you will have to use a strip of cloth. There will be no one to serve you as will be a maid yourself. So you will have to do it yourself.'

Thus, the entire mission of our living incognito was planned with minute details under Krishna's guidance. Everybody handed over their weapons to Bhimsena. He was going to keep them in a safe secret place on the border of the Matsya kingdom before entering Viratanagar. Krishna bade farewell to us and left for Dwaraka along with Bhama and Uddhavadeva. Within a few days, our period of staying in the forest was over.

As decided, Yudhishthira first entered Viratanagar alone and presented himself in the service of King Virata. Following him, Bhimsena, Arjuna and all of us entered the city one after the other. All of us assumed our roles and began our work cautiously. Yudhishthira barely managed to send a messenger to Dwaraka to let Krishna know that we had safely reached Viratanagar. It was the last contact with Krishna and Dwaraka. Now, not even by mistake was any messenger or message from Dwaraka going to come to Viratanagar. We were going to hear news of Dwaraka only from the chief minister of the Viratas, that, too, very rarely.

Six months of our incognito life passed by uneventfully. Then the first news of Dwaraka arrived in Viratanagar – that of the wedding of Samba, the son of our Jambavati, to Lakshmana, the daughter of Duryodhana, who was the reason of our misery. Word was that Balaramadada had taken all the initiative in this marriage alliance. I was shocked by that news. Various thoughts crossed my mind. How come Krishna, who had been the best friend to us Pandavas, accepted Lakshmana, the daughter of Duryodhana, who had humiliated me, as his own daughter-in-law? And had Krishna befriended Duryodhana, just like he had befriended us? If he had indeed become Duryodhana's friend, then what was going to happen to us? Who was going to be our patron in this incognito life planned by him?

We were all shocked. We could not meet each other openly. We could not even talk in detail during the short meetings that we had in the kitchen. We were going through a big emotional turmoil.

Krishna himself released us soon from this tension. For the first time, his messenger came to Viratanagar and met with Kanka, the expert astrologer of the Viratas. Indeed, it was Krishna's speciality that he would think of an event from all angles, take into consideration its effect everywhere, and find a perfect solution.

In short, the story of the Samba–Lakshmana marriage went like this – Samba had abducted Duryodhana's daughter Lakshmana from Hastinapura. The only reason for that was that he really liked her. Actually,

Duryodhana should have prudently accepted the relation with Krishna through this bond – like Rukmini's brother Rukmi had tried to patch up by giving his daughter Rukmavati's hand in marriage to Pradyumna. But, despite everything that had happened, Duryodhana still considered Krishna as a lowlife cowherd. Duryodhana chased Samba and Lakshmana and put Samba in prison, and sent Lakshmana back to the royal palace. Due to all this, there was agitation in Dwaraka. Balaramadada brandished the Samvartaka plough on his shoulders and attacked Hastinapura with the army. He ferociously fought with Duryodhana's army and left Hastinapura shaken. Defeating his disciple, he freed Samba from prison. He brought Samba to Dwaraka, along with Lakshmana, and got them married with grandeur. Krishna watched everything silently. Why? I was wondering about that. He probably did not find it right to hurt his big brother while we were living incognito. He had sent a special message only for me with his messenger. It said, 'Krishney, I have no relation with Duryodhana whatsoever. You should harbour no doubt in your heart. Once the incognito life ends and your five husbands come out in the open, I have plans to get much bigger things done by them. It's up to you to convince them to remain calm.'

Nowadays, I was clearly becoming aware that my love for him as a friend was transforming into a devotion that could not be defined. It was his doing, after all. He was a true king of the Chandravansha. His legacy was that of the moon, which stays far away in the sky but makes the lotus flowers bloom in a lake. It was indeed a blessing to feel Krishna's closeness with such intensity while he was far away.

During this period of living incognito, while combing the long black hair of Virata princess Uttaraa, I would automatically go into a trance. At such times, occasionally the princess would reprimand me, saying, 'Sairandhri, you are being so careless – where are you looking and what are you doing? Do you even know how to braid hair? If you cannot handle my thick, black hair, I will choose another maid. You can just leave.' I would have to take her upbraiding in my stride.

Then, to alleviate her anger, I would tell her stories of Krishna of Dwaraka, Arjuna–Draupadi of Indraprastha and Subhadra and her son Abhimanyu, as if I were a third person and had just heard all those stories from someone else. She would listen to those tales attentively. As I had a watchful disposition, I had already noted a subtle thing about her. She paid extra attention to the tales of Arjuna more than anybody else.

I would frequently visit the dance school and the kitchen of the Viratas under some pretext or the other. I would see Brihannadaa in the dance school, wearing the special Matsya-style costume. The sound of jingling anklets on her feet at the rhythm of the dance beat 'Ta Thai Tak Thai' would leave me heartbroken. Arjuna was the best man among my five husbands. He possessed many rare qualities. Probably that is why, more than the others, he was the one who had to go through this difficult test of living as an insignificant maid.

While wiping the drops of sweat on her forehead, she would glance at me for a glass of water. I could never forget that look in his eyes. When Ballava would meet me in the kitchen, he would first convey the well-being of his four brothers to me in a whisper. He would put some special dish that he had prepared that day in my hand and say, 'Sairandhri, take care of your health.' I had the least contact with Kanka. He would always accompany Maharaja Virata. How could a maid from the inner chambers of Princess Uttaraa appear before them directly? I had to devise many ideas to meet Yudhishthira, and convey his instructions to his brothers safely. For that, I would create some fictitious problems for Princess Uttaraa and go to Maharaja Virata along with her to get them resolved. While the princess talked with her father, I would enquire about Kanka's well-being and seek instructions from him. It was comparatively easy to meet my husbands Nakula–Sahadeva, or Granthika and Tantipala, as they were known, in the stable and the cow pen.

The second half of our incognito life was also coming to an end. Now just the last week remained. After that, we were going to be free. But we were not as fortunate to have our lives going on so smoothly. As usual, to meet Kanka, I went to Maharaja Virata along with Uttaraa. Virata's commander Kichaka was in a confidential meeting with his king in the royal chamber. After seeing us, Maharaja Virata smiled and said to his daughter, 'Come, Uttaraa, have you heard what our commander is saying? He has received news that the Pandavas of Indraprastha, who lost the gambling game, are living secretly in our kingdom. Prince Duryodhana of Hastinapura has requested to search for them thoroughly. The message is that as soon as they are found, they should be imprisoned. The commander is working on the same plan.' I was horrified on hearing those words. Our plan had worked successfully throughout the year but it was about to be exposed in the last phase. If somebody recognised us, we would be immediately imprisoned. I felt dizzy. I kept staring at Maharaja Virata with my mouth open. I did not even realise that Commander Kichaka had been staring at me with unblinking eyes. He asked Uttaraa, 'Is this your maid, Princess? What is her name?'

'Malini,' replied Uttaraa.

It was impossible for me to wait there even for a moment. It was necessary to warn my husbands of the impending grave danger without wasting a moment.

First, I met Kanka in his room. 'Duryodhana has come to know that we are living in the Matsya kingdom. He is searching for us.' As soon as he heard my words, his face turned white with fear. He stood silent for a long time. 'Go and meet Bhima and Arjuna immediately. We will have to do what they say.'

As per his instruction, first I met Bhima and Arjuna, and informed them of the impending calamity. I also warned Nakula and Sahadeva. I did this very astutely, and at the end of the day, returned to my room. While wiping the sweat from my forehead, I sat on a mat in front of a big mirror. I freed my tied hair and started running my fingers through it. Just then, Madhulika, another maid, entered my chamber hurriedly. 'Malini, the commander is coming to visit you,' she said with frightened eyes.

It did not occur to me that I should gather and tie my hair. Only Krishna's warning kept ringing in my ears and mind, 'Draupadi, do not ever go in front of the Viratas' commander Kichaka, even by mistake.' Just the memory of these words left me trembling. I could not think of anything.

While I stood bewildered like a statue in front of the mirror, the tall Virata commander Kichaka came in, stomping his feet, bearing his huge mace on the shoulder, and stood right in front of me. For a moment, I felt as if the entire world around me was spinning. His eyes wide, he kept staring strangely at my heel-long hair. Then, laughing sarcastically, he said, 'Indeed, you are Malini – a garland of beautiful flowers – but you are also Sukesha – the one with beautiful, long hair – just like Draupadi of Indraprastha.'

I stood stupefied in front of him, as if struck by lightning. He kept muttering further, 'Such a ravishingly beautiful maid should exercise the power of her beauty on the commander instead of serving the princess. I am going to make such arrangements by telling the king, so that even I will be able to adorn your thick hair with flowers.'

Suddenly my fear vanished into thin air. I delicately brought my hair over my shoulder. While making playful gestures with a strand of my hair in a shameless way that surprised even my own self, I invitingly said, 'Oh how fortunate this lowlife maid Sairandhri would be to serve the commander. Whenever you want, Malini will be at your service.'

He said in a whisper, 'Sairandhri – Malini, get all dressed up and ready. I will spend tonight in your fragrant company.'

I blurted out the words of response as if pushed by someone, 'As the commander wishes. This maid is at your service.' Hearing that, the commander of the Viratas was pleased with himself, laughed aloud and left just as he came in, like a storm. I was scared to death looking at his retreating figure. First of all, I remembered Krishna. It was as if he was telling me from every direction, 'Go to Bhimsena without wasting a moment.' As if pulled by an unknown force, I rushed towards the kitchen of the Viratas. The moment he saw me, just by looking at my face, Bhimsena surmised that I was in big trouble. I immediately told him what had happened. For a moment, he was lost in thought. Then he said, 'He seems like the Jayadratha of the Viratas. Do not worry. I am here. I will take good care of him. What did he say to you – that he wanted to plant flowers in your hair, didn't he? Let me sever that rugged tree of his body itself. And that, too, in front of you. Do not worry at all. Just as you have promised him, get all decked up and sit on your bed.'

Night descended on Viratanagar. During the evening, Bhimsena met all his brothers and instructed them to wait near my bedroom throughout the night. It was a perfect arrangement to make sure that not a single warrior of the Viratas would be able to enter my bedroom even if it was on fire.

As per Bhimsena's instruction, I sat on my bed, all decked up. The night progressed. Kichaka had not yet arrived. Many suspicions stirred in my mind. Had the commander come to know something about our incognito life? Was he planning to capture us? What if his armed warriors came in instead of him? Just when I was getting restless with each passing moment, Kichaka entered my bedroom. There was no crown on his head, no mace on his shoulder. His eyes were overflowing with lust.

To appear inviting to him, I portrayed shyness. I had purposefully let my thick, long hair hanging down the bed like a serpent, their tips directly touching the carpet on the floor.

Kichaka – the lecherous commander of the Viratas – came and sat by my side while stammering something like 'M – Malini – Sa – Sairandhri – dear'. In the gambling hall, when Dushasana had grabbed my saree, I had seen his eyes burning with revenge. I raised my head and looked at Kichaka's eyes too. They looked so different. There was no trace of revenge in them, but the uncontrollable, flared-up inferno of bare lust. At that moment, I strongly felt deep in my heart that one's eyes give away one's character. Impatient Kichaka moved closer to me to take me into his embrace. I got terrified. Exactly at that moment, my hair got tugged. I became fearless. I dropped my jade-studded, serpent hood-shaped ring on the floor. It made a clunking sound. I bent down saying, 'Where did my ring go?', and as planned, crawled under my bed. Lascivious Kichaka got restless on the bed. He put his muscular, hairy hand under the bed and grabbing the hair that came into his hand, and said, 'Come on, dear – come outside'.

The one he pulled out was my mighty husband Bhimsena. He stammered, 'You…Ba…Ba…Ballava…how come you are here?' Bhimsena was not in a state of mind to listen to anything. He shouted, 'You scoundrel, she is not Sairandhri!' He put the first powerful strike on Kichaka's neck. Kichaka lurched to one side. I crawled out from under the bed. Leaning against the wall, I kept staring. I had only heard of Bhimsena's unmatched wrestling power. I had never seen it in person.

'You sinful soul… She is not Malini either.'

Bhimsena leapt on the tall commander like a soaring falcon.

'She is Draupadi – the wife of us Pandavas of Indraprastha – you foul creature.' He struck Kichaka's neck from the other side.

By this time, Kichaka had also regained his composure. He thumped his arms loudly. Like two massive wild elephants colliding with each other, both began fighting right in front of me. Within a short time, they began perspiring profusely. Bhimsena was throwing Kichaka down on the ground, using various wrestling tactics, like a washerman striking wet twisted clothes on the stone steps of the Yamuna's ghat. Half an hour passed. Kichaka looked half dead now. 'Malini, see how your Ballava is beating the crap out of him.' Bhimsena sat on Kichaka's belly and began landing strikes one after the other with his iron fist on Kichaka's big, hairy chest, shouting wildly. With every strike, Kichaka would shut his eyes in agonising pain and writhe.

Finally, the invincible wrestler of the Pandavas put his arms around Kichaka's neck and held it tightly in the Bahukantaka hold. Bhimsena began tightening his grip every moment, gnashing his teeth in anger. As Kichaka suffocated, he started to flounder like a fish out of water and tried to break free. Bhimsena ultimately killed him.

As Maharaja Virata came to know of the death of Commander Kichaka, initially, he got scared. But when he came to know that Bhimsena had done it, he regained his composure. He came to the kitchen in person to meet us, along with gift salvers of royal costumes. His speech indicated regret that the Pandavas, who had conquered the world, had to work as lowly servants in his kingdom.

As per Maharaja Virata's wish, we all put on royal costumes again. That day, I strongly realised a special quality of Yudhishthira's. In the last thirteen years, twelve years of forest life and one year of incognito life, he had spoken in a dismal, pathetic, piteous manner. But when we wore royal costumes, the kingship and spirit of a Kshatriya within him resurfaced with a flourish. He assumed leadership of the Pandavas for further action. My mind was concerned about one thing, though. Would he create a problematic situation again? Where was he going to lead us, after all? But he had transformed. He said to Maharaja Virata, 'Maharaja, send an urgent message to Srikrishna – the Lord of Dwaraka –

that we Pandavas are coming out of our incognito life.' I was happy that he had remembered Krishna first. It was obvious now that the Viratas were going to be in trouble due to us. It was necessary for us to leave the city as soon as possible. We held a council at night. It was unanimously decided that we should go to one of the towns on the borders of Virata and Indraprastha, choosing such a place with the permission of Maharaja Virata. According to the condition put forward in the second gambling game, the Kauravas were supposed to return the Indraprastha kingdom to us after the completion of our incognito life.

But the very next day, we received a message from a special messenger of Krishna that left all of us wary again. The message was, 'The army of Hastinapura with all prominent warriors has left to attack the Viratas to capture their cattle. Duryodhana has unerringly surmised that you are located in Viratanagar due to the execution of Kichaka. He has presumed that you will show up for the protection of the cattle. Grandsire Bhishma, Guru Drona, Kripa, Karna – the king of Anga – his brother Shona, Ashwatthama, Duryodhana himself with a few chosen brothers, and Shakuni are coming with the army. You should fight against them along with the Virata army, showing yourself up on the day of Vijayadashami. Arjuna should lead your army.'

The veil of whitish fog that had spread over Viratanagar lifted as the day progressed. The citizens began their daily routine. Herds of pure white, brown, blackish, greyish cows were taken out of their corrals and to the incline of Mount Arbuda nearby for grazing. As the day advanced, a big commotion was heard from the inclines of Mount Arbuda. Following that, Maharaja Virata, who was gasping for breath, entered the kitchen along with a newly assigned commander. My five husbands, dressed as warriors, and I had gathered there under the leadership of Bhimsena. My husbands had already prepared their minds as per Krishna's timely instruction. But none of them had a single weapon with them. Maharaja Virata brought his palms together in prayer and implored them earnestly, 'You are mighty warriors. Please protect the cattle of my subjects. You should immediately get into the chariots, chase and protect our cattle and save our honour.'

Maharaja Virata continued, 'You can take whatever weapons you want from our armoury and leave immediately.'

I realised the problem was that my valiant husbands did not have their weapons charged with mantras and said, 'They have kept their weapons in the hollow of a Shami tree on the border of your kingdom. They will have to use those weapons only.'

'Tell Prince Uttara to get the chariot ready. We are all set. Maharaja should command him to steer the chariot as per my instruction. We will take care of the rest.' Arjuna's face brightened at the thought of seeing his favourite Gandiva bow after a year.

Bidding farewell to us, under the leadership of Arjuna, the brigade of chariots of the Viratas marched forward. The mammoth Virata army followed them. Throughout that day of Vijayadashami, I kept moving about restlessly, remembering Krishna. I was imploring to him in my heart, 'You have protected the honour of the Pandavas till today. Protect it today too. Let my invincible archer Arjuna be successful in the mission.'

Dusk descended over Viratanagar. Flocks of birds that had gone to Mount Arbuda to feed themselves were returning to the city. Then, the indistinct mooing of hundreds of cows was heard from far away. I became alert. Followed by that, I heard acclaim of Maharaja Virata. My face brightened. I pricked up my ears. Now, I could clearly hear only one victorious slogan – 'Hail invincible archer Arjuna! Well done, Partha – protector of the cows. Master of the Gandiva bow, Dhananjaya – victory to him! Victory!' My face brightened with the brilliance of millions of lights.

My triumphant husbands had returned after a sweeping victory over the Kauravas. It was a small compensation to the Viratas, who had given us invaluable support by offering us shelter for one year. My five husbands came to visit me with radiant, victorious faces. The account they gave was thrilling. It was hopeful of the future.

The Kaurava army comprising thousands of horse riders had reached the inclines of Mount Arbuda and chased the cattle of the Viratas. They had come to surround the cattle and steal it. Grandsire Bhishma, the son of Ganga, a lifetime celibate, who had acquired the Prasvapaastra from Bhagvan Parashurama, Acharya Drona and Kripa, who had taught archery to the Kauravas and Pandavas, Ashwatthama who had acquired the Brahmastra from his father, world conqueror Karna – the king of Anga – his brother Shona, many Kaurava brothers and brothers of

Shakuni were all there. And who was leading them? It was Duryodhana, who had shown his bare thigh to me in an assembly full of people, and Shakuni, who had played the deceptive gambling game.

In the chariots of the Viratas, my husbands had reached the Shami tree where the weapons were kept. Everyone offered flowers and paid obeisance to the weapons.

Now the change on their faces was noticeable. Their faces displayed fearlessness. Their eyes became radiant like the sun. Physically, they were five armed warriors, but their hearts were united in a powerful fist in which Goddess Ida resided. Unanimously, they hailed the name of Goddess Ida.

They approached the Kauravas, who were fleeing with the cattle of the Viratas. Near Mount Arbuda, amidst the cacophony of war drums, a fierce battle broke out between the Kauravas and the Pandavas, along with the Viratas, to obtain the cattle. Arjuna was possessed by the spirit of war that day. His grit erupted uncontrollably. By evening, he had undeniably defeated Grandsire Bhishma, Guru Drona, Kripa, Karna and everyone else. One of his sharp arrows hit Karna's brother Shona in the chest and he fell in battle. Karna collapsed, crying over his lifeless body.

In the evening, Arjuna projected the Sammohanastra – the weapon of hypnosis – on all the Kaurava warriors whom he had disarmed. Due to the effect of the astra, the Kaurava warriors, who were exhausted from fighting, got hypnotized first, then delusional and finally fainted.

Maharaja Virata was very pleased with Arjuna and my other husbands for defeating the Kauravas. Even Princess Uttaraa's opinion had changed when she came to know that her dance teacher Brihannadaa was not a woman but valiant Arjuna himself. She had openly expressed her desire to have Arjuna as her husband to her father. Oh, she was so young. If I had had a daughter, she would have been of the same age. She was attracted to my husband – master archer Arjuna – with romantic ideas suitable to a teenage girl who worshipped valour.

Her strange wish, which was inappropriate for her age, reached my ears. I was baffled. She was a princess. Her father loved her very much. He might have even granted her wish. And I knew Arjuna very well. He went on a pilgrimage and returned after marrying twice! This needed to stop somewhere. Whenever I faced any emotional problem, I did not remember anybody but Krishna.

I met the royal messenger who was carrying Yudhishthira's message to Dwaraka in person and told him, 'Tell Krishna to leave immediately. Or else Arjuna will get married to Uttaraa, who is suitable to be his daughter.'

Now, as the news that my husbands, the Pandavas, had come out of incognito life spread, kings from various kingdoms neighbouring the Matsya kingdom began visiting Viratanagar with their commanders and chief ministers. The first to visit us was my brother Dhrishtadyumna, who came along with the army. One messenger of the Viratas was also sent to Hastinapura to Kuntidevi and Vidura.

We had strictly fulfilled the condition of 'twelve years of forest life and one year of incognito life', as agreed with the Kauravas. There shouldn't have been any obstacle in getting the Indraprastha kingdom back, just as the Pandavas had previously obtained Khandavavana through Krishna's mediation. I was dreaming about re-entering Indraprastha in a grand manner and honourably along with all my husbands.

Viratanagar was bedecked with garlands, festoons and arches decorated with flowers. Everyone was eager to see Krishna in person. Within a few days, his triumphant, embellished Garudadhwaja chariot, driven by Daruka, stood in front of the gate on the southern border of Viratanagar. My beloved friend Krishna descended from the chariot. With a smile on his face and palms joined together, he politely offered respects to the men and women who had gathered there. I simply kept staring at his radiant face. All my tensions vanished into thin air. I was seeing him in person after a long time, but to me it felt like yesterday. He walked briskly and whispered in a soft voice which only I could hear, 'Krishnee, I have received your message. Do not worry about anything at all. How are you doing?' Within a moment, he bowed down to Maharaja Virata and Sudeshnadevi, and disappeared among the Pandavas.

A meeting of the royal circle of the Viratas, Yadavas and Pandavas took place at night. Before that meeting, Krishna met only Arjuna in private and discussed something important. Maharaja Virata enquired about the well-being of all and then presented his heart's desire. He said, 'The Pandavas, especially master archer Arjuna, have fought courageously and protected our cattle as well as our honour. Therefore, I have taken a decision with the Maharani's consent, to offer our one and only beautiful daughter Uttaraa, who is an expert in dance and music, in marriage to valiant Arjuna! Arjuna should accept her hand in front of all present at this meeting.'

All eyes turned to Arjuna now. Without wasting any time, he said, 'The Maharaja's daughter Uttaraa is my disciple in dance and music. I am her guru. A marriage between these two great relations will be against Dharma. Any guru can look at his disciple only as his child, and not from any other perspective. We Pandavas cannot forget the affectionate treatment that we got from the Viratas during our incognito life. Therefore, with respect, I am accepting the Maharaja's offer. His daughter Uttaraadevi will become part of the Pandava royal family, not as my wife but as my daughter-in-law. My son Abhimanyu is young and handsome. He is well suited to be a son-in-law to the Maharaja and all the citizens of Virata. I propose the Virata princess's marriage to him in front of all.'

Arjuna had cautiously and skilfully diverted the arrow coming towards him. He was a master archer, after all. He had spoken everything that Krishna had told him. Abhimanyu and Uttaraa's wedding was fixed and it was decided that it would take place in Viratanagar itself.

Priests from both sides found an auspicious date for the wedding. This was the first wedding ceremony of the third generation of the Pandavas. The aged Maharaja Vasudeva and both his queens wished to attend this wedding but were going to be unable to do so due to the long journey. They had already given their blessings to Abhimanyu before he left Dwaraka.

Rajmata Kuntidevi arrived from Hastinapura along with the armed guards that Mahatma Vidura had sent with her. Nobody else was coming. Even the Viratas had not invited anybody else.

Krishna affectionately embraced young and handsome Abhimanyu, who looked like him except for the blue complexion, and gave him an appropriate blessing, 'May your glory reach the corners of the world.' While blessing Uttaraa, he said, 'May you live long!'

The faces of the newly married Abhimanyu and Uttaraa beamed with a unique radiance.

On the day after the wedding, a council of the Viratas was held. I sat in this meeting next to Maharani Sudeshnadevi, along with the eight queens of Krishna. Whatever Krishna said in front of the Viratas, the Yadavas, the Panchalas and the Pandavas, who had gathered together for the wedding was indeed unforgettable – it exhibited concern for justice that he had demonstrated throughout his life. It was full of his pure love for the Pandavas. More than that, it contained a prudent vision, as if he could vividly see the events in the future. He said in his clear, spellbinding speech, 'The five valiant and virtuous Pandava brothers have completed the time of twelve years of forest life and one year of incognito life, and have come out in the open now. From this royal altar of the Viratas, I am directly questioning the Kurus of Hastinapura – are you, at least now, going to do justice to the Pandavas?

'Right since childhood, Duryodhana and his brothers, Shakuni and his brothers, and all their allies have been tormenting the Pandavas. Why? Did they seem defenceless to them? From the royal city of the Viratas, I proclaim openly that I regard the Pandavas to be the undoubted leaders of future Aaryavarta.

'But as much as I have understood Duryodhana and Shakuni, I am quite sure that they will never readily do justice to the Pandavas. The Pandavas will have to go to war with all the support that they can gather to obtain their rightful share of power. They will have to elicit justice on the battlefield itself. If at all such an occasion arises, I appeal today that the Matsya kingdom of the Viratas should firmly stand behind the Pandavas, along with their army. Maharaja Virata should dispatch a mature, wise and experienced envoy today to Hastinapura to meet Maharaja Dhritarashtra of the Kurus. Also, send a clear message to the Kauravas that they should honourably return the Indraprastha kingdom to the Pandavas.

'Dwaraka and I have belonged to the Pandavas right since our very first meeting. I would say only one thing with the experience that life has offered me – that life's problems never get resolved by fighting destructive wars on the battlefield. In fact, they multiply and get more complicated. The only way to make human life happier and more bearable is – love. For that undoubted love, I appeal to Hastinapura openly on behalf of the Pandavas and the kingdoms of the Viratas, the Panchalas and the Yadavas who are present in this council, that they should resolve the matter of Indraprastha with conciliatory means and love. I appeal to the Kurus – give justice to the Pandavas.'

He decided to send the newly married Uttaraa–Abhimanyu back to Dwaraka along with a few chosen relatives. I asked Krishna a question that had been pressing on my mind for quite a few days, 'Oh Lord of Dwaraka, I have heard that you have raised a staircase in your royal capital with golden steps in memory of the people that you have met in your life. I have heard the acclaim of this grand Srisopana from many people. Word is that there has been the addition of many steps to it. Krishna, you never said anything about it, so I have to ask you myself now – is there at least a single step among the golden steps of this Srisopana for this disgraced sakhi of yours living in the forest?' My question was completely unexpected to him. He kept looking at me with a weird expression. Then he gave me a charming smile and said, 'Krishney, who told you that there is only one Sopana? You are my sakhi. Think about it. Is there another Srisopana? If there is, then at what number will there be a jewel-studded step in your name?'

His answer left me confused. I kept thinking – a second Sopana? Where could it be?

'Can't find it? Shyamale, silly girl, the other Sopana is right here in the heart of this dear friend of yours. You yourself have to decide which step will be yours in that sopana. Nobody else, not even I can do that.' He smiled and casually walked away from me – like the fragrant autumnal breeze coming from the Yamuna.

Now it was certain that we were going to Indraprastha. For that Krishna presented a proposal to Maharaja Virata – to raise an encampment for the Pandavas in a town called Upaplavya on the border of the Matsya kingdom, which was close to Indraprastha.

The royal envoy of the Viratas had already left for Hastinapura. It was time to say goodbye to the city where we had spent the hardest and most testing year in disguise. I met each one of the maids who worked as sairandhris. When I went to say goodbye to them, they were overwhelmed with emotion, some of them even started sobbing. Their pure love brought tears to my eyes too.

Bhimsena's kitchen mates cooked his favourite dishes while bidding farewell to him. Yudhishthira and Nakula–Sahadeva had similar experiences with their mates who worked with them throughout the year. We came to Upaplavya, a small town, along with Krishna. As per Maharaja Virata's order, a luxurious encampment with all sorts of amenities was raised there for us. Satyaki and few chosen warriors of Dwaraka accompanied Krishna. Once we settled in this camp, Krishna organised an important meeting with us. In this meeting, he looked quite serious. I had never seen him like this before. He said, 'The Kurus of Hastinapura have not given any response to the royal envoy of the Viratas. They have conveniently kept silent. Now, I will have to compel them to speak. For a final attempt to reconcile relations between you and the Kurus, I will go to Hastinapura as a mediator. I will put my intelligence and eloquence to test. I have stood up for justice throughout my life. I will try my best to get you justice by means of reconciliation.' Hearing that, Yudhishthira said, 'Vasudeva, I also want to put an end to this by means of reconciliation. War will bring permanent enmity between us cousins. We have followed all the conditions of the gambling game to the letter, now they should return Indraprastha to us, just as they had taken it from us. That is what we want to insist upon. To go to war for that and sacrifice many more lives who have nothing to do with it will not be right. Try to reconcile as much as possible. You may ask for the opinion of my brothers if you wish.'

Bhima spoke, leaving me appalled, 'Just tell them to give our Indraprastha kingdom back without any retaliation. That is all we are asking for.'

Unexpected to me, Arjuna seconded him and said, 'Our own people will be killed in war – instead, in my opinion, mending fences is better.'

I was upset about the delusional behaviour of those upon whom I was relying the most, and said, 'Krishna, looks like these valiant husbands of mine have forgotten my humiliation in front of all the seniors in the overcrowded gambling hall of the Kurus. That was so shameful for all of us. They have also forgotten about my open hair and their vows. They do not consider me their own and hence do not realise the intensity of my sorrow. Even if they have forgotten it, I will never forget the humiliation of my honour. I will not even allow you to forget it. If you forget it, then my father Drupada and brother Dhrishtadyumna will seek revenge for my humiliation. If they do not, then remember that all my valiant sons, including Abhimanyu, will seek it.'

Even after listening to my words, he calmly said, 'Krishney, I understand how you feel, but first calmly listen to what I say. It is not necessary that I will succeed in my good intentions of reconciliation. One should always keep trying. One should not be adamant to expect any particular outcome of one's attempts. If I succeed in my efforts of reconciliation, you will regain the kingdom of Indraprastha. If not, your husbands will have to be ready with their weapons charged with mantras for a grand battle.' It was now becoming clear why he had become so serious.

From his manner of speaking and grave attitude, I reckoned that he was thinking about something more than negotiation. He sent his loyal Yadava messenger to Maharaja Dhritarashtra with a message, 'I am coming to Hastinapura.' We were waiting for his return. He returned within a few days. But he returned with Sanjaya. Sanjaya was not just a minister, he was the chief of the Kurus' chariot troop. He was an ardent devotee of Krishna. It was a political ploy of the Kurus to send a message through him. Instead of directly saying that the Pandavas would not get the Indraprastha kingdom back, Duryodhana and Shakuni had sent a hypocritical message in the name of Maharaja Dhritarashtra.

It was, 'If the Pandavas want to go to war, they should consider that war is never beneficial to anybody. Innumerable gallant warriors and soldiers will be killed. Kingdoms will get destroyed. A philosophical and stable-minded person like Yudhishthira should think about it. Instead of participating in such a war, where his own relatives will be destroyed, wouldn't it be better to spend life in a holy place like Kurukshetra, on the alms given by religious pilgrims? He should remember that his name is Dharmaraja, hence he and his brothers should act according to Dharma. They should give up the idea of going to war.'

In the capacity of a minister, Sanjaya delivered the exact message that he carried as a loyal servant, to all of us. I was benumbed to hear that message. The Kauravas were directly telling the Pandavas to seek alms. A murmuring disquiet buzzed among the Pandavas. Krishna was the only one who was calm. He got up from his seat and went close to Sanjaya and put his right hand on his shoulder. Patting him for a moment, Krishna said, 'Sanjaya, my brother Yudhishthira is indeed Dharmaraja. He will definitely follow Dharma as his name connotes, and his brothers will also do as he tells them to do. They will never be divided. Just convey to Kuru Maharaja Dhritarashtra and Grandsire Bhishma that Krishna is coming to visit them – to meet them and to seek their blessings.'

As his friend Sanjaya understood the hidden meaning in his response, he simply kept staring at Krishna while holding his hands for a moment. The next moment he muttered, 'Oh, what a situation am I caught in?'

Kuru minister Sanjaya stayed for a day at our camp and left for Hastinapura.

Now in Upaplavya, preparations for Krishna's departure for Hastinapura began with the assistance of Maharaja Virata. Satyaki and select Yadava warriors were to accompany him. Ten well-equipped and embellished chariots stood in a queue behind the Garudadhwaja chariot. Behind them were rows of cavalry and infantry. Krishna left our grand pavilion, along with Maharaja Virata and my five husbands. As soon as Maharaja Virata moved forward and signalled Krishna with his hand, he quickly got into his chariot. I was standing near his chariot. He looked deep into my eyes, as if saying, 'Krishney, do not worry. Everything will be all right. You will ascend the throne of Indraprastha as the Maharani again.' Raising his right hand, he signalled Daruka to depart.

Krishna did not succeed in the mediations. Let alone the Indraprastha kingdom, Duryodhana flatly refused to give even the five towns of Avisthala, Vrikasthala, Makanda, Varanavati and Shalibhavana, which Krishna asked for the Pandavas. Not only that, he replied insolently, saying, 'Without war, the Pandavas will not get even a small particle of the dust that rests on the tip of a needle.'

I felt deeply hurt by one of his thoughtless utterances. In the crowded Kuru assembly, he dismissed Krishna, degradingly saying, 'I would have ordered my servants to get back even the dust particles of the holy land of Kurus stuck to your soles, you cowherd, who is going back donning the tatters of my denial. But I do not wish even my servants to touch your feet, which are always soiled with cow dung and urine. Get out of this assembly hall quietly. Or else, you insolent bull of Gokul, I will get you all tied up with ropes and put you in prison.'

Yadava commander Satyaki could not control himself after hearing those words and ran towards Duryodhana brandishing a sword. Krishna stopped him with a gesture of his hand.

I was enraged even while listening to that disgraceful news.

Krishna, when he returned from Hastinapura, was not the same person at all. The mischievous, playful, charming smile with the dimple that easily blossomed on his cheek, had disappeared beyond the banks of the Yamuna. He spoke as less as possible now. He was thinking more and more. For me, this was the most trying period, the period of his unbearable silence, even more than what I had had to endure already.

After the unsuccessful attempt at negotiations, Krishna himself took the decision on behalf of all of us – that of a conclusive war. It was going to be a war of Truth against Untruth.

Krishna came from Hastinapura and immediately left for Dwaraka after telling us Pandavas resolutely to begin 'preparations for war'. During this time, living in Upaplavya, I kept thinking about the downfall of the Pandavas as a family. Rajmata was in Hastinapura. Subhadra was in Dwaraka, along with her newly married son and daughter-in-law, and my sons were in Kampilyanagar with their mama, Dhrishtadyumna. Even if we would have thought of sending a message to each other, it would take a month to reach. Once Krishna decided that war was inevitable, my five husbands spread in all directions to seek military support from other kingdoms, just as they had done before conquering the world. The only thing I could do was wait to hear any news from them. In Upaplavya, Maharaja Virata did everything possible to comfort me. For the first time in my entire life, I was experiencing this kind of heart-wrenching loneliness.

Right beyond the Matsya kingdom was the border of Indraprastha. But Indraprastha was now under the rule of the Kauravas. The news that the Pandavas were staying in the Upaplavya city of the Matsya kingdom had already reached Hastinapura. Because of that, armed Kaurava troops began hovering around Upaplavya.

Just as my husbands and Krishna tried to seek military support, Duryodhana–Shakuni did the same for Hastinapura. In fact, groups of ten brothers of Duryodhana accompanied by one of Shakuni's ten brothers had already dispersed in different directions of Aaryavarta. Duryodhana himself went with Shakuni to meet the rulers of kingdoms such as Panchanada, Gandhara, Vahika and Kamboja with salvers full of lavish gifts.

As all kingdoms of Aaryavarta showed interest in this war, its significance increased manifold. It was not just a war any more. Unintentionally, it had turned into the Great War. News started arriving that armies of some kingdoms were on their way to Hastinapura. A shocking news arrived for us in Upaplavya: 'Duryodhana has left for Dwaraka from Hastinapura along with Shakuni and few chosen Kuru warriors. He is going to meet his guru, Prince Balarama, to seek the support of the Yadavas in the war. Then he is going to meet Krishna and after reminding him about their relationship due to the marriage alliance between his son and Duryodhana's daughter, he is going to request Krishna to support him.'

We were shaken when we heard that. We had been taking it for granted that the entire Dwaraka kingdom, along with Balaramadada and Krishna, was going to support us. We arranged an urgent council to take a decision in this matter. In that council, Yudhishthira insisted on only one thing –Arjuna should immediately go to Dwaraka on behalf of the Pandavas. He should remind Krishna about their friendship, and take every precautionary measure to make sure that in any case, the mammoth Yadava army should not offer its support to Duryodhana, but only to us.

Arjuna returned from Dwaraka with a very bizarre fact.

Arjuna and Duryodhana visited Krishna in his resting chamber on the same morning. Krishna was in a blissful slumber on a rosewood bed. Duryodhana, who had arrived first in the chamber, sat on a seat near his head so as to not disturb his sleep. Arjuna, who arrived later, was startled to see Duryodhana there. He was about to turn back when he remembered my words, 'Do not come back without Krishna's blessings.' He gently sat on the bed near Krishna's feet. Taking enough caution not to disturb his sleep, Arjuna took the opportunity of gently pressing his legs. The moment he touched his leg, Arjuna immediately realised that Krishna was not asleep. He was just lying down with his eyes closed. After some time, Krishna opened his eyes. He smiled gently at Arjuna and said,

'Partha, when did you come?' Immediately, Duryodhana smiled and attracted his attention by saying, 'Pranama, Lord of Dwaraka, I have also come to visit you. Is everything fine?'

Krishna stretched and twisted his body, as if he was just waking up from sleep, and sat up. Duryodhana did not give Arjuna a chance to speak and said, 'Oh Lord of Dwaraka, I arrived in your chamber first. I came to ask for your forgiveness for having ignorantly called you a lowlife cowherd in the Kuru council. Kindly forgive me and listen to what I have to say first.'

Each word was full of deceitful diplomatic strategy. Krishna recognised it and, winking to Arjuna, smilingly said to Duryodhana, 'Oh Prince of the Kurus, I had forgiven you even as I was leaving the assembly hall of Hastinapura. But today morning I saw Dhananjaya of the Pandavas first. Besides, he is younger to you. Therefore, I should listen to him first. Tell me Arjuna, why have you come?' Krishna did not give Duryodhana a chance to complain about it.

By this time, Arjuna had got up from the bed and, with his palms brought together in prayer, said, 'Your sakhi Draupadi has conveyed her affectionate pranama to you. Oh Hrishikesha, as per your wish, the war between the Kauravas and the Pandavas is now inevitable. It is with your blessings that we raised our kingdom of Indraprastha. In this war, the Pandavas want your blessings along with the blessings of Balaramadada, Uddhavadeva, Maharaja Vasudeva and Rajmata. I have come here to obtain those blessings.'

Krishna smiled. In his special style, he said, 'Oh Arjuna, I can offer only my blessings to you and the Pandavas. Yesterday itself, in our Sudharma royal assembly, Dada and I had a serious difference of opinion over the problem of the Pandavas and the Kauravas. He said that all senior Yadava warriors, including him and I, should support Kaurava Maharaja Dhritarashtra, along with the entire army. Or else stay aloof from the war. Prince Duryodhana had already visited him promptly and convinced him so. I told the Sudharma assembly, "Let the senior warriors decide for themselves whose side they want to choose in this war between the Kauravas and the Pandavas. The Yadava army will go to the side that Prince Balaramadada decides to join. But I am not at all going to participate in this war as an armed warrior. If need be, all I will be able to do is supply weapons to the warriors, look after the injured or maybe steer someone's chariot.

'Dear friend Arjuna, you have come as a representative of the Pandavas and as you are the first in line, you tell me undoubtedly and clearly, what do you want? Do you want me, who will be unarmed and will share his experience and wisdom with you, or the Yadava army, which is huge and equipped with weapons? If you want the Yadava army, then you will have to go right away and visit Balaramadada.'

Arjuna did not think about anything else and without an iota of doubt in his mind, bent down. He put his head on Krishna's feet and politely said, 'In any case, it is only your blessing that I want, Achyuta!'

Krishna put his hand on the crown Arjuna was wearing and said smilingly, 'As you wish.' He immediately looked at Duryodhana and spoke in Yudhishthira's style, 'Oh Suyodhana, you have no alternative but to accept the Yadava army. What is your decision?'

Duryodhana bent a little, brought his palms together and hiding his joy, said with sly courtesy, 'As the Yadava Lord wishes. The Kauravas are ready to accept the Yadava army. I have already obtained such permission from Balaramadada yesterday. I know it fully well that a word from the Lord of Dwaraka has the power to change it. That is why I came here to seek permission from you too. I am contented that you granted it to me. I have only one polite request.'

Hearing praise for his words from Duryodhana, Krishna smiled suggestively. He surmised what Duryodhana was going to request and said, 'Kaurava, do not be afraid. I am not going to hold any weapon in my hands. I have taken such a vow. The only thing I will hold in my hands is the whip for the horses. It does not make any difference whether I am there or not in this war between the Kauravas and the Pandavas.'

He was Duryodhana, after all. He knew Krishna of Dwaraka very well. He said, 'It is not about the weapons, it is about your silence.'

At that point, Krishna got up and patting Duryodhana on his shoulders, said, 'Your expectation for even a charioteer to keep silent is really strange, Suyodhana. You will shout as you please to encourage your soldiers. Then isn't it unfair that a charioteer should keep silent and not utter anything at all to encourage his horses? I never asked you for justice. I ask it today. Let me speak freely to encourage innocent beings. Do not insist on the silence, Suyodhana.'

'All right. As you wish.' Remembering the fact that he was older than Krishna, Duryodhana raised his right hand as if in blessing.

Krishna smiled. Arjuna had never seen him smile like that before. As Duryodhana had turned his back, he didn't get to see it.

But a strange thing happened in this period due to the events that took place. When Balaramadada, who had insisted that the Yadavas should side with the Kauravas in the war, heard Krishna's final decision, he disagreed with it and actually went to the Himalayas. After that, Uddhavadeva, who was completely against war, also left and went to some place in the same region. Uddhavadeva visited his dear brother Krishna before leaving. But Balaramadada did not meet him. This was, of course, in accordance with his nature.

Maharaja Virata sent special messengers to places like Chedi, Madra, Manipura and Girivraja, and invited all Pandava ladies scattered in various cities to Upaplavya. All Pandava ladies, except the forest-dwelling Hidimba, who was Bhimsena's wife, gathered in Upaplavya. The small town of Upaplavya was now transformed into a royal city. Maharaja Virata made sure that the guests of the Pandavas coming to the city were comfortable.

News came that the Yadava army of Dwaraka was on its way to Kurukshetra. The fourfold army of Hastinapura had already reached Kurukshetra. The Kaurava army was inflating like the inundated River Ganga that bloated by the moment in a great flood. And we received the final instruction from Dwaraka, 'All warriors and ladies should now leave Upaplavya and go to Kurukshetra towards the encampment of the Pandava army on the banks of River Drishadwati.'

As per Krishna's instructions, I arrived at the Pandava base on the banks of River Drishadwati along with Subhadra and a pregnant Uttaraa. The wives of major Pandava warriors also accompanied us. Automatically, the responsibility of the care of these ladies fell on me.

Dhrishtadada arrived from Kampilyanagar along with Shikhandi, other brothers and the armed Panchala army. Kurukshetra bustled with action with his arrival. Every day the number of warriors in our encampment kept growing. Kekeya king Brihatkshatra came along with his army. Subahu, the king of Kashi, arrived with Shaibya. His army consisted of thirty thousand chariots. From Shuktimati, the city of the Chedis, Shishupala's son Dhrishtaketu arrived with his son Veetahotra and a huge army. Krishna himself had appointed him as the ruler of the Chedis after Shishupala. The Vatsas came along with their army. Notably, commander Satyaki joined the Pandava base along with his troops. He had declined the appeal and orders of Balaramadada, Anadhrishti and Krutavarman to join the Kaurava camp. He said, 'I will go wherever Krishna goes', and came to our camp. But Krutavarman, the other valiant Yadava warrior, was going to join the Kauravas. Of course, the entire Yadava army was not with these two. Some troop leaders of the Yadava army had decided not to participate in the war as per Balaramadada's wish. They had stayed back in Dwaraka. Every day, Dhrishtadada came to the royal ladies' pavilion and reported the day's happenings to us.

Now all of us were waiting for Krishna. After all, he was the charioteer of all of us. Arjuna had gone to Dwaraka to meet him.

Meanwhile, at the Kaurava base located opposite ours, a colossal army had united. It was one-and-a-half times larger than the Pandava army. From the Gandhara kingdom of Shakuni, a proficient army had arrived. There was a big group of the Yavana and Shaka clans from the western region comprising the Kapisha, the Kamboja, the Vahika and the Gandhara kingdoms. All of them had gathered at Kurukshetra in support of the Kauravas. This was all Shakuni's skill. Shalya, the mama of the Pandavas, had left from Shakalnagar along with son Hritayana to join our camp. But Duryodhana visited him on the way and convinced him to join the Kaurava camp by giving him grand gifts. Ashmakeshwara of the Ashmaka kingdom had arrived at the Kaurava camp. Krishna's chariot, steered by Daruka, was the last to arrive on the holy land of Kurukshetra, where about forty million soldiers had gathered to showcase their gallantry.

Krishna's chariot entered Kurukshetra from the side of the Kaurava base. As soon as it entered, many people recognised it. By now everybody knew that he was backing the Pandavas. Still, to get a glimpse of him, even from a distance, soldiers eagerly gathered at the entrance of their pavilions.

The news of his arrival in Kurukshetra spread rapidly, like wildfire, and reached my camp. When I heard it, I got so restless that I did not know what to do. I was very angry with him. We had expected that he would support us with the entire Yadava army. But he had proved that nobody could take anything about him for granted. Therefore, though everybody went to visit him, I did not go. After meeting everyone, he himself came to my pavilion. He had already reckoned the reason for my anger. He saw me with my back turned to him, and tried to convince me, 'Krishney, I know why you are angry. But have some patience. Just keep watching what happens next. Success in war never depends on the number of soldiers. All my vows and your wishes will be fulfilled. Arjuna told me in Dwaraka what you had instructed him to do. I am very much contented that the Pandavas accepted me despite my vow of being unarmed. I will never let your faith get shattered. Trust me. Victory will be only yours. May I take your leave now?'

His last words were a direct blow to my heart. Though I was younger than him in every sense, he was asking for my permission. Oh, how foolish I was to get angry with him. I quickly turned my face towards him, briskly moved forward and touched his feet. I got up and looked at him. He was smiling. His face looked resplendent like never before. Before commencing the Great War that would be remembered for years to come, he said to me, 'Krishney, I know very well how to defuse your anger. I take your bow as permission granted and take your leave.' He turned and left. I kept wondering, 'Who is my best friend Krishna, after all?'

Finally, the second day of the dark fortnight of Margashirsha dawned. Since before dawn, commanders on both sides had already arranged their armies in particular formations. The commander of the Pandava army was my brother Dhrishtadyumna, who was formally appointed with rituals at the hands of Krishna. The Pandava army, ready to fight, stood behind him. Grandsire Bhishma was the Kaurava commander. The Kuru army stood behind him. I was in my pavilion far away. We could not see any proceedings on the battlefield at all. The only audible sound was the clamour of elephant cries in the distance, the neighing of horses and the faint hubbub of the warriors blending with it.

The resplendent disc of the sun gradually ascended in the sky on the eastern horizon of the holy land of Kurukshetra. In our pavilion, we eagerly pricked up our ears in anticipation of hearing a loud commotion. Everyone's mind had already reached the battlefield. I first heard the familiar sound of Krishna's Paanchjanya conch. It was followed by the sound of Dhrishtadada's conch. Probably, Grandsire Bhishma responded to it by blowing his own conch. Then there were familiar sounds of the conches of my five husbands. After that, a loud, thrilling cacophony of conch sounds was heard, which gave us goosebumps. The trumpeting of elephants and the neighing of horses was heard from both sides. Suddenly, nobody knew what happened, but all the sounds gradually reduced and stopped completely. Utter silence prevailed, leaving all of us bewildered. I just could not control myself. I got up from the circle of ladies and went to the entrance of the pavilion. I stared madly in the direction of the battlefield that was not in sight. What had happened? Did the war stop? In that case, what about my vows? What about my long hair that I had left open? For whatever reason, if the war did not take place, if the scoundrels who dared to touch the saree on my body and the shameless people who watched it helplessly did not get punished, then Pandava Maharani Draupadi's honour would be reduced to nothing. It would be stained. About half an hour passed by in that miserable and tormenting silence. Once again, Kurukshetra reverberated with the commotion of the sound of conches, elephants, horses and camels, the clinking sounds of various weapons and the encouraging loud shouts of 'Get set…rise…attack'.

The unprecedented, thrilling Great War between the Kauravas and the Pandavas had begun.

I breathed a sigh of relief. The Himalayan tension in my mind abated immediately.

The evening of the thirteenth day of the war descended on our camp. All the news that the war messenger had brought so far was hopeful with respect to the outcome of the war. So far none of the major Pandava warriors had fallen.

But today, at the centre of the 'Chakravyuha' formation arranged by Guru Drona, a fierce battle took place between Duryodhana's son

Lakshmana and our Abhimanyu. Lakshmana had struck a blow with a mace on unconscious Abhi and killed him.

Jayadratha had asked 'Where is your mace?' and insolently kicked the lifeless body of dead Abhi. Abhi's head remained on the ground, only his torso turned around.

My entire body flushed with rage on hearing that news. Holding back my grief, I tried to console Subhadra, who was beating her chest and lamenting, 'Abhi – my Abhi'. Just then Krishna and Arjuna came into our pavilion to console Subhadra. I was moved to see Arjuna for the first time with his head hung low. I composed myself again and went to him. I held both his arms tightly and shook him frantically. I shouted, 'I want to see Jayadratha's head. That scoundrel has kicked the lifeless body of my Abhi. Tell me, oh archer, are you going to do it or not?'

Composing himself, grief-stricken Arjuna said, 'Krishney, I have already taken a vow in the Chakravyuha formation itself that I will kill Jayadratha before tomorrow's sun sets or else will enter into a fire myself. Be calm.'

Krishna and Arjuna consoled Subhadra and me, and went to their camp. Subhadra still sobbed with the grief of losing her son. I kept patting her, saying, 'Calm down. Compose yourself, Subhadra'. She had lost her only son. I could not even imagine what she was feeling. I remembered what Krishna had once said, 'Yajnasena, war is like a great yajna. No one can tell what kind of sacrifice one will have to offer in it.' I wondered from whom and how many more sacrifices this great yajna was going to claim.

ARJUNA

I am Arjuna. One of the five famous Pandava brothers. In my life, I regarded only Srikrishna as supreme. Everyone prides the 'self'. I took pride in the fact that I had surrendered my 'self' at Srikrishna's feet.

Initially, I used to address him as 'Srikrishna' like the others.

But when Draupadi came into my life, I gradually realised how appropriate it was to call him 'Krishna'. And it was he who taught me that life means actual experience. Nothing else.

I got into the habit of inadvertently calling him 'Srikrishna', whenever I wanted him to realise that he was much greater than me, and whenever I realised that I had made a mistake and wanted to indicate that I was a being much smaller than him, unwittingly, I would call him 'Krishna'. Such was Krishna and Srikrishna, who was so great that he occupied the whole of my life and yet remained much more beyond it.

It was Krishna who clearly explained the meaning of my name 'Arjuna' to me. During our very first meeting at Kurukshetra near the Suryakunda, he looked deep into my eyes and said, 'The name "Arjuna" befits only you. Try to understand the meaning of your name clearly and always remember it. "Arjuna" means to acquire – to obtain. Your life's fruitfulness lies in acquiring all selective knowledge in the world that takes one to the zenith of honour.' Sometimes, he would call me 'sakha' with affection. It was my experience that whenever he called me 'sakha', my entire day would be filled with extreme joy. I had noted subtly that he addressed and considered only a few more chosen people as 'sakha'. The list included his charioteer Daruka, his best friend Sudama of Sudampuri, Mahatma Vidura and minister Sanjaya of Hastinapura. And the most important person was Uddhavadada.

I had heard him address only Draupadi as 'sakhi'. Sometimes, from Kuntimata or Balaramadada I had heard that in his childhood, in Gokul, he called Radhika 'sakhi'. He himself had told me that in remembrance of Radhika, he used to wear a fresh, white Vaijayanti garland on his chest every day. As I reflected on Draupadi and Radhika being his 'sakhi's,

I would inadvertently remember Rukmini. She was Krishna's favourite wife. After Kuntimata, I revered her the most. Kuntimata herself had told me once, 'Arjuna, observe minutely how my Krishna treats every woman that he meets. Cultured behaviour is nothing but this. You should never forget it.'

When I look back at my life in this way, I vaguely remember Mount Gandhamadana. As Kuntimata had told us, all of us Pandavas were born on Mount Gandhamadana. While offering us the region of Khandavavana as our share of the kingdom, Shakuni had said, meanly, in Krishna's presence, 'The Pandavas are used to a life in the forest.' What he said as political sarcasm was in fact the truth of life that we had experienced. Today, I feel very proud of that life in the forest. Later, I had to spend nine years on Mount Gandhamadana. As kings, we ruled Khandavavana. We spent our years in the forest in the Kamyaka and Dvaita vanas. After the unprecedented Great War of Kurukshetra, we ruled Indraprastha for a few years and then for our final journey we went to the forest of Himavana – the snow forest. The Pandavas and forests were inseparable right from birth till the end. It must be because we were constantly in touch with the forests that our hearts remained simple, artless and pure, even in all adverse conditions.

As the five of us looked different – we appeared different to the world. It is also true that our temperaments were different. Yet, the five of us were a united, unbreakable entity like a mighty fist. Kuntimata played a crucial role in keeping it that way. Her daughter-in-law Draupadi also played an equally important role in that. But we knew very well that an invaluably large share of this credit went to Srikrishna – our beloved friend.

Some events in our lives were unforgettable and proved to be turning points. The very first event was that of the house of lacquer. The second was that of the swayamwar of Draupadi. Then many more events like the burning of Khandavavana, the creation of Indraprastha, the killing of Jarasandha, the Rajasuya yajna, the killing of Shishupala, Yudhishthira's mindless gambling game and the calamity, Draupadi's humiliation, and so on. Any of these events could have caused a rift in our unity. But it did not happen. What was the reason behind that? It was the life-giving guidance of Kuntimata that we received in the first phase of our lives, and the gift of Srikrishna's invaluable blessings that we obtained in the second phase of our lives. Sometimes even the thought, 'What if Srikrishna had never met us?' leaves me numb and at a loss for words. I feel terrified and restless.

Personally, I was indeed his best friend. That is why later he counselled me during the Great War to help me wise up to my duty when I felt despondent and was veering away from it.

Why did he choose only me for that eternal advice? In fact, Dhrishtadyumna of the Panchalas was the commander of the Pandavas in that war. When he noticed that I was despondent and not ready to do my duty, he should have actually approached Commander Dhrishtadyumna. He could have just transferred the leadership of my army to him and continued with the war. He did not do so at that time. The reason behind that was his pure love for me.

In his mind, he surely must have assessed the suitability of my elder brothers Yudhishthira and Bhimsena, before imparting the timeless and indispensable philosophy of the Gita to me. Why must Yudhishthira have not passed this acid test of his? I feel it was because Yudhishthira had proved that he could get obsessed with an addiction like gambling – an addiction that makes one forget one's humanity. Krishna had not forgotten that despite being the eldest, instead of sacrificing his right, Yudhishthira had expressed his wish to get married to Draupadi after the swayamwar. Yudhishthira has always spoken in the philosophical way that Krishna preached in the Gita to me. But those words never made any impression on the minds of the four of us who were younger to him. Why was it so? It was because whatever Yudhishthira preached throughout his life, he never practised himself whenever faced with a trying situation. In fact, as the eldest brother, it was his responsibility to showcase gallantry. He had become the Maharaja of Indraprastha because he was the eldest. But he never expressed any desire to visit the Dwaraka of Srikrishna, with whose invaluable assistance Indraprastha was erected. He never actually went there. That is why I occasionally addressed Srikrishna as 'Dada', but I always called Yudhishthira as 'Yudhishthira' or 'Maharaja'.

Sometimes, I wondered what if either Bhimsena or I were born as the eldest? If either of us had become the Maharaja of Indraprastha, how would things have been? But I never expressed this thought openly. Was my behaviour hypocritical? Not at all. I always respected the word of Kuntimata and Srikrishna as final – from the bottom of my heart. My utmost devotion to them was the strength of my life. It was, in fact, the essence of my life.

Yudhishthira had a bit of an inconspicuous royal pride about the fact that his brothers would never disobey his word. Krishna was completely aware of that. If he would have preached the timeless philosophy of life in the Gita to Yudhishthira, then Yudhishthira would have moved about from temple to temple giving shallow discourses on it.

Then why did he not choose mighty and powerful Bhimsena? Everybody knew that Bhimsena was mighty. But when he was overpowered by valour, at times he would become uncontrollable. It was easy to puff up his pride about his strength but difficult to control him. Srikrishna himself was a mighty wrestler. Everybody thought he made Bhimsena take on Jarasandha himself. I never had that misconception. What would have happened if Bhimsena would have lost control during the wrestling bout in Girivraja that lasted so many days? Invincible Jarasandha would have definitely taken advantage of that. Bhimsena put the Bahukantaka hold around Jarasandha's neck in the end. What if the opposite had happened? Srikrishna would have come forward exactly at that moment. He would have openly indicated Bhimsena to seek pardon by raising his thumb. And in the same wrestling pit, he would have challenged Jarasandha to fight with him. It was with this Bahukantaka hold that Krishna had killed Kansa, who was much younger and more powerful than Jarasandha. Although everybody had forgotten about it, I remembered it well. Bhimsena's hunger and sleep were his other weak points. That is why he had not chosen Bhimsena for the Gita.

Then why did he choose only me to preach the Gita? To tell you the truth, this question never came to my mind. I was never 'myself'. I was the breath of Srikrishna. Therefore, my life cannot be complete if he is omitted. In another sense, talking about him is like revealing myself. It is like a shadow trying to describe the actual figure in its entirety.

I am narrating this story of Krishna and Arjuna as I recall it. I am fully aware that his life is like the everlasting quiver that I got along with the Gandiva bow, overflowing with events.

No matter what angle I look at him from, what I essentially feel is that he is vast and limitless – just like the clear blue skies. The piece of sky that one can see from the roof of a cottage and the vastness of sky that one sees when one comes out of the cottage – it is the same experience with him.

Of late, I frequently remember his first visit with us on the land of Kurukshetra near the Suryakunda.

In our childhood, we first appeared in Hastinapura from Mount Gandhamadana along with Kuntimata. He received the news about us in Dwaraka within a few days. After that, he used to gather detailed information about us, on Vasudevababa's instruction. On the occasion of the solar eclipse, he met us at Kurukshetra along with Uddhavadeva. Since that day, not a single day has passed without us remembering him and Uddhavadeva.

The second time he met us was at the time of Draupadi's swayamwar. I had no idea that he, too, had come to participate. Three major happenings during the swayamwar are deeply etched in my heart. The first was that Karna, the charioteer's son, stepped forward with pride and picked up the bow of Shiva that was kept for the swayamwar. At that moment, I intensely felt that Karna was also a Jalapurusha like Srikrishna and Grandsire Bhishma. But the next moment, I discarded that thought promptly. In no way could a charioteer's son be on an equal footing with Grandsire and Srikrishna. After quite a while, I came to know that Karna's son Sudamana had been killed by an arrow of mine. Word was that Karna had therefore taken a vow to execute me. Draupadi's words were what I recalled vividly next. It was unheard of for a Kshatriya lady to ever speak of her own accord, during a swayamwar. But Draupadi said with clear determination, 'I will never become the wife or the daughter-in-law of a charioteer.' And the third event was Srikrishna, Balaramadada and Uddhavdeva's visit at the potter's house in Kampilyanagar where we were residing. Really, what if Srikrishna had not met us Pandavas on that day? The way Draupadi had looked at me on that day might have perhaps prompted me to vehemently oppose sharing her with my four brothers. I had strongly thought of doing so. That day, a unique facet of Srikrishna and Kuntimata got imprinted permanently on my mind. It taught me never to disobey the word of these two.

Srikrishna convinced us about how it was appropriate that Draupadi become the wife of all five of us.

It was only after that event during Draupadi's swayamwar that the firm bond between Krishna and me was initiated. Had there been any other gallant Kshatriya in my place, he would have mistakenly harboured a grudge against Srikrishna for supporting the sharing of his wife. Later, Draupadi became Krishna's beloved sakhi. Even that did not bother me at all. In fact, as time passed, I came to understand my wife Draupadi more through Krishna. Not only Draupadi, I also came to understand Kuntimata more as a 'mother' than my brothers. It was at the time of the burning of Khandavavana that I grew closer to Srikrishna. Duryodhana and Shakuni, the leaders of the Kurus, pretended to be generous, and offered us the region of Khandavavana, full of thick forests, as our share of the kingdom. Here I must tell you clearly what I understood of Duryodhana. He was very difficult to win over in a war, just as his name suggested. Even in normal life, he was difficult to comprehend. In front of the citizens of Hastinapura, he made a great show of his deep love for his ninety-nine brothers, but in his heart, he had no love and affection for any of them except for five to six of his favourite brothers. He considered the other brothers only as his obedient servants. He was well aware of the fact that he did not hold any right over the Kuru throne. He knew it quite well that our eldest brother Yudhishthira was the rightful heir. Except for his subtle pride and addiction to gambling, Yudhishthira was a loving person who treated the Pandavas and Kauravas with affection. He was loved by the citizens of Hastinapura. They also considered him their prince. Grandsire Bhishma also thoughtfully supported him as the prince.

Shakuni, the son of the Gandhara king Subala, was the one who was the thorn between the Kauravas and the Pandavas. Shakuni made the blind king Dhritarashtra and Maharani Gandharidevi, who had blindfolded herself for the sake of her husband, dance to his tunes, along with Duryodhana and his ninety-nine brothers. Shakuni had ten brothers. They moved about freely in Hastinapura as his loyal spies. All of them were supported by a shrewd politician called Kanaka. Duryodhana treated his beloved brother Dushasana, who was born after him, like his own shadow. The four of them always tried to drag world conqueror

Karna into their crafty plans. Duryodhana had obliged Karna by making him the king of the Anga kingdom. But for some reason, Karna had insisted on only one thing, 'Challenge the Pandavas directly. Let us fight them on the battlefield.'

The house of lacquer was the first ordeal for us Pandavas. We escaped that because of the timely warning from Mahatma Vidura. Only one good thing came out of that calamity. Our Bhimsena got associated with the rakshasa clan due to his marriage with Hidimba. Her son Ghatotkacha was growing up in the forests. The second ordeal in our lives was the burning Khandavavana. Krishna had given as much importance to the construction of the well-planned royal city of Indraprastha by clearing Khandavavana as he had given to the construction of Dwaraka. During the construction of Indraprastha, many a time, he had come to visit us and had guided us. Each one around him felt that they were the only ones Srikrishna loved the most. That was his speciality indeed. His close brothers Balaramadada and Uddhodeva thought him to be closest to them. But his feelings of love for both of them were quite different. Just as those two brothers thought that he was closest to them, all of us, too, thought the same. Not only that, the young and old Yadavas of the eighteen clans of Dwaraka also thought of him as their own brother. During each and every visit of ours, Uddhodeva and I talked about him. These talks were a delightful experience. He had two fathers – his biological father Vasudevababa and his foster father Nandababa from Gokul, who had nurtured him. He also had two mothers, his biological mother Devakimata and his foster mother Yashodamata, the gopa woman who had taken care of him diligently and inculcated sansakaras in him.

Just as he had two mothers and two fathers, he also had two gurus. The first was Acharya Sandipani and the other was Ghor Angirasa. Acharya Sandipani had given him the fundamental knowledge of Brahmacharyashrama, comprising the Shastras and the Astras, fourteen Vidyas and sixty-four fine arts. Ghor Angirasa had imparted the complete knowledge of Brahman to him.

As I happened to come into his company, no one else but I realised that though Guru Drona and Acharya Kripa imparted the knowledge of the Shastras and Astras to us, we never got a guru who imparted brahmavidya to us. We never went to any ashrama at all. We never experienced that ashrama life was a powerful centre for imparting values. Lately, I had started to strongly feel that the reason for the enmity that grew between the Kauravas and us was probably because we were deprived of the ashrama life.

I do not know if my brothers felt it but while talking to him, I always felt that Krishna was my greatest guru.

At the time of burning Khandavavana and erecting Indraprastha in its place, I developed a more affectionate and close relationship with Srikrishna. I will always remember what he said to me while setting the forest on fire, 'Oh Arjuna, my heart breaks while destroying such a beautiful treasure of Mother Nature created after years of penance. I have experienced it once before on Mount Gomanta, how agonising it is for a heart that longs for creation. I will never forget these two events in my life. That is why I could never forgive Jarasandha, who left me no choice but to destroy the forests of Mount Gomanta. We are having to set Khandavavana afire to erect the royal city of Indraprastha for you Pandavas; I will never forgive Duryodhana and Shakuni for that. Remember that just as sometimes one is required to set ablaze thick forests clearly visible to the eyes, one also has to destroy the forests of insolence, injustice and arrogance in human life. Without that the flow of life does not proceed. Even in the new royal city one has to raise well-planned, beautiful forests.

It was in this Khandavavana that I obtained the Nandighosha chariot of four pure white horses with the pennant of Kapi, and a very auspicious bow named Gandiva along with two inexhaustible quivers. I could never forget the extreme joy that he felt when I received it, which was even more than what I felt. Now, after so many years today, I realise his face was like that at the time of the Rajasuya yajna when he projected the Sudarshan chakra towards Shishupala. He always emphasised the significance of the Gandiva bow that I had obtained. One time he told me firmly, 'You should guard this difficult-to-obtain Gandiva bow just as vigilantly as you protect Draupadi.' After that, many a time, the thought of the divine Sudarshan chakra that he had obtained kept spinning in my mind. I would wonder what the association between his twelve-spoked, Vajra-centred Sudarshan and the bow string of my Gandiva bow, the hair-raising sound of which can be vividly heard at a faraway distance, could be? Why was my complexion blue just like his – like the multicoloured shades congealed on a hot iron rod after splashing water on it? Whenever such a question arose in my mind, I would simply keep looking at him for a long time. At that time, it felt as if I was looking into a mirror. Ultimately, I would ask him only one question, 'Oh Hrishikesha, who exactly are you? Tell me at least once, who exactly am I to you?'

Then he would give me a charming smile and say, 'You are my beloved friend. There is one more like you.' I would look deep into his eyes and say promptly, 'Uddhodeva!' Then he would give me a very different kind of smile and say, 'Right. You correctly guess what is on my mind. That is why you are my beloved friend.'

It was only as per his instructions that I went to the Shiva temple of Somanatha near Dwaraka at the time of Subhadra's abduction. I was disguised in saffron robes as an ascetic. My beard had grown long. During the mission of Subhadra's abduction, I obeyed all his instructions to the letter. There was only one thing I did spontaneously. Leaving the Shiva temple of Somanatha, I crossed the creek in a boat and reached Dwaraka. That was to visit his Srisopana to my heart's content before abducting Subhadra. No citizen of Dwaraka could recognise me due to my saffron attire. Passing by the check posts one after the other, I reached the Srisopana. Oh, how sparkling and grand it looked. It was so tall with so many steps. I bowed down to the Srisopana from the bottom of my heart and touched my head to the step. I raised my head while thinking only about Krishna and simply kept looking. On the highest step of the Srisopana he stood – so tall. Srikrishna himself. Climbing down the steps one by one he came closer. No one else had recognised me yet, but he recognised me on the very first glance. He spoke something that only I would understand and not any of the attendants who were around, 'Yogiraja, I know you. Of late, the Raivatakas are in strong need of an ascetic like you. You should immediately go there. Tomorrow itself, my sister Subhadra will leave here to visit the temple of the family deity before her wedding to the great Kuru, Duryodhana. I have instructed her to visit you as well. I am sure you will give her appropriate blessings. You should.' I received my clue from the person I wanted it from. For me, it was like his blessing. From that moment, the Srisopana occupied a precious spot in my heart – just as Subhadra did later.

There are so many such incidents that are engraved in my heart, as Krishna's beloved friend. For the naming ceremonies of our sons, he came from Dwaraka to Indraprastha without fail. Kuntimata named Yudhishthira's son 'Prativindhya'. Prativindhya means resembling Mount Vindhya. For the naming ceremony of Bhima's son, he came to Indraprastha along with Balaramadada, his son Pradyumna, two more of his brothers and two stepbrothers. This big and healthy child of Bhimsena was named 'Sutasoma'. Balaramadada himself gave him this name, saying, 'Bhima is my disciple. I will name his son'. He also gave a funny and convincing explanation to the name 'Sutasoma'. Dada said, 'We Yadavas always love Soma. He is the son of this Soma – hence Sutasoma.' Hearing that, Srikrishna smiled and said, 'Dada, Soma means the Moon. So, you mean to say that he is the son of the Pandavas who belong to the Chandravansha. Right?'

For my son's naming ceremony, he came along with Uddhodeva, Rukmini and Balaramadada. Srikrishna himself named my son 'Shrutakirti'. He explained the name in the following way, 'His father – our Arjuna - has struggled through days and nights to obtain great acclaim. He had to travel throughout Aaryavarta for conquering kingdoms. This son of his will receive acclaim right from birth. He cannot be anybody else but "Shrutakirti"! Born with acclaim!'

He also came for the naming ceremonies of the sons of my two younger brothers, Nakula and Sahadeva. Our Uddhodeva named both of them. That was also as per Srikrishna's wish. Uddhodeva himself named Nakula's son 'Shatanika' and Sahadeva's son 'Shrutasena'. Those two names were also meaningful.

All the five brothers wholeheartedly loved all the five sons of Draupadi. We had been bereft of our father's love since childhood. All of us strongly felt that our sons should not miss what we had. Whenever the subject of 'fatherly love' was discussed, my heart would fill with deep respect for two people. The first was Kuntimata. Whether it was in the forest or at the royal palace of Indraprastha, she never let us feel the lack of anything. The second person was Srikrishna. He was our mentor and guru. My brothers may not have felt it but I strongly felt that he was also our loving father.

His love for me had so many facets. No matter how hard I tried, I could not comprehend them all.

The way he protected me with vigilance gave me the feeling of his fatherly love. It was impressed on my mind the most during the mission of Jarasandha's killing in Girivraja. In the royal palace of the Magadhas, he put forth Bhimsena and himself, not me.

He could have easily fulfilled the condition of Draupadi's swayamwar but refrained from it. He recognised me correctly, just by the Virasana pose that I took and assumed the position of a silent spectator. This act of his befitted only a father. He had silently loved me like a son. Many times, he behaved in a way that only I could understand. I also reciprocated his fatherly love with appropriate respect.

His elder brother Balaramadada was like an elder brother to us too. I used to call him 'Dada'. I had subtly noticed that Krishna called him 'Dada' in many different ways. Whenever he wanted to point out a mistake to his Balaramadada, he would act more humbly. Occasionally, he stood in complete opposition to him. But even while opposing him, he never spoke with disrespect.

Srikrishna's favourite, beloved wife Rukminidevi was my favourite too. Many a time I felt that it was as a result of Rukimini's influence that Srikrishna's speech became so charming. When I would ask him so, he would simply smile. If I tried to get an answer from Rukmini, she would say, 'Oh Arjuna, is it ever possible for anybody to do that? How can anyone bring high tide to the ocean by pouring a bowl of water in it?'

He said once, 'Our Abhimanyu has complete knowledge of breaking into the Chakravyuha formation. He has learnt it from me. But he does not know how to break out from the centre, towards the first ring of the formation. Why don't you bring him to Dwaraka sometime? I will give him the demonstration in person.'

Abhimanyu was unique among all the Pandava sons. He was passionate about learning to use new shastras and astras. He was also very humble. He was Srikrishna's favourite nephew. Abhimanyu also loved his mama very deeply. He never disobeyed his mama's word.

Since my first meeting with Srikrishna at Kurukshetra, I had experienced a truth about him – his life was like a lotus flower with a thousand petals that blossomed gradually day by day and looked different every day.

I often wondered why he took so much interest in Subhadra's marriage with me even in the face of Balaramadada's wrath. The reason for that was not only his absolute love for me but also his boundless love for his sister. It was a big surprise for me as to how he had discovered the love between Subhadra and me, without asking me anything at all. I tried to dig it out of Subhadra later. The answers she gave were completely unexpected. She told me, 'Before the abduction, Krishnadada kept complaining about you. He used to say, "That Arjuna of the Pandavas is very reserved. Karna, the king of Anga who possesses the kavacha-kundala, and Ekalavya, the son of Hiranyadhanu, are better archers than him. That master archer is a womaniser more than the other brothers. Wherever he goes, he gets married and brings a new wife." While hearing Subhadra's words, I would keep smiling. Once she finished, I would say, 'Silly Subhadra, it was a unique trick of your Krishnadada to find out how strong and firm your love for me was. The world does not consider each and every action and every word of your Dada's as Krishnalila for no reason.'

He was a master of acting. The title of his drama was 'Premayoga'. Whether it was for the gopa–gopis of Gokul, for the Yadavas of Mathura, for the disciples in the ashrama of Acharya Sandipani, or for the Yadavas and the Pandavas while creating Dwaraka and Indraprastha, or while travelling continuously throughout Aaryavarta to eliminate the unjust kings of various kingdoms – every time and in every event, he practised and worshipped only Premayoga.

Due to his prudent vision, he made me abduct Subhadra, resulting in the strengthening of relations between the Pandavas and the Yadavas of Dwaraka. After getting married to Subhadra, the frequency of my visits to Dwaraka increased.

I recall a funny incident that took place during one of my visits to Dwaraka. Our guru's son, Ashwatthama, also came to Dwaraka from Hastinapura. In the evening, Ashwatthama and Srikrishna went to the ocean shore in Srikrishna's Garudadhwaja chariot, for offering evening oblations to the Sun god. Later, Srikrishna and Ashwatthama sat in the sand, chatting. The platter-sized disc of the sun was about to set. While looking at it intently, god knows what came over Ashwatthama and suddenly he said to Srikrishna, 'Oh Lord of Dwaraka, I always keep thinking about the Sudarshan that you have – the radiant chakra that looks like the sun disc. I have travelled so far to meet you just for that. Oh Yadava, will you please appear in front of me in your form carrying that Sudarshan chakra?' Krishna looked at him and smiled gently, despite his strange request. While he continued sitting, he looked at the platter-sized sun disc for a few moments, closed his eyes and chanted the divine mantras of the chakra of brilliance. His face started looking much brighter. Ashwatthama kept staring with his eyes wide. He could see the radiant chakra revolving rapidly on Krishna's raised right index finger. Krishna's face glowed with the same brilliance as that of the Sudarshan. Ashwatthama shut his eyes automatically, as they could not bear that light. Now, the cacophony of instruments reduced gradually and ceased. From his index finger, Srikrishna put the chakra on his right in the sand. Ashwatthama just kept staring at the Sudarshan chakra with astonishment. He himself was the master of powerful astras such as Brahmastra and Narayanastra. Without moving his eyes away from the Sudarshan, he asked Srikrishna, 'Oh Lord of Dwaraka, if you find me worthy of it, then give your divine Sudarshan chakra along with its mantras to me. If you possess a heart as big as the western ocean in front of us, then give away this Sudarshan to this Ashwatthama today.'

The son of the guru had put Srikrishna in a tight spot. Yet, Srikrishna was calm. He got up gently and walked towards the ocean. Krishna bent forward and picked some ocean water in his cupped palms. He walked back and offered the water in his palm on the Sudarshan yantra lying in the sand, chanting the mantras with his eyes closed. He smiled as usual and said to the guru's son, 'Oh Ashwatthama, you can take the Sudarshan with you if it is possible for you to carry it and take care of it. From today, it belongs to you.'

Ashwatthama bent down and tried to pick up the Sudarshan chakra. He could not even move it a little despite applying all his might. That maharathi warrior made many efforts in different ways to pick up the Sudarshan and got all soaked in sweat in the process. Exhausted, he dropped on his knees in the sand itself. He was at his wit's end and embarrassed. The sun had sunk in the west. Srikrishna came forward and patted his back gently for a few moments and said, 'Come, let's go!'

Without a word, Ashwatthama got up obediently. He moved forward and fell at Srikrishna's feet, saying, 'Oh Hrishikesha, you are the only one worthy of this Sudarshan. Nobody else can possess it but you. Be kind to me and take it back.'

Krishna pulled him up lovingly, patted his shoulders and smiled. He closed his eyes, chanted some mantras and said, 'Done.' Both of them started walking towards his chariot. Krishna stopped and turned back. He saw that the Sudarshan lying on the sand had disappeared in the dim light of dusk. Maybe it went to visit the sun that had set.

When Sikrishna himself told me this incident, I got to see a petal of his incredible personality. He did not share this incident with anybody else. I had actually seen him project the Sudarshan chakra in the Rajasuya yajna. I possessed the auspicious Gandiva bow along with the inexhaustible quiver. I was the master of Narayanastra and Pashupatastra. Yet I never felt greedy for Srikrishna's Sudarshan. Such a thought never occurred to me and would never occur in future either, even unknowingly. In fact, I would have happily surrendered my bow and the astras at his feet if required. Whenever I saw Ashwatthama and talked to him, I always remembered his father Guru Drona. Guru Drona was indeed Dhanurveda incarnate! His knowledge about weaponry was as vast as the ocean. His love for the Kauravas and the Pandavas was befitting of a guru. The only two weaknesses in him were his love for his son and the desire for revenge. Ashwatthama was his only son. Maybe because of that, he was as dear to him as his own life. Amongst all his pupils, he taught the great Brahmastra only to the two of us. Ashwatthama and me. He deemed nobody else worthy.

Guru Drona's urge for revenge was so strong that he had vowed to avenge the refusal by King Drupada to acknowledge him as a friend in spite of their former friendship, the reason being Drona's poverty. The Kauravas and the Pandavas completed training in weaponry under his guidance. As his Gurudakshina, he had asked us to capture king

Drupada and present him as a prisoner. I captured Drupada and presented him in front of my guru. Later, the same Panchala king, Draupadi's father, became my father-in-law. I had thought that he might have held a grudge against me as I had taken him captive. But there was no trace of that at all. The exact reason for that was not known to me for quite a long time, though. Sometime later I came to know about it from Draupadi. Panchala king Drupada had an intense hatred for me due to some past events. How did his hatred transform into love, not only for me but for all of us brothers? It was all due to Krishna's magic.

Draupadi becoming the wife of all five of us was also not agreeable to Drupada. Dhrishtadyumna had clearly stated his father's disagreement. But subsequently, the marriage of the five of us with Draupadi took place in Kampilyanagar, one a day, at the hands of Drupada himself. The credit for this also goes only to Krishna's magic.

At both times, Krishna had used Dhrishtadyumna for making it happen. Srikrishna had visited the Panchala kingdom many times in person along with Uddhava and Balaramadada. He had invited Draupadi's brother Dhrishtadyumna to Dwaraka for various reasons. He had felicitated Dhrishtadyumna often, offering him fine vesture and selective weapons in the royal assembly of the Yadavas. Further, Srikrishna constantly kept iterating to him, 'Panchala Prince Dhrishtadyumna, your valour has not been acclaimed appropriately yet. Despite being a young leader to lakhs of Panchalas, you have not been bestowed with the honour that you deserve. I will give you that honour, which will make you eternal and immortal.' He kept saying such things mysteriously. I came to know about all these things sometimes from Draupadi and at other times from Dhrishtadyumna. One such sentimental incident related to Draupadi took place in Indraprastha. Krishna himself told me about it. That time he was visiting Indraprastha with Rukmini. He loved our Abhi very much. One day, he took Abhi with him and toured the entire royal city of Indraprastha in his Garudadhwaja chariot. Our Indraprastha had just been inhabited then. Our chief minister would show each room in our royal palace to any visiting guests while explaining the architectural intricacies. In the end, they all arrived in the armoury, where many of the Pandavas' favourite weapons were lined up. In my section of the armoury, many bows were placed in a line. A quiver filled with arrows was placed near each bow. Srikrishna was very enthusiastically giving information about various arrows to Abhi. Finally, he came to the quiver filled with Bastika arrows. Krishna picked up a Bastika arrow from the quiver to demonstrate how the tip of the arrow gets embedded in its target.

The screw of that arrow was tight and was not turning easily as it had not been handled for a long time. He handed that arrow to Abhimanyu and told him to unscrew the nut. Abhi also tried his best, but to no avail. The screw was tight as it had rusted. Now Srikrishna took that arrow back in his hand. Biting his lower lip with his teeth, Krishna tried to unscrew the rusted Bastika arrow.

The nut came loose but the tip of the sharp blade pierced Krishna's index finger. Blood started trickling from it. Everyone panicked. Subhadra said to Rukmini, 'Hold the finger tight to stop the bleeding. I will be back with a bandage.' She ran towards her chamber. Rukmini stopped the trickle of blood with her thumb.

But Draupadi tore a strip of her rich saree without any hesitation at all. Coming forward, she removed Rukmini's thumb from her dear friend's index finger. She immediately tied the strip of the rich cloth tightly over the wound and stopped the bleeding.

Looking at Draupadi, he said, 'You realised that blood is more valuable than garments. At the right time, you will also realise that sometimes blood needs to flow for the sake of garments.'

Srikrishna occupied the whole of my mind when he executed Shishupala.

At that time, I saw him in his resplendent form, holding the Sudarshan.

The condemnations Shishupala hurled at him were unpardonable. Srikrishna's forbearance was on display then. He warned Shishupala from time to time and tolerated ninety-nine of his offences. Throughout his life, he had been enduring the vilifying name-calling as a 'lowlife cowherd' by his mama Kansa, Jarasandha, Narakasura and many more kings. Yet, he tolerated it calmly with a smile.

At the time of Shishupala's execution, I realised that once he was determined about something, his face dazzled with the brightness of hundreds of suns. The moment when he closed his fish-shaped eyes while his intensely brilliant form held the Sudarshan chakra is imprinted on my mind forever. At that very moment, I earnestly and resolutely surrendered myself at his feet. The second incident that brought me even closer to Srikrishna was the abduction of Subhadra and my marriage to her. At that time, I was on a pilgrimage as I had violated a rule in the code of conduct decided by us brothers. During that journey, I had got married to Uloopi and Chitrangada. Before each marriage, I had not forgotten to seek permission through his messengers, who met me every now and then. It was probably due to this reason that he invited me to Dwaraka when he got wind of Subhadra's proposed marriage with Duryodhana. After Subhadra's abduction, I returned to Indraprastha. I was worried about proud and dignified Draupadi's reaction with respect to Subhadra. It was obvious that as per her outspoken nature, she was going to rebuke me. She would have probably reprimanded Srikrishna too. I had prepared myself to face her wrath. But she welcomed Subhadra wholeheartedly as Srikrishna's sister. At that time, I realised how difficult it is to predict what goes on in a woman's mind. Subhadra became Draupadi's sister as much as she became my wife.

After getting married to Subhadra, I had come to Dwaraka to celebrate my first Diwali as the son-in-law of Dwaraka. Oh, how the Yadava men and women showered me with affection.

I met Kuntimata as soon as I returned to Indraprastha. Krishna had put the Vaijayanti garland around my neck during Diwali, something he had never done before with anybody else. She smiled slightly when she heard that. I felt that her smile reflected a tinge of Krishna's. She said, 'Do you clearly understand the meaning of him putting the garland around your neck in the presence of all the Yadavas?'

'What does it mean?' I asked her.

'Arjuna, he is going to conduct some kind of grand spectacle in the future. You will have the responsibility of playing the main role in that. Remember, while conferring commandership on a Kshatriya, a garland is put around his neck. He has quietly announced you as his future commander without performing any formal rituals.'

Just like Kuntimata, Acharya Drona had also inculcated deep sanskaras in us, which were useful in actual life. Once he told all of us to shoot the eye of a stuffed bird hanging on a tree, only with a single arrow.

Just when each disciple took the stance, the guru asked him, 'What do you see at the tip of your arrow?' As no one realised the intent of the question, everybody answered something like, 'I see the leaves of the tree', 'I see the branches', 'I see many other birds', 'I see the sky' and such.

I told him, 'I can clearly see the tip of my arrow touching the bird's eye.' Hearing that, Gurudeva was very pleased with me. He had taken efforts to teach me how to pierce a target just by hearing its sound. I knew only two other master archers who were experts in sound targeting. One was Ekalavya and the other was the charioteer's son Karna.

We spent our adolescent days in the royal city of the Kurus. The citizens of Hastinapura revered our world-conquering father – Emperor Pandu. We received the same affection in abundance from the men and women of Hastinapura during this period.

All of us, the members of the Kuru family, lived in the royal palace that was erected by Maharaja Kuru a long time ago. Grandsire Bhishma was Dhanurveda incarnate. He was a celibate for life. He had attained the eminence of a staunch Rajayogi despite living in the royal palace of the Kurus. Whenever he entered the armoury, Acharya Drona and Kripa would welcome him with a smile. The armoury would get filled with his presence. He would thoroughly check the progress of all hundred and five of us. Along with us, he would also enquire about the radiant Karna, son of a charioteer, who was one of the disciples of Acharya Kripa. Drona's son Ashwatthama was his favourite.

During adolescence, our ideal was the son of Ganga, Grandsire Bhishma. He was free from jealousy and therefore had no enemies. My subconscious mind was greatly influenced by him.

Perhaps because of that, I could never forget that it was he who had first addressed Srikrishna, who was my perfect ideal, as 'Vasudeva'.

Maharaja Dhritarashtra of the Kurus was a grand mystery that no one could fathom. Among all the members of the royal circle that I had seen, the lives of Grandsire Bhishma and Srikrishna were eventful with respect to thoughts and actions. Their lives were like prodigious volumes of literature. Still, I could read and understand every single page. Maharaja Dhritarashtra was the only piece of literature where I could not move beyond the first chapter – the chapter of greed for power and blind love for a son. It was Srikrishna who safely pulled me out of it many years later.

Was Maharaja Dhritarashtra blind? I think not. The million eyes of his mind saw one and only dream in various manifestations – that of his eldest son Duryodhana being formally enthroned as the ruler of Hastinapura. I am quite sure that had it happened, he would have left Hastinapura the very next day for vanaprasthashrama. Maharaja Dhritarashtra was the one and only person in my life who I felt was constantly telling me with his lamenting, wet and blinking eyes, 'Oh Arjuna, son, you are the master of sound targeting. How can you not hear this lamentation of my heart. It is my only wish that my son Duryodhana inherits the throne of Hastinapura after me. You Pandavas, who unexpectedly showed up here and are becoming an obstacle in achieving that goal, should return to the forest, just as you came.' People become blind with greed, but this king of the Kurus always had his eye on the royal throne due to his selfish desire. He kept dreaming of only one thing – the coronation of his son.

The glory of our Kuru dynasty was eclipsed by only one person – Shakuni Mama of Gandhara. He was a sly fox. Maharaja Dhritarashtra had a sixth sense – that of the greed for the royal throne. Shakuni, too, had a sixth sense – that of innate subterfuge. Only one example can correctly describe his deceitfulness – a scorpion's deadly poison is hidden in its crooked pincers. Shakuni was the master of slander. I could never understand how a virtuous sister like Gandharimata got a wicked, crafty brother like him? The only place of respite in Hastinapura for me, my brothers and Srikrishna was Mahatma Vidura and his simple but neat residence on the border of Hastinapura. His heart was as simple and pure as his home. His wife Parasavidevi was a perfect match for him. Mahamantri Vidura was extremely learned, pure at heart by penance and very pragmatic. His face reflected the brilliance of his wisdom. It always reminded me of Uddhodeva in Dwaraka.

As a Kshatriya warrior and a disciple, whenever I think of Guru Drona, I am reminded of the vast Yamuna under the sprawling Kadamba tree, the waters of which glisten in the rays of the sun and the depth of which is immeasurable. I could never comprehend three things in his life. The first was the discrimination he practised between Ashwatthama and me. I was his best disciple and merit-wise a bit better than his son. I could never forget that he silently observed these qualities and secretly offered the Brahmastra to his son.

The second thing was the incident of the disgusting game of dice. At that time, Draupadi had implored him, wailing and spreading both her hands in front of him. Even today it is chilling to remember her words. At that time, she had said to him, 'Acharya Drona, you are their guru. Practise your right as the guru and control Duryodhana and Dushasana. Bring my husband, who was foolish enough to play the game of dice, to his senses. This daughter-in-law of the Kurus – your daughter – begs you to save her honour.' But Guru Drona simply kept staring at Grandsire Bhishma. She gave out a heart-wrenching cry that I could never forget. When she saw the helplessness in his eyes, she realised that 'the men in this hall are slaves of wealth'.

The third thing that I could not comprehend was his refusal to accept Karna and Ekalavya as his disciples based on their caste by birth. Both of them were dynamic youth who were seekers of knowledge. Eventually, they proved their incredible mettle, though they did not receive any guidance from him as a guru. Ekalavya had erected an earthen statue of the guru and rigorously practised archery in front of it. Just like me, he had achieved mastery over the skill of hitting a target only by hearing its sound. One day, during a hunting expedition, Guru Drona got to witness this feat of his archery while we were all present. Ekalavya had consecutively shot five arrows with different pressures in the mouth of a continuously barking dog with such skill that it had stopped barking without causing the slightest injury to the dog's tongue. This was indeed an ultimate matchless feat of archery. While witnessing it, I felt like surrendering my bow at Ekalavya's feet.

But Guru Drona demanded gurudakshina at that very instant from that phenomenal disciple, whom he had never trained. I found it bizarre. Guru Drona asked his tribal disciple to give his right thumb as gurudakshina. Ekalavya cut it immediately in front of us with his left hand and offered it at the guru's feet. I could never forget the brilliance with which his eyes shone while offering that unique gurudakshina at the feet of his guru.

Later, I came to know from Guru Drona himself that the unprecedented event had taken place because of me and for my sake. He stated that it had been done as a precaution against letting anyone else getting better than me in archery.

I came to know that Karna was also becoming an expert at hitting a target by its sound. He was the disciple of Kripacharya and not Drona. What if, coerced by Drona, Kripacharya had demanded Karna's impenetrable kavacha-kundala as gurudakshina? I do not know why but I certainly believed that he would have removed it from his body and offered it at his guru's feet. Had Acharya Drona, instead of Acharya Sandipani, been Krishna's guru, would he have demanded something like this from Srikrishna? What would have Krishna done as a staunch, obedient disciple? I am quite sure he would have just given a naughty smile and said, 'As far as my knowledge goes, a guru would never accept a bloodsoaked gurudakshina. I wish to offer my thumb at my guru's feet, but it would not be possible for me to cut it with the left hand. Besides, I would not like to spill my blood on the guru's feet. Therefore, the guru should be so kind as to cut my thumb himself. Emancipate me from the "sanskar" of gurudakshina and give me blessings for a successful life.'

Two of Guru Drona's relatives made distinct impressions on my mind. One was his brother-in-law Kripacharya. He was not just a guru but also the family priest of the Kurus. The other person was his son Ashwatthama. From birth, he possessed a very precious gift that no one else had. A fleshy red gem was located on the crown of his head. He used to cover his head with a strip of cloth to prevent it from being seen by anyone. He spent most of his time in Karna's company. I always found Ashwatthama to be different from others. I even asked Srikrishna once, 'Madhava, how do you find the guru's son Ashwatthama? What do you think of him?' At that time, he did not respond with his usual playful irony. His face became solemn as it rarely did and he said, 'To tell you the truth, he is not the guru's son and not even Ashwatthama. He is like that permanent blemish on the moon.' I did not understand a single word that he had said then. So, with the innate perseverance of an archer, I pushed him further and asked one more time, 'I did not understand a single word of what you said.' Then he smiled playfully as usual and said, 'Dhananjaya, is it really necessary to understand everything? Arjuna, sometimes ignorance is bliss.' That further confused me.

After the coronation of our elder brother Yudhishthira in Indraprastha, some years passed blissfully. Under Srikrishna's guidance, our newly built kingdom thrived progressively and judiciously. Within the first six years, Draupadi had borne us five brilliant sons. The royal palace of Indraprastha bustled with their lively presence. During this time, we had decided to follow certain rules with regard to spending private time with our wife. Once I broke one of those rules. Therefore, I had to leave Indraprastha and go on a pilgrimage for one year. At that time, I travelled in the eastern region of Aaryavarta. After visiting many places, I finally entered River Ganga, which was considered the holiest of all.

Seeing me bathing, the Naga daughter Uloopi, who had come there to fetch water, approached me. In a very sweet voice, she requested, 'I have recognised who you are. Please do me a favour and come to the Naga kingdom with me. Accept the hospitality of the Nagas and then continue on your pilgrimage.' She was indeed incredibly good-looking. I could not refuse her offer.

Her father, Kauravya Naga, put forth a marriage proposal as soon as he saw me. Meanwhile, all the Nagas who had gathered there had realised that I was Kunti's son Dhananjaya. They made a din and pleaded me to accept the proposal. I could not refuse. Finally, I agreed to get married to the Naga daughter Uloopi. Uloopi had been married to the son of a Naga called Airavata during childhood. As her husband passed away when she was still a child, she became a 'child widow'. Now she became my lawful wife.

I continued on my journey and, in the end, I came to Mount Mahendra which had been blessed because Bhagvan Parashurama, who had bestowed the Sudarshan upon Srikrishna, had stayed there. I visited the summit there and the Bhrigu ashrama on it and descended into the Manipura kingdom. The ruler of this kingdom was Chitravahana. His daughter, Chitrangada of Manipura, became my third wife after Draupadi. She loved dancing. She would make me sit in the dance hall and present her splendid dancing skills for hours. After some time, while wiping the beads of perspiration on her forehead and neck, she would come and sit next to me. Like an innocent, naive young girl she would ask, 'Did you like my dance? Am I making any mistakes? Among the citizens of Manipura, even men dance along with women. It is our tradition. Will you dance freely with me?'

Hearing that, I would smile and say, 'I like watching dance. I also like to make my enemy dance to the beat of my arrows!' Hearing my reply, she would get disheartened.

One day she zealously approached me along with an informer from Dwaraka. Since the beginning of my pilgrimage, my best friend Srikrishna had been sending his expert informers one after the other and was always in touch with me. Chitrangada presented the informer of Dwaraka and said, 'Oh master archer, listen to what he says. It looks like the right person has taken it upon himself to make you understand what is good for you. He has brought a message from the Lord of Dwaraka that as long as you are in Manipura, you should take dance lessons from Chitrangada every day. Dance is an art form that keeps one fit. Learning any form of art never goes waste.'

Srikrishna's message was a command for me. This training in dance that I took in the Manipura kingdom came in handy later, during the year of living incognito in Viratanagar while teaching dance to Princess Uttaraa, in the disguise of Brihannadaa. It was proof of Krishna's words that 'learning any art form never goes waste'. Later, when Chitrangada gave birth to a son, I named him 'Babhruvahana'. Babhru's hair was brown. In his youth, instead of a horse, he used to ride an animal which was also brown in colour. The citizens of Manipura called it Yak.

There was not a single event in my life that was not connected with Madhusudana of Dwaraka. I always addressed him with different names, suitable to the occasion. When I found him extremely composed and showing a great deal of self-control, I called him 'Hrishikesha' – the one who has control over his senses. Whenever he talked to me about his life in Gokul, I addressed him by names such as 'Gopala', 'Muralidhara', 'Damodara', 'Nandanandana', 'Mohana', and 'Govinda'. Whenever he talked about the lakhs of Yadavas of Dwaraka, I called him 'Lord of Dwaraka', 'Vasudeva' and 'Yadava'. From whatever angle I looked at my life, I saw only Srikrishna there.

Among the royal circle of Dwaraka, Balaramadada's personality was a bit difficult to understand. I should have, in fact, felt resentment towards him because of the stand he took during Subhadra's wedding. But I did not feel that way. That was also due to Srikrishna's ingenuity. Whenever Balaramadada's name was mentioned in my presence, he would always say casually, 'Our Balaramadada is hot-tempered but also calms down quickly. Just as quickly as he gets emotional, he also forgets his own actions. The Yadavas do not mind it. Others also should not.'

I always had the same respect for him as Srikrishna did. The Yadavas had two commanders – Anadhrishti and Satyaki. Anadhrishti had become old now. A true pillar and guide of the Yadava army was maharathi Satyaki, who was experienced and had travelled throughout Aaryavarta with Srikrishna. Satyaki's disposition was a bit like Balaramadada's. As long as he was in Srikrishna's company, he seemed very energetic and radiant. Away from him, he looked lustreless and dull. Just like him, I was also Srikrishna's sakha. But he was a sakha dependent on Srikrishna while I was a sakha surrendered to Srikrishna.

This submission of mine knew no boundaries. On various occasions, Srikrishna had assessed the extent of my submission to him through many tests. He had chosen only me as his 'paramsakha' among us Pandava brothers. He never addressed any of my brothers as sakha.

There was a huge difference between the Yadava ladies and the Kaurava-Pandava ladies. All the Kaurava ladies, except for Gandharidevi, unknowingly carried the pride of their riches. Such women included Duryodhana's wife Bhanumati and his sister Dushala. As our Pandava women had to struggle constantly with difficult circumstances, they had automatically developed a kind of forbearing maturity. Kuntimata was their esteemed ideal. Draupadi also perfectly suited her as a daughter-in-law. After that disgraceful incident in the gambling hall, Draupadi's place in my heart was elevated to a much higher position. Bhima had openly taken some vows. My way of doing things was different. Therefore, at that moment, in the gambling hall itself I had taken a vow in my heart to avenge the dishonour of her chastity. Draupadi was Srikrishna's beloved sakhi. Other than Draupadi, he had not regarded any other woman as his sakhi, except for Radhika of Gokul. Draupadi was closer to me than my other wives.

I frequently thought of the Yadava ladies of Srikrishna's Dwaraka. I also used to think about how Draupadi felt about each of them. The leading ladies of the Yadavas of Dwaraka were Devaki and Rohinimata. Srikrishna had very thoughtfully refrained from accepting the royal throne of Dwaraka and had conferred that honour on Vasudevababa instead. He knew that this would cast aside Rukmini's right to be the Maharani of Dwaraka. He had discussed matters with Rukmini and only then planned the administrative system of the Dwaraka kingdom.

Srikrishna's seven wives in Dwaraka apart from Rukmini had completely different dispositions. Like seven kinds of flowers with different fragrances. It was Rukmini who had successfully carried out the tough and unmatched task of being the thread that strung them together in one Vaijayanti garland. That is why Draupadi and I had boundless respect for her.

I could never forget Karna's vow of killing me during Draupadi's swayamwar. I had heard that he had the impenetrable kavacha-kundala on his body. My brothers and I had already witnessed his expertise in archery. Yudhishthira had clearly expressed concern about Karna at our meeting the same evening after the contest. I had consoled him, saying, 'You do not have to worry about that son of a charioteer.' But the throbbing pain of his terrible vow was always there at the back of my mind. I would particularly discuss this subject in my meetings with Srikrishna. He would not usually get solemn. But whenever we discussed the topic of Karna, he would initially fall silent for a few moments. After some time, he would smile as charmingly as usual and say, 'You just maintain your unbreakable unity. Then you have no reason to worry about his kavacha-kundala.'

After Indraprastha, Hastinapura and Dwaraka, the most important places in my life were the Panchala kingdom as my father-in-law's place and Viratanagar as Abhimanyu's father-in-law's place. Dhrishtadyumna, who was born out of the yajna fire, had a great influence over Kampilyanagar of the Panchalas. He was valiant, had a complexion like hot gold and spoke passionately. The Panchalas were abundant in number. As their Maharaja Drupada – my father-in-law – belonged to the same generation as Grandsire and Maharaja Dhritarashtra, he was now aged and weary. The enormous kingdom of Panchala was under the rule of Dhrishtadyumna. This brother-in-law of mine regarded me very highly, not only because I was his sister's husband but also because in his eyes, I was a master archer.

I had never dreamt that I would have to stay in Viratanagar of the Matsyas for an entire year. But I had realised and agreed to what Srikrishna had always said – one could never tell who would enter one's life and where one would have to go. The five of us, along with Draupadi, had to spend the initial period of our stay in the forest in Kamyakavana. It was in this Kamyakavana that we met Srikrishna for the first time during our forest stay. We had directly come to the Kamyakavana from Hastinapura without meeting him after the gambling incident, and without going to Indraprastha, as per the conditions of the game. None of us mentioned anything about gambling to Krishna in this first visit. But Draupadi said it all. As usual, he heard it silently. He guided us with minute details of how to spend the twelve years of living in a forest and one year of living incognito with unity and self-control. He stayed in our hut in the Kamyakavana for two days and returned to Dwaraka.

It was in this forest that an unforgettable truth of my life came to be. In the council in the forest, it was decided that I should go to the Himalayas. As Srikrishna had told us, henceforth, we would not be able to sustain ourselves unless we obtained a powerful Astra. In his opinion, only I was suitable for that purpose. Therefore, I had to leave the company of all my brothers and Draupadi to obtain the Pashupatastra. For that, I had consciously prepared my mind. I stood in front of Draupadi to bid farewell to her. It felt as if the entire hut was full of emotion like never before. But she was very strong. She said, 'Oh master archer, do not come back without obtaining the astra. Whenever you miss me, remember only Srikrishna. He will never desert you under any circumstances.' I gave her the response that she expected, 'It is because of him that I exist. Do not worry about me, Shyamale. Goodbye.'

I reached Mount Gandhamadana in the Himalayas. It was filled with such appealing and fresh natural beauty. Kuntimata had told us that we were born on the Shatashringa summit here. I went to the summit and found our birthplace.

For two days. I stayed in the hut where we were born. According to Krishna, a pilgrim should not live in one place for more than two days. I experienced so much in those two days.

After two days, I bade farewell to the pure-of-heart, affectionate natives and arrived on the plateau on Mount Gandhamadana. I had carried my Gandiva bow with me, along with the two inexhaustible quivers. On this airy plateau of Gandhamadana, I built a neat hut.

Here, I lived alone not for a few days but for five years.

I had come here to obtain the Pashupatastra. But it was with Lord Shiva. It was very difficult to please him. Obtaining the astra from him was indeed an extremely difficult task.

Every morning, I used to get up before dawn to bathe in the river and return. I would take a light fruit snack and then sit for meditation and recitation. Without fail, I would remember dear friend Krishna first. His face with the peacock-feathered golden crown on his head would appear in front of my closed eyes. Krishna, wearing a yellow silk dhoti, with the fresh Vaijayanti garland and pearl necklaces with the Kaustubh jewel resting on his chest, holding the mace and chakra, would manifest in front of my closed eyes.

I would get entranced, and begin singing the hymn of Sri in my mind. I would surrender to him and earnestly implore – 'Oh Lord Vasudeva, save me!'

Whenever I would start such a prayer and become one with him, I would hear the clear words coming from his divine lips. Unknowingly, I would imitate him.

I would automatically start singing Shiva's hymn. Now, Srikrishna, who was earlier wearing the peacock-feathered crown, would appear in the form of Shivashankara. He looked like Shiva sitting in the meditative pose on the Kailasa summit of Mount Himavana, bearing Ganga and the crescent-shaped moon in his matted hair, wearing necklaces of serpents around his blue throat and holding the small drum in his hand. I would plead to him from the bottom of my heart, 'Oh Lord Shivashankara, save me!'

This life on Mount Gandhamadana, during which I did penance, lasted for four years. Autumn was now over on Mount Gandhamadana and summer had begun. It was the thirteenth day of the dark fortnight in the month of Magha. As usual, with the Gandiva bow on my shoulders, I went hunting, balancing the two inexhaustible quivers on my back. For a long time, I did not see any deer. I entered the thick forests. There was a grassy meadow there with several deer grazing in it. I aimed at a tall male deer with wide antlers and shot an arrow at him. The deer leapt, ran desperately for a few feet and collapsed. Meanwhile, all the others had disappeared from the meadow. I moved forward. When I was about to touch it, I heard intimidating words from behind a thick bush, 'I have shot that deer. That arrow stuck in his chest is mine. It is my kill. Do not touch it.' He was a Kirata – a tribal man. He was tall, muscular, bearded, had covered his matted hair by tucking wild bird feathers in it and had fully covered his chest with a tiger skin. I was taken aback by his appearance for a moment. Of course, I still had complete faith in my perfect aim. I said, 'The arrow that has pierced the chest of the deer is mine. The kill is mine.'

He challenged me, saying, 'I am the Kirata king. I have complete authority over Mount Gandhamadana – and also the Himalayas. You, a worthless human being who carries a trivial bow on his shoulders, get ready to fight with me.'

I was agitated on hearing his challenge. I said, 'I am Kunti's son, master archer Arjuna of Indraprastha. I am Dhananjaya, the best sakha of Srikrishna. I may tolerate my own insult but not that of my Gandiva bow. Kirata, get ready, I have accepted your challenge.'

A fierce battle began in the forest. For a long time, our battle remained inconclusive. His expertise of archery was unique among all the archers I had met so far. I did not fail to remember Srikrishna while counterattacking each of his arrows. Hours passed. Evening was approaching. We were surrounded by heaps of arrows. Wild flies began hovering over the kill that lay in the middle. Suddenly, the arrows coming from the opposite side stopped. The Kirata had hung his bow on his shoulder and was approaching me. I stopped too. He stood right in front of me. In a melodious voice he said, 'Oh Krishna devotee, Kunti's son Partha, you have recognised yourself. You have also recognised your best sakha Krishna. How come you did not recognise me?'

Stunned, I kept looking at him. His words fell on my ears as if echoing from the valleys of Shatashringa, 'I am the Lord of Kailasa!'

The lord of Kailasa – Shivashankara – whose name itself has tremendous power – was standing in front of me. Promptly, I prostrated at his feet. I could not speak a word. My whole body was covered with goosebumps.

Shiva picked me up just as gently as Srikrishna would. Just like Krishna, Shiva held me in a deep embrace. There are no words to describe that touch of Lord Shiva. It was unforgettable. After some time, he looked deep into my eyes and said, 'I am pleased by your expertise in archery with the Gandiva bow. I am going to bestow upon you the Pashupatastra along with its mantras, for which you came here with such determination. Remember that you have to fulfil a mission that will benefit the entire human race. You are born as "Narashreshtha", the best of men, and you have Srikrishna – Narayana himself by – your side. Wherever he will be, there will be Dharma, and wherever there is Dharma, there will be victory. You will be victorious. You have my blessings. Listen to the divine mantras of Pashupatastra –'

Shiva closed his eyes. The flow of mantras in his voice started cascading like a torrent of Ganga gushing down the Himalayas. I, too, closed my eyes and began repeating the mantras. In the end, Shiva said, 'Tathastu'– May your wish be fulfilled.

When I opened my eyes, he had disappeared.

That night I slept peacefully, like never before. From the very next day, I could feel a tremendous change within me. I was free from thoughts of being separated from my family. I began seeing Shiva everywhere on Mount Gandhamadana.

My four brothers, along with Draupadi, came to Mount Gandhamadana to meet me. Meeting them after five years gave me inexpressible joy. Bhimsena embraced me so tightly that I felt as if he was going to crush my body. Their faces blossomed like sunflowers when they heard that I had obtained the Pashupatastra.

We selected the distant summit Kubera for our next stay. There, on a sizeable circular area, we built a small colony of huts having separate chambers for each one of us like in the royal palace of Indraprastha. Next to our colony, a colony of ashramas for Dhaumya Rishi and his disciples was also built. It had been six years since we had left to live in the forest. It was unanimously decided that we would stay here for the next three–four years. Mount Gandhamadana was quite far away from Hastinapura. Therefore, Duryodhana and Shakuni, who were responsible for pushing us into this situation, were not going to know about our further movements. All this planning was obviously Srikrishna's.

Now, it was ten years since we had left Hastinapura. At the beginning of the eleventh year, we had a meeting. It was unanimously decided that we would leave Mount Gandhamadana. We were leaving this mountain for the second time. During the first time we had left it with Kuntimata as children. This time we were leaving with the contentment of having fulfilled a duty. Kuntimata was living alone at Vidurakaka's house in Hastinapura. All of us were desperately longing to see her. We knelt and prayed to the mountain god. During our return journey, we were going to take a halt at Badri-Kedara. We arrived at this holy place on the Ganga and stayed on the veranda of a charitable rest house of a Shiva temple. I went to the banks of the Ganga with an earthen pot to fetch water. I finished my bath and came out. Holding the earthen pot on my shoulders, I began climbing the steps of the ghat. I was lost in thought when I heard a voice calling me, 'Dhananjaya, is that you?' That voice was as sweet as a pot of honey. I knew that voice quite well. A radiant-looking man was standing on a step in front of me. He was wearing simple white clothes. His thick, curly, open hair rested on his shoulders. He was our Uddhodeva!

Exclaiming 'Uddhodeva, you?', I put the earthen pot down and touched his feet. He pulled me up and held me in a deep embrace. I promptly questioned him, 'How come you are here? And that, too, dressed like this?' He smiled and said, 'Are you surprised, Arjuna? I will tell you. Where are your brothers? Where is Draupadi? How are you all?'

I was overwhelmed with the realisation that I had met someone so dear after so many years.

'Deva, please come with me. They are all staying at the charitable rest house of the Shiva temple.' As I had assumed, no one recognised him at first. Then within a few moments Draupadi got up from near the stove. Narrowing her eyes, she stared at Uddhodeva and almost screamed, 'Oh, this is our Uddhodeva! How come he is here?' She came forward. She paid obeisance to him by touching his feet three times. The next moment, she asked, 'How is Krishna? Where is he? When is he coming to meet us?' My brothers, too, paid obeisance by touching Deva's feet. Yudhishthira held his hand with utmost respect and seated him on his own mat. He asked, 'How come you are here, Deva?'

Uddhodeva smiled and said, 'I will tell you everything at leisure. But I see that all of you have not been keeping good health during this period of living in the forest. Look after your health first. I am here in Badri-Kedara as per my Dada's instructions. I relinquished the royal attire of Dwaraka's Yadavas in the Ganga when I first saw her on my way here. For many years – since the time we spent at the ashrama of Acharya Sandipani – only one thought has been lingering in my mind – to find the meaning of human life. I realised that I would never be able to do it while living in Dwaraka and carrying weapons.

'Dada probably has plans to construct something here in Badri-Kedara. Therefore, he had sent me here to survey this area thoroughly. He has counted the years of your forest stay precisely. You should directly go to Kamyakavana. Dada will meet you there and tell you the further plan.'

Uddhodeva's visit left us feeling much gratified. He stayed with us for two days. As soon as we reached Kamyakavana, Bhimsena surveyed the forest and selected a beautiful area near Trinabindu sarovar for our stay. This was our last halt before we went to live incognito for one year. This was the twelfth year of forest-living. Here, too, we erected a capacious colony of huts.

Our daily routine in the forest began. During this last year of our forest stay, some significant events took place.

A messenger that Srikrishna had sent brought some very significant news. It was with reference to Karna, who had begun a charity session in Hastinapura. He had offered his impenetrable kavacha-kundala to a Brahmin mendicant, who had asked for it. The mendicant was not a Brahmin – he was Indra, the king of Gods. I had tremendous respect in my heart for Indra. But I did not like Indra's act of disguising as a Brahmin mendicant to rob Karna of his kavacha-kundala by deception. Despite the fact that Karna had disgraced Draupadi in the crowded gambling hall and was my prime enemy.

The second event was that of the Kauravas' Ghoshayatra. During the Ghoshayatra, Bhimsena and I fought valiantly to rescue Duryodhana, Dushasana and Karna, who were captured by Chitrasena Gandharva. We spared their lives and sent them back to Hastinapura.

The most significant event that took place here was our last meeting with Srikrishna in Kamyakavana. When he met us with select Yadava leaders on the banks of Trinabindu sarovar, the weariness which had come upon us due to living in the forest vanished into thin air. The unbearable tension in our minds was released instantly.

He presented to us a detailed picture of his meticulous plan of how and where we should spend the entire year of living incognito. As per Srikrishna's instructions, we had to go to Viratanagar. I can never forget the year spent at Viratanagar.

I had to get out of my warrior's attire during this year. I had to wear the dress of a female dance teacher. I had to wear a bodice on my chest in place of an iron armour. It was most painful when I had to hand over my cherished Gandiva bow to Bhima for hiding. Even more painful was the realisation that for the sake of safety, my beloved best friend Srikrishna was not going to meet us even once.

I felt the same agonising pain while putting on a woman's dress that Draupadi must have felt when her saree was being pulled. None of my brothers ever had to face the harrowing situation of dressing up like a woman that I had to, in spite of being a warrior and the master of Pashupatastra. We came to know about the nature of the Matsya people because Srikrishna had maintained friendly relations with them. For one year, we lived in Viratanagar safely.

The ruler of this city, King Virata, Maharani Sudeshna, Uttaraa, who later became my daughter-in-law, and her brother Uttara entered my emotional circle. Uttaraa became dear to me like a daughter, just as Srikrishna's daughter Charumati.

I felt that I had changed considerably since obtaining the mantras of the Pashupatastra. Whenever the mantras echoed in my mind, I strongly remembered Shiva, whom I had seen in the form of a Kirata.

After our period of living incognito was over, things moved with much speed. It was confirmed that many of the problems between the Kauravas and us were not going to be resolved without a war on the battlefield. I had been to Dwaraka and met Srikrishna. To his seemingly difficult question, 'Do you want the armed Yadava army or unarmed me?', I had instantly and clearly answered, 'It is you that we want, as is. Kuntimata, all my brothers and I, along with Draupadi, want Srikrishna and his invaluable blessings.'

He had given detailed information to Duryodhana about the exact numbers of rathis – maharathis, chariot warriors, infantry and horse riders of the Yadava army. He had convinced him and sent him back to Hastinapura with a smiling face. He took only Yadava commander Satyaki and select warriors with him and left Dwaraka along with me. We came to Upaplavya.

As soon as we came to Upaplavya, he turned the wheels with his ingenious intellect. He tried his best to avoid the catastrophic war between the Kauravas and us. As the first attempt, he told my father-in-law Drupada to send the family priest of the Panchalas to Hastinapura for negotiations of compromise with Maharaja Dhritarashtra and Grandsire Bhishma. He came back unsuccessful.

Knowing that Kaurava minister Sanjaya was one of Srikrishna's sakhas, Duryodhana, Shakuni and Kanaka sent him for negotiations on behalf of the Kauravas to our encampment in Upaplavya. Minister Sanjaya presented the message of the Kauravas, which he himself disapproved of, to Srikrishna in my presence. It was not a message of compromise at all. It was a crooked denial in a hypocritical message.

Sanjaya had to deliver that spiteful royal message to Srikrishna because it was his duty, but was overcome with emotion after doing so and fell at Srikrishna's feet. The saviour of the Pandavas patted him, pulled him up while smiling and, holding him in an affectionate embrace, said, 'Sanjaya, be calm. Control yourself. You have done your duty. You are not at fault at all. This does not change my love for you even the slightest bit. As a friend, convey my message to your maharaja. Tell him that the Pandavas have endured a lot. As a caretaker, make a conciliatory move and return the kingdom that their father, Maharaja Pandu, had won. As they have precisely fulfilled all the conditions of the game of dice, at least return the kingdom of Indraprastha to them. Let him also know that to settle this matter, I am coming to Hastinapura in person as a mediator.'

Sanjaya went back to Hastinapura. He delivered the exact message to the Kaurava maharaja. We all waited for some time, expecting some response from Hastinapura. Nothing happened. Finally, all of us, along with Draupadi, had a last meeting in Upaplavya under Srikrishna's leadership. It was unanimously decided that Srikrishna should go as a mediator.

On reaching Hastinapura, Srikrishna first observed the formalities of meeting the elders like Grandsire Bhishma and Dhritarashtra, and enquired about their well-being.

In the evening, he told Daruka to steer the Garudadhwaja chariot towards Duryodhana's chamber in the royal palace of the Kurus. Duryodhana and Shakuni had no idea that he was coming to meet them. At first, both the cunning diplomats got flustered. This was Srikrishna's special quality indeed that no one around him could anticipate when and what he would do and how he would behave. Duryodhana and Shakuni welcomed him with awkward smiles. Krishna had, in a discussion with Mahatma Vidura, already picked up clues about the views of Dhritarashtra, Duryodhana, Shakuni and Chief Minister Vrishavarma on the matter. He realised that Grandsire Bhishma was frustrated with the father-son duo of Dhritarashtra and Duryodhana.

The very next day, peace negotiations began. Grandsire Bhishma, Mahatma Vidura and the chief minister seated Srikrishna on the high seat arranged especially for him in the assembly hall. Satyaki and select armed Yadava-Pandava warriors were behind him. In that ancient royal assembly, full of people, Srikrishna spoke for the sake of us Pandavas. Only Satyaki from among us was fortunate enough to hear that exquisite speech.

But his words had no impact whatsoever on Maharaja Dhritarashtra, Duryodhana and Shakuni. They rebuffed his peace proposal. Duryodhana spoke like a demented person, 'Pandavas will not get even the smallest particle of dust that could rest on the tip of a needle, without war. Not only that, I am going to imprison this lowlife cowherd, who is the basic cause of this dispute. That will solve all the problems.' That demented soul, who had reached the peak of arrogance, blurted out exactly like Shishupala.

He even gave commands to his various troop leaders in the assembly hall. Srikrishna had closed his eyes and incanted the divine mantras of the

Sudarshan. With each mantra that he incanted, an instrumental sound, which the Kurus had never heard before, started reverberating in the hall, making it tremble. It was so piercing that every single person in the assembly hall got terrified and stood up. Initially, only three people kept sitting. Maharaja Dhritarashtra, Maharani Gandharimata, as they were unable to see, and Grandsire Bhishma. The Sudarshan chakra with twelve spokes had manifested on Srikrishna's right index finger. The waves of its bright light had dazzled everyone in the assembly hall. Not a single person had the strength to bear the blinding light. Eventually, Maharaja Dhritarashtra and Rajmata also stood up. Maharaja pleaded in a faint voice, 'Oh Lord of Dwaraka, please forgive him, my son is not in his senses.'

Only Grandsire Bhishma, who continued to be seated, had brought his palms together and was whispering some mantras.

He let the Kurus see him in this divine form only for a few moments. He spoke very little, 'Duryodhana, I dare you to bring all the ropes in your kingdom, arrest me with all your armed soldiers and imprison me.' Then he walked out of the hall, planting every step with determination. The Sudarshan chakra gradually disappeared. Duryodhana had collapsed in his seat helplessly while Srikrishna left the assembly hall with Satyaki.

Insolent Duryodhana had rebuffed Srikrishna's prudent peace proposal. The Great War was inevitable now. It was in no one's control to stop it. I was confident that it was only Srikrishna who would control the way in which it would be fought. When he returned to Upaplavya, he had transformed. After meeting him only one thought was confirmed in everyone's mind – 'war, a desperate, unprecedented war which will set the final judgement of justice and injustice'. We all were in the encampment on the battlefield of Kurukshetra. Srikrishna was in Upaplavya. He confirmed the date of the commencement of the Great War in a meeting with Dhaumya Rishi of the Pandavas, Gargamuni of the Yadavas, Yaaja Upayaaja of the Panchalas and many more experienced sages. The date confirmed was the second day of the dark fortnight of the month of Margashirsha. It was essential to seek the blessings of the elders. But all my venerable elders were in Hastinapura. Therefore, two days before the war, I came to Hastinapura along with all my brothers. First, we visited Kuntimata and Mahatma Vidura. When I humbly put my head at the feet of Kuntimata, my heart became fearless. She pulled me up and embraced me, and said to me like the noble Kshatriya lady she was, 'Put up a fight that will make the Kuru dynasty proud. Never disobey Krishna's word. Remember he is not a mere charioteer. Do not forget to put your head at his feet and seek his blessings every day before entering the battlefield. Make all your brothers do the same. It is your invincible valour on which the Pandavas are relying the most. May you have a long life, be victorious and earn acclaim.'

All of us took the blessings of Vidura. We went to meet Grandsire Bhishma. He immediately pulled me up. Grandsire said to me, 'Arjuna… son, do as Srikrishna says. May you live long. May you be victorious. As the last Kuru, I give my blessings to you, as you are the most virtuous of the next generation.'

All of us also sought the blessings of Guru Dronacharya, Kripacharya, Maharaja Dhritarashtra and Maharani Gandharidevi. When we returned to Kurukshetra from Hastinapura, my mind was ready to go to war and determined. This war was no longer a battle between cousins for the sake of ruling a kingdom. It was going to be a historical battle between Truth and Untruth, to be remembered by generations. A great part of its responsibility lay with me. My role was going to be crucial.

Finally, the second day of the dark fortnight of Margashirsha dawned. After performing morning rituals, my brothers and I arrived at Krishna's encampment. Yudhishthira washed his feet and worshipped him with full rituals. The rest of us put our heads on his feet one by one and sought his blessings. He said to Yudhishthira, 'May you be victorious. May you be the king.' He blessed Bhimsena with 'May you be victorious and glorious'. I approached him for blessings. Without uttering any words, he immediately embraced me. I had obtained my desired blessing. He blessed Nakula–Sahadeva with 'May you live a long and glorious life'.

The Panchala prince Dhrishtadyumna was with us. As per Srikrishna's advice, the day before, we had entrusted him with the commandership of our army. As the commander, he was wearing a fresh white garland around his neck, which suited him perfectly. Srikrishna's chest, as usual, was adorned with the Vaijayanti garland.

With Srikrishna leading, we followed Dhrishtadyumna and left his pavilion. Everyone mounted their own chariots. I also followed Srikrishna and climbed into my embellished chariot Nandighosha, which was equipped with many weapons. The Kapidhwaja pennant on the flagpole was fluttering in the wind. The ocean of our army, neatly organised in sections, was spread out behind us.

In front of us was the mammoth ocean of the Kaurava army, organised in a similar manner. Leading it was the Gangaudha chariot of Grandsire Bhishma, who had been instated as the Kaurava commander today. On his right, Guru Drona was seen leading the troop of chariots with Acharya Kripa on his right. On the left of Grandsire Bhishma were the guru's son Ashwatthama, Bhurishrava and Vikarna.

Srikrishna had not yet taken the seat of the charioteer on my Nandighosha chariot. He took the eight reins used for controlling, turning and boosting the horses in his hands and assessed them. He threw a glance at me and smiled. He untied the Paanchjanya conch from the blue shawl tied around his waist and held it in his hands. Raising his head high towards the sky, the veins in his throat protruding, he blew it. Goosebumps prickled on my entire body. Meanwhile, the Grandsire blew his Ganganabha conch in a similar manner. Acharya Drona and Kripa followed and blew their conches. A cacophony of war instruments arose in the Kaurava army.

Innumerable conflicting thoughts began resonating in my mind like the conch sounds. Seeing white-bearded, aged Grandsire I trembled. How could I shoot arrows at Grandsire, who took care of me as a child? How could I kill the person whom I paid my respects to? How could I slay Acharya Drona and Kripa, who loved me a lot as their disciple? Only for the sake of getting a kingdom? Instead, what is wrong with surviving on alms, like Sanjaya's message said? Isn't staying in the forest better than the war that takes lakhs of lives?

I could imagine the lifeless bodies of Grandsire, Guru Drona and Kripacharya, killed by my arrows.

Darkness surrounded me instantly. My throat felt dry, my mouth was parched. I began perspiring profusely. My soul ached like it was being pierced by innumerable spears. Tears filled my eyes. I began seeing many blood-soaked corpses killed by my arrows. My legs got heavy.

I did not even realise when my Gandiva bow, which had never slipped from my hands, fell down. 'No... No...Hrishikesha. I am not going to fight at all.'

As I uttered these words, my legs gave way and I just sat down in the back of the Nandighosha chariot. Uncontrollable streams of tears started rolling down my cheeks. My head hung low like a blue lotus with a broken stem.

Hrishikesha was stunned for a few moments. Then he jumped to the ground and came to the back of the chariot. He affectionately put his hands on my shoulders and said, 'What happened, Arjuna? Why is it that you are so dispirited? Why did your beloved Gandiva bow slip from your hands?' I replied in a devastated voice, 'Madhusudana, how can I kill esteemed and venerable Grandsire and Acharya Drona-Kripa? How can I aim my arrows at the throats of those whose feet I touch with respect? It is better to live on alms than kill such great souls. It is acceptable to me. It is the right thing to do.'

To this reply of mine, the advice that he offered was so invaluable that every man should always remember it.

He spoke very little. But those words were full of the essence of life. Many people have told my life's story, exaggerating it as they liked and glorifying it unduly. Similarly, this advice has also been magnified beyond the limits of truth. I have always valued the essence of this advice more than such elaborations. When he asked me, 'Why are you quiet, why don't you say something?', I said to him, 'Venerable guru, elders and my own cousins are standing in front of us on the battlefield and I have no desire to live by killing them. The innate quality of being a Kshatriya within me has ceased to exist. At this moment, I am caught in a terrible conflict of what is right and what is wrong. Herefore, tell me only the determinate truth. Madhava, I am your best sakha, your disciple. Give me the right guidance. I do not really see anything that will remove this confusion and grief that has absorbed all my senses.'

Srikrishna patted me with immense affection and said, 'Arjuna, you are lamenting in vain for things that should not be lamented over. Wise men never mourn, whether someone's life is lost or saved. It is not that you, I and these warriors did not exist before. It is also highly unlikely that we will not exist in the future. The soul, that has occupied this whole world, is indestructible. It is immortal. No one can destroy it.

'Oh Kaunteya, the one who thinks that he can slay such a soul, or the one who believes that it can be slain, both lack true knowledge. It never takes birth, nor does it ever die. It is indestructible, perpetual, everlasting and ancient.' I simply kept staring at him with tearful eyes and a distraught mind. Explaining it to me again, he said, 'Just as one discards one's old clothes and dons new ones, the soul, that is the master of the body, discards old bodies and takes on new ones.'

He continued, 'Dhananjaya, weapons cannot break the soul; fire cannot burn it; water cannot soak it; and wind cannot dry it. It is stable, perpetual, immovable, ancient and everlasting. Oh Parakrami Partha, this soul is invisible. It cannot be seen easily. It is highly impossible to perceive it only with one's intellect and mind.

'Oh Gudakesha, you are a Kshatriya. Remember that there is nothing more appropriate for a Kshatriya than to fight a war that upholds Dharma. If you lose courage at this point and abandon the battlefield, you will be condemned as a runaway and a coward for generations to come. And remember well that for a man of honour, infamy is worse than death. All maharathis standing here will think that you retreated from this holy land of Kurukshetra because of fear. The enemies standing against you will spread unspeakable gossip about you. Indeed, if you die fighting this war, you will attain heaven, which a true Kshatriya deserves, and if you win this war you will enjoy the kingdom on earth with honour.

'Therefore, Arjuna, rise and fight the war determinedly. Regard joy and sorrow, loss and gain, victory and defeat as the same, and get ready to fight. If you do this, you will not be committing any sin.

'Oh Kaunteya! You must remember, throughout your life, that you have a right only on your karma – performing your duty; it should never be over the fruits of your actions. Never become a person who performs his duties in anticipation of the fruitful results of his actions. Remember, karma is inevitable for every living being, even during one's sleep.'

Now I was much composed. Pulling myself together, I asked, 'Oh Keshava, Hrishikesha, you mentioned a "sthitaprajna" – one who possesses a steady mind – how should I recognise him? Tell me at least once how such a person talks, walks and behaves?' He gave me the sweetest smile. Caressing the thick Vaijayanti garland on his chest, he said, 'Oh Jishnu Arjuna. Listen carefully to the characteristics of a sthitaprajna that you are so intent upon knowing. He who abandons all desires of the heart and finds satisfaction in his own self is called a sthitaprajna.

'He who does not get upset by miseries, is free from the yen for happiness, and free from the feelings of attachment, fear and anger is called a sthitaprajna.

'The man who withdraws his senses from material pleasures and keeps his desires under control like a turtle drawing its limbs within its shell is called a sthitaprajna.

'He whose mind is stable and does not get elated or dejected when he receives good or bad – such a person is called a sthitaprajna.

'Many a time a person observing abstinence refrains from enjoyment of the senses, yet the taste for material objects remains.

'The one who experiences the taste of divine consciousness and thus attains freedom from both, the enjoyment of the senses and the desire for such enjoyment, is called a sthitaprajna.

'Understand it well that a person who pursues material pleasures develops an attachment for the objects of enjoyment. Such attachment generates lust towards the desired object. And when there are obstructions in the path of satisfying that lust, it gives rise to anger.

'Oh my Savyasachi! Such anger eventually leads to delusion. Delusion leads to loss of memory and then to loss of intellect and finally to destruction of self.'

His speech was now getting more and more interesting. 'Remember well that when anger and hatred end, all senses come under one's control. One remains in a blissful state, despite living among material pleasures. He whose senses refrain from material desires is called a sthitaprajna.

'The person who never loses his peace of mind by the incessant flow of desires, just as the ocean never gets disturbed when rivers merge into it from all sides, is called a sthitaprajna. When a person is devoid of ego and pride, and performs his worldly duties selflessly, only then does he attain peace of mind.

'This is how a sthitaprajna attains the state of spirituality. He does not go astray even at the end of life, and thus attains moksha.'

At this point, I came to realise subtly and strongly that he had been living like a sthitaprajna throughout his life. I stretched my memory to see if I could find a single moment in the flow of his life when he had acted in anticipation of getting something in return. The 'Sri' in the name of Srikrishna that I could not comprehend before began to unravel slowly with each word. My limitations as an ordinary man were becoming clearly apparent to me. Half the truth was clear to me – that I was a confused man. The other half was not yet clear – who was He?

I joined my palms humbly and asked him, 'Oh Janardana, you say that balanced intellect is superior to karma. Then oh venerable Keshava, why do you want me to engage in this ghastly karma of war? Madhava, please be kind to me and tell me decisively what exactly is most beneficial for me.'

He looked at the confusion on my face and again gave me a sweet smile. Looking deep into my eyes, in his inspiring tone, he said, 'Oh Arjuna, merely abstaining from work does not give one the freedom from it. One cannot achieve perfection only by renunciation of karma. No one can live without doing something even for a moment. He who outwardly restrains his senses and organs but dwells on material desires in his heart is called a hypocrite. He who controls his senses and keeps them engaged in activity without any attachment is considered superior. And oh Partha, he who takes pleasure in the self, rejoices in and is contented with the self, is free from duty.

'In the Prayaga ashrama, my guru Ghor Angirasa, who had attained divine knowledge, said to me once, "Dear Keshava, Achyuta, I have no duties to be fulfilled in the world any more. I have nothing to gain. Still, I am engaged in my duty. Why so?" Since then I have been thinking about it and have come to understand it now, that if I do not shake away laziness and do my duty, then, oh Gudakesha, all the people will follow in my footsteps and become inactive and lazy.

'The delusional, egotistical man believes that he is the doer of things. That is why he who has complete knowledge of the self is considered a great being.'

I asked, 'Why is one impelled to do sinful acts against his own will?'

Now he became solemn, which was rare, and said, 'Understand clearly that lust and anger are the all-consuming enemies in that regard. Just as smoke covers fire, dust covers a mirror, lust and anger cover truth. Therefore, you should first conquer the unyielding enemy of lust.'

'Keshava, you were born quite recently. Many great yogis are senior to you by birth. How am I to understand it when you say that you are the one who preached the truth of yoga to mankind?'

Then he gave me a meaningful smile as usual and said, 'I know of all the previous lives that you and I have lived. But, oh Parantapa, you do not know them. I have to elevate you to my level. Understand that I am unborn and the master of all beings. Whenever there is decline in the practice of Dharma and a predominant rise in the practice of Adharma, I take birth. To protect the righteous people and destroy the immoral, and to re-establish the principles of Dharma, I reincarnate in every era.'

He smiled once again and said, 'Arjuna, you are also one of my reincarnations. Just focus your attention on me. Be my devotee and worship me. Leave everything else and surrender yourself to me. I will emancipate you from every sin.' His eyes opened wide, and he sternly commanded me, 'Arjuna … rise. Pick up your Gandiva bow and blow your Devadutta conch. Inspire the Pandava army with a resolve to go to war. I am not going to listen to anything that you say now.'

He provoked the combatant Kshatriya within me. I got up at once like a puppet. I was holding the Gandiva bow that I had instinctively picked up. I hung it on my shoulders, untied the Devadutta conch wrapped in a shawl around my waist and took it in my hands. I looked only once at Krishna. His face was blooming with a striking, deeply meaningful smile that no one must have ever seen. It felt as if he was commanding me – 'Blow the conch, Arjuna – let the Great War of Bharata commence.'

I closed my eyes, paid obeisance to him and Kuntimata and blew my Devadutta conch. Dhrishtadyumna also blew his Yajnaghosha conch as the commander of the Pandava army. After that, I heard the familiar sound of Bhimsena's Paundra conch. From both sides a cacophony of inspiring war cries arose from lakhs of throats of valiant warriors – 'Mount! Onward! Attack!'

Troops of lakhs of warriors from the Kaurava and Pandava army fell upon each other, clanging their weapons. The battle went on vigorously for thirteen days. I could never forget the thirteenth and fourteenth days in my entire life. On the thirteenth day, the battle stopped for the day after sunset as per the rules of war. The Chakravyuha – discus – formation arranged by Guru Drona had wreaked havoc on our army. I was utterly exhausted after fighting the whole day. Every evening, while returning to our camp, my charioteer, Srikrishna, would continuously talk to me while reporting the events of the day. I never saw him tired. But today, he was silent. I felt it very strongly. I was about to ask him something, when he brought the Nandighosha chariot to the centre of the battlefield. Yudhishthira and all my brothers, Commander Dhrishtadyumna, Satyaki and major Pandava warriors had gathered there for the first time today. Definitely one of the Pandava warriors had died a hero's death today. Srikrishna brought the chariot near the circle of warriors and, without saying a word, leapt down from his seat. He broke through the circle towards the centre. I followed him, drawn like a magnet. A corpse of a valiant warrior lay at the centre of the circle. His face was thrust into the ground. It was unrecognisable as it was smeared with mud.

Srikrishna gently picked up the face hidden in the lap of Kurukshetra and kept it next to the torso.

I was struck by a bolt. He was my most beloved son Abhimanyu. The apple of Subhadra's eyes, the husband of Uttaraa and Srikrishna's favourite nephew 'Abhi'.

Krishna spread his blue shawl on the severed face of his dear Abhi. Commander Dhrishtadyumna placed a garland that somebody handed over to him on Abhi's body.

Krishna was benumbed. I was speechless. Composing himself, commander Dhrishtadyumna briefed us about the incident, 'Bold Abhi performed incredible matchless feats today. Breaking six chains of the Chakravyuha military formation while intimidating major Kaurava warriors such as Drona, Shakuni, Dushasana, Jayadratha, Kritavarma, Kripa, Ashwatthama and Duryodhana, this valiant Pandava warrior infiltrated the Kuru army like a serpent entering a hole. Bhimsena, who was protecting him, eventually fell behind. Fighting against thousands of chariot warriors, elephant riders and horse riders, Abhimanyu singlehandedly broke seven chains of the formation and reached the eighth chain at the centre. He fought alone at the centre of the formation. The Kauravas, who were feeling utterly helpless, behaved treacherously for the first time in the war. Commander Drona, Kripa, Kritavarma, Ashwatthama, Brihadbala and Karna – six maharathis – attacked Saubhadra at the same time. In fact, as per the rules of engagement, even though it is a double-chariot war, the fight has to be one against one. The Kauravas heartlessly broke this rule for the first time today.'

'What – what did the six of them do?' Krishna asked Commander Dhrishtadyumna.

Commander Dhrishtadyumna said with his chest swollen with pride for Abhimanyu's valour, 'Abhimanyu did not surrender to the six warriors. He made them retreat from the battlefield one after the other. In the end, Duryodhana's son Lakshmana and Abhi fought a fierce mace fight at the exact centre of the formation. Both of them struck each other fiercely at the same time and lost consciousness after that. Abhimanyu was lying face down. As the Kaurava warriors made Duryodhana's son Lakshmana sniff medicinal herbs, he regained consciousness first. Without a second thought, he hit a strong, wicked blow of his mace on the head of Abhimanyu who had lost consciousness and was lying face down. He thus violated all rules of engagement.

'Abhi whimpered indistinctly before dying, indicating some consciousness. Meanwhile, the six warriors who had retreated earlier gathered there again. Even their strong hearts were shaken for a moment, hearing Abhi's last distressed call.'

Benumbed and speechless, I was staring at Krishna's blue shawl. Tears flowed continuously from my eyes. I was wailing in agony, 'Abhimanyu – dear Abhi…'

The concluding words of the commander fell on my ears, 'At that time, only Jayadratha came forward like a monster. He wanted to check whether Abhimanyu was really dead or not. But the brave warrior's body was lying face down. More than half of his severed face was detached and stuck in the ground of the holy battlefield of Kurukshetra. Insolent Jayadratha kicked his body to straighten it. Gallant Abhi's crushed head remained stuck in the ground. Only his torso turned around. Maybe that mighty warrior did not want to see the faces of the Kuru warriors.'

Commander Dhrishtadyumna was so courageous but even he could not control his tears.

Each word of his felt like embers on my body. For a moment, my entire body trembled with rage. My eyes dilated with anger. I stood up at once, raised my Gandiva bow as high as I could towards the skies of Kurukshetra and took a fierce vow, 'I will kill the uncultured, insolent Jayadratha, who ruthlessly kicked my dear son's lifeless body, before sunset tomorrow. Or else I will enter the fire pit myself and reach heaven to be with my dear son.'

While my body was shaking with uncontrollable rage, I had taken a ferocious vow that everyone could hear clearly. My ear lobes were hot with rage. I could not think of anything. Srikrishna was patting my sweaty back and saying to me, 'Arjuna, the first part of your vow befits you. But the second part is going to be difficult.' At that time, I did not understand the meaning of his words. It had happened many times before. We could not always comprehend the meaning of his words immediately.

Something that had not happened in the last thirteen days happened that night. Srikrishna sent an attendant and invited me to his pavilion. A royal astrologer was seated in front of Srikrishna's seat and had spread the birch parchment of an almanac. Both were discussing something in low voices. Srikrishna was whispering something to him while counting on his fingers. I did not understand anything at all.

My heart, devastated by Abhimanyu's death, was writhing in pain with millions of his memories. I was unable to sleep. I just lay down on the bed with my eyes closed and my mind fatigued. As per Srikrishna's instruction, I was going to stay in his pavilion tonight.

Around midnight, I woke up hearing the fleeting words of the royal astrologer. They seemed quite irrelevant to me. He said, 'Yes Yadavaraja, there is a total solar eclipse on the new moon day tomorrow. After the third prahar of the day!' The fourteenth day of the war, which I could never forget in my life, dawned. The battlefield of Kurukshetra echoed with a cacophony of sounds of various war instruments. So far, every day, a new battlefield had been chosen for the war. It was essential to do so to make arrangements to dispose the dead bodies, weapons, chariots, dead horses, camels and elephants fallen on the battlefield. No battle was to be fought at night.

Today, Srikrishna steered my Nandighosha chariot among various troops till the third prahar of the day. We could not see Jayadratha anywhere. Duryodhana and Shakuni had taken the decision to not bring him to the battlefield at all. He was resting in a secured pavilion guarded by a thousand armed soldiers. My body started seething with fury as I could not find Jayadratha even after searching for him. In frustration, I slaughtered troop after troop. Shouting loudly, 'Show me Jayadratha – who humiliated my dear Abhi's lifeless body – show me that scoundrel Jayadratha', I made Srikrishna run my Nandighosha chariot all over the battlefield. All of a sudden, after the third prahar of the day, the skies got murky. No one understood what was happening. Within a few moments, the sun was eclipsed completely. Due to the darkness, flocks of chirping birds started returning to their nests. Crickets started chirping loudly. Kurukshetra was illuminated by night attendants with hundreds of burning torches. Everyone thought the day was over. The Kaurava army arranged a funeral pyre of sandalwood logs for me as I had been unable to fulfil my vow. It was arranged at the centre of the encampments of both the armies so that it would be visible to all.

I was feeling confused and extremely ashamed. I felt as if furious Abhimanyu was standing at heaven's gate and sending me back. I was benumbed with the thought of what everyone, including Yudhishthira, Bhimsena, Draupadi and especially Subhadra would think of me. With tearful eyes, I touched the feet of Yudhishthira, Bhimsena and aged Kuntimata. With deep grief, I embraced Nakula and Sahadeva. Lakhs of distressed warriors gathered to say their final goodbyes to me. I raised my hands and humbly bowed down to them.

In the end, I approached my dear Krishna, who had counselled me so wisely about life. My heart was flooded with varied emotions. Going away from Srikrishna? Forever? How was it possible? But I had taken a vow and to fulfil it, I had to go away from everyone. I steadied my heart with resolve. I removed the Gandiva bow from my shoulders and kept it at his feet. He promptly said with a solemn expression, 'Oh Veera, Arjuna, even in heaven, the Kshatriyas cannot enter without their weapons. Who else is going to handle the Gandiva bow but you? Even I cannot do it.' He forcefully put the quiver on my back and tied its strings tight over my chest. The next moment, he held me in a deep embrace, and whispered in my ears, 'Very soon you are going to have to put your exceptional archery skills to use and use the Gandiva bow as never before. Focus your attention on my index finger.' He patted my shoulders effusively. I became vigilant.

I climbed the steps to get on the tall and huge funeral pyre with my head hanging low in utter humiliation. Keeping my eyes on Srikrishna's feet, I closed my eyes.

An attendant touched a burning oil torch to the pyre with his trembling hands. I was still looking around for Jayadratha. He was standing silently behind Duryodhana with a shawl covering his face, like women do. He had come to quench the fire in his cruel eyes and vicious mind, by witnessing his foremost enemy, Arjuna, entering the fire. My body seethed with rage.

Suddenly, the darkness of the eclipse started lifting. The rays of the sun started streaming on to the holy land of Kurukshetra like water slowly running from a crack in an earthen pot. Smiling at the bleak torches on the battlefield, the bright Sun god appeared on the western horizon like before.

A familiar voice fell on my ears, raising goosebumps on my body, 'Oh Savyasachi, Partha, look there – the sun in the sky – and there – the scoundrel Jayadratha on Kurukshetra. Take aim and shoot your arrow.' Pointing the index fingers of both his hands in two different directions, he stood tall, like Mount Kailasa in the Himalayas. His right index finger was pointed at the sun and left index finger was pointed right at Jayadratha's throat. I promptly mounted an arrow on my Gandiva bow and shot it in the exact direction of his left index finger. It was narrow with a zigzag shaft and a crescent moon-shaped blade at the tip. Taking many twists and turns and avoiding others in the path, it unmistakably cut through Jayadratha's throat. Even I did not understand what happened and how.

The Pandava army put Jayadratha's corpse on the huge funeral pyre that the Kauravas had prepared for me. The fourteenth day of battle tricked everyone with the solar eclipse and ended with Jayadratha's funeral pyre.

When offering advice, Srikrishna had firmly told me, 'Keep your mind focused on me. Be my devotee. Bow only to me. I will emancipate you from every kind of sin.'

While responding to that, I had just said to him as determinedly, 'I promise you, I will do as you say.'

I had come to understand the priceless truth of life – that I was just a simple man, Nara, and he was the Almighty, Narayana.

SATYAKI

I am Satyaki. From the renowned Vrushni clan among the eighteen clans of the Yadavas. I am the grandson of Shini and the son of Satyaka. My father Satyaka was one of the ten ministers in the Sudharma royal assembly. My grandfather Shini was a close friend of Maharaj Vasudeva.

I was lucky enough to get the rare opportunity to offer my services throughout life to the great Yadava, the Lord of Dwaraka, who was born in Kansa's prison, raised in Gokul as Krishna and later attained epithets like Srikrishna, Achyuta, Vasudeva and Bhagvan.

I was veracious by nature. It was only because of this singular quality that I always got to be part of the inner circle of Maharaja Srikrishna. I was one of his many sakhas who were dear to his heart. Maybe the last one – yet, one of them. I always felt proud of it.

I was as fearless as I was truthful. Today, I feel that it was in the company of this great Yadava that this fearlessness was instilled in me and kept on increasing.

One more quality that the great Yadava had noted about me was the way I destroyed my foes. I fought many battles along with the Lord of Dwaraka. I never faced failure even in one of those battles. I must clarify today that apart from my dauntless fighting, his mere presence, too, was a strong reason for my success. Forthrightness was an innate quality in me. Many of the Yadavas had it. Balaramadada was the best example of that among the Yadavas. My disposition was much like him – short-tempered with a tendency to calm down quickly. There was only one difference between us. Maybe because of his seniority or due to his position as a prince, Balaramadada would quickly get furious any time. He would also cool down quickly. My rage would flare up on the battlefield. It would not abate until I had destroyed my enemy.

One day, while in Indraprastha, I implored Arjuna, joining my palms, 'Oh valiant Partha, though you are younger to me, please initiate me as your humble disciple in warfare and archery.' He said to me, 'Oh mighty commander of the Yadavas, are you making fun of me? I know that there are only two valiant warriors with knee-long arms among the Yadavas, the Kauravas and the Pandavas – our Krishna and you. I am much younger. How can I teach you anything?'

Forgetting my seniority for the sake of learning, I pleaded earnestly with appropriate modesty. I became Arjuna's initiated disciple. Just as I became the humble disciple of Arjuna, in Dwaraka I was already a disciple of the great Yadava Srikrishna for learning astravidya. Krishnadeva and Arjuna were already a pair of guru and disciple. In entire Aaryavarta, I was the only person who was a disciple of both Krishna and Arjuna. But as Arjuna was younger to me, he would address me using an honorific. Krishnadeva casually called me 'Satyaki'. In other words, as guru and disciple, the three of us were clearly bound in an emotional triangular relationship. I insist that our lives be looked at from that point of view.

Only Uddhavadeva got to see the emotional life of the Lord of Dwaraka in depth. His most beloved sakha, Arjuna, got to witness his entire life. What did I see? As a combative commander, I witnessed his ingenious heroic mind with expertise in warfare and his incomparable Kshatriya splendour. The greatest speciality that I noted about his mind was that he fought each of his wars for the betterment of mankind and not merely for the desire to achieve acclaim as a matchless, valiant commander. If it was for that, he would never have participated in the Great War of Bharata unarmed. In his entire life, he never claimed the right to any royal throne. And yet, why did he compel innumerable kings to fight vehemently against each other for both the Kauravas and the Pandavas, who claimed such a right?

Whenever such questions arose in my mind, I remembered the first night of the dark fortnight of Margashirsha on Kurukshetra, when he expressed his thoughts to all Pandava warriors.

That night, warriors such as Commander Dhrishtadyumna, the five Pandavas, Drupada, Virata, Abhimanyu, Ghatotkacha, Dhrishtaketu, Chekitana, Iravana and I, had gathered in the Pandava camp. I can never forget a single word that the Lord of Dwaraka spoke that night. 'I know that war cannot be the ultimate truth. A war neither solves any problems, nor answers any questions. On the contrary, there is danger of the society becoming degraded. The cultural foundation of a nation's civilisation may get uprooted. The dreams that mankind harboured for generations could be destroyed. Then why am I going to ignite the great Yajna of Death itself, in which lakhs of warriors will sacrifice their lives?

'Are we doing this to punish Duryodhana, Dushasana and Karna, who dishonoured Draupadi's pure, spotless character? To make selfish Dhritarashtra's blind eyes see the blazing truth? If that were my only intent, my job would have been easy. Was it impossible for me to teach a lesson to each one of them separately and destroy them? Then why am I initiating this thrilling great yajna?

'Life means expression. Sometimes, the human race needs to witness the cataclysmic form of this expression, because it becomes greedy beyond the knowledge in books, sane advice and moralistic principles. It develops a fondness for rest and inactivity. It gets smeared with blind selfishness. It needs to be stopped at some point. And for that purpose, there is no other effective option but war. The Great War that is going to begin tomorrow is for this purpose alone.'

That night a question arose in my mind, 'When did I meet the Lord of Dwaraka for the first time?' I saw him closely for the first time during Kansa's execution. At that time, I was sitting near Yadava commander Anadhrishti. For me, the way young Balaramadada and Krishna finished off the mighty elephant Kuvalayapida was amazing. I still vividly remember the days of Jarasandha's attacks on Mathura. After I was appointed the co-commander, the first thing I had to face was the truth of war. Not just once or twice, these attacks took place seventeen times. During that period, Krishnadeva had given me the responsibility of guarding the western gate of the royal city of Mathura. There was a reason for that. Mathura was located directly on the western side of the royal city of Girivraja of Emperor Jarasandha. Therefore, his assaults on Mathura should have fallen on the eastern gate of Mathura first. But that was not possible due to a geographic reason. The Yamuna surrounded Mathura in a crescent shape. The eastern bed of the Yamuna was not convenient for the enemy ships to enter. To guard Mathura, I had to be vigilant by frequently sailing on the crescent-shaped Yamuna from the western gate to the eastern gate. Sometimes, during such trips, Krishnadeva also accompanied me. While sailing on the waters of the Yamuna, I could strongly feel the abundant love in his heart for it. Eventually, I came to realise that he was a 'Jalapurusha'. Right after his birth, he had travelled on the waters in Gokul, and in Mathura he lived near the banks of the Yamuna. The city of Dwaraka that he had erected was surrounded by water. It was his vision that lakhs of Yadavas should be blessed with the bountiful Jala principle. That is why he had developed Dwaraka into a well-planned harbour.

As a commander, I experienced the deep-rooted Jalapurusha in him during the seventeenth and last mighty attack of Jarasandha. At that time, he had annihilated two of Jarasandha's powerful commanders, Hansa and Dimbhaka. For that he had taken advantage of the bountiful Yamuna.

The great Yadava would always say to me, 'Satyaki, you have recognised me correctly as a Jalapurusha. There are two more like me in Kuru's Hastinapura – just as you have knee-long arms like me, they have knee-long arms too. Can you guess who they are?'

Grandsire Bhishma's name would immediately come to mind, as he was the son of Ganga. He was also a disciple of Bhagvan Parashurama. I would say, 'It is clear that one of them is the Grandsire – the son of Ganga. Who could be the second one? I cannot guess.' When I would look at him with a frown, he would smile mischievously as usual and say, 'You will come to know at the right time.' That right time came too late in my life.

Just as he loved the Yamuna and the water bodies, he also loved the trees, the vines and the forests. He deeply regretted the fact that the rich forest of Mount Gomanta had to be burnt for a safe escape from Jarasandha's siege in the south. He felt remorse throughout his life that a magnificent forest like Khandavavana had to be set ablaze to erect the well-planned royal city of Indraprastha for the Pandavas.

His feet bore chakra symbols. He had travelled all over the Bharatavarsha from Mathura to Dwaraka, Dwaraka to Indraprastha, Pragjyotishapura, Dwaraka to Kundinpura, and Karvir, Sauvira to Jagannathpuri.

While travelling with him throughout Bharatavarsha as a commander, I noticed many of his qualities. The most notable was his altruistic nature. For instance, he never desired the royal throne of Dwaraka. The mission of his life was to emancipate the masses from the unrestrained tyrannical rule of unjust and arrogant emperors. While working towards that end, it would have been easy for him to seize the defeated kingdoms, but he never did that.

In the beginning, he had eradicated the unjust and uncontrollable king, Shrugala of Karvir. For that, he had projected the Sudarshan chakra for the first time. But he did not claim any right over the royal throne of Karvir. In Shrugala's place, he appointed his son Shakradeva. He won the hearts of thousands of citizens there because of his actions.

Krishnadeva launched an armed attack on the insolent and arrogant Narakasura of the Kamarupa kingdom. It was an ambitious mission – directly charging on Pragjyotishapura in the eastern region from the Dwaraka kingdom, located on the shores of the western ocean.

During this prolonged mission, many of his qualities dazzled me. He killed the unjust and autocratic Narakasura of Kamarupa and offered the kingdom to his son Bhagdutta. At that time, all of us Yadava warriors were astonished to see the pure respect he had for women. He offered mangalsutras in his name to the sixteen thousand Kamarupa women victims through Uddhavadeva. He rehabilitated all those helpless women in Dwaraka with honour. He became the very first man in ancient Aaryavarta to do something like this.

I clearly remember the day when he entered the Sudharma royal assembly without speaking a word to me. On the same day, Satrajita, who later became his father-in-law, had accused him of stealing the Syamantaka jewel. That day Krishnadeva gave his word, and after trying everything possible brought the Syamantaka jewel back and handed it to Satrajita in the assembly full of people.

All the Yadavas marvelled at the Syamantaka jewel. But I admired the lady jewel that came to Dwaraka because of the Syamantaka jewel. She was our queen Jambavatidevi. Krishnadeva had married a tribal woman in the forests of Mount Hrikshawana and brought her to Dwaraka as a queen of the Yadavas.

I came to witness a very unique quality of his at the time of Shishupala's execution during the Rajasuya yajna of the Pandavas. Patience was an innate quality he possessed. He had tolerated ninety-nine of Shishupala's offences with tremendous patience. But he could not forgive his hundredth offence. He launched the Sudarshan and cut off his head, along with his foul-speaking tongue. All the invitees in the yajna pandal were too dazed to bear his divine form.

But I was greatly astonished to see him after the yajna. On that day in Indraprastha, on the banks of the Yamuna, multitudes of people feasted on the delicious food offered by the Pandavas. The Lord of Dwaraka, master of the Sudarshan, who was just moments ago honoured with the agrapooja in the Rajasuya yajna, picked up the soiled plates of invited guests afterwards. I was astonished to see him, in a golden silk dhoti, in the pandal of the Rajasuya yajna, picking up the used plates of the invitees. Each of his manifestations was like the sun in the month of Shravana, sometimes hiding behind the clouds and sometimes making the whole world shine with its dazzling brightness. Everyone saw him differently according to their ability. It is indeed difficult for me to talk about so many shades of his manifestations.

A gallant man may not necessarily be merciful. But Yadavaraja Srikrishna was. He reinstated minister Akrura, who had deserted Dwaraka. He kind-heartedly forgave the inexcusable offence by him with regard to the Syamantaka jewel. At that time, I had realised that he would never let the merits of a person go waste in his new kingdom. He had a specific political objective in mind and the Kuru kingdom of Hastinapura was a significant part of it. Hastinapura was the second-most powerful kingdom after Jarasandha's Magadha. Krishnadeva had not been to Hastinapura often. He may have visited it three–four times at the most. Yet, he had precise evaluations of all men and women of political significance in Hastinapura at his fingertips. In his opinion, the most significant person in the Hastinapura kingdom was Grandsire Bhishma. After Bhishma, he gave importance to Karna, the king of Anga.

'Grandsire Bhishma is the only person in Hastinapura who knows and cares about the Truth. But he is helpless due to old age. No one in Hastinapura understands that even if an ember is covered with ashes, it is not extinguished. Even today, Grandsire Bhishma is incredibly valiant.

'The most difficult and complicated mind is that of Maharaja Dhritarashtra. Two different Dhritarashtras are hiding in his mind. One is a greedy father who, in spite of being blind, is shrewdly dreaming of Duryodhana's coronation. The second is a hypocritical king who pretends to follow royal protocol. Maharaja Dhritarashtra is clearly divided into two puppets. One is controlled by Shakuni and the other by Duryodhana. Duryodhana's and Shakuni's crafty diplomatic machinations are honed by the brain of Kanaka, the astute minister of the Kurus.

'All of them are trying their best to involve the mighty Karna, the king of Anga, in every plot of theirs. He has full confidence in his own valour. The minds of all these have been revealed with all their shades at the time of the incident that Draupadi had to face in the gambling hall.

Rajmata Gandharidevi is the most virtuous lady among the Kaurava women. She is the one who has somehow controlled ambitious Duryodhana with her harsh reprimands.

Mahatma Vidura and Sanjaya are my devotees. If at all, they are the only hope to obtain some kind of justice for the Pandavas.'

Just as the great Yadava knew everything about the Kauravas, so also did he have all the information about the Pandavas. He regarded Rajmata Kuntidevi with utmost respect. He would regard Kuntidevi in the place of Yashodamata, who had been left behind in distant Gokul. He would say, 'This aunt of mine has proved herself by making her five sons' lives blossom in all adversities. Each one of the Pandavas is blessed with different qualities. Draupadi has the knack to unite their power in one strong fist. The Pandavas are ideal not only today but will remain so in future. We should actively support them with all our might whenever necessary.'

The true treasure of opulent Dwaraka, which had reached the zenith of acclaim, was one royal lady. Rukminidevi now graced Dwaraka like Mahalakshmi, the goddess of wealth. She never returned to Kundinpura even after being repeatedly invited by her Rukmidada, who had now developed cordial relations with Krishnadeva. From time to time, she sent letters of her well-being to her mother Shuddhamatidevi. Gift salvers were also exchanged. Rukminidevi considered all the children of her seven co-wives as her own.

After Krishnadeva, Uddhavadeva was the one whom the citizens of Dwaraka held in the highest regard. He had gained that place due to the virtuous qualities he possessed. Right since birth, he was different from all the other Yadavas. He was a sanyasi by disposition, unmarried and celibate. That is why his father Devabhaga had got both his brothers, Chitraketu and Brihadbala, married to expand the family. Their families had also blossomed with children. Uddhavadeva was the only Yadava in Dwaraka who everybody, including Krishnadeva, felt close to.

I frequently visited Indraprastha with Krishnadeva. During the visits to Indraprastha, I gradually came to know the five Pandava brothers one by one. The five brothers had very different temperaments. But one thing was common to all of them. They all had the utmost devotion to Krishnadeva.

Yudhishthira – the eldest among the Pandavas – was a complex mixture of good and bad qualities. He was valiant but did not have any feats of gallantry to his credit. He was sacrificing but also covetous. He was senior by birth but not necessarily so in action. From Yudhishthira he became Dharmaraja due to the knowledge he obtained. But he did not necessarily implement Dharma with full understanding. Does that mean he did any adharma? It was not that either. He was responsible for the unforgivable blunder of playing the game of dice. Bhimsena – the second among the Pandavas – was like Balaramadada. Bhimsena's prowess was dazzling in the way he killed Jarasandha. He was not just gallant, but also thoughtful and intelligent. It was just that he frequently displayed his physical power and not so much his intelligence. In the entire journey of the Pandavas' life, the armour of Bhimsena's valour was of great value. The notable thing about Bhimsena was that he himself never claimed to be the armour of his brothers. Draupadi always sought support in quiet Bhimsena. Keeping this quality of Bhimsena in mind, I once asked Krishnadeva, 'Would you find Bhimsena to be an apt Pandava commander in the future if such an occasion arises?'

He smiled casually and answered, 'Bhimsena is perfectly suited to be the commander of any army. But I would not do it if such a need arises. Because just as it is quite hard to motivate Bhimsena's valour, it is even harder to control him once he is motivated. And to tell you the truth, my wish is that Bhimsena should be uncontrollably valiant instead of being the commander of the Pandavas. The responsibility of being a commander sets limitations on one's valour.'

I would ask him the next question, 'Then master archer Arjuna is the only one who remains as the commander of lakhs of Pandava warriors of Indraprastha. What do you think of him?' Hearing my question, he would give his usual pure, charming smile. He would put his arm around my shoulder and say, 'Satyaki, there are many reasons why Arjuna is my favourite. I cannot think of the Pandavas, Indraprastha and even the entire world, including Dwaraka, without Arjuna. He is not only Savyasachi, who uses both hands equally skilfully for brandishing all kinds of weapons, but is also a cautious and humble disciple who exercises the most potent weapon of his intellect with all its facets. I like his attitude of being a perpetual student from the bottom of my heart. That is why whatever I want to convey to all people, I say only to Arjuna, as I consider him their representative.' Then I would ask Krishnadeva many things only about Arjuna. I would feel convinced that just like commander Skanda was the perfect commander for the gods, master archer Arjuna could be the perfect commander of the Pandavas, Yadavas and Kauravas. Still, I wanted to know more about the remaining two Pandava brothers from Krishnadeva. So, I would ask him, 'What do you think of Nakula and Sahadeva, the sons of Madri?' Here, too, correcting my unintentional mistake, he would say, 'Satyaki, they are not only Madreyas or sons of Madri but also of Kunti. They are twins. Both are experts in horses. Nakula is exquisitely handsome, like our Pradyumna, and therefore very attractive. If you observe carefully, you will come to know that Aunt Kunti brought them up as "Pandavas", inculcating the same sanskaras in them.'

Whenever the topic of Kuntimata would come up in discussion, the Lord of Dwaraka would talk abundantly about her. The whole world knew that Krishnadeva had two mothers. His biological mother Devakidevi and foster mother Yashodadevi, who nurtured him. Very few people had realised that Kuntidevi was like his third mother; Bhavamata – the one emotionally connected with him. Krishnadeva was her nephew but she herself was also an ardent devotee of his. She always said to him, 'Krishna, whenever there is adversity, I remember you without fail. I know that your other aunts forgot you as they were always happy and faced no problems. Some of their sons even went against you. I do not mind if the whole world does not support me, but your blessings should always be with me and my sons.'

Just as Krishnadeva had three mothers, he also had three sisters. As he and Uddhavadeva used to say, Ekananga, the daughter of Nandababa and Yashodadevi of Gokul, was his first sister. Subhadradevi from Dwaraka was already well known as the beloved sister of the two great Yadavas – Balaramadada and Krishnadeva. The third sister was Draupadidevi. She was more fortunate than the first two sisters. She was not only his sister but had also become his beloved sakhi. She was lucky to have achieved what no other woman could – to be the wife of five great men and the sister-sakhi of the one and only Narayana. It was because of this fortune of hers that I had utmost respect for Draupadidevi, as much as I had for the mother of the Pandavas.

Nowadays, the Lord of Dwaraka had started sitting on the stone seats located near the western Aindra gate of Dwaraka for hours together. Often, Uddhavadeva and Daruka would accompany him. Staring at the foaming, continuous waves of the western ocean in high tide, he would say to me, 'Commander Satyaki, human life is also like this ocean. It is characterised by change every single moment.' At such times, I would keep silent and just listen to him. During one such talk, he asked me, 'Commander, in the Kuru army, how exactly would you place the world conqueror, Maharathi Karna, who has donated his kavacha-kundala?'

'After giving away the kavacha-kundala, Karna, the charioteer's son, went to Mount Mahendra and obtained the divine astra called "Brahma" from Bhagvan Parashurama. But a holy cow named Shubhada was killed by his arrow unknowingly while hunting. The Brahmin owner of the cow inflicted a heart-breaking curse on him: "Mother earth will consume the wheel of your chariot right at the time of war, just like you have consumed my ashrama by killing this cow." Even before that, after he obtained the Brahmastra, Gurudeva Parashurama had cursed him, saying, "You will not remember the mantras of Brahmastra during war." The reason behind this curse was that Karna had lied about his caste to gain the Brahmastra. The cursed Karna, today, without the kavacha-kundala, is just like the king of the jungle, the lion, with his claws removed. In my opinion, he does not have any significant standing in the Kuru army.' I put forth all the details about Karna that I knew as a commander.

He looked at the western ocean and then at me and smilingly said, 'Commander Satyaki, you are wrong. This ocean in front of us is also bound by high tides and low tides, but could it be considered any less powerful because of that? Karna is also the same in the Kuru army. What if the Kauravas appoint him as their commander? Then it is going to be very tough for the Pandavas. That is why I am going to try my best to see that the Pandavas get all their rights in a peaceful manner. For that, I will have to go to Hastinapura for diplomatic talks. During that visit, Satyaki, as my loyal escort, I want you, with your troop of extremely loyal bodyguards with me. I am telling you right now that as per his nature, Duryodhana will not listen to my diplomatic advice. The arrogant, mighty, insolent kings whom I have obliterated were nothing compared to Duryodhana. It is going to be Duryodhana who we will have to deal with. It cannot be said now how things will turn out eventually.'

A royal envoy arrived in Dwaraka from Upaplavya with a message from Yudhishthira. As per the wish of the great Pandava Yudhishthira, who had come out of incognito living, the Lord of Dwaraka left for Upaplavya. Upaplavya was a town in the Matsya kingdom located on the southern border of Indraprastha and the western border of Hastinapura. Sanjaya, the royal minister of Hastinapura, arrived in Upaplavya. He had brought a persuasive message from Maharaja Dhritarashtra for the great Pandava Yudhishthira. In the council at Upaplavya, Sanjaya presented that message to Krishnadeva in the presence of all five Pandavas, Draupadidevi and Kuntimata. As he was a Krishna devotee, Sanjaya had to harden his heart and read the message in a very low voice. The so-called kind-hearted Maharaja Dhritarashtra had an atrocious and merciless message for his nephews, who had just come into the open after spending twelve years in forests and one year incognito. But it was in a deceptively sweet diplomatic language, 'Pandavas are used to forest living. They are used to living on alms. They should spend their remaining lives in forests seeking alms and praying to God. They should not bother to come to Hastinapura.'

Hearing that hypocritical and humiliating message, Draupadidevi burst out in rage as per her nature. She spoke directly in clear words, 'Who are the people of Hastinapura to decide whether we should seek alms or make others seek alms?'

Kuntimata, trying to abate the sharp response of her daughter-in-law, said, 'Oh Sanjaya, we are not seeking alms from the Kurus. We are asking that justice be served. If we ask for the kingdom of Hastinapura, Maharaja Dhritarashtra should dutifully return it to us, as he was appointed the trustee of the kingdom. My sons have completed twelve years of living in the forest and one year of incognito life as per the conditions. Now he should honourably return the kingdom to my sons. His actions will safeguard the pride of his kingdom and the honour of my sons.'

But Krishnadeva sent a message through Sanjaya to Dhritarashtra, 'If we are to seek alms, we will begin from Hastinapura. Oh Sanjaya, let the great Kuru know that I am coming to Hastinapura in person for mediation.'

Krishnadeva said to all the Pandavas, 'Brothers, on your behalf, I am going to appeal for your rightful share of the kingdom in the ancient royal assembly of the Kurus. Whatever I will speak, it will be in your favour. Still, I want to know clearly whether I have your unconditional permission including that of your wife and mother, for this mediation. Would every word that I say be agreeable to you? What do you think?'

The eldest Pandava Yudhishthira said, 'Srikrishna, we will all accept whatever mediations you do.'

Krishnadeva, Daruka and I entered the royal capital of the Kurus along with an escort of select Yadava warriors.

Today, the citizens of Hastinapura were going to see Krishnadeva after a long time. That is why the entire city was bursting with energy and vigour. The news of our arrival at Vrikasthala had reached the royal capital. Grandsire, Vidura, minister Sanjaya, Chief Minister Vrishavarma and Acharya Drona arrived in Vrikasthala to welcome the Lord of Dwaraka. Karna, the king of Anga, and the guru's son Ashwatthama also accompanied them.

White-bearded Grandsire spread both his arms wide, called him 'Vasudeva' and held Krishnadeva in a deep embrace. The other three also enquired about his well-being. Karna directly touched Krishnadeva's feet, saying 'my respects to you, Yadavaraja'. I clearly heard Krishnadeva whisper, 'May you be victorious, Karna.'

Duryodhana was the only one who had not come to see Krishnadeva. And neither had Shakuni or his brothers. How unfortunate all of them were.

In the scorching midday heat, Daruka brought the Garudadhwaja chariot to the gates of the ancient royal palace of Hastinapura. Krishnadeva calmly descended from the chariot with a smile.

We left for the assembly hall with all the Kuru warriors. While climbing the staircase in the grand royal palace of the Kurus, he stopped on a step. I was standing right behind him. Unknowingly, I was counting every step. I remembered the esteemed 'Srisopana' in Dwaraka. The step that he had stopped on was the one-hundred-and-fifth. Krishnadeva momentarily waited on the step and glanced at Karna, the king of Anga, with a smile. Then he stepped on the last and one-hundred-and-sixth step of the staircase.

As soon as he entered the assembly hall, he paid obeisance to the ancient renowned royal throne of the Kurus. He calmly took the seat allotted to him.

Vrishavarma raised the royal sceptre and presented the agenda of the council. He welcomed Krishnadeva saying, 'Now Yadavaraja Bhagvan Srikrishna himself will share the purpose of his visit. All Kurus should think about it carefully. This is a very crucial time. It is going to be decisive.'

Krishnadeva calmly got up from his seat and gathered his shawl. In his sharp, keen voice, he began speaking. 'Grandsire Bhishma, Maharaja Dhritarashtra, Maharani Gandharidevi, world conqueror Karna, Acharya Drona, Kripa, Mahatma Vidura, Ashwatthama, Gandhara king Shakuni, Chief Minister Vrishavarma, expert politician Kanaka, Dushasana, Duryodhana and all the Kuru warriors who are present here and the citizens of Hastinapura. Today, I have not come to your city as a Yadavaraja. I have also not come as the cousin of the Pandavas. And not at all as Srikrishna, the Lord of Dwaraka. I have come here today as a supporter of a fair party to seek justice from this ancient royal throne. You have stretched the tolerance of the Pandavas beyond limits. Will the eldest Kaurava Duryodhana explain to me today who taught him the warfare of setting the Pandavas on fire in the lacquer house? Will Shakuni Mama, who offered the freakish kingdom of Khandavavana – full of thick and thorny trees and creepers, echoing with the loud roars of wild animals – to the Pandavas, leave the royal capital of his Gandhara kingdom and go to the Dandakaranya and build a new royal city there if I offer it to him as his new kingdom? If I sit today to play the game of dice putting my Dwaraka at stake, would he play the game with me and put his Gandhara kingdom at stake? Would he put his wife at stake and, after losing her in the game of dice, allow me to bring her in this assembly hall in front of all, even if she were menstruating? What if my commander Satyaki touches her vesture to remove it in this hall full of people? Would Shakuni Mama just watch, along with Duryodhana and Dushasana? Would he endure thirteen years of forest life and incognito living? Would you accept it if the lakhs of Yadava warriors in Mathura and Dwaraka attack Hastinapura to seize your cows just like all of you Kuru warriors did? Each one of you possesses an eternal pure voice within you. With that voice as witness, tell me honestly, what justice have you offered to the Pandavas so far? Are you even aware today of what meting out justice means?

'Still, I consider the Kauravas and the Pandavas equals, as two sides of the same royal seal. I consider all of you as Kurus of the Chandravansha. That is why I am ready to forget all the bitter events of the past. Give half of the kingdom to the Pandavas, which is rightfully theirs, and put out the mammoth inferno of destruction that is looming in the future. In fact, Maharaja Pandu appointed you as the trustee of the kingdom for its protection, and so you should return the entire kingdom as it is to his sons. So, tell me, are you ready to do justice in this matter?'

The entire assembly hall was filled with a terrifying silence with his sharp words sounding like the cracking of a whiplash. Maharaja Dhritarashtra was not ready to give him an answer. Many great men were sitting in the assembly hall but no one dared to utter a single word.

Breaking that silence, Krishnadeva roared again, 'Come on. Can any one of you stand up and tell me what your final decision is?' His eyes kept moving rapidly around the entire assembly hall.

A stunned silence enveloped the assembly hall. 'I will do that. Once and for all, I will tell you the final decision of all the Kuru warriors who are benumbed by your preposterous speech here. The Pandavas will not get even half of the kingdom,' Duryodhana stood up and spoke, raising his eyebrows. He waved his short and stubby fingers in the air in negation.

'They have nothing to do with this kingdom. Not even if they are the sons of Maharaja Pandu. Dividing the kingdom today will break it into a hundred pieces tomorrow and a thousand pieces later. Do the Pandavas think of the kingdom as a coconut that ten ashrama disciples can share among themselves?'

'If not half the kingdom, would you at least return the Indraprastha kingdom that they raised and brought to prosperity in Khandavavana, as per the conditions of the second gambling game? Duryodhana, do not shut out justice and truth with your arrogance,' Krishnadeva said in a very persuasive tone.

Discarding his entreaty, Duryodhana said, 'No. They have lost the kingdom in the game of dice. They have not completed a year of incognito life. There are still two more days for the year to get over. They have come out in the open before that.'

'No. They have completed one year in incognito. You have made a mistake in the calculation of time. You did not take into consideration the extra lunar month, Duryodhana. Return Indraprastha to the Pandavas.' Krishnadeva was not going to let him get away with any excuse today.

'Never.' The already stubborn son of Dhritarashtra was not going to give in today.

'Why not?'

'They are not the sons of our Maharaja Pandu. They may be the sons of Kunti and the sons of Madri but they are not Pandavas.'

These detestable words of Duryodhana caused a commotion in the ancient royal assembly of the Kurus. Duryodhana was thoughtlessly trying to tarnish the esteemed character of Kuntidevi openly and without any shame.

Now Grandsire Bhishma stood up at once. Tightly holding the shawl resting on his chest, he roared, 'Reckless Duryodhana, shut your mouth. I know exactly what you want to say. You know nothing about politics and ethics. It was impossible for Maharaj Pandu to bear a son in the forest due to the curse of Kindama rishi. Pandu, who could not bear the thought of an emperor dying without bearing a son, shared his pain with wife

Kuntidevi. To save him from going to hell, Kunti, as a dutiful wife, agreed to bear him a son by way of niyoga. Both sent such a message to us with Maharishi Vyasa. After receiving that message, Maharaja Dhritarashtra, Vidura and I held an urgent meeting. We sent them our approval for the niyoga. Pandavas are the sons of Maharaja Pandu borne by way of niyoga, which is approved by Dharma. They belong to the Kuru dynasty. They are the rightful heirs of this kingdom.'

Duryodhana had already surmised that the Grandsire was going to attack him in the assembly. He wanted to spit out his deep-rooted hatred for the Pandavas in front of all the people in the assembly. He raised his stubby finger again and said, 'Then what status do my brothers and I hold in Hastinapura? Grandsire should clearly tell the assembly what our status as Kurus is, after all.'

Aged Grandsire stood up again. He said, 'Duryodhana, indeed you are quite ignorant. You Kauravas and Pandavas – none of you are born in the Kuru dynasty.' This was the second powerful shock to the royal assembly of the Kurus. Now a buzz of whispers started in the Kaurava section among Duryodhana, Dushasana, Shakuni Mama, their brothers and Karna. Gandhara king Shakuni rose and said, 'The Maharaja's sons Duryodhana and his brothers are not Kurus. Yudhishthira and his brothers born by way of niyoga are also not Kurus. Then who are the Kurus, after all? Who does this kingdom belong to?' Grandsire Bhishma said firmly, 'I am that last Kuru. The son of Shantanu, Gangeya Bhishma. Long ago, the Kuru dynasty had adapted the niyoga system with the permission of my mother Satyavatidevi to avoid its extinction. Maharaja Dhritarashtra, Maharaja Pandu and Mahatma Vidura are all sons of Vyasa by way of niyoga, which is sanctioned by Dharma. So, I am the last and only Kuru. I earnestly request you Kauravas and Pandavas to not let a single word of Srikrishna go unheeded. At this moment, it will be an unforgivable blunder that can never be fixed. You—Kauravas and Pandavas—are fortunate enough that he has come in person in this assembly hall today to mediate between you. I earnestly feel that you should not disrespect his words.'

Absolute silence spread in the assembly hall now. Taking advantage of the silence, Krishnadeva said, 'Duryodhana, if not the kingdom of Hastinapura and not the kingdom of Indraprastha, then where should your brothers go? Are you at least ready to give five towns to the five brothers just for shelter?' It broke the hearts of all the warrior members to hear that desperate appeal.

Duryodhana instantly discarded Krishnadeva's proposal with arrogance and said, 'No. Never ever. We are not the heirs of this Kuru kingdom. Because we are not Kurus. The Pandavas born by way of niyoga are also not the heirs. They are also not Kurus. Grandsire Bhishma is the only Kuru. But he has taken a vow of lifelong celibacy. Then should this ancient throne of the Kurus be left without any heir? Only the battlefield will now decide who is going to inherit the kingdom on the basis of strength.

'Forget five towns – without a battle, the Pandavas will not get even the tiniest dust particle trembling on the tip of a needle.'

With extreme disrespect, rejecting Krishnadeva's authority as the esteemed Vasudeva, he insanely raved, 'Not only that, I would have even told my servants to wipe the dust particles sticking to your feet when you go back with this denial, so that they do not fall in the hands of the Pandavas. But even for that, I would not want my servants to touch your dirty feet smeared in cow dung. Go, wrap these tatters of your deal of compromise around yourself and leave the borders of Hastinapura as soon as possible. Or else –'

Krishnadeva's lips quivered with rage now. His fish-shaped eyes became blood-red. I stood up at once as if struck by lightning. My whole body was trembling with rage. I did not even know when my hands clasped the scabbard of my sword tied around my waist. Shouting loudly, I promptly pulled the sword out. The ninety-nine brothers of Duryodhana and all the brothers of Shakuni were also standing now. Duryodhana raved deliriously, 'Karna, I am going to capture this cowherd, who is the reason for all this chaos, today! This cowherd, born in the prison of Mathura, should perish in the darkness of the prison of Hastinapura. That is the place he deserves.'

His words fell on my ears like molten iron. They began stinging my brain like a lethal slithering serpent. A lightning of thought flashed through my mind. Now, I clearly understood why the Lord of Dwaraka had instructed me to bring escorts along with us for this mission.

I urgently walked out of the hall, holding the scabbard of my sword tightly in my fist – to command the escorts to encircle Deva. Suddenly, I could hear the same unclear mixed sounds that I had heard in the Rajasuya yajna – those of various musical instruments. After that, the last fleeting words of the Lord of Dwaraka fell on my ears, 'Oh Karna, tell him that I dare him to gather all the chains that he has in his kingdom and detain me if he can.'

The very next moment, the armed Yadava warriors in the escort troop burst into the assembly hall, brandishing their naked weapons. They surrounded Krishnadeva from all sides. Fortunately, the Sudarshan was not launched that day. Whose luck was that? Only Krishnadeva knew. Brandishing the bare sword in my hand, moving around Krishnadeva like a whirligig, I brought him safely out of the assembly hall with the assistance of the escort troop.

He walked briskly and mounted the Garudadhwaja chariot that Daruka had brought to the front. There were a few men who followed him as if they were being dragged behind him due to a bond through ages. Among them were Grandsire Bhishma, Mahatma Vidura, Karna and Sanjaya. Krishnadeva accepted all their salutations and said only to Karna, 'Come, king of Anga, there is something I have to tell you.' He gently pulled Karna into his chariot with a smile. Daruka steered the chariot. We also got into our chariots. A line of chariots followed the Garudadhwaja towards the border of Hastinapura. Krishnadeva's mediation was over!

That day, under a sprawling banyan tree, on the border of Hastinapura, Karna and Krishnadeva discussed something of utmost importance for half an hour on the shores of River Ganga. It was only between the two of them and completely confidential. I waited under a tree along with the escort troops until the discussion between the two warriors was over. After some time, both returned. Karna bowed respectfully and bade farewell to Krishnadeva. He pulled that son of a charioteer into a deep embrace. I looked back with curiosity. Karna disappeared towards Hastinapura, alone and lonely. We came to Upaplavya. The very next day, a messenger of the Kurus came to Upaplavya. A special meeting had been arranged on the holy land of Kurukshetra. It was to decide the date and rules of engagement between both parties for the inevitable war between the Kauravas and the Pandavas. In this meeting, Grandsire Bhishma, Acharya Drona, Kripa, Ashwatthama, Duryodhana and Karna were going to represent the Kauravas, and Krishnadeva, Virata, King Drupada and his son prince Dhrishtadyumna, and I were going to represent the Pandavas.

We left for Kurukshetra on the decided day. The Kaurava representatives came directly to Kurukshetra. The meeting began in a very solemn environment. Grandsire announced the first rule of engagement, 'Every day, the war will commence exactly at sunrise.'

'And will end exactly at sunset,' Krishnadeva completed the rule.

'The entire war will be fought in the form of a duel,' Grandsire said. Hearing that, Krishnadeva nodded in approval and said, 'Nobody will attack an unarmed warrior or charioteer with any weapon or astra.' Acharya Drona added, 'The group wars should also be defined in this council itself.'

I said, 'Where many warriors are fighting with the same kind of weapon, it will be considered a group war for that particular weapon. Where a group of chariots of one party are fighting another group of chariots, it would be considered a group war of chariots. Similarly, for any other such form.'

The council now got engrossed in detailing the subtle rules of war.

'A group of warriors will be prohibited from surrounding a single warrior. It will be considered against the rules of engagement,' said Grandsire Bhishma.

'The holy land of Kurukshetra will serve as the battleground for this Great War. It is expected that no disregard for Dharma will take place here. The battlefield should always be clear. Therefore, both armies will have to arrange their military formations on a cleared out battlefield every day.'

The Lord of Dwaraka had mentioned an unarmed charioteer. 'What about an unarmed warrior?' Karna, king of Anga questioned Krishnadeva.

'Good question, Karna.' Krishnadeva said smilingly and continued, 'Weaponry as well as astras will be used in this war. Therefore, it will have to be defined as to who should be considered unarmed. I think it should be decided according to the situation.'

'Unchorioted and injured warriors should be permitted to retire from the battlefield.' Acharya Drona looked expectantly at Krishnadeva.

'Indeed, it should be allowed. But Acharya, a real warrior does not retire even in his sleep,' The Lord of Dwaraka answered smilingly.

We bade farewell to Grandsire and returned to Upaplavya with Yadavaraja. Krishnadeva summoned the expert astrologer of the Viratas and after having a thorough discussion with him, finalised the day for the commencement of the war.

The Lord of Dwaraka summoned Maharaja Virata and Drupada, and gave them final instructions. Drupada's son Dhrishtadyumna began huge preparations in Kampilyanagar with the assistance of his brothers Shikhandi, Sumitra, Priyadarshana, Chitraketu, Suketu, Dhwajaketu, Viraketu, Suratha and Shatrunjaya.

The Matsya kingdom of the Viratas was much closer to Kurukshetra than the Panchala kingdom. It was possible only for the Matsyas to supply food to the Pandava army. Though Indraprastha was the closest kingdom to Kurukshetra, it was now under the rule of the Kauravas. It was going to be advantageous for Hastinapura to supply food for their mammoth army from Indraprastha. As the final authority on the Pandava side, Krishnadeva took charge of the Great War in his hands. I came to Dwaraka along with him to find ourselves facing a very difficult situation. Balaramadada had become irate over all the events that had taken place. He came to his young brother's chamber, stomping his feet. Castigating his brother, he said, 'Srikrishna, what are you up to? Both the Kauravas and the Pandavas are closely related to us. You went there for reconciliation. And came back after fixing a catastrophic Great War between them. I am tired of your political games. You should have just left and come back to Dwaraka once you realised that reconciliation was not possible. Instead, you have also dragged the Yadavas into this old dispute between the Kauravas and the Pandavas. Our Yadava kingdom itself has clearly got divided into two factions. Why are you doing all this?'

Dada's questions were apparently appropriate but the objective of the war was no longer just the right of the Kauravas and the Pandavas over Hastinapura. Almost all of Aaryavarta and the region from Kapisha to Kamboja were involved in it. In such a situation, would Dwaraka have been able to protect itself in future by staying aloof from the war? Once Duryodhana had defeated the Pandavas, was he not going to swindle the remaining eastern, central and northern parts of Aaryavarta by the end of the war? If that happened, was it not going to create a risk for our allies in the east – the Magadha and the Kamarupa kingdoms? How long would we have been able to keep the Dwaraka kingdom safe? Before forcing entry into one's home, the enemy first takes over the front yard. This is what Dada did not understand. He always considered Duryodhana, his best disciple, as his friend. Due to his short-tempered nature, no one could stand up to him and explain this.

The Lord of Dwaraka could think of only one person who could be assigned that task – Uddhavadeva. The three of them decided to organise a final conclusive royal assembly of the Yadavas before leaving Dwaraka for Kurukshetra.

The Sudharma royal assembly in Dwaraka that day was unprecedented. Every single Yadava had made it a point to be present there.

As per tradition, Chief Minister Vipruthu stated the objective of the assembly. He said, 'Recently, Duryodhana on behalf of the Kauravas and Arjuna on behalf of the Pandavas had come to Dwaraka to meet Krishnadeva to seek military assistance from the kingdom of Dwaraka. During this visit, Duryodhana accepted the assistance of the Yadava army. But Arjuna selected only Srikrishnadeva as his charioteer. He will chariot without carrying any weapons. He will only offer his wise advice to the Pandavas if need be. He will only hold the whip to steer Arjuna's Nandighosha chariot. Only time will decide who will be the winner between the whip and the Yadava army.

'The Lord of Dwaraka has granted freedom to all Yadava warriors to choose whichever side they deem appropriate between the Kauravas and the Pandavas. That is why mighty Satyaki is going to fight on behalf of the Pandavas with his troops, and gallant Kritavarma is going to fight on behalf of the Kauravas. All sons of Krishnadeva are going to remain in Dwaraka for its protection with the remaining Yadava army. Prince Pradyumna will lead them. Balaramadada's sons and brothers will also stay in Dwaraka and assist him.

'Prince Balarama and Krishna's sakha Uddhavadeva have not expressed their views about this Great War. I request them to share their views about this.'

Balaramadada got up to speak. He cleared his throat. Then, in a husky voice, he said, 'Politics is not my forte. I am just an unsophisticated Yadava warrior. I lay bare my heart so all my Yadava brothers will understand my clear views about the war. In my opinion, the Yadavas should take no part at all in this dispute between the Kauravas and the Pandavas. Both sides are equally close to us. No good will come of it if we participate. Therefore, today itself I am leaving Dwaraka and going towards the Himalayas. I will come back only when I feel like doing so. I might not come back at all. Therefore, I pay obeisance to everyone from the bottom of my heart. If I have unwittingly insulted anybody so far due to my short-tempered nature and straight talk, I request them to kindly forgive me.' Hearing Balaramadada's firm decision, the assembly hall fell silent.

Now Uddhavadeva got up from his seat. His face was tranquil. There was no turbulence whatsoever on his face and in his eyes. He said, 'Oh Yadava brothers, I am also going to the Himalayas like Balaramadada. But there is a difference in his leaving and mine. Both of us have talked about it. We will leave Dwaraka together. Both of us will travel together till the holy place of Badri-Kedara on the banks of River Ganga. I will stay at that holy place. Balaramadada will travel further to go wherever he wants.

'I am going to Badri-Kedara as per the wish and command of the Lord of Dwaraka. Krishnadada wants to set up an ashrama like that of Acharya Sandipani's Ankapada ashrama there. Krishnadada will certainly succeed in the Great War. He is going to participate in it as an unarmed charioteer. Yet, I have full confidence that whatever he does with master archer Arjuna will guide many future generations of Aaryavarta. I believe that Dharma and victory will prevail where master archer Arjuna and Sudarshan-wielder Srikrishna are present.'

Finally, Krishnadeva stood up. Only three words came out of his mouth. Those inspirational words were, 'Hail Goddess Ida.' The entire assembly hall shouted again and again, 'Hail Goddess Ida.' The conclusive Sudharma royal assembly in Dwaraka was over.

Krishnadeva left Dwaraka after seeking the blessings of all elders, and meeting all his queens and sons and daughters. Daruka, a few Yadava warriors that he himself had selected, and I were with him. As per Krishnadeva's wish, the royal priest Gargamuni had already gone ahead to the Shiva temple at Somanath with Acharya Sandipani. We came to the square in front of the Somnath temple.

Krishnadeva stopped near a stone statue of a tortoise at his feet. Putting his arm around my shoulders, he said, 'Satyaki, one should regard the tortoise as his ideal. It has drawn in six enemies such as lust, anger, pride, greed and envy, along with its legs. It is sitting at Shiva's feet with a stable mind. In a similar manner, one should also go with a stable and pure mind to seek the blessings of the cosmic dancer, Shiva.'

Gargamuni, Acharya Sandipani and many more sages who were standing at the entrance of the shrine approached Krishnadeva respectfully when they saw him. Krishnadeva descended into the shrine along with everybody. Daruka and I stood in a corner of the shrine with palms joined in prayer. The shrine echoed with the inspirational hymns of Shiva's praise.

From there, we came to another Shiva temple at Nageshwara in Aanarta. After worshipping Shiva at both these places, Krishnadeva's virtuous face began looking very different. I clearly felt that his blue throat had become dark blue now.

Our first stopover was in Kuntibhojanagar. We intentionally did not halt in the Avanti kingdom. Vinda and Anuvinda of Avanti were brothers of Mitravindadevi. They were Krishnadeva's paternal cousins. But they were going to participate in this war on behalf of Duryodhana's Kaurava army. They had already left for Kurukshetra with their army.

Our last stopover was in Upaplavya of the Matsyas. The Matsya king Virata had also reached Kurukshetra with his army and his sons Uttara, Shweta, Shatanika and Vasudana.

Towards the end of the month of Kartika, our troop entered Kurukshetra along with Krishnadeva. First, we came across the huge camp of the Kauravas' united army. Krishnadeva said, 'Satyaki, for sure, the Kuru army is massive. This war is not going to be easy for the Pandavas.'

Our charioteer Daruka had to stop the chariot in front of the pavilion of Grandsire Bhishma, who had been appointed the commander of the Kaurava army. He was standing right in the middle of the path with his attendants. Seeing Grandsire in warrior's attire and armour, Krishnadeva promptly descended the chariot. He started to bend down to touch

Grandsire's feet. Without allowing him to do so, Grandsire quickly pulled him up, embraced him and muttered, 'Vasudeva…! I do not care if I die on the battlefield of Kurukshetra now. I got to see you first. The Kurus have formally appointed me as the commander. I am going to appoint the rathis and maharathis today.'

We bade farewell to Grandsire and arrived at the Pandava base. The Pandavas, Dhrishtadyumna and many other warriors welcomed Krishnadeva. With them, we finally reached the tallest and most capacious pavilion raised for Krishnadeva at the centre of the Pandava base. Maharaja Virata and Drupada were inside the pavilion. Krishnadeva politely offered obeisance to them.

For the duration of the Great War, all military tactics of the Pandava army were going to be determined from this pavilion.

The important council to choose the commander of the Pandava army began. Krishnadeva said, 'Considering all aspects, Satyaki of the Yadavas and master archer Arjuna of the Pandavas are both perfectly fit to be the commander of the Pandava army. But in war, the end result is considered important. So, taking all this into consideration, I think we should appoint Panchala's young prince Dhrishtadyumna as the commander of the Pandava army.'

All mighty warriors in the council unanimously hailed Dhrishtadyumna and accepted him as the commander. Dhrishtadyumna politely offered obeisance to aged Drupada and Virata. As per Krishnadeva's instructions, a simple sandalwood seat was placed for him on the right of the commander's seat.

Taking his seat, Dhrishtadyumna brought his hands together and requested, 'As the commander of the army of the Pandavas, I request the Lord of Dwaraka to announce the leaders of the seven regiments of our army.' I looked at Commander Dhrishtadyumna with the utmost pride. He was undoubtedly proving to be a perfect commander by making this request to Krishnadeva. Krishnadeva smilingly stood up and said, 'As per our commander's instruction, I am announcing the names of the leaders of the seven regiments. They would be Dhrishtadyuma himself, Panchala king Maharaja Drupada, Matysa king Maharaja Virata, Drupada's son Shikhandi, Satyaki, Maharathi Chekitana and Bhimsena.'

Krishnadeva and I walked towards the area at the far back of the army encampment. The pavilions for the Pandava army's royal ladies were located here. We arrived at Kuntidevi's pavilion. Draupadidevi was also there. As soon as we entered, Krishnadeva bent down to touch the feet of Kuntidevi. Holding him in a deep embrace just like Grandsire, she said, 'Krishna, it is good that you did not yoke my Arjuna with the responsibility of a commander. He should always remain free and unrestrained to fight dauntlessly.'

Krishnadeva enquired after Draupadidevi's. Putting his hand on Subhadradevi's head, he blessed her, 'May you live long.'

Krishnadeva assigned me a special task as soon as we returned to his pavilion. He said, 'Satyaki, you meet the Kuru commander Bhishma and let him know that the Panchala prince Dhrishtadyumna has been unanimously chosen as our commander.'

Right at the entrance of Grandsire's pavilion, an armed guard stopped me. I heard Karna's fleeting words, 'Until this old and egotistic Bhishma, who calls me an ardhrathi, falls on the battleground, I will not step on to the battleground at all. I will remain in my pavilion worshipping the Sun god.'

I saw Karna come out of the Kuru commander's pavilion and walk briskly towards his own. From the whispering discussions among the kings and gallant warriors who had assembled there, I came to know the situation.

Grandsire Bhishma had just announced the list of maharathi, rathi and ardharathi warriors in the Kaurava army. While doing that, he had mentioned World Conqueror Karna, who had obtained the Brahmastra from Bhagvan Parashurama, as a mere ardharathi. Karna's reaction spoke for itself. He had left declaring that he would not enter the battleground until Bhishma fell. I met Bhishma, shared news of the Pandava commander's appointment with him and came back. I directly went to Krishnadeva's pavilion and shared this information with him. He let out a sigh of relief and said, 'Has Karna refrained? That is good for Arjuna. Satyaki, I tried so hard for exactly this to happen. I had sent a message to Grandsire through Vrishavarma, saying, "I do not see any other maharathi in the Kuru army except for Karna. That is why your Kaurava army is not going to be able to survive against our maharathis." Grandsire has responded to that message as expected. He has kept his word. I may have to keep his word in the future. Let's see how Goddess Ida helps me at that time.' He spoke very mysteriously. I did not understand anything. He asked me to summon Daruka. Now I realised why he had made sure to bring Daruka, Garudadhwaja and all his horses to Kurukshetra. He said to Daruka, 'Tomorrow you are to groom all the four horses of our Garudadhwaja, feed them well, adorn them and harness them with your own hands to Arjuna's Nandighosha chariot. From tomorrow, I will not feel that I am steering the Nandighosha chariot. I will feel that I am steering my own Garudadhwaja. Duryodhana has not put yjr condition of not bringing the Garudadhwaja chariot and charioteer to Kurukshetra.'

Our commander Dhrishtadyumna's pavilion was very close to my tent. Within the night, the tents for other five regiment leaders were also raised around the pavilion of the commander. After the midnight hour, some kind of commotion was heard from the direction of our commander's pavilion. The commander was standing right at the entrance and actually embracing Duryodhana's brother Yuyutsu. Yuyutsu, who was Dhritarashtra's son born to a maid, had taken the decision of his own accord to leave their side and join hands with the Pandava army. Dhrishtadyumna welcomed him genially.

The first day of the Great War dawned. Commander Bhishma himself stood at the mouth of the crocodile-shaped formation of the Kaurava army, bearing his bow on his shoulder. His thick, white beard was flowing gently in the wind. Behind Grandsire were his mammoth camel and cavalry unit in the shape of a crocodile's midriff. The infantry unit and a few single horse riders were positioned at the tail end of the crocodile.

Except for the white beard resting on his iron armour, no signs of his age were apparent anywhere.

Our Pandava army was also ready under the guidance of Panchala prince Dhrishtadyumna. All five regiment leaders, including me, had taken their places on the battlefield. The yajna pit formation of our army was in position.

Now, two gigantic, continuously roaring oceans of Kaurava and Pandava armies stood facing each other for a blood-thirsty war.

Millions of combative, armed warriors from both sides were awaiting Krishnadeva. As soon as Arjuna's Nandighosha chariot came into sight from a distance, a wave of energy arose in our Pandava army.

As Krishnadeva tugged at the reins in his hands, the four horses responded by raising their front hooves high and neighed loudly. Within a trice, he took the big, auspicious Paanchjanya conch tied to his shawl. From the Nandighosha chariot, master archer Dhananjaya moved his glance over the twenty-five-lakh-strong army that stood in front. And then, suddenly, I saw the Gandiva bow literally slip out of his hands. Not only that, in the next moment, he stopped Krishnadeva from blowing the Paanchjanya conch, shook his head in negation and said something like 'No…no… I cannot fight.' He just sat down at once.

Everyone could see that valiant Arjuna was nervous and literally sitting in the back of the Nandighosha chariot. He was constantly shaking his head in negation and saying something to Krishnadeva. He was seen bringing his palms together in request and pleading. Nobody could understand what kind of drama was unfolding in the Nandighosha. Forty lakh armed warriors from both armies were restlessly waiting. Everyone saw Krishnadeva dropping the reins of his horses. Now he had turned towards dejected and dispirited Arjuna. He had focused his all-encompassing eyes on Arjuna's distressed, teary ones. Krishnadeva was occasionally patting Arjuna's strong shoulders covered in iron armour. At times, he was pointing his index finger towards him and speaking something rapidly.

Almost ten–fifteen minutes had passed. Lakhs of warriors on both sides started getting more anxious. The horses became uncontrollable and started neighing. The elephants swaying in their places started trumpeting. Nobody could understand the sudden cessation of war activity.

Krishnadeva was exhausted trying to boost Arjuna's morale. It had been almost half an hour. He had turned towards the horses again and picked up the reins in his hands. A heart-wrenching suspicion tormented me. Was he going to steer Nandighosha out of the battleground now? I frantically leapt out of my chariot and ran towards Nandighosha. As I approached Nandighosha, Krishnadeva's determined words fell on my ears, 'Keep your mind focused on me. Be my devotee. Bow down only to me. I will emancipate you from every kind of sin.'

Hearing those words of Vasudeva, Arjuna's face lit up like before. His face was again overflowing with the passion of a valiant archer. I clearly heard him saying with resolve while picking up the Gandiva bow, 'Oh Achyuta, your advice has removed all my attachments now. I have become aware of my duty again. I will certainly fight the war as per your wish.' As Krishnadeva heard these words befitting a warrior, his face brightened in a way that I had never seen before.

He signalled me to get into my chariot. Then he determinedly cupped his hands around the big, auspicious Paanchjanya conch and blew it with ultimate resolve and all his might.

The resonating sound was so inspirational that the lakhs of horses from both armies puffed their chests and pricked their ears. The elephants raised their trunks high like war horns and trumpeted excitedly.

As soon as he heard the sound of the Paanchjanya, Grandsire also blew his Ganganabha conch with equal profoundness. Following this, an uproar of mixed sounds of the soldiers' sky-rending peals, weapons, war drums, slogans and animal shouts permeated the atmosphere of Kurukshetra.

The chariots of commander Grandsire Bhishma and Dhrishtadyumna raced forward with flags fluttering atop them.

On the holy land of Kurukshetra, the inferno of an unprecedented great yajna kindled by Krishnadeva, flared up passionately. It was going to evaluate Justice and Injustice, and bring mankind face to face with Truth and Untruth.

Like two catastrophic, hideous and roaring dark clouds clashing against each other, both well-equipped armies finally fell upon each other. Even in such a tumult of war, I could clearly hear the penetrating roar that Bhimsena gave while wielding his heavy mace. The first shock of it was so unbearable that his own charioteer Vishoka got startled. His whole body trembled for a moment. In that fit itself, he propelled Bhimsena's well-equipped chariot in front of everybody else.

First, a fierce battle eclipsing even the sun took place between Duryodhana and him.

Draupadidevi's five youthful sons, who had had no opportunity to showcase their valour so far, started fiercely wedging through the Kaurava army.

From Bhishma's Gangaugha chariot, hundreds of arrows started swiftly swooshing from his flower-bedecked bow that was as tall as him. Their only target was Pandava warrior and master archer Arjuna. First, Arjuna greeted him with a humble bow from a distance. Then he brandished his Gandiva bow in his hands. He twanged its taut bow string once. While doing this, he skilfully dodged Bhishma's arrows by turning his neck around. As if he were respectfully paying homage to the initial eight–ten arrows shot by venerable Grandsire Bhishma. He was indeed Arjuna. He had also acquired the noble virtue of humility. He was a grandson that befitted Grandsire Bhishma.

Now the invincible Gandiva bow in his hands was not going to rest till a clear result was in sight. For the first half an hour, he simply blocked Bhishma's non-stop arrows and rendered them ineffective.

My troop and I had the primary responsibility of protecting the wheels of Arjuna's Nandighosha chariot. Therefore, my chariot was constantly going to be moving around, keeping a keen eye on the pennant of the Nandighosha. I was going to get the opportunity to closely watch all his subtle movements on the battleground. So far, I had closely observed many of his qualities on life's battlefield. Our own maharathi Kritavarma was the first to attack Nandighosha. I blocked him by moving forward with my chariot troop. A fierce fight took place between us.

Duryodhana attacked Bhimsena with years of pent-up rage. Bhimsena overthrew his assault within a short time, just like the ocean in high tide repels the incoming water of a stream. Arjuna's son young Abhimanyu began fighting tenaciously with the experienced Kosala king. Dushasana hounded our handsome Nakula with his arrows. Nakula's body, bloody with Dushasana's arrows, started looking like a blooming palash tree in summer. Krishnadeva deftly steered the Nandighosha chariot within his vicinity. Making wounded Nakula aware of his self, Krishnadeva said from the Nandighosha chariot, 'Nakula … you look exactly as your name suggests. Like a Nakula – a mongoose that has just bitten a snake.

That snake called Dushasana is also biting you like he bit Draupadi. Do not be afraid.' Those words of Krishnadeva worked like magic. Injured Nakula prepared his bow and, within moments, hurled Dushasana's crown into the air and tossed it on the ground with his arrows.

The afternoon of the first day was now on the decline. Commander Grandsire Bhishma began damaging the Pandava army irreparably in front of our eyes. Like the gusty winds of the Mriga constellation thrashing a sprawling mango tree, instantly knocking down hundreds of mangoes, infuriated Grandsire Bhishma started knocking down Pandava soldiers with his unerring arrows. Just as its name denoted, his Gangaugha chariot began moving amidst our Pandava army like the torrent of the Ganga's waters flowing unrestricted through the valleys and mountains of the Himalayas. Abhimanyu, who was enraged to see that, moved forward. With a single arrow, he broke the pennant of the chariot of Kritavarma, who was covering Grandsire Bhishma. He restrained Shalya with five arrows. Shooting a Sannathparva arrow, he cut off the head of Durmukha's charioteer. He shot a Jidma arrow and broke Kripacharya's bow unerringly. That broke the wall of protection around Grandsire.

Watching the breath-taking valour of young Abhimanyu, Grandsire Bhishma stood still for a moment in his chariot. Throwing an admiring glance at Abhimanyu, he exclaimed, 'Bless you Partha's son, gallant Abhimanyu, victory to you.' During this time, he had moved nimbly and rendered many arrows coming from various directions ineffective by bearing them on his iron armour.

On the left of Grandsire, a fierce battle was going on between Virata's son Uttara and Madra king Shalya. Uttara was sitting in a canopied seat on a giant elephant. The army of the Viratas was fighting behind him. Uttara's elephant grabbed Shalya's charioteer in his trunk, whirled him in a circular motion and threw him away. From the broken chariot, Shalya shot a snake-like iron arrow at Uttara. It tore the iron armour on Uttara's chest and pierced his heart. He collapsed from the back of the elephant, squirmed in pain and died. His death caused chaos in our army.

Uttara's brother Shweta attacked Shalya furiously. Jayatsena, Rukmaratha and Anuvinda blocked him. A fight broke out between Grandsire Bhishma, who had come to assist Shalya, and Uttara's brother Shweta.

Virata's son valiant Shweta performed a remarkable feat of valour on this day on behalf of the Pandavas. First, he broke the bow of the Kaurava commander Bhishma – the disciple of invincible master archer Parashurama. That got the Pandava soldiers excited and they let out slogans of 'Hail Virata's son Shweta – victory to you'. Those slogans infuriated Grandsire Bhishma. He picked up another bow. In the very first attack, he killed all the horses of Shweta's chariot. Then, with an arrow, he beheaded Shweta's charioteer too. Injured Shweta launched a very potent shakti at Bhishma. Bhishma recognised it unmistakably and shot eight arrows in such a formation that they confined that shakti and rendered it useless on the ground.

Evening was approaching now. The splendid disc of the sun touched the western horizon. A few moments before the end of the first day of battle, Bhishmacharya shot Virata's son Shweta with a shining arrow charged with Brahma mantra. It pierced Shweta's chest and he collapsed dead in his chariot. The sun set and the day's battle came to an end.

The elongated evening shadows of the second day stretched on Kurukshetra. Many generations of Kshatriyas had regarded this place as auspicious and offered charities on the day of the solar eclipse after bathing in the suryakunda there. Every year, on the day of the solar eclipse, countless charity-offering platforms were raised along the shore of the lake. In the same place, today many rows of funeral pyres were prepared by troops on both sides. The Viratas had prepared two elevated sandalwood funeral pyres for Uttara and Shweta. The aged Matsya king Virata had to ignite the funeral pyres of his valiant sons. The reflection of the blazing funeral pyres along the shore of the lake made the lake itself look like it was on fire.

After dinner, a meeting of the seven regiment leaders, rathis, atirathis and maharathis and the Panadavas was arranged in Krishnadeva's capacious pavilion.

With a crestfallen, gloomy expression, the eldest Pandava Yudhishthira said to Krishnadeva, 'If Grandsire keeps slaughtering the Pandava army like this, our defeat is certain.' Krishnadeva smiled on hearing that. He said to Yudhishthira, 'Dharma, do not give up just yet. Do not worry. We will lose some battles for sure, but the ultimate victory will certainly be ours. Our army has warriors like maharathi Satyaki, valiant Virata and courageous Dhrishtadyumna.'

Hearing those reassuring words, all assembled warriors bowed to him devotedly. I could not resist asking, 'Is the Panchala prince Dhrishtadyumna going to remain our commander tomorrow too?' He smiled again. 'The valiant commander of an army never changes until he falls on the battleground. My guess is that the Kauravas will follow the same. Grandsire Bhishma's grit is not stagnant. He has the experience that comes with age. Everyone should boldly stand ground against his impeccable arrows. Right now, I am thinking of only one thing – how to face him tomorrow.'

I noticed something that many had missed. There was not a single scratch on Krishnadeva's body. By declaring himself to be an unarmed charioteer, he had secured himself completely, according to the rules of engagement. No one, including Duryodhana, had realised the genius of his intellect.

The third day dawned. Our commander Dhrishtadyumna arranged our army in the Krauncharuna, or heron, formation.

Grandsire Bhishma arranged the Kuru army in the arrow formation. At the triangular tip of this arrow, Duryodhana himself stood on the right of Commander Bhishma along with his ten brothers.

Raising thick and crooked eyebrows, he threw a contemptuous glance at the heron bird of our army and roared, 'Oh Kuru warriors. Today, we will pierce the heart of this worthless heron of the Pandavas.' Bhimsena, Abhimanyu, Dhrishtadyumna, Virata and I attacked Grandsire but he confined all of us in one place with rapid-fire arrows. He cast a trap of seven Naracha arrows around me. I broke it with much effort. He separated the two impenetrable parts of the beak of our Krauncharuna formation. Our chariot warriors and horse riders began retreating. Master archer Arjuna, who was watching all this from a distance, got enraged. He said to Krishnadeva, 'Vasudeva, now you must take Nandighosha right in front of Grandsire.'

It was the same Arjuna who had earlier been tormented by the thought of shooting deadly arrows at Grandsire Bhishma. Krishnadeva smiled naughtily and asked, 'Dhananjaya, are you sure?'

'Yes, certainly. Otherwise those five warriors will not stand a chance in front of Grandsire.'

A fierce battle ensued between Grandsire Bhishma and Arjuna. Duryodhana, Shalya, Jayadratha and Shakuni came to assist Grandsire. There was now a crowd of fights between pairs of chariots on the battlefield near Grandsire. Hundreds of arrows littered around on the land of Kurukshetra. Injured and dead soldiers on both sides lay amidst them. Great archer Dhananjaya stood his ground like a mountain, fighting against four great warriors, including Grandsire.

Gallant Abhimanyu was besieged by many, including Duryodhana. Seeing him in trouble, Krishnadeva steered the Nandighosha chariot closer to Abhimanyu. Arjuna showered rains of arrows from his Gandiva bow to free his son. It made Duryodhana and the others flee helter-skelter. The sun soon set on the horizon of Kurukshetra.

After dinner, as usual, our meeting was arranged in Krishnadeva's pavilion. Master archer Arjuna started explaining the next day's crescent-moon formation to all of us. Suddenly, our surveillance team leader Vaayusena entered the pavilion and presented an important piece of news that he had picked up from the pavilion of the Kaurava commander.

'Duryodhana rebuked Commander Bhishma severely in the Kaurava camp: "Lakhs of Kuru soldiers got killed within two days. We made you the commander because you are senior and have experience. You have not demonstrated any real valour yet. You are partial to the Pandavas. You are not being fierce enough with them on purpose." Thus, he clearly accused Grandsire with sharp, humiliating words.

'On hearing that, Bhishma, who was humiliated and angry, furiously took a vow that "Tomorrow I will compel unarmed Srikrishna, the Lord of Dwaraka, to hold a weapon in his hands. Or else I will die on the battlefield."

'Once the Lord of Dwaraka holds a weapon in his hands, Duryodhana is planning to raise a hue and cry that "A rule of engagement has been broken. Srikrishna, who is supposed to be an unarmed participant of the war, has held a weapon in his hands. Now he is disqualified to enter the battlefield. He should be removed from his position as the charioteer of Arjuna's Nandighosha."'

On hearing that news, our council became utterly solemn. Kurukshetra without Krishnadeva meant clear defeat for us. No one could even imagine that.

Baffled Arjuna said, 'In my opinion, Srikrishna should not enter the battlefield at all tomorrow. Then taking up a weapon will be out of question.' Many people seconded him. All knew very well that Grandsire's promise was like a promise carved in stone.

But Krishnadeva was calm.

After some time, he said, 'I will see how to handle Bhishma's promise. You get back to the daily preparations of war as usual. Have a good night's sleep. Hail Goddess Ida.' He concluded the meeting at that.

The day was yet to break. The Kaurava commander today looked like the Sun god dispersing thousands of rays. His face was emitting a glow of determination. With all the warriors, he walked to the battlefield to survey the disciplined formation of his army. Under the command of Grandsire, the Kaurava army had gathered in a Garuda formation – the shape of an eagle, the king of birds. The most vital part of this eagle was its beak at the foremost end, where Bhishma would be standing. This formation of Grandsire's army was indeed ingenious, impenetrable and aggressive.

With his warriors, Grandsire walked through the throat of the eagle formation, both its wings and came into its abdomen. He said to Duryodhana, who stood there, 'Suyodhana, today I will compel Krishna to break his vow. Then it will be up to you to see how to drive him out of the battlefield. Once he leaves the battleground, victory will certainly be yours.' Hearing that, Duryodhana's chest puffed up with pride and he insanely ranted, 'If that happens, Grandsire, then I am going to send the sinful Pandavas to the forest again, without playing any game of dice. This time I am going to send them even beyond the Himalayas.'

Grandsire put his arm around his shoulders and, smiling weakly, said, 'As per my information, the Pandavas are going to structure the army in the shape of a crescent moon. Think about how you can eclipse that moon. I am telling you firmly that as long as Vasudeva is on the side of the Pandavas, it is going to be highly impossible for you to gain victory.'

While talking to everyone, Grandsire came to the tail end of the eagle formation. Here, Shalya was a bit upset. He had left the Madra kingdom to join the Pandavas. But Duryodhana had intercepted him and offered him countless gifts, and with his sweet words convinced him to join the Kaurava side. In yesterday's council, Duryodhana had instructed Grandsire to keep him at the tail end of the Kuru army.

The Kaurava army of Duryodhana was full of rifts. I did not have the slightest doubt that Krishnadeva was astutely going to take advantage of these rifts. Krishnadeva steered Arjuna's chariot, overflowing with weapons, and brought it to the centre of the Pandava army. We surveyed the crescent-moon shape of our army, which had two edges – one on the inside and one on the outside.

The distinctive feature of this crescent-moon shape was its two end points facing each other. If agile, expert war soldiers were posted at both these endpoints, then at the right time they could be brought together by the commander's orders and our whole army could swallow any bird entirely, whether it was a hawk, a vulture or an eagle.

As the radiant sun disc appeared on the horizon, Krishnadeva held his head high and blew the divine Paanchjanya. Bhishma and Drona were unyielding today. They strongly tried breaking open the crescent-moon formation but Bhimsena and Ghatotkacha overthrew them effortlessly. Then furious Duryodhana came forward. He covered Ghatotkacha under a shower of arrows. As Bhima could not see his son anywhere, he got furious and lost his temper.

He shot a powerful arrow at Duryodhana's chest. It penetrated his iron armour and pierced his chest. Duryodhana's flower-bedecked bow slipped from his wounded hands. He lost consciousness and collapsed in his chariot. Seeing their leader collapse, the terrified Kaurava army started running helter-skelter. Raising both his hands, Dushasana tried to stop them in vain. His charioteer pulled aside unconscious Duryodhana's huge chariot.

Abhimanyu and I infiltrated Shakuni's Gandhara army, shouting war slogans. Master archer Arjuna's army was supporting us strongly.

By this time, Duryodhana's charioteer had brought him back to consciousness. The moment he regained consciousness, Duryodhana roared, 'Where is that gluttonous Pandava? Why are our soldiers running away like this?' As the charioteer made him aware of the situation, he composed himself. Hastily racing his chariot through his army, raising both his hands, he howled at the top of his lungs, addressing his soldiers, 'You cowards, where are you running? I am your master. Don't you feel ashamed of running away like this, leaving me unconscious? Come back and fight.' His howling made his soldiers stop and come back with their weapons. Duryodhana sighed in relief and commanded his charioteer to take the chariot right in front of Grandsire and Drona.

He admonished Grandsire in harsh words, saying, 'Grandsire, despite phenomenal archers like you and Acharya Drona being present in our army, terrified soldiers are running everywhere. Do you think that is right? Are you really fighting for me or just pretending to do so? Watching my soldiers run away, I am convinced that you are the advocate of the Pandavas. Both of you are not fighting from the bottom of your hearts today. Every action of yours is full of charade. Your body is in my service but your heart longs for the Pandavas.

'Grandsire, if you would have told me this right at the beginning, I would have appointed Karna as the commander. I would not have faced such humiliation then.'

Grandsire Bhishma remained calm despite Duryodhana's harsh words. 'Stop talking nonsense. Bhishma's vow is like an indelible line carved on the black boulder of Time.'

Grandsire Bhishma commanded his charioteer sternly to take his chariot directly in front of Arjuna's. Indomitable Bhishma's arrows unerringly killed my charioteer. He collapsed on the battlefield from his seat. My chariot was now stuck in one place. Furthermore, seeing my charioteer getting killed, many charioteers in my chariot troop protecting Arjuna's chariot started running away. Bhishma grabbed this opportunity and commanded the chariot warriors behind him to besiege Nandighosha. Furious master archer Arjuna was telling Krishnadeva, 'Take the chariot forward. No one can stand against me.' Saying thus, he showered a rain of arrows on Bhishma.

That offensive attack of Arjuna provoked Bhishma.

After all, in his eyes, our master archer Arjuna was just a youngster. Bhishma's face started looking like a tempestuous ocean at the time of a catastrophe. He began tossing the heads of Arjuna's soldiers in the air like balls. The Kaurava commander was indeed proving his epithet Bhishma, meaning 'ghastly'.

Grandsire Bhishma made Arjuna drop his bow in the chariot itself by showering arrows at him. Disabled by Bhishma's arrows, which had pierced his body at many places, Arjuna leaned against the flagpole of Nandighosha and slid down as he lost consciousness. Chaos erupted in his division. Krishnadeva had no choice but to get down from Nandighosha. Meanwhile, I had found another charioteer and come closer to Nandighosha to help Arjuna. My foremost duty was to bring Arjuna back to consciousness. For that, I made him sniff divine herbs. He regained his consciousness. As soon as he came around, he asked, 'Where is Krishna?' We began looking everywhere on the battlefield. There, even in Grandsire's mind, a commotion ensued as he could not see Krishnadeva anywhere on the Nandighosha chariot. He had dropped his bow and stopped shooting arrows. He was also asking his charioteer, 'Where is Krishna?' He had also got out of his chariot on to the battlefield.

Krishnadeva saw Bhishma walking slowly towards him. The moment he saw Bhishma, he picked up a chariot wheel lying on the battlefield and furiously rotated it using both his palms. He tossed it in the air for a moment and caught it in both his hands again. When he was about to rush fiercely towards Bhishma, Arjuna, who was walking next to me, leapt forward and grabbed his feet in his arms. 'Achyuta. Please do not use this chakra.' Krishnadeva balanced the chakra in his hands and looked smilingly at Arjuna.

Looking at Bhishma standing still in front of him, Krishnadeva smiled and dropped the chariot wheel on the ground. Spreading both his arms wide, he held Grandsire Bhishma, who was the first to unmistakably recognise him and address him with the epithet 'Vasudeva', in a deep embrace.

Both great men separated from each other without speaking a single word.

At that moment, the sun set on the western horizon of Kurukshetra. The battle stopped. Both great men started walking calmly towards their pavilions.

That night, in the meeting that took place in Krishnadeva's pavilion, the only thing discussed was the formation of our army for the next day.

Duryodhana, on the other hand, was loudly telling his commander, 'That cowherd has broken his promise. Send a messenger promptly to his pavilion and reprimand him that he has broken the rule of engagement and hence has been removed from his position as Arjuna's charioteer. Rising from the elevated seat of the commander and patting his muscular shoulders as an elder, Grandsire said to him, 'Duryodhana, you can still stop this catastrophic, atrocious war. Neither you nor any of your brothers, and no one of whatever is remaining of our army, can be compared to Srikrishna even remotely. You are making a mistake in understanding him. Compose and control yourself. Srikrishna has not broken any rule. He had held a chariot wheel in his hands – not a weapon. Why did he even do that? Only I can understand it. By holding it, he allowed me to keep my promise. That, too, without breaking his own promise. That is why I am telling you firmly for the last time as your elder – stop this war now. Return the kingdom of Indraprastha to the Pandavas. Only then will that cowherd go back to Dwaraka. But he will do so only after sending us Kauravas to Hastinapura and the Pandavas to Indraprastha.' It was impossible for Duryodhana to accept this.

As per precise instructions of Commander Bhishma, the Kaurava army was ready at dawn in the formation of a bull, ready to attack. Bhishma himself stood at the end of its tapering mouth. When our spies brought in news about the bull formation, Krishnadeva advised Commander Dhrishtadyumna to lay out the Pandava army in the formation of an elephant. With its head tilted forward, this elephant stood ready to slam into anyone that approached.

Amidst the cacophony of war drums, a gruesome battle ensued. Grandsire Bhishma's chariot, surrounded by the chariots of Drona, Duryodhana, Balhika, Durmarshana and Jayadratha, sped forward. All of them attacked Arjuna. Five warriors besieged gallant Abhimanyu. Dhrishtadyumna beheaded the son of King Chala, which wreaked havoc on that side. Chala and Shalya, with each other's support, surrounded Dhrishtadyumna and broke his bow. Seeing Dhrishtadyumna unarmed, valiant Abhimanyu promptly came to support him. He confined Shalya with his swift arrows. Duryodhana steered the elephants of Jayadratha's Sindhu troops to assist Shalya. His loud war cries blended with the trumpeting sounds of the elephants raising their trunks high – 'Attack … trample the troops of Abhimanyu, Dhrishtadyumna and destroy them.'

Bhimsena realised that Abhimanyu would not be able to hold it against the elephantry of Duryodhana and descended from his chariot. He swung the gold-plated heavy iron mace around his head and so skilfully and quickly struck the temple of any elephant that approached him that many elephants who bore the strike went wild and turned back. In all that commotion, no one realised where Duryodhan was lost.

Bhima saw eight sons of Dhritarashtra moving forward in chariots to confront him. As soon as the eight brothers of Duryodhana came within sight, Bhimsena continuously shot arrows at them with lightning speed. They all fell just the way ripened mangoes fall from the tree in the hot summer wind.

Seeing not one but eight of his brothers killed, Duryodhana got furious and attacked Bhima. A potent shakti arrow hit Bhima and he took support of the flagpole to sit down. Seeing his father unconscious for the first time, Hidimba's son Ghatotkacha came to his assistance. He spread terror in Duryodhana's army using his demonic illusive technique of war. At that time, Bhishma said to Duryodhana, 'Kaurava, the rakshasas are most powerful in the evening. Ghatotkacha is from the rakshasa family. The sun is setting now. So stop the war.'

Duryodhana stopped the war according to Grandsire's instruction. The fourth day of the war was over. Krishnadeva helped Bhimsena recover using his medicinal herbs.

At night, as usual, our council took place in Krishnadeva's pavilion. Our surveillance presented news that he had picked up from Bhishma's pavilion. Grandsire Bhishma was going to arrange the Makara or crocodile, formation again tomorrow for the fifth day of the war.

Krishnadeva gave instructions to Bhimsena and other regiment leaders about how to arrange the army in the Shyena hawk formation tomorrow. He wrapped up that day's meeting a bit sooner. As others left, he asked me to stay back. 'Yadava commander, do you have any idea how many soldiers we have lost in the war so far?' This question was unexpected. I answered, 'No sire, no idea.'

He got up from his seat, put his arm around my shoulder and said, 'About fifteen lakh soldiers have got received a hero's death in battle. What must their families, their wives be feeling? Sakha Satyaki, in a war, we lose control over everything. The end result of the war is only whatever is agreeable to Kala – Time. You must act in a way befitting of a Yadava commander tomorrow in the hawk formation of our army. Go now, and have a good night's sleep.'

I wondered why he had addressed me as 'sakha' and I thought it must be because I was closest to him amongst all the commanders. The fifth day dawned. At the sound of Krishnadeva's Paanchjanya, the hawk of our army collided against the crocodile of the Kaurava army. Along with my ten gallant sons, five on my right and five on my left, I attacked Bhurishrava. His brothers Bhuri and Shala were protecting him. This Bhurishrava was the son of Somadutta.

He was the grandson of the great Kuru Balhika and nephew of Grandsire Bhishma himself. He was a gutsy and invincible Kuru warrior in the duel of swords.

A tenacious bow-and-arrow fight ensued between my sons and Bhurishrava and his brothers. With my chariot at the centre, my ten sons kept fighting without getting tired. Within moments they encircled Bhurishrava. My sons were determined to kill Bhurishrava but his skilled archer brothers Bhuri and Shala offered him strong protective cover. A while later, infuriated Bhurishrava commanded both his brothers to move aside and sprinted forward. He was not only an invincible swordsman but also an expert archer, well trained by Grandsire Bhishma himself. He acutely shot ten rapid-fire Sarpamukha arrows in quick succession at my ten sons. Those arrows pierced the chest of one, the neck of another and directly pierced the heads of some. My ten valiant sons collapsed one by one. I was benumbed for a moment to witness that carnage. My heart, a father's heart, was shattered into a hundred pieces.

Controlling the tears in my eyes, I put down the head of my eldest son on the battleground. Around him, soldiers had arranged the heads of my other nine sons. I looked at each son's face for the last time. I intensely felt that at that moment I needed Srikrishnadeva, the Lord of Dwaraka, to console me. But he was at the other end, on the other wing of the hawk, with Arjuna, who was fighting with Dronacharya.

'Bhurishrava, you scoundrel, this Yadava commander, Satyaka's son Satyaki declares that I will not rest until I kill you on the battlefield today. Hail Idamata.' I held my bow and mounted my chariot.

In a fit of fury, I collided my chariot with Bhurishrava's and destroyed his chariot wheels first. His chariot broke. With the thought that as long as he was holding the bow and arrow in his hands, it was fair to hit him with an arrow as per the rules of war, I told my charioteer to circle around his chariot. Bhurishrava realised my intention and immediately dropped his bow. Holding a bare sword in his hand, he jumped on to the battleground. Challenging me to a sword duel, he said, 'I have already killed your ten sons. You are the eleventh one, dear friend of the runaway leader of the savage Yadavas; you coward, who claims to be a gallant commander.'

Hearing those words, my entire body seethed. It did not bother me that he had called me a coward, it did not bother me that he had called the Yadavas savage – I could not stand the fact that he had called my beloved Krishnadeva a 'runaway'.

I challenged him fiercely, 'You descendant of the Kuru dynasty – a cajoler of Duryodhana, who gave the loathsome command of undressing a royal lady in her menses in a crowded hall – today, with the corpses of the ten sons that you killed as my witnesses, I will teach you a lesson.' A duel took place. It continued even when the sun was about to set.

Suddenly, blood-soaked Bhimsena emerged, holding his mace on his shoulder and stood between us like a mountain. Our duel came to a halt. Bhurishrava could not strike Bhimsena as he was holding a mace and both of them did not have the same weapon in their hands. Bhimsena patted my back, saying, 'Let's go, commander.' The sun set. The battle had ended for the day.

While returning to my pavilion in Bhimsena's chariot, I realised why Krishnadeva had asked me to wait last night. Why he had called me 'sakha' with so much affection.

As I was mourning the death of my sons, I did not attend the nightly meeting in Krishnadeva's pavilion. Benumbed, I stayed in mine.

Around midnight, Krishnadeva himself came to meet me in my pavilion, along with a Yadava soldier holding a torch.

Seeing him in person, my heart ached with the agony of the death of my sons. Yet, I stood in my place to show him respect.

Without saying a word, he opened both his arms and held me in a deep embrace. The warm tears flowing from my eyes went streaming down his back. Just the touch of his hand had gently calmed my heart.

On the sixth day of the war, the Kuru commander organised his army in the Krauncha – heron-formation. In response to that, Dhrishtadyumna arranged the Pandava army in the shape of an arrow. Duryodhana was hell-bent on destroying Bhimsena. Bhimsena had killed more than twenty of Duryodhana's brothers. Within moments, along with ten of his brothers, he besieged Bhimsena's chariot. Bhimsena jumped on to the battleground brandishing his huge mace. Dhrishtadyumna approached to support Bhimsena. He used an astra called Sammohanastra for the first time in the war. The arrows he shot released such torrents of smoke that the sons of Dhritarashtra lost consciousness after inhaling them and collapsed one after the other. They lay motionless. Dronacharya came to their assistance. Launching Prajnastra with the first set of arrows, he dissipated the smoke. With the next set of arrows, he dispersed a fragrance of divine herbs and brought Duryodhana's brothers back to consciousness. Mighty mace warrior Bhima and Pandava commander Dhrishtadyumna could not face Dronacharya, who was possessed by the war spirit, for long. They called Arjuna's young son Abhimanyu for help.

Evening was approaching, so Bhurishrava caught hold of a wide-bladed bare sword and got down from his chariot. Throwing me a challenge of a sword duel again, he shouted, 'You were saved yesterday because of Bhimsena. Let me see who comes to save you today.' Hearing the electrifying sounds of the clanging of our swords, the soldiers around us stopped fighting and assumed the role of spectators. Both our bodies were bathed in blood. Severely wounded, I knelt down on the battleground. My sword had slipped out of my hands and fallen at a distance. Bhurishrava raised his blood-soaked sword to behead me while I was unarmed. I realised what was going to happen the next moment. Closing my eyes, I remembered Krishnadeva, whom I had followed like a shadow and served my whole life. Bhurishrava's sword was going to fall upon my neck and cut my head off any moment. That moment passed. I heard a loud thud on the ground and opened my eyes. Krishnadeva was standing in front of me in the Nandighosha chariot, holding the whip in his hand just the way I had envisioned him. In the back of the chariot, Arjuna stood smiling at me with the Gandiva bow in his hand. He had shot a potent Chandramukha arrow and cut off Bhurishrava's raised arm holding the sword, with which he was about to cut off my head. That day I returned to my pavilion in the Nandighosha chariot.

In our nightly meeting, we heard that Duryodhana had created a big scene in the Kuru camp. He had raised the objection that Arjuna had broken a rule of engagement by shooting an arrow at Bhurishrava from behind. He wanted a royal envoy to be promptly dispatched to the Pandava camp to force him to retire from the war.

Bhishma listened to his tantrums calmly for a long time and then answered, 'When ten sons of Dhritarashtra first surrounded Bhimsena who was alone and started a group mace, that itself was against the rules of engagement. You yourself led that attack, Duryodhana. Would you be the first one to retire from the war? Besides, Bhurishrava was going to kill an unarmed Satyaki. Did Arjuna not stop him from breaking that rule?' Hearing that, an upset Duryodhana left the meeting in frustration.

Yudhishthira organised our army in the Vajra formation with the assistance of Dhrishtadyumna on the seventh day of war. This formation was in the shape of the well-known Vajra weapon of Indra, the king of Gods. In response to that, Grandsire had arranged the Kuru army in a Mandal formation – in the shape of a circle.

At the frontal serrated sharp edge of our Vajra formation, Bhimsena's son Ghatotkacha and I stood guard. Behind us, in the central part of the Vajra, Matsya king Virata and Panchala king Drupad stood guard with Arjuna and the army. The tail end of the Vajra was occupied by warriors such as Arjuna's son Iravana, Chekitana, Nakula and Sahadeva. Bhimsena was going to guard the edges of the Vajra moving throughout the army, roaring loudly in his chariot.

Our army's Vajra fell upon Grandsire's Mandal with a roaring sound. From amongst the leading Kauravas, Bakasura's brother, rakshasa

Alambusha, collided with me and Ghatotkacha. Alambusha was proficient in the deceptive war technique of the rakshasas. In a moment, he was seen on the east side and in the next moment he would appear on the west side. Our fight went on resolutely till noon.

Realising that the tenacious fighter, Narakasura's son Bhagadutta, was getting out of control, Ghatotkacha shot a Mayavee Shakti at him. Asura son Bhagadutta broke it into three pieces and dropped them on the battlefield. Terrified, Ghatotkacha left the battlefield and started running towards the camp. The sun of the seventh day set, witnessing Bhima's son running away from the battlefield.

A detailed account of the daily encounters on various battlefields was being reported daily to Hastinapura, Dwaraka and the royal cities of other kingdoms. In Hastinapura, it was first conveyed to Kuru minister Sanjaya – the charioteer chief. He would then convey it to Maharaja Dhritarashtra and Gandharidevi with detailed descriptions. So far about forty sons of Dhritarashtra had been killed. Most of them were killed by Bhimsena alone. Maharaja Dhritarashtra would tremble with anger and curse Bhima.

The eighth and ninth days of war witnessed sky-high valour by Bhishma alone.

Bhishma had performed incredible feats of valour in the last eight days, destroying lakhs of Pandava soldiers. But except for the death of Virata's sons Uttara and Shweta, none of the prominent Pandava warriors had been killed. That is why Bhishma himself was dissatisfied with his performance as commander. The sound of his conch was so terrifying on the eighth day that just on hearing it, Krishnadeva surmised that no one would be able to control Grandsire that day. And that is exactly what happened. In just one day, by evening, along with maharathis like Dronacharya, Duryodhana, Susharma and Bhagadutta, Grandsire slaughtered thousands of soldiers of the Pandavas. Terrified by the thought that if Grandsire was not controlled, the Pandava army would be annihilated, all four brothers of Arjuna gathered around his chariot. Yudhishthira pleaded to Krishnadeva, 'Oh Great Yadava, now only you can save the Pandava army.'

Krishnadeva brought the Nandighosha chariot in front of Grandsire's Gangaugha.

Krishnadeva was astounded to see master archer Dhananjaya standing idle, just holding his Gandiva bow in his hands. Krishnadeva reminded him, 'Partha, have you forgotten my advice given before the commencement of the war so soon? Are you afraid of Grandsire's potent arrows or what is it?'

Arjuna simply shook his head. He had got confused again. He was debilitated due to his attachment. Krishnadeva resolutely said to him, 'Fine then. For the sake of Grandsire, I broke my vow of not holding any weapon in my hands. It seems that I will have to break it again for you.'

Putting down the reins in his hand, the Lord of Dwaraka held the whip in his hand and leapt down.

Arjuna was baffled now. He, too, left his Gandiva bow in the chariot and jumped down. Spreading both arms and blocking Krishnadeva's way he pleaded, 'Hrishikesha, wait! Please do not break your vow. Tomorrow I will fight with Grandsire determinedly.' The sun had set on the ninth day on the battleground of Kurukshetra.

Grandsire watched the commotion that went on between Krishnadeva and Arjuna with a smile.

Krishnadeva wrapped up the night council quickly.

As all Pandavas were leaving the pavilion, he said, 'Arjuna, wait. I want to talk to you about something.'

Arjuna was preparing himself for a severe admonition. 'Do not worry. I am not going to ask you about your confusion. Just go to the royal ladies' camp right away and ask sakhi Draupadi to meet me.'

I was also about to leave, wondering, 'What could a woman do in war?' He stopped me and said, 'Sakha Satyaki, you have to wait for some time. You have to fulfil a duty – as a Yadava commander.'

In the Kaurava camp, an infuriated Duryodhana had stormed into Kuru commander Bhishma's pavilion in a frenzy along with Shakuni and Dushasana. He had only one question – why had the Grandsire left a confused Arjuna alive? Speaking in his usual haughty way, he asked, 'Grandsire, is this a war or just an entertaining cock fight going on? It has been nine days. Bhima and Arjuna have slaughtered more than half our army. More than fifty of my brothers have died on the battlefield. But not a single Pandava has got even a scratch of an arrow. What is this?

Have you forgotten your duty as a commander due to your love for the Pandavas? Or is this just a stroke of bad luck for me? I have come here to request you that if you cannot give up your love for the Pandavas, then resign from commandership. Then we can summon world conqueror Karna and appoint him as our commander. I am confident that he will bring victory to us for sure. What should I do? Please feel free to speak your mind openly.'

Bhishma was saddened. He advised Duryodhana with extreme patience, 'Duryodhana, you are making a mistake in recognising Krishna and Arjuna. You have forgotten that I myself have addressed Krishna as "Vasudeva". As an experienced elder, I am telling you, return the Indraprastha kingdom to the Pandavas. That will be beneficial for all.'

Discarding Grandsire's advice, Duryodhana said, 'That time is well past. I have lost more than half my army in war. Are you going to resign as the commander or are you going to wholeheartedly fight for the undoubted victory of the Kauravas?'

This was rather too much for this master of the Brahmastra. Bhishma said very calmly and determinedly, 'Tomorrow, I will annihilate all Pandavas. Else, I will offer my own body as a sacrifice in the yajna of this war. You may go now.'

After all, it was 'Bhishma's vow'. It could not remain a secret for long. Riding on the winds, it reached Krishnadeva's pavilion. I noticed that on hearing that news, he became restless like never before.

The midnight of the ninth day was approaching. Draupadidevi, who had received the message through Arjuna, arrived. As soon as he saw her, Deva said in his usual loving tone, 'Sakhi Draupadi, at this moment, you have to carry out a big task to protect your husbands and the Pandava army. You have to leave immediately with our Satyaki to meet Kuru commander Grandsire Bhishma. Take only one precaution while going there. Make sure that your face is covered with your shawl while seeking Grandsire's blessings. Due to old age, he will not be able to see your face clearly in the dim light of the torches. You have to take only one precaution - not to speak a single word before he says anything to you. Do not forget to make the clear tingling sound of your golden bangles when you bend down to seek his blessings. Once he speaks, you will automatically know what to say next.'

I left with Draupadidevi towards the pavilion of Kuru commander Grandsire Bhishma. I was given strict instructions to wait outside the pavilion and tell Grandsire's guard that 'a lady wishes to meet Grandsire'.

The chirping sounds of crickets echoed around the battleground of Kurukshetra. The hooting of owls could be heard in between. Far away, the cries of jackals and wolves that were clawing at the organs of human bodies were audible. As decided, when we came near Grandsire Bhishma's pavilion, I delivered the message to the guard and waited outside. Draupadidevi covered her face with her shawl and went inside. Bhishma came out from the inner chamber, wondering, 'A lady? To meet me? On the battlefield? Who could she be?' In the dim light of the torches, Draupadidevi scurried and bowed down to seek his blessings, making clear sounds using her golden bangles.

Words of blessing slipped out of Grandsire's mouth, 'May you be a saubhagyavati, fortunate to enjoy married life forever. May you have a long life.'

I pricked up my ears in curiosity to hear what Draupadidevi was going to say now.

Draupadidevi said clearly, 'Grandsire, today itself you have taken a vow to annihilate all Pandavas. And just now you have blessed me to be a saubhagyavati forever. Forgive me if I sound disrespectful, as I am younger to you in age. Which of these is true?'

The gallant warrior smiled pleasantly and said, 'The blessing that I have given you is real. Convey only one message of mine to Krishna, that I am extremely happy that I have given him the perfect epithet of "Vasudeva". Draupadi, this is Bhishma's promise – that you will remain a saubhagyavati forever.

'To keep your husbands safe, tell Krishna only one thing. Take the Panchala son Shikhandi, who has a woman's soul in a man's body, on the Nandighosha chariot tomorrow as Arjuna's protection. The whole world knows that Bhishma, the disciple of Parashurama, the son of Shantanu and Ganga, would never shoot an arrow at a woman.

'Go, Draupadi, the manliness of Shikhandi, whom you and your brothers ridiculed as effeminate, is going to be Arjuna's protective shield tomorrow.' He raised his hand and, with a broad smile on his face, blessed Draupadi.

Draupadidevi, speechless and overwhelmed with emotion, touched the feet of the tall Kuru commander.

I returned to Krishnadeva's pavilion with Draupadidevi. How easily Krishnadeva had found a solution to this impossible problem!

At that hour of midnight, I had to go to Panchala son Shikhandi's pavilion and present him to Krishnadeva. Krishnadeva discussed the details of the next day's battle and advised Shikhandi on how to handle things the next day.

The tenth day of war dawned. While blowing the Paanchjanya conch, Krishnadeva's blue face reddened. Tears collected on the long thick lashes of his fish-shaped eyes. I clearly saw him wipe those tears with the shawl on his chest. Such a thing had not happened with him before.

At the front line of our army, Shikhandi stood with his bow, between Krishnadeva and Arjuna.

An incredibly intense and catastrophic battle ensued between Grandsire Bhishma and Arjuna. Seeing a line of arrows shot by Grandsire targeting Arjuna, iron-armoured Shikhandi would quickly cover Arjuna by putting himself in between. Seeing him in the line of target, Grandsire would lower his bow and stop shooting arrows. Shikhandi grabbed that opportunity unerringly and killed Grandsire's charioteer first with six arrows. With the next set of arrows, he broke Grandsire's pennant and with the third set of arrows, Shikhandi destroyed the Grandsire's bow. That mighty old man quickly picked up another bow. Evening was fast approaching. Only a few fleeting arrows had pierced Arjuna's blue body. When Shikhandi got an opportunity, he pulled them out and threw them on the ground. He quickly put medicinal herbs on the wounds. When the sun touched the western horizon, Arjuna shot two sets of ten different arrows, showering them on Bhishma. Some of those arrows broke through the iron armour and pierced his chest. Grandsire Bhishma, whose bow was destroyed and charioteer was killed, who had many arrows pierced in his valiant body, and who looked like a blood-soaked radiant sun disc on the western horizon, collapsed from his chariot on to the battleground. Seeing him fall, news spread in the Kuru army – Commander Bhishma has fallen.

Soldiers of both armies dropped their weapons to the ground and got around in long lines to take a last look at the aged, gallant commander.

I followed Krishnadeva, along with all the Pandavas, to see Grandsire. He was calmly lying on the bed of shara grass. As soon as he saw Krishnadeva, he said in a feeble voice, 'Come here, Vasudeva. Whatever you wish will happen. Do not worry. I will not leave my body right now.

'Just like you are, I am also a devotee of the sun. I will leave my body only when the sun starts moving towards the summer solstice from the winter solstice.'

Krishnadeva lovingly pressed Grandsire's hand in his and said, 'It will be fifty-six more days till the sun's position moves towards summer solstice.'

Grandsire, who had become feeble due to continuous bleeding, smiled slightly and said, 'You can explain to those present here why this son of Ganga is waiting for that moment. Bestow your grace on me, Vasudeva, of hearing your melodious speech at this moment.'

Krishnadeva said, 'Every human body has two poles – the south and the north. The south pole is in the lower part of the body below the waist. In the north pole of the body is the brain, controlling the seventy-two thousand nadis in the body – the holy abode of the intellect.

'In this north pole of the body is the Brahmarandhra, which has been considered holy by sages. Grandsire wants to draw the vital energy in his lower body from his toes to the crown of his head and unite it with the sun's energy. And he wants to do it only after the sun starts its journey towards summer solstice. Am I correct, oh disciple of Parashurama?'

'Sudarshana, how can you be wrong? Do one thing now. Arrange for my meeting with Karna, who has been sitting inactive in his pavilion for the last ten days because I called him an ardharathi. I have to tell him something in private.'

'As you wish, Grandsire.' Krishnadeva gently let go of his hand and stood up. He put his head on Grandsire's feet for a few moments.

Karna met Grandsire sometime in the night and went back to his pavilion. Neither I nor anybody else ever came to know what both of them conversed about. That was because Grandsire had told the armed guards to go away, and met Karna in complete privacy.

Now maharathi, world conqueror Karna, the master of the Brahmastra was going to participate in the war. He was indeed capable of recovering the loss of military strength in the Kuru army due to Grandsire's fall.

In our nightly meeting, there was a long discussion about doing something before the eleventh day broke and Karna entered the battlefield. As usual, to make me stay behind, he said, 'Sakha Satyaki, you stay here.'

'Commander, take Daruka and the Nandighosha chariot with you and go to the Pandava royal ladies' camp. You have to fetch Aunt Kunti urgently.'

Kunti was just as confused as I was. As soon as she came, she said, 'Krishna, how come my valiant sons need me today when you are present here in person? Is everything fine?'

'Tomorrow, your first-born son Karna will enter the battlefield for the first time. You know as well as I do that none of your five sons will be able to survive in front of his valour.

'He has taken a vow to kill Arjuna. Will you or I be able to live without Arjuna? That is why you have to do one thing, setting aside the pride of a Kshatriya lady.'

'What should I do?' Kuntidevi stuttered.

'Karna has left Kurukshetra to bathe in the Ganga. You will have to catch up with him on the banks of the Ganga as a common supplicant.'

She could not help but ask, 'I have to go to my son as a supplicant?'

'Yes. If you want your five sons, including Arjuna, alive.'

Kuntidevi was lost in thought for some time. Then she made up her mind, looked at me and said, 'Come, Yadava commander, I am ready to go with you.'

I left Rajmata Kuntidevi in her pavilion after she was promised by Karna that he would spare the lives of at least four of her sons, except Arjuna.

Acharya Drona, who was appointed as the new commander during the night, mounted his chariot on the eleventh day.

Duryodhana made a plea that Guru Drona capture Yudhisthira alive.

Gandhara king Shakuni stood behind Duryodhana, fixed his eyes on Drona and said, 'Commander should capture the eldest Pandava alive and present him to us. We will send him to the forest again.'

Guru Drona could not bear Shakuni's senseless rambling and simply ignored him. Yet, he reassured Duryodhana that he would capture Yudhishthira alive. During the night, we had decided that all of us would guard Yudhishthira with our lives.

The eleventh day of war dawned. For the first time, today, Karna had entered the battlefield as the head of the chariot regiment under the leadership of Drona. He looked splendid, like the soaring peak of Mount Kailasa, in his shining pure golden Jaitra chariot embellished with vines and creepers. His fine saffron royal pennant with the emblem of an elephant's chain was fluttering in the wind.

Acharya Drona fell upon Yudhishthira first. As per Krishnadeva's instruction, I went to assist him. Like the God of Death himself, Drona stood in front of Yudhishthira's chariot. The Pandava soldiers who had heard of his vow were terrified and started screaming, 'Eldest Pandava Dharmaraja is surrounded. He is going to be captured now. Drona is going to kill him. Run…help…!'

Hearing their loud bawling, Arjuna pleaded with Krishnadeva to protect his elder brother, 'Madhava, take the chariot in front of Acharya Drona first.'

Krishnadeva had smilingly obeyed his command.

Till Karna, with his potent valour like a latent volcano, was going to move unobstructed in the battlefield, it was dangerous to bring Arjuna in front of him. That is why, through me, he had instructed Bhimsena to strike Karna. It was while witnessing the relentless battle between the two of them that the eleventh day of the war ended.

On the twelfth day, the Sanshaptakas, who had vowed to kill or be killed, besieged Arjuna. Krishnadeva pointed the whip in his hand towards Yudhishthira and ordered me to go there.

Along with Panchala warrior Satyajita and Virata's sons Shatanika and Vasudana, I began fighting with all my might to protect Yudhishthira from Drona. Within moments, Drona had beheaded all three of them in front of my eyes.

Arjuna fought with the Sanshaptakas ferociously and beheaded them all.

Then, Krishnadeva rushed the Nandighosha chariot towards Yudhishthira. Here, Narakasura's son Bhagadutta had surrounded Yudhishthira and confined him from all sides.

Bhagadutta was an asura. His thick, long eyebrows would hang over his eyelashes, covering his eyes. He had tied his eyebrows with a strip of cloth around his forehead to prevent obstruction to his vision.

Krishnadeva was the only one who knew of this weakness. He told Arjuna to tear off that strip of cloth first. Arjuna succeeded in doing that with just one arrow. As the strip of cloth was torn off, Kurukshetra was barely visible to Bhagdutta. Dhananjaya then shot a crescent-moon-shaped arrow at the temple of his elephant. The giant elephant collapsed, and Bhagadutta, who had fallen to the ground, got up and started running.

Arjuna shot one more Chandramukha arrow and beheaded him. Shakuni was furious at that and charged at Arjuna with his staunch Gandhara soldiers. Arjuna launched the Aditya Astra and chased away Shakuni, along with his Gandhara army.

Closer to evening, Karna's Jaitra chariot came in front of Arjuna for the first time that day. Both barely got a chance to shoot arrows at each other before the sun set.

The news that our surveillance chief had gathered from the Kuru camp was indeed alarming. Duryodhana had admonished Commander Drona in front of all, discarding all the proprieties of their sacred relationship, saying, 'Within twelve days, we have lost twelve lakh soldiers and yet not a single Pandava is dead. More than half of my brothers have been killed but not a single Pandava has got even a scratch. You made me a promise that you will capture Yudhishthira alive. Then what is going on? Is this a war or a feast for Vishnuyaga yajna? Oh, Guru Drona ... if your bow is incapable of slaying the Pandavas, then hand over the royal pennant on your royal chariot to Karna tomorrow. We will fight the war our way.'

Guru Drona, who could not bear the harsh words of ignominy, got up from his seat and took a solemn vow, 'Tomorrow, the sun will not set until it witnesses the body of at least one of the Pandavas lying lifeless inside the Chakravyuha.'

Krishnadeva sat quiet in the meeting for a long time. The question was how to break open the extremely complex circles of the wheel formation.

After some time, with a solemn face, the great Yadava ordered me, 'Commander, summon valiant Abhimanyu here.'

I caught up with maharathi Abhimanyu in his pavilion. He had just removed his attire and was resting. I hesitated even while giving the message to that sixteen-year-old young warrior. 'Your Mama has summoned you.' As soon as he heard my words, he promptly got up, saying, 'Let's go, commander'.

As soon as he entered the pavilion, Krishnadeva called him in a voice drenched in love, 'Come, Abhi….' I had never heard Krishnadeva speak in such a voice before.

That perceptive son of Arjuna also instantly realised that his Mama had called him 'Abhi' instead of 'Abhimanyu'. He touched Krishnadeva's feet, held his hands together and stood politely with a smile. Just a year ago, this young son of Arjuna's had got married. His pregnant wife Uttaraa was staying in the ladies' camp.

Noting everyone sitting in silence, Abhimanyu asked, 'Why are you all so quiet? So tense?'

Krishnadeva got up from his elevated seat, put his arm around Abhimanyu's shoulders and said, 'Guru Drona is going to arrange his army in the complicated Chakravyuha tomorrow. The mission of breaking it open …' Even Krishnadeva could not say anything further.

'It would be my honour if that responsibility falls on my shoulders. With blessings from all of you, I will be glad to accept it.' He paid obeisance to all humbly and immediately left the pavilion graciously as he did not have the immodesty of taking a seat among his elders and seniors.

Overwhelmed, I kept staring at his disappearing figure.

The thirteenth day of war became memorable due to the indomitable, sky-high prowess of Abhimanyu. To break open the Chakravyuha that Drona had arranged, Abhimanyu entered along with Bhimsena. Breaking open circle after circle of the enemy's formation, he directly went to the centre of the wheel formation. There, a violent mace fight took place between him and Duryodhana's son Lakshmana. Both of them fell unconscious at the same time. Lakshmana, who regained consciousness first, killed unconscious Abhimanyu with a strike of his mace. Insolent Jayadratha literally kicked dead Abhimanyu to roll his body over. As Arjuna heard about the disgraceful treatment meted out to his son, he took a vow 'to kill Jayadratha by the end of the next day or enter the sandalwood funeral pyre himself.'

On the fourteenth day, the Kurus had taken thorough precautions not to bring the Sindhu king Jayadratha on the battlefield at all.

Arjuna, enraged with the grief of losing his son, was lamenting irately, 'Show me Jayadratha! Where is Jayadratha?' His unarmed charioteer steered his chariot all over the battlefield throughout the day. But in vain …

In the evening, according to his solemn vow, Arjuna ascended the sandalwood funeral pyre. He took advantage of the clearing of the eclipse, looked precisely in the direction that Krishnadeva pointed his forefinger at and shot an arrow, which beheaded insolent Jayadratha.

Due to the unanticipated killing of Jayadratha, all Kuru warriors, including Drona, Kripa, Karna, Ashwatthama and Duryodhana, were furious. That was the beginning of the night wars. Karna, who was surrounded by the Pandavas on all sides, began showering them with arrows. Yudhishthira, who had been defeated and chased away by him, stood in front of Drona. Nakula faced Shakuni. Arjuna and Karna came face to face for the first time that day – that, too, in a night war.

Karna was familiar with night war too. He shot at Arjuna over and over again. Bhima, Arjuna, Yudhishthira, Dhrishtadyumna and I – none of us could hold our ground in front of him. Terrified, Yudhishthira was asking every warrior, 'Is this Radheya going to spare anyone from our army till morning or not? Or is he going to turn it into a silent river of blood like River Drishadwati?' If Karna was not stopped, the Pandava army would not be able to see the next day.

Dhrishtadyumna and I, along with the four Pandavas, approached Arjuna's chariot. Joining our palms together, we pleaded charioteer Krishnadeva, 'Oh Yogayogeshwara, do whatever is required but please stop Karna.'

He called Bhimsena. Since we were engaged in a night war, there was no time for a secret meeting. The Lord of Dwaraka spoke loudly and said to Bhimsena, 'Tell your son Ghatotkacha to confront Karna with his rakshasa army.'

Bhimsena found him and mounted his chariot. Both father and son approached Karna. Their massive chariot with fourteen hefty, dark black horses looked ghastly. That blood-red rakshasa pennant was decorated with wet intestine garlands. Ghatotkacha, with conical ears, big, beady eyes, thick eyebrows and a hairy stomach, looked frightening.

Ghatotkacha roared, 'Hail Hidimbamata!' A breathtaking night battle ensued between Karna, shielded by rakshasa Alayudha at the frontline, and Ghatotkacha, covering Bhimsena. Finally, at midnight, Ghatotkacha slew Alayudha in a horrifying, violent way. Then the panic-stricken Kuru army began wailing in fear, raising their arms in the air, 'Oh world conqueror Karna, the king of Anga, save us from this rakshasa. Offer us your charity.'

Charity. That word had always enticed that munificent warrior. Karna acceded. For a moment, he closed his eyes and chanted something. Then, from his quiver, he pulled out the Vaijayanti Shakti that Indra had blessed him with when he had offered his kavacha-kundala to him. Closing his eyes, he charged it with a mantra and shot it at Ghatotkacha. It was the only Shakti that he was left with to protect himself. The moment he shot it, his life became like an empty quiver.

As that Shakti pierced Ghatotkacha's chest, he screamed horribly in agony. While falling down, he magnified his body enormously and many Kuru soldiers got crushed under his gigantic body and died. The night war was over.

As per Krishnadeva's plan, Ghatotkacha's life mission to leave Karna devoid of the Vaijayanti Shakti was also over.

The day had not yet dawned. Exhausted soldiers from both armies dropped their weapons and went to various lakes on the land of Kurukshetra to take a bath. While they were performing their morning rituals, I presented the eldest Pandava Yudhishthira alone in front of Krishnadeva.

Krishnadeva advised Yudhishthira to beware of Karna. He suggested that Yudhishthira go and meet Bhishma on the deathbed once. I did not understand one thing: why had he summoned Yudhishthira alone to discuss all those things? Why hadn't he asked for Dhrishtadyumna, when he was the commander? Finally, Yudhishthira got ready to leave for his pavilion. At that time, Krishnadeva got up, put his arm around Dharmaraja's shoulder and said, 'Yudhishthira, keep in mind two things that I am going to tell you now. There are many large elephants in our army. There is also an elephant named 'Ashwatthama' in the Kuru army. Do not forget to send Bhimsena to attack him tomorrow. If anyone asks you in the battlefield tomorrow, just say 'Ashwatthama has been killed – human or elephant, no idea'.

I did not understand a thing. Yudhishthira, too, looked confused.

On the fifteenth day, Guru Drona organised his army in the shape of a hawk. For hours, Guru Drona fought tenaciously. But suddenly somebody gave out a fake cry, 'Ashwatthama has fallen.' In fact, it was the Malava king Indravarma's elephant Ashwatthama that Bhima had slain. To check the authenticity of the news, Drona steered his chariot all over the battlefield and finally brought it near truth-loving Yudhishthira. In agony, he pleaded with Yudhishthira, saying, 'Oh Yudhishthira, everyone is screaming that Ashwatthama has fallen. Tell me if it is true that my dear Ashu has been killed? I believe in your veracity.'

'Gurudeva, it is true that Ashwatthama has fallen. But I do not know if it is the man or the elephant.' For the first time in his life, Yudhishthira had uttered a lie. He had whispered the second sentence, barely audible even to himself.

Grieving Drona, mourning the death of his son, threw away his bow, sat down in his chariot and began meditating in Padmasana. Meanwhile, Dhrishtadyumna, with bloodshot eyes, descended from his chariot and ran towards Drona with his sword. Before anyone could comprehend what was happening, he tightly held the long, matted hair of the old man, chopped his head off in a single strike and threw it on the ground between both armies. The venerable guru who had taught hundreds of young men in Hastinapura and ruled their hearts with love lay dead in the dust.

The dawn of the second day of the bright fortnight descended on the land of Kurukshetra with the sprinkling of golden sunrays like showers of Prajakta flowers. The Lord of the sky had nothing to do with the atrocity or compassion of mankind.

Duryodhana gathered the Kuru army and appointed Karna as the commander. The original battlefield where the war had commenced was now a few miles away to the north. Battlefields were being changed every day and the location kept moving. Commander Karna selected a place convenient for the formation of his army.

Our Pandava army marched forward on that day under Arjuna's leadership in a half-moon formation.

As Karna could not see Arjuna's Kapidhwaja pennant anywhere, he got confused momentarily. Krishnadeva signalled to take his chariot towards Karna.

But the commander that he was dealing with was like a bolt of lightning. Easily rendering Nakula's arrows ineffective, Karna broke Nakula's chariot to pieces and, with a smile, said to unarmed Nakula, 'Go and send your elder brother Arjuna. I am sparing your life just for that.'

Contrite Nakula turned back with his head hanging low.

Krishnadeva brought Arjuna's Nandighosha in front of Karna's Jaitra chariot just as evening set in. Seeing each other, both became fiercely aggressive, and loudly screamed at each other. Fiery sparks flew from the iron tips of their arrows. Those sparks scorched Karna's charioteer Satyasena. In the end, he was killed by Arjuna's arrows. The second day of the bright fortnight of Pausha, the tough sixteenth day of the war, ended with difficulty.

That night Duryodhana asked him, 'Oh king of Anga, you have lost your charioteer. Who is going to be your charioteer tomorrow?' Karna answered, 'Oh Prince, get me an expert and loyal charioteer. Then you will see that my chariot will storm through the battlefield tomorrow with such speed that it will put the wind to shame.'

Then Duryodhana said, 'If you do not mind, I would like to recommend only one such warrior who is perfect to be your charioteer.'

'Madra king Shalya,' Duryodhana continued.

'Shalya? Are you forgetting that Shalya is the Pandavas' mama? He is Rajmata Madridevi's brother.'

'Karna, even before this war began, I gave Shalya more distinct and honourable treatment than other kings. He had left the Madra kingdom and was travelling towards Kurukshetra to join hands with the Pandavas. But I erected luxurious camp sites, appointed royal envoys on his way and, by offering him many valuable gifts, convinced him to join our side. For the last sixteen days, he has been fighting for us genuinely, and with loyalty. Trust me, Shalya will not go back now.'

The news of Madra king Shalya being appointed as Karna's charioteer reached our camp.

For the first time, Krishnadeva ordered me to summon Nakula. 'Nakula, you are to go to your mama Madra king Shalya's pavilion right now,' Krishnadeva told Nakula.

As a Yadava commander, I expressed my doubt, 'For the last sixteen days, Madra king Shalya has sincerely fought on behalf of the Kurus. Why will he take the Pandavas' side now?'

Krishnadeva looked at me smilingly and said, 'We do not want him to fight on our behalf as such. Nakula is supposed to meet his mama and request only one thing – he should frequently remind Karna in the battlefield tomorrow that he is the son of a charioteer, and dependant on Duryodhana. Nakula should astutely seek such a promise from his mama and come back.'

Nakula left to meet Shalya. He returned after successfully accomplishing his task.

The seventeenth day of war dawned. The number of soldiers on both sides had gone down to less than half.

The Kuru army was in the formation of a circle like the sun disc.

Krishnadeva had arranged the Pandava army behind Arjuna's Nandighosha chariot in the form of a buffalo – the vehicle of Yama, the Lord of Death. As Karna mounted his chariot, charioteer Shalya took his seat.

For the first time, both armies hailed only two names? 'Hail Arjuna – the son of Kunti'; 'Hail generous Karna – the king of Anga – the son of Radha.'

Nobody understood when Karna's Jaitra chariot infiltrated the Panchala troops at the frontline of the Pandava army.

Karna had broken through and faced Yudhishthira in the inner circle. He harassed Yudhishthira for quite some time and finally made his charioteer Indrasena drop down. Utterly helpless, Yudhishthira ran away from the battlefield.

Bhima held a grudge against Karna, who had killed his mighty son Ghatotkacha. He was looking for an opportunity to get hold of Karna's son so he could strangle him.

Karna's valiant son Prasena fought with Bhima for a while but was felled by Bhima's arrow. He writhed in pain and died.

Yudhishthira, grudgingly seeking vengeance for his defeat, again stood in front of Karna along with select Dravida and Nishadha troops. But Karna, fuming with anger over his son's death, immediately slaughtered Yudhishthira's chariot wheel guards, Dandadhara and Chandradeva. As Karna's arrows got unbearable, Yudhishthira, Yuyutsu and I got into a chariot and fled from the battlefield. Yudhishthira shot a Suchi arrow that precisely hit a vital point near Radheya's right ear, and he fell down, unconscious.

Yudhishthira fled from the battlefield and sat still in his pavilion. As Arjuna was extremely worried about his elder brother's safety, he started missing his targets. He was not going to regain composure until he was convinced about Yudhishthira's safety. Krishnadeva gradually reduced the speed of Nandighosha and snuck Arjuna out of the battlefield. He brought the chariot to Yudhishthira's pavilion.

When Arjuna told him with his head hanging low that he had not met Karna on the battlefield yet, he lost his temper.

In a fit of fury, Yudhishthira said, 'Arjuna, why don't you throw your Gandiva bow away?' Arjuna made a solemn vow, 'I will not return to the campsite until I kill Karna.'

Dushasana and Bhima fought a fierce battle. For about half an hour, they were oblivious to lakhs of other warriors on the battlefield. Finally, Bhima struck Dushasana down with a powerful blow. He threw the mace on the ground. Running forward swiftly, the son of Vayu seized Dushasana's right arm, which was holding a mace, in a tight grip with both his hands. He pressed his heavy right foot on Dushasana's muscular right armpit. The mace had already slipped from Dushasana's hands.

Screaming wildly, 'I am tossing into the sky this sinful arm of yours that dared to touch Draupadi's sacred vesture!', that incredibly mighty mace fighter wrenched out Dushasana's arm in one swift jerk. He looked skywards as if possessed and whirled the blood-stained arm before tossing it far away.

That did not satisfy the enraged Bhima. He picked up Dushasana's mace, raised it high above his head and struck a powerful blow on the whimpering Dushasana's insolent chest, shattering both the mace and the iron armour on his body.

Dushasana let out a sky-shattering final scream.

Bhimsena flung the mace far away and knelt on the ground. 'Come, I dare you to stop me,' he screamed dreadfully, addressing the Kaurava warriors such as Duryodhana, Shakuni, Kripa, Ashwatthama and Karna.

He thrust his round, tiger-like face in the blood flowing from Dushasana's chest and gulped this down. Everyone was horrified by that sight, including me. Only Krishnadeva descended from the Nandighosha chariot and controlled him. Now I realised why Krishnadeva had refrained from appointing him as the Pandava commander. Krishnadeva himself wiped his blood-stained face and sent him towards Draupadidevi's pavilion to tie her open hair with his hands covered in Dushasana's blood as per his vow.

The battlefield was now divided into two parts. On the north side were Bhima, Dhrishtadyumna, Sahadeva, Yudhishthira and I, fighting with Duryodhana's brothers, Kripa and Saindhava, and on the south side were Nakula, Uttamauja and Arjuna, who were targeting Vrishasena, Karna's son, from among the circle of Ashwatthama, Shakuni and Duryodhana.

Karna had barely reached the circle surrounding Vrishasena when Arjuna shouted loudly, 'Son of a charioteer. Here I am killing your son in front of all of you, just like all of you killed my dear Abhi', and shot a Chandramukha arrow in such a way that Vrishasena's head, already pinned behind the fence of arrows around his chariot, instantly fell to the ground with a thud.

Karna got down from the Jaitra chariot, cradled Vrishasena's head for some time and let out a sky-shattering war cry.

Reuniting survivors of the Kuru army, Karna was now approaching Arjuna's Nandighosha chariot like the sea wind.

Krishnadeva positioned the Nandighosha chariot at a strategic location where Shalya could not bring Karna's chariot in front of Arjuna without entering the marshland on the south. Proficient Shalya circled the fringe of the marshland for a long time to check if he could find at least a small dry patch in the mud. Finally, he stopped as there was no other choice and said to Karna, 'Radheya, today is not a good day to fight with Arjuna. It is risky to put the chariot into this marsh.'

Without uttering a word, Karna pointed his finger and commanded Shalya to steer the chariot into the middle of the bog.

Now Arjuna's Nandighosha and his Jaitra chariot stood face to face.

Silence prevailed for a moment. Then, at once, they began shouting ear-splitting war slogans and shooting arrows at each other. Even I had not seen such a gripping war of arrows in the last sixteen days. Their battle was much more catastrophic than those of Bhishma, Drona and Abhimanyu. It was a hair-raising experience for everyone.

The bog around the chariot had started to thicken now. Warm blood trickled from the wounds on their open arms. They had no time to think about it. An agitated Karna had now forgotten that their blood had delicate familial ties.

Arjuna showered arrows and confined Karna's charioteer Shalya in one place like a caged hawk. The dexterous charioteer could no longer move. The Jaitra chariot was grounded in one place now.

Karna's arrows were flying over Krishnadeva's crown. During the course of the fierce battle, he did not shoot a single arrow at Krishnadeva even by mistake.

As Shalya saw the Nandighosha approaching their chariot, he tried to steer it by motivating the horses. The horses dug their hooves in and with all their might tried to turn the chariot around but could not.

'Oh, King of Anga, the chariot is not moving. The left wheel is stuck in the ground,' Shalya shouted in fear.

'King of Madra, do not worry. I will pull the chariot wheel out.' He descended in one leap, with the quiver on his back and the Vijaya bow in his hands.

He thrust his right hand out and held a strong spoke of the left wheel and used all his strength to pull it out. The wheel did not budge.

Arjuna was still shooting arrows and those arrows pierced Karna's bare arms. He sat down and thrust his bow in the ground as far as he could to make it stand firmly. Now, he assumed the shooting posture in a sitting position.

With one scathing arrow, he rendered Arjuna unconscious. Seeing that, Karna put down his Vijaya bow for a moment. Using both his hands, he was now struggling with all his might to pull the wheel out. The wheel did not budge.

Krishnadeva held the wooden tube with medicinal herbs near Arjuna's nose. He revived in an instant and stood up.

But seeing Karna unarmed, Arjuna also lowered his Gandiva bow.

Krishnadeva pointed his right forefinger towards Karna, who was struggling to release the chariot wheel, and said, 'Arjuna, pick up a crescent moon-shaped Anjalika arrow.'

'But – he is unarmed, and standing on the ground. I am in my chariot.' Arjuna hesitated. He was confused again.

'Arjuna, this is an order,' Krishnadeva's voice was harsh and sharp.

Obedient Arjuna swiftly pulled an Anjalika arrow from the quiver and twanged the bow string once to test its tautness.

Hearing that faint sound, Karna turned his eyes towards Nandighosha. Seeing Arjuna prepare his bow to shoot, he shouted, 'Wait, Arjuna. I am unarmed, standing on the ground. It is against the rules of engagement to attack an unarmed opponent on foot.' Meanwhile, he must have tried his best to recall the mantras of the Brahmastra that he had obtained on Mount Mahendra. No matter how hard he tried, they eluded him.

'Radheya, do you even know what Dharma is? Son of a charioteer, where was this sacred Dharma of yours when you called Panchali a prostitute in the crowded ancient hall of the Kurus? Why didn't your Dharma object when you heard the news of the Pandavas being burnt to ashes in the lacquer house? Son of a charioteer, when the six of you besieged the sixteen-year-old Abhimanyu, why didn't you recall the same Dharma then that you mention now? Son of Radha, where was your Dharma then? Arjuna, take aim.' Krishnadeva pointed his forefinger straight at Karna's throat.

The Anjalika arrow zoomed from Arjuna's bow, sliced through the iron armour covering his thick neck and embedded itself in his throat piercing it half way. That maharathi slid into the mud beside the chariot wheel.

As soon as Karna collapsed, Krishnadeva blew his conch to indicate the end of the day's battle. The sun set, witnessing Karna and his divine conch Hiranyagarbha lying in the slush of flesh and blood. The battle had ended for the day.

While I was getting out of my war costume, Krishnadeva's attendant came. He had immediately summoned me. He had just returned after meeting Karna, who had fallen on the battlefield a short while ago. Just as Grandsire Bhishma had told Krishnadeva why he was waiting for the sun to begin its journey towards the summer solstice, Karna had told something in Krishnadeva's ear in a low voice. Only they knew what it was.

As I approached Krishnadeva, he said, 'Sakha Satyaki, come with me.' I followed him silently. We came to the place where Karna's lifeless body was being guarded by armed soldiers of the Anga kingdom. His favourite horse – the white Vayujita – stood nearby. The circle of soldiers around him moved away on Krishnadeva's signal. Both of us picked up Karna's body, which looked as if it was in a state of slumber, and put it horizontally on Vayujita's back.

Krishnadeva said to me, 'It was the final wish of the generous king of Anga, Karna, that I be the one to light his funeral pyre on a virgin piece of land. I am going alone. You wait here at the base till I return.' He had already made arrangements to send sandalwood logs on the hill through his attendants.

For the first time, Krishnadeva himself was going to perform the final rites of a fallen warrior, the son of a charioteer, that, too, on a virgin piece of land. I just could not fathom what was happening.

I waited at the base of the hill. Krishnadeva began climbing the hill holding a torch in one hand and the reins of Vayujita in the other. After some time, I vividly saw a sandalwood funeral pyre burning on the summit of the hill and a woman dressed in white running towards it from the Kuru campsite. Who could she be? I could not guess.

In a short while, Krishnadeva came back alone to the base of the hill. He had no torch in his hand. He was silent. I just followed him. Both of us came to his pavilion. He came close to me, held my arm in his and gently said, 'Sakha Satyaki, inform all the regiment leaders in person that I am not going to arrange any war-related meeting today. In the relentless battle between Karna and Arjuna, both sides have lost almost their entire armies. Duryodhana, who is the root cause of all this, is still alive. I will handle him tomorrow. So only you stay back in my pavilion tonight.'

We heard that Duryodhana had appointed Madra King Shalya as the commander. Following that, a competent surveillance chief named Malaya, who had come from the royal ladies' pavilion of the Kurus stood in front of Vasudeva. He said, 'I have picked up significant news from the royal ladies' pavilion of the Kurus. But it is of such confidentiality that I should share it only with Hrishikesha. So…'

Krishnadeva reassured him, 'Malaya, feel free to share the news. Commander Satyaki is my right hand. My best friend.'

Gathering his courage, Malaya said, 'The Kuru Maharani Gandharidevi has summoned Duryodhana for a meeting. "Come and see me immediately – just as you took birth from my womb, naked, like the sky." Duryodhana is preparing to leave for this meeting.'

I was utterly perplexed. Why would such a pious lady send such a strange message to her own son? Without giving me a chance to ponder over it, Krishnadeva said to me, 'Come on, commander.' We left and came to a spot on the border from where the camp of the royal ladies of the Kuru dynasty began. I was holding a burning torch in my hand. Within a short time, we saw Duryodhana approaching, dressed in his usual royal attire, followed by torch-bearing guards.

Krishnadeva moved forward. Catching up with Duryodhana, he said casually, 'Kaurava, I know where you are going in such a hurry. I can also reckon why you are so confused at this moment. Gandharidevi has summoned you to meet her in the same state that you were born – that is, stark-naked. She is not at fault. She still considers you an innocent child. It looks like she wants to advise you to stop the war, just like all the others did. Are you going to really meet her all naked just because she insists?'

Fixing his cat-like eyes on Krishnadeva, Duryodhana said, 'You are well known for your crafty schemes. Except for Arjuna, no one has benefitted from your advice. I have a gut feeling that you are playing some game. Yet, I am also confused about how to meet my mother completely naked, even though I am her son. As I cannot think of a solution, I might as well fend off the meeting.'

'It will be a big mistake to disobey her. It is indeed possible for you to go and meet Rajmata alone the way she wants you to – it is also possible for you to keep her respect as a mother.'

'How? Tell me clearly without any political machinations,' Duryodhana asked hastily. Stressing every word, Krishnadeva calmly told him, 'Wear your regular royal attire till you reach the door of Rajmata's inner chamber. Take a big banana leaf with you. Before entering the chamber, remove all your royal attire and wrap the banana leaf around your waist. That way, you will be completely undressed as per Rajmata's instructions and you will be remembered for generations to come as an idol of devotion to your mother because a banana leaf is not an article of clothing.'

Duryodhana's eyes shone brightly with the joy of relief from a terribly awkward situation. He said, 'Indeed, if I had had only you in the royal council of the Kurus instead of the many people like Kanaka and Shakuni Mama, all my wishes would have already been fulfilled. I will go and meet Rajmata exactly as you have suggested.'

He indeed went to meet Rajmata Gandharidevi as discussed. Later, we came to know Rajmata Gandharidevi admonished her son severely, 'Duryodhana, you are not only stupid but also utterly unfortunate. You believed in Krishna more than the mother who gave birth to you. You moron, seeing you as you were born in front of me, I was going to bless you with the boon of an indestructible body with the potent power of my pure eyesight. Now, you have got the boon only partially. All your body upon which my motherly eyesight fell has become indestructible. The part hidden behind the banana leaf has remained destructible.'

The eighteenth day of war arrived. Balaramadada, who had gone to the Himalayas, had come to Kurukshetra along with Uddhavadeva. The Kaurava army now had only a few thousand combative soldiers left. The Pandava army had even fewer soldiers. There was no question of arranging any Chakravyuha. Duryodhana formally appointed Madra king Shalya as the commander. A notable fight took place between Yudhishthira and Shalya. On the other side, a ruthless battle took place between Dhrishtadyumna and Ashwatthama, who was infuriated due to the gruesome killing of his father Drona. Yudhishthira fought relentlessly for a few hours and beheaded Shalya, his mama.

At the southern end of the battlefield, Gandhara King Shakuni, along with his remaining brothers, was fighting Sahadeva. Sahadeva was not going to let him off the hook today. He struck two fatal intersecting blows of his sword on Shakuni's chest, on which the cord of his quiver was fastened. Fountains of blood spurted out. The vicious villain of the Gandhara kingdom, who had destroyed the lives of lakhs, fell in the mud. A chapter of villainy had come to an end.

As soon as Kaurava commander Shalya and Shakuni fell in battle, Duryodhana disappeared from the battlefield along with his chariot. He went and hid in the suryakunda, in which lakhs of warriors had taken their baths.

Mace warrior Bhima, who had taken a stern vow – 'I will break Duryodhana's lap, which he had shamelessly shown to Draupadi in front of the crowded gambling hall' – searched for him, shouting, 'Show me Duryodhana – where is Duryodhana?'

Unable to find Duryodhana, Bhima approached Krishnadeva. He shouted angrily, 'Hrishikesha, I want to destroy the root of all this destruction. I want to kill that deadly snake of the Kurus, vile Duryodhana. He has run away from the battlefield. Where should I find him?'

For the first time, Krishnadeva instructed Arjuna to follow him and alighted from the chariot. He approached Bhimsena's chariot and signalled Arjuna to steer the Nandighosha himself and follow him. He sent Bhima's charioteer Vishoka to the back and took his place. With Yudhishthira and Arjuna following him, he manoeuvred Bhimsena's chariot towards the Suryakunda shore. Duryodhana was hiding in the centre of the lake and unwilling to climb out, despite being called out to several times. To force Duryodhana out of the lake, Yudhishthira, on Krishnadeva's advice, shouted, 'Duryodhana, get out of the water and fight a duel with any one of us five brothers. If you do not do that, we will have to mix safflower toxins in the waters of Brahma sarovar and Jyoti sarovar and all our soldiers will have to pour jars filled with those waters in this lake. Then not only will you be forced out but all innocent life in the lake will also die in vain.'

This had an immediate effect on that vicious Kuru. To confirm the proposition, Duryodhana asked Yudhishthira again, 'Will you give me a chance to fight a duel?' And when he nodded in affirmation, Duryodhana expectantly glanced at Balaramadada on the shore. Balaramadada had full confidence in Duryodhana's mace-fighting skills. As he nodded in affirmation, Duryodhana swam out of the suryakunda. He challenged

Bhimsena, who had killed his ninety-nine brothers, to a mace duel, saying, 'My dead brothers will not get the offerings of tarpana unless I break open the chest of this gluttonous, vile son of Pandu, who killed all ninety-nine of them. My dearest brother Dushasana's soul will not feel contented until I drink the hot blood from his ruptured chest like the Maireyaka wine. I, Duryodhana, the prince of the Kurus, challenge this gluttonous Bhima for a conclusive mace duel.'

A breathtaking, riveting mace duel ensued between the two princes on the shore of Suryakunda. 'You coward, who always acted under Shakuni's influence – the wicked villain who shamelessly ordered the disrobing of my beloved wife in the gambling hall in front of all elders. You savage beast, who showed his bare thigh to my wife in a crowded hall! This Bhimsena, son of Pandu, accepts your challenge.'

Their heavy maces clashed and made loud clanging sounds. Streams of blood mixed with sweat began trickling from both their muscular bodies. Both their headgears had been tossed aside in the dust. Bhimsena's strikes did not affect Duryodhana at all and they were not going to. He was provoking Bhimsena while roaring out loudly, 'Have you lost the power that crushed the temples of elephants? You gluttonous eater, where is the strength of a thousand elephants that you possess?'

Confused, Bhimsena frequently kept looking at Krishnadeva under the pretext of wiping the sweat on his forehead. Krishnadeva had been giving him some kind of a hint by thumping on his thigh. But Bhimsena simply could not understand.

Gandharimata had rendered Duryodhana's body indestructible with whatever power she had gained as a dutiful wife by her virtuous conduct. Bhimsena knew nothing about it. Naïve Bhimsena was fighting the mace duel relentlessly in credulous expectation that he would be able to crush Duryodhana's chest with the blessings of Gurudeva Balarama and the grace of Krishnadeva. He did not understand why Krishnadeva was thumping his thigh frequently. All Pandavas had fallen silent with the fear that if the duel continued the way it was going, Duryodhana would succeed in killing Bhimsena by evening.

It was essential to do what Duryodhana had done in the gambling hall of the Kurus. Krishnadeva pulled his yellow dhoti aside, bared his thigh and indicatively thumped his tight fist on it. Now Bhimsena precisely understood what Krishnadeva meant. The next moment, mammoth Bhimsena fiercely struck a powerful blow on Duryodhana's muscular thigh. 'Oh, mata,' Duryodhana moaned loudly, flung his mace away in the air and collapsed. Fountains of blood spurted out. The other thigh was also crushed. With both his thighs smashed completely, Duryodhana fell face down on the battlefield of Kurukshetra. Balaramadada, who was the guru of both the mace fighters, trembled with fury as he saw what had happened. Brandishing his mace, he dashed towards Bhimsena, saying, 'You fool of a disciple. By hitting below the waist, you have broken a vital rule of a mace duel. Now I will have to kill you to offer tarpana to my beloved disciple. Hail Goddess Ida.' Krishnadeva controlled him by spreading both his arms wide, and said, 'This mace fighter bared his thigh in front of a noble lady in a gambling hall full of people. Isn't it fair to crush his thigh or should the noble lady Draupadi be brought back and made to sit on his lap? Dada, if I were in your place, I would have proudly offered the Kaumodaki mace on my shoulder to my valiant disciple Bhimsena.'

'You are the reason behind all this. In fact, you should be punished before Bhima – but what to do? After all, you are my younger brother,' Balaramadada said helplessly. He rushed towards his wounded disciple, who had fallen face down.

Krishnadeva leaned forward towards Duryodhana, and giving him an ultimatum, asked, 'Duryodhana, do you feel even an iota of remorse for all your sins now? If yes, tell me, I will still emancipate you from all your sins.'

Duryodhana looked at Krishnadeva with utter contempt and said in clear words, 'How would a lowly cowherd like you with feet soiled in cow dung and urine understand what kind of honour it is for a Kshatriya to die while fighting a battle?' All of us were stunned to hear his words.

Looking at his venerable gurudeva Balarama, he said, 'Gurudeva, I bow down to you for the last time. Please explain the rules of a duel to this younger brother of yours, who is smaller in every sense – this cowherd Srikrishna.'

Balaramadada said, 'Bhimsena has broken the rule of a mace duel by hitting below the waist.'

'Dada, what kind of brotherly duty did this best disciple of yours fulfil when, in childhood, he dumped Bhimsena in the waters of the Ganga in the name of swimming after he poisoned him by feeding him toxic sweets? In the gambling hall of the Kurus, he ordered that Draupadi be disrobed in front of all elders. What kind of royal duty did this so-called prince fulfil at that time? This favourite disciple of yours, utterly lacking in discretion, did he not reinvite the Pandavas to play the game of dice again through Shakuni? With whose support did the six warriors collectively dare to besiege our beloved Abhimanyu? Dada, consider it lucky that this gallant Bhimsena has not drunk the blood from the crushed thighs of Duryodhana.'

'Whatever excuse you want to give, a rule of war has indeed been broken. And it has happened in my presence. I do not want to see your face or his any more. Feel free to continue the war. I am going to Dwaraka,' Balaramadada spoke harshly and immediately left Kurukshetra.

The sun set. All of us returned to our tents. In the meeting held during the night, Krishnadeva had a discussion with Dhrishtadyumna. 'With Duryodhana's death, the war has come to an end. The remaining soldiers should take down their tents and leave Kurukshetra.' While he was having the discussion, surveillance chief Malaya presented Krishnadeva with news.

Before Duryodhana had passed away, he had earnestly beseeched Kripacharya, who had come to meet him, to formally appoint Ashwatthama as the last commander of the Kurus. Though both his thighs were crushed, his indomitable, enraged royal heart was not – he was not yet ready to accept defeat. He was still daydreaming about seeking revenge.

Kripacharya appointed Ashwatthama as commander and Duryodhana himself had put the crown of commander on his head while lying down. Even Drona's son Ashwatthama had become overwhelmed with emotion due to Duryodhana's faith in him. Duryodhana, who was at death's doorstep, fixed his eyes on Ashwatthama's and said, 'Oh, son of our guru, Kuru commander Ashwatthama, you are our last valiant commander. Even though Krishna is the master of the Sudarshan chakra, the mantras of that divine astra have escaped his memory as he has not launched it for a long time. If that was not the case, there have been many occasions during the last several years when he should have used the Sudarshan. He is in the same state that the cursed Karna, who had given away his kavacha-kundala in charity, was, and in which I am today, like a powerless lion whose claws have been clipped. You have with you the divine Brahmastra that our acharya, your father Guru Drona, has given you. You will be the ultimate source of our success. As the last Kuru, I instruct you, and as a friend I request you, to wipe out the Pandavas completely.'

'Kaurava, I will fulfil your wish. I will destroy the Pandava family line completely.' The son of the guru gently pressed Duryodhana's hand to reassure him.

'Hail Gandhari ...' Before he could even say 'mata', Duryodhana breathed his last on the banks of Surya sarovar, still holding Ashwatthama's hand in his.

A ghastly night descended on Kurukshetra. Except for half a mile or so, the rest of the battlefield was defiled with the blood of more than forty lakh warriors from both sides, and lakhs of elephants, horses and camels. Around the vast battlefield, many funeral pyres had been set ablaze every day. The river beds of Drishadwati, Sharavati and Saraswati, and lakes such as Brahma sarovar, Surya sarovar and Jyoti sarovar had turned black as the ashes of the dead soldiers were dumped into them. The entire battlefield was littered with piles of broken chariot wheels, broken parts of weapons like swords, maces, spears and iron clubs, scattered body parts of human corpses, cut-off elephant trunks and horse tails. Some funeral pyres were still burning near the waterfront. The entire land of Kurukshetra was filled with the cries of vultures, hyenas, foxes, wolves, wild dogs and tigers. The ghastly hooting of owls echoed in the hollows of trees. The torches burning in the night were dimming as there were no soldiers to put oil in them. Kurukshetra was no longer a holy land. It had become a vast crematorium.

I was lying on a rug in my tent along with a few Yadava soldiers who had survived. I was constantly tossing and turning. The images of the war over the last eighteen days were dancing frantically in front of my eyes. No matter how hard I tried, I could not sleep that night. How could one sleep in an atmosphere filled with the growling of wild animals and bizarre sounds?

It was about midnight. I heard the heart-wrenching cry of a woman coming from a distance. Sharp words like the pointed tip of Suchi arrows fell on my ears, 'Achyuta … Madhava … Milinda … Madhusudana … betrayal. The scoundrel did not spare any of my sleeping sons. Oh Hrishikesha, you are awake when all beings are asleep, how come you are asleep today? Arise, Krishna … Get up.'

I sat on the rug at once. That wailing woman was none other than Draupadidevi herself. I lifted a burning torch and rushed in the direction of the voice. The wailing sound seemed to come from the direction of Krishnadeva's pavilion. I entered Krishnadeva's pavilion. His peacock-feathered crown was still sitting in the salver. Uddhavadeva, dressed in a saffron cloak, was standing on his right. Both were trying to console Draupadidevi, who was beating her chest, 'What is it, Krishney? What happened, Panchali?'

The royal lady could barely speak as she was beating her chest in uncontrollable agony. She was just crying loudly in distress, 'My Prativindhya … Shrutakirti … my Sutasoma … Shatanika … my Shrutasena.' All we could comprehend was that she was talking about all the five sons of the Pandavas. Why? For what reason? We had no clue. Her wailing would not stop. Krishnadeva sat next to her, lovingly patted her hair made by Bhimsena and even more affectionately asked her, 'Sakhi Shyamale, what happened? Be calm. Get a hold on yourself. What happened to your sons?'

Still sobbing, with tears streaming down her eyes, Draupadidevi said, 'That scoundrel killed my five sons while they were asleep. He has also beheaded my brother Dhrishtadyumna.'

By this time, all five Pandavas had entered Krishnadeva's pavilion and circled their wife. Bhimsena said, stroking her back, 'Draupadi, be calm. Tell us clearly, who committed such a sinful act?'

Overwhelmed with sorrow, Draupadidevi looked at Bhimsena and said, 'They touched my saree in the gambling hall full of people – I kept quiet. I should have been sitting on the royal throne of Indraprastha but they sent me barefoot to live in a forest – I endured that without protest. Today, that vicious villain has beheaded my beloved sons – your own progeny–leaving me, a mother, bereft of her children. Yet you ask me to stay calm?'

Finally, shaking Draupadidevi frantically, Bhimsena spoke harshly, 'Who committed this sin? Tell me his name.' Srikrishnadeva also patted her head and asked, 'Give us his name, Draupadi.'

'Your – your guru Drona's son – that – scoundrel Ashwatthama.'

'What?' All five Pandavas exclaimed unanimously in shock. As soon as he heard the name of the killer of his sons, Bhimsena put his huge mace on his muscular shoulders and immediately left the pavilion. Krishnadeva promptly followed him. Uddhavadeva and I rushed after him.

Bhimsena entered the pavilion of Dhrishtadyumna, who had been the Pandava commander from the beginning. A gruesome scene that would have benumbed anyone's senses lay in front of him. Pandava commander Dhrishtadyumna's head had been cut off in his sleep, and his torso lay askew in a pool of blood. Corpses of his beloved nephews, all five sons of the Pandavas, sleeping on both sides, lay cluttered chaotically in a pool of blood. Most of them had long brutal strokes of the sword visible on their chests. After watching his sons and the commander in such a dreadful state, even Bhimsena, so hefty and strong, covered his face with his hands and slumped for a moment. The next moment, he got up and in that dim light of the early morning, went towards the west side of the battlefield in search of Ashwatthama, shouting loudly, 'Somebody just show me the merciless killer Ashwatthama – show me Ashwatthama...' He was oblivious to the elephant trunks, skulls of dead soldiers, body parts and horse tails being crushed under his feet. Ashwatthama was nowhere to be found. In the end, exhausted Bhimsena helplessly sat on a boulder near the trunk of a tree. We caught up with him. Seeing that he was almost on the verge of crying, Krishnadeva said to him, 'Oh son of Vayu, get a hold on yourself. I can understand your rage. Ashwatthama's time has not yet come. I cannot tell you when it will come.'

The next day dawned on Kurukshetra. Krishnadeva, who was bringing Bhimsena back to his pavilion, saw a human figure far away near the base of a hill, sitting on a boulder in the shadow of a sprawling tree. At that point, he said to Bhimsena, 'Pandava, look ahead. How that tree has bloomed.'

Bhimsena looked in front with his big tearful eyes, as if he were looking through a veil. His sight fell on the tree blooming with red flowers and then on the boulder. He recognised Ashwatthama even from such a long distance. Immediately, he howled loudly, 'Ashwatthama...you merciless killer of the sleeping sons of Pandavas. I appeal to you in the name of your father. Wait where you are. I dare you to strike me with your sword.'

Taking long leaps, Bhimsena reached him in no time. The blood-stained clothes that Ashwatthama was wearing were parched as the blood had dried, but his eyes still reflected the same indomitable rage of war. A mace duel ensued between the two of them. We all encircled them and kept watching. Though the Sun god had ascended high up in the sky, their duel did not appear close to concluding. The sun was now directly overhead. Bhimsena tossed the sword in his hand aside and challenged Ashwatthama for a conclusive wrestling bout. Even though Ashwatthama was aware of the reputation of invincible Bhimsena he accepted the challenge. Srikrishnadeva stood in the middle of the two and said, 'Bhimsena, this challenge of yours will never come to an end. You fought the wrestling bout with Jarasandha for twenty-seven days. It will be pointless if you fight with Ashwatthama for not one but even for twenty-seven years. Ashwatthama is immortal, he will not die.'

Turning towards Ashwatthama, he tried to convince him as well, 'There is no other wrestler like Bhimsena in Aaryavarta after Jarasandha. Do not try to dare him. If both of you still do not want to listen, then I will hand you both the soil to commence the bout.'

Both stood facing each other like a snake and a mongoose. They were unaffected by Krishnadeva's words.

Both accepted the soil from Krishnadeva to commence the wrestling bout and got into a simple pit. Finally, in the last hour of the day, Bhimsena fastened the Bahukantaka hold around Ashwatthama's neck. But it was clear that Ashwatthama was not going to die. This went on for a long time. Then Krishnadeva moved forward, put a sword near Bhimsena and whispered in his ears, 'Son of Kunti, listen to me carefully. Ashwatthama is immortal. He will never die. There are two ways a human being can die – one is physical death and the other is public humiliation. He has a bead of flesh on his head since birth. Cut it off with the sword I have given you. The wound on his head will never heal. It will keep bleeding forever. Ashwatthama will live forever carrying the perpetually bleeding wound.

That humiliation will be like death to him. Hurry up and cut off the bead of flesh on his head with the sword.'

Sweating Bhimsena did exactly as Krishnadeva told him. Holding Ashwatthama's neck with his left hand, he removed the bead of flesh on Ashwathhama's head using the sword.

Flinging the blood-stained sword on the battlefield, he returned to the Pandava pavilion with the precious bead of flesh in his hand.

He handed it to beloved wife Draupadidevi and described to her what had happened. Consoling her, Krishnadeva also told her about Ashwatthama's immortality to reduce the sorrow of her sons' deaths.

The evening of the nineteenth day approached. The Lord of Dwaraka commanded us to uproot the poles of his spacious pavilion and wrap it up. A troop leader counted the remaining Pandava army. It numbered only a few hundreds. In the Kaurava army, there were only three warriors alive now – Kripacharya, Kritavarma and Ashwatthama.

The religious duty of offering final tarpana to all the dead soldiers was still to be performed. For that purpose, we all came to the shore of River Drishadwati. Krishnadeva had invited Dhaumya rishi to perform the final rites. All of us breathed a sigh of relief that the Great War was over. River Drishadwati, which had been flowing for ages, was tranquil. She had nothing to do with the human disaster on her banks.

While Uddhavadeva, Daruka, all Pandavas, Achyuta and I were observing preparations for the rituals, surveillance chief Malaya reached the banks, gasping for breath. Bowing down to Krishnadeva, he said while trembling, 'Oh Lord, I have bad news. Before Ashwatthama disappeared into the forest with his bleeding wound, he launched the Brahmastra.'

'What? Brahmastra?' Krishnadeva got up at once. 'Yes, my Lord, Brahmastra. That missile has killed all our remaining soldiers who were packing up their tents, as the war had come to end. It also descended upon the foetus in the womb of Uttaraadevi in our ladies' camp. All Pandava women are beating their chests and wailing loudly because they have lost the one and only scion of the third generation of the Pandavas. They are calling for you. The Pandavas are lucky enough to be alive only because they were with you. I was also spared because I went to summon

Dhaumya rishi.' All of us were stunned and stared at Krishnadeva. Uddhavadeva tightly held both his arms and said, 'Vasudeva, only you can save the Pandava clan from this destruction now. It is now inevitable for you to recall the sadhana of your life and sip Drishadwati's water to remove the effect of the Brahmastra on Uttaraa's unborn child. Or else the Pandava clan will be wiped out from the world. Let's go.'

With Krishnadeva walking behind him, Uddhavadeva went towards the bed of River Drishadwati. He spread a small rug. Krishnadeva sat on it. He closed his fish-shaped eyes. Uddhavadeva picked up a palm full of water thrice and released it in Krishnadeva's cupped hands. Releasing it on the ground, he spoke in clear words, audible to everyone, 'If I am the son of renowned Maharaja Vasudeva and Devakimata, if I am entitled to be called the son of Nandadeva and Yashodamata of Gokul, if I am the true disciple of renowned Acharya Sandipani and sage Ghor Angirasa in every sense, if I did not act selfishly in any manner whatsoever while uprooting injustice from Aaryavarta to emancipate justice, if I did not perform any kind of sin whatsoever during any event in my life through the day or night, then as I sip this, the scion of the Pandavas' third generation growing in the womb of noble Pandava lady Uttaraa will take his first breath of life.' Narayana took a sip of water and opened his eyes. Looking at Uddhavadeva, he smiled and said, 'Udho, dear friend, go straight to the Pandava ladies' camp, and come back with news about Uttaraa's foetus.'

'As you wish, Dada,' said Uddhavadeva and hastily climbed the stairs of Drishadwati's ghat. Uddhavadeva returned hurriedly with a smile on his face. All of us except Krishnadeva surrounded him with utmost curiosity. 'Uttaraa's foetus has begun moving again. The scion of the Pandavas' third generation is safe.

'Only ten warriors have survived the Great War. Kritavarma, Kripa and Ashwatthama on the Kaurava side, and all the Pandavas and maharathi Satyaki on the Pandavas' side.'

Breathing a sigh of relief that their clan had been saved, none of the Pandavas realised who the tenth warrior was. I could never forget him. To make sure that everyone heard his name from Uddhavadeva's mouth,

I asked him, 'Uddhavadeva, you said ten warriors, but told us only nine names. Who is the tenth warrior?'

Then Krishnadeva's closest friend Uddhavadeva smiled, put his hand on my shoulder and exclaimed, 'Yugandhar Srikrishna.'

UDDHAVA

I am Uddhava, son of Devabhaga and Kansaa. My father Devabhaga was Maharaja Vasudeva's brother. My mata Kansaa was the sister of Maharaja Kansa, king of Mathura. Thus, I was Krishna's paternal as well as maternal cousin. More than any of these relations, I was Srikrishna's favourite 'paramsakha' – his confidant. This relation with Krishna was the most valuable for me throughout my life.

In fact, he had casually conferred that epithet upon me.

As Srikrishna was my elder brother, I used to earnestly address him as 'Dada' with respect. In fact, so many other emotions were involved in it. There was not a single event in his life that he did not share with me. He spoke to me as if he were speaking to himself.

Everyone asked why I did not want to get married. But my Dada never questioned me about that. That was the prominent reason why I had so much respect for him.

I did not have the temperament of a warrior. What I acknowledged was the tug of war that goes on in a human mind day and night. Dada was aware that I was the only one amongst lakhs of Yadavas in whose mind such a war would go on. That is why, among all his favourite sakhas, including Grandsire Bhishma, Mahatma Vidura, dear friend Sudama, Sanjaya, Balidada, Jalapurusha Karna and master archer Arjuna, whom he gave the advice of a lifetime on the battlefield, he considered me his 'paramsakha'. He was aware of what I was, and I tried throughout my life to understand who he was, whatever I could. He was just like the wind that is invisible but occupies the entire world rapidly with tremendous speed. He was blue-complexioned, like the endless sky above us. His blue colour had a darkish tinge to it, like the limitless dark space beyond the vast skies. In the Ankapada ashrama, Acharya Sandipani had explained the difference between aakasha, the sky, and avakasha, the space in so many ways to all of us. It was later that I came to realise why Gurudeva addressed him as 'Krishna, Shyama' on many occasions and especially on the day of Gurudakshina.

Only recently, I realised that each time his smile was different – like the earth. The earth never shows the same beauty of colours during all seasons. Every season has its own beauty. He was indeed like the earth – merciful.

I witnessed first hand, his natural attraction towards water – right from Mathura to Dwaraka, Hastinapura and Indraprastha.

His life, that was like the river Yamuna, had some prominent and elegant turns. Gokul, where he spent his childhood, was the very first, most elegant milestone that would have made a deep and lasting impression on anybody's mind. The second equally beautiful turn was life in the Ankapada ashrama of Acharya Sandipani in the forest of Avanti, where he absorbed knowledge. When he arrived in Mathura from Gokul, I was the only Yadava of Mathura to meet him first. Since then, I have constantly lived in his company till the commencement of the Great War of Bharata. I witnessed how he overthrew Magadha emperor Jarasandha's assaults on Mathura.

With the support of innumerable dexterous Yadavas, he erected the new kingdom of golden Dwaraka on the turbulent, roaring, vivacious western ocean.

When he left Mathura and came to Dwaraka, he taught me something without uttering a word. It was an invaluable lesson – that at times one has to leave behind even one's beloved motherland for the sake of fulfilling one's duty. Every event in his life has taught me something or the other that was pro life.

Despite living and enjoying a comfortable life in Dwaraka with lakhs of Yadavas, he consciously took interest in the life of the displaced Pandavas. The Great War of Bharata that he masterminded was the zenith of his divine genius. It became a great yajna where forty lakh soldiers were sacrificed in the war. He participated in this war for eighteen days without holding any weapon in his hand. It is because of his unarmed participation that this war turned out to be a great yajna.

Because of that, he became 'Yugandhar' – the epoch-maker.

Whatever I understood from all these turns in the life of my Dada 'Srikrishna' is what I am going to share as per my intellectual ability. I am aware that no matter how much I try, it cannot be shared in its entirety.

It was his hearty wish to erect an ashrama at Badri–Kedara near the base of the Himalayas. I had gone to Badri–Kedara to make preparations for that. It was many days before the commencement of the Great War. I selected an appropriate place for an ashrama. During my travels in the Himalayas, I met many yogis, ascetics, sages and hermits. I did not make any of them my guru. As I had taken formal initiation from Acharya Sandipani and spent my whole life in the company of Dada, I did not find any necessity to do that. But now, I have donned saffron clothes after a great deal of thought.

While returning to Dwaraka, I kept receiving news of the war in Kurukshetra from time to time from sages and hermits I met during the journey. My feet inadvertently turned towards Kurukshetra with only one yearning in my heart – checking on the well-being of Dada.

I reached Kurukshetra in the last phase of the war. Just like me, Balidada, too, had come there straight from the Himalayas.

For the sake of the offspring of the Pandavas' third generation – Uttaraa's unborn child – Srikrishna Dada took a sip of water and prayed with all earnestness on the strength of his virtuous merits on the bank of River Drishadwati. As a result, Uttaraa's foetus came back to life. The Pandavas' third generation was safe – their lineage was saved.

Only one ritual was left to be performed now for the cessation of the war that lasted eighteen days like a great yajna. It was of performing the last rites, the ceremonial tarpana offering for more than forty lakh soldiers slain in the battle from both sides. For that purpose, the Pandava family priest, Dhaumya rishi, who was invited by Dada, was present at Kurukshetra along with his disciples. Yudhishthira, as the eldest of the Pandavas, was going to perform the last rites on behalf of all. All Pandava women, including Draupadi, all Kaurava ladies who could come, except for Gandharidevi, had arrived at Kurukshetra. Dhaumya rishi commenced the ceremony. First, Yudhishthira paid homage to all the ancestors and performed the rites. Grandsire Bhishma was still alive on the shara grass bed surrounded by guards.

All rituals were performed with the chanting of mantras. As per Dhaumya rishi's instructions, Yudhishthira left his seat from near the fire pit and walked towards River Drishadwati. First, he was going to worship the river. After that, he was to mention the names of all relatives who had died as heroes according to their seniority.

At that exact moment, Kuntidevi signalled to Dada to come close. She whispered something in his ear. Hearing that, Dada nodded and whispered something in the ear of Dhaumya rishi. Dhaumya rishi then hurriedly got up from his grass mat. To stop Yudhishthira, who had meanwhile reached River Drishadwati, he loudly called, 'Pandava, wait.' Yudhishthira stopped. Hurrying towards him, Dhaumya rishi said, 'It is Krishnadeva's instructions that the very first rite be offered to Karna, the king of Anga. He was the eldest brother amongst all the Pandavas.'

Yudhishthira began trembling in his place with an overwhelming volley of emotions. The golden salver in his hands started rattling. Wondering why Yudhishthira had stopped, first Bhima and Arjuna and later Nakula–Sahadeva rushed forward.

Yudhishthira had not yet recovered from the shock. He was still shaking. Bhima asked him, 'What happened?'

Looking at Bhima with tearful eyes and in a trembling voice Yudhishthira said, 'Do not call me "elder one". I was not elder then and I am not elder now.'

Arjuna came forward and lovingly asked, 'What is wrong, Yudhishthira? Are you not our elder brother? Is it not because you are the eldest that you performed all these rituals?'

'No. I am not. The world conqueror, maharathi king of Anga, was the eldest. Karna, who we disparaged all the time as the son of a charioteer.'

'What?' Bhima and Arjuna both took a step back in shock with their eyes opened wide. Arjuna went to Yudhishthira and, violently shaking his shoulders, asked in a heart-wrenching voice, 'What are you saying, Yudhishthira? Have you gone crazy because of the carnage of lakhs of lives?'

'Bhimsena, did I not tell you just now? Our older brother was Karna. I am going to offer the very first jalanjali of tarpana to him now – as per Krishna's instructions. Each one of you will have to do the same after me,' said Yudhishthira.

Arjuna, who was disconcerted by all this, stood silent for a few moments as if hit by lightning. He turned around and rushed towards the ladies sitting near the fire pit. Within moments, he reached Kuntidevi. He pulled out the divine Gandiva bow from around his shoulder. Looking at the expression on his face, terrified Kuntidevi stood up, trembling in fear.

'You sinful woman. You made me murder my own brother.' Shouting thus, he put his divine Gandiva bowstring around the neck of his own mother like a noose. Shaking it violently, regretting the fact that he had killed his own brother's sons Sudamana, Vrishasena and Karna's foster brother Shona, Dhananjaya raved insanely. He shouted at her, 'Evil woman, I used this Gandiva bow to kill my own elder brother and many others. Now I, who have reached the gates of hell by committing the sin of killing my own brother, will tighten this bowstring around your neck and take your life too.'

Everyone was stunned to see Arjuna's violent emotional outburst. The fear that the religious ritual might turn into a bloody scene confounded me too. In one leap, I grabbed Arjuna's hand holding the Gandiva bow and said to him, 'Pandava, be calm. Compose yourself.'

Dada came from behind me, put his arm on Arjuna's back and gently patted him for a few moments with affection. Then, in his usual sharp and sarcastic style that brought many arrogant people to their senses, he said, 'Well done, my pupil. You are going to kill my venerable aunt, whose blessings I do not consider myself worthy of seeking even today. Sakha Arjuna, without even hearing her side of the story, you assaulted her with uncontrollable rage. Then how are you going to console my sister Subhadra, who lost her son, my beloved nephew Abhi? How are you going to offer her solace?'

With each of his words, Arjuna's boiling anger gradually subsided like the western ocean retreating in low tide. Exhausted, he leaned on Dada's shoulder. Seeing the trickle of warm tears running down his eyes, I, too, gently kept patting his back. Arjuna sought the blessings of Kuntimata and offered jalanjali in the waters of Drishadwati. From the river, we came to the camp of the Pandava ladies. Those tents had not yet been dismantled. Aunt Kunti had returned along with all the women in the chariots of the Pandavas and was sitting in her pavilion. As I entered the pavilion with Dada, Subhadra came running and threw her arms around Dada's neck, crying convulsively, 'Krishnadada, where is my Abhi – show me his face at least once.' For a few moments, Dada's fingers gently stroked her back with affection, as if silently telling her, 'My dear sister Subhadra, compose yourself and listen to me carefully.'

The next moment, he said in a very calm and steady voice, 'Subhadra, our Abhi has attained the zenith of glory. He was the only one who performed such a valiant feat at such a young age in the great yajna of war. He has brought acclaim not only to the Kuru dynasty of the Pandavas but also to us Yadavas because of you. Do not cry over his death – be proud of him.' Each word of his, especially his divine touch, had so much strength that very soon, Subhadra calmed down. More than anybody else, I was curious to know what Dada was going to say to his dear aunt. He touched her right foot with his fingers. Then moving them over the crown on his head respectfully, he sat on a mat near her right foot. A few moments passed in utter silence. Finally, Dada spoke in his mellifluous voice that completely transformed the atmosphere.

With utmost tenderness, he brought his palms together and said, 'Pardon me. Consider me in his place and forgive me.' All of us sitting around did not understand what he was referring to. But Aunt Kunti probably understood it. She said, 'Forgive you and for what? Am I even worthy of forgiving you? You have not done anything wrong.'

All of us – at least I – thought that he was seeking pardon from Kunti for getting Karna killed by Arjuna by expounding to him what Dharma is.

To clear the misapprehension from our minds, including Aunt Kunti's, he said, 'I am seeking forgiveness for the fact that my dear friend Arjuna forgot his duty as a son and assaulted you out of ignorance, in front of me. As for your eldest son Karna – he has achieved even higher acclaim than our Abhi. You are indeed great – as a mother and as a grandmother.'

At that point Aunt Kunti rose from her seat. Exclaiming 'Oh Krishna', she spread both her arms and embraced him with the satisfaction that at least one person understood her completely.

All the Pandavas left for Hastinapura along with their wives. Kritavarma had already left for Dwaraka. Nobody came to know when and towards which forest Ashwatthama left with his bleeding wound.

In the very end, Daruka, Satyaki, Dada and I – the four of us left the desolated land of Kurukshetra.

Soon, we entered the city of Hastinapura. When Dada had come here for the mediation, how zealously the citizens of Hastinapura had welcomed him with pomp and splendour. Now there wasn't a single soul on either side of the road. At least one person from each household in Hastinapura had died a hero's death in the war of Kurukshetra. Those left behind were the aged, women and children. And they, too, were drowned in grief behind closed doors.

We came near Vidura's residence on the border of the city. I do not know how but even without knowing of our arrival, Mahatma Vidura was standing there to welcome Dada with his palms joined in greeting. Dada said to him, 'Sakha Vidura, join us in the chariot. We are here to meet the Kuru Maharaja. You are his mahamantri.'

'As you wish, oh Lord of Dwaraka.'

I noticed that Dada had addressed him as 'sakha'. That was because all four of us – Daruka, Satyaki, Vidura and I – standing in Garudadhwaja today, at that moment were his sakhas. The magnificent ancient royal palace of the Kurus built with reddish stone came into sight. All of us descended from the chariot. All five Pandavas, who had already reached there as per Dada's instructions, came forward to greet him. Dada whispered something in Vidura's ear.

Vidura left towards Maharaja Dhritarashtra's chamber to convey the news of their arrival. As soon as he left, Dada called all the Pandavas and instructed, 'Dear brothers, as a duty, you are to bow down to your kaka and meet him from a distance. No one should go close to him. Especially you, Bhimsena – you should stay farthest. Whatever curse he inflicts upon you in the agony of losing his hundred sons, you are to hear them quietly without fidgeting with your mace.'

All the Pandavas heard Dada attentively. There was a single iron statue standing on the west side. It looked like a replica of Bhima holding his mace on his shoulder. Dada stood right in front of that iron statue with all of us.

Bhimsena could not restrain his curiosity and asked, 'An iron statue resembling me – how come it is located in the wrestling pit of the Kurus' armoury, Srikrishna? Who placed it here?'

Dada looked at him and smiled, 'Do not feel flattered, Kaunteya. It is not placed here for your worship or to offer flowers. Duryodhana himself got it made by proficient ironsmiths by getting a mould of your size created. For practising mace fighting daily. Every day, he practised mace fighting here for hours. If you observe closely, you will see many dents on the statue caused by heavy strikes that he rained on the statue when he was angry.'

Not just Bhimsena but the other Pandavas, too, were stunned.

Just then Mahamantri Vidura entered the armoury holding Kuru Maharaja Dhritarashtra's hand, guiding him, saying, 'This way, Maharaja.' Then Dada signalled us as decided earlier. All of us scattered around. Only Dada stood in front of Bhimsena's iron statue. Mahamantri Vidura, who had brought the blind king of the Kurus holding his hand, said, 'The Lord of Dwaraka, who has returned from Kurukshetra, seeks your blessings, Maharaja.' Dada promptly moved forward and touched his feet. That cunning diplomatic Maharaja asked, 'Who is it?', to determine the voice. 'Maharaja, I am Srikrishna – the son of Vasudeva–Devaki of Dwaraka.' Still, the shrewd maharaja touched the crown on Dada's head to check if it had a peacock feather. Then, in his usual pretentious manner, he said, 'Srikrishna? You are not at fault. You were unarmed. A charioteer. Srikrishna, I understand that you have come to offer your condolences to me as my hundred sons have not returned at all. But whether it is you Yadavas of Dwaraka or us Kurus of Hastinapura, we are, after all, Kshatriyas.' For a moment, the wily king paused to gauge Dada's opinion.

'Yes, Maharaja, I have come to offer my condolences. I should have visited Rajmata Gandharidevi first but I know how afflicted you are due to the bereavement of your hundred sons. I thought it was appropriate to meet you first as the ruler of this ancient royal throne, hence I am here. Maharaja, please be calm and compose yourself.'

'I am calm already. If my dear brother Pandu's sons rule the kingdom of Hastinapura, it would be like my own sons ruling the kingdom. I am anxious to meet the Pandavas. I am especially looking forward to meeting Bhimsena and holding him in my embrace. It is true that as a father I do lament the death of foolish Duryodhana and all his brothers. But I have drowned my sorrows in River Ganga already. Our sages and hermits have taught us that enmity should end with the death of the enemy.

'Oh Srikrishna, dear son, have you come alone? Vidura told me that my beloved Pandavas have also come with you. Where are they? Where is my dear Bhimsena?' Meanwhile, Dada quickly moved behind Bhimsena's iron statue. From there, he said, 'Maharaja, now that you have pardoned them, they are feeling relieved. They have been silently standing here in front of you wondering what and how to speak. Bhimsena is standing right in front of you. Please take him in your deep, loving embrace. He is yearning to seek your blessings.'

Hearing that, Maharaja Dhritarashtra left Vidura's hand at once. Spreading both his strong arms, he said in clear, loud words, 'Oh dear Bhimsena… Come here, son. Let me embrace you tightly.' With our eyes dilated, we all witnessed an unprecedented thrilling drama. The aged father, lamenting the death of his hundred sons, embraced Bhimsena's iron statue so tightly that even the mace-holding arm of the iron statue came loose from the socket and fell on the floor. Hearing its clanging sound, he thought that Bhimsena had dropped his mace. In that delusion, the mournful Kuru father embraced the remainder of the statue even harder. The left hand of the statue, too, fell down. The mournful father kept embracing the iron statue continuously, calling Bhimsena, 'Bhima… son, oh warrior Bhima…' He crushed the upper body of the iron statue into small pieces, which fell clanging to the stone floor.

While crushing the statue of iron thinking it was Bhimsena, the aged Kuru's body also got stained with blood. With the warm touch of his own blood, he came to his senses, sank on the floor and screamed strangely, 'Oh my hundred sons, I have crushed your killer, vile Bhimsena, to pieces. Come and see them. Where are you, my boys?'

Mahatma Vidura affectionately patted his blind brother's back first. Then, giving him support, Vidura slowly carried him towards his chamber.

I approached Dada with all the five Pandavas. Satyaki was standing by my side. But Daruka was waiting in the chariot outside.

I picked up one of the pieces of Bhimsena's iron statue fallen on the stone floor. It had a few drops of blood on it. Looking at those pieces, I said to Dada, 'From Satyaki, I have heard accounts of various tactics of your ingenious intellect on Kurukshetra during the eighteen days of war. But today, I witnessed the culmination of your genius in person. Indeed, what would have happened to mighty Bhimsena if you were not here today?'

That night all of us stayed at Vidura's residence on the border of Hastinapura.

Dada said to Vidura, 'Sakha Vidura, all these years you were the mahamantri of the Kauravas and you performed your duties devotedly. Henceforth, you will have to carry out the same task for the Pandavas. First, get all the preparations done for Yudhishthira's coronation. Grandsire Bhishma is still awaiting the start of the sun's journey towards the northern solstice to breathe his last. When he breathes his last, immediately inform me in Dwaraka.'

'As you wish, Lord of Dwaraka. I will follow your instructions to the letter,' said Mahamantri Vidura, bowing slightly with utmost respect.

'Let Yudhishthira rest here for a couple of days. Then send him to Kurukshetra immediately. Grandsire is waiting for him. He wants to speak to Yudhishthira in private about something important.'

I remembered that even when Karna had gone to meet Grandsire, he had sent all the others away. Probably, he was going to impart some advice from his experience, about politics, Dharma, warfare and the duties of a king, to Yudhishthira. All the Pandavas had anyway left Kurukshetra only after meeting him. Notably, Rajmata Kuntidevi had met Grandsire along with Draupadi and all other Pandava ladies. He had advised, 'Once Yudhishthira is crowned as the king of Hastinapura, you should take up vanaprasthashrama the very next day. Maharaja Dhritarashtra and Gandhari will never stay in Hastinapura after that. They will strongly insist on living in the forest. You should not leave the company of your brother-in-law and his wife, irrespective of whatever has happened in the war. You should accompany the desolate couple in the forest.'

Kuntidevi had put her head on Grandsire's feet and nodded in affirmation, agreeing to his instructions.

When I came to know all this, it became crystal-clear to me why my Dada had so much respect for Kuntidevi. Some men and women were indeed difficult to comprehend, irrespective of whether they were Kurus or Yadavas. As for Dada, I had not yet understood him at all. My only satisfaction was that he had undoubtedly considered me his paramsakha. While talking to many people, he had undoubtedly mentioned my name as his confidant.

The next morning, our skilled charioteer Daruka steered the chariot and brought it right in front of Rajmata Gandharidevi's residential palace. The chariots of the Pandavas followed. All of us followed Vidura into the Kuru royal palace. We reached Rajmata's chambers. Royal charioteer Sanjaya was standing right there. Rajmata sat on a polished rosewood settee in the inner chamber. Many Kuru ladies, including Duryodhana's wife Bhanumati, Duryodhana's sister and Jayadratha's wife Dushaladevi, and Guru Drona's wife Kripidevi, sat on a rug spread near the settee.

Seeing Dada and all of us coming, all of them except Rajmata stood up, covering their faces with their shawls. A few clear and a few muffled sobs were heard. But Rajmata Gandharidevi, who had for years blindfolded herself with a white strip of cloth, sat motionless on the settee – calm, like a marble statue. As Dada saw her, his feet hesitated for a moment. The very next moment, he quickly stepped forward, put his head straight on Rajmata's feet and said, 'I, Srikrishna – son of Vasudeva–Devaki – bow down to you, Rajmata.'

Rajmata Gandharidevi got flustered for a moment.

In the next instant, that royal lady, heartbroken due to the death of her hundred sons, hastily pulled both her feet up and sobbed uncontrollably. To avoid the touch of Dada's hands, she sat cross-legged on the settee. Many men and women from various kingdoms of Aaryavarta had passionately fallen at Dada's imperial feet just to touch them. This was his very first experience of being snubbed by someone.

I was shaken to witness such a scene. All the Pandavas and Dada's sakhas felt the same. The entire room was now packed with many suppressed emotions. When Dada, who had spoken so charmingly all his life, was dumbfounded and could not open his mouth, who else could dare to speak?

Everyone's eyes were fixed on Rajmata, who was sobbing uncontrollably. She cried with convulsive gasps for quite some time and finally stopped, getting calmer on her own. She composed herself and spoke something vaguely, as if she were speaking to herself, 'I do not – I do not understand what is on your mind. You have destroyed my one hundred sons, killed them ruthlessly, and on top of that you have come to meet me.' My dear Dada held Rajmata's wrinkled hand resting on the settee, took them in his own, and affectionately said, 'No, Rajmata – never. Even when a son becomes a bad son, a mother can never be a bad mother. I have really come to only see you and not to offer solace. I have given so many philosophical speeches but even I have no words at all to console you.'

'Do you think you can fool me with your web of words like you fooled others? Once I had removed my blindfold and blessed my son Duryodhana with an invincible body. If I wish so today, at this moment, I can remove my blindfold again and in a single glance burn you to ashes in front of all those who are present here. You are under the illusion that all the words of the world have surrendered themselves to you – you wrongly imagine that you are the only one who knows politics,' Gandharidevi roared.

Even Dada, who could otherwise guess precisely what was going on in anyone's mind, got confused. Still, he said politely, 'I know that too. Still, I have come to see you with respect, earnestly.'

Now Rajmata Gandharidevi rose from the settee and stood erect. Gathering all the strength of her meditative powers, the rajmata uttered a terrifying curse on Dada in clear, sharp words that raised the hair on the skin of all present, in fear, 'You are the one who ignited the Great War that got my hundred sons killed mercilessly; you left the Kuru clan bereft of an heir. You are the one who got all my daughters-in-law widowed. Obliterating you alone is not going to give any solace to a mother's heart. Therefore, this daughter of the Gandharas, Rajmata of the Kurus and devotee of Shiva, Gandhari, curses you from the bottom of her excruciated heart. Oh Srikrishna, the Yadava leader of Dwaraka, son of Vasudeva–Devaki, within thirty-six years from now, you will also be destroyed like us with the entire Yadava clan. The Yadava women will also be widowed like our women. Oh Srikrishna, you who told Arjuna proudly that if he got killed in war, he would attain heaven, and if he won the war he would become the king of Hastinapura, I, the mother of one hundred sons, curse you profoundly that you will not achieve the death of a hero, fighting as a brave warrior. You will die worthlessly, alone, in some unknown forest, and no one will even know about it. Both Devakimata and Rohinimata will be left heartbroken for you just as I am heartbroken in grief for my sons. Your eight wives will become widows like all my daughters-in-law.' The old rajmata, who was trembling, pressed her thin fingers against her temples and cracked her knuckles loudly. Dada heard the curse with extreme composure while sitting on the rug at her feet. Even more calmly, he said, 'Oh rajmata, please calm down. Despite knowing that I will receive some kind of a terrible curse from you, I have come here to see you. Do not worry. I am not going to seek any kind of remission from your curse. I have accepted your curse with a composed mind. Even at this moment, I respect you as much as I respect Devakimata and Rohinimata. I regard you like Goddess Ida herself. Taking that into consideration, give me your blessings now – which will give me the strength to bear your curse.' With the utmost humility, Dada put his head again on her feet. The Rajmata who had considerably calmed down now, leaned forward and with trembling hands pulled Dada up. The Rajmata, who had achieved sky-high greatness with her penance and veracity, held Dada in a deep embrace effusively, just like she would have held Duryodhana. For a few moments, both of them stood silently in each other's embrace.

Without speaking another word, Dada left the chamber. The rest of us, moved by overwhelming emotion, touched Rajmata's feet while lost in thought and automatically followed him. Once we came out to the square, he told Yudhishthira, 'All of you should go to Vidura's residence and stay at the feet of your mother. She will also be leaving for the forest later as per Grandsire's instructions.' The Garudadhwaja then began its journey towards Dwaraka. We arrived at the western ocean creek near Dwaraka.

Dada sent Satyaki by boat to go across the creek to intimate Pradyumna of our arrival. We sailed to the Shuddhaksha gate of Dwaraka on the east side. Our entry into Dwaraka this time was so very different. We had returned after losing over our Yadava soldiers on the battlefield of Kurukshetra. For a few moments, Dada kept gazing at the royal insignia on the gate. He stepped on the shore with his right foot, touched it with his hand and began walking calmly. I realised that from this moment, a new chapter in his life had begun – because never before had he touched the step of the Shuddhaksha gate while entering from the east side and chanted the name of Idamata.

Detailed news of the war at Kurukshetra had already reached Dwaraka. More than feeling jubilant for the Pandavas' victory, everyone was feeling dejected due to the sacrifice of lakhs of our soldiers in the war. No one had come to the Shuddhaksha gate. It was the first time that Dada was entering Dwaraka in such a dismal atmosphere. But he was calm. He greeted everyone along the way with a smile and a polite bow. But this smile was not his usual one. The citizens of Dwaraka felt it strongly.

Dada first went to meet Devakimata and Vasudevbaba. Then we met Rohinimata, Balidada, Revativahini, Acharya Sandipani and his wife. As they all saw Dada in person, their depressed faces were refreshed. Only Balidada was still upset with his dear brother – due to the unlawful death of his beloved disciple Duryodhana. He spoke to Dada using the same words as Gandharidevi, 'You are the sole reason of the catastrophic war of Kurukshetra. That poor rajmata lost one hundred sons. What must she be feeling? He may have been egoistic but Duryodhana was still the father-in-law of your own son. It was I who had taken the initiative to get Samba married to Duryodhana's daughter Lakshmanaa, with only one objective in mind – that at least sometime in the future, Duryodhana and you will come together as friends.'

Hearing his naïve Dada's political calculations, Krishnadada smiled with amusement. He said, 'I met Gandharidevi and have returned to Dwaraka only after calmly receiving the terrible curse that she has put upon me. As my elder brother, you will also have to bear the brunt of that curse. If you are upset about it and if you, too, want to curse me, I am ready to accept that too – with the same calm mind.'

'A curse? What kind of curse?' Balidada widened his big eyes.

'That of the extinction of the Yadava race.'

Balidada was speechless.

Seeing him dumbstruck, Dada said,

'Balabhadradada, everything that comes to exist in this world is ultimately bound to be destroyed some time or the other. It is going to be consumed by fire. Can you tell me confidently that venerable Rajmata Gandharidevi who cursed me will never be engulfed by the flames of fire? I would advise only one thing to you as a brother…'

'What advice? It has been already proven that your advice always involves some wily politics. Go on, what is it?'

'Dada, you should control your temper. You get angry very quickly – and of late you have lost your old habit of calming down quickly. Just give a thought to whether you can get rid of both these habits and be stable-minded.'

Dada turned around to leave the chamber without giving Balidada any chance to raise doubts or objections as usual. Within two days, Balidada summoned the Sudharma royal assembly in his capacity as the crown prince of the Yadavas. The royal assembly was overflowing with Yadava men and women. Everyone was curious as to what Balidada was going to say.

As old Vipruthu took the place of the chief minister and raised the jewel-studded royal sceptre of the Yadavas, the assembly hall fell silent, as if someone had switched off the volume except for the roaring sound of the western ocean.

Vipruthu commenced the council in broken words, saying, 'This is an auspicious occasion for the citizens of Dwaraka to see the Lord of Dwaraka in person after so many days.

'Since the time of Jarasandha's attacks, we Yadavas are used to fighting battles. We have already prepared our hearts to bear the loss of lakhs of lives. One truth has been ingrained in every drop of our blood – that lakhs may die while protecting Truth and Dharma, but their patron should remain safe.

'On behalf of all Yadavas and my own self, I pray to Goddess Ida that Krishnadeva may live a long and healthy life. And I request Haladhara Balarama to take charge of the assembly.'

Yadava prince Balidada rose from his grand golden seat. He glanced over the crowded assembly hall once and said, 'Yadava brothers, giving speeches is not my forte. In fact, I am not going to speak at all today. I am only going to listen. Your Lord of Dwaraka, my younger brother Srikrishna, should lay his heart bare in front of us today.' Balidada sat down while looking at us.

Now all eyes in the Sudharma royal assembly were fixed only on my dear Dada. He stood up. With his peaceful eyes, he glanced around the Sudharma assembly once. He said, 'My dear Yadava brothers, the descendants of eighteen families, I can clearly see only one curious question in your eyes. That question is what did the war of Kurukshetra achieve? What did the Lord of Dwaraka gain by sending lakhs of soldiers of Aaryavarta to the jaws of death, putting forth the cause of the Kauravas and the Pandavas? Who is going to console the lakhs of widows of Hastinapura, Dwaraka and Aaryavarta, and how? Was this war really necessary for Bharatavarsha. Why was this great yajna of death ignited?' He clearly worded the question lingering in everyone's mind. He intentionally stopped for a moment and glanced around the Sudharma assembly.

He continued, 'My dear brothers. Whether it is you or I, we tend to think about life from only one angle. All of you should also think - what if the war had not taken place at all? What would have been the state of affairs in the various kingdoms of Aaryavarta?

'Couldn't it have been that kings of various kingdoms would have followed in Yudhishthira's footsteps and played a game of dice by putting anyone – even their own mothers – at stake? Wouldn't they have? What if the rulers of various kingdoms had felt inspired by Duryodhana's arrogant attitude and self-centredness to behave in the same manner? In what condition would Aaryavarta have been then? What if cunning outsiders would have come here to settle down, taking inspiration from Shakuni, who came to Hastinapura from the distant kingdom of Gandhara, and created political turmoil in Hastinapura?

'I have always told my dear friend Arjuna, and my brother Uddhava, that whether it be Duryodhana, Dushasana, selfless Grandsire Bhishma or world conqueror Karna, no one can experience eternal truth by staying confined in their lives. To experience that, sometime or the other, everyone will have to enter the battle of life under the glowing sun in the sky.

'Who knows, tomorrow, all of you and even I may have to enter a battlefield.

You should never forget the experience of the lakhs of warriors who died at Kurukshetra. Lakhs of you here might have to face even more heart-rending circumstances in future. That is why I am going to repeat only a select part of the advice that I imparted to Arjuna on the battlefield to understand the philosophy of life. The only and easiest way to understand life efficiently is to do one's duty without expecting anything in return. It is indeed difficult to put into practice but it is as beneficial as a bitter medicinal herb that works wonders.

'I do not want to tell you anything more than that at this point. But I intend to do two things for sure. The first thing is a radical reform to improve the Sudharma royal assembly. I recommend that the aged members of the Sudharma assembly be relieved from duty. Prince Balaramadada will appoint the new ministers.

'The most important thing that I am going to do today concerns my best friend, my brother Uddhava. I find him perfectly suitable for it among lakhs of you Yadavas. In the presence of and with the permission of all my Yadava brothers and sisters, I confer the epithet of "Avadhuta" upon him.

'Avadhuta means one who is detached from all kinds of desires, like the lotus leaf – a truly emancipated soul. A sanyasi also yearns for moksha. But an Avadhuta has no desire even for that.'

With his declaration, thousands of assembled Yadavas showered a roaring round of applause. Dada rose from his seat and approached me. I stood up due to my respect for him. Then, quite unpredictably, he removed the fresh white Vaijayanti garland from around his neck and put it around mine. Looking at the assembly hall, he said, 'I could never forget the Kadamba garland that this Avadhuta Uddhava had put around my neck on the Yamuna's shore when we met for the first time on the day that I came from Gokul to Mathura.'

Slogans arose from all sides, 'Hail Avadhuta Uddhavadeva… glory to you.' 'Say something, Avadhuta Uddhavadeva. Go ahead and speak,' everyone insisted.

Respectfully honouring the request of all, I bowed down humbly and said, 'First, let me offer obeisance to my dear Dada and your Lord of Dwaraka. All my life, I was seeking the answer to the question, "Who am I?" I could not find the right path to self-realisation. Many a time, I was stuck at a particular point of contemplation. Today, I have come to know exactly who I am. What Dada says is true. I lived my life to attain the epithet of "Avadhuta". I earnestly yearned for it. I have the exact same feeling right now, on hearing the word "Avadhuta" from Dada's mouth that he must have felt at the time when he was addressed as "Vasudeva" by the right person, Grandsire Bhishma. I am privileged to accept the epithet of "Avadhuta" affectionately conferred upon me. But, honestly, I do not think I am worthy enough to wear this Vaijayanti garland that he has put around my neck for more than a few moments. That right is solely his, as I know very well who has given it to him. From today, I sincerely accept the responsibility of all the duties that he has assigned to me as "Avadhuta". But this Vaijayanti garland, which belongs to him and is loved by his best friends and devotees, I humbly offer at his feet.' I quickly removed the garland from around my neck and put it at Dada's feet. Dada smiled, picked it up and held it close to his heart. Once again, exhilarated Yadavas gave a big round of applause.

News came from Hastinapura that Grandsire Bhishma, lying on the bed of shara grass, had breathed his last on Kurukshetra at the auspicious time when the sun began its journey for the summer solstice. Yudhishthira had been visiting him for some time every day and had received guidance from him about the duties of a king. Just like Arjuna had felt blessed by hearing the advice of the Gita from Dada, Yudhishthira felt blessed by obtaining the advice of Grandsire Bhishma. The Pandava brothers had performed the final rites of Grandsire at Kurukshetra itself, near the shore of Brahma sarovar. All brothers were now occupied with preparations for Yudhishthira's coronation. When Dada heard the news, he dispatched Satyaki to Hastinapura. Now, after performing his daily duties, every evening, he began to go to the Aindra gate on the west side and sit on the stone seat located near it with me. During one such meeting, he said to me, looking at the continuously roaring waves of the western ocean, 'Avadhuta, you must have wondered why I did not go for the funeral of Grandsire Bhishma but cremated Karna on the hill?

'Let me tell you why – it is only you who has the capacity to understand it. All three of us have spent our lives as Jalapurushas. Bhishma, who had taken the profound vow of lifelong celibacy, was an emancipated soul right from birth. He had no need for any formalities of jalanjali. But Karna, who was engulfed by Duryodhana's cunning political friendship, needed it. That is why I offered it only to Karna from among the lakhs of soldiers. Brother Udho, only you can understand that if Kunti would not have abandoned him after birth – if he would not have come into the company of Duryodhana during his lifetime – Grandsire Bhishma would have addressed him as "Vasudeva" just like he addressed me.' Seeing me silent, Dada held my arm and said, 'Oh Avadhuta! You have to go to

Gokul – just like you went to the people of Gokul with my message when I came to Mathura for the first time.'

I kept looking into his dark and deep eyes. He smilingly said, 'Udho, brother, you, and only you, have to go to Gokul – as my representative – as Avadhuta – as me.'

As per Dada's instructions, I left for Mathura the next day with Daruka in the Garudadhwaja chariot. How much it had transformed now. I strongly realised what Vasudeva Krishna had been telling me was so true. The world around us keeps changing constantly. It is characterised by growth and progress. Mathura had flourished a lot as there were no longer any threats of Magadha attacks. Maharaja Ugrasena was too old to attend the royal council any more. The king appointed by him was looking after the administration of Mathura. After meeting Maharaja Ugrasena and taking a tour of our royal palace once, I entered Gokul along with Daruka. I could see the gopas of the second and third generations after Nandababa. Our Garudadhwaja chariot, harnessed with four white horses, stood in front of the western gate of the same old residence of Nandababa. A young gopa from the third generation conveyed the news of my arrival to Nandababa, who was now very tired and stooped. Hearing the news of my arrival, Nandababa and Yashodamata came with a group of gopas. Yashodamata, with a wrinkled body and face and hair turned completely white, stood in front of me, shielding her eyes in the sunlight. Narrowing her tired eyes, she kept staring at me for a long time. Then she said in a trembling voice, 'He is not our Kanhaiya.' Nandababa also seconded her opinion, saying, 'Definitely not. He is not our Kanha. He would never don such saffron clothing.'

I promptly went forward, touched their feet and said, 'I am not your Kanhaiya. He is doing well in Dwaraka. I am his cousin, Uddhava. I have come here as per his instructions. I had come once before too, a long time ago. He has sent a message: Do not worry. I am fine. Very soon, I will come to visit you.'

Hearing my words, the faces of that aged couple instantly glowed with joy. A large crowd of gopas who had assembled in front of me whispered among themselves, 'Kanha is coming soon – the great Lord of Dwaraka is coming!' While hearing their whispers, I only kept thinking of one thing that Dada had said. He had said that sometimes the illusion of the truth of life is more fascinating than the truth itself – it can be really life giving.

By this time, the news of my arrival had already spread all over small Gokul. I took a seat on a platform covered by a blanket in the main square of Nandababa's residence. Daruka was sitting next to me. Just then a gopa woman, of about the same age as Revati, entered with searching eyes. Her hair had also turned grey now. As soon as she came near me, she did not get confused like the others, and said, 'Paramsakha Avadhuta, do you recognise this sakhi of your Dada's?' I quickly moved forward and touched the feet of the gopa woman and said, 'Not recognising you is like not recognising my own reflection in the mirror. Dada has sent a message of his well-being to you. What is your message for him?'

She smiled slightly. Her smile reflected a tinge of Dada's. She was Radhika. She said, 'Tell him that even I am fine by his grace. I have stopped waiting for him long ago. My heart is in Dwaraka all the time.

'I have taken care of his gift with all sincerity so far. Now tell him to take care of it himself.' She pulled out a flute from the folds of her dress and handed it to me.

The next day, I visited every place in Gokul associated with the divine memories of Dada. In the end, I came to the same place on the banks of the Yamuna where he had played with friends and had raised a shivapindi from sand along with Balidada.

In that same place, there was now a small stone Shiva temple built by Nandababa.

After staying in Gokul for two days, I returned to Dwaraka. I presented a detailed report of everything that had happened in Gokul to Dada. I handed over his beloved flute that his gopa-sakhi Radhika had given me. He stopped there for a moment and said, 'Brother Avadhuta, listen to this.' He closed his fish-shaped eyes and, becoming one with the flute, played such canorous tunes one after another that it felt as if many rolls of fine-textured fabric were unrolling in front of my closed eyes. Then he put the flute in a wooden casket in the treasury and closed it. We went back to his chamber. The Srisopana came into sight. The staircase, made up of glistening gold-plated sheets, looked very tall and grand.

He called for an attendant and summoned Gargamuni and Vipruthu's son Sukrita, who had now become the chief minister. Climbing one step at a time, both of us went into his chambers. He was not speaking at all. He was lost in thought.

In a short while, Gargamuni arrived with Vipruthu's son. He greeted both of them with a smile and shared his plan with them. He said, 'Chief Minister, summon architect Maya from Indraprastha along with his team. Gargamuni, we have to make some changes in the structure of this staircase. We have to add some steps to it in memory of some great warriors of the Great War of Bharata. You should look after the preparations personally.'

Architect Maya, and his assistants Taraksha, Kamalaksha and Vidyunmali, arrived in Dwaraka accompanied by Vishwakarma. Renovation of the Srisopana commenced as per Dada's instructions under the guidance of Gargamuni. Dada himself supervised this project. He was giving minute directions to the craftsmen. That is when I realised that the Srisopana was going to be Dada's favourite treasured memory henceforth.

Amidst this, a servant brought news that Sudamadeva had come to visit. Dada immediately sent him back to fetch Sudama and present him there respectfully.

Servants brought Sudama to us near the Srisopana. He looked quite old now. But his frame was still the same – thin and sinewy. He still carried a cloth bag on his shoulder, as usual, with his dear-to-heart sandalwood slippers in it.

Dada instantly spread both his arms and pulled him into a deep embrace. Sudama whispered as if he were talking to himself, 'What a Great War. I could not get any news about you. That is why I could not resist and came here in person. Oh Keshava, how are you?'

Releasing him from the embrace, Dada held him in front by both his shoulders, smiled and said, 'This is how I am – how are you doing? Where is the cloth bundle containing my favourite treat?'

Sudama pulled out the cloth bundle with a sentimental gift for his friend. He then glanced at me. Dada realised what he was wondering about and putting his hand on my shoulder, said, 'Sudamana, this is our Uddhava – my Udho – he has become Avadhuta now!'

My saffron dress had confused Sudama. At first, he did not recognise me. Then he spread his arms and embraced me just as he had embraced Dada. None of us spoke for a while. Well, we spoke volumes with each other, silently!

For about a month, Maya, his team and Vishwakarma worked diligently following Gargamuni's instructions for the grand renovation of the Srisopana. The Srisopana now had more than one hundred steps with gold-plated copper sheets. It meant that Dada had at least these many men and women, maybe more, in his life, who were close to his heart and whom he had chosen and remembered. No one around him knew in whose memory all those steps were being built and in what order. Even I did not know. And Arjuna was so far away – in Hastinapura.

There, in Hastinapura, preparations were completed for Yudhishthira's coronation. Pandava horse riders had dispersed in various directions to distribute invitations for Yudhishthira's coronation. The Pandavas had organised this ceremony in consultation with Dada. Therefore, the Yadavas had received the very first invitation from the Pandavas. To deliver the invitation, master archer Arjuna had arrived in person along with Vrishavarma, who was the former chief minister of the Kurus but had now become the Pandava chief minister, and Dhaumya rishi.

Eager to meet Dada, Arjuna had already boarded the boat to cross the creek. But Dada sent him a message and instructed him to wait near the coast. Dada crossed the creek and went to welcome him in person along with Balidada, me and the new chief minister. He had accepted to be Arjuna's charioteer not only in war but for life.

Lakhs of Yadava men and women cheered and welcomed him. When Arjuna placed the invitation for his elder brother's coronation at the feet of Maharaja Vasudeva, the royal assembly reverberated with a roaring round of applause.

In a few days, we reached the border of the Hastinapura kingdom located on the banks of the Ganga. Yudhishthira and all the four Pandavas had come to greet us at the border with Aunt Kunti and Draupadidevi. Mahatma Vidura and Sanjaya were also with them. As we entered Hastinapura, the men and women welcomed us appropriately.

Despite Yudhishthira's repeated requests, this time too, Dada decided to stay with sakha Vidura. Obviously, Satyaki, Daruka and I accompanied him.

The rituals for Yudhishthira's coronation as the king of Hastinapura commenced. When the golden crowns of the Maharaja and the Maharani of the Kurus, blessed with mantras, were placed on the heads of Yudhishthira and Draupadidevi, Dada's eyes reflected great satisfaction at having fulfilled his duty. After the coronation, Maharaja Yudhishthira and Maharani Draupadi came to seek his blessings.

After seeking blessings of all elders, Maharaja Yudhishthira and Maharani Draupadidevi ascended the royal throne. Blind Maharaja Dhritarashtra and Gandharidevi were nowhere in this grand coronation ceremony. The couple had not come in spite of a formal invitation by Yudhishthira and Draupadidevi. Aunt Kuntidevi had also urged them a lot. But the blind father had sent her back, saying, 'Both of us are blind. What are we going to see there? It makes no difference whether we come there or stay here in our chambers. May you rule the kingdom happily. May your sons live long.'

But Dada did not forget to visit the old couple before leaving Hastinapura. Touching the feet of the old king, he said, 'I, Srikrishna of Dwaraka, the son of Maharaja Vasudeva, pay my respects to you with my wife Rukmini.' But this time, old Maharaj Dhritarashtra groped with his hands for Dada's shoulders, holding him passionately. The tears lingering at the edges of his blind eyes trembled.

The blind father tightly squeezed Dada's upper arms and heart-wrenchingly said, 'Oh Krishna...!' Till date, as an imperial ruler, he had always addressed Dada as the 'Lord of Dwaraka', 'Son of Vasudeva' or 'Srikrishna'. Today, the father who had lost a hundred sons instinctively called him 'Krishna' with affection.

'Krishna, you have been doing so many things for so many people all your life. Now, do only one thing for this father with a devastated heart, mourning his one hundred sons. Tell Yudhishthira to arrange for my vanaprasthashrama along with Gandhari. We cannot stay in Hastinapura even for a moment now.'

Dada had surmised what he was going to say. He calmly said, 'I urge both of you to remain in Hastinapura. I am going to leave Hastinapura only after instructing Pandava Maharaja Yudhishthira that Maharaja Dhritarashtra and Maharani Gandharidevi should always be treated honourably and respectfully by everyone. The moment you feel insulted, you are free to leave Hastinapura and go to the forest. Elders should not ask something in favour, they should give. I urge you to do me this favour.'

Dada had no room for argument. He inadvertently ended up saying, 'As you wish Krishna….'

As Dada had surmised, when we touched Kuntidevi's feet and said our goodbyes, she firmly said, 'Krishna, you have fulfilled all your duties. My Yudhishthira has been crowned the ruler of Hastinapura. My daughter-in-law has become the Maharani. Now, I will go to the forest for vanaprasthashrama.'

I knew for sure that Dada would not be able to convince his determined aunt. Dada let a few moments pass. After that, he spoke in his usual playful manner, 'You are so eager to go to the forest. Is it such a bad idea to spend some time amidst royal riches? It will not hurt the forests in any way.'

Aunt Kunti said, 'You are always spinning a web with your words. But I am not going to listen to any of it. I am going for sure.'

He asked, 'Will you be going alone or is anybody else coming with you?'

This strategy worked perfectly. Aunt Kunti casually said, 'As per Grandsire's instructions, I am going to spend the remainder of my life serving my brother-in-law and his wife in the forest. I am going to accompany them. Nothing is going to change my decision.'

Dada's job was done. He said, 'As you wish. Whenever they leave, you can go with them. But for now, give me all your blessings.'

We sailed across the creek and arrived in Dwaraka, where Dada faced a new issue. Banasura, the king of Shonitpura, had captured Dada's grandson – young Aniruddha – and imprisoned him. Banasura was from the rakshasa clan. His daughter Usha had fallen in love with Aniruddha, the son of Pradyumna and Rukmavati. Rukmavati was the daughter of sister-in-law Rukmini's brother, Rukmi. Aniruddha was already married to Rochana, the daughter of Rukmi's son. They also had a son named Vajra. During Rochana and Aniruddha's wedding ceremony, Rukmi had said something bad about the Yadavas of Dwaraka. At that point, Balaramadada had got furious with Rukmi and had hit him with the dice board itself, killing him on the spot. That is why Rochana had lost contact with her parental home in Bhojakataknagar forever.

Rochana was agitated as Banasura had imprisoned Aniruddha and had come to see Dada with Vajra. She said, 'My husband is in the prison of Shonitpura. Banasura's daughter Usha is behind all this. I am ready to accept Usha as my sister, my co-wife. But the Lord of Dwaraka should liberate my husband and bring him back to Dwaraka.'

Once before, Jambavativahini's son Samba had also gotten involved in a similar situation. Samba, who had gone to Hastinapura for the swayamwar ceremony of Duryodhana's daughter Lakshmanaa, had tried to abduct her from the ceremony hall itself. And Duryodhana had caught up with him at the border of the city and imprisoned him. Balaramadada had travelled to get him liberated, brought him back to Dwaraka and got him married to Lakshmanaa.

Dada summoned Satyaki and the new chief minister Sukrita and gave them detailed information about the mission at Shonitpura. This was going to be the last battle of his life. In this war, he intentionally did not take Balidada with him. But he did not forget to take Aniruddha's father, Pradyumna. Both father and son attacked Shonitpura with their army. A great battle took place between Dada and Banasura. Rakshasas always considered themselves to be very powerful. As they were experts in the strategy of deceitful war, they considered the Kshatriyas to be feeble. That is why Banasura vehemently opposed the idea of getting his dear daughter Usha married to a Kshatriya. The fierce battle continued till evening. Ultimately, Banasura surrendered. He was compelled to surrender, as valiant Satyaki, along with Pradyumna, had vehemently beaten up countless rakshasas. In the evening, he handed over Aniruddha and Usha to Satyaki.

Once, Dada and I were sitting on the stone veranda of the Shiva temple located near the Bhallata gate on the north side. Daruka was also with us. Dada said to the men gathered there, 'Our Uddhavadeva – our Avadhuta – has been travelling through the Himalayas. He is thinking of raising an ashrama in future at Shiva's feet in Badri–Kedara. All of you should listen attentively to what he says. If possible, each of you should try to practise at least one of his thoughts in real life.'

As I was about to begin, Chief Minister Sukrita entered hastily, along with Satyaki and a few Yadava soldiers. The eyes of the audience turned to him. Seeing Dhaumya rishi and his disciples with the chief minister, I automatically stopped. As they approached him, Dada rose. He asked, 'Oh venerable rishi, is everything fine at Hastinapura?'

'I have brought an invitation and a message with me. Maharaja Dhritarashtra and Gandharidevi have left for vanaprasthashrama.' Dada surmised what the rishi was going to say further and said, 'Surely, some kind of altercation must have taken place between Bhimsena and Maharaja Dhritarashtra. Bhimsena must have lost his temper and said something humiliating. That is why he must have gone to the forest and, following in their footsteps, Aunt Kunti must have also left for the forest.'

Dhaumya rishi stopped for a moment and looked at Dada in surprise and said, 'Yes, that is exactly what has happened. Kuntidevi has sent a message for the Lord of Dwaraka.' The sage stopped.

'What message?' Dada asked.

While going to the forest, Pandavamata Kuntidevi said, 'Tell Krishna, "You have done everything possible. I am going to the forest to serve the elders. Whether it is the royal palace of Hastinapura or the forest, both are the same for me. We are going towards the forest at the foothills of the Himalayas. Just as you had come to visit us in the Kamyakavana, come and visit us here too, sometimes."'

Dada was lost in deep thought. Then composing himself, he said, 'What is the invitation for, oh sage?'

'The Maharaja has invited both you and Baladeva. The Pandavas are organising an Ashwamedha yajna. I have come here on their behalf with a formal invitation.'

After some time, Dada said, 'Oh rishi, hereafter, I am not going to leave Dwaraka. Take Commander Satyaki with you as our representative. I will also send my blessings and gifts for the Pandavas for their Ashwamedha yajna. Please check with Balaramadada on what he wants to do.'

As Dada was not going, Balidada, too, declined the invitation. As decided, Commander Satyaki left for Hastinapura with gifts and a few soldiers along with Dhaumya rishi.

I had started noticing that Dada had been taking more interest in sages, hermits, yogis and ascetics than soldiers, warriors, troop leaders and fighters. Dada had a new time-indicating disc installed near Shuddhaksha gate. It was to be used whenever a special guest arrived in Dwaraka. Thereafter, one day, the first toll was struck on the new disc.

The moment he heard the clear tolls, Dada closed his eyes for a moment. 'Bandhu Avadhuta, who could be the special guest? Let's go and see.'

A tall bearded rishi, clad in white, stood on the stone platform of the iron disc. The dark-complexioned rishi was surrounded by ten–fifteen disciples. Dada walked forward briskly. He prostrated at the feet of the aged Maharishi Vyasa.

Balaramadada honoured the maharishi and his disciples.

After staying for two days, the maharishi was to depart. Only Dada, Balaramadada and I walked with the maharishi and came near the big boat in which he was going to sail across the creek with his disciples. Maharishi put his right hand on Dada's shoulder, glanced at me and said, 'The three of you will have to face a testing truth way more severe than the war of Kurukshetra.' Maharishi said to Balaramadada, 'Prince Balabhadra, my disciples have given me detailed information about your kingdom. Since your return from the Himalayas, you have not left the royal palace much. Srikrishna, you are extremely disturbed ever since your return from Kurukshetra. This Avadhuta Uddhava is occupied in serving you day and night. Your subjects – the lakhs of Yadavas – have no true ruler. They are rapidly becoming inclined towards fun and frolic. They are forgetting their daily rituals and chores. This is the biggest threat to your kingdom. The three of you should get alert well in time. You should practise strict administrative rules without fearing the so-called status among your subjects. If you fail to do so, you will not even have the time to regret it.

'I have also come to know that your subjects are increasingly getting addicted to alcohol, which is resulting in the disrespect of women's honour.

Your previously valiant Yadava soldiers are now becoming womanisers. Look at the facts and take appropriate action. You have my blessings.'

Maharishi Vyasa turned around and stepped on to the boat.

Time passed. A while later, the tolls indicated the arrival of yet another special guest. On the platform, among his disciples and our Yadava soldiers, stood Acharya Ghor Angirasa of Prayaga in person.

Like Maharishi Vyasa, he, too, embraced Dada, Balabhadradada and me deeply. He had a white strip of cloth covering his mouth, like before. He had also grown very old now and spoke much lesser than before. He told Dada in a very calm and steady voice, 'I have come here to see for myself how well and how much you have practised and treasured the knowledge of Brahmavidya that I gave you in the Prayaga ashrama. The war that you started in Kurukshetra was a great yajna. I know that it was required. I can also understand that if it had not taken place, this Aaryavarta would have become a very ugly place. But now, I am not here to give you any advice. In fact, I have come here hoping to hear your words and understand the real meaning of life at this juncture of my life.'

'You are putting me in a great quandary, Acharya.' Ghor Angirasa was not ready to go to the Sudharma royal assembly directly like Maharishi Vyasa. In very few words, he said, 'I am no longer interested in felicitation ceremonies. I only wish to speak freely with you, and only you. My disciples Uddhava and Daruka can also join in, just for listening. After talking to you, I will visit Vasudevababa, both your mothers and Acharya Sandipani, who moulded you, and then I will leave for Mount Raivataka.'

As soon as we entered Dada's chambers, he made Dada sit on his right and signalled us to sit down. Patting Dada's back, he said, 'Whatever you told Arjuna at Kurukshetra, tell me. I am only going to listen. Speak freely.'

Dada spoke and we listened. This speech was such that one could go on listening to it forever. We did not even realise how two days had passed in the company of Acharya Ghor Angirasa.

After the acharya left us, we felt an emotional vacuum for several days.

The conversations between Dada and me always included the subject of the Pandavas. They had established amicable and cordial alliances with all neighbouring kingdoms. Their administration was running smoothly under the guidance of Mahatma Vidura and experienced minister Sanjaya.

Due to the successful Ashwamedha yajna, plenty of riches were being sent to the Pandavas' royal city by all surrounding kingdoms every year. Abhimanyu and Uttaraa's son, Parikshita, was being trained under the guidance of Dhaumya rishi and was learning weaponry, astra vidya, royal customs and formalities under expert acharyas from various kingdoms.

The advice that Dada had offered to Arjuna on the battlefield had spread far and wide. It was because anyone who went to Hastinapura would meet Arjuna and request him very politely to share the advice that Dada had given him on the battlefield. Arjuna, too, would share it as he remembered, with a lot of passion. While being passed from person to person, it was inadvertently getting augmented. The people in the valley of Brahmavarta, including the kingdoms of Kurujangala, Hastinapura and Indraprastha, were now acknowledging it as 'Srikrishnagita'.

Once we were having a chat in Dada's chamber. Just then, some commotion was heard from the direction of the Srisopana. A gasping troop leader came with news of a 'munibaba' who had refused to strike the iron disc to announce his arrival and had pushed past to come and meet Dada.

The troop leader, who had come running to share this information, barely breathed a sigh of relief when a tall, dark-complexioned, bearded rishi with matted hair and a crooked staff in his hand entered Dada's chambers.

The moment Dada saw him, he stood up. Briskly moving forward, he prostrated at the feet of the rishi, who was rolling his eyes in anger. Seeing him prostrate, all of us in the chamber prostrated at his feet. Dada lovingly held his frail hand and asked him politely, 'When did you come to Dwaraka, oh rishi? Please let us know the purpose of your visit.'

The lanky sage glowered with his angry red eyes at all of us. Then, raising the staff in the air once, he roared, 'Alas, what a sad state you and your Dwaraka are in, self-proclaimed Lord of Dwaraka. I travelled through the entire city. In every square, liquor shops have been opened. Your heroic Yadavas keep fighting with each other arrogantly over trivial matters, getting drunk day and night, and forgetting their Kshatriya lineage. They remain quiet temporarily when they see your armed squad leaders. They pretend to be innocent.'

I kept staring at Dada. He did not react.

The guests who had come to meet Dada became nervous. They wondered who the sage was and raised their eyebrows questioningly.

At that, the rishi roared, 'Who wants to know who I am? And what for? I am Durvasa. Son of venerable Sage Atri.' Immediately fixing his eyes on Dada, Durvasa roared again, 'Lord of Dwaraka, from where and why have you collected such a bunch of idiots? Get rid of all of them. You ignited such a great war! What is the outcome of that? Instead, you should have spent your life in improving the hearts of the people of your golden Dwaraka. Now, neither are you are keeping tabs on Indraprastha, nor Hastinapura, and not even Dwaraka. Thousands of your Yadava citizens have become insolent due to your victory in the war of Kurukshetra. They don't respect anyone. Even a human body, which is just thrice the length of an arm, does not work properly if it is not disciplined, then how will a kingdom run? Even though it is made of gold, how long will it take to turn it into dust? Who do you think you are? Vasudeva? Bhagvan? The one who does everything?'

Shocked, all of us only kept listening. Dada listened without interrupting him. Durvasa got angrier and roared, 'Do you have any idea what happened to Kuntidevi, who had served me and was the possessor of the Devahuti mantra?'

Dada was now startled and looked up.

'Kuntidevi, who had gone to the forest to serve her blind brother-in-law Dhritarashtra and his wife Gandhari has been consumed by a sudden wildfire in the forest. Blind Dhritarashtra, who built a lacquer house in the forest of Varanavata to burn Kunti's five sons to ashes, has now turned into ashes himself along with his virtuous wife. And Hastinapura has no clue about this.'

Hearing this devastating news, Dada's eyes brimmed with tears.

Sage Durvasa softened a bit. He said, 'As her nephew, you should perform her final rites. Send a message to the Pandavas to perform the final rites for all three of them immediately. I have come to you first, taking the shortest path from the Himalayas, travelling along the foothills of Mount Aravali.'

'Who is this saffron-clad man?' he pointed at me.

Before Dada could answer, I leaned forward with joined palms and answered, 'I am the son of Devabhaga and Kansaa, cousin of the Lord of Dwaraka.'

'It is good that you did not introduce yourself as "Avadhuta" to me. But let me tell you that you have indeed achieved the status of an Avadhuta. Your eyes reflect it. I will see you later in Badri–Kedara.

'Krishna, I will visit your parents, Prince Balarama and Acharya Sandipani and go back tomorrow. On my way back, at the holy place of Prabhasa, I am going to perform the ritual of my last rites with my own hands and return to the Himalayas.'

Durvasa had now calmed down quite a bit. He looked at Dada, held both his arms lovingly in his hands and said, 'Vasudeva, I spoke as per my irascible nature. If I have hurt you, forgive this dispassionate, crazy man who has been constantly walking throughout his life.'

Dada held both his feeble hands and patted them with a lot of affection. With a smile, he said, 'I am not hurt at all, venerable rishi. If you hadn't said something like this, I would have been concerned. You should go with Avadhuta and meet my parents. I am going to send for all my queens and sons and daughters right away. Please grant them permission to get your blessings. My brother Avadhuta will accompany you to the holy place of Prabhasa to make all the arrangements for you there.'

Durvasa Rishi rose from Dada's seat and blessed him, 'Oh Lord of Dwaraka, may all be well.'

After giving him blessings, the rishi casually said, 'Krishna, even the greatest of rishis like me have not understood the meaning of life the way you have. To tell you frankly, I am not worthy of giving you my blessings. What I have given you are only my best wishes as your senior in age.'

Durvasa Rishi met everyone and was now ready to leave for the holy place of Prabhasa. Along with me, Dada's son Samba and about twenty of his half-brothers accompanied the sage to the holy place.

At Prabhasa, Samba and his brothers played a prank that spelt doom for the Yadava dynasty. Sage Durvasa was approached by a supposedly pregnant woman, who asked him if she was going to give birth to a boy or a girl.

The woman who had approached Durvasa was, in fact, not a woman at all. It was Samba. He had got a sudden impulse of teaching Durvasa rishi a lesson for throwing tantrums and defiantly giving orders to everybody. It was all Samba's idea - the drama of dressing up as a pregnant woman, pretentiously asking for Sage Durvasa's blessings, asking him about the gender of the unborn child to ridicule his wisdom, and he had made all his brothers participate in this scheme..

Shaking with rage, Sage Durvasa went closer to the three pieces of pestle that Samba had used inside the woman's clothing he was wearing. He struck a few blows of his staff on them. He then poured some water on his right palm from the kamandalu he was holding, closed his eyes, whispered something quickly and sprinkled the water on them. He then roared loudly, 'You stupid Yadavas who dared to humiliate a rishi like me, this same pestle will soon become the cause of your destruction. It will lead to your annihilation. I will not stay here a moment now.'

Durvasa Rishi did not even bother to throw a glance at me or anyone else. He turned in the direction of the north and marched on. His disciples dragged behind him. Benumbed, I ran after him to see if I could pacify him. Durvasa Rishi did not pay any attention to my pleadings and left without a word.

I came back to the tree under which Dada's sons had gathered, along with Samba. They were not there; nor was the destructive pestle to be seen. All of them had made one more unforgivable mistake. Samba had ground the wet pestle into powder using stones. He thought that if he destroyed the source of the problem, it would be solved. He and his brothers had dumped the powder in the frothing waves of the western ocean.

When I returned alone to Dwaraka from Prabhasa, I was dejected. Not just because the Yadavas were going to be annihilated but because I could not do anything to stop it. And more than that, it was me who had to break this devastating news to my dear Dada.

When Dada asked me, 'Did Sage Durvasa return safely?', I just said 'Yes' and stopped short. He patted my shoulders and said, 'Avadhuta, you will never be able to hide anything from me. Tell me what happened, no matter how unpropitious it is.' I hesitated for a moment, wondering what to say. How was I going to tell him news of their total annihilation?

Finally, I hardened my heart and told him everything that had taken place on the holy land of Prabhasa.

He was solemn for a long time. For quite a long time, he did not say anything to me. Then he just smiled and stopped. After some time, he asked me, 'Uddhava, what would you have done if you were in my place?'

I answered, 'I would have spoken in the Sudharma assembly as candidly as you would have.'

Now he gave me his usual smile. 'That's what is going to happen. Ask Chief Minister Sukrita to meet me.'

An announcement was made: 'The Lord of Dwaraka wants to say something of crucial importance to all the citizens of Dwaraka. No one will ever be able to hear him talk in the Sudharma royal assembly or any other assembly after this. Anyone who is interested in listening to his speech should make sure to attend the Sudharma assembly this Wednesday.'

Everyone was present. Yes, even Samba, who had brought this calamity upon all due to his naughtiness, was sitting along with his brothers and half-brothers.

The huge hall of the Sudharma royal assembly was overflowing. Not even an ant could enter in there.

Now everyone, including the chief minister, was waiting for the Lord of Dwaraka and Rukmini. The Sudharma royal assembly was quite close to Dada's palace. Yet, as per Dada's instructions, Daruka had embellished his Garudadhwaja chariot and kept it ready. We boarded the chariot and moved towards the Sudharma assembly. On our way, we passed the time-indicating iron disc platform. Dada alighted from the chariot alone. Walking slowly, he climbed the stairs of the platform and went close to the broad and tall gold-plated iron disc. He landed three successive powerful strikes with the heavy hammer. The echoing sound was so piercing that it subdued even the roaring sound of the ocean.

Dada entered the assembly, raised both his arms and, smiling politely, signalled to the crowd to take their seats. Sukrita, the newly appointed young chief minister of the Yadavas, spoke briefly in his sharp voice, 'Dear Yadava brothers, this assembly today is of crucial importance. The Lord of Dwaraka himself has called it. Never has he himself called a Sudharma assembly before. It was always done by the order of Vasudeva Maharaja and Prince Balaramadada from time to time. I humbly request Bhagvan Vasudeva to take over.'

Silence prevailed inside the assembly hall.

'Dear people, who love me unconditionally, I am going to speak very little. It is my first-hand experience that excess talk is always futile. This western ocean has been speaking, roaring for lakhs of years now. Has anybody ever heard him? He is roaring and telling us, "deep within me there is a treasure of many jewels and pearls, but what everyone sees is only my saline water. The one with intelligence and the power of distinction can make use of even the saline water, by obtaining salt from it and making it beneficial for life."

'My speech today is not advice. It is my duty to share with you whatever life has given me. I told Arjuna all kinds of yogas of life on the land of Kurukshetra. Today I assert that the essence of life is Premayoga. Love has no limit. It is endless. The human race has been created only for spreading love. Hatred comes to an end. When one person hates another, that hatred ends with the death of the other person. In short, hatred ends at some point of time. Till it comes to an end, the individuals, castes, groups and kingdoms on both sides suffer tremendous irrecoverable loss. That is not the case with love. The more one gives love, the more it multiplies. It never gets reduced by giving.

'Wars take place due to the immeasurable greed for power, wealth and women. It leads to utter destruction. The war between the Kauravas and the Pandavas has proved it. I tried my best to avoid that war. Finally, when the war became inevitable, I had to turn it into a great yajna.

'All of you who are listening to me now should learn a lesson from the great war. The biggest war or the greatest yajna is actually going on in everyone's heart. The one who understands his own spirit, and its good and bad powers, understands life. The meaning of life is to live and let live. Only when one recognises one's own ego and the hundreds of tentacles of one's greed will one understand the cause-and-effect relationship between every small event that takes place in the surroundings.

'Each one of you carries a tiny reflection of the gigantic expanse outside. When you obtain the strength to look at it with an aloof mind, you will be able to see the grandeur within yourself.

'Due to the everlasting bond, which is present between you and me, I assert over and over again that Samba, who insulted venerable Durvasa rishi, was your representative. That Samba is hiding within each one of us. You better recognise him in time and obliterate him. Do not hate each other. Do not fight with each other, falling prey to your egocentric nature. Do not fall prey to addictions like alcohol, which incites the pride within. Gluttony, addiction, indulgence, inertia, apathy, dishonesty and corruption are all falsities that were present yesterday, are present today and will be present tomorrow.

'Similarly, love, the lust for knowledge, the passion to live and let others live, earnestness towards one's duty and the urge to study for that, a penchant for sincerity and hatred for corruption are truths existing in the past, present and future.

'The one who considers that he is the doer or undoer of things that are happening around, he makes the sun and the moon shine, makes rivers, streams and wind flow, makes the ocean roar, causes lightning to flash, makes farms grow, makes fruits grow on trees, makes flowers breathe fragrance and is the cause of every such thing, is far removed from the Truth.

'No matter how hard we try, we cannot create a mere drop of blood or milk at our whim. We cannot even tell how a mother's body produces blood from the food she eats and how a cow's body creates milk in its udder from the fodder that she eats. Then why should we indulge in self-conceit?

'I know all your virtues and vices quite well as I grew up among you. You should renounce your ego, which is destructive, let go of your short temper and keep addiction at bay, like venom.

'I have fulfilled my duty of telling you this assertively in front of Acharya Sandipani, who is present in this assembly hall. Nowadays, Acharya frequently expresses his desire to leave Dwaraka and go back to his Ankapada ashrama in the forests of Avanti. I also intuitively feel that this is the right time for him to do so. I announce that Acharya Sandipani should bless all of us and happily leave for the ashrama with his family. Prince Balaramadada should go to his residence later and felicitate him in a way that is befitting the status of the Yadavas.

'What I am going to announce now will be the most difficult thing to digest for my beloved wife Rukmini and her seven sisters, who are present in this assembly hall.'

A curious buzz of whispers spread through the assembly hall. The chief minister raised the royal sceptre and pounded it on the floor. Immediately, silence prevailed.

Dada expressed his intention in clear words, 'Oh Yadava brothers, from tomorrow, I will not accept any services from anyone except my confidant and best friend Avadhuta Uddhava. Not even from my beloved wife Rukmini and the other seven wives. This does not mean that they cannot come to meet me. They can come to my residential chambers any time to see me. The people of Dwaraka should not make any changes in the royal treatment towards them. But from tomorrow, I will not visit the island of the queens' mansion.

'Just as I will not go there, I will not come to the Sudharma royal assembly of the Yadavas ever again. Prince Balaramadada will solve all your political, military, social and individual problems. No one should present them to me any more. As I knew beforehand that someday I was going to have to take this decision, I had intentionally not accepted any position in the royal assembly.

'I am saying this in front of my venerable acharya, who is soon going to leave Dwaraka, that this is the beginning of my vanaprasthashrama, without going to any forest at all. This is not physical or verbal – it is mental, and spiritual.

'The most important thought that I shared with Arjuna on Kurukshetra was of a stable mind. That of keeping your heart detached while performing the duties of your life. From tomorrow, my mental and spiritual vanaprasthashrama symbolising that thought is going to commence. I reside among thousands of you Yadavas, and of course, in every one of you, and yet I am not in anything.

'From tomorrow, only my most beloved sakha Uddhava will serve all my needs.' The last Sudharma royal council in Dada's life was over. He politely saluted everyone by joining his palms. Benumbed members of the assembly, Yadava men and women began silently leaving the assembly hall one by one. They knew very well that those were Krishna's words of determination. No one could ever alter them in any way.

Now, my life's important Karmayoga, of serving Dada, began. One day, while we were chatting in Dada's chambers, a guard at the gate brought news. 'A guard from the holy land of Prabhasa has come to see the Lord of Dwaraka. He is carrying a bunch of grass blades under his arms and wants to show it to the Lord of Dwaraka in person. He insists on meeting you.' Hearing that news, a web of wrinkles appeared on Dada's forehead.

I got up and went outside to meet the guard of Prabhasa. He greeted and implored me, 'Oh Avadhuta, do anything, but let me meet the Lord of Dwaraka for a few moments. Take a look at this.'

He pulled some blades of grass out of the bunch he was holding under his arm and handed them to me. They were of an arm's length, just like the ones used for regular religious rituals. But they were not green. They were black like burnt iron. Their tips were not like those of regular grass blades. They were sharp and triangular like the tip of an arrow.

The guard said, 'Uddhavadeva, these grass blades are not like the regular ones. See if you can break them. They only bend like an iron wire and straighten back to their original shape.'

Terrified, the guard continued, 'In my entire life, I have not seen such a terrifying iron grass blade. These are signs of doom. As soon as my servants showed these to me, I pulled out a couple of grass blades from each of the meadows as a sample and brought them. Please let me visit him once.'

I realised the gravity of his speech. Holding the bunch of grass blades that he had handed to me, I said to him, 'Come with me.' I entered Dada's chambers with him.

The moment the blades touched his hands, his wide forehead creased.

Dada held its triangular sharp tip closer and observed it thoroughly.

'No. This is not an iron grass blade. This is an arrow blade. An iron arrow blade. Even more powerful than our regular Suchi arrow.'

I asked the guard to leave. Dada was restlessly moving around in his chamber, chanting only one thing, 'Oh Idamata, save us. Oh Lord Shambho, save us!'

Days were passing leisurely. More than thirty-six years had passed since the war at Kurukshetra. Many memories related to it had been forgotten. I, too, had forgotten the meeting with the guard of Prabhasa. One day, Dada told Daruka to take the Garudadhwaja chariot towards Balaramadada's palace. Dada and I waited in the chariot. Daruka went to inform the prince of our arrival but returned with his head hanging low. 'He is there, but the guards did not even let me inside. He is castigating someone severely in his chamber. The guards said that I should not approach him at such a time. So, I waited for some time and came back.'

Hearing that, Dada alighted from the chariot in a single leap.

I followed him.

Balidada was standing with his back to us. But we could feel that he was trembling with rage. In front of him stood Kritavarma, who looked much more older than him.

Since the end of the Kurukshetra war, Kritavarma had stopped attending the Sudharma assembly. He also avoided Dada and saw me very rarely. Though he was a member of the Yadava ministry, he remained intoxicated day and night. Gradually, this addiction had spread among all Yadava soldiers in the whole of Dwaraka. Intoxicated Yadava soldiers were insanely fighting with each other.

Since the time Dada had announced that he would take to vanaprasthashrama, he had stopped attending the Sudharma assembly. Prince Balabhadradada was fed up of drawing decrees and making announcements. The Yadavas refused to conform to any kind of rules.

Balabhadradada, who otherwise spoke very less, was saying, 'You vile traitor. You are cunningly trying to do what you could not do at Kurukshetra. We should have recognised it that very night when Ashwatthama slew all the sons of Draupadi. That night, you were the one holding your bare sword and keeping a watch outside the pavilion along with Kripa. After that, you spoilt all the combative Yadava soldiers left in Dwaraka. You turned them into addicts, alcoholics. You are a traitor. You better leave Dwaraka today or else I will behead you in front of the crowd with my own hands.'

At that point, Dada came forward. He said, 'I can understand your rage. It is too late for your severe actions now. In my opinion, you yourself should go to the holy land of Prabhasa and pray to the Almighty for the betterment of the Yadavas. You decide and do whatever seems right to you.' Without uttering a single extra word, he left Balaramadada's chamber.

The Yadavas had a tradition of visiting the holy land of Prabhasa on a full moon day. Accordingly, all the major Yadavas left for Prabhasa in boats. Only the elderly Yadavas and children were left behind. A special caravan, of about one hundred boats, carrying pitchers full of Maireyaka wine and jars full of Somarasa for the entertainment of thousands of Yadavas, also left. Dada had given up attending such public festivities long ago.

As it was the night of the full moon, the two of us, along with Daruka, sat on the stone seats near the Aindra gate in the clear, beautiful starlit night. The waves of the western ocean were dancing in front of us. We sat there in silence for a long time. When we came back, it was past midnight.

Two days went by. On the third day, early in the morning, we heard three sharp tolls on the time-indicating iron disc after a long time, asking for a special meeting with the Lord of Dwaraka. Dada and I looked at each other questioningly.

After some time, the same guard of the holy land of Prabhasa came. Shaking with fear, he directly prostrated at Dada's feet and began sobbing.

Both of us wondered what had happened. I sat down and tried to console him.

But Dada stood still instead of pulling him up quickly, as he usually did when someone prostrated at his feet. Wiping the tears continuously streaming down his eyes, he barely uttered one word at a time, after gathering all his courage, 'Oh Lord of Dwaraka – Avadhuta – a devastating thing has happened. A disaster took place on the night of the full moon. All major Yadavas of the eighteen royal families got drunk and under the influence of alcohol, fought with each other and destroyed themselves.'

'What...?' I almost screamed.

But Dada was still calm. He spoke firmly as if talking to himself, 'Oh guard, calm down and tell us everything that has happened and how it happened, in detail.'

'As the full moon rose in the sky, thousands of Yadavas began drinking from the cauldrons full of wine. By the time the moon reached overhead, all of them got uncontrollably drunk.

'First, Kritavarma provoked commander Satyaki by bringing up the subject of the Symantaka jewel. He literally called the Lord of Dwaraka a "thief". Hearing that, Satyaki got infuriated and began hurling the iron grass arrows from the nearby meadows at Kritavarma, with his bare hands. It was hard to figure out how quickly and how many grass arrows Satyaki was uprooting and shooting. Samba got enraged to see Kritavarma wounded. He attacked Satyaki and shot countless grass arrows at him. Pradyumna could not tolerate this attack on the commander. He killed Samba first. Bhadradevi's eldest son Sangramjita was killed by his own brother Subhadra.

'For a long time, all intoxicated Yadavas fell upon each other noisily, forgetting their age, relations and morals.

'Prince Balaramadada got exhausted running around, raising both his hands while shouting and pleading, "Wait! Stop it in the name of Goddess Ida." No one bothered to pay any attention to him. The yelling and hurling of arrows by the drunk Yadavas continued till late night. The benumbed prince sat on a boulder, holding his head in his hands.

'All the Yadavas killed their own brethren ruthlessly with grass arrows. By sunrise, the holy land of Prabhasa had turned into Kurukshetra. The dead bodies of the Yadavas had scattered all over the place. All the meadows of grass arrows were wiped out. There was not even a tiny portion on the ocean shore near the meadows where a corpse of a Yadava did not lie.

'Dejected, Prince Balarama took the support of a young Yadava who had escaped and came near the shore of the western ocean. In the ocean sand, he sat in padmasana and went into a meditative trance. Just then, the high tide came in. The young Yadava who was with him told me later that a white flame came out of Dada's closed eyes and disappeared far away among the ocean waves.

'Seeing the roaring high tide of the ocean, the young Yadava accompanying him ran away in fear. We could not find the prince's body.

'Oh, Lord of Dwaraka – our prince Balabhadradada has left us, he was swept away by the ocean.'

The guard hid his face in his shawl and trembled.

Benumbed, I held my head in my hands and slipped to the floor.

Dada spoke only one sentence and went inside, 'Dear Dada, once you got angry with me and left me. So, I sent my peacock feather and brought you back. But now, this younger brother of yours has nothing to bring you back with.'

Dada got Daruka to get the Garudadhwaja chariot ready. Dada, Revati and I left for the holy land of Prabhasa. He had left only after instructing the chief minister to bring Vasudevababa and Rohinimata to Prabhasa. He had also instructed that informers be sent with the news to places such as Hastinapura, Kampilyanagar, Indraprastha, Viratanagar and Raivataknagar.

Now all of us were going to stay there till all the final rites of Balabhadradada were performed. Dada got eighteen huge funeral pyres arranged for all Yadava warriors who had lost their lives in the fight. He had brought one elderly person from each royal family of the Yadavas. Those seniors performed the final rites of all the dead together. He was steady and calm even while igniting Balaramdada's funeral pyre.

To offer their respects, Yudhishthira and Draupadi had come from Hastinapura along with the other Pandavas. Mahatma Vidura and Sanjaya also accompanied them.

Dada later took Arjuna aside from among the Pandavas. I accompanied them. Very calmly, he asked, 'Did you perform the final rites of Aunt Kunti properly in the forest of the Himalayas?'

With moist eyes, he simply kept staring at Dada. Even he looked much older now. He just nodded, indicating that they had performed all the final rites. He did not know what to say.

Dada put his right arm around Arjuna's broad shoulders and, patting him gently, said, 'My elder brother is gone. Everyone has to go. I will also have to go tomorrow. In memory of Aunt Kunti and Balabhadradada, promise me something right now.'

Dada had never asked for anything from anyone – not even a promise. Arjuna felt even more overwhelmed with tears. He gently put his hand on Dada's palm.

Dada said to Arjuna slowly, 'Partha, you are to protect all the Yadava women after I am gone.'

I shivered at those words. I did not expect him to say something like that at all. Arjuna was utterly stunned. Soon it was time for the Pandavas to return to Hastinapura. While bidding farewell, Dada knelt down on the ground and prostrated at the feet of eldest Pandava Yudhishthira and Bhimsena, like he did at the feet of Acharya Sandipani and Sage Ghor Angirasa. But both were so shaken that they hardly noticed what he did.

Draupadi, who always spoke openly with him without any reservations, was speechless now. As Dada approached her, she leaned forward to touch his feet. With utmost affection, Dada held both her hands and stopped her.

She thought Dada was going to give her some advice but he spoke only a single sentence, 'Sakhi … you want my words right now. I am giving you my love – in the form of a garment. Take good care of it.' And he handed over the orange shawl wrapped around his throat to her.

The Pandavas left for Hastinapura with Draupadi. We came back to Dwaraka with Vasudevababa and both the matas. Now I could clearly see the disorder in Dada's daily routine. He had stopped going to the ocean shore to offer his oblations to the Sun god. He had particularly stopped meeting any sages, ascetics or hermits visiting Dwaraka. But he still visited Vasudevababa and both rajmatas twice a day without fail. Just as I could feel his reticence, Rukmini felt it too. Whenever both of us met, we spoke only about this subject. While concluding such discussions, she would say, 'Do not worry. I am sure that Sri will talk only to you and when he does, he will talk to his heart's content.'

I kept waiting for that day. My heart was getting numb inside. Meanwhile, the naval chief brought news that made everyone solemn. Something akin to an earthquake had taken place underwater in the western ocean. Due to that, the Kroshtu lighthouse guiding the harbour of Dwaraka had sunk at the base. Dada did not even mention this to me. And finally, the day dawned – the day Dada spoke – the day of the end of an era.

That day, very early in the morning, I woke up to melodious tunes of the flute, one after the other. I witnessed him playing the flute in Dwaraka for the first time. Even the bards had not yet arrived. Before they could wake Dada up with their songs, he woke me up with the unforgettable, unknown tunes on his flute.

We performed our morning chores. Dada sent a Yadava servant to summon Daruka. Daruka arrived with the Garudadhwaja chariot in the front yard.

He had decorated the already embellished chariot with garlands of Dada's favourite Kadamba flowers. We left for Dada's morning visit to Vasudevababa and both the mothers. Daruka brought the chariot to the palace of Maharaja Vasudeva.

Before climbing down, he said, 'Sakha Daruka, looks like you have not groomed my beloved horses for two days.'

'Yes, my Lord. I did not get the chance to collect the thorny wild creepers to groom them. They look a bit fatigued today. Or else they would have neighed in ecstasy as soon as they saw you.' Daruka gave a detailed explanation abashedly.

'That is fine. I will go and bring the thorny wild creepers myself this afternoon.' Dada smiled and descended from the Garudadhwaja. The three of us entered the royal palace and went to see Vasudevababa and the mothers in their chamber. Dada prostrated in front of them. Daruka and I followed suit. Dada did not leave their chamber in a hurry. He sat on Devakimata's bed. A few moments passed. No one spoke. Dada said to Devakimata, 'It has been so long since I drank milk from your hands. Will you give me some today?' He gave her such a charming smile that she could not say anything. 'Yes, I will', she said and went into the inner chambers rather than ordering the maid to bring it. Dada came and stood in front of Rohinimata. Both were overwhelmed with emotion as memories of Balabhadradada flooded their minds. Rohinimata began sobbing. Dada held her wrinkled hands in his palms and said, 'Calm down, mata. In fact, I should be grieving more than you. Oh, how much I troubled my elder brother your son.' Dada savoured the sweet taste of milk that Devakimata had brought for him and drank it with closed eyes.

The chief minister had arranged golden salvers with various gifts on the charity platform at the centre of the city on Dada's instructions. I did not realise that those were considerably higher in number today.

Dada respectfully offered vermilion and flowers on all the salvers. People, who felt satisfied simply by seeing him in person, were raising their hands and offering their blessings to him, 'Long live the Lord of Dwaraka. May all be well.'

We came back to his residential chambers. It was about lunchtime now. Usually, Daruka would go to his residence at this time. Dada asked Daruka to join him for lunch and the three of us sat on three wooden seats. We finished our meal while chatting about various subjects. Dada got up first. While getting up, he picked up the golden jar of water that was usually kept in front of him with his left hand.

We came out for washing our hands. I realised that for the last forty years or more, I had been pouring water on his hands after the meal. I quickly moved forward and tried to take the jar from Dada's left hand. He promptly pulled his hand back, gave me a charming smile and said, 'No … Avadhuta, today is your day. Till today, you have been pouring water on my hands. Today, I am going to pour water on your as well as Daruka's hands. Both of you have served me till today. Let me serve you at least today.'

While wiping his hands with the dry cloth that I handed him, he asked Daruka, 'Daruka, from which forest do you collect the thorny wild creepers that you need for grooming the horses?'

'From the forest of Bhalaka Tirtha near Veravala,' Daruka answered.

'Do one thing, Daruka. You take rest today. After taking my afternoon nap, Uddhava and I will go there and bring the wild creepers. Do not release the horses from the chariot. You have decorated the chariot very well today. Leave it as is in the stable.'

He touched Dada's feet and was about to leave. Dada gently pulled him up and held him in a deep embrace. Daruka left wondering why the Lord had honoured him with a deep embrace and lunch.

Bhalaka Tirtha was in the forest near Somanatha–Veravala. This forest was about twenty miles away after crossing the creek. We would have to go there in the Garudadhwaja, and it needed to be carried in a boat to go across the creek.

I was stunned to look at Dada. He had donned the attire of an unarmed charioteer for the first time after returning from Kurukshetra. It had never been worn in the last thirty-six years. He had worn the peacock-feathered, decorative golden crown on his thick white hair. It was not the crown that he used to wear daily. His favourite iridescent peacock feather was still tucked into that dazzling golden crown. Even at this moment, his face had lit up with the dazzling brilliance of a hundred suns. A white Vaijayanti garland that looked as fresh as if he had just worn it, was resting on his chest, reaching below his knees. Underneath it, he wore pearl necklaces with a shining pendant of the Kaustubh jewel. Beneath these, on his broad chest, he was wearing his usual gold-plated iron armour. His favourite orange shawl with a gold border was hanging from his broad shoulders. On both his upper arms and wrists were intricately designed golden armlets. He wore a shining golden dhoti. A sky-blue shawl was tied over it. His auspicious white Paanchjanya conch was tied in the shawl. In his left hand, he was holding a fresh, long-stemmed orange lotus. He had now added only two more new things to this earlier attire. He had tucked the colourful bamboo flute that he had played heartily in the morning today into his dhoti. On his right wrist, he was wearing the silver bracelet – the symbol of the Abhirbhanu dynasty – that his grandfather Chitrasena had gifted him when he had left Gokul.

Even today his handsomeness was indeed eye-catching. Even today, he was the Krishna who attracted others – Srikrishna who possessed the qualities of Sri, befitting his name.

Seeing me staring at him, he said, 'Shall we leave? This is your day. I am going to tell you everything about this Srisopana.' He walked towards the first step of the Srisopana along with me. He stopped for a moment and closed his fish-shaped eyes. 'This first step of the Srisopana is in the name of my biological mother Devakimata, who endured the excruciating pain of seeing her six newborn sons being killed in Kansa's prison.' He lingered on the step for a moment.

'The second one is in the name of my beloved wife Rukmini – the Lakshmi of Dwaraka. The third is in the name of my biological father, Maharaja Vasudevababa – the emperor of Dwaraka.' Looking at the fourth step, he said, 'I am not going to tell you in whose name this fourth step is. You have to find out for yourself.' We lingered for a moment, then climbed down the step. Standing on the fifth step, he said, 'This one is in the name of my guru – Ghor Angirasa – who conferred the knowledge of Brahmavidya upon me.' Looking at the sixth and seventh steps, he said, 'These are in the names of my two Jala brothers – the first one is for Grandsire Gangeya Bhishma and the next is for the first Kaunteya – Radheya – the munificent. As you already know, eight is my favourite number since birth. This one is in the name of my beloved sakha Arjuna.' The following steps were serially in the names of Balabhadradada, all the remaining Pandavas, our favourite nephew Abhimanyu, Yashodamata, Nandababa, Rohinimata, Aunt Kunti, sakhi Radhika, Draupadi, Subhadra and Revati.

After them were all of Dada's queens – Jambavati, Satyabhama, Kalindi, Lakshmanaa, Bhadra, Mitravinda and Satya.

Then came the Kauravas' mother, Gandharidevi, followed by his daughter Charumati.

The steps following those were in the name of Dada's sakhas – Mahatma Vidura, dear friend Sudama, Daruka, Sanjaya and Satyaki.

By this time, we had climbed down more than half the Srisopana. I was wondering right after the first two steps whether Dada had forgotten Acharya Sandipani.

Now, he began uttering the names of each of his closest relatives. Among the closest relatives, the first name he took was that of my father – Devabhagababa. Then grandfather Chitrasena of Gokul, Vikarna from the Kauravas, my mother Kansaamata. Then quickly mentioning names such as Virata, Drupada, Dhrishtadyumna, Drona, Kripa, Dhaumya Rishi, Gargamuni, Vishwakarma and Maya, he went down the stairs briskly. Among close relatives, he mentioned the name of Kubja towards the very end.

He did not forget to mention the names of the seven first-born sons of his seven wives, but before them, he mentioned the name of his grandson, Aniruddha. Then he mentioned the names of Pradyumna, Bhanu, Sangramjita, Vrika, Veer, Shruta, Praghosha and great grandson Vajra.

Jambavati's son Samba – who became the cause of the destruction of the Yadavas – was not among them. His name was among the people who became a hurdle for Dada throughout his life.

Yes. He did not forget to remember even the arrogant, insolent and tyrannical people.

Among those, the first was Kansa. Then came Shrugala, Narakasura, Kalayavana, Jarasandha, Shishupala, Dantavakra, Viduratha, Paundraka

Vasudeva, Shalva, Duryodhana, Dhritarashtra, Dada's son Samba, Kritavarma and Shakuni.

Now only the last step of the Srisopana remained. I could not resist and asked, 'Dada, how come you forgot our venerable Acharya Sandipani and Guru Drona's son Ashwatthama?' He looked at me and said with a smile, 'Udho, Avadhuta, is it ever possible for me to forget him? The one that we are standing on – this last step – is in the name of my venerable Acharya Sandipani, who moulded my personality and made me the man I am today. Brother, a man is born not once but twice. First, he takes physical birth from the womb of his mother and he is born again when his guru transforms him into a complete man through virtues and sanskaras. The staircase of everybody's life is contained within these two stages of life. Is it not?'

He did not allow me to ponder over that for a long time and asked me promptly, 'My beloved sakha Avadhuta, brother Uddhava – Udho, now you tell me, in whose name is the fourth step?'

'In my name.' I responded promptly. Then we laughed heartily just like we used to laugh in the Ankapada ashrama. I asked him the last question, 'And what about Ashwatthama?' He gave me a pure smile as usual and said, 'He is immortal. In the form of human pain.' He lingered for a moment, then turned around and stood still in front of the Srisopana silently. He brought his palms together and offered obeisance to the Srisopana.

We started walking towards the stable – to get ready for our travel to Bhalaka Tirtha. Usually, I would not give Dada any hint about Rukmini standing in the gallery. But today I stopped and said, 'It would have been just fine if you had not taken a look at the Srisopana today, but I feel that you should take a look at the gallery of Rukmini's palace on the right.' Coming out of his reverie, he stopped and glanced at the gallery. The moment Rukmini's and Dada's eyes met, she got flustered. She had experienced such a thing for the first time. She immediately hid herself behind the window. Dada gently patted his rosy palm on my shoulder and said, 'You are such a mind reader.'

We entered the stable. As Daruka was not with us, I moved forward to take the charioteer's seat on the Garudadhwaja. Dada stopped me.

He said with a smile, 'This is your day. I am going to drive the chariot for you while talking to my horse friends. I am going to serve you today – just like I served Arjuna. You are more fortunate than him. Look at me carefully. I have donned this charioteer's costume only to serve you.'

He held the eight golden-bordered reins tightly in his hands and affectionately called out the names of the third generation of his horse friends – 'Megha, Bala, Shaibya, Sugriva'. The wise animals turned the chariot around and took it out of the stable.

We passed through the Shuddhaksha gate on the east side of Dwaraka and embarked on a huge boat along with the chariot, riding it over wooden planks. The boat started to cross the creek of Bhrigukachchha in the western ocean. The jalapurusha was sailing on the vast expanse of water, going towards the 'other end'. The great Yadava kept feasting his eyes on the view of the golden Dwaraka that was moving farther and farther away. As the other end of the shore approached, Dada held both his palms together and offered obeisance to his beloved royal city, Dwaraka, along with its golden reflection swaying on the waves. Now, he disembarked from the chariot on the opposite shore, which was in Saurashtra. He removed one pearl necklace from among the many resting on his chest, handed it to the fishermen chief and said to him, 'Hail Goddess Ida.' The chief and his assistants prostrated at Dada's feet. Our chariot began speeding in the direction of Somanatha. We first arrived at the small stone temple of Shiva at Somanatha. From there we proceeded and reached a very small village called Veravala. Soon, we entered the thick forest near Bhalaka Tirtha. Dada said, 'Come, let us collect the thorny wild creepers.' I followed him. We stopped under the cooling shade of a sprawling banyan tree nearby. This tree was just as huge and had many branches, shoots and leaves as the Bhandirvriksha in Gokul that Dada had told me about many times. Even our chariot was clearly visible from here. From the deepest recesses of my heart, I strongly felt that this was the time to ask him an important question that had been nagging at me constantly for the last thirty-six years.

Moving forward with a sudden urge, I held his hand and said, 'Dada, whatever you say, it is certain that Arjuna is a much more beloved sakha to you than me. If that were not the case, you accepted all kinds of services from me for the last thirty-six years – but – but -' I hesitated, not knowing how to speak my mind.

'But what? Say it, brother Udho, speak freely.'

'If that were not the case, then you would have given me advice like you gave Arjuna before the war at Kurukshetra, which people know as the "Gita" now. You would have considered me suitable for such advice. Arjuna is indeed your best sakha. Not I. I am simply your best servant.' Abashed, I stood in front of him with my head lowered. I had never spoken so openly in front of him.

He removed his hand from mine and patted my shoulders with utmost love. I clearly felt the genuine love in that touch. He smiled and said, 'That is not true, Uddhava. You are silly. Arjuna is my sakha, after all, my cousin. In the war of Kurukshetra, he was the confidant of my worldly life. You are my only confidant in my spiritual life. You insist on hearing, so let me tell you. 'He looked around and chose a boulder to sit on. He rested his mace against it, dusted the boulder with his orange shawl and sat on it. He asked, 'What is your name?'

'Uddhava,' I said, getting a little flustered.

He asked, 'What does Uddhava mean?'

'"Uddhava" means the being that longs to ascend,' I answered. He gave me a very sweet smile and said, 'Let me explain it to you in simple words, because this is your day and you are my paramsakha, closest confidant, and my cousin, Avadhuta. Listen carefully. Let me explain what parmatma is.' He had read my mind and continued, 'Paramatma is the weightless unhindered energy that continuously flows through the universe around us, the vast skies and the space beyond it. It is eternal, perpetual and unending. With the help of time, that energy always keeps creating or destroying things. It keeps control over everything.'

I asked him to clarify, 'Then does this mean that human beings should just rely on this paramatma and do nothing?'

Holding his head high as sometimes he did while speaking in the Sudharma assembly, he said, 'Not at all. For generations, this is where people have been going wrong. You are looking at only half of the complete truth that I told you. You are making it one-sided and convenient to suit your purpose. A part of that great paramatma resides in every being.

And you yourself said that life means the consciousness of one's existence. To explore that consciousness day and night from every angle is life.'

I kept staring at him. No matter how hard I tried, I could not fathom the depth of his eyes. I asked, 'So what exactly happens when one explores it?'

He said, 'Once you discover the connection between you and the paramatma, then the revelation of what life is comes to you like unrolling a bundle of a fine, soft cloth. You gain the unending knowledge of not just your own self but of all animate, inanimate beings around you, the visible as well as the invisible world around you, the vast expanse of the sky, the space beyond it and the unhindered, weightless brilliance that flows through all these.'

'What is the best way to comprehend this?' I asked with utmost curiosity now.

'Complete surrender with utmost devotion and loving all beings without any expectations is the only way.' A few moments ago, I had seen him embrace the horses of his chariot. I began to understand the meaning of that action of his – his Ashwagita.

'I have come to realise why, in the Srisopana, the steps in the name of Ganga's son Bhishma and the first-born Kaunteya, the munificent Karna, are at such a higher level. They always strived to reach your level throughout their lives. You knew it very well.

'You were always a level higher than both of them. That is why the Grandsire first addressed you as "Vasudeva" and considered you as Narayana. Even Karna said so when he met you and regarded you in the same way.'

He gave me a sweet smile, like the one that he had given me only in the Ankapada ashrama before, and said, 'Udho, brother, you are as pure as a lotus blooming in a lake. Because Arjuna is a complete nara, he got attracted to more women than his other brothers. Despite being a Yadava, you kept yourself detached from such kind of attachments, like Guru Ghor Angirasa. That is why I addressed you as "Avadhuta" in the Sudharma assembly. Even Guru Ghor Angirasa approved it in his last visit, even though I did not ask him. You know very well that he is my guru of Brahmavidya.'

Now most of my doubts had been cleared. I still had a couple more. I asked him, 'You said that seeking the energy that resides within oneself is life and the best way to seek it is through complete surrender with utmost devotion and pure love without any expectation. I want to ask you what exactly is devotion and love.'

'Devotion is selfless faith, service and worship. Love is respectful attraction without any kind of expectation.'

He continued after a pause. 'To make people understand the feminine aspect of the paramatma clearly, I bore this peacock feather in my crown with honour throughout my life. It is the matchless symbol of the fertile female yoni – the essence of womanhood. Today, more than the Sudarshan chakra that I have renounced completely, this peacock feather on my head is my message to the world.' He had left me spellbound and speechless. I had obtained a complete blessing from him whom I had served wholeheartedly for the last thirty-six years. Exactly at that moment, he spread the rosy palm of his right hand in front of me just like he had spread it in front of Arjuna. I clearly saw the brilliant rare symbols of a pennant, chakra, conch, swastika, triangle and square on his hand, which I had never seen on anybody else's. Looking deep into my eyes, he said, 'Avadhuta, do you understand now how you are the confidant of my spiritual life? Promise me that whatever I have told you just now, you will pass on to the generations to come, by raising an ashrama in Badri–Kedara and teaching it to them yourself.'

I put my palm on his. He smiled and said, 'Uddhava, people will like even this Avadhutagita of yours from the bottom of their hearts. Come now, let's go.' I moved forward with respect and handed him his Kaumodaki mace. He put it on his shoulder and casually said, 'You go back to the royal city with the Garudadhwaja chariot. Think carefully about everything that I told you now. Go ahead.'

'Your wish is my command, Narayana.' I touched his feet. He put his left arm around me and took me into a deep embrace. Then I left the forest. He entered the forest in the direction of Bhalaka Tirtha.

I was completely lost in the many thoughts that he had shared with me, every thought more amazing than the other. I did not even realise when the chariot passed Veravala. To comprehend the depth of the thoughts that he shared with me, it was necessary to find a tranquil place and contemplate. What better place could there be than the Shiva temple of Somanatha to do that?

A long time passed while I contemplated and tried to understand each and every word that I had heard from Dada. It was evening now. It was essential to return to the royal city. I had still not come out of the web of thoughts that Dada had spun. Engrossed in those thoughts, I drove the chariot and came on the Dwaraka side of the creek in front of the Shuddhaksha gate. The Garudadhwaja chariot entered the royal city of Dwaraka from the Shuddhaksha gate. Pondering over the thoughts that Dada had shared, I came near the Srisopana. With my right hand, I touched the step in the name of Acharya Sandipani, touched my hand to my forehead respectfully and began climbing the tall staircase in front of me. I was lost in myself. Many of Dada's thoughts had become quite clear to me now. I had already begun planning when and how to go to Badri–Kedara as per his wish. Just then –

Just then Chief Minister Sukrita, climbing down the stairs, stood in front of me, saying, 'Avadhuta, there is bad news. The lifeless body of the Lord of Dwaraka is lying under an ashwattha tree in the forest of Bhalaka Tirtha. A hunter named Jara, whose fatal Suchi arrow pierced the sole of his left foot, came here some time ago, along with a couple of his young friends. He himself brought the news to the city. The whole of Dwaraka, along with Rukminidevi, has gone there. There is no one in the city. I – I was waiting only for you. Avadhuta, our Lord of Dwaraka has left us!' The chief minister wiped his eyes with the edge of his shawl and gave out an uncontrollable sob. Then he kept weeping; his entire body trembled with sorrow. The jewel-studded royal Yadava sceptre that he was holding slipped from his hand. Clanging on each step of the staircase, it tumbled down to the last step, lingered there for a moment and fell down further.

My mind, which had just about cleared, was again overcast with black clouds. I was stunned, dumbfounded and benumbed as if lightning had struck me. I could not understand where I was standing, what the meaning of me being the closest confidant was … Nothing, nothing made any sense.

It was just a few moments ago that he had shared so many wonderful thoughts about life.

The chief minister had already left. I was unable to cry. My eyes were completely dry. I turned around and climbed down the stairs, leaping over three-four steps at a time. I did not even realise when I reached the end of the staircase. I darted towards the Shuddhaksha gate like an arrow shot from a bow. I could not even think of going to the stable first. The creek shore was overcrowded with people of Dwaraka. Seeing me run barefoot, the crowd automatically made way for me. The moment we approached the other shore, I leapt out of the boat. Climbing in the chariot that came in front of me, I commanded the charioteer impatiently, 'Hurry up – do not stop anywhere. Go to Bhalaka Tirtha directly.' I leapt out of the chariot as soon as we reached Bhalaka Tirtha and rushed into the forest. I did not even realise that the shawl on my chest had flown away.

I reached the ashwattha tree soon to find that it was surrounded by Yadava men and women.

They made way for me, whispering, 'Uddhavadeva is here'.

I came near Dada's lifeless body. I was feeling suffocated. I could not understand why I was unable to cry. Looking at the foot that was stuck to the pool of blood, I intensely felt that the vast expanse of the celestial sky above was contained in his tall body.

His friend Sudama had implored him in a similar forest – Aanarta – while bidding him farewell, saying, 'Give me something as your gift.' Sudama had moved his glance from the peacock feather in the golden crown on his head to his feet. In the end, he had embraced his sandalwood slippers and asked for those as a gift.

My eyes moved over his body, from his toes up to his rosy lips. My heart said agonisingly, 'Let me hear a word of yours. Call me "Udho Avadhuta" once. Give me a teardrop.'

He did not say anything. He was not going to say anything ever! Just a while ago, he had shared a lot with me. And he still had so much more worth sharing, but no one was ever going to be able to hear it.

'Dada...!' I gave out a cry and collapsed. The cocoon of tears in my eyes broke open. My whole body shook with uncontrollable sobs. I calmed down only when Rukminidevi patted me on my back.

I composed myself. Considering what he would have liked me to do, I consoled all seven queens along with Rukmini. With the assistance of a few Yadavas, the chief minister erected a funeral pyre of sandalwood. sunset was approaching now. A few senior Yadavas came forward to assist me. Dada's body was put on the sandalwood funeral pyre, along with the things that he had carried with him throughout his life – the Paanchjanya conch, his mace, a lotus, the Vaijayanti garland, the Kaustubh jewel, his crown with the peacock feather tucked in it, and the Nandaka sword. I could clearly see two more things from Gokul added to them – the flute tucked into his yellow dhoti and the silver bracelet on his wrist. Along with the chief minister, a few old Yadavas, sitting under a tree at a distance, brought Vasudevababa, Devakimata and Rohinimata, who were composed by now, to the sandalwood funeral pyre. I put the very last sandalwood log on his body. Somebody handed me an ignited sandalwood torch.

Then, amidst the incantation of mantras, I ignited the funeral pyre as his close relative 'Avadhuta'. The birds of fiery flames soared above to touch the sky. The chief minister made arrangements for Vasudevababa, both mothers and all other seniors to go back to the royal city. In the end, I tossed the sandalwood torch I was holding into the funeral pyre, and left for Dwaraka along with a few select Yadavas. It was necessary for me to console his horse friends in the stable.

Everyone was speechless. After walking a considerable distance, we approached a blue lake. I saw a few peacock feathers lying on the thick green meadows. Their sight produced goosebumps on my whole body. A few peacocks had shed these feathers sometime in the morning while dancing to their heart's content.

I just could not walk ahead. Bending down, I picked up one peacock feather. I kept staring at the iridescent feather reflecting dark green, dark purple and rich golden shades of colour. My mind was flooded with many of his colourful reminiscences. The tears streaming down my eyes tried to brighten the bluish shade of the peacock feather in vain.

Overwhelmed by emotion, my heart was constantly wondering, 'Dada, who were you really? Did your mother – Devakimata - who gave you birth, ever understand you? Did Rohinimata? Did Vasudevababa ever realise it? Did Balabhadradada, who accompanied you throughout your entire life? Acharya Sandipani and Guru Ghor Angirasa, who gave you second birth, as you had said – did they at least get some idea? Grandsire Bhishma and Karna, whom you considered Jalapurushas – could they ever trace who you were? Grandfather Chitrasena, Yashodamata and Nandababa, who nurtured you and inculcated sanskaras in you – did they ever understand you completely? Did Kuntidevi, who sought grief to keep you in her memory always, at least understand you completely? Did the terrible curse of the Kauravas' mother Gandharidevi have the power to bring an end to you?

'Did Gargamuni, Dhaumya Rishi, Devabhagababa, Virata, Drupada and Dhrishtadyumna, whom you considered your intimate associates, ever reach the depths of your heart? Weren't the lives of vicious men blessed because they got the honour of being finished by you? Daruka, Sanjaya, Mahatma Vidura, Sudama and Satyaki, whom you considered to be your sakhas, and Radha and Draupadi, whom you considered your sakhis, sister Subhadra, Ekananga, Abhimanyu and his wife Uttaraa – did any one of them understand precisely who you were?

'Could even one among all your sons, including Pradyumna, try to learn who you were? Your beloved daughter Charumati and all her sisters – could they pursue that search?

'Except for Rukmini, did the other seven queens ever realise how fortunate they were to be your wives?

'All the Pandavas including Yudhishthira, whom you mentored – were they ever able to assess who you were?

'Leave aside the others, could master archer Arjuna, whom you bestowed with the invaluable knowledge of the Gita and whom you considered your best sakha, comprehend all the facets of your life?

'Forget everyone else, have I – who have been continuously serving you in every way for the last thirty-six years – understood you completely?

'I think it was only Rukmini who probably understood you somewhat. Oh my Dada, 'Yugandhara', whenever, whoever understands you completely from every angle and every perspective, that day will be a golden day not only for Aaryavarta but for the entire world.'

My heart was still wailing, 'My brother – Srikrishna, Yugandhara – who were you, really?'

The boundless, endless blue colour of the peacock feather I had held was shining brightly due to the continuous flow of tears streaming down my eyes.

On the western horizon of Bhalaka Tirtha in Aanarta, Saurashtra, the sun had now set. An era had come to an end!

Glossary

Ô	the sacred sound composed of three sounds 'A-U-M'. It spoken at the beginning and end of each mantra
Aachamana	the act of swallowing water three times while chanting mantras in praise of God
Aamra	mango tree
Aate bandhu	father's sister's son
Aatmavidya	knowledge of the Self and the Soul
Aatya	paternal aunt, father's sister
Aatyapatya	a game played between two teams of nine players each, where players from one team try to cross over nine trenches and the opposing team tries to block their progress from one trench to the next
Abhishek	a ceremonious holy bath offered to a deity or a person of royalty
Agrapooja	the guest of honour at a yajna is given the highest mark of reverence or respect by being asked to perform the pooja at the very beginning of the yajna
Akshauhini	a mammoth army containing approximately twenty-two thousand elephants, twenty-two thousand chariots, sixty-six thousand horses, eleven thousand foot soldiers

Ananta	a white flower, also known as gardenia
Arghya	offering water to God, oblations
Asharan	one who does not seek protection, one who does not surrender
Ashwattha	Pipal tree
Asura	a demon
Audumbara	Indian fig tree
Aukshan	a religious ritual where lighted lamps are placed on a plate, which is then circled around a person on auspicious occasions
Barabandi dress	a traditional dress for men with twelve small strips of cloth to tie it at twelve places and therefore called bara (twelve) bandee (knots)
Bela	a sacred leaf that has three leaflets, offered to Lord Shiva
Bhacha	a man's sister's son or a woman's brother's son
Bhache	plural of Bhacha
Bhandirvriksha	Banyan tree
Bharadwaja	the greater coucal or crow pheasant with a long tail and coppery brown wings
Bharata	descendant of king Bharata
Bharatashreshtha	best among the descendants of king Bharata
Bhauji	husband's brother, brother-in-law
Bibhatsu	one who creates terror among the enemy during a war
Brahmakamala	white lotus flower
Brahma Muhurta	the early part of the day, dawn
Brahmavidya	knowledge of the Brahman
Chakravarti	an ideal ruler who rules over the entire world ethically and benevolently

Champaka	a yellow flower known for its fragrance, also called magnolia
Chandola	wood lark, a singing bird, brown above and pale below
Chandravansha	lunar dynasty, a dynasty descended from the Moon or Chandra
Chataka	pied crested cuckoo, also known as Jacobin cuckoo.
Chitrahuti	food offered to deities before beginning a meal
Chulat bandhu	father's brother's son
Damaru	a small drum shaped like an hourglass; an instrument of Lord Shiva
Dhairyashil	courageous
Dhananjaya	another name of Arjuna, meaning one who can conquer over riches
Dhanurdhara	expert archer
Dhanurveda	the knowledge of archery
Dharma	in Hinduism, Dharma signifies the 'right way of living'. The term includes behaviours that are in accord with the cosmic law and order, such as duties, conduct, virtues and rights that one is supposed to follow throughout life
Dhirodatta	courageous, brave and noble-minded
Digvijayi	world conqueror
Falguni	another name of Arjuna, born in the Uttara Falguni nakshatra
Ghatika	a measure of time, a period of twenty-four minutes
Gopalakala/gopabhoga	the feast of Krishna's gopa friends, prepared by mixing everyone's food together and distributed equally

Gudakesha	an epithet of Arjuna, one who has conquered sleep
Gurudakshina	a tradition in Hinduism where a student repays a guru after the completion of his formal education
Himalinga	Shivalingam made with snow
Hututu	a game played between two teams, where a single player from one team seeks the players of the opposing team while holding his/her breath and saying 'Hu tu tu'. The players of the other team try to catch the seeker and confine him/her to their play area till the seeker runs out of breath
Ingudi	oil made from the seeds of the desert date tree
Jalanjali	an offering of water made to deceased ancestors
Jamun	Indian black plum
Jaswanda	hibiscus flower
Jayishnu	one who conquers
Jishnu	victorious, triumphant
Jnanlobhi	knowledge-hungry
Jyeshtha	eldest brother
Kadamba	common Bur flower tree. It is a fast-growing, large, evergreen tree
Kajal	dark eyeliner, collyrium
Kaka	paternal uncle, father's brother
Kaku	father's brother's wife
Kamandalu	An oblong water pot used by Hindu ascetics for storing drinking water
Karanjel	oil made from the seeds of the Indian beech tree
Karmabhumi	the place where one builds one's life by performing one's duty, the sphere of one's duty
Kaunteya	son of Kunti
Khaira	Cutch tree, black cutch

Kharja	Bass, lowest tone
Kho-kho	a tag game played between two teams, where runners from one team avoid getting caught by the tagger of the opposing team by giving each other 'kho' (tapping on the back of one's player and saying 'kho')
Kiritin	wearing a celestial crown given by Lord Indra
Kirtivan	renowned, celebrated
Kojagiri paurnima	the full-moon night of the month of Ashwin, when people spend the night in a variety of festivities and drink warm milk
Kokila	a species of the cuckoo class Kokum – the fruit of mangosteen tree
Kosa	ancient Indian unit of length; one kosa is about 3.2 kilometres or 2 miles
Kotwala	black drongo, also known as the king crow
Lagori	a game played between two teams, where a seeker from one team knocks out a small tower of stones with a ball. The seeker's team then tries to restore the tower of stones while the opposing team tries to hit the seekers with the ball and get them out
Lezim	a musical instrument with jingling cymbals chained together and attached at both ends of a small wooden stick, used in folk dance
Mahabaho	mighty armed
Maharathi	great warrior, a war hero
Mahaskandha	broad-shouldered
Mallakhamba	a traditional sport where a gymnast performs feats on a vertical wooden pole
Mame bandhu	mother's brother's son
Mavas bandhu	mother's sister's son
Mavashi	maternal aunt, mother's sister

Mayura	Indian peacock
Muhurta	an auspicious time to begin a ceremony or an enterprise
Nadi	a vein
Namana	singing a psalm in praise of God
Nandi	the sacred bull, the carrier of Lord Shiva
Nidrajayi	one who has conquered sleep
Nishpaap	sinless
Niyoga	this was a practice prevalent in ancient times that permitted a childless woman to bear a child by having intercourse with any kinsman of her husband, to continue the family line
Padar	the end or border of a saree
Palash	a tree with red/orange flowers, also known as the flame of the forest
Parakrami	valiant
Parantapa	subduer of enemies
Paras	a stone that has the quality of turning metal into gold by its touch
Parijata	white flower with an orange centre
Partha	name of Arjuna, the son of Pritha
Pindadana	the offering of a rice ball at a funeral; the funeral oblation made to dead ancestors on the evening of the newmoon
Prahar	eighth part of the day, the period of three hours
Pranayama	'Prana' meaning life force or breath, and 'Yama' meaning to control or restrain one's breath to produce a particular result
Purashcharana	repeating a mantra for a particular number of times and for a certain period of time

Purusha	a linear measure used in ancient India to measure length. It literally means 'the measure of man' with both arms stretched upwards
Purushottama	Supreme man or Supreme being
Putanya	a man's brother's son or the son of a woman's brother-in-law
Putane	plural of Putanya
Rasa	Lord Krishna's divine dance with Radha and other gopikas in Gokul. This practice was also prevalent in the Yadava dynasty
Rudraksha	the seed of a particular tree found in the Himalayan region. It is considered significant in a spiritual seeker's life
Saga	teak tree
Sakha	a best friend, confidant
Sakhi	a best friend, confidante
Salunki	mynah
Samaasa	composition of words; compound words
Sandhya prayer	the morning, noon and evening prayers a Brahmana is supposed to do everyday
Sanyami	one who keeps his passions under control
Sanyasi	a person who has renounced material desires and detached himself/herself from the material world
Saptak	the octave
Satshil	truthful, virtuous, honest person
Sattva, Rajas and Tamas Gunas	Sattva (good, constructive, harmonious), Rajas (passionate, active, confused) and Tamas (dark, destructive, chaotic). According to Hinduism, these are the three basic qualities of Nature. They exist forever in all beings

Savitru mantra	a mantra from the Rigveda dedicated to the Sun god. It is composed in the Gayatri meter, hence also known as Gayatri mantra
Savyasachi	another epithet of Arjuna, meaning ambidexterous, a person who is able to use both right and left hands equally well
Shaligrama	a fossilised shell used as a symbol of Lord Vishnu in Hinduism
Shalunka	the base or part of Shivapindi that bears the lingam
Shisam	rosewood or blackwood tree
Shivapindi	symbol of Lord Shiva
Suryavansha	solar dynasty, a dynasty descended from the Sun or Surya
Swastika	an ancient symbol of auspiciousness and good luck
Tandava dance	a vigorous divine dance performed by Lord Shiva, which is the source of creation, preservation and dissolution of life
Tarpana	offering water to deceased ancestors to satisfy them
Tilanjali	A handful of sesame seeds with water offered daily to manes until the tenth day of their death
Típrya	playing sticks used in traditional Indian dances
Tirtha-Prasada	holy water and food offered to devotees in the temple after performing the worship of God
Upanayana	a traditional ceremony of initiation, marking the acceptance of a student by a teacher and the student's entrance to a school
Upanishadas	collections of texts containing central philosophical concepts of Hinduism, such as Karma (action), moksha (salvation), Brahman (ultimate reality) and Atman (soul)

Vahini	brother's wife
Vandana	a namaskar, bowing down to God by bringing both palms together
Vanaprasthashrama	in the Vanaprasthashrama, or hermit stage, a man's duties as a family man come to an end and he retires from social and professional life
Veera	brave
Vijayadashami	the tenth day of the month of Ashwin, celebrated in India as the day of Rama's victory over Ravana
Vijigishu	desirous of victory
Vikrami	heroic, valiant
Yajna	a ritual in Hindu Dharma to propitiate deities where sacrificial offerings are made into a pit of fire
Yajnavetta	a person who is well versed in the matters of a yajna
Yogi	an ascetic, a monk, or a person who follows the yoga system of philosophy; a practitioner of yoga
Yoganidra	Deepest state of relaxation while sleeping but still maintaining full consciousness
Yogayogeshwara	the greatest yogi of all who has complete control over all senses and is not attached to any worldly karmas
Yojana	unit of measuring distance in ancient India; one yojana is about nine miles